PRAISE FOR WILBUR SMITH

'Wilbur Smith rarely misses a trick'
Sunday Times

'The world's leading adventure writer'
Daily Express

'Action is the name of Wilbur Smith's game
and he is a master'
Washington Post

'The pace would do credit to a Porsche, and the invention
is as bright and explosive as a fireworks display'
Sunday Telegraph

'A bonanza of excitement'
New York Times

'. . . a natural storyteller who moves confidently and
often splendidly in his period and sustains a flow of
convincing incident'
Scotsman

'Raw experience, grim reality, this is a story laced
with mystery a

'A

D1350688

THE SEVENTH SCROLL
&
GOLD MINE

Wilbur Smith was born in Central Africa in 1933. He was educated at Michaelhouse and Rhodes University. He became a full-time writer in 1964 after the successful publication of *When the Lion Feeds*, and has since written thirty novels, all meticulously researched on his numerous expeditions world-wide. His books are now translated into twenty-six different languages.

Also by Wilbur Smith

THE COURTNEYS

When the Lion Feeds
The Sound of Thunder
A Sparrow Falls
Birds of Prey
Monsoon
Blue Horizon
The Triumph of the Sun

THE COURTNEYS OF AFRICA

The Burning Shore
Power of the Sword
Rage
A Time to Die
Golden Fox

THE BALLANTYNE NOVELS

A Falcon Flies
Men of Men
The Angels Weep
The Leopard Hunts in Darkness

THE EGYPTIAN NOVELS

River God
Warlock
The Quest

Also

The Dark of the Sun
Shout at the Devil
The Diamond Hunters
The Sunbird
Eagle in the Sky
The Eye of the Tiger
Cry Wolf
Hungry as the Sea
Wild Justice
Elephant Song

WILBUR SMITH

THE SEVENTH
SCROLL
&
GOLD MINE

PAN BOOKS

The Seventh Scroll first published 1995 by Macmillan.
First published in paperback 1996 by Pan Books.
Gold Mine first published 1970 by William Heinemann.
First published in paperback 1974 by Pan Books.

This omnibus first published 2008 by Pan Books
An imprint of Pan Macmillan
A division of Macmillan Publishers Limited
Pan Macmillan, 20 New Wharf Road, London N1 9RR
Basingstoke and Oxford
Associated companies throughout the world
www.panmacmillan.com

ISBN 978-0-330-45793-4

3 5 7 9 8 6 4 2

A CIP catalogue record for this book is available from
the British Library.

Typeset by SetSystems Ltd, Saffron Walden, Essex
Printed and bound in the UK by
CPI Mackays, Chatham ME5 8TD

THE SEVENTH SCROLL
&
GOLD MINE

THE SEVENTH SCROLL

This book is for my wife and the jewel of my life, Mokhiniso, with all my love and gratitude for the enchanted years that I have been married to her

The dusk crept in from the desert, and shaded the dunes with purple. Like a thick velvet cloak it muted all sounds, so that the evening was tranquil and hushed.

From where they stood on the crest of the dune they looked out over the oasis and the complex of small villages that surrounded it. The buildings were white with flat roofs and the date palms stood higher than any of them except the Islamic mosque and the Coptic Christian church. These bastions of faith opposed each other across the lake.

The waters of the lake were darkling. A flight of duck slanted down on quick wings to land with a small splash of white close in against the reed banks.

The man and the woman made a disparate couple. He was tall, though slightly bowed, his silvering hair catching the last of the sunlight. She was young, in her early thirties, slim, alert and vibrant. Her hair was thick and curling, restrained now by a thong at the nape of her neck.

'Time to go down now. Alia will be waiting.' He smiled down at her fondly. She was his second wife. When his first wife died he thought that she had taken the sunlight with her. He had not expected this last period of happiness in his life. Now he had her and his work. He was a man happy and contented.

Suddenly she broke away from him, and pulled the thong from her hair. She shook it out, dense and dark, and she laughed. It was a pretty sound. Then she plunged down the steep slip-face of the dune, her long skirts billowing around her flying legs. They were shapely and brown. She kept her balance until halfway down, when gravity over-whelmed her and she tumbled.

From the top he smiled down on her indulgently. Sometimes she was still a child. At others she was a grave and dignified woman. He was not certain which he pre-ferred, but he loved her in both moods. She rolled to a halt at the bottom of the dune and sat up, still laughing, shaking the sand out of her hair.

'Your turn!' she called up at him. He followed her down sedately, moving with the slight stiffness of advanc-ing age, keeping his balance until he reached the bottom. He lifted her to her feet. He did not kiss her, although the temptation to do so was strong. It was not the Arab way to show public affection, even to a beloved wife.

She straightened her clothing and retied her hair before they set off towards the village. They skirted the reed beds of the oasis, crossing the rickety bridges over the irrigation canals. As they passed, the peasants returning from the fields greeted him with deep respect.

'*Salaam aleikum, Doktari!* Peace be with you, doctor.' They honoured all men of learning, but him especially for his kindness to them and their families over the years. Many of them had worked for his father before him. It mattered little that most of them were Moslem, while he was a Christian.

When they reached the villa, Alia, the old house-keeper, greeted them with mumbles and scowls. 'You are late. You are always late. Why do you not keep regular hours, like decent folk? We have a position to maintain.'

'Old mother, you are always right,' he teased her gently. 'What would we do without you to care for us?' He sent her away, still scowling to cover her love and concern for him.

They ate the simple meal on the terrace together, dates and olives and unleavened bread and goat's milk

2

cheese. It was dark when they finished, but the desert stars were bright as candles.

'Royan, my flower.' He reached across the table and touched her hand. 'It is time to begin work.' He stood up from the table and led the way to his study that opened out on to the terrace.

Royan Al Simma went directly to the tall steel safe against the far wall and tumbled the combination. The safe was out of place in this room, amongst the old books and scrolls, amongst the ancient statues and artefacts and grave goods that were the collection of his lifetime.

When the heavy steel door swung open, Royan stood back for a moment. She always felt this prickle of awe whenever she first looked upon this relic of the ages, even after an interval of only a few short hours.

'The seventh scroll,' she whispered, and steeled herself to touch it. It was nearly four thousand years old, written by a genius out of time with history, a man who had been dust for all these millennia, but whom she had come to know and respect as she did her own husband. His words were eternal, and they spoke to her clearly from beyond the grave, from the fields of paradise, from the presence of the great trinity, Osiris and Isis and Horus, in whom he had believed so devoutly. As devoutly as she believed in another more recent Trinity.

She carried the scroll to the long table at which Duraid, her husband, was already at work. He looked up as she laid it on the tabletop before him, and for a moment she saw the same mystical mood in his eyes that had affected her. He always wanted the scroll there on the table, even when there was no real call for it. He had the photographs and the microfilm to work with. It was as though he needed the unseen presence of the ancient author close to him as he studied the texts.

Then he threw off the mood and was the dispassionate

scientist once more. 'Your eyes are better than mine, my flower,' he said. 'What do you make of this character?'

She leaned over his shoulder and studied the hiero-glyph on the photograph of the scroll that he pointed out to her. She puzzled over the character for a moment before she took the magnifying glass from Duraid's hand and peered through it again.

'It looks as though Taita has thrown in another cryptogram of his own creation just to bedevil us.' She spoke of the ancient author as though he were a dear, but sometimes exasperating, friend who still lived and breathed, and played tricks upon them.

'We'll just have to puzzle it out, then,' Duraid declared with obvious relish. He loved the ancient game. It was his life's work.

The two of them laboured on into the cool of the night. This was when they did their best work. Sometimes they spoke Arabic and sometimes English; for them the two languages were as one. Less often they used French, which was their third common language. They had both received their education at universities in England and the United States, so far from this very Egypt of theirs. Royan loved the expression 'This very Egypt' that Taita used so often in the scrolls.

She felt a peculiar affinity in so many ways with this ancient Egyptian. After all, she was his direct descendant. She was a Coptic Christian, not of the Arab line that had so recently conquered Egypt, less than fourteen centuries ago. The Arabs were newcomers in this very Egypt of hers, while her own blood line ran back to the time of the pharaohs and the great pyramids.

At ten o'clock Royan made coffee for them, heating it on the charcoal stove that Alia had lit for them before she went off to her own family in the village. They drank the sweet, strong brew from thin cups that were half-filled with the heavy grounds. While they sipped, they talked as old friends.

For Royan that was their relationship, old friends. She had known Duraid ever since she had returned from England with her doctorate in archaeology and won her job with the Department of Antiquities, of which he was the director.

She had been his assistant when he had opened the tomb in the Valley of the Nobles, the tomb of Queen Lostris, the tomb that dated from about 1780 BC.

She had shared his disappointment when they had discovered that the tomb had been robbed in ancient times and all its treasures plundered. All that remained were the marvellous murals that covered the walls and the ceilings of the tomb.

It was Royan herself who had been working at the wall behind the plinth on which the sarcophagus had once stood, photographing the murals, when a section of the plaster had fallen away to reveal in their niche the ten alabaster jars. Each of the jars had contained a papyrus scroll. Every one of them had been written and placed there by Taita, the slave of the queen.

Since then their lives, Duraid's and her own, seemed to have revolved around those scraps of papyrus. Although there was some damage and deterioration, in the main they had survived nearly four thousand years remarkably intact.

What a fascinating story they contained, of a nation attacked by a superior enemy, armed with horse and chariot that were still alien to the Egyptians of that time. Crushed by the Hyksos hordes, the people of the Nile were forced to flee. Led by their queen, Lostris of the tomb, they followed the great river southwards almost to its source amongst the brutal mountains of the Ethiopian highlands. Here amongst those forbidding mountains, Lostris had entombed the mummified body of her husband, the

5

Pharaoh Mamose, who had been slain in battle against the Hyksos.

Long afterwards Queen Lostris had led her people back northwards to this very Egypt. Armed now with their own horses and chariots, forged into hard warriors in the African wilderness, they had come storming back down the cataracts of the great river to challenge once more the Hyksos invader, and in the end to triumph over him and wrest the double crown of upper and lower Egypt from his grasp.

It was a story that appealed to every fibre of her being, and that had fascinated her as they had unravelled each hieroglyph that the old slave had penned on the papyrus.

It had taken them all these years, working at night here in the villa on the oasis after their daily routine work at the museum in Cairo was done, but at last the ten scrolls had been deciphered – all except the seventh scroll. This was the one that was the enigma, the one which the author had cloaked in layers of esoteric shorthand and allusions so obscure that they were unfathomable at this remove of time. Some of the symbols he used had never figured before in all the thousands of texts that they had studied in their combined working lives. It was obvious to them both that Taita had not intended that the scrolls should be read by any eyes other than those of his beloved queen. These were his last gift for her to take with her beyond the grave.

It had taken all their combined skills, all their imagination and ingenuity, but at last they were approaching the conclusion of the task. There were still many gaps in the translation and many areas where they were uncertain whether or not they had captured the true meaning, but they had laid out the bones of the manuscript in such order that they were able to discern the outline of the creature it represented.

Now Duraid sipped his coffee and shook his head as he had done so often before. 'It frightens me,' he said. 'The responsibility. What to do with this knowledge we have gleaned. If it should fall into the wrong hands . . .' He sipped and sighed before he spoke again. 'Even if we take it to the right people, will they believe this material that is nearly four thousand years old?'

'Why must we bring in others?' Royan asked with an edge of exasperation in her voice. 'Why can we not do alone what has to be done?' At times like these the differences between them were most apparent. His was the caution of age, while hers was the impetuosity of youth.

'You do not understand,' he said. It always annoyed her when he said that, when he treated her as the Arabs treated their women in a totally masculine world. She had known the other world where women demanded and received the right to be treated as equals. She was a creature caught between those worlds, the Western world and the Arab world.

Royan's mother was an Englishwoman who had worked at the British Embassy in Cairo in the troubled times after World War II. She had met and married Royan's father, who had been a young Egyptian officer on the staff of Colonel Nasser. It was an unlikely union and had not persisted into Royan's adolescence.

Her mother had insisted upon returning to England, to her home town of York, for Royan's birth. She wanted her child to have British citizenship. After her parents had separated, Royan, again at her mother's insistence, had been sent back to England for her schooling, but all her holidays had been spent with her father in Cairo. Her father's career had prospered exceedingly, and in the end he had attained ministerial rank in the Mubarak government. Through her love for him she came to look upon herself as more Egyptian than English.

It was her father who had arranged her marriage to Duraid Al Simma. It was the last thing that he had done for her before his death. She had known he was dying at the time, and she had not found it in her heart to defy

7

him. All her modern training made her want to resist the old-fashioned Coptic tradition of the arranged marriage, but her breeding and her family and her Church were against her. She had acquiesced.

Her marriage to Duraid had not proved as insufferable as she had dreaded it might be. It might even have been entirely comfortable and satisfying if she had never been introduced to romantic love. However, there had been her liaison with David while she was up at university. He had swept her up in the hurly-burly, in the heady delirium, and, in the end, the heartache, when he had left her to marry a blonde English rose approved of by his parents.

She respected and liked Duraid, but sometimes in the night she still burned for the feel of a body as firm and young as her own on top of hers.

Duraid was still speaking and she had not been listening to him. She gave him her full attention once more. 'I have spoken to the minister again, but I do not think he believes in me. I think that Nahoot has convinced him that I am a little mad.' He smiled sadly. Nahoot Guddabi was his ambitious and well-connected deputy. 'At any rate the minister says that there are no government funds available, and that I will have to seek outside finance. So, I have been over the list of possible sponsors again, and have narrowed it down to four. There is the Getty Museum, of course, but I never like to work with a big impersonal institution. I prefer to have a single man to answer to. Decisions are always easier to reach.' None of this was new to her, but she listened dutifully.

'Then there is Herr von Schiller. He has the money and the interest in the subject, but I do not know him well enough to trust him entirely.' He paused, and Royan had listened to these musings so often before that she could anticipate him.

'What about the American? He is a famous collector,' she forestalled him.

'Peter Walsh is a difficult man to work with. His passion to accumulate makes him unscrupulous. He frightens me a little.'

'So who does that leave?' she asked.

He did not reply, for they both knew the answer to her question. Instead, he turned his attention back to the material that littered the work table.

'It looks so innocent, so mundane. An old papyrus scroll, a few photographs and notebooks, a computer printout. It is difficult to believe how dangerous these might be in the wrong hands.' He sighed again. 'You might almost say that they are deadly dangerous.'

Then he laughed. 'I am being fanciful. Perhaps it is the late hour. Shall we get back to work? We can worry about these other matters once we have worked out all the conundrums set for us by this old rogue, Taita, and completed the translation.'

He picked up the top photograph from the pile in front of him. It was an extract from the central section of the scroll. 'It is the worst luck that the damaged piece of papyrus falls where it does.' He picked up his reading glasses and placed them on his nose before he read aloud.

'"*There are many steps to ascend on the staircase to the abode of Hapi. With much hardship and endeavour we reached the second step and proceeded no further, for it was here that the prince received a divine revelation. In a dream his father, the dead god pharaoh, visited him and commanded him, 'I have travelled far and I am grown weary. It is here that I will rest for all eternity.'"*' Duraid removed his glasses and looked across at Royan, '"*The second step*". It is a very precise description for once. Taita is not being his usual devious self.'

'Let's go back to the satellite photographs,' Royan suggested, and drew the glossy sheet towards her. Duraid came around the table to stand behind her.

'To me it seems most logical that the natural feature that would obstruct them in the gorge would be something

9

like a set of rapids or a waterfall. If it were the second waterfall, that would put them here—' Royan placed her finger on a spot on the satellite photograph where the narrow snake of the river threaded itself through the dark massifs of the mountains on either hand.

At that moment she was distracted and she lifted her head. 'Listen!' Her voice changed, sharpening with alarm.

'What is it?' Duraid looked up also.

'The dog,' she answered.

'That damn mongrel,' he agreed. 'It is always making the night hideous with its yapping. I have promised myself to get rid of him.'

At that moment the lights went out.

They froze with surprise in the darkness. The soft thudding of the decrepit diesel generator in its shed at the back of the palm grove had ceased. It was so much a part of the oasis night that they noticed it only when it was silent.

Their eyes adjusted to the faint starlight that came in through the terrace doors. Duraid crossed the room and took the oil lamp down from the shelf beside the door where it waited for just such a contingency. He lit it, and looked across at Royan with an expression of comical resignation.

'I will have to go down—'

'Duraid,' she interrupted him, 'the dog!'

He listened for a moment, and his expression changed to mild concern. The dog was silent out there in the night.

'I am sure it is nothing to be alarmed about.' He went to the door, and for no good reason she suddenly called after him.

'Duraid, be careful!' He shrugged dismissively and stepped out on to the terrace.

She thought for an instant that it was the shadow of the vine over the trellis moving in the night breeze off the desert, but the night was still. Then she realized that it was a human figure crossing the flagstones silently and swiftly, coming in behind Duraid as he skirted the fishpond in the centre of the paved terrace.

'Duraid!' She screamed a warning and he spun round, lifting the lamp high.

'Who are you?' he shouted. 'What do you want here?'

The intruder closed with him silently. The traditional full-length *dishdasha* robe swirled around his legs, and the white *ghutrah* headcloth covered his head. In the light of the lamp Duraid saw that he had drawn the corner of the headcloth over his face to mask his features.

The intruder's back was turned towards her so Royan did not see the knife in his right hand, but she could not mistake the upward stabbing motion that he aimed at Duraid's stomach. Duraid grunted with pain and doubled up at the blow, and his attacker drew the blade free and stabbed again, but this time Duraid dropped the lamp and seized the knife arm.

The flame of the fallen oil lamp was guttering and flaring. The two men struggled in the gloom, but Royan saw a dark stain spreading over her husband's white shirt front.

'Run!' he bellowed at her. 'Go! Fetch help! I cannot hold him!' The Duraid she knew was a gentle person, a soft man of books and learning. She could see that he was outmatched by his assailant.

'Go! Please! Save yourself, my flower!' She could hear by his tone that he was weakening, but he still clung desperately to his attacker's knife arm.

She had been paralysed with shock and indecision these few fatal seconds, but now she broke free of the spell and ran to the door. Spurred by her terror and her need to bring help to Duraid she crossed the terrace, swift as a cat, and he held the intruder from blocking her way.

She vaulted over the low stone wall into the grove, and almost into the arms of the second man. She screamed and twisted away from him as his outstretched fingers raked across her face, and almost broke free, but his fingers hooked in the thin cotton stuff of her blouse.

This time she saw the knife in his hand, a long silvery flash in the starlight, and it goaded her to fresh effort. The cotton tore in his grip and she was free, but not quickly enough to escape the blade. She felt the sting of it across her upper arm, and she kicked out at him with all the strength of panic and her hard young body behind it. She felt her foot slam into the softness of his lower body with a shock that jarred her knee and ankle, and her attacker cried out and fell to his knees.

Then she was away and running through the palm grove. At first she ran without purpose or direction. She ran simply to get as far from them as her flying legs would carry her. Then gradually she brought her panic under control. She glanced back, but saw nobody following her. As she reached the edge of the lake she slowed her run to conserve her strength, and she became aware of the warm trickle of her own blood down her arm and then dripping from her fingertips.

She stopped and rested her back against the rough bole of one of the palms while she tore a strip of cloth from her ripped blouse and hurriedly bound up her arm. She was shaking so much from shock and exertion that even her uninjured hand was fumbling and clumsy. She knotted the crude bandage with her teeth and left hand, and the bleeding slowed.

She was uncertain of which way to run, and then she saw the dim lamplight in the window of Alia's shack across the nearest irrigation canal. She pushed herself away from the palm trunk and started towards it. She had covered less than a hundred paces when a voice called from the grove behind her, speaking in Arabic, 'Yusuf, has the woman come your way?'

Immediately an electric torch flashed from the darkness ahead of her and another voice called back, 'No, I have not seen her.'

Another few seconds and Royan would have run full into him. She crouched down and looked around her desperately. There was another torch coming through the grove behind her, following the path she had taken. It must be the man she had kicked, but she could tell by the motion of the torchbeam that he had recovered and was moving swiftly and easily again.

She was blocked on two sides, so she turned back along the edge of the lake. The road lay that way. She might be able to meet a late vehicle travelling on it. She lost her footing on the rough ground and went down, bruising and scraping her knees, but she jumped up again and hurried on. The second time she stumbled, her out-thrust left hand landed on a round, smooth stone the size of an orange. When she went on she carried the stone with her; as a weapon it gave her a glimmer of comfort.

Her wounded arm was beginning to hurt, and she was driven by worry for Duraid. She knew he was badly wounded, for she had seen the direction and force of the knife thrust. She had to find help for him. Behind her the two men with torches were sweeping the grove and she could not keep her lead ahead of them. They were gaining on her – she could hear them calling to each other.

She reached the road at last, and with a small whimper of relief climbed out of the drainage ditch on to the pale gravel surface. Her legs were shaking under her so that they could hardly carry her weight, but she turned in the direction of the village.

She had not reached the first bend before she saw a set of headlights coming slowly towards her, flickering through the palm trees. She broke into a run down the centre of the road.

'Help me!' she screamed in Arabic. 'Please help me!'

The car came through the bend and before the

headlights dazzled her she saw that it was a small, dark-coloured Fiat. She stood in the centre of the road waving her arms to halt the driver, lit by the headlights as though she were on a theatre stage.

The Fiat stopped in front of her, and she ran round to the driver's door and tugged at the handle. 'Please, you must help me—'

The door was opened from within, and then was thrown back with such force that she staggered off-balance. The driver leapt out into the roadway and caught her by the wrist of the injured arm. He dragged her to the Fiat and pulled open the back door.

'Yusuf! Bacheet!' he shouted into the dark grove. 'I have her.' And she heard the answering cries and saw the torches turn in their direction. The driver was forcing her head down and trying to push her into the back seat, but she realized then that she still had the stone in her good hand. She turned slightly and braced herself, and then swung her fist with the stone still clenched in it against the side of his head. It caught him squarely on the temple. Without another sound he dropped to the gravel surface and lay motionless.

Royan dropped the stone and pelted away down the road, but she found that she was running straight down the path of the headlights, and they lit her every movement. The two men in the grove shouted again and came up on to the gravel roadway behind her, almost shoulder to shoulder.

Glancing back, she saw them gaining on her swiftly, and she realized that her only chance was to get off the road and back into the darkness. She turned and plunged down the bank. Immediately she found herself waist-deep in the waters of the lake.

In the darkness and the confusion she had become disorientated. She had not realized that she had reached the point where the road skirted the embankment at the water's edge. She knew that she did not have time to climb back on to the road, and she knew also that there were thick clumps of papyrus and reeds ahead of her, that might give her shelter.

She waded out until the bottom sloped away steeply under her feet, and she found herself forced to swim. She broke into an awkward breast-stroke, hampered by her skirts and her injured arm. However, her slow and stealthy movements created almost no disturbance on the surface, and before the men on the road had reached the point where she had descended the bank, she reached a dense stand of reeds.

She eased her way into the thick of them and let herself sink. Before the water covered her nostrils she felt her toes touch the soft ooze of the lake bottom. She stood there quietly, with just the top of her head above the surface and her face turned away from the bank. She knew her dark hair would not reflect the light of a probing torch.

Though the water covered her ears, she could make out the excited voices of the men on the road. They had turned their torches down towards the water and were shining them into the reeds, searching for her. For a moment one of the beams played full on her head, and she drew a deep breath ready to submerge, but the beam moved on and she realized that they had not picked her out.

The fact that she had not been seen even in the direct torchlight emboldened her to raise her head slightly until one ear was clear and she could make out their voices.

They were speaking Arabic, and she recognized the voice of the one named Bacheet. He appeared to be the leader, for he was giving the orders.

'Go in there, Yusuf, and bring the whore out.'

She heard Yusuf slipping and sliding down the bank and the splash as he hit the water.

'Further out,' Bacheet ordered him. 'In those reeds there, where I am shining the torch.'

'It is too deep. You know well I cannot swim. It will be over my head.'

'There! Right in front of you. In those reeds. I can see her head.' Bacheet encouraged him, and Royan dreaded that they had spotted her. She sank down as far as she could below the surface.

Yusuf splashed around heavily, moving towards where she cowered in the reeds, when suddenly there was a thunderous commotion that startled even Yusuf, so that he shouted aloud, 'Djinns! God protect me!' as the flock of roosting duck exploded from the water and launched into the dark sky on noisy wings.

Yusuf started back to the bank and not any of Bacheet's threats could persuade him to continue the hunt.

'The woman is not as important as the scroll,' he protested, as he climbed back on to the roadway. 'Without the scroll there will be no money. We always know where to find her later.'

Turning her head slightly, Royan saw the torches move back down the road towards the parked Fiat whose headlights still burned. She heard the doors of the car slam, and then the engine revved and pulled away towards the villa.

She was too shaken and terrified to make any attempt to leave her hiding-place. She feared that they had left one of their number on the road to wait for her to show herself. She stood on tiptoe with the water lapping her lips, shivering more with shock than with cold, determined to wait for the safety of the sunrise before she moved.

It was only much later when she saw the glow of the fire lighting the sky, and the flames flickering through the trunks of the palm trees, that she forgot her own safety and dragged herself back to the bank.

She knelt in the mud at the water's edge, shuddering and shaking and gasping, weak with loss of blood and shock and the reaction from fear, and peered at the flames through the veil of her wet hair and the lake water that streamed into her eyes.

'The villa!' she whispered. 'Duraid! Oh please God, no! No!'

She pushed herself to her feet and began to stagger towards her burning home.

Bacheet switched off both the headlights and the engine of the Fiat before they reached the turning into the driveway of the villa and let the car coast down and stop below the terrace.

All three of them left the Fiat and climbed the stone steps to the flagged terrace. Duraid's body still lay where Bacheet had left it beside the fishpond. They passed him without a glance and went into the dark study.

Bacheet placed the cheap nylon tote bag he carried on the tabletop.

'We have wasted too much time already. We must work quickly now.'

'It is Yusuf's fault,' protested the driver of the Fiat. 'He let the woman escape.'

'You had a chance on the road,' Yusuf snarled at him, 'and you did no better.'

'Enough!' Bacheet told them both. 'If you want to get paid, then there had better be no more mistakes.'

With the torchbeam Bacheet picked out the scroll that still lay on the tabletop. 'That is the one.' He was certain, for he had been shown a photograph of it so that there would be no mistake. 'They want everything – the maps and photographs. Also the books and papers, everything on the table that they were using in their work. Leave nothing.'

Quickly they bundled everything into the tote bag and Bacheet zipped it closed.

'Now the *Doktari*. Bring him in here.'

The other two went out on to the terrace and stooped over the body. Each of them seized an ankle and dragged Duraid back across the terrace and into the study. The back of Duraid's head bounced loosely on the stone step at the threshold and his blood painted a long wet skid mark across the tiles that glistened in the torchlight.

'Get the lamp!' Bacheet ordered, and Yusuf went back to the terrace and fetched the oil lamp from where Duraid had dropped it. The flame was extinguished. Bacheet held the lamp to his ear and shook it.

'Full,' he said with satisfaction, and unscrewed the filler cap. 'All right,' he told the other two, 'take the bag out to the car.'

As they hurried out Bacheet sprinkled paraffin from the lamp over Duraid's shirt and trousers, and then he went to the shelves and splashed the remainder of the fuel over the books and manuscripts that crowded them.

He dropped the empty lamp and reached under the skirts of his *dishdasha* for a box of matches. He struck one of them and held it to the wet run of paraffin oil down the bookcase. It caught immediately, and flames spread upwards and curled and blackened the edges of the manuscripts. He turned away and went back to where Duraid lay. He struck another match and dropped it on to his blood- and paraffin-drenched shirt.

A mantle of blue flames danced over Duraid's chest. The flames changed colour as they burned into the cotton material and the flesh beneath it. They turned orange, and sooty smoke spiralled up from their flickering crests.

Bacheet ran to the door, across the terrace and down the steps. As he clambered into the rear seat of the Fiat, the driver gunned the engine and pulled away down the driveway.

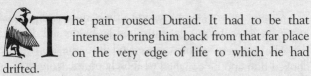The pain roused Duraid. It had to be that intense to bring him back from that far place on the very edge of life to which he had drifted.

He groaned. The first thing he was aware of as he regained consciousness was the smell of his own flesh burning, and then the agony struck him with full force. A violent tremor shook his whole body and he opened his eyes and looked down at himself.

His clothing was blackening and smouldering, and the pain was as nothing he had ever experienced in his entire life. He realized in a vague way that the room was on fire all around him. Smoke and waves of heat washed over him so that he could barely make out the shape of the doorway through them.

The pain was so terrible that he wanted it to end. He wanted to die then and not to have to endure it further. Then he remembered Royan. He tried to say her name through his scorched and blackened lips, but no sound came. Only the thought of her gave him the strength to move. He rolled over once, and the heat attacked his back that up until that moment had been shielded. He groaned aloud and rolled again, just a little nearer to the doorway.

Each movement was a mighty effort and evoked fresh paroxysms of agony, but when he rolled on to his back again he realized that a gale of fresh air was being sucked through the open doorway to feed the flames. A lungful of the sweet desert air revived him and gave him just sufficient strength to lunge down the step on to the cool stones of the terrace.

His clothes and his body were still on fire. He beat feebly at his chest to try to extinguish the flames, but his hands were black burning claws.

Then he remembered the fishpond. The thought of plunging his tortured body into that cold water spurred him to one last effort, and he wriggled and wormed his way across the flags like a snake with a crushed spine.

The pungent smoke from his still cremating flesh choked him and he coughed weakly, but kept doggedly on. He left slabs of his own grilled skin on the stone coping as he rolled across it and flopped into the pond. There was a hiss of steam, and a pale cloud of it obscured his vision so that for a moment he thought he was blinded. The agony of cold water on his raw burned flesh was so intense that he slid back over the edge of consciousness.

When he came back to reality through the dark clouds he raised his dripping head and saw a figure staggering up the steps at the far end of the terrace, coming from the garden.

For a moment he thought it was a phantom of his agony, but when the light of the burning villa fell full upon her, he recognized Royan. Her wet hair hung in tangled disarray over her face, and her clothing was torn and running with lake water and stained with mud and green algae. Her right arm was wrapped in muddy rags and her blood oozed through, diluted pink by the dirty water.

She did not see him. She stopped in the centre of the terrace and stared in horror into the burning room. Was Duraid in there? She started forward, but the heat was like a solid wall and it stopped her dead. At that moment the roof collapsed, sending a roaring column of sparks and flames high into the night sky. She backed away from it, shielding her face with a raised arm.

Duraid tried to call to her, but no sound issued from his smoke-scorched throat. Royan turned away and started down the steps. He realized that she must be going to call for help. Duraid made a supreme effort and a crow-like croak came out between his black and blistered lips.

Royan spun round and stared at him, and then she screamed. His head was not human. His hair was gone, frizzled away, and his skin hung in tatters from his cheeks and chin. Patches of raw meat showed through the black crusted mask. She backed away from him as though he were some hideous monster.

'Royan,' he croaked, and his voice was just recognizable. He lifted one hand towards her in appeal, and she ran to the pond and seized the outstretched hand.

'In the name of the Virgin, what have they done to you?' she sobbed, but when she tried to pull him from the pond the skin of his hand came away in hers in a single piece, like some horrible surgical rubber glove, leaving the bleeding claw naked and raw.

Royan fell on her knees beside the coping and leaned over the pond to take him in her arms. She knew that she did not have the strength to lift him out without doing him further dreadful injury. All she could do was hold him and try to comfort him. She realized that he was dying – no man could survive such fearsome injury.

'They will come soon to help us,' she whispered to him in Arabic. 'Someone must see the flames. Be brave, my husband, help will come very soon.'

He was twitching and convulsing in her arms, tortured by his mortal injuries and racked by the effort to speak.

'The scroll?' His voice was barely intelligible. Royan looked up at the holocaust that enveloped their home, and she shook her head.

'It's gone,' she said. 'Burned or stolen.'

'Don't give it up,' he mumbled. 'All our work—'

'It's gone,' she repeated. 'No one will believe us without—'

'No!' His voice was faint but fierce. 'For me, my last—'

'Don't say that,' she pleaded. 'You will be all right.'

'Promise,' he demanded. 'Promise me!'

'We have no sponsor. I am alone. I cannot do it alone.'

'Harper!' he said. Royan leaned closer so that her ear touched his fire-ravaged lips. 'Harper,' he repeated. 'Strong

21

– hard – clever man—' and she understood then. Harper, of course, was the fourth and last name on the list of sponsors that he had drawn up. Although he was the last on the list, somehow she had always known that Duraid's order of preference was inverted. Nicholas Quenton-Harper was his first choice. He had spoken so often of this man with respect and warmth, and sometimes even with awe.

'But what do I tell him? He does not know me. How will I convince him? The seventh scroll is gone.'

'Trust him,' he whispered. 'Good man. Trust him—' There was a terrible appeal in his 'Promise me!'

Then she remembered the notebook in their flat at Giza in the Cairo suburbs, and the Taita material on the hard drive on her PC. Not everything was gone. 'Yes,' she agreed, 'I promise you, my husband, I promise you.'

Though those mutilated features could show no human expression there was a faint echo of satisfaction in his voice as he whispered, 'My flower!' Then his head dropped forward, and he died in her arms.

The peasants from the village found Royan still kneeling beside the pond, holding him, whispering to him. By that time the flames were abating, and the faint light of dawn was stronger than their fading glow.

All the senior staff from the museum and the Department of Antiquities were at the funeral service in the church of the oasis. Even Atalan Abou Sin, the Minister of Culture and Tourism and Duraid's superior, had come out from Cairo in his official black air-conditioned Mercedes.

He stood behind Royan and, though he was a Moslem, joined in the responses. Nahoot Guddabi stood beside his uncle. Nahoot's mother was the minister's youngest sister, which, as Duraid had sarcastically pointed out, fully made up for the nephew's lack of qualifications and experience in archaeology and for his ineptitude as an administrator.

The day was sweltering. Outside, the temperature stood at over thirty degrees, and even in the dim cloisters of the Coptic church it was oppressive. In the thick clouds of incense smoke and the drone of the black-clad priest intoning the ancient order of service Royan felt herself suffocating. The stitches in her right arm pulled and burned, and every time she looked at the long black coffin that stood in front of the ornate and gilded altar, the dreadful vision of Duraid's bald and scorched head rose before her eyes and she swayed in her seat and had to catch herself before she fell.

At last it was over and she could escape into the open air and the desert sunlight. Even then her duties were not at an end. As principal mourner, her place was directly behind the coffin as they walked in procession to the cemetery amongst the palm groves, where Duraid's relatives awaited him in the family mausoleum.

Before he returned to Cairo, Atalan Abou Sin came to shake her hand and offer her a few words of condolence. 'What a terrible business, Royan. I have personally spoken to the Minister of the Interior. They will catch the animals responsible for this outrage, believe me. Please take as long as you need before you return to the museum,' he told her.

'I will be in my office again on Monday,' she replied, and he drew a pocket diary from inside the jacket of his dark double-breasted suit. He consulted it and made a note, before he looked up at her again.

'Then come to see me at the Ministry in the afternoon. Four o'clock,' he told her. He went to the waiting Mercedes, while Nahoot Guddabi came forward to shake hands. Though his skin was sallow and there were coffee-coloured stains beneath his dark eyes, he was tall and elegant with thick wavy hair and very white teeth. His suit was impeccably tailored and he smelt faintly of an expensive cologne. His expression was grave and sad.

'He was a good man. I held Duraid in the highest esteem,' he told Royan, and she nodded without replying to this blatant untruth. There had been little affection between Duraid and his deputy. He had never allowed Nahoot to work on the Taita scrolls; in particular he had never given him access to the seventh scroll, and this had been a point of bitter antagonism between them.

'I hope you will be applying for the post of director, Royan,' he told her. 'You are well qualified for the job.'

'Thank you, Nahoot, you are very kind. I haven't had a chance to think about the future yet, but won't you be applying?'

'Of course,' he nodded. 'But that doesn't mean that no one else should. Perhaps you will take the job out from in front of my nose.' His smile was complacent. She was a woman in an Arab world, and he was the nephew of the minister. Nahoot knew just how heavily the odds favoured him. 'Friendly rivals?' he asked.

Royan smiled sadly. 'Friends, at least. I will need all of those I can find in the future.'

'You know you have many friends. Everyone in the department likes you, Royan.' That at least was true, she supposed. He went on smoothly, 'May I offer you a lift back to Cairo? I am certain my uncle will not object.'

'Thank you, Nahoot, but I have my own car here, and I must stay over at the oasis tonight to see to some of Duraid's affairs.' This was not true. Royan planned to travel back to the flat in Giza that evening but, for reasons that she was not very sure of herself, she did not want Nahoot to know of her plans.

'Then we shall see you at the museum on Monday.'

Royan left the oasis as soon as she was able to escape from the relations and family friends and peasants, so many of whom had worked for Duraid's family most of their lives.

24

She felt numbed and isolated, so that all their condolences and pious exhortations were meaningless and without comfort.

Even at this late hour the tarmac road back through the desert was busy, with files of vehicles moving steadily in both directions, for tomorrow was Friday and the sabbath. She slipped her injured right arm out of the sling, and it did not hamper her driving too much. She was able to make reasonably good time. Nevertheless, it was after five in the afternoon when she made out the green line against the tawny desolation of the desert that marked the start of the narrow strip of irrigated and cultivated land along the Nile which was the great artery of Egypt.

As always the traffic became denser the nearer she came to the capital, and it was almost fully dark by the time she reached the apartment block in Giza that overlooked both the river and those great monuments of stone which stood so tall and massive against the evening sky, and which for her epitomized the heart and history of her land.

She left Duraid's old green Renault in the underground garage of the building and rode up in the elevator to the top floor.

She let herself into the flat and then froze in the doorway. The sitting room had been ransacked – even the rugs had been pulled up and the paintings ripped from the walls. In a daze she picked her way through the litter of broken furniture and smashed ornaments. She glanced into the bedroom as she went down the passage, and saw that it had not escaped. Her clothes and those of Duraid were strewn over the floor, and the doors of the cupboards stood ajar. One of these was smashed off its hinges. The bed was overturned, and the sheets and bolsters had been flung about.

She could smell the reek of broken cosmetic and perfume bottles from the bathroom, but she could not yet bring herself to go in there. She knew what she would find. Instead she continued down the passage to the large room that they had used as a study and workshop.

In the chaos the first thing that she noticed and mourned was the antique chess set that Duraid had given her as a wedding present. The board of jet and ivory squares was broken in half and the pieces had been thrown about the room with vindictive and unnecessary violence. She stooped and picked up the white queen. Her head had been snapped off.

Holding the queen in her good hand she moved like a sleepwalker to her desk below the window. Her PC was wrecked. They had shattered the screen and hacked the mainframe with what must have been an axe. She could tell at a glance that there was no information left on the hard drive; it was beyond repair.

She glanced down at the drawer in which she kept her floppy disks. That and all the other drawers had been pulled out and thrown on the floor. They were empty, of course; along with the disks, all her notebooks and photographs were missing. Her last connections with the seventh scroll were lost. After three years of work, gone was the proof that it had ever existed.

She slumped down on the floor, feeling beaten and exhausted. Her arm started to ache again, and she was alone and vulnerable as she had never been in her life before. She had never thought that she would miss Duraid so desperately. Her shoulders began to shake and she felt the tears welling up from deep within her. She tried to hold them back, but they scalded her eyelids and she let them flow. She sat amongst the wreckage of her life and wept until there was nothing more left within her, and then she curled up on the littered carpet and fell into the sleep of exhaustion and despair.

By the Monday morning she had managed to restore some order into her life. The police had come to the flat and taken her statement, and she had tidied up most of the disarray. She had even glued the head back on her white queen. When she left the flat and climbed into the green Renault her arm was feeling easier, and, if not cheerful, she was at least a great deal more optimistic, and sure of what she had to do.

When she reached the museum she went first to Duraid's office and was annoyed to find that Nahoot was there before her. He was supervising two of the security guards as they cleared out all Duraid's personal effects.

'You might have had the consideration to let me do that,' she told him coldly, and he gave her his most winning smile.

'I am sorry, Royan. I thought I would help.' He was smoking one of his fat Turkish cigarettes. She loathed the heavy, musky odour.

She crossed to Duraid's desk, and opened the top right-hand drawer. 'My husband's day book was in here. It's gone now. Have you seen it?'

'No, there was nothing in that drawer.' Nahoot looked at the two guards for confirmation, and they shuffled their feet and shook their heads. It did not really matter, she thought. The book had not contained much of vital interest. Duraid had always relied on her to record and store all data of importance, and most of it had been on her PC.

'Thank you, Nahoot,' she dismissed him. 'I will do whatever remains to be done. I don't want to keep you from your work.'

'Any help you need, Royan, please let me know.' He bowed slightly as he left her.

It did not take her long to finish in Duraid's office. She had the guards take the boxes of his possessions down the corridor to her own office and pile them against the wall.

She worked through the lunch-hour tidying up all her own affairs, and when she had finished there was still an hour until her appointment with Atalan Abou Sin.

If she was to make good her promise to Duraid, then she was going to be absent for some time. Wanting to take leave of all her favourite treasures, she went down into the public section of the huge building.

Monday was a busy day, and the exhibition halls of the museum were thronged with groups of tourists. They flocked behind their guides, sheep following the shepherd. They crowded around the most famous of the displays. They listened to the guides reciting their well-rehearsed spiels in all the tongues of Babel.

Those rooms on the second floor that contained the treasures of Tutankhamen were so crowded that she spent little time there. She managed to reach the display cabinet that contained the great golden death-mask of the child pharaoh. As always, the splendour and the romance of it quickened her breathing and made her heart beat faster. Yet as she stood before it, jostled by a pair of big-busted and sweaty middle-aged female tourists, she pondered, as she had so often before, that if an insignificant weakling king could have gone to his tomb with such a miraculous creation covering his mummified features, in what state must the great Ramessids have lain in their funeral temples. Ramesses II, the greatest of them all, had reigned sixty-seven years and had spent those decades accumulating his funerary treasure from all the vast territories that he had conquered.

Royan went next to pay her respects to the old king. After thirty centuries Ramesses II slept on with a rapt and serene expression on his gaunt features. His skin had a light, marble-like sheen to it. The sparse strands of his hair were blond and dyed with henna. His hands, dyed with the same stuff, were long and thin and elegant. However, he was clad only in a rag of linen. The grave robbers had even unwrapped his mummy to reach the amulets and scarabs beneath the linen bandages, so that his body was almost naked. When these remains had been discovered in 1881 in the cache of royal mummies in the cliff cave at Deir El Bahari, only a scrap of papyrus parchment attached to his breast had proclaimed his lineage.

There was a moral in that, she supposed, but as she stood before these pathetic remains she wondered again, as she and Duraid had done so often before, whether Taita the scribe had told the truth, whether somewhere in the far-off, savage mountains of Africa another great pharaoh slept on undisturbed with all his treasures intact about him. The very thought of it made her shiver with excitement, and goose pimples prickled her skin and raised the fine dark hair at the nape of her neck.

'I have given you my promise, my husband,' she whispered in Arabic. 'This will be for you and your memory, for it was you who led the way.'

She glanced at her wrist-watch as she went down the main staircase. She had fifteen minutes before she must leave for her appointment with the minister, and she knew exactly how she would spend that time. What she was going to visit was in one of the less-frequented side halls. The tour guides very seldom led their charges this way, except as a short-cut to see the statue of Amenhotep.

Royan stopped in front of the glass-fronted display case that reached from floor to ceiling of the narrow room. It was packed with small artefacts, tools and weapons, amulets and vessels and utensils, the latest of them dating from the twentieth dynasty of the New Kingdom, 1100 BC, whilst the oldest survived from the dim ages of the Old Kingdom almost five thousand years ago. The cataloguing of this accumulation was only rudimentary. Many of the items were not described.

At the furthest end, on the bottom shelf, was a display of jewellery and finger rings and seals. Beside each of the seals was a wax impression made from it.

Royan went down on her knees to examine one of these artefacts more closely. The tiny blue seal of lapis lazuli in the centre of the display was beautifully carved. Lapis was a rare and precious material for the ancients, as it had not occurred naturally in the Egyptian Empire. The wax imprint cut from it depicted a hawk with a broken wing, and the simple legend beneath it was clear for Royan to read: 'TAITA, THE SCRIBE OF THE GREAT QUEEN'.

She knew it was the same man, for he had used the maimed hawk as his autograph in the scrolls. She wondered who had found this trifle and where. Perhaps some peasant had plundered it from the lost tomb of the old slave and scribe, but she would never knew.

'Are you teasing me, Taita? Is it all some elaborate hoax? Are you laughing at me even now from your tomb, wherever it may be?' She leaned even closer, until her forehead touched the cool glass. 'Are you my friend, Taita, or are you my implacable adversary?' She stood up and dusted off the front of her skirt. 'We shall see. I will play the game with you, and we shall see who outwits whom,' she promised.

The minister kept her waiting only a few minutes before his male secretary ushered her into his presence. Atalan Abou Sin wore a dark, shiny silk suit and sat at his desk, although Royan knew that he preferred a more comfortable robe and a cushion on the rugs of the floor. He noticed her glance and smiled deprecatingly. 'I have a meeting with some Americans this afternoon.'

She liked him. He had always been kind to her, and she owed him her job at the museum. Most other men in

30

his position would have refused Duraid's request for a female assistant, especially his own wife.

He asked after her health and she showed him her bandaged arm. 'The stitches will come out in ten days.'

They chatted for a while in a polite manner. Only Westerners would have the gaucherie to come directly to the main business to be discussed. However, to save him embarrassment Royan took the first opportunity he gave her to tell him, 'I feel that I need some time to myself. I need to recover from my loss and to decide what I am to do with the rest of my life, now that I am a widow. I would be grateful if you would consider my request for at least six months' unpaid leave of absence. I want to go to stay with my mother in England.'

Atalan showed real concern and urged her, 'Please do not leave us for too long. The work you have done has been invaluable. We need you to help carry on from where Duraid left off.' But he could not entirely conceal his relief. She knew that he had expected her to put before him her application for the directorship. He must have discussed it with his nephew. However, he was too kind a man to relish having to tell her that she would not be selected for the job. Things in Egypt were changing, women were emerging from their traditional roles, but not that much or that swiftly. They both knew that the directorship must go to Nahoot Guddabi.

Atalan walked with her to the door of his office and shook her hand in parting, and as she rode down in the lift she felt a sense of release and freedom.

She had left the Renault standing in the sun in the Ministry car park. When she opened the door the interior was hot enough to bake bread. She opened all the windows and fanned the driver's door to force out the heated air, but still the surface of the driver's seat burned the backs of her thighs when she slid in behind the wheel.

As soon as she drove through the gates she was

engulfed in the swarm of Cairo traffic. She crawled along behind an overloaded bus that belched a steady blue cloud of diesel fumes over the Renault. The traffic problem was one that seemed to have no solution. There was so little parking available that vehicles lined the verge of the road three and four deep, choking the flow in the centre to a trickle.

As the bus in front of her braked and forced her to a halt, Royan smiled as she recalled the old joke that some drivers who had parked at the kerb had to abandon their cars there, for they were never able to extricate them from the tangle. Perhaps there was a little truth in this, for some of those vehicles she could see had not been moved for weeks. Their windscreens were completely obscured with dust and many of them had flat tyres.

She glanced in the rear-view mirror. There was a taxi stopped only inches from her back bumper, and behind that the traffic was backed up solidly. Only the motor-cyclists had freedom of movement. As she watched in the mirror, one of these came weaving through the congestion with suicidal abandon. It was a battered red 200 cc Honda so covered with dust that the colour was hardly recognizable. There was a passenger perched on the pillion, and both he and the driver had covered the lower half of their faces with the corners of their white headcloths as protection against the exhaust fumes and dust.

Passing on the wrong side, the Honda skimmed through the narrow gap between the taxi and the cars parked at the kerb with nothing to spare on either side. The taxi-driver made an obscene gesture with thumb and forefinger, and called on Allah to witness that the driver was both mad and stupid.

The Honda slowed slightly as it drew level with Royan's Renault, and the pillion passenger leaned out and dropped something through the open window on to the passenger seat beside her. Immediately the driver accelerated so abruptly that for a moment the front wheel was lifted off the ground. He put the motorcycle over into a tight turn and sped away down the narrow alleyway that opened off the main thoroughfare, narrowly avoiding hitting an old woman in his path.

As the pillion passenger looked back at her the wind blew the fold of white cotton from his face, and with a shock she recognized the man she had last seen in the headlights of the Fiat on the road beside the oasis.

'Yusuf!' As the Honda disappeared she looked down at the object that he had dropped on to the seat beside her. It was egg-shaped and the segmented metallic surface was painted military green. She had seen the same thing so often on old TV war movies that she recognized it instantly as a fragmentation grenade, and at the same moment she realized that the priming handle had flown off and the weapon was set to explode within seconds.

Without thinking, she grabbed the door handle beside her and flung all her weight against the door. It burst open and she tumbled out in the road. Her foot slipped off the clutch and the Renault bounded forward and crashed into the back of the stationary bus.

As Royan sprawled in the road under the wheels of the following taxi, the grenade exploded. Through the open driver's door blew a sheet of flame and smoke and debris. The back window burst outwards and sprayed her with diamond chips of glass, and the detonation drove painfully into her eardrums.

A stunned silence followed the shock of the explosion, broken only by the tinkle of falling glass shards, and then immediately there was a hubbub of groans and screams. Royan sat up and clasped her injured arm to her chest. She had fallen heavily upon it and the stitches were agony.

The Renault was wrecked, but she saw that her leather sling bag had been blown out of the door and lay in the street close at hand. She pushed herself unsteadily to her feet and hobbled over to pick it up. All around her was confusion. A few of the passengers in the bus had been injured, and a piece of shrapnel or wreckage had wounded a little girl on the sidewalk. Her mother was screaming and mopping at the child's bloody face with her scarf. The girl struggled in her mother's grip, wailing pitifully.

Nobody was taking any notice of Royan, but she knew the police would arrive within minutes. They were geared up to respond swiftly to fundamentalist terror attacks. She knew that if they found her here she would be tied up in days of interrogation. She slung the bag over her shoulder and walked as swiftly as her bruised leg would allow her to the alleyway down which the Honda had disappeared.

At the end of the street was a public lavatory. She locked herself in one of the cubicles and leaned against the door with her eyes closed, trying to recover from the shock and to get her confused thoughts in order.

In the horror and desolation of Duraid's murder she had not until now considered her own safety. The realization of danger had been forced upon her in the most savage manner. She remembered the words of one of the assassins spoken in the darkness beside the oasis 'We always know where to find her later!'

The attempt on her life had failed only narrowly. She had to believe that there would be another.

'I can't go back to the flat,' she realized. 'The villa is gone, and anyway they would look for me there.'

Despite the unsavoury atmosphere she remained locked in the cubicle for over an hour while she thought out her next movements. At last she left the toilet and went to the row of stained and cracked washbasins. She splashed her face under the tap. Then in the mirror she combed her hair, touched up her make-up, and straightened and tidied her clothing as best she was able.

She walked a few blocks, doubling back on her tracks

and watching behind her to make sure she was not being followed, before she hailed a taxi in the street.

She made the driver drop her in the street behind her bank, and walked the rest of the way. It was only minutes before closing time when she was shown into the cubicle office of one of the sub-accountants. She withdrew what money was in her account, which amounted to less than five thousand Egyptian pounds. It was not a great sum, but she had a little more in her Lloyds Bank account in York, and then she had her Mastercard.

'You should have given us notice to withdraw an article from safe deposit,' the bank official told her severely. She apologized meekly and played the helpless little-girl-lost so convincingly that he relented. He handed over to her the package that contained her British passport and her Lloyds banking papers.

Duraid had numerous relatives and friends who would have been pleased to have her to stay with them, but she wanted to remain out of sight, away from her usual haunts. She chose one of the two-star tourist hotels away from the river where she hoped she could remain anonymous amongst the multitudes of the tour groups. At this type of hotel there was a high turnover of guests, for most of them stayed only for a few nights before moving on up to Luxor and Aswan to view the monuments.

As soon as she was alone in her single room she phoned British Airways reservations. There was a flight to Heathrow the following morning at ten o'clock. She booked a one-way economy seat and gave them the number of her Mastercard.

It was after six o'clock by then, but the time difference between Egypt and the UK meant that it would still be office hours there. She looked up the number in her notebook. Leeds University was where she had completed her studies. Her call was answered on the third ring.

'Archaeology Department. Professor Dixon's office,' said a prim English school-marm voice.

'Is that you, Miss Higgins?'

'Yes, it is. To whom am I speaking?'

'It's Royan. Royan Al Simma, who used to be Royan Said.'

'Royan! We haven't heard from you for an absolute age. How are you?'

They chatted for a short while, but Royan was aware of the cost of the call. 'Is the Prof in?' she cut it short.

Professor Percival Dixon was over seventy and should have retired years ago. 'Royan, is it really you? My favourite student.' She smiled. Even at his age he was still the randy old goat. All the pretty ones were his favourite students.

'This is an international call, Prof. I just want to know if the offer is still open.'

'My goodness, I thought you said that you couldn't fit us in, what?'

'Change of circumstances. I'll tell you about it when I see you, if I see you.'

'Of course, we'd love to have you come and talk to us. When can you manage to get away?'

'I'll be in England tomorrow.'

'My goodness, that's a bit sudden. Don't know if we can arrange it that quickly.'

'I will be staying with my mother near York. Put me back to Miss Higgins and I will give her the telephone number.' He was one of the most brilliant men she knew, but she didn't trust him to write down a telephone number correctly. 'I'll call you in a few days' time.'

She hung up and lay back on the bed. She was exhausted and her arm was still hurting, but she tried to lay her plans to cover all eventualities.

Two months ago Prof Dixon had invited her to lecture on the discovery and excavation of the tomb of Queen Lostris, and the discovery of the scrolls. It was that book, of course, and more especially the footnote at the end of it, that had alerted him. Its publication had caused a great deal of interest. They had received enquiries from Egyptologists, both amateur and professional, all around the world, some from as far afield as Tokyo and Nairobi, all of them questioning the authenticity of the novel and the factual basis behind it.

At the time she had opposed letting a writer of fiction have access to the transcriptions, especially as they had not been completed. She felt that the whole thing had reduced what should have been an important and serious academic subject to the level of popular entertainment, rather like what Spielberg had done to palaeontology with his park full of dinosaurs.

In the end her voice had been over-ruled. Even Duraid had sided against her. It had been the money, of course. The department was always short of funds to conduct its less spectacular work. When it came to some grandiose scheme like moving the entire Temple of Abu Simbel to a new site above the flood waters of the Aswan High Dam, then the nations of the world had poured in tens of millions of dollars. However, the day-to-day operational expenses of the department attracted no such support.

Their half share of the royalties from *River God*, for that was the book's title, had financed almost a year of research and exploration, but that was not enough to allay Royan's personal misgivings. The author had taken too many liberties with the facts contained in the scrolls, and had embroidered historical characters with personalities and foibles for which there was not the least evidence. In particular she felt he had portrayed Taita, the ancient scribe, as a braggart and a vainglorious poseur. She resented that.

In fairness she was forced to concede that the author's brief had been to make the facts as palatable and readable as possible to a wide lay public, and she reluctantly agreed that he had succeeded in doing so. However, all her scientific training revolted against such a popularization of something so unique and wonderful.

But she sighed and put these thoughts out of her head. The damage was done, and thinking about it only served to irritate her.

She turned her thoughts to more pressing problems. If she was to do the lecture that the Prof had invited her to deliver, then she would need her slides and these were still at her office in the museum. While she was still working out the best way to get hold of them without fetching them in person, exhaustion overtook her and she fell asleep, still fully clothed, on top of the bed.

In the end the solution to her problem was simplicity itself. She merely phoned the administration office and arranged for them to collect the box of slides from her office and send it out to the airport in a taxi with one of the secretaries.

When the secretary handed them over to her at the British Airways check-in desk, he told her, 'The police were at the museum when we opened this morning. They wanted to speak to you, Doctor.'

Obviously they had traced the registration of the wrecked Renault. She was pleased that she had her British passport. If she had tried to leave the country with her Egyptian papers she might have run into delays: the police would probably have placed a restriction order on all passport control points. As it was, she passed through the checkpoint with no difficulty and, once she was in the final departure lounge, she went to the news-stand and studied the array of newspapers.

All the local newspapers carried the story of the

bombing of her car, and most of them had resurrected the story of Duraid's murder and linked the two events. One of them hinted at fundamentalist religious involvement. *El Arab* had a front-page photograph of herself and Duraid, which had been taken the previous month at a reception for a group of visiting French tour operators.

It gave her a pang to see the photograph of her husband looking so handsome and distinguished, with herself on his arm smiling up at him. She purchased copies of all the papers and took them on board the British Airways flight.

During the flight she passed the time by writing down in her notebook everything she could remember from what Duraid had told her of the man that she was going to find. She headed the page: 'Sir Nicholas Quenton-Harper (Bart).' Duraid had told her that Nicholas's great-grandfather had been awarded the title of baronet for his work as a career officer in the British colonial service. For three generations the family had maintained the strongest of ties with Africa, and especially with the British colonies and spheres of influence in North Africa: Egypt and the Sudan, Uganda and Kenya.

According to Duraid, Sir Nicholas himself had served in Africa and the Gulf States with the British army. He was a fluent Arabic and Swahili speaker and a noted amateur archaeologist and zoologist. Like his father, grandfather and great-grandfather before him, he had made numerous expeditions to North Africa to collect specimens and to explore the more remote regions. He had written a number of articles for various scientific journals and had even lectured at the Royal Geographical Society.

When his elder brother died childless, Sir Nicholas had inherited the title and the family estate at Quenton Park. He had resigned from the army to run the estate, but more especially to supervise the family museum that had been started in 1885 by his great-grandfather, the first baronet. It housed one of the largest collections of African fauna in private hands, and its ancient Egyptian and Middle Eastern collection of artefacts was equally famous.

However, from Duraid's accounts she concluded that there must be a wild, and even lawless, streak in Sir Nicholas's nature. It was obvious that he was not afraid to take some extraordinary risks to add to the collection at Quenton Park.

Duraid had first met him a number of years previously, when Sir Nicholas had recruited him to act as an intelligence officer for an illicit expedition to 'liberate' a number of Punic bronze castings from Gadaffi's Libya. Sir Nicholas had sold some of these to defray the expenses of the expedition, but had kept the best of them for his private collection.

More recently there had been another expedition, this time involving an illegal crossing of the Iraqi border to bring out a pair of stone bas-relief friezes from under Saddam Hussein's nose. Duraid had told her that Sir Nicholas had sold one of the pair for a huge amount of money; he had mentioned the sum of five million US dollars. Duraid said that he had used the money for the running of the museum, but that the second frieze, the finest of the pair, was still in Sir Nicholas's possession.

Both these expeditions had taken place years before Royan had met Duraid, and she wondered idly at Duraid's readiness to commit himself to the Englishman in this way. Sir Nicholas must have had unique powers of persuasion, for if they had been apprehended in the act there was no doubt that it would have meant summary execution for both of them.

As Duraid had explained to her, on each occasion it was only Nicholas's resourcefulness and his network of friends and admirers across the Middle East and North Africa, which he had been able to call on for help, that had seen them through.

'He is a bit of a devil,' Duraid had shaken his head with evident nostalgia at the memory, 'but the man to have with you when things are tough. Those days were all very exciting, but when I look back on it now I shudder at the risks we took.'

She had often pondered on the risks that a true in-the-blood collector was prepared to take to slake his passion. The risk seemed to be out of proportion to the reward, when it came to adding to his accumulations; and then she smiled at her own pious sentiments. The venture that she hoped to lead Sir Nicholas into was not exactly without risk, and she supposed that a circumlocution of lawyers might debate the legality of it endlessly.

Still smiling, she fell asleep, for the strain of these last few days had taken their toll. The air hostess woke her with an admonition to fasten her seat-belt for the landing at Heathrow.

Royan phoned her mother from the airport. 'Hello, Mummy. It's me.'

'Yes, I know that. Where are you, love?' Her mother sounded as unflappable as ever.

'At Heathrow. I am coming up to stay with you for a while. Is that all right?'

'Lumley's B and B,' her mother chuckled. 'I'll go and make your bed. What train will you be coming up on?'

'I had a look at the timetable. There is one from King's Cross that will get me into York at seven this evening.'

'I'll meet you at the station. What happened? Did you and Duraid have a tiff? Old enough to be your father. I said it wouldn't work.'

Royan was silent for a moment. This was hardly the time for explanations. 'I'll tell you all about it when I see you this evening.'

Georgina Lumley, her mother, was waiting on the

platform in the gloom and cold of the November evening, bulky and solid in her old green Barbour coat with Magic, her cocker spaniel, sitting obediently at her feet. The two of them made an inseparable pair, even when they were not winning field trials cups. For Royan they painted a comforting and familiar picture of the English side of her lineage.

Georgina kissed Royan's cheek in a perfunctory manner. 'Never was one for all that sentimental fiddle-faddle,' she often said with satisfaction, and she took one of Royan's bags and led the way to the old mud-splattered Land Rover in the car park.

Magic sniffed Royan's hand and wagged his tail in recognition. Then in a dignified and condescending manner he allowed her to pat his head, but like his mistress he was no great sentimentalist either.

They drove in silence for a while and Georgina lit a cigarette. 'So what happened to Duraid, then?'

For a minute Royan could not reply, and then the floodgates within her burst and she let it all come pouring out. It was a twenty-minute drive north of York to the little village of Brandsbury, and Royan talked all the way. Her mother made only small sounds of encouragement and comfort, and when Royan wept as she related the details of Duraid's death and funeral, Georgina reached across and patted her daughter's hand.

It was all over by the time they reached her mother's cottage in the village. Royan had cried it out and was dry-eyed and rational again as they ate the dinner that her mother had prepared and left in the oven for them. Royan could not remember when last she had tasted steak and kidney pie.

'So what are you going to do now?' Georgina asked as she poured what remained in the black bottle of Guinness into her own glass.

'To tell the truth, I don't know.' As she said it, Royan

wondered ruefully why so many people used that particular phrase to introduce a lie. 'I have six months' leave from the museum, and Prof Dixon has arranged for me to give a lecture at the university. That is as far as it goes for the moment.'

'Well,' said Georgina as she stood up, 'there is a hot-water bottle in your bed and your room is there for as long as you wish to stay.' From her that was as good as a passionate declaration of maternal love.

Over the next few days Royan arranged her slides and notes for the lectures, and each afternoon she accompanied Georgina and Magic on their long walks over the surrounding countryside.

'Do you know Quenton Park?' she asked her mother during one of these rambles.

'Rather,' Georgina replied enthusiastically. 'Magic and I pick up there four or five times a season. First-class shoot. Some of the best pheasant and woodcock in Yorkshire. One drive there called the High Larches which is notorious. Birds so high they baffle the best shots in England.'

'Do you know the owner, Sir Nicholas Quenton-Harper?' Royan asked.

'Seen him at the shoots. Don't know him. Good shot, though,' Georgina replied. 'Knew his papa in the old days before I married your father.' She smiled in a suggestive way that startled Royan. 'Good dancer. We danced a few jigs together, not only on the dance floor.'

'Mummy, you are outrageous!' Royan laughed.

'Used to be,' Georgina agreed readily. 'Don't get many opportunities these days.'

'When are you and Magic going to Quenton Park again?'

'Two weeks' time.'

'May I come with you?'

'Of course – the keeper is always looking for beaters.

43

Twenty quid and lunch with a bottle of beer for the day.'
She stopped and looked at her daughter quizzically. 'What
is all this about, then?'

'I hear there is a private museum on the estate. They
have a world-renowned Egyptian collection. I wanted to
get a look at it.'

'Not open to the public any more. Invitation only. Sir
Nicholas is an odd chap, secretive and all that.'

'Couldn't you get an invitation for me?' Royan asked,
but Georgina shook her head.

'Why don't you ask Prof Dixon? He is often one of the
guns at Quenton Park. Great chum of Quenton-Harper.'

 t was ten days before Prof Dixon was ready for
her. She borrowed her mother's Land Rover and
drove to Leeds. The Prof folded her in a bear hug
and then took her through to his office for tea.

It was nostalgic of her days as a student to be back in
the cluttered room filled with books and papers and ancient
artefacts. Royan told him about Duraid's murder, and
Dixon was shocked and distressed, but she quickly changed
the subject to the slides that she had prepared for the
lecture. He was fascinated by everything she had to show
him.

It was almost time for her to leave before she had an
opportunity to broach the subject of the Quenton Park
museum, but he responded immediately.

'I am amazed that you never visited it while you were
a student here. It's a very impressive collection. The family
has been at it for over a hundred years. As a matter of fact,
I am shooting on the estate next Thursday. I'll have a word
with Nicholas. However, the poor chap isn't up to much at
the moment. Last year he suffered a terrible personal
tragedy. Lost his wife and two little girls in a motor accident
on the M1.' He shook his head. 'Awful business. Nicholas

was driving. I think he blames himself.' He walked her out to the Land Rover.

'So we will see you on the twenty-third,' he told Royan as they parted. 'I expect that you will have an audience of at least a hundred, and I have even had a reporter from the *Yorkshire Post* on to me. They have heard about your lectures and they want to do an interview with you. Jolly good publicity for the department. You'll do it, of course. Could you come a couple of hours early to speak to them?'

'Actually I will probably see you before the twenty-third,' she told him. 'Mummy and her dog are picking up at Quenton Park on Thursday, and she has got me a job as a beater for the day.'

'I'll keep an eye open for you,' he promised, and waved to her as she pulled away in a cloud of exhaust smoke.

The wind was searing cold out of the north. The clouds tumbled over each other, heavy and blue and grey, so close to earth that they brushed the crests of the hills as they hurried ahead of the gale.

Royan wore three layers of clothing under the old green Barbour jacket that Georgina had lent her, but still she shivered as they came up over the brow of the hills in the line of beaters. Her blood had thinned in the heat of the Nile valley. Two pairs of fisherman's socks were not enough to save her toes from turning numb.

For this drive, the last of the day, the head keeper had moved Georgina from her usual position behind the line of guns, where she and Magic were expected to pick up the crippled birds that came through to them, into the line of beaters.

Keeping the best for last, they were beating the High Larches. The keeper needed every man and woman he could get into the line to bring in the pheasant from the huge piece of ground on top of the hills and to push them off the brow, out over the valley where the guns waited at their pegs far below.

It seemed to Royan a supreme piece of illogical behaviour to rear and nurture the pheasants from chicks, and then, when they were mature, go to such lengths to make them as difficult to shoot as the keeper could devise. However, Georgina had explained to her that the higher and harder to hit the birds passed over the guns, the more pleased the sportsmen were, and the more they were willing to pay for the privilege of firing at them.

'You cannot believe what they will pay for a day's shooting,' Georgina had told her. 'Today will bring in almost £14,000 to the estate. They will shoot twenty days this season. Work that out and you will see that the shoot is a major part of the estate's income. Quite apart from the fun of working the dogs and beating, it gives a lot of us local people a very useful bit of extra money.'

At this stage of the day, Royan was not too certain just how much fun there was to be had from the job of beating. The walking was difficult in the thick brambles, and Royan had slipped more than once. There was mud on her knees and elbows. The ditch ahead of her was half-filled with water and there was a thin skin of ice across the surface. She approached it gingerly, using her walking-stick to balance herself. She was tired, for there had already been five drives, all as onerous as this one. She glanced across at her mother and marvelled at how she seemed to be enjoying this torture. Georgina strode along happily, controlling Magic with her whistle and hand signals.

She grinned at Royan now, 'Last lap, love. Nearly over.'

Royan was humiliated that her distress had been so obvious, and she used her stick to help her vault the muddy ditch. However, she miscalculated the width and fell short

46

of the far bank. She landed knee-deep in the frozen water and it poured in over the top of her wellington boots.

Georgina laughed at her and offered her the end of her own stick to pull her out of the glutinous mud. Royan could not hold up the line by stopping to empty her flooded boots, so she went on, squelching loudly with each pace.

'Steady on the left!' the order from the head keeper was relayed over the walkie-talkie radio, and the line halted obediently.

The art and skill of the keeper was to flush the birds from the tangled undergrowth, not in one massed covey, but in a steady trickle that would pass over the waiting guns in singles and pairs, giving them the chance, after they had fired two barrels, to take their second gun from the loader and be ready for the next bird to appear in the sky high above them. The size of the keeper's tip and his reputation depended on the way he 'showed' the birds to the waiting guns.

During this respite Royan was able to regain her breath, and to look around her. Through a break in the grove of larches that gave the drive its name, she could see down into the valley.

There was an open meadow at the foot of the hills, the expanse of smooth green grass broken up by patches of dirty grey snow from the previous week's fall. Down this meadow the keeper had set a line of numbered pegs. At the beginning of the day's sport the guns had drawn lots to decide the peg number from which each of them would shoot.

Now each man stood at his allotted peg, with his loader holding his second gun ready behind him, ready to pass it over when the first gun was empty. They were all looking up expectantly to the high ground from which the pheasant would appear.

'Which is Sir Nicholas?' Royan called to her mother, and Georgina pointed to the far end of the line of guns.

'The tall one,' she said, and at that moment the keeper's voice on the radio ordered, 'Gently on the left. Start tapping again.' Obediently the beaters tapped their sticks. There was no shouting or hallooing in this delicate and strictly controlled operation.

'Forward slowly. Halt to the flush of birds.'

A step at a time the line moved ahead, and in the brambles and bracken in front of her Royan could hear the stealthy scuffle of a number of pheasants moving forward, reluctant to take to the air until they were forced to do so.

There was another ditch in their path, this one choked with an almost impenetrable thicket of brambles. Some of the larger dogs, like the Labradors, balked at entering such a thorny barrier. Georgina whistled sharply and Magic's ears went up. He was soaked and his coat was a matted mess of mud and burrs and thorns. His pink tongue lolled from the corner of his grinning mouth and the sodden stump of his tail was wagging merrily. At that moment he was the happiest dog in England. He was doing the work that he had been bred for.

'Come on, Magic,' Georgina ordered. 'Get in there. Get them out.'

Magic dived into the thickest and thorniest patch, and disappeared completely from view. There was a minute of snuffling and rooting around in the depths of the ditch, and then a fierce cackle and flurry of wings.

A pair of birds exploded out of the bushes. The hen led the way. She was a drab, nondescript creature the size of a domestic fowl, but the cock bird that followed her closely was magnificent. His head was capped with iridescent green and his cheeks and wattles were scarlet. His tail, barred in cinnamon and black, was almost as long again as his body and the rest of his plumage was a riot of gorgeous colour.

As he climbed he sparkled against the lowering grey

sky like a priceless jewel thrown from an emperor's hand. Royan gasped with the beauty of the sight.

'Just look at them go!' Georgina's voice was thick with excitement. 'What a pair of crackerjacks. The best pair today. My bet is that not one of the guns will touch a feather on either of them.'

Up, and then on up, the two birds climbed, the hen drawing the cock after her, until suddenly the wind boiling over the hills like overheated milk caught them both and flung them away, out over the valley.

The line of beaters enjoyed the moment. They had worked hard for it. Their voices were tiny and faint on the wind as they urged the birds on. They loved to see a pheasant so high and fast that it could beat the guns.

'Forward!' they exulted. 'Over!' and this time the line came involuntarily to a halt as they followed the flight of the pair that were twisting away on the wind.

In the valley bottom the faces of the guns were turned upwards, pale specks against the green background. Their trepidation was almost palpable as they watched the pheasant reach their maximum speed, so that they could no longer beat their wings, but locked them into a back-swept profile as they began to drop down into the valley.

This was the most difficult shot that any gun would face. A high pair of pheasant with a half gale quartering from behind, dropping into the shot at their terminal rate of flight, set to pass over the line at the extreme effective range of a twelve-bore shotgun. For the men below it was a calculation of speed and lead in all three dimensions of space. The best of shots might hope to take one of them, but who would dare to think of both?

'A pound on it!' Georgina called. 'A pound that they both get through.' But none of the beaters who heard her accepted the wager.

The wind was pushing the birds gently sideways. They

49

started off aimed at the centre of the line, but they were drifting towards the far end. As the angle changed, Royan could see the men at the pegs below her brace themselves in turn as the birds appeared to be heading straight for them, and then relax as the wind moved them on. Their relief was evident as, one after the other, each of them was absolved from the challenge of having to make such an impossible shot with all eyes fastened upon him.

In the end only the tall figure at the extreme end of the line stood in their flight path.

'Your bird, sir,' one of the other guns called mockingly, and Royan found that instinctively she was holding her breath with anticipation.

Nicholas Quenton-Harper seemed unaware of the approach of the pair of pheasant. He stood completely relaxed, his tall frame slouching slightly, his shotgun tucked under his right arm with the muzzles pointing at the ground.

At the moment that the leading hen bird reached a point in the sky sixty degrees out ahead of him he moved for the first time. With casual grace he swung the shotgun up in a sweeping arc. At the instant that the butt touched his cheek and shoulder he fired, but the gun never stopped moving and went on to describe the rest of the arc.

The distance delayed the sound of the shot reaching Royan. She saw the barrels kick with the recoil, and a pale spurt of blue smoke from the muzzle. Then Nicholas lowered the gun as the hen suddenly threw back her head and closed her wings. There was no burst of feathers from her body, for she had been hit cleanly in the head and killed instantly. As she began the long plummet to earth Royan heard the thud of the shot.

By then the cock was high over Nicholas's head. This time as he mounted the gun in that casual sweeping gesture he arched his back to point upwards, his long frame bending from the waist like a drawn bow. Once again at the apex of the swing the weapon kicked in his grasp.

'He has missed!' Royan thought with a mixture of satisfaction and disappointment, as the cock sailed on seemingly unscathed. Part of her wanted the beautiful bird to escape, while part of her wanted the man to succeed. Gradually the profile of the high cock altered as the wings folded back and it rolled over in flight. Royan had no way of knowing that his heart had been struck through, until seconds later he died in mid-air and the locked wings lost their rigid set.

As the cock tumbled to earth, a spontaneous chorus of cheers ran down the line of beaters, faint but enthusiastic on the icy north wind. Even the other guns added their voices with cries of, 'Oh, good shot, sir!'

Royan did not join in the cheering, but for the moment her fatigue and cold were forgotten. She could only vaguely appreciate the skill that those two shots had called for, but she was impressed, even a little awed. Her very first glimpse of the man had fulfilled all the expectations that Duraid's stories about him had raised in her.

By the time the last drive ended it was almost dark. An old army truck came rumbling down the track through the forest along which the tired beaters and their dogs waited. As it slowed they scrambled up into the back. Georgina gave Royan a boost from behind before she and Magic followed her up. They settled thankfully on one of the long hard benches, and Georgina lit a cigarette as she joined in the chat and banter of the under-keepers and beaters around her.

Royan sat silently at the end of the bench, enjoying the sense of achievement at having come through such a strenuous day. She felt tired and relaxed, and strangely contented. For one whole day she had not thought either of the theft of the scroll or of Duraid's murder and the unknown and unseen enemy who threatened her with a violent death.

The truck ground down the hill and slowed as it reached the bottom, pulling in to the verge to let a green Range Rover pass. As the two vehicles drew level, Royan turned her head and looked down into the open driver's window of the expensive estate car, and into the eyes of Nicholas Quenton-Harper at the wheel.

This was the first time she had been close enough to him to see his features. She was surprised at how young he was. She had expected him to be a man of Duraid's age. She saw now that he was no older than forty, for there were only the first strands of silver in the wings of his thick, rumpled hair. His features were tanned and weatherbeaten, those of an outdoors man. His eyes were green and penetrating under dark, beetling brows. His mouth was wide and expressive, and he was smiling now at some witticism that the driver of the truck called to him in a thick Yorkshire accent, but there was a sense of sadness and tragedy in the eyes. Royan remembered what the Prof had told her of his recent bereavement, and she felt her heart go out to him. She was not alone in her loss and her mourning.

He looked directly into her eyes and she saw his expression change. She was an attractive woman, and she could tell when a man recognized that. She had made an impression on him, but she did not enjoy the fact. Her sorrow for Duraid was still too raw and painful. She looked away and the Range Rover drove on.

Her lecture at the university went off extremely well. Royan was a good speaker and she knew her subject intimately. She held them fascinated with her account of the opening of the tomb of Queen Lostris and of the subsequent discovery

52

of the scrolls. Many of her audience had read the book, and during question time they pestered her to know how much of it was the truth. She had to tread very carefully here, so as not to deal too harshly with the author.

Afterwards Prof Dixon took Royan and Georgina to dinner. He was delighted with her success, and ordered the most expensive bottle of claret on the wine list to celebrate. He was only mildly disconcerted when she refused a glass of it.

'Oh, dear me, I forgot that you were a Moslem,' he apologized.

'A Copt,' she corrected him, 'and it's not on religious grounds. I just don't like the taste.'

'Don't worry,' Georgina counselled him, 'I don't have the same odd compulsion to masochism as my daughter. She must get it from her father's side. I'll give you a hand to finish the good stuff.'

Under the benign influence of the claret the Prof became expansive, and entertained them with the accounts of the archaeological digs he had been on over the decades. It was only over the coffee that he turned to Royan.

'Goodness me, I almost forgot to tell you. I have arranged for you to visit the museum at Quenton Park any afternoon this week. Just ring Mrs Street the day before, and she will be waiting to let you in. She is Nicholas's PA.'

Royan remembered the way to Quenton Park from when Georgina had driven them to the shoot, but now she was alone in the Land Rover. The massive main gates to the estate were made of ornate cast iron. A little further on, the road divided and a cluster of road signs pointed the way to the various destinations: 'Quenton Hall. Private', 'Estate Office' and 'Museum'.

The road to the museum curved through the deer park

where herds of fallow deer grazed under the winter-bare oaks. Through the misty landscape she had glimpses of the big house. According to the guidebook that the Prof had given her, Sir Christopher Wren had designed the house in 1693, and the master landscapist, Capability Brown, had created the gardens sixty years later. The results were perfection.

The museum was set in a grove of copper beech trees half a mile beyond the house. It was a sprawling building that had obviously been added to more than once over the years. Mrs Street was waiting for her at the side door, and introduced herself as she let Royan in. She was middle-aged, grey-haired and self-assured. 'I was at your lecture on Monday evening. Fascinating! I have a guidebook for you, but you will find the exhibits well catalogued and described. I have spent almost twenty years at the job. There are no other visitors today. You will have the place to yourself. You must just wander around and please yourself. I shall not leave until five this evening, so you have all afternoon. If I can help you in any way my office is at the end of the passage. Please don't hesitate.'

From the first moment that Royan walked into the display of African mammals she was enthralled. The primate room housed a complete collection of every single species of ape and monkey from that continent: from the great silver-backed male gorilla to the delicate colobus in his long flowing mantle of black and white fur, they were all represented.

Although some of the exhibits were over a hundred years old, they were beautifully preserved and presented, set in painted dioramas of their natural habitat. It was obvious that the museum must employ a staff of skilled artists and taxidermists. She could guess what this must have cost. Wryly she decided that the five million dollars from the sale of the plundered frieze had been well spent.

She went through to the antelope room and stared

around her in wonder at the magnificent beasts preserved here. She stopped before a diorama of a family group of the giant sable antelope of the now extinct Angolan variety, *Hippotragus niger variani*. While she admired the jet black and snowy-chested bull with his long, back-swept horns, she mourned his death at the hand of one of the Quenton-Harper family. Then she checked herself. Without the strange dedication and passion of the hunter-collector who had killed him, future generations might never have been able to look upon this regal presence.

She passed on into the next hall which was given over to displays of the African elephant, and paused in the centre of the room before a pair of ivory tusks so large that she could not believe they had ever been carried by a living animal. They seemed more like the marble columns of some Hellenic temple to Diana, the goddess of the chase. She stooped to read the printed catalogue card:

> *Tusks of the African Elephant,* Loxodonta africana.
> *Shot in the Lado Enclave in 1899 by Sir Jonathan Quenton-Harper. Left tusk 289 lb. Right tusk 301 lb. Length of larger tusk 11' 4". Girth 32". The largest pair of tusks ever taken by a European hunter.*

They stood twice as high as she was tall, and they were half as thick again as her waist. As she passed on into the Egyptian room she marvelled at the size and strength of the creature that had carried them.

She came up short as her eyes fell upon the figure in the centre of the room. It was a fifteen-foot-high figure of Ramesses II, depicted as the god Osiris in polished red granite. The god-emperor strode out on muscular legs, wearing only sandals on his feet and a short kilt. In his left hand he carried the remains of a war-bow, with both the upper and lower limbs of the weapon broken off. This was the only damage that the statue had suffered in all those

thousands of years. The rest of it was perfect – the plinth
even bore the marks of the mason's chisel. In his right fist
Pharaoh carried a seal embossed with his royal cartouche.
Upon his majestic head he wore the tall double crown of
the upper and lower kingdoms. His expression was calm
and enigmatic.

Royan recognized the statue instantly, for its twin
stood in the grand hall of the Cairo museum. She passed it
every day on her way to her office.

She felt anger rising in her. This was one of the major
treasures of her very Egypt. It had been plundered and
stolen from one of her country's sacred sites. It did not
belong here. It belonged on the banks of the great river
Nile. She felt herself shaking with the strength of her
emotion as she went forward to examine the statue more
closely and to read the hieroglyphic inscription on the
base.

The royal cartouche stood out in the centre of the
arrogant warning: '*I am the divine Ramesses, master of ten
thousand chariots. Fear me, O ye enemies of Egypt.*'

Royan had not read the translation aloud; it was a soft,
deep voice close behind her that spoke, startling her. She
had not heard anyone approaching. She spun round to find
him standing close enough to touch.

His hands were thrust into the pockets of a shapeless
blue cardigan. There was a hole in one elbow. He wore
faded denim jeans over well-worn but monogrammed
velvet carpet slippers – the type of genteel shabbiness that
certain Englishmen often cultivate, for it would never do
to seem too concerned with one's appearance.

'Sorry. Didn't mean to startle you.' He smiled a lazy
smile of apology, and his teeth were very white but slightly
crooked. Suddenly his expression changed as he recognized
her.

'Oh, it's you.' She should have been flattered that he
remembered her from so fleeting a contact, but there was

that flash of something in his eyes again that offended her. Nevertheless, she could not refuse the hand he offered her. 'Nick Quenton-Harper,' he introduced himself. 'You must be Percival Dixon's old student. I think I saw you at the shoot last Thursday. Weren't you beating for us?'

His manner was friendly and forthright, so she felt her hackles subsiding as she responded, 'Yes. I am Royan Al Simma. I think you knew my husband, Duraid Al Simma.'

'Duraid! Of course, I know him. Grand old fellow. We spent a lot of time in the desert together. One of the very best. How is he?'

'He's dead.' She had not meant it to sound so bald and heartless, but then there was no other reply she could think of.

'I am so terribly sorry. I didn't know. When and how did it happen?'

'Very recently, three weeks ago. He was murdered.'

'Oh, my God.' She saw the sympathy in his eyes, and she remembered that he also had suffered. 'I telephoned him in Cairo not more than four months ago. He was his old charming self. Have they found the person who did it?'

She shook her head and looked around the hall to avoid having to face him and let him see that her eyes were wet. 'You have an extraordinary collection here.'

He accepted the change of subject at once. 'Thanks mostly to my grandfather. He was on the staff of Evelyn Baring – Over Bearing, as his numerous enemies called him. He was the British man in Cairo during—'

She cut him short. 'Yes, I have heard of Evelyn Baring, the first Earl of Cromer, British Consul-General of Egypt from 1883 to 1907. With his plenipotentiary powers he was the unchallenged dictator of my country for all that period. Numerous enemies, as you say.'

Nicholas's eyes narrowed slightly. 'Percival warned me you were one of his best students. He didn't, however, warn me of your strong nationalistic feelings. It is clear that you didn't need me to translate the Ramesses inscription for you.'

'My own father was on the staff of Gamal Abdel Nasser,' she murmured. Nasser was the man who had toppled the puppet King Farouk and finally broken the British power in Egypt. As president he had nationalized the Suez Canal in the face of British outrage.

'Ha!' he chuckled. 'Different sides of the track. But things have changed. I hope we don't have to be enemies?'

'Not at all,' she agreed. 'Duraid held you in the highest esteem.'

'As I did him.' He changed the subject again. 'We are very proud of our collection of royal *ushabti*. Examples from the tomb of every pharaoh from the old Kingdom onwards, right up to the last of the Ptolemys. Please let me show it to you.' She followed him to the huge display case that occupied one complete wall of the hall. It was lined with shelf after shelf of the doll-like figures which had been placed in the tombs to act as servants and slaves for the dead kings in the shadow world.

With his own key Nicholas opened the glazed doors of the case and reached up to bring down the most interesting of the exhibits. 'This is the *ushabti* of Maya who served under three pharaohs, Tutankhamen, Ay and Horemheb. It is from the tomb of Ay who died in 1343 BC.'

He handed the doll to her and she read aloud the three thousand-year-old hieroglyphics as easily as though they had been the headlines of that morning's newspaper. 'I am Maya, Treasurer of the two Kingdoms. I will answer for the divine Pharaoh Ay. May he live for ever!' She spoke in Arabic to test him, and his reply in the same language was fluent and colloquial.

'It seems that Percival Dixon told me the truth. You must have been an exceptional student.'

Engrossed now in their common interest, speaking alternately Arabic and English, the initial sharp prickles of antagonism between them were dulled. They moved slowly round the hall, lingering before each display case to handle and examine minutely each object that it contained.

It was as though they were transported back over the millennia. Hours and days seemed of no consequence in the face of such antiquity, and so it startled both of them when Mrs Street returned to interrupt them, 'I am off now, Sir Nicholas. Can I leave it to you to lock up and set the alarm? The security guards are on duty already.'

'What time is it?' Nicholas answered his own question by glancing at the stainless steel Rolex Submariner on his wrist. 'Five-forty already, what on earth happened to the day?' He sighed theatrically. 'Off you go, Mrs Street. Sorry we kept you so long.'

'Don't forget to set the alarm,' she warned him, and then to Royan, 'He can be so absent-minded when he is off on one of his hobby-horses.' Her fondness towards her employer was obviously that of an indulgent aunt.

'You've given me enough orders for one day. Off you go,' Nicholas grinned, as he turned back to Royan. 'Can't let you go without showing you something that Duraid was in on with me. Can you stay for a few minutes longer?' She nodded and he reached out as if to take her arm, and then dropped his hand. In the Arab world it is insulting to touch a woman, even in such a casual manner. She was aware of the courtesy, and she warmed to his good manners and easy style a little more.

He led her out of the exhibition halls through a door marked 'Private. Staff Only', and down a long corridor to the room at the end.

'The inner sanctum.' He ushered her in. 'Excuse the mess. I must really get around to tidying up in here one of these years. My wife used to—' He broke off abruptly, and he glanced at the silver-framed photograph of a family group on his desk. Nicholas and a beautiful dark-haired woman sat on a picnic rug under the spreading branches of an oak. There were two little girls with them and the family resemblance to the mother was strong in both of them. The youngest child sat on Nicholas's lap while the elder girl stood behind them, holding the reins of her Shetland pony. Royan glanced sideways at him and saw the devastating sorrow in his eyes.

So as not to embarrass him she looked around the rest of the room, which was obviously his study and workshop. It was spacious and comfortable, a man's room, but it illustrated the contradictions of his character – the bookish scholar set against the man of action. Amongst the muddle of books and museum specimens lay fishing reels and a Hardy split cane salmon rod. On a row of wall hooks hung a Barbour jacket, a canvas shotgun slip and a leather cartridge bag embossed with the initials N.Q.-H.

She recognized some of the framed pictures on the walls. They were original nineteenth-century watercolours by the Scottish traveller David Roberts, and others by Vivant Denon who had accompanied Napoleon's *L'armée de l'Orient* to Egypt. They were fascinating views of the monuments drawn before the excavations and restorations of more modern times.

Nicholas went to the fireplace and threw a log on the fading coals. He kicked it until it flared up brightly and then beckoned her to stand in front of the floor-to-ceiling curtains that covered half of one wall. With a conjuror's flourish he pulled the tasselled cord that opened the curtains and exclaimed with satisfaction, 'What do you make of that, then?'

She studied the magnificent bas-relief frieze that was mounted on the wall. The detail was beautiful and the rendition magnificent, but she did not let her admiration show. Instead she gave her opinion in offhand tones.

'Sixth King of the Amorite dynasty, Hammurabi, about 1780 BC,' she said, pretending to study the finely chiselled features of the ancient monarch before she went on, 'Yes, probably from his palace site south-west of the ziggurat at Ashur. There should have been a pair of these friezes. They are worth in the region of five million US dollars each. My guess is that they were stolen from the saintly ruler of modern Mesopotamia, Saddam Hussein, by two unprincipled rogues. I hear that the other one of the pair is at present in the collection of a certain Mr Peter Walsh in Texas.'

He stared at her in astonishment, and then burst out laughing. 'Damn it! I swore Duraid to secrecy but he must have told you about our naughty little escapade.' It was the first time she had heard him laugh. It seemed to come naturally to his lips and she liked the sound of it, hearty and unaffected.

'You are right about the present owner of the second frieze,' he told her, still laughing. 'But the price was six million, not five.'

'Duraid also told me about your visit to the Tibesti Massif in Chad and southern Libya,' she remarked, and he shook his head in mock contrition.

'It seems I have no secrets from you.' He went to a tall *armoire* against the opposite wall. It was a magnificent piece of marquetry furniture, probably seventeenth-century French. He opened the double doors and said, 'This is what Duraid and I brought back from Libya, without the consent of Colonel Muammar al Gadaffi.' He took down one of the exquisite little bronzes and handed it to her. It was the figure of a mother nursing her infant, and it had a green patina of age.

'Hannibal, son of Hamilcar Barca,' he said, 'about 203 BC. These were found by a band of Tuareg at one of his old camps on the Bagradas river in North Africa. Hannibal must have cached them there before his defeat by the Roman general Scipio. There were over two hundred bronzes in the hoard, and I still have fifty of the best of them.'

'You sold the rest of them?' she asked, as she admired the statuette. There was disapproval in her tone as she went on, 'How could you bear to part with something so beautiful?'

He sighed unhappily, 'Had to, I am afraid. Very sad, but the expedition to retrieve them cost me a fortune. Had to cover expenses by selling some of the booty.'

He went to his desk and brought out a bottle of Laphroaig malt whisky from the bottom drawer. He placed the bottle on the desk top and set two glasses beside it. 'Can I tempt you?' he asked, but she shook her head.

'Don't blame you. Even the Scots themselves admit that this brew should only be drunk in sub-zero weather on The Hill, in a forty-knot gale, after stalking and shooting a ten-point stag. May I offer you something a little more ladylike?'

'Do you have a Coke?' she suggested.

'Yes, but that is really bad for you, even worse than Laphroaig. It's all that sugar. Absolute poison.'

She took the glass he brought to her and returned his toast with it.

'To life!' she agreed, and then she went on, 'You are right. Duraid did tell me about these.' She replaced the Punic bronze in the *armoire*, then came to face him at the desk. 'It was also Duraid who sent me to see you. It was his dying instruction to me.'

'Aha! So none of this is coincidence then. It seems I am the unwitting pawn in some deep and nefarious plot.' He pointed to the chair facing his desk. 'Sit!' he ordered. 'Tell!'

He perched above her on the corner of the desk, with the whisky glass in his right hand and with one long, denim-clad leg swinging lazily as the tail of a resting leopard. Though he was smiling quizzically, he watched her face with a penetrating green gaze. She thought that it would be difficult to lie to this man.

She took a deep breath, 'Have you heard of an ancient Egyptian queen called Lostris, of the second intermediate period, co-existent with the first Hyksos invasions?'

He laughed a little derisively and stood up, 'Oh! Now we are talking about the book *River God*, are we?' He went to the bookcase and brought down a copy. Although well thumbed, it was still in its dust-jacket, and the cover illustration was a dreamy surrealistic view in pastel shades of green and rose purple of the pyramids seen over water. He dropped it on the desk in front of her.

'Have you read it?' she asked.

'Yes,' he nodded. 'I read most of Wilbur Smith's stuff. He amuses me. He has shot here at Quenton Park a couple of times.'

'You like lots of sex and violence in your reading, obviously?' She pulled a face. 'What did you think of this particular book?'

'I must admit that he had me fooled. Whilst I was reading it, I sort of wished that it might be based on fact. That was why I phoned Duraid.' Nicholas picked up the book again and flipped to the end of it. 'The author's note was convincing, but what I couldn't get out of my mind was the last sentence.' He read it aloud. '"*Somewhere in the Abyssinian mountains near the source of the Blue Nile, the mummy of Tenus still lies in the unviolated tomb of Pharaoh Mamose.*"'

Almost angrily Nicholas threw the book down on the desk. 'My God! You will never know how much I wanted it to be true. You will never know how much I wanted a shot at Pharaoh Mamose's tomb. I had to speak to Duraid. When he assured me it was all a load of bunkum, I felt cheated. I had built up my expectations so high that I was bitterly disappointed.'

'It's not bunkum,' she contradicted him, and then corrected herself quickly, 'well, at least not all of it.'

'I see. Duraid was lying to me, was he?'

'Not lying,' she defended him hotly. 'Just delaying the truth a little. He wasn't ready to tell you the whole story then. He didn't have the answers to all the questions that he knew you would ask. He was going to come to you when he was ready. Your name was at the top of the list of potential sponsors that he had drawn up.'

'Duraid did not have the answers, but I suppose you do?' He was smiling sceptically. 'I was caught once. I am not likely to fall for the same cock and bull a second time.'

'The scrolls exist. Nine of them are still in the vaults at the Cairo museum. I was the one who discovered them in the tomb of Queen Lostris.' Royan opened her leather sling bag and rummaged around in it until she brought out a thin sheaf of glossy 6 × 4 colour photographs. She selected one and passed it to him. 'That is a shot of the rear wall of the tomb. You can just make out the alabaster jars in the niche. That was taken before we removed them.'

'Nice picture, but it could have been taken anywhere.'

She ignored the remark and passed him another photograph. 'The ten scrolls in Duraid's workroom at the museum. You recognize the two men standing behind the bench?'

He nodded. 'Duraid and Wilbur Smith.' His sceptical expression had turned to one of doubt and bemusement. 'What the hell are you trying to tell me?'

'What the *hell* I am trying to tell you is that, apart from a wide poetic licence that the author took unto himself, all that he wrote in the book has at least some foundation in the truth. However, the scroll that most concerns us is the seventh, the one that was stolen by the men who murdered my husband.'

Nicholas stood up and went to the fireplace. He threw on another log and bashed it viciously with the poker, as if to give release to his emotions. He spoke without turning around, 'What was the significance of that particular scroll as opposed to the other nine?'

'It was the one that contained the account of Pharaoh Mamose's burial and, we believe, directions that might enable us to find the site of the tomb.'

'You believe, but you aren't certain?' He swung around to face her with the poker gripped like a weapon. In this mood he was frightening. His mouth was set in a tight hard line and his eyes glittered.

'Large parts of the seventh scroll are written in some sort of code, a series of cryptic verses. Duraid and I were in the process of deciphering these when—' she broke off and drew a long breath, 'when he was murdered.'

'You must have a copy of something so valuable?' He glared at her, so that she felt intimidated. She shook her head.

'All the microfilm, all our notes, all of it was stolen along with the original scroll. Then whoever killed Duraid went back to our flat in Cairo and destroyed my PC on to which I had transposed all our research.'

He threw the poker into the coal scuttle with a clatter, and came back to the desk. 'So you have no evidence at all? Nothing to prove that any of this is true?'

'Nothing,' she agreed, 'except what I have here.' With a long slim forefinger she tapped her forehead. 'I have a good memory.'

He frowned and ran his fingers through his thick curling hair. 'And so why did you come to me?'

'I have come to give you a shot at the tomb of Pharaoh Mamose,' she told him simply. 'Do you want it?'

Suddenly his mood changed. He grinned like a naughty schoolboy. 'At this moment I cannot think of anything I want more.'

'Then you and I will have to draw up some sort of working agreement,' she told him, and she leaned forward in a businesslike manner. 'First, let me tell you what I want, and then you can do the same.'

It was hard bargaining, and it was one in the morning

when Royan admitted her exhaustion. 'I can't think straight any more. Can we start again tomorrow morning?' They still had not reached an agreement.

'It's tomorrow morning already,' he told her. 'But you are right. Thoughtless of me. You can sleep here. After all, we do have twenty-seven bedrooms here.'

'No, thanks.' She stood up. 'I'll go on home.'

'The road will be icy,' he warned her. Then he saw her determined expression and held up his hands in capitulation. 'All right, I won't insist. What time tomorrow? I have a meeting with my lawyers at ten, but we should be finished by noon. Why don't you and I have a working lunch here? I was supposed to be shooting at Ganton in the afternoon, but I will cancel that. That way I will have the afternoon and evening clear for you.'

Nicholas's meeting with the lawyers took place the next morning in the library of Quenton Park. It was not an easy nor a pleasant session, but then he never expected it to be. This had been the year in which his world began to fall to pieces around his head. He gritted his teeth as he remembered how the year had opened with that fatal moment of fatigue and inattention at midnight on the icy motorway, and the blinding headlights of the truck bearing down on them.

He had not recovered from that before the next brutal blow had fallen. This was the financial report of the Lloyd's insurance syndicate on which Nicholas, like his father and grandfather before him, was a 'Name'. For half a century the family had enjoyed a regular and substantial income from their share of the syndicate profits. Of course, Nicholas had been aware that liability for his share of any losses that the syndicate suffered was unlimited. The enormity of that responsibility had weighed lightly; for there had never been serious losses to account for, not for fifty years, not until this year.

With the California earthquake and environmental pollution claims awarded against one of the multinational chemical companies, the syndicate's losses had amounted to over twenty-six million pounds sterling. Nicholas's share of that loss was two and a half million pounds – some of which had been settled, but the rest was due for payment in a little over eight months' time – together with whatever nasty surprises next year might hold.

Almost immediately after that the Quenton Park estate's crop of sugar beet, almost a thousand acres in total, had been hit by *rhizomania*, the mad root disease. They had lost the lot.

'We will need to find at least two and a half million,' said one of the lawyers. 'That should be no problem – the Hall is filled with valuable items, and what about the museum? What could we reasonably expect from the sale of some of the exhibits?'

Nicholas winced at the thought of selling the Ramesses statue, the bronzes, the Hammurabi frieze or any item of his cherished collection at the Hall or the museum. He acknowledged that their sale would cover his debts, but he doubted that he could live without them. Almost anything was preferable to parting with them.

'Hell, no,' Nicholas cut in, and the lawyer looked across at him coldly.

'Well, let's see what else we've got,' he continued remorselessly. 'There's the dairy herd.'

'That will bring in a hundred thousand, if we are lucky,' Nicholas grunted. 'Leaves only two point four million to find.'

'And your racing stud,' the accountant came into the conversation.

'I have only six horses in training. Another two

67

hundred grand.' Nicholas smiled without humour, 'Brings us down to two point two. We are getting there slowly.'

'The yacht,' suggested the youngest lawyer.

'It's older than I am,' Nicholas shook his head, 'belonged to my father, for heaven's sake. You probably wouldn't be able to give it away. Sentimental is the only value it has. My shotguns would be worth more.'

Both lawyers bent their heads over their lists, 'Ah, yes! We have those. A pair of Purdey sidelock ejectors in good condition. Estimate forty thousand.'

'I also have some secondhand socks and underpants,' Nicholas admitted. 'Why don't you list those also?'

They ignored the jibe. 'Then there is the London house,' the elder lawyer went on unperturbed, inured to human suffering. 'Good address. Value one point five million.'

'Not in this financial climate,' Nicholas contradicted him. 'A million is more realistic.' The lawyer made a note in the margin of his document before going on, 'Of course we want to avoid, if at all possible, putting the entire estate up for sale.'

It was a hard and difficult meeting which ended with nothing definitely decided, and Nicholas feeling angry and frustrated.

He saw the lawyers off, and then went up to the family quarters to take a quick shower and change his shirt. As an afterthought, and for no good reason, he shaved and splashed aftershave on his cheeks.

He drove across the park and left the Range Rover in the museum car park. The snow had turned to sleet, and his bare head was sprinkled with cold droplets by the time he had crossed the car park.

Royan was waiting in Mrs Street's office. The two of them seemed to be getting along well together. He stopped outside the door to listen to her laughter. It made him feel a little better.

The cook had sent across a hot lunch from the main house. She seemed to believe that a substantial meal would keep this foul weather at bay. There was a tureen of thick, rich minestrone and a Lancashire hotpot, with a half bottle of red Burgundy for him and a jug of freshly squeezed orange juice for her. They ate in front of the fire, while the rain whipped against the windowpanes.

While they ate he asked her to give him the details of Duraid's murder. She left out nothing, including her own injuries, and drew back her sleeve to show him the dressing over the knife wound. He listened intently as she told him of the second attempt on her life in the streets of Cairo.

'Any suspicions?' he asked, when she had finished. 'Anybody you can think of who might be responsible?' But she shook her head.

'There was no warning of any kind,' she said.

They finished the meal in silence, each of them thinking their own thoughts. Over the coffee he suggested, 'All right, then. What about our agreement?'

They argued back and forth for nearly an hour.

'It's difficult to agree on your share of the booty, until I know just what your contribution is going to be,' Nicholas protested as he topped up their coffee cups. 'After all, I am going to be called on to finance and conduct the expedition—'

'You will just have to trust that my contribution will be worthwhile, otherwise there will simply be no booty, as you call it. Anyway you can be certain I am not going to tell you one thing more until we have an agreement, and have shaken hands on it.'

'A bit harsh?' he asked, and she gave him a wicked smile.

'If you don't like my terms, there are three other names on Duraid's list of possible sponsors,' she threatened.

'All right,' he cut in with a contrived look of martyr-

69

dom, 'I agree to your proposal. But how do we calculate equal shares?'

'I shall choose the first item of any archaeological artefacts we are able to retrieve, and you the next, and so on, turn about.'

'How about I choose first?' He raised an eyebrow at her.

'Let's spin for it,' she suggested, and he fished a pound coin from his pocket.

'Call!' He flipped the coin, and while it was in the air she called, 'Heads.'

'Damn!' he exclaimed, as he retrieved the coin and shoved it back into his pocket. 'So, you get first choice of the booty, if there ever is any.' He held out his hand across the lunch table. 'It will be yours to do exactly what you want to do with it. You can even donate it to the Cairo museum, if that is still your particular aberration. Deal?' he asked, and she took his hand.

'Deal!' she agreed, and then added, 'Partner.'

'Now let's get down to it. No more secrets between us. Tell me every detail that you have been holding back.'

'Bring that book,' she pointed to the copy of *River God*, and while he fetched it she pushed the dirty dishes aside. 'The first thing we should go over is the sections of the book that Duraid edited.' She turned to the last pages. 'Here. This is where Duraid's obfuscation begins.'

'Good word,' Nicholas smiled, 'but let's keep it simple. You have obfuscated me enough already.'

She did not even smile. 'You know the story to this point. Queen Lostris and her people are driven out of Egypt by the Hyksos and their superior chariots. They journey south up the Nile until they reach the confluence of the White and Blue Niles. In other words, present-day Khartoum. All this is reasonably faithful to the scrolls.'

'I recall. Go on.'

'In the holds of their river galleys they are carrying the mummified body of Queen Lostris's husband, Pharaoh Mamose the Eighth. Twelve years previously she has sworn to him as he lay dying of a Hyksos arrow through his lung that she would find a secure burial site for him, and that she would lay him in it with all his vast treasure. When they reach Khartoum she determines that the time has at last come for her to make good her promise to him. She sends out her son, the fourteen-year-old Prince Memnon, with a squadron of chariots to find the burial site. Memnon is accompanied by his mentor, the narrator of the history, the indefatigable Taita.'

'Okay, I remember this section. Memnon and Taita consult the black Shilluk slaves they have captured, and on their advice decide to follow the left-hand fork of the river, or what we know as the Blue Nile.'

Royan nodded and continued the story. 'They travelled eastwards and were confronted by formidable mountains, so high that they were described as a blue rampart. So far what you read in the book is a fairly faithful rendition of the scrolls, but at this point,' she tapped the open page, 'we come to Duraid's red herring. In his description of the foothills—'

Before she could continue, Nicholas interjected, 'I remember thinking when I originally read it that it didn't accurately describe the area where the Blue Nile emerges from the Ethiopian highlands. There are no foothills. There is only the sheer western escarpment of the massif. The river comes out of it like a snake out of its hole. Whoever wrote that description doesn't know the course of the Blue Nile.'

'Do you know the area?' Royan asked, and he laughed and nodded.

'When I was younger and even more stupid than I am now, I conceived the grandiose plan of boating the Abbay

71

gorge from Lake Tana down to the dam at Roseires in the Sudan. The Abbay is the Ethiopian name for the Blue Nile.'

'Why did you want to do that?'

'Because it had never been done before. Major Cheesman, the British consul, had a shot at it in 1932, and nearly drowned himself. I thought I could make a film, and write a book about the voyage and earn myself a fortune from the royalties. I talked my father into financing the expedition. It was the kind of mad escapade that appealed to him. He even wanted to join the expedition. I studied the whole course of the Abbay river, not only on maps. I also bought myself an old Cessna 180 and flew down the gorge, five hundred miles from Lake Tana to the dam. As I said, I was twenty-one years old and crazy.'

'What happened?' She was fascinated. Duraid had never told her about this, but it was the type of adventure that she would have expected this man to launch into.

'I recruited eight of my friends from Sandhurst, and we devoted our Christmas holidays to the attempt. It was a fiasco. We lasted two days on those wild waters. The gorge is the most hellish corner of this earth that I know of. It's almost twice as deep and as rugged as the Grand Canyon of the Colorado river in Arizona. It smashed up our kayaks before we had covered twenty miles out of the five hundred. We had to abandon all our equipment and climb the walls of the gorge to reach civilization again.'

He looked serious for a moment, 'I lost two members of our party. Bobby Palmer was drowned, and Tim Marshall fell on the cliffs. We were not even able to recover their bodies. They are still down there somewhere. I had to tell their parents—' he broke off as he remembered the agony of it.

'Has anybody ever succeeded in navigating the Blue Nile gorge?' she asked, to distract him.

'Yes. I went back a few years later. This time not as

leader, but as a very junior member of the official British Armed Forces Expedition. It took the army, the navy and the air force to beat that river.'

She stared at him with a feeling of awe. He had actually rafted the Abbay. It was as though she had been led to him by some strange fate. Duraid was right. There was probably no man in the world better qualified for the work in hand.

'So you know as much as anybody about the real nature of the gorge. I will try to give you a general indication of what Taita actually set down in the seventh scroll. Unfortunately this section of the scroll had suffered some damage and Duraid and I were obliged to extrapolate from parts of the text. You will have to tell me how this agrees with your own knowledge of the terrain.'

'Go ahead,' he invited her.

'Taita described the escarpment very much the way you did, as a sheer wall from which the river emerged. They were forced to leave their chariots, which were unable to cover the steep and rugged terrain of the canyon. They were forced to go forward on foot, leading the pack horses. Soon the gorge grew so steep and dangerous that they lost some of these animals, which fell from the wild goat tracks they were following and plunged into the river far below. This did not deter them and they pressed on at the orders of Prince Memnon.'

'I can see it exactly as he describes it. It's a fearsome bit of countryside.'

'Taita then describes coming to a series of obstacles, which he describes as "steps". Duraid and I could not decide with certainty what these were. But our best guess was that they were waterfalls.'

'No shortage of those in the Abbay gorge, either,' Nicholas nodded.

'This is the important part of his testimony. Taita tells us that after twenty days' travel up the gorge they came upon the "second step". It was here that the prince received a fortuitous message from his dead father, in the form of a dream, in which he chose this as the site of his own tomb. Taita tells us that they travelled no further. If we are able to determine what it was that stopped them, that would give us an accurate measurement of just how far into the gorge they penetrated.'

'Before we can go any further we will need maps and satellite photographs of the mountains, and I will have to go over my expedition notes and diary,' Nicholas decided. 'I try to keep my reference library up-to-date, and so we should have satellite photographs and the most recent maps on file here in the museum. If they are Mrs Street is the one to find them.'

He stood up and stretched, 'I will dig out my diaries this evening and read over them. My great-grandfather also hunted and collected in Ethiopia in the last century. I know he crossed the Blue Nile near Debra Markos in 1890-something. I'll get out his notes as well. They are preserved in our archives. The old boy may have written something there that could help us.'

He walked with her to the old green Land Rover in the car park, and as she started the engine he told her through the open window, 'I still think that you should stay over here at the Hall. It must be an hour-and-a-half's drive across to Brandsbury — each way that's three hours a day. We are going to have a lot of work to do before we can even think of leaving for Africa.'

'What would people think?' she asked, as she let out the clutch.

'I have never given a damn about people,' he called after her. 'What time will I see you tomorrow?'

'I have to stop off to see the doctor in York. He is going to take the stitches out of my arm. I won't be here before eleven,' she stuck her head out of the window to yell back at him.

The wind tossed her dark hair around her face. His fancy had always run towards dark-haired women. Rosalind had had that mysterious Eastern look. He felt guilty and disloyal making the comparison, but the memory of Royan was hard to shake off.

She was the first woman who had interested him since Rosalind had gone. The admixture of her blood drew him. She was exotic enough to pique his taste for the oriental, but English enough to speak his language and understand his sense of humour. She was educated and knowledgeable about those things that interested him, and he admired her spirit. Usually Eastern women were trained from birth to be self-effacing and compliant. This one was different.

Georgina had phoned her doctor in York to make an appointment to have the stitches removed from Royan's arm. They left after breakfast from the cottage in Brandsbury. Georgina was driving and Magic sat between them on the bench seat.

As they turned into the village street, Royan noticed a large MAN truck parked down near the post office, but she thought no more about it.

Once they were out in the countryside they found there were patches of heavy fog that in places reduced visibility to thirty yards, but Georgina made no concessions to the weather, and sent the Land Rover rattling and whining through it at the top of its speed, which Royan reflected thankfully was on the right side of sixty miles an hour.

She glanced over her shoulder to check the road behind them, and saw that the MAN truck was following them. Only the cab rose above the sea of low mist that surrounded it like the conning tower of a submarine. Even as she watched it, a bank of fog intervened and swallowed it up. She turned back to listen to her mother.

'This government is a troop of incompetent nincompoops.' Georgina squinted her eyes against the smoke from the cigarette that dangled from her lips. She drove single-handed, stroking Magic's flowing silken ear with her free hand, 'I don't mind ministers boffing themselves into a stupor, but when they start fiddling around with my pension I get really mad.' Her mother's pension from the foreign service was her sole source of income, and it wasn't much.

'You don't truly want a Labour government, now tell the truth, Mummy,' Royan teased her. Her mother had always been the arch Conservative.

Georgina wavered, and then avoided the choice, 'All I say is, bring back Maggie.'

Royan turned slightly in her seat and glanced through the dirty rear window again. The truck was still behind them, looming out of the fog and the trail of blue exhaust smoke that Georgina was laying behind her like the vapour trail of a jet aircraft. Up until now it had hung back, but suddenly it accelerated up behind them.

'I think he wants to pass you,' Royan told Georgina mildly.

The massive bonnet of the truck was only twenty feet from their rear bumper. The radiator was emblazoned with the chrome logo 'MAN' and stood taller than the cab of the Land Rover, so that she could not see the face of the driver from where she sat.

'Everybody wants to pass me,' lamented Georgina. 'Story of my life.' She held the centre of the narrow road doggedly.

Royan glanced back again, and saw that the truck was creeping still closer. It filled the rear window completely. The driver declutched and revved the gigantic engine menacingly.

'You'd better give over. I think he means business.'

'Let him wait,' Georgina grunted around her cigarette butt. 'Patience is a virtue. Anyway, can't let him through here. There is a narrow stone bridge ahead of us. Know this stretch of road like the way to my own bathroom.'

At that moment the truck-driver sounded his klaxon so close that it was deafening. Magic jumped up on the rear seat and barked in outrage.

'Stupid bastard,' Georgina swore bitterly. 'What does he think he is playing at? Write down his number plate. I am going to report him to the York police.'

'His plates are covered with mud. Can't make it out, but it looks like a continental registration. German, I think.'

As if the driver had heard her protest he slowed slightly and fell back until a gap of twenty yards opened between the two vehicles. Royan had swivelled right round in the seat to watch him.

'That's better,' Georgina said smugly. 'Ruddy Hun learning some manners.' She peered ahead through the fog, 'There is the bridge—'

For the first time Royan was able to see up into the driver's cab of the truck. The driver wore a balaclava helmet that covered all but his eyes and nose with dark blue wool. It gave him a sinister and evil aspect.

'Look out!' Royan screamed suddenly. 'He is coming straight at us!' The engine beat of the great truck rose to a bellow that engulfed them like the sound of a gale-driven sea. For a moment Royan saw nothing but glittering steel and then the front of the truck smashed into them from behind.

She was thrown half over the back of her seat by the impact. She dragged herself up and saw that the truck had picked them up like a fox with a bird in its jaws. It carried the Land Rover forward on the steel bull bars that protected the shining chromed radiator.

Georgina wrestled with the wheel, trying to maintain control, but the effort was futile. 'Can't hold her. The bridge! Try and get clear—'

Royan hit the quick-release buckle on her safety-belt and reached for the door handle. The stone walls of the bridge were racing towards them at a terrifying pace. The Land Rover was slewing across the road, completely out of control.

The door burst open in Royan's grip, but she could not push it all the way before the Land Rover was flung into the solid stonework columns that guarded the approaches to the bridge.

The two women screamed in unison as the vehicle crumpled, and the impact hurled them forward. The windscreen shattered as they bounced off the stone columns, and the body of the Land Rover flipped over as it went down the embankment and began to roll.

Royan was catapulted through the open door and flung clear. The slope of the bank broke her fall, but it knocked the wind out of her. She bounced and rolled down the incline and then dropped into the icy waters of the stream below the bridge.

Just before her head went under, she found herself looking up at the sky and the bridge above her. She caught one last glimpse of the truck before it roared away. It was towing two huge cargo trailers. The tall bodywork of the trailers stood higher than the guard rail of the bridge.

Both of the trailers were covered by a heavy green nylon tarpaulin roped down to the lugs on the body. She had only a subliminal glimpse of a large red trademark and company name painted on the side of the nearest trailer, but before she could register the name she was plunged below the surface of the stream and the cold and the force of her fall drove the air from her lungs.

She fought her way to the surface of the river, and found she had been washed some way downstream. Impeded by her sodden clothing, she floundered to the bank and used the branch of a tree to haul herself out.

She knelt in the mud, coughing up the water she had

swallowed and trying to assess what injury she had suffered in the collision. Then her own plight was forgotten as she heard the terrible sounds of her mother's agony from the overturned wreck of the Land Rover.

In frantic haste she clawed herself to her feet and stumbled through the wet and frosted grass to where the Land Rover lay on its back at the foot of the embankment. The bodywork was crumpled and torn, and the bright silver aluminium metal shone through where the dark green paint had been stripped away. The engine had stalled, and the front wheels were still spinning aimlessly as she reached it.

'Mummy! Where are you?' she cried, and the terrible sounds never checked. She used the metal body of the vehicle to steady herself as she dragged herself towards the sound, dreading what she might find.

Georgina sat on the wet earth with her back against the side of the car. Her legs were thrust out straight ahead of her. The left one was twisted so that the toe of the booted foot was pointed down into the mud at an unnatural angle. The leg was obviously broken at the knee or very close to it.

This was not the cause of Georgina's distress. She held Magic in her lap, and was bowed over him in an attitude of abandoned grief; the sound of it bubbled up unchecked from deep inside her. The spaniel's chest had been crushed between metal and earth. His tongue lolled from the corner of his mouth in his last smile, but the blood dripped steadily from the pink tip and Georgina was using her scarf to wipe it away.

Royan sank down beside her mother and placed one arm around her shoulders. She had never before seen her mother weep. She hugged her hard and tried by main strength to quell the sound of her sorrow, but it went on and on.

She never knew how long they sat together like that.

But at last the sight of her mother's maimed leg, and an awakening fear that the driver of the truck might return to finish the job, roused her. She crawled up the bank and tottered into the centre of the road to stop the next car that arrived on the scene.

Not until Royan was two hours late for their meeting did Nicholas become sufficiently worried to phone the police in York. Fortunately he had noticed the licence plate of the Land Rover. It was an easy one for him to remember. The registration number was his mother's initials combined with an unlucky 13.

There was a delay while the woman constable checked her computer, and then she came back. 'I am sorry to have to tell you, sir, that Land Rover was involved in an accident this morning.'

'What happened to the driver?' Nicholas demanded brusquely.

'The driver and one passenger have been taken to the York Minster Hospital.'

'Are they all right?'

'I am sorry, sir. I don't have that information.'

It took Nicholas forty minutes to reach the hospital and almost as long again to trace Royan. She was in the women's surgical ward, sitting beside her mother's bed. Her mother had not yet come round from the anaesthetic.

She looked up when Nicholas stood over her. 'Are you all right? What the hell happened?'

'My mother – her leg is badly smashed up. The surgeon had to put a pin in her thigh – the femur.'

'How are you?'

'A few bruises and scrapes. Nothing serious.'

'How did it happen?'

'A truck – it pushed us off the road.'

'Not deliberate?' Nicholas felt something inside him quail as he remembered another truck on another road on another night.

'I think so. The driver wore a mask, a balaclava. He crashed into us from behind. It must have been deliberate.'

'Did you tell the police?'

She nodded. 'Apparently the truck was reported stolen early this morning, long before the accident, while the driver was stopped at one of those Little Chef cafés. He is German. Speaks no English.'

'That is the third time they have tried to kill you,' Nicholas told her grimly. 'So I am taking over now.'

He went out into the hospital waiting room and used the telephone there. The chief constable of the county was a personal friend, as was the hospital administrator.

By the time he returned, Georgina had come round from the anaesthetic. Although still woozy she was comfortable as they wheeled her off to the private ward that Nicholas had arranged. The orthopaedic surgeon arrived a few minutes later.

'Hello, Nick, what are you doing here?' he greeted Nicholas. Royan was surprised how many people knew him.

Then he turned his attention to Georgina. 'How are you feeling? We have got ourselves a nice little compound fracture. Looks like confetti in there. We've managed to put it all together again, but you're going to be with us for ten days at the very least.'

'Right you are, young lady,' Nicholas told Royan as they left Georgina sleeping. 'What more do you need to convince you? My housekeeper has made up a room for you at the Hall. I am not letting you wander around on your own any more. Otherwise, next time they try to cull you they may have a little more luck.'

She was still too shaken and upset to argue, and she climbed meekly into the front seat of the Range Rover and let him drive her first to have her stitches removed and then back to Quenton Park. As soon as they arrived, he sent her up to her bedroom.

'The cook will send dinner up to you. Make sure you take the sleeping pill that the doc gave you. Somebody will fetch your gear from Brandsbury if you give the key to your mother's cottage to Mrs Street. In the meantime my housekeeper has set out some nightclothes and a toothbrush in your room for you. I don't want to hear from you again before tomorrow morning.'

It was good to have him take control of her life. For the first time since that terrible night at the oasis she felt secure and safe. Still, she made one last gesture of independence and self-reliance; she flushed the Mogadon sleeping tablet down the toilet.

The nightdress that was laid on her pillow was full-length sheer silk with finest Cambrai lace at the cuffs and throat. She had never worn anything so luxurious and sensual against her skin before. She realized that it must have belonged to his wife, and the knowledge stirred mixed emotions in her. She climbed up into the four-poster bed, but even that lonely expanse of over-soft mattress and her unfamiliar surroundings did not keep her too long from sleep.

I n the morning a young housemaid woke her with a copy of *The Times* and a pot of Earl Grey tea, then returned a few minutes later with her holdall.

'Sir Nicholas would like you to take breakfast with him in the dining room at eight-thirty.'

While she showered Royan inspected her naked body in the full-length mirror that covered one wall of the bathroom. Apart from the knife wound on her arm, which was still livid and only partially healed, there was a dark bruise on her thigh and another down her left flank and buttock, legacies of the car crash. Her shin was scraped raw, and gingerly she pulled a pair of slacks over the injury. She limped a little as she went down the main staircase to find the dining room.

'Please help yourself.' Nicholas looked up from his newspaper to greet her as she hesitated in the doorway. He waved at the display of breakfast dishes on the sideboard. As she spooned scrambled eggs on to her plate, she recognized the landscape on the wall in front of her as a Constable.

'Did you sleep well?' He didn't wait for an answer, but went on, 'I have heard from the police. They found the MAN truck abandoned in a lay-by near Harrogate. They are going over it now but they don't expect to find much. We seem to be dealing with someone who knows what he is doing.'

'I must phone the hospital,' she said.

'I have already done so. Your mother had an easy night. I left a message that you would visit her this evening.'

'This evening?' She looked around sharply. 'Why so late?'

'I intend to keep you busy until then. I want to get my money's worth out of you.'

He stood as she came to the table, and drew back her chair to seat her. She found the courtesy made her feel slightly uncomfortable, but she made no comment.

'The first attack on you and Duraid at your villa in the oasis – we can draw no conclusions from that, apart from the fact that the assassins knew exactly what they were after, and where to look for it.' She found the abrupt change of subject disconcerting. 'However, let's give some thought to the second attempt in Cairo. The hand grenade. Who knew you were going to the Ministry that afternoon, apart from the minister himself?'

She reflected as she chewed and swallowed a mouthful of egg. 'I am not sure. I think I told Duraid's secretary, maybe one of the other research assistants.'

He frowned and shook his head. 'So half the museum staff knew about your appointment?'

'That is about it, yes. Sorry.'

He pondered a moment, 'All right. Who knew you were leaving Cairo? Who knew you were staying at your mother's cottage?'

'One of the clerks from administration brought my slides out to the airport.'

'Did you tell him what flight you were leaving on?'

'No, definitely not.'

'Did you tell anybody at all?'

'No. That is—' she hesitated.

'Yes?'

'I told the minister himself during our interview, when I asked for leave of absence. Not him – surely not?' her expression reflected her horror at the thought.

Nicholas shrugged, 'Some funny things happen. Of course, the minister knew all about the work that you and Duraid were doing on the seventh scroll?'

'Not all the details, but – yes – in general terms he knew what we were up to.'

'All right. Next question, tea or coffee?' He poured coffee into her cup, and then went on, 'You said that Duraid had a list of possible sponsors for an expedition. Might give us some ideas as to a short-list of suspects?'

'The Getty Museum,' she said, and he smiled.

'Cross one from the list. They don't go around tossing grenades in the streets of Cairo. Who else was there on the list?'

'Gotthold Ernst von Schiller.'

'Hamburg. Heavy industry. Metal and alloy refineries. Base mineral production.' Nicholas nodded. 'Who was the third name on the list?'

'Peter Walsh,' she said. 'The Texan.'

'That's the one,' he nodded. 'Lives in Fort Worth. Fast-food franchising. Mail order retail.' There were very few collectors with the substance to compete with the major institutions when it came to making significant acquisitions of antiquities or to financing archaeological exploration. Nicholas knew them all, for it was a mutually antagonistic circle of no more than a couple of dozen men. He had competed with each of them at one time or another on the auction floors of Sotheby's and Christie's, not to mention other less salubrious venues where 'fresh' antiquities were sold. The adjective 'fresh' was used in the context of 'fresh out of the ground'.

'Those are two beady-eyed bandits. They would probably eat their own children if they felt peckish. What would they do if they thought you stood in their way to the tomb of Mamose? Do you know if either of them contacted Duraid after the book was published, the way I did?'

'I don't know. They may have.'

'I cannot imagine that either of those beauties would have missed such an easy trick. We must believe that they both know that Duraid had something going on. We will put their names on our list of suspects.' Then he inspected her plate. 'Enough? Another spoonful of egg? No? Very well, let's go down to the museum and see what Mrs Street has found for us to work on.'

When they walked into his study, she was impressed by the amount of organization that he had accomplished in such a short time. He must have been busy at it all last night, turning the room into a military-type headquarters. In the centre of the room stood a large easel and blackboard on which were pinned a set of overlapping satellite photographs. She went across to study them, and then glanced at the other material pinned on the board.

Along with a large-scale map covering the same area of south-western Ethiopia as the satellite photographs there were lists of names and addresses, lists of equipment and stores which he had obviously used on previous African expeditions, sheets of calculations of distance and what looked like a preliminary financial budget. At the top of the board was a schedule headed 'Ethiopia – General Information'. There were five closely typed foolscap sheets, so she did not read through the entire schedule, but she was impressed by his thoroughness in preparation.

Royan determined to study all this material at the earliest opportunity, but now she crossed to one of the two chairs he had set up at a table facing the board. He stood at the board and picked up a silver-topped swagger stick from the table, brandishing it like a schoolmaster's pointer.

'Class will come to order.' He rapped on the board. 'The first thing you have to do is convince me that we will be able to pick up the spoor of Taita again after it has had several thousand years to cool. Let us first consider the geographical features of the Abbay gorge.'

Nicholas described the course of the river on the satellite photograph with his pointer. 'Along this section the river has cut its way through the flood basalt plateaux. In places the cliffs of the sub-gorge are sheer, as high as four or five hundred feet on each side. Where there are intrusive strata of harder igneous schists the river has not been able to erode them. They form a series of gigantic steps in the course of the river. I think you are correct in your assumption that Taita's "steps" are actually waterfalls.'

He came to the table and picked out a photograph from amongst the bundles of papers that covered it. 'I took this in the gorge during the Armed Forces Expedition in 1976. It will give you an idea of what some of those falls are like.'

He passed her a black and white riverscape of towering cliffs on either hand and a cascade of water that seemed to fall from the heavens to dwarf the tiny figures of half-naked men and boats in the foreground.

'I had no idea it was like that!' She stared at it in awe.

'Doesn't do justice to the splendid desolation down there in the gorge,' he told her. 'From a photographer's point of view there is no place to stand from which you can get it all into perspective. But at least you can see how that waterfall would halt a party of Egyptians coming upriver on foot, or at least with pack horses. There is usually some sort of path alongside the cataracts made by elephant and other wild game over the ages. However, there is simply no way to bypass waterfalls such as this one, and to get around those cliffs.'

She nodded, and he went on, 'Even coming downstream we had to lower the boats and all our equipment down each set of waterfalls on ropes. It wasn't easy.'

'Let us agree that it was a waterfall that stopped them going further – the second waterfall from the westerly approaches,' she conceded.

Nicholas picked up the swagger stick and on the satellite photograph traced the course of the river up from the dark wedge shape of the Roseires dam in central Sudan. 'The escarpment rises on the Ethiopian side of the border, that is where the gorge proper begins. No roads or towns in there, and only two bridges far upstream. Nothing for five hundred miles except racing Nile waters and savage black basalt rock.' He paused to let that sink in.

'It is one of the last true wildernesses on earth, with an evil reputation as the haunt of wild animals and even wilder men. I have marked the main falls that show in the gut of the gorge here on the satellite photo.' With the pointer he picked them out, each circled neatly in red marker pen.

'Here is waterfall number two, about a hundred and twenty miles upstream from the Sudanese border. However, there are a number of factors we have to consider, not least the fact that the river may have altered its course during the last four thousand years since our friend, Taita, visited it.'

'Surely it could not have escaped from such a deep canyon, four thousand feet,' she protested. 'Even the Nile must be held captive by that?'

'Yes, but it would certainly have altered the existing bed. In the flood season the volume and force of the river exceeds my ability to describe it to you. The river rises twenty metres up the side walls and bores through at speeds of ten knots or more.'

'You navigated that?' she asked doubtfully.

'Not in the flood season. Nothing could survive that.'

They both stared at the photograph in silence for a minute, imagining the terrors of that mighty stretch of water in its full fury.

Then she reminded him, 'The second waterfall?'

'Here it is, where one of the tributary rivers enters the main flow of the Abbay. The tributary is the Dandera river and it rises at twelve thousand feet altitude, below the peak of Sancai Mountain in the Choke range, here about a hundred miles north of the gorge.'

'Do you remember the spot where it joins the Abbay from when you were there?'

'It was over twenty years ago, and even then we had been almost a month down there in the gorge, so it all seemed to merge into a single nightmare. The memory blurred with the monotonous surroundings of the cliffs and the dense jungle of the walls, and our senses were dulled by the heat and the insects and the roar of water and the repetitive, unremitting toil at the oars. But, strangely, I do remember the confluence of the Dandera and the Abbay for two reasons.'

'Yes?' She sat forward eagerly, but he shook his head.

'We lost a man there. The only casualty on the second expedition. Rope parted and he fell a hundred feet. Landed on his back across a spur of rock.'

'I am sorry. But what was the other reason you remember the spot.'

'There is a Coptic Christian monastery there, built into the rock face about four hundred feet above the surface of the river.'

'Down there in the depths of the gorge?' She sounded incredulous. 'Why would they build a monastery there?'

'Ethiopia is one of the oldest Christian countries on earth. It has over nine thousand churches and monasteries, a great many of them in similarly remote and almost inaccessible places in the mountains. This one at the Dandera river is the reputed burial site of St Frumentius, the saint who introduced Christianity to Ethiopia from the Byzantine Empire in Constantinople in the early third century. Legend has it that he was shipwrecked on the Red Sea shore and taken to Aksum, where he converted the Emperor Ezana.'

'Did you visit the monastery?'

'Hell, no!' he laughed. 'We were too busy just surviving, too eager to escape from the hell of the gorge to have any time for sightseeing. We descended the falls and kept on downriver. All I remember of the monastery are the excavations in the cliff face high above the pool of the river, and the distant figures of the troglodytic monks in their white robes lining the parapet of the caves to watch impassively as we passed. Some of us waved up to them, and felt quite rebuffed when they made no response.'

'How would we ever reach that spot again, without a full-scale river expedition?' she wondered aloud, staring disconsolately at the board.

'Discouraged already?' He grinned at her. 'Wait until you meet some of the mosquitoes that live down there. They pick you up and fly with you to their lairs before they eat you.'

'Be serious,' she entreated him. 'How would we ever get down there?'

'The monks are fed by the villagers who live up on the highlands above the gorge. Apparently, there is a goat track down the wall. They told us that it takes three days to get down that track into the gut of the gorge from the rim.'

'Could you find your way down?'

'No, but I have a few ideas on the subject. We will come to that later. Firstly, we must decide what we expect to find down there after four thousand years.' He looked at her expectantly. 'Your turn now. Convince me.' He handed her the silver-headed pointer, dropped into the chair beside her and folded his arms.

'First you have to go back to the book.' She exchanged the pointer for the copy of *River God*. 'You remember the character of Tanus from the story?'

'Of course. He was the commander of the Egyptian armies under Queen Lostris, with the title of Great Lion of Egypt. He led the exodus from Egypt, when they were driven out by the Hyksos.'

'He was also the Queen's secret lover and, if we are to believe Taita, the father of Prince Memnon, her eldest son,' she agreed.

'Tanus was killed during a punitive expedition against an Ethiopian chief named Arkoun in the high mountains, and his body was mummified and brought back to the Queen by Taita,' Nicholas expanded the story.

'Precisely.' She nodded. 'This leads me on to the other clue that Duraid and I winkled out.'

'From the seventh scroll?' He unfolded his arms and sat forward in his seat.

'No, not from the scrolls, but from the inscriptions in the tomb of Queen Lostris.' She reached into her bag and brought out another photograph. 'This is an enlargement of a section of the murals from the burial chamber, that part of the wall that later fell away and was lost when the alabaster jars were revealed. Duraid and I believe that the fact that Taita placed this inscription in the place of honour, over the hiding-place of the scrolls, was significant.' She passed the photograph to him, and he picked up a magnifying glass from the table to study it.

While he puzzled over the hieroglyphics Royan went on, 'You will recall from the book how Taita loved riddles and word games, how he boasts so often that he is the greatest of all bao players?'

Nicholas looked up from the magnifying glass, 'I remember that. I go along with the theory that bao was the forerunner of the game of chess. I have a dozen or so boards in the museum collection, some from Egypt and others from further south in Africa.'

'Yes, I would also subscribe to that theory. Both games have many of the same objects and rules, but bao is a more rudimentary form of the game. It is played with coloured stones of different rank, instead of chess men. Well, I believe that Taita was not able to resist the temptation to display his riddling skills and his cleverness to posterity. I believe that he was so conceited that he deliberately left clues to the location of the Pharaoh's tomb, both in the scrolls and amongst the murals that he tells us he painted with his own hands in the tomb of his beloved Queen.'

'You think that this is one of those clues?' Nicholas tapped the photograph with the glass.

'Read it,' she instructed him. 'It's in classical hieroglyphics – not too difficult compared to his cryptic codes.'

'"*The father of the prince who is not the father, the giver of the blue that killed him,*"' he translated haltingly, '"*guards eternally hand in hand with Hapi the stone testament of the pathway to the father of the prince who is not the father, the giver of blood and ashes.*"'

Nicholas shook his head, 'No, it doesn't make sense,' he protested, 'I must have made an error in the translation.'

'Don't despair. You are making your first acquaintance with Taita, the champion bao player and consummate riddler. Duraid and I puzzled over it for weeks,' she reassured him. 'To work it out, let's go back to the book. Tanus was not the father of Prince Memnon in name, but, as the Queen's lover, was his biological father. On his deathbed, he gave Memnon the blue sword that had inflicted his own mortal wound during the battle with the native Ethiopian chief. There is a full description of the battle in the book.'

'Yes, when I first read that section, I remember thinking that the blue sword was probably one of the very earliest iron weapons, and in an age of bronze would have been a marvel of the armourer's art. A gift fit for a prince,' Nicholas mused, and went on, 'So "*the father of the prince who is not the father*" is Tanus?' He sighed with resignation. 'For the moment I accept your interpretation.'

'Thank you for your trust and confidence in me,' she said sarcastically. 'But to proceed with Taita's riddle – Pharaoh Mamose was Memnon's father in name only, but not his blood father. Again the father who was not the father. Mamose passed down to the prince the double crown of Egypt, the red and white crowns of Upper and Lower Kingdoms – the blood and the ashes.'

'I am able to swallow that more easily. What about the rest of the inscription?' Nicholas was clearly intrigued.

'The expression "hand in hand" is ambiguous in ancient Egyptian. It could just as well mean very close to, or within sight of, something.'

'Go on. At last you have me sitting up and taking notice,' Nicholas encouraged her.

'Hapi is the hermaphroditic god or goddess of the Nile, depending on the gender he or she adopts at any particular moment. Throughout the scrolls Taita uses Hapi as an alternative name for the river.'

'So if we put the seventh scroll and the inscription from the Queen's tomb together, what then is your full interpretation?' he insisted.

'Simply this: Tanus is buried within sight of, or very close to, the river at the second waterfall. There is a stone monument or inscription on, or in, his tomb that points the way to the tomb of Pharaoh.'

He exhaled through his teeth. 'I am exhausted from all this jumping to conclusions. What other clues have you ferreted out for me?'

'That's it,' she said, and he looked at her with disbelief.

'That's it? Nothing else?' he demanded, and she shook her head.

'Just suppose that you are correct so far. Let us suppose that the river is recognizably the same in shape and configuration as it was nearly four thousand years ago. Let us further suppose that Taita was indeed pointing us towards the second waterfall at the Dandera river. Just what do we look for when we get there? If there is a rock inscription, will it still be intact or will it be eroded away by weather and the action of the river?'

'Howard Carter had an equally slender lead to the tomb of Tutankhamen,' she pointed out mildly. 'A single piece of papyrus, of dubious authenticity.'

'Howard Carter had only the area of the Valley of the Kings to search. It still took him ten years,' he replied. 'You have given me Ethiopia, a country twice the size of France. How long will that take us, do you think?'

She stood up abruptly, 'Excuse me, I think I should go and visit my mother in hospital. It's fairly obvious that I am wasting my time here.'

'It is not yet visiting hours,' he told her.

'She has a private room.' Royan made for the door.

'I will drive you to the hospital,' he offered.

'Don't bother. I will call a taxi,' she replied in a tone that crackled with ice.

'A taxi will take an hour to get here,' he warned, and she relented just enough to let him lead her to the Range

Rover. They drove in silence for fifteen minutes, before he spoke.

'I am not very good at apologies. Not much practice, I am afraid, but I am sorry. I was abrupt. I didn't mean to be. Carried away by the excitement of the moment.'

She did not reply, and after a minute he added, 'You will have to talk to me, unless we are to correspond only by note. It will be a bit awkward down in the Abbay gorge.'

'I had the distinct impression that you were no longer interested in going down there.' She stared ahead through the windscreen.

'I am a brute,' he agreed, and she glanced sideways at him. It was her undoing. His grin was irresistible, and she laughed.

'I suppose I will just have to come to terms with that fact. You are a brute.'

'Still partners?' he asked.

'At the moment you are the only brute I have. I suppose that I am stuck with you.'

He dropped her off at the main hospital entrance. 'I will pick you up here at three o'clock,' he told her and drove on into the centre of York.

From his university days Nicholas had kept a small flat in one of the narrow alleys behind York Minster. The entire building was registered in the name of a Cayman Island company, and the unlisted telephone there did not route through an internal switchboard. No ownership could be traced to him personally. Before he had met Rosalind the flat had played an important part in his social life. But nowadays Nicholas only used it for confidential and clandestine business. Both the Libyan and the Iraqi expeditions had been planned and organized from here.

He hadn't used the flat for months, and it was cold and musty-smelling and uninviting. He put a match to the gas fire in the grate and filled the kettle. With a mug of steaming tea in front of him he placed a call to a bank in

Jersey, followed immediately by another to a bank in the Cayman Islands.

'A wise rat has more than one exit from its burrow.' This was a family maxim, passed down through the generations. There should always be a little something tucked away for the day the heavens opened. He was going to need funds for the expedition, and the lawyers had most of those locked up already.

He gave the passwords and account numbers to each of the bank managers and instructed them to make certain transfers. It always amazed him how easily matters could be arranged, as long as you had money.

He checked his watch. It was still early morning in Florida, but Alison picked up the phone on the second ring. She was the blonde feminine dynamo who ran Global Safaris, a company that arranged hunting and fishing expeditions to remote areas around the world.

'Hello, Nick. We haven't heard from you in over a year. We thought you didn't love us any more.'

'I have been out of it for a while,' he admitted. How do you tell people that your wife and two little girls had died?

'Ethiopia?' She did not sound at all disconcerted by the request. 'When did you want to go?'

'How about next week?'

'You have to be joking. We only work with one hunter there, Nassous Roussos, and he is booked two years in advance.'

'Is there nobody else?' he insisted. 'I have to be in and out again before the big rains.'

'What trophies are you after?' she hedged. 'Mountain nyala? Menelik's bushbuck?'

'I am planning a collecting trip for the museum, down the Abbay river.' It was as much as he was prepared to tell her.

She hedged a little longer and then told him

reluctantly, 'This is without our recommendation, do you understand. There is only one hunter who may take you on at such short notice, but I don't even know if he has a camp on the Blue Nile. He is a Russian, and we have had mixed reports about him. Some people say he is ex-KGB and was one of Mengistu's bunch of thugs.'

Mengistu was the 'Black Stalin' who had deposed and then murdered the old Emperor Haile Selassie, and in sixteen years of despotic Marxist rule had driven Ethiopia to its knees. When his sponsor, the Soviet Empire, had collapsed, Mengistu had been overthrown and fled the country.

'I am desperate enough to go to bed with the devil,' he told her. 'I promise I won't come back to you with any complaints.'

'Okay, then, no come-backs—' and she gave him a name and a telephone number in Addis Ababa.

'I love you, Alison darling,' Nicholas told her.

'I wish,' she said, and hung up on him.

He didn't expect that it would be easy to telephone Addis, and he wasn't disappointed in his expectations. But at last he got through. A woman with a sweet lisping Ethiopian accent answered and switched to fluent English when he asked for Boris Brusilov.

'He is out on safari at present,' she told him. 'I am Woizero Tessay, his wife.' In Ethiopia a wife did not take on her husband's name. Nicholas remembered enough of the language to know that the name meant Lady Sun, a pretty name.

'But if it is in connection with safari business I can help you,' said Lady Sun.

icholas picked Royan up outside the hospital entrance.

'How is your mother?'

'Her leg is doing well, but she is still distraught about Magic – about her dog.'

'You will have to get her a puppy. One of my keepers breeds first-class springers. I can arrange it.' He paused and then asked delicately, 'Will you be able to leave your mother? I mean, if we are going out to Africa?'

'I spoke to her about that. There is a woman from her church group who will stay with her until she is well enough to fend for herself again.'

Royan turned fully around in her seat to examine his face. 'You have been up to something since I last saw you,' she accused him. 'I can see it in your face.'

He made the Arabic sign against the evil eye, 'Allah save me from witches!'

'Come on!' He could make her laugh so readily, she was not sure if that was a good thing or not. 'Tell me what you have up your sleeve.'

'Wait until we get back to the museum.' He would not be moved, and she had to bridle her impatience.

As soon as they entered the building he led her through the Egyptian room to the hall of African mammals, and then stopped her in front of a diorama of mounted antelope. These were some of the smaller and medium-sized varieties – impala, Thompson's and Grant's gazelle, gerenuk and the like.

'*Madoqua harperii*.' He pointed to a tiny creature in one corner of the display. 'Harper's dik-dik, also known as the striped dik-dik.'

It was a nondescript little animal, not much bigger than a large hare. The brown pelt was striped in chocolate over the shoulders and back, and the nose was elongated into a prehensile proboscis.

'A bit tatty,' she gave her opinion carefully, unwilling

97

to offend him, for he seemed inordinately proud of this specimen. 'Is there anything special about it?'

'Special?' he asked with wonder in his voice. 'The woman asks if it is special.' He rolled his eyes heavenward and she had to laugh again at his histrionics. 'It is the only known specimen in existence. It is one of the rarest creatures on earth. So rare that it is probably extinct by now. So rare that many zoologists believe that it is apocryphal, that it never really existed. They think that my sainted great-grandfather, after whom it is named, actually invented it. One learned reference hinted that he may have taken the skin of the striped mongoose and stretched it over the form of a common dik-dik. Can you imagine a more heinous accusation?'

'I am truly appalled by such injustice,' she laughed.

'Darned right, you should be. Because we are going to Africa to hunt for another specimen of *Madoqua harperii*, to vindicate the honour of the family.'

'I don't understand.'

'Come with me and all will be explained.' He led her back to his study, and from the jumble on the tabletop picked out a notebook bound in red Morocco leather. The cover was faded and stained with water marks and tropical sunlight, while the corners and the spine were frayed and battered.

'Old Sir Jonathan's game book,' he explained, and opened it. Pressed between the pages were faded wild flowers and leaves that must have been there for almost a century. The text was illuminated by line drawings in faded yellow ink of men and animals and wild landscapes. Nicholas read the date at the top of one page.

2nd of February 1902. In camp on the Abbay river. All day following the spoor of two large bull elephants. Unable to come up with them. Heat very intense. My men played out. Abandoned the chase and returned to camp. On the return march spied a small antelope grazing on the river-bank, which I brought down with one shot from the little Rigby rifle. On close examination it proved to be a member of the genus Madoqa. *However, it was of a species that I had never seen before, larger than the common dik-dik and possessing a striped body. I believe that this specimen may be new to science.*

He looked up from the diary. 'Old great-grandpa Jonathan has given us the perfect excuse for going down into the Abbay gorge.' He closed the book, and went on, 'As you pointed out, to cater for our own expedition would require months of planning and organization, not to mention the expense. It would mean having to obtain approval and permission from the Ethiopian government. In Africa that can take months, if not years.'

'I don't imagine that the Ethiopian government would be too cooperative if they suspected our real intentions,' she agreed.

'On the other hand, there are a number of legitimate hunting safari companies operating throughout the country. They have all the necessary permits, governmental contacts, vehicles, camping equipment and logistic back-up necessary to travel and stay in even the remotest areas. The authorities are quite accustomed to foreign hunters arriving and leaving with these companies, whereas a couple of *ferengi* nosing around on their own would have the local military and everybody else down on them like a herd of angry buffalo.'

'So we are going to travel as a pair of dik-dik hunters?'

'I have already made the booking with a safari operator in Addis Ababa, the capital. My plan is to look upon the whole of our project in three distinct and separate stages.

The first stage will be this reconnaissance. If we find the lead we are hoping for, then we will go back again with our own men and equipment. That will be stage two. Stage three, of course, will be getting the booty out of Ethiopia, and that I assure you from past experience will not be the easiest part of the operation.'

'How will you do that—' she began, but he held up his hands.

'Don't ask, because at this stage I don't have even the vaguest idea how we will do it. One stage at a time.'

'When do we leave?'

'Before I tell you when, let me ask you one more question. Your interpretation of the Taita riddle – did you explain that in the notes that were stolen from you at the oasis?'

'Yes, everything was either in those notes or on the microfilm. I am sorry.'

'So the uglies will have it all neatly laid out for them, just the way you laid it out for me.'

'I am afraid they will, yes.'

'Then to reply to your question as to when, the answer is *tout de suite*, and the tooter the sweeter! We must get into the Abbay gorge before the competition beats us to it. They have had your conclusions and suppositions for almost a month. For all we know they are on their way already.'

'When?' she repeated eagerly.

'I have booked two seats on the British Airways flight to Nairobi this Saturday – that is, in two days' time. We will connect there with an Air Kenya flight to Addis that will get us in on Monday at around midday. We will drive down to London this evening and stay over at my digs there. Are your yellow fever and hepatitis shots up to date?'

'Yes, but I have no equipment and hardly any clothing with me. I left Cairo in rather a hurry.'

'We will see to that in London. Trouble with Ethiopia is it's cold enough to emasculate a brass monkey in the highlands, and like a sauna bath down in the gorge.'

He crossed to the board and began to check off the items on his list. 'We will both start malarial prophylactics immediately. We are going into an area of chloroquine-resistant *P. falciparum* mosquitoes, so I will put you on Mefloquine—' He worked swiftly through the list.

'Of course all your travel documents are in order, or you wouldn't be here. We will both need visas for Ethiopia, but I have a contact who can arrange that in twenty-four hours.'

As soon as he completed the list he sent her up to her room to pack the few personal items she had brought with her from Cairo.

By the time they were ready to leave Quenton Hall it was dark outside, but still he stopped for an hour at the York Minster Hospital to allow her to say goodbye to her mother. He waited in the Red Lion pub across the road, and he smelt of Theakston's Old Peculier when she climbed back into the Range Rover beside him. It was a pleasant, yeasty aroma, and she felt so much at ease in his company that she lay back in the seat and fell asleep.

His London house was in Knightsbridge, but despite the fashionable address it was much less grand than Quenton Hall, and she felt more at home there, even if it was only for two days. During that time she saw little of Nicholas, for he was busy with all the last-minute arrangements, which included a number of visits to government offices in Whitehall. He returned with wads of letters of introduction to high officials and British Embassies and High Commissions throughout East Africa.

'Ask any Englishman,' she smiled to herself. 'There is

no such thing as upper-class privilege any longer, nor is there an old-boy network that runs the country.'

While he was away, she went off with the shopping list he had given her. Even walking the streets of the safest capital city in the world she found herself looking back over her shoulder, and ducking in and out of ladies' rooms and tube stations to make certain that she was not being followed.

'You are acting like a terrified child without its daddy,' she scolded herself.

However, she felt a quite disproportionate sense of relief each evening when she heard his key in the street door of the empty house where she waited, and she had to control herself so as not to rush down the stairs to welcome him.

On Saturday morning, when a taxi cab deposited them at the departures level of Heathrow Terminal Four, Nicholas surveyed their combined luggage with approval. She had only a single soft canvas bag, no larger than his, and her sling bag over her shoulder. His hunting rifle was cased in travel-worn leather, with his initials embossed on the lid. A hundred rounds of ammunition was packed in a separate brass-bound magazine and he carried a leather briefcase that looked like a Victorian antique.

'Travelling light is one of the great virtues. Lord save us from women with mountains of luggage,' he told her, refusing the services of a porter and throwing it all on to a trolley, which he pushed himself.

She had to step out to keep up with him as he strode through the crowded departures hall. Miraculously the throng opened before him. He tilted the brim of his panama hat over one eye and grinned at the girl at the check-in counter, so that she came over all girlish and flustered.

It was the same once they were aboard the aircraft. The two stewardesses giggled at everything he said, plied him with champagne and fussed over him outrageously, to the obvious irritation of the other passengers, including Royan herself. But she ignored him and them and settled back to enjoy the unaccustomed luxury of the reclining first-class seat and her own miniature video screen. She tried to concentrate on the screen images of Richard Gere, but found her attention wandering to other images of wild canyons and ancient stelae.

Only when Nicholas nudged her did she look around at him a little haughtily. He had set up a tiny travelling chessboard on the arm of the seat between them, and now he lifted an eyebrow at her and inclined his head in invitation.

When they landed at Jomo Kenyatta airport in Kenya they were still locked in combat. They were level at two games each, but she was a bishop and two pawns up in the final deciding game. She felt quite pleased with herself.

At the Norfolk Hotel in Nairobi he had booked a pair of garden bungalows, one for each of them. Within ten minutes of her flopping down on the bed, he called her from next door on the house phone.

'We are going to dinner with the British High Commissioner tonight. He is an old chum. Dress informal. Can you be ready at eight?'

One did not have to rough it too onerously when travelling around the world in this man's company, she thought.

It was a relatively short haul from Nairobi up to Addis Ababa, and the landscape below them unfolded in fascinating sequences that kept her glued to the cabin window of the Air Kenya flight. The hoary summit of Mount Kenya was for once free of cloud, and the snow-clad double peaks glistened in the high sunlight.

The bleak brown deserts of the Northern Frontier District were relieved only by the green hills that surrounded the oasis of Marsabit and, far out on the port side, the flashing waters of Lake Turkana, formerly Lake Rudolf. The desert finally gave way to the highlands of the great central plateau of the ancient land of Ethiopia.

'In Africa only the Egyptians go back further than this civilization,' Nicholas remarked as they watched it together. 'They were a cultured race when we peoples of northern climes were still dressing in untanned skins and living in caves. They were Christians when Europeans were still pagans, worshipping the old gods, Pan and Diana.'

'They were a civilized people when Taita passed this way nearly four thousand years ago,' she agreed. 'In his scrolls he writes of them as almost his cultural equals, which was rare for him. He disparaged all the other nations of the old world as his inferiors in every way.'

From the air Addis was like so many other African cities, a mixture of the old and the new, of traditional and exotic architectural styles, thatched roofs alongside galvanized iron and baked tiles. The rounded walls of the old *tukuls* built with mud and wattle contrasted with the rectangular shapes and geometrical planes of the brick-built multi-storeyed buildings, the blocks of flats and the villas of the affluent, the government buildings and the grandiose, flag-bedecked headquarters of the Organization of African Unity.

The distinguishing features of the surrounding countryside were the plantations of tall eucalyptus trees, the ubiquitous blue gums that provided firewood. It was the only fuel available to so many in this poor and war-torn land, which over the centuries had been ravaged by marauding armies and, more recently, by alien political doctrines.

After Nairobi the high-altitude air was cool and sweet when Royan and Nicholas left the aircraft and walked across the tarmac to the terminal building. As they entered, before they had even approached the row of waiting immigration officers someone called his name.

'Sir Nicholas!' They both turned to the tall young woman who glided towards them with all the grace of a dancer, her dark and delicate features lit by a welcoming smile. She wore full-length traditional skirts which enhanced her movements.

'Welcome to my country of Ethiopia. I am Woizero Tessay.' She looked at Royan with interest, 'And you must be Woizero Royan.' She held out her hand to her and Nicholas saw that the two women liked each other immediately.

'If you will let me have your passports, I will see to the formalities while you relax in the VIP lounge. There is a man from your British Embassy waiting there to greet you, Sir Nicholas. I don't know how he knew that you were arriving.'

There was only one person waiting in the VIP lounge. He was dressed in a well-cut tropical suit and wore the orange, yellow and blue diagonally striped old Sandhurst tie. He stood up and came to greet Nicholas immediately, 'Nicky, how are you? It's good to see you again. Must be all of twelve years, isn't it?'

'Hello, Geoffrey. I had no idea they had stuck you out here.'

'Military attaché. His Excellency sent me down to meet you as soon as he heard that you and I had been at Sandhurst together.' Geoffrey looked at Royan with marked interest, and with a resigned air Nicholas introduced them.

'Geoffrey Tennant. Be careful of him. Biggest ram north of the equator. No girl safe within half a mile of him.'

'I say, steady on,' Geoffrey protested, looking pleased

with the reference that Nicholas had given him. 'Please don't believe a word the man says, Dr Al Simma. Notorious prevaricator.'

Geoffrey drew Nicholas aside and quickly gave him a résumé of conditions in the country, particularly in the outlying areas. 'HE is a little worried. He doesn't like the idea of you swanning around out there on your own. Lots of nasty men down there in the Gojam. I told him that you knew how to look after yourself.'

In a remarkably short time Woizero Tessay was back. 'I have cleared all your luggage, including the firearm and ammunition. This is your temporary permit. You must keep it with you at all times whilst you are in Ethiopia. Here are your passports – the visas are stamped and in order. Our flight to Lake Tana leaves in an hour, so we have plenty of time to check in.'

'Any time you need a job, come and see me,' Nicholas commended her efficiency.

Geoffrey Tennant walked with them as far as the departures gate, where he shook hands, 'Anything I can do, it goes without saying. "*Serve to Lead*", Nicky.'

'"*Serve to lead*"?' Royan asked, as they walked out to the waiting aircraft.

'Sandhurst's motto,' he explained.

'How nice, Nicky,' she murmured.

'I have always considered Nicholas to be more dignified and appropriate,' he said.

'Yes, but Nicky is so sweet.'

 In the high, thin air the Twin Otter aircraft that took them on the last, northern, leg pitched and yawed in the updraughts from the mountains below.

Although they were at fifteen thousand feet above sea level, the ground was close enough for them to make out the villages and the sparse areas of cultivation around them. Subjected for so many centuries to primitive agricultural methods and to the uncontrolled grazing of domestic herds, the land had a thin, impoverished look, and the bones of rock showed through the thin red fleshing of earth.

Abruptly ahead of them the plateau over which they were flying was rent through by a monstrous chasm. It was as though the earth had received a mighty sword-stroke that struck through to her very bowels.

'The Abbay river!' Tessay leaned forward in her seat to tap Royan's shoulder.

The rim of the gorge was clear-cut, and then the slope dropped away at an angle of over thirty degrees. The bare plains of the plateau gave way immediately to the heavily forested walls of the gorge. They could make out the candelabra shapes of giant euphorbia rising above the dense jungle. In places the walls had collapsed in scree slopes of loose rock, and in others they were up-thrust into bluffs and needles that erosion had sculpted with a monstrous artistry into the figures of towering humanoids and other fantastic creatures of stone.

Down and down it plunged, and they winged out over the void until they could look directly down, a mile and more, on to the glittering snake of the river in the depths. The funnel shape of the upper walls formed a secondary rim as they reached the sheer cliffs of the sub-gorge five hundred feet above the Nile water. Deep down there between its terrible cliffs the river gouged dark pools and long slithering runs through the red sandstone. In places the gorge was forty miles across, in others it narrowed to under ten, but through all its length the grandeur and the desolation were infinite and eternal. Man had made no impression upon it.

'You will soon be down there,' Tessay told them in a voice so awed that it was almost a whisper, and they were both silent. Words seemed superfluous in the face of such raw and savage nature.

Almost with relief they watched the northern wall rise to meet them, and the high mountains of the Choke range stood up against the tall blue African sky, higher than their fragile little craft was flying.

The aircraft banked into its descent and Tessay pointed over the starboard wingtip.

'Lake Tana,' she told them. It was a wide and lovely body of water, over fifty miles long, studded with islands on each of which stood a monastery or an ancient church. As they dropped in over the water on the final approach, they could make out the white-robed priests plying between the islands on their traditional little boats made from bundles of papyrus.

The Otter touched down on the dirt strip beside the lake and rolled out in a long trailing cloud of dust. It swung in and stopped engines beside the run-down terminal building of thatch and daub.

The sunlight was so bright that Nicholas pulled a pair of sunglasses from the breast pocket of his khaki jacket and placed them on his nose as he stood at the top of the boarding ladder. He took in the pock-marks of bullets and shrapnel on the dirty white walls of the terminal, and the burnt-out hull of a Russian T35 battle tank standing in the grass on the verge of the runway. The barrel of its turret gun pointed earthwards, and grass had grown up between the rusted tracks.

The other passengers pushed forward impatiently behind him, jostling him and jabbering with excitement as they saw friends and relatives waiting to greet them under the eucalyptus trees that shaded the building. There was only one vehicle parked out there, a sand-coloured Toyota Land Cruiser. The roundel on the driver's door had at its centre the painted head of a mountain nyala, with long corkscrew horns, and in a ribbon below it the title 'Wild Chase Safaris'. A white man lounged behind the wheel.

As Nicholas came down the ladder behind the two women, the driver slipped out of the truck and strode out on to the strip to meet them. He was dressed in a faded khaki bush suit, and he was tall and lean and walked with a spring to his step.

'Fortyish,' Nicholas judged his age from the grizzling in his short beard. 'One of the hard men,' Nicholas thought. His ginger hair was cropped short, his eyes were pale killer blue. There was a puckered white scar that ran across one cheek and up to twist and deform his nose.

Tessay introduced Royan to him first, and he made a short, choppy bow as he shook her hand. '*Enchanté*,' he told her in an execrable French accent and then looked at Nicholas.

'This is my husband, Alto Boris,' Tessay introduced him. 'Boris, this is Alto Nicholas.'

'My English is bad,' Boris said. 'My French is better.'

'Not much to choose between them,' Nicholas thought, but he smiled easily and said, 'So we will speak French then. *Bonjour*, Monsieur Brusilov. I am delighted to make your acquaintance.' He offered the Russian his hand.

Boris's grip was hard – too hard. He was making a contest out of the greeting, but Nicholas had expected it. He knew this type of old, and he had taken a deep grip so Boris could not crush his fingers. Nicholas held him without allowing any strain or effort to show on his lazy smile. Boris was the first to break the handshake, and there was just the trace of respect in those pale eyes.

'So you have come for a dik-dik?' he asked, just short of a sneer. 'Most of my clients come for big elephant, or at least for mountain nyala.'

'Bit rich for my nerves,' Nicholas grinned, 'all that big stuff. Dik-dik will suit me fine.'

'Have you ever been down in the gorge?' Boris demanded. His Russian accent overpowered the French words and made them difficult to follow.

'Sir Nicholas was one of the leaders of the 1976 river expedition,' Royan intervened sweetly, and Nicholas was amused by her unexpected intervention. She had picked up the antagonism between them very quickly, and come to his rescue.

Boris grunted, and turned to his wife. 'Have you got all the stores I ordered?' he demanded.

'Yes, Boris,' she answered meekly. 'They are all on board the aircraft.' She is afraid of him, Nicholas decided, probably with good reason.

'Let's get loaded up, then. We have a long journey ahead of us.'

The two men rode in the front seats of the Toyota, and the women sat behind them with many of the packages of stores packed in around them. Good African protocol, Nicholas smiled to himself: men first, women fend for themselves.

'You don't want to do the tourist run, do you?' Boris made it sound like a threat.

'The tourist run?'

'The outlet from the lake, and the power station,' he explained. 'The Portuguese bridge over the gorge and the point where the Blue Nile begins,' he added. But before they could accept he warned them, 'If you do, we won't get into camp until long after dark.'

'Thanks for the suggestion,' Nicholas told him politely, 'but I have seen it all before.'

'Good.' Boris made his approval evident. 'Let's get out of here.'

The road swung away into the west, below the high mountains. This was the Gojam, the land of the aloof mountaineers. It was well-populated country, and they passed many tall, thin men along the roadside as they strode along behind their herds of goats and sheep, with their long staffs held crossways over their shoulders. Both men and women wore *shammas*, woollen shawls, and baggy white jodhpur pants, with their feet in open sandals.

They were people with proud and handsome features, their hair dressed out into thick, bushy halos, and their eyes fierce as those of eagles. Some of the younger women in the villages they passed through were truly beautiful. Most of the men were heavily armed. They carried two-handed swords in chased silver scabbards, and AK-47 assault rifles.

'Makes them feel like big men,' Boris chuckled. 'Very brave, very macho.'

The huts in the villages were circular walled *tukuls*, surrounded by plantations of eucalyptus and spiky-headed sisal.

Bruised purple storm clouds boiled over the high peaks of the Choke and swept them with squalls of rain. Like silver coins, the huge drops rattled against the windscreen of the Land Cruiser and turned the road to a running river of mud under their wheels.

The condition of the road surface was appalling; in places it deteriorated into a rocky gully which even the four-wheel drive Toyota could not negotiate, and Boris was forced to make his own track across the rocky hillside. Often reduced to walking speed, they were nevertheless tossed about in their seats as the wheels bounced over the rough terrain.

'These damn blacks don't even think to repair the roads,' Boris grunted. 'They are happy to live like animals.' None of them replied, but Nicholas glanced up into the rear-view mirror at the faces of the two women. They were closed and neutral, hiding any hurt that either of them might have felt at the remark.

As they went on, the road, bad as it had been originally, became even worse. From here onwards the soft muddy surface had been torn up by the tyres and tracks of heavy traffic.

'Military traffic?' Nicholas raised his voice above the buffeting rain squalls, and Boris grunted.

'Some of it. There is a lot of *shufta* activity along the gorge – bandits and dissident warlords. However, most of this traffic is mineral-prospecting. One of the big mining companies has got concessions in Gojam and they are moving in to begin drilling.'

'We have passed no civilian vehicles,' Royan remarked, 'not even public buses.'

'We have just come through a terrible period in our long and troubled history,' Tessay explained to her. 'We are an agrarian-based economy. Once we were known as the bread basket of Africa, but when Mengistu seized power he drove us right over the edge of poverty. He used starvation as a political weapon. We are still suffering terribly. Very few of our people can afford the luxury of a motor vehicle. Most of them are worried how they will be able to afford food for their children.'

'Tessay has an economics degree from Addis University,' Boris chuckled. 'She is very clever. She knows everything. You ask her, she will tell you. History, religion, economics – just ask her.' Tessay relapsed into silence at the rebuff.

In the middle of the afternoon the rain at last eased and a timid sun peered through the cloud banks. Boris stopped the Toyota in a deserted stretch of countryside. 'Pinkel pause,' he announced. 'Wee-wee stop. Pee-pee time.'

The two girls left the truck and wandered away amongst the rocks. When they returned to the vehicle they had changed their clothing. Both of them now wore the *shammas* and the jodhpur trousers of the country.

'Tessay has made me a gift of a traditional Tigrean costume,' said Royan, pirouetting for Nicholas's approval.

'Looks good, too,' he gave his opinion. 'You will be a lot more comfortable in pants.'

The sun was lowering as the road dropped into another rocky valley, down the length of which ran a river with steep, eroded banks. Above the river nestled a circular, white-walled church with a wooden Coptic cross set high on its reed-thatched roof. The village of *tukuls* huddled around the church.

'Debra Maryam,' Boris announced with satisfaction, 'the hill of the Virgin Mary, and the river is the Dandera. I sent my men on ahead in the big truck. They will have the camp ready and be waiting for us. We will sleep here tonight, and tomorrow we will follow the river downstream until we reach the rim of the gorge.'

Boris's camp staff had set up the tents in a eucalyptus grove just beyond the village.

'The second tent is yours,' Boris pointed it out.

'That will do fine for Royan,' Nicholas agreed. 'I will need a tent on my own.'

'Dik-dik and separate tents,' Boris looked at him with a flat, pale stare. 'A hell of a man. You impress me.'

He shouted for his men to erect Nicholas's tent alongside the other, the side walls almost touching.

'You may get up your courage during the night,' he leered at Nicholas. 'Don't want you to have too far to walk.'

The shower under which they bathed was a drum hung in the lower branches of one of the blue gum trees, with a roofless canvas screen set up around it. Royan used it first and came back looking cheerful and refreshed, and with a damp towel wrapped around her hair.

'Your turn, Nicky!' she called to Nicholas as she passed his tent. 'The water is beautifully hot.'

It was dark by the time Nicholas had showered and changed. He walked across to the dining tent where the rest of the party were already seated in camp chairs around the fire. The two women sat a little to one side, talking quietly, and Boris had his feet propped on the low table as he leaned back in his chair with a glass in one hand.

He indicated the vodka bottle on the table, as Nicholas stepped into the circle of firelight, 'Get yourself a drink. Ice in the bucket.'

'I prefer a beer,' Nicholas told him. 'Thirsty drive.' Boris shrugged and bellowed for his camp butler to bring a brown bottle from the portable gas refrigerator.

'Let me tell you something, a little secret.' He grinned at Nicholas as he poured himself another vodka. 'There is no such animal as a striped dik-dik these days, even if there ever was one. You are wasting your time and your money.'

'Fine,' Nicholas agreed mildly. 'It's my time and my money.'

'Just because some old fart shot one back in the Dark Ages, doesn't mean you are going to find another now. We could go up into the tea plantations for elephant. I saw three bulls there only ten days ago. All with tusks over a hundred pounds a side.'

As they argued, the level in Boris's vodka bottle fell like the Nile at the end of the inundation. When Tessay told them that the meal was ready, Boris carried the bottle with him; he stumbled on his way to the table. During the meal his only contribution to the conversation was to snarl at Tessay.

'The lamb is raw. Why don't you see to it that the cook does it properly? Damn monkeys, you have to watch everything they do.'

'Is your lamb under-cooked, Alto Nicholas?' Tessay asked without looking at her husband. 'I can have them cook it longer.'

'It's perfect,' he assured her. 'I like mine pink.'

By the end of dinner the vodka bottle at Boris's elbow was empty, and his face was flushed and swollen. He got up from the table without a word and disappeared into the darkness in the direction of his tent, swaying on his feet and occasionally catching his balance with a two-step jig.

'I apologize,' Tessay told them quietly. 'It is only in the evenings. In the day he is fine. It is a Russian tradition, the vodka.' She smiled brightly; only her eyes stayed sad.

'It is a lovely night, and too early yet for bed. Would you like to walk up to the church? It is very old and famous. I will have one of the servants bring a lantern, so that you may admire the murals.'

The servant walked ahead of them, lighting their way, and an ancient priest waited to welcome them on the portico of the circular building. He was thin and so very black that only his teeth flashed in the gloom. He carried a magnificent Coptic cross in massive native silver, set with carnelians and other semi-precious stones.

Both Royan and Tessay dropped on their knees in front of him to ask for his blessing. He slapped their cheeks lightly with the cross and genuflected over them, mumbling his benediction in Amharic. Then he ushered them into the interior.

The walls were covered with a magnificent display of paintings in brilliant primary colours. In the lantern light they blazed like gemstones. There was a strong Byzantine flavour to the style: the saints' eyes were huge and slanted, with great golden halos over their heads. Above the altar, with its tinsel and brass furnishing, the Virgin cradled her infant while the three wise men and a host of angels knelt in adoration. Nicholas slipped his Polaroid camera from the pocket of his jacket and adjusted the flash. He wandered around the church photographing these murals, while Tessay and Royan knelt before the altar side by side.

Once he had finished his photography Nicholas found a seat on the hand-hewn wooden pews and sat quietly watching their intent faces which the candlelight touched with golden highlights, and he was moved by the beauty of the moment.

'I wish I had that kind of faith,' he thought, as he had so often before. 'It must be a comfort in the hard times. I wish I were able to pray like that for Rosalind and the girls.' He could not stay longer, and he went out and sat on the church portico where he watched the night sky.

In these high altitudes, in the thin unpolluted air, the stars were such a dazzling blaze that it was difficult to pick out the individual constellations. After a while his sadness abated. It was good to be back in Africa.

When the two women emerged at last from the dark interior, Nicholas gave the old priest a one hundred birr note and a Polaroid photograph of himself which the old man clearly valued above the money. Then the three of them walked back down the hill together in companionable silence.

'Nicky!' Royan shook him awake. When he sat up and switched on his torch, he saw that she had thrown the woollen shawl over a pair of men's striped pyjamas before she had come into his tent.

'What is it?' he asked, but before she could answer he heard the sound of a hoarse and angry voice shouting invective in the night, and then the unmistakable thud of a clenched fist striking flesh and bone.

'He's beating her.' Royan's voice was tight with outrage. 'You have to make him stop.'

There was a cry of pain after the blow, and then sobs.

Nicholas hesitated. Only a fool interferes between a man and his wife, and his reward usually is to have them unite and turn savagely upon him.

'You must do something, Nicky, please.'

Reluctantly he swung his legs out of the cot and stood up. He slept in boxer shorts, and he did not bother to find his shoes. She followed him, also on bare feet, to the end

116

of the grove where Boris's tent stood beyond the dining tent.

There was a lantern still burning within, and it threw magnified shadows on the canvas walls. He saw that Boris had his wife by the hair and was dragging her across the floor, roaring at her in Russian.

'Boris!' Nicholas had to shout his name three times to get his attention, and then they saw the shadow play on the canvas as he dropped Tessay and flung open the tent flap.

He was dressed only in a pair of underpants. His torso was lean and muscular, the chest flat and hard-looking, covered with coppery curls. On the floor behind him Tessay lay face down, sobbing into her cupped hands. She was naked, and the planes of her body were sleek as those of a panther.

'What the hell is going on here?' Nicholas demanded, his anger only just beginning to stir as he witnessed the gracious, gentle woman's distress and humiliation.

'I am giving this black whore a lesson in good manners,' Boris gloated, his face still swollen and flushed with drink and passion. 'It's none of your business, English, unless you want to pay some money and have a bit of pork for yourself.' He laughed, an ugly sound.

'Are you all right, Woizero Tessay?' Nicholas looked directly into Boris's face, sparing the woman the further humiliation of another man's eyes on her nudity.

Tessay sat up, lifted her knees against her chest, and hugged them with both arms to cover her body.

'It's all right, Alto Nicholas. Please go away before there is real trouble.' Blood was trickling from one nostril into her mouth, and dyeing her teeth pink.

'You heard my wife, English bastard. Go away! Mind your own business. Go away, before I give you a little lesson in good manners also.'

Boris staggered forward and thrust his open hand

against Nicholas's chest. Nicholas moved as smoothly and as effortlessly as a matador avoiding the first wild charge of the bull. He swayed to one side, and used Boris's own momentum to send him on in the direction in which he was already committed. Completely off balance, the Russian reeled across the open ground in front of the tent until he collided with one of the camp chairs and went down in a sprawling heap.

'Royan, take Tessay to your tent!' he ordered softly. Royan ran into the tent and pulled a sheet from the nearest cot. She spread it over Tessay's shoulders and lifted her to her feet.

'Please, don't do this,' Tessay sobbed. 'You don't know him when he gets like this. He will hurt somebody.'

Royan dragged her, still protesting and weeping, out of the tent, but by now Boris was on his feet again. He bellowed with rage and picked up the camp chair that had tripped him. With a single jerk he tore off one of the legs and hefted it in his bunched fist.

'You want to play games, English? All right, we play!' He rushed at Nicholas, swinging the chair leg like a Ninja baton, so that it hissed with the force with which he aimed it at his head. As Nicholas ducked under it Boris reversed the swing, going for the side of his chest, under his upraised arm. It would have staved in his ribs if it had landed, but again Nicholas twisted away.

They circled each other warily, and then Boris charged again. If it had not been for the effect of the vodka on the Russian's reflexes Nicholas would never have taken a chance with an adversary of this calibre, but Boris was just loose enough in his control to allow him to duck in under the swinging chair leg. He straightened, with all his weight rolling into the punch, and his fist slogged into the pit of Boris's belly just under the sternum. The Russian's breath was driven out of him in a great gusty belch.

The chair leg flew from his grip, and he doubled over

and collapsed. Clasping his middle, and heaving and wheezing for breath, Boris lay curled in the dust. Nicholas stooped over him and told him softly in English, 'This sort of behaviour simply isn't good enough, old chap. We don't bully girls. Please don't let it happen again.'

He straightened up and spoke to Royan, 'Get her to your tent and keep her there.' He combed his hair back from his face with his fingers. 'And now, if you have no serious objections, may we get a little sleep?'

I t rained again during the early hours. The heavy drops drummed down on the canvas and the lightning lit the interior of the tents with an eerie brilliance. However, by the time that Nicholas went through to the dining tent for breakfast the next morning, the clouds had cleared and the sunshine was bright and cheering. The sweet mountain air smelt of wet earth and mushrooms.

Boris greeted Nicholas with hearty good fellowship. 'Good morning, English. We had some fun last night. I still laugh to remember it. Very good jokes. One day soon we will have some more vodka, then we will make some more good jokes.' And he bellowed through to the kitchen tent, 'Hey! Lady Sun, bring your new boyfriend something to eat. He is hungry from all the sport last night.'

Tessay was quiet and withdrawn as she supervised the servants handing round breakfast. One eye was swollen almost closed, and her lip was cut. She did not look at Nicholas once during the meal.

'We will go on ahead,' Boris explained jovially as they drank coffee. 'My servants will break camp, and follow us in my big truck. With luck, we will be able to camp tonight on the rim above the gorge, and tomorrow we will begin the descent.'

As they were climbing into the truck, Tessay was able

to speak to him softly for a moment, without danger of Boris overhearing her. 'Thank you, Alto Nicholas. But it was not wise. You don't know him. You must be careful now. He does not forget, nor does he forgive.'

From the village of Debra Maryam Boris took a branch road that ran alongside the Dandera river directly south-wards. The road they had followed the previous day from Lake Tana was shown on the map as a major highway. It had been bad enough. But this track that they were now on was marked as a secondary road 'not passable in all weather'. To compound matters, it seemed that most of the heavy traffic that had torn up the main road had followed this same track. They came to a place where some huge vehicle had become bogged down in the rain-saturated earth, and the efforts to free it had left areas of ploughed land and an excavation like a bomb crater that resembled an old photograph of the battlefields of First World War Flanders.

Twice during the day the Toyota too became stuck in this foul ground. Each time this happened, the big truck that was following them came up and all the servants swarmed down from the cargo body to push and heave the Toyota through. Even Nicholas stripped to the waist to work with them in the mud to free it.

'If you had only listened to my advice,' Boris grumbled, 'we would not be here. There is no game where you want to go, and there are no roads worth the name either.'

In the early afternoon they stopped beside the river for an alfresco lunch. Nicholas went down to the pool beside the road to wash off the mud and filth of the morning's labours. He had been in the forefront of the efforts to keep the truck moving. Royan followed him down the slope and perched on a rock above the pool while he stripped off his shirt and knelt at the verge to splash himself with the cold mountain water. The river was muddy yellow and swollen from the rainstorms.

'I don't think Boris believes your story about the striped dik-dik,' she warned him. 'Tessay tells me that he is suspicious of what we are up to.' She watched with interest as he sluiced his chest and upper arms. Where the sun had not touched it, his skin was very white and unblemished. His chest hair was thick and dark. She decided that his body was good to look at.

'He is the type that would go through our luggage if he gets a chance,' Nicholas agreed. 'You didn't bring anything with you that has any clues for him? No papers or notes?'

'Only the satellite photograph, and my notebooks are all in my own shorthand. He won't be able to make anything of them.'

'Be very careful of what you discuss with Tessay.'

'She is a dear. There is nothing underhand about her.' Heatedly Royan came to the defence of her new friend.

'She may be all right, but she's married to my chum Boris. Her first allegiance lies there. No matter what your feelings towards her, don't trust either of them.' He dried himself on his shirt, slipped it on and then buttoned it over his chest. 'Let's go and get something to eat.'

Back at the parked truck Boris was pulling the cork from a bottle of South African white wine. He poured a tumblerful for Nicholas. Chilled in the river, it was crisp and fruity. Tessay offered them cold roast chicken and *injera* bread, the flat, thin sheets of stone-ground unleavened bread of the country. The trials and labours of the morning's travels faded into insignificance as Royan lay beside Nicholas in the grass and they watched a bearded vulture sailing high against the blue. It saw them and drifted overhead curiously, twisting its head to look down at them. Its eyes were masked in black like those of a highwayman, and the distinctive wedge-shaped tail feathers flirted with the wind the way the fingers of a concert pianist would stroke the ivories of the keyboard.

When it was time to go on, Nicholas gave her his

hand to lift her to her feet. It was one of their rare moments of physical contact, and she held on to his fingers for just a second or two longer than was strictly necessary.

There was no improvement in the surface of the track as they drew nearer to the rim of the gorge, and the hours passed in this bone-jarring, teeth-rattling progress. The track snaked over a rise and then dog-legged down the far slope. Halfway down Boris swore in Russian as they came round the hairpin bend of a high earthen bank to find a huge diesel truck slewed across the track, almost blocking it.

Even though they had been following the tracks of this convoy of vehicles since the previous day, this was the first of them that they had encountered, and it took Boris by surprise. He hit his brakes so suddenly that his passengers were almost catapulted from their seats, but on the steep incline in the mud the brakes did not bring them to a complete halt. Boris was forced to change down into his lowest gear and steer for the narrow gap between the bank and the truck.

From the back seat Royan looked out of the window beside her, up the high side of the diesel truck. There was a company name and logo emblazoned in scarlet on the green background.

A strong feeling of *déjà vu* overcame her as she stared at the image. She had seen this sign recently, but her memory cheated her: she could not recall the time or the place. She only knew that it was of vital importance that she should remember.

The side of the Toyota scraped against the metal of the truck, and then they were past it. Boris leaned out of his window and shook his fist at the driver of the larger vehicle.

He was a local man, probably recruited in Addis by the owner of the truck. Grinning at Boris's antics, he leaned out of his own cab to return the clenched fist salute, adding a nice little touch by jerking a raised forefinger upwards.

'Dung-eater!' Boris roared with outrage at being bested in the exchange, but he did not stop. 'No use even talking to them. What do they know? Black chimps!'

For the rest of the wearisome journey Royan remained silent and withdrawn, shaken and troubled by the conviction that she had seen the trademark of the winged red horse before, with, set above it in a pennant, the name of the company: 'PEGASUS EXPLORATION'.

As they approached the end of the day's journey at last they passed a signpost beside the track. The supporting legs of the sign were solidly set in concrete, and the artwork was of such high quality that it could only have been that of a professional signwriter.

Across the top of the board an arrow indicated a newly bulldozed road that headed off to the right, and the directions read:

PEGASUS EXPLORATION
BASE CAMP – ONE KILOMETRE
PRIVATE ROAD
NO ENTRY TO UNAUTHORIZED TRAFFIC

The scarlet horse reared in the centre of the board with its wings spread wide, on the point of flight.

Now she gasped aloud as the elusive memory came upon her with stunning clarity. She remembered where she had last seen the flying red horse. In an instant she was transported back into the icy waters of an English salmon river, flung from the rolling body of the Land Rover, the huge MAN truck roaring over the bridge above her, and, for a subliminal pulse of time, the prancing red horse upon its side.

'It's the same!' she almost shouted aloud, but controlled herself. The terror of the moment returned to her with full force, and she found herself breathing hard and her heart racing as though she had run a long way.

'It cannot be a coincidence,' she assured herself silently, 'and I am not mistaken. It is the same company. Pegasus Exploration.'

She was withdrawn and distracted for the last few miles of the journey, until the track they were following ended abruptly on the brink of the sheer cliffs of the escarpment. Here Boris pulled on to the grassy verge and stopped the engine.

'This is as far as we ride. We camp here tonight. My big truck is not far behind. They will make camp as soon as they arrive. Tomorrow we will go down into the gorge on foot.'

As they dismounted, Royan tugged at Nicholas's arm, 'I must speak to you,' she whispered urgently, and she followed him as he led her along the bank of the river.

He found a place for them to sit side by side, with their legs dangling over the drop. Beside them the swollen yellow river seemed to sense what lay ahead of it. The cold mountain waters speeded up, swirled amongst the rocks, and gathered themselves for that dizzying leap out into empty space. The cliff below them was a sheer wall of rock almost a thousand feet deep. It was so high that in the evening light the abyss far below was a dark, mysterious place, its bottom hidden from them by shadow and spray from the falls. As Royan looked down into it her sense of balance swirled with vertigo. She cringed back from the edge and found herself instinctively leaning against Nicholas's shoulder to steady herself. Only when they touched did she realize what she was doing, and she pulled away from him self-consciously.

The muddied waters of the Dandera river leaped from the brink, and were miraculously transformed into curtains of ethereal lacework as they fell. Like the skirts of a waltzing bride they shimmered and swirled, and rainbows of light played through them as though from an embroidery of seed pearls. Still falling, the columns of white spray twisted and changed into lovely but ephemeral shapes, until they struck the lower ledges of glistening black rock and exploded outwards into fresh clouds of white that at last screened the dark depths of the abyss with an opalescent veil.

It was with a conscious effort that Royan pulled her mind away from the awe-inspiring scene and back to the troubled present.

'Nicky, do you remember I told you about the truck that forced my mother and me over the bridge in the Land Rover?'

'Of course.' His expression was mystified as he studied her face. 'You are upset. What is it, Royan?'

'The truck had signwriting down the sides of the trailers that it was towing.'

'You told me, yes. Green and red. You told me that you didn't get a good enough look to read the sign.'

'It was the same as the truck we passed this afternoon. I saw the sign at the same angle as before and it came back to me. The red Pegasus, the flying horse.'

He studied her face for a while, 'Are you absolutely certain?'

'Absolutely!' She nodded vehemently.

Nicholas stared out over the magnificent panorama of the gorge spread below them. It was forty miles to the far wall of the canyon, but in the brilliant rain-washed air it seemed so close that he could reach across and touch it.

'A coincidence?' he wondered at last.

'Do you think so? A very strange and wonderful coincidence, then. Pegasus in both Yorkshire and Gojam? Do you accept that?'

'It doesn't make sense. The truck that hit you was stolen—'

'Was it?' she demanded. 'Are we sure of that?'

'If it wasn't, then let's hear your ideas.'

'If you were planning an assassination, would you rely on stealing a truck conveniently left at a Little Chef for you?'

He shook his head, 'Go on.'

'Suppose you arranged for your own truck to be placed there for you, and for your driver to report it stolen only after you had a good head start on the police.'

'It's possible,' he agreed without enthusiasm.

'Whoever murdered Duraid, and made two further attempts to kill me, obviously has considerable resources at his disposal. He is able to make arrangements in Egypt and England. On top of that, he has the seventh scroll in his possession. He has our notes and all our workings and translations which point him clearly to this spot on the Abbay river. Just suppose that he has control of a company like Pegasus – is there any reason why he can't be here in Ethiopia, just as we are, right at this moment?'

Nicholas was silent for a while. He picked up a stone from the ledge beside him and tossed it out over the cliff. They both watched it drop away, dwindling in size until it vanished in the veils of spray far below where they sat.

Abruptly Nicholas stood up and reached for her hand to pull her to her feet beside him. 'Come on,' he said.

'Where are we going?'

'Pegasus base camp. Let's go and have a chat to the site foreman.'

Boris protested angrily and hurried to intervene when Nicholas climbed into the Toyota and started the engine, 'Where the hell do you think you are going?'

'Sight-seeing.' Nicholas let in the clutch. 'Back in an hour.'

'Hey, English, my truck!' He ran to catch up with them, but Nicholas accelerated away.

'Charge me for the hire.' He grinned back at Boris in the rear-view mirror.

They reached the signposted turn-off and followed the side track over the ridge. The Pegasus camp lay on the far side. Nicholas braked to a halt on the crest of the rise and they studied it in silence.

An area of about ten acres had been cleared and levelled. It was surrounded by a barbed-wire security fence, with a single closed gate. Three of the massive diesel trucks in their green and red livery were parked in a rank inside the fence. There were also several smaller vehicles and a tall mobile drilling rig in the line. The rest of the yard was filled with prospecting equipment and stores. There were stacks of drilling rods and steel core boxes, wooden crates of spares, and several hundred forty-four-gallon drums of diesel and oil and drilling mud. The drums and the stores were stacked with a neatness and sense of good order that was startling in this wild and rocky landscape. Just inside the gate stood a small village of a dozen buildings made of corrugated sheet sections, of the Quonset type. They too were set out in a street of military precision.

'A big, well-organized outfit,' Nicholas commented. 'Let's go down and see who is in charge.'

There were two armed guards on the gate, dressed in the camouflage uniform of the Ethiopian army. They were clearly surprised by the arrival at the gate of the strange Land Cruiser, and when Nicholas sounded his horn one of them came forward suspiciously with his AK-47 rifle at the ready.

'I want to speak to the manager here,' Nicholas told him in Arabic, with enough haughty authority to make the sentry uncertain and uneasy.

The soldier grunted, went back and consulted his colleague, then lifted the handset of the two-way radio and spoke earnestly into the mouthpiece. There was a five-minute delay after he finished speaking, and then the door of the nearest Quonset building opened and a white man came out.

He was dressed in khaki coveralls and a soft bush cap. His eyes, covered by mirrored sunglasses, were set in a deeply tanned, leathery face. His physique was short and chunky, and his sleeves were rolled up over hairy, work-thickened arms. After speaking a few words to the guards at the gate he came out to the Toyota.

'Yeah? What's going down here?' he demanded in a Texan drawl, speaking around the stub of an unlit cigar.

'The name is Quenton-Harper.' Nicholas dismounted from the truck to greet him, and held out his hand. 'Nicholas Quenton-Harper. How do you do?'

The American hesitated, and then took the hand as though he had been offered an electric eel to squeeze.

'Helm,' he said. 'Jake Helm, from Abilene, Texas. I am the foreman here.' His hand was that of an artisan, with calloused palms and lumpy scar tissue over the knuckles, and half moons of black grease under the fingernails.

'Terribly sorry to worry you. I am having some trouble with my truck. I wondered if you had a mechanic who could have a look at it for me.' Nicholas smiled winningly, but received no encouragement from the man.

'Not company policy.' He shook his head.

'I am prepared to pay for any—'

'Listen, buddy, I said no.' Jake removed the cigar from his mouth and examined it minutely.

'Your company – Pegasus. Can you tell me where your head office is situated? Who is your managing director?'

'I am a busy man. You are wasting my time.' Helm returned the cigar to his mouth and began to turn away.

'I will be hunting in this area over the next few weeks. I would not like to endanger any of your employees with a stray shot. Can you give me some idea of where you will be working?'

'I am running a prospecting outfit here, mister. I don't give out news flashes on my movements. Beat it!'

He turned and walked to the gate and gave brusque orders to the guards before marching back to his office building.

'Satellite disc on the roof,' Nicholas remarked. 'I wonder who our lad Jake is speaking to at this very moment.'

'Somebody in Texas?' Royan hazarded.

'Doesn't follow, necessarily,' Nicholas demurred. 'Pegasus is probably a multinational. Just because Jake is one, doesn't mean his boss is Texan also. Not a very instructive conversation, I am afraid.' He started the engine and U-turned the Toyota. 'But if someone at Pegasus is the ugly mixed up in this, he will recognize my name. We have given them notice of our arrival. Let's see what we have flushed out of the bushes.'

When they got back to the Dandera river falls, they found that Boris's truck had arrived, the tents had been erected, and the chef had brewed tea for them. Boris was less welcoming than his chef, and maintained a sullen silence while Nicholas tried to placate him for commandeering his truck. It was only after his first vodka of the evening that he mellowed sufficiently to speak again.

'The mules were supposed to be waiting for us here. Time means nothing to these people. We cannot start down into the gorge until they arrive.'

'Well, at least while we are waiting for them I will have a chance to sight in my rifle,' Nicholas remarked with resignation. 'In Africa it never pays to be in a hurry. Too wearing on the nerves.'

After a leisurely breakfast the next morning, when

there was still no sign of the mules, Nicholas fetched his rifle case.

When Nicholas lifted the weapon out of its nest of green baize, Boris took it from him and examined it minutely.

'An old rifle?'

'Made in 1926,' Nicholas nodded. 'My grandfather had it made for himself.'

'They knew how to make them in those days. Not like the mass-produced crap they turn out today.' Boris pursed his lips critically. 'Short Mauser Oberndorf double square-bridge action, beautiful! But it has been rebarrelled, no?'

'The original barrel was shot out. I had it replaced with a Shilen match barrel. It will shoot the wings off a mosquito at a hundred paces.'

'Calibre 7 × 57, is it?' Boris asked.

'275 Rigby, as a matter of fact,' Nicholas corrected him, but Boris snorted.

'It is exactly the same cartridge – just your English bloodiness must call it something else.' He grinned. 'It will push a 150 grain bullet out there at 2800 feet per second. It is a good rifle, one of the best.'

'You will never know, my dear fellow, how much your approval means to me,' Nicholas murmured in English, and Boris chuckled as he handed the rifle back to him.

'English jokes! I love your English jokes.'

When Nicholas left camp carrying the little rifle in its slip case, Royan followed him down to the river and helped him fill two small canvas bags with white river sand. He laid them on top of a convenient rock and they formed a firm but malleable rest for the rifle as he settled it over them.

Using the open hillside as a safe back-stop, he stepped out two hundred yards and at that range set up a cardboard carton on which he had taped a Bisley-type target. He came back to where Royan waited and then settled down behind the rock on which the weapon lay.

Royan was unprepared for the report of the first shot from the dainty, almost feminine-looking rifle. She jumped involuntarily, and her ears sang.

'What a horrible, vicious thing!' she exclaimed. 'How can you bring yourself to kill lovely animals with a high-powered gun like that?' she demanded.

'Rifle,' he corrected her, as he noted the strike of the shot through his binoculars. 'Would it make you feel better if I used a low-powered rifle, or beat them to death with a stick?'

The shot had struck three inches right and two inches low. As he adjusted the telescopic sight he attempted to explain. 'An ethical hunter does everything in his power to kill as swiftly and as cleanly as is possible, and that means stalking in as close as he is able to do, using a weapon of adequate power and sighting it the best way he knows how.'

His next shot struck exactly on line but only an inch above the bullseye. He wanted it to shoot three inches high at that range. He worked on the sight again.

'Gun or rifle, but I don't understand why you would want to deliberately kill any of God's creatures,' she protested.

'That I can never explain to you.' He aimed deliberately and fired once. Even through the lower magnification of the sight lens he could see that the bullet had struck exactly three inches high.

'It is something to do with an atavistic urge that few men, no matter how cultured and civilized they deem themselves, can deny completely.' He fired a second time. 'Some of them work it out in the board room, others on the golf course or the tennis court, and some of us on a salmon river, in the ocean deeps or in the hunting field.'

He fired a third shot, merely to confirm the previous two, and then went on, 'As for God's creatures, he gave them to us. You are the believer. Quote me Acts 10, verses 12 and 13.'

'Sorry.' She shook her head. 'You tell me.'

'". . . *all manner of fourfooted beasts of the earth, and wild beasts, and creeping things, and fowls of the air,*"' Nicholas obliged her. '"*And there came a voice to him, Rise, Peter; kill, and eat.*"'

'You should have been a lawyer,' she moaned in mock despair.

'Or a priest,' he suggested, and went forward to retrieve the target. He found that his last three shots had punched a tiny symmetrical rosette three inches above the bull, all three bullet holes just touching each other.

He patted the butt stock of the little rifle, 'That's my lovely darling, Lucrezia Borgia.' He had named the rifle for her beauty and for her murderous potential.

He slid the rifle back into its leather slip case and they walked back together. As they came in sight of the camp, Nicholas pulled up short.

'Visitors,' he said, and raised his binoculars. 'Aha! We have flushed something out of the undergrowth. That is a Pegasus truck parked there and, unless I am much mistaken, one of our visitors is the charming laddie from Abilene. Let's go down and find out what is going on.'

As they drew closer to camp, they realized that there were a dozen or more heavily armed, uniformed soldiers clustered around the red and green Pegasus truck, and that Jake Helm and an Ethiopian army officer were seated under the awning of the dining tent in serious and intent conversation with Boris.

As soon as Nicholas entered the tent, Boris introduced him to the bespectacled Ethiopian officer. 'This is Colonel Tuma Nogo, the military commander of the southern Gojam region.'

'How do you do?' Nicholas greeted him, but the colonel ignored the pleasantry.

'I want to see your passport, and your firearms licence,' he ordered arrogantly, while Jake Helm chewed complacently on the evil-smelling butt of an extinguished cigar.

'Yes, of course,' Nicholas agreed, and went to his own tent to fetch his briefcase. He opened it on the dining table, and smiled at the officer. 'I am sure you will also want to see my letter of introduction from the British Foreign Secretary in London, and this one from the British Ambassador in Addis Ababa. Here is another from the Ethiopian Ambassador to the Court of St James, and this *firman* is from your own Minister of Defence, General Siye Abraha.'

The colonel stared in consternation at this fruit salad of ornate official letterheads and scarlet beribboned seals. Behind the gold-rimmed glasses his eyes were bemused and confused.

'Sir!' He jumped to his feet and saluted. 'You are a friend of General Abraha? I did not know. Nobody informed me. I beg your pardon for this intrusion.'

He saluted again, and his embarrassment made him awkward and ungainly. 'I came to warn you only that the Pegasus Company is conducting drilling and blasting operations. There may be some danger. Please be alert. Also there are many bandits and outlaws, *shufta*, operating in this area.' Colonel Nogo was flustered and barely coherent. He stopped and drew a deep breath to steady himself. 'You see, I have been ordered to provide an escort for the employees of the Pegasus Company. If you yourself experience any trouble while you are here, or if you need assistance for any reason you have only to call on me, sir.'

'That is extremely civil of you, colonel.'

'I will detain you no longer, sir.' He saluted a third time and backed off towards the Pegasus truck, taking the Texan foreman along with him. Jake Helm had not uttered a word since their arrival, and now he left without a farewell.

Colonel Nogo gave Nicholas his fourth and final salute through the cab window as the truck pulled away.

'Deuce!' Nicholas told Royan, as he acknowledged the salute with a nonchalant wave. 'I think that point was definitely ours. Now at least we know that, for whatever reason, Mr Pegasus definitely does not want us in his hair. I think we can expect his next service fairly promptly.'

They walked back to where Boris sat in the dining tent and Nicholas told him, 'All we need now are your mules.'

'I have sent three of my men to the village to find them. They should have been here yesterday.'

The mules arrived early the next morning, six big sturdy animals, each accompanied by a driver dressed in the ubiquitous jodhpurs and shawl. By mid-morning they were loaded and ready to begin the descent into the gorge.

Boris paused at the head of the pathway, and looked out over that valley. For once even he seemed to be subdued and awed by the immensity of the drop and the rugged splendour of the gorge.

'You will be passing into another land in another age,' he warned them in an uncharacteristically philosophical mood. 'They say that this trail is two thousand years old, as old as Christ.' He spread his hands in a deprecating gesture. 'The old black priest in the church at Debra Maryam will tell you that the Virgin Mary passed this way when she fled from Israel after the crucifixion.' He shook his head. 'But then these people will believe anything.' And he stepped out on to the pathway.

It clung to the cliff, descending at such an angle that

each pace was down a rock step so deep that it stretched the tendons and the sinews in their groins and knees, and jarred their spines. They were forced to use their hands to scramble the rougher and steeper sections, where it was almost as though they were descending a ladder.

It seemed impossible that the mules under their heavy packs could follow them down. The plucky beasts lunged down each of the rock steps, landing heavily on their forelegs, then gathered themselves for the next drop. The trail was so narrow that the bulky packs scraped against the rock wall on one hand, while on the other hand the drop sucked at them giddily.

When the path dog-legged and changed direction, the mules could not make the turn in one attempt. They were forced to back and fill, edging their way round the narrow trail, sweating with terror and their eyes rolling until the whites flashed. The drivers urged them on with wild cries and busy whips.

At places the pathway entered the body of the mountain, passing behind butts and needles of rock that time and erosion had prised away from the cliff face. These rocky gateways were so narrow that the mules had to be unloaded and the packs carried through by the drivers, and then the mules were reloaded on the far side.

'Look!' Royan cried in astonishment and pointed out into the void. A black vulture rose up out of the depths on widespread pinions and floated past them almost within arm's length, turning its gruesome naked head of pink lappeted skin to stare at them with inscrutable black eyes before sailing away.

'He is using the thermals of heated air from the valley for lift,' Nicholas explained to her. He pointed out along the cliff to an overhanging buttress on the same level as themselves. 'There is one of their nests.' It was a shaggy mound of sticks piled on an inaccessible ledge. The excrement of the birds that had inhabited it over the ages had painted the cliff face below with streaks of brilliant white, and even at this distance they could catch whiffs of rotting offal and decaying flesh.

All that day they clung to the precipitous track as they eased their way down that terrible wall. It was late afternoon, and they were only halfway down, when the trail turned back upon itself once more and they heard the rumble of the falls ahead. The sound grew louder and became a thunderous roar as they moved around the corner of another buttress and came in full sight of the falls.

The wind created by the torrent tugged at them and forced them to clutch for handholds. The spray blew around them and wetted their upturned faces, but the Ethiopian guide led them straight on until it seemed that they must be washed away into the valley still hundreds of feet below.

Then, miraculously, the waters parted and they stepped behind the great translucent curtain into a deep recess of moss-covered and gleaming wet rock, carved from the cliff by the force of water over the aeons. The only light in this gloomy place was filtered through the waterfall, green and mysterious like some undersea cavern.

'This is where we sleep tonight,' Boris announced, obviously enjoying their astonishment. He pointed to bundles of firewood piled at the rear of the cave, and the smoke-blackened wall above the stone hearth. 'The mule-teers carrying food and supplies down to the priests in the monastery have used this place for centuries.'

As they moved deeper into the cavern, the sound of falling water became muted to a dull background rumble and the rock underfoot was dry. Once the servants had lit the fire, it became a warm and comfortable, not to say romantic, lodging.

With an old soldier's eye for the most comfortable spot, Nicholas laid out his sleeping bag in a corner at the back of the cave, and quite naturally Royan unrolled hers beside his. They were both tired out by the unusual exertion of climbing down the cliff wall, and after supper they stretched out in their sleeping bags in companionable silence and watched the firelight playing on the roof of the cave.

'Just think!' Royan whispered. 'Tomorrow we will be retracing the footsteps of old Taita himself.'

'To say nothing of the Virgin Mary,' Nicholas smiled.

'You are a horrid old cynic,' she sighed. 'And what is more, you probably snore.'

'You are about to find out the hard way,' he told her, but she was asleep before him. Her breathing was gentle and even, and he could just hear it above the sound of the water. It was a long time since he had had a lovely woman lying at his side. When he was sure she was deeply under, he reached across and touched her cheek gently.

'Pleasant dreams, little one,' he whispered tenderly. 'You have had a busy day.' That was the way he had often bid his younger daughter sleep.

The muleteers were stirring long before the dawn, and the whole party was on the pathway again as soon as the light was strong enough to reveal their footing. When the early sun struck the upper walls of the cliff face, they were still high enough above the valley floor to have an aerial view of the terrain. Nicholas drew Royan aside and they let the rest of the caravan go on down ahead of them.

He found a place to sit and unrolled the satellite photograph between them. Picking out the major peaks and features of the scene, they orientated themselves and began to make some order out of the cataclysmic landscape that rioted below them.

'We can't see the Abbay river from here,' Nicholas

pointed out. 'It's still deep in the sub-gorge. We will probably only get our first glimpse of it from almost directly above.'

'If we have identified our present position accurately, then the river will make two ox-bow bends around that bluff over there.'

'Yes, and the confluence of the Dandera river with the Abbay is over there, below those cliffs.' He used his thumb knuckle as a rough scale measure. 'About fifteen miles from here.'

'It looks as though the Dandera has changed its course many times over the centuries. I can see at least two gullies that look like ancient river beds.' She pointed down: 'There, and there. They are all choked with jungle now.' She looked crestfallen, 'Oh, Nicholas, it is such a huge and confused area. How are we ever going to find the single entrance to a tomb hidden in all that?'

'Tomb? What tomb is this?' Boris demanded with interest. He had come back up the trail to find them. They had not heard his approach, and now he stood over them. 'What tomb are you talking about?'

'Why, the tomb of St Frumentius, of course,' Nicholas told him smoothly, showing no concern at having been overheard.

'Isn't the monastery dedicated to the saint?' Royan asked as smoothly, as she rolled up the photograph.

'*Da.*' He nodded, looking disappointed, as though he expected something of more interest. 'Yes, St Frumentius. But they will not let you visit the tomb. They will not let you into the inner part of the monastery. Only the priests are allowed in there.'

He removed his cap and scratched the short, stiff bristles that covered his scalp. They rasped like wire under his fingernails. 'This week is the ceremony of Timkat, the Blessing of the Tabot. There will be a great deal of excitement down there. You will find it very interesting, but you will not be able to enter the Holy of Holies, nor will you be able to see the actual tomb. I have never met any white man who has seen it.'

He squinted up at the sun. 'We must get on. It looks close, but it will take us two more days to reach the Abbay. It is bad ground down there. A long march, even for a famous dik-dik hunter.' He laughed delightedly at his own joke, and turned away down the path.

As they approached the bottom of the cliff, the gradient of the trail smoothed out and the steps became shallower and further apart. The going became easier and their progress swifter, but the air had changed in quality and taste. It was no longer cool, bracing mountain air but the languid, enervating air of the equator, with the smell and taste of the encroaching jungle.

'Hot!' said Royan, shrugging out of the woollen shawl.

'Ten degrees hotter, at least,' Nicholas agreed. He pulled his old army jersey over his head, leaving his hair in curly disarray. 'And we can expect it to get hotter before we reach the Abbay. We still have to descend another three thousand feet.'

Now the path followed the Dandera river for a while. Sometimes they were several hundred feet above it, and shortly afterwards they splashed waist-deep through a ford, hanging on to the panniers of the mules to keep themselves from being swept away on the flood.

Then the gorge of the Dandera river was too deep and steep to follow any longer, as sheer cliffs dropped into dark pools. So they left the river and followed the track that squirmed like a dying snake amongst eroded hills and tall red stone bluffs.

A mile or two further downstream they rejoined the river in a different mood as it rippled through dense forest. The dangling lianas swept the surface and tree moss brushed their heads as they passed, straggling and unkempt as the beard of the old priest at Debra Maryam. Vervet monkeys chattered at them from the treetops and ducked their heads in wide-eyed outrage at the human intrusion into these secret places. Once a large animal crashed away through the undergrowth, and Nicholas glanced across at Boris.

The Russian shook his head, laughing. 'No, English, not dik-dik. Only kudu.'

On the hillside above them the kudu paused to look back. He was a large bull with full twists to his wide corkscrew horns, a magnificent beast with a maned dewlap and pricked ears shaped like trumpets. He stared at them with huge, startled eyes. Boris whistled softly and his attitude changed abruptly.

'Those horns are over fifty inches. They would get a place right at the top of *Rowland Ward*.' He was referring to the register of big game which was the Bible of the trophy hunter. 'Don't you want to take him, English?' He ran to the nearest mule and pulled the Rigby rifle from its slip case, then ran back and offered it to Nicholas.

'Let him go.' Nicholas shook his head. 'Only dik-dik for me.'

With a flirt of his white powder-puff tail, the bull was gone over the ridge. Boris shook his head disgustedly and spat into the river.

'Why did he try to insist that you kill it?' Royan demanded as they went on.

'A photograph of a record pair of horns like that would look good on his advertising brochure. Suck in more clients.'

All day they followed the winding trail, and in the late afternoon they camped in a clearing above the river where it was evident that other caravans had camped many times before them. It seemed obvious that this road was divided into time-honoured stages: every traveller took three full days from the top of the falls to reach the monastery, and they all camped at the same sites.

'Sorry. No shower here,' Boris told his clients. 'If you want to wash, there is a safe pool around the first bend upstream.'

Royan looked appealingly at Nicholas, 'I am so hot and sweaty. Please won't you stand guard for me, where you can hear me call if I need you?'

So he lay on the mossy bank just below the bend, out of sight but close enough to hear her splash and squeal at the cold embrace of the water. Once when he turned his head he realized that the current must have drifted her downstream, for through the trees he caught a flash of a naked back, and the curve of a buttock, creamy and glistening wet with water. He looked away again guiltily, but he was startled by the intensity of his physical arousal brought on by that brief glimpse of lambent skin dappled with the late sunlight through the trees.

When she came downstream along the bank, singing softly, towelling her wet hair, she called to him, 'Your turn. Do you want me to stand guard for you?'

'I am a big boy now.' He shook his head, but as she passed him he noticed the saucy glint in her eye, and he wondered suddenly if she had been fully aware of just how far downstream she had swum, and how much he had seen. He was titillated by the thought.

He went upstream to the pool alone, and as he stripped he looked down at himself and felt guilty when he saw how she had moved him. Since Rosalind, no other woman had had this effect on him.

'A nice cold plunge won't do you any harm, my lad.' He threw his jeans over a bush, and dived into the pool.

As they sat at the campfire after the evening meal, Nicholas looked up suddenly and cocked his head.

'Am I hearing things?' he wondered.

'No,' Tessay laughed. 'That is singing you hear. The priests from the monastery are coming to welcome us.'

They saw the torches then, winding up the hillside in procession, flickering through the trees as they approached the camp. The muleteers and the servants crowded forward, singing and clapping rhythmically to greet the deputation from the monastery.

The deep male voices soared and then dropped away, almost to a whisper, then rose again in descant, haunting and beautiful, the sound of Africa in the night. It drove icy thrills down Nicholas's spine, so that he shivered involuntarily.

Then they saw the white robes of the priests, flitting like moths in the torchlight as they wound along the trail. The camp servants fell on their knees as the first of the holy men entered the perimeter of the camp. They were young acolytes, bare-headed and bare-footed. They were followed by the monks, wearing long robes and tall turbans. Their ranks wheeled aside and opened up, an honour guard for the phalanx of deacons and fully ordained priests in their gaudy embroidered robes and vestments.

Each of them carried a heavy Coptic cross, set on a tall staff and intricately chased and worked in native silver. They in turn opened into two ranks, still chanting, and allowed the canopied palanquin to be carried forward by four hefty young acolytes and placed in the centre of the camp. The crimson and yellow silk curtains shimmered in the light of the camp lanterns and the torches of the procession.

'We must go forward to welcome the abbot,' Boris told Nicholas in a stage whisper. 'His name is Jali Hora.' As they stepped up to the litter, the curtains were drawn dramatically aside and a tall figure stepped down to earth.

Both Tessay and Royan sank to their knees respectfully, and clasped their hands at the breast. However,

Nicholas and Boris remained on their feet, and Nicholas inspected the abbot with interest.

Jali Hora was skeletally thin. Beneath the skirts of his robe his legs were like sticks of cured tobacco, tar-black and twisted, with desiccated sinew and stringy muscle. His robe was green and gold, worked with gold thread that glittered in the firelight. On his head he wore a tall hat with a flat top embroidered with a pattern of crosses and stars.

The abbot's face was dead sooty black, the skin wrinkled and riven with the deep etchings of age. There were few teeth behind his puckered lips, and even those were yellowed and askew. His beard was startling silver white, breaking like storm surf on the old bones of his jaw. One eye was opaque blue and blinded with tropical ophthalmia, but the other eye glistened like that of a hunting leopard.

He began to speak in a high, quavering voice. 'A blessing,' Boris warned Nicholas, and they both bowed their heads respectfully. The assembled priests came in with the chanted response each time the old man paused.

When at last he had finished giving his blessing Jali Hora made the sign of the cross in four directions, rotating slowly towards each point of the compass, while two altar boys swung their silver censers vigorously, deluging the night with pungent clouds of incense smoke.

After the blessing the two women came forward to kneel before the abbot. He stooped over them and struck them lightly on each cheek with his silver cross, chanting a falsetto blessing over them.

'They say the old man is over a hundred years old,' Boris whispered to Nicholas.

Two white-robed *debteras* brought forward a stool of African ebony, so beautifully carved that Nicholas eyed it acquisitively. He guessed that it was probably centuries old, and would have made a handsome addition to the museum collection. The two *debteras* took Jali Hora's elbows and gently seated him on the stool. Then the rest of the company sank to the earth in a congregation around him, their black faces lifted towards him attentively.

Tessay sat at his feet, and when her husband spoke she translated quietly for him into Amharic. 'It is a great pleasure and an honour for me to greet you again, Holy Father.'

The old man nodded, and Boris went on, 'I have brought an English nobleman of royal blood to visit the monastery of St Frumentius.'

'I say, steady on, old boy!' Nicholas protested, but all the congregation studied him with expectant interest.

'What do I do now?' he asked Boris out of the corner of his mouth.

'What do you think he came all this way for?' Boris grinned maliciously. 'He wants a gift. Money.'

'Maria Theresa dollars?' he enquired, referring to the centuries-old traditional currency of Ethiopia.

'Not necessarily. Times have changed. Jali Hora will be happy to take Yankee green-backs.'

'How much?'

'You are a nobleman of royal blood. You will be hunting in his valley. Five hundred dollars at least.'

Nicholas winced and went to fetch his bag from one of the mule panniers. When he came back he bowed to the abbot and placed the sheaf of currency in his outstretched, pink-palmed claw. The abbot smiled, exposing the yellow stumps of his teeth, and spoke briefly.

Tessay translated for him, 'He says, "Welcome to the monastery of St Frumentius and the season of Timkat." He wishes you good hunting on the banks of the Abbay river.'

Immediately the solemn mood of the devout company changed. They broke out in smiles and laughter, and the abbot looked expectantly at Boris.

'The holy abbot says it has been a thirsty journey,' Tessay translated.

'The old devil loves his brandy,' Boris explained, and shouted to the camp butler. With some ceremony a bottle of brandy was brought and placed on the camp table in front of the abbot, shoulder to shoulder with the bottle of vodka in front of Boris. They toasted each other, and the abbot tossed back a dram that made his good eye weep with tears, and his voice husky as he directed a question at Royan.

'He asks you, Woizero Royan, where do you come from, daughter, that you follow the true path of Christ the Saviour of man?'

'I am an Egyptian, of the old religion,' Royan replied. The abbot and all his priests nodded and beamed with approval.

'We are all brothers and sisters in Christ, the Egyptians and the Ethiopians,' the abbot told her. 'Even the word Coptic derives from the Greek for Egyptian. For over sixteen hundred years the Abuna, the bishop, of Ethiopia was always appointed by the Patriarch in Cairo. Only the Emperor Haile Selassie changed that in 1959, but we still follow the true road to Christ. You are welcome, my daughter.'

His *debtera* poured another dram of brandy and the old man swallowed it at a gulp. Even Boris looked impressed, 'Where does the skinny old black tortoise put it?' he wondered aloud. Tessay did not translate, but she lowered her eyes and the hurt she felt for the insult to the holy man showed on her madonna features.

Jali Hora turned to Nicholas. 'He wants to know what animals you have come to hunt here in his valley,' Tessay told him.

Nicholas steeled himself and then replied carefully. There was a long moment of disbelief, then the abbot cackled happily and the assembled priests shouted with incredulous mirth.

'A dik-dik! You have come to hunt a dik-dik! But there is no meat on an animal that size.'

Nicholas let them get over the first shock, and then produced a photograph of the mounted specimen of *Moquoda harperii* from the museum. He placed it on the table in front of Jali Hora.

'This is no ordinary dik-dik. It is a holy dik-dik,' he told them in portentous tones, nodding at Tessay for the translation. 'Let me recount the legend.' They were silenced by the prospect of a good story with religious overtones. Even the abbot arrested the glass on its way to his lips and replaced it on the table. His one eye swivelled from the photograph to Nicholas's face.

'When John the Baptist was dying of starvation in the desert,' Nicholas began, and a few of the priests crossed themselves at the mention of the saint's name, 'he had been thirty days and thirty nights without a morsel passing his lips—' Nicholas spun out the yarn for a while, dwelling on the extremities of hunger endured by the saint, details savoured by his audience who liked their holy men to suffer in the name of righteousness.

'In the end the Lord took mercy on his servant and placed a small antelope in a thicket of acacia, held fast by the thorns. He said unto the saint: "I have prepared a meal for you that you shall not die. Take of this meat and eat." Where John the Baptist touched the small creature, the marks of his thumb and fingers were imprinted upon its back for all time, and all generations to come.' They were silent and impressed.

Nicholas passed the photograph to the abbot. 'See the prints of the saint's fingers upon it.'

The old man studied the print avidly, holding it up to his single eye, and at last he exclaimed, 'It is true. The marks of the saint's fingers are clear to see.'

He passed it to his deacons. Encouraged by the abbot's endorsement, they exclaimed and wondered over the picture of the insignificant creature in its coat of striped fur.

'Have any of your men ever laid eyes upon one of these animals?' Nicholas demanded, and one after the other they shook their heads. The photograph completed the circle and was passed to the rank of squatting acolytes.

Suddenly one of them leaped to his feet prancing, brandishing the photograph and gibbering with excitement.

'I have seen this holy creature! With my very own eyes, I have seen it.' He was a young boy, barely adolescent.

There were cries of derision and disbelief from the others. One of them snatched the print from the boy's grasp and waved it out of his reach, taunting him with it.

'The child is soft in the head, and often possessed by demons and fits,' Jali Hora explained sorrowfully. 'Take no notice of him, poor Tamre!'

Tamre's eyes were wild as he ran down the rank of acolytes, trying desperately to recapture the photograph. But they passed it back and forth, keeping it just out of his reach, teasing him and jeering at his antics.

Nicholas rose to his feet to intervene. He found this taunting of a weak-minded lad offensive, but at that moment something tripped in the boy's mind, and he fell to the ground as though struck down by a club. His back arched and his limbs twitched and jerked uncontrollably, his eyes rolled back into his skull until only the whites showed, and white froth creamed on his lips that were drawn back in a grinning rictus.

Before Nicholas could go to him, four of his peers picked him up bodily and carried him away. Their laughter dwindled into the night. The others acted as though this was nothing out of the ordinary, and Jali Hora nodded to his *debtera* to refill his glass.

It was late when at last Jali Hora took his leave and

was helped into the palanquin by his deacons. He took the remains of the brandy with him, clutching the half-empty bottle in one clawed hand and tossing out benedictions with the other.

'You made a good impression, Milord English,' Boris told him. 'He liked your story of John the Baptist, but he liked your money even more.'

W hen they set out the next morning, the path followed the river for a while. But within a mile the waters quickened their pace, and then raced through the narrow opening between high red cliffs and plunged over another waterfall.

Nicholas left the well-trodden trail and went down to the brink of the falls. He looked down two hundred feet into a deep cleft in the rock, only just wide enough to allow the angry river to squeeze through. He could have thrown a stone across the gap. There was no path nor foothold in that chasm, and he turned back and rejoined the rest of the caravan as it detoured away from the river and into another thickly wooded valley.

'This was probably once the course of the Dandera river, before it cut a fresh bed for itself through the chasm.' Royan pointed to the high ground on each side of the path, and then to the water-worn boulders that littered the trail.

'I think you are right,' Nicholas agreed. 'These cliffs seem to be an intrusion of limestone through the basalt and sandstone. The whole area has been severely faulted and cut up by erosion and the ever-changing river. You can be certain that those limestone cliffs are riddled with caves and springs.'

Now the trail descended rapidly towards the Blue Nile, falling away almost fifteen hundred feet in altitude in the last few miles. The sides of the valley were heavily covered with vegetation and at many places small springs of water oozed from the limestone and trickled down the old river bed.

The heat built up steadily as they went down, and soon even Royan's khaki shirt was stained with dark patches of sweat between her shoulder blades.

At one stage a freshet of clear water gushed from an area of dense bush high up the hillside and swelled the stream into a small river. Then they turned a corner of the valley and found that they and the stream had rejoined the main flow of the Dandera river. Looking back up the gorge, they could see where the river had emerged from the chasm through a narrow archway in the cliff. The rock surrounding the cleft was a peculiar pink in colour, smooth and polished, folded back upon itself, so that it resembled the mucous membrane on the inside of a pair of human lips.

The rock was of such an unusual colour and texture that they were both struck by it. They turned aside to study it while the mules went on downwards, the clatter of their receding hoofbeats and the voices of the men echoing and reverberating weirdly in this confined and unearthly place.

'It looks like some monstrous gargoyle, gushing water through its mouth,' Royan whispered, looking up at the cleft and at those strange rock formations. 'I can imagine how the ancient Egyptians, led by Taita and Prince Memnon, would have been moved if they had ever reached this place. What mystical connotations would they have attributed to such a natural phenomenon!'

Nicholas was silent, studying her face. Her eyes were dark with awe, and her expression solemn. In this setting she reminded him strongly of a portrait that he had in his collection at Quenton Park. It was a fragment of a fresco from the Valley of the Kings, depicting a Ramessidian princess.

'Why should that surprise you?' he asked himself. 'The very same blood runs in her veins.'

She turned to face him, 'Give me hope, Nicky. Tell

me that I have not dreamed all this. Tell me that we are going to find what we are looking for, and that we are going to vindicate Duraid's death.'

Her face was up-turned to his, and it seemed to glow under the light dew of perspiration and the strength of her commitment. He was seized by an almost overwhelming urge to take her up in his arms and kiss those moistly parted lips, but instead he turned away and started down the trail.

He dared not look back at her until he had himself fully under control. After a while he heard her quick, light tread on the rock behind him. They went on down in silence, and he was so preoccupied that he was unprepared for the sudden stunning vista that opened abruptly before them.

They stood high on a ledge above the sub-gorge of the Nile. Below them was a mighty cauldron of red rock five hundred feet deep. The main flow of the legendary river plunged in a green torrent into the shadowy abyss. It was so deep that the sunlight did not reach down into it. Beside them the sparser waters of the Dandera river took the same leap, falling white as an egret's feather, twisting and blowing in the false wind of the gorge. In the depths the waters mingled, churning and roiling together in a welter of foam, turning upon themselves like a great wheel, weighty and viscous as oil, until at last they found the exit gorge and tore away down it with irresistible force and power.

'You sailed through that in a boat?' Royan asked, with awe in her voice.

'We were young and foolish, then,' Nicholas said with a sad little smile that was haunted by old memories.

They were silent for a long while. Then Royan said softly, 'One can see how this would have stopped Taita and his prince as they came upstream.' She looked about her, and then pointed down the gorge towards the west.

'They certainly could never have come up the sub-gorge itself. They must have followed the line of the top of the cliffs, right along here where we are standing.' Her voice took on an edge of excitement at the thought.

'Unless they came up the other side of the river,' Nicholas suggested to tease her, and her face fell.

'I hadn't thought of that. Of course it's possible. How would we ever cross over, if we find no evidence on this side?'

'Let's consider that only when it's forced upon us. We have enough to contend with as it is, without looking for more hardships.'

Again they were silent, both of them considering the magnitude and uncertainty of the task that they had taken on. Then Royan roused herself.

'Where is the monastery? I can see no sign of it.'

'It's in the cliff right under our feet.'

'Will we camp down there?'

'I doubt it. Let's catch up with Boris and find out what he intends to do.'

They followed the trail along the edge of the cauldron, and came up with the mule caravan at a spot where the track forked. One branch turned away from the river into a wooded depression, while the other still hugged the rimrock.

Boris was waiting for them, and he indicated the track that led away from the river. 'There is a good campsite up there in the trees where I stayed last time I hunted down here.'

There were several tall wild fig trees throwing shade across this glade, and a spring of fresh water at the head. To minimize the loads, Boris had not carried tents down into the gorge. So as soon as the mules were unloaded he set his men to building three small thatched huts for their accommodation, and to digging a pit latrine well away from the spring.

While this work was going on, Nicholas beckoned to Royan and Tessay, and the three of them set off to explore the monastery. Where the trail forked, Tessay led them along the path that skirted the cliff top, and soon they came to a broad rock staircase that descended the cliff face.

There was a party of white-robed monks coming up the stone stairway, and Tessay stopped briefly to chat to them. As they went on she told Nicholas and Royan, 'Today is Katera, the eve of the festival of Timkat, which begins tomorrow. They are very excited. It is one of the major events of the religious year.'

'What does the festival celebrate?' Royan asked. 'It is not part of the Church calendar in Egypt.'

'It's the Ethiopian Epiphany, celebrating the baptism of Christ,' Tessay explained. 'During the ceremony the *tabot* will be taken down to the river to be rededicated and revitalized, and the acolytes will receive baptism, as did Jesus Christ at the hand of the Baptist.'

They followed the staircase down the sheer cliff face. The treads of the steps had been dished by the passage of bare feet over the centuries. Down they went, with the great cauldron of the Nile boiling and hissing and steaming with spray hundreds of feet below them.

Suddenly they came out on to a wide terrace that had been hewn by man's hand from the living rock. The red rock overhung it, forming a roof to the cloister with arches of stone left in place by the ancient builders to support it. The interior wall of the long covered terrace was riddled with the entrances to the catacombs beyond. Over the ages the cliff face had been mined and burrowed to form the halls and cells, the vestibules, churches and shrines of the monastic community which had inhabited them for well over a thousand years.

There were groups of monks seated along the length of the terrace. Some of them were listening to one of the deacons reading aloud from an illuminated copy of the scriptures.

'So many of them are illiterate,' Tessay sighed. 'The Bible must be read and explained to even the monks, for most of them are unable to read it for themselves.'

'This was what the Church of Constantine was like, the Church of Byzantium,' Nicholas pointed out quietly. 'It remains the Church of cross and book, of elaborate and sumptuous ritual in a predominantly illiterate world today.'

As they wandered slowly down the cloister they passed other seated groups who, under the direction of a precentor, were chanting and singing the Amharic psalms and hymns. From the interior of the cells and caves there came the hum of voices raised in prayer or supplication, and the air was thick with the smell of human occupation that had taken place over hundreds of years.

It was the smell of wood smoke and incense, of stale food and excrement, of sweat and piety, of suffering and of sickness. Amongst the groups of monks were the pilgrims who had made the journey, or been carried by their relatives, down into the gorge to make petition to the saint, or to seek from him a cure for their disease and suffering.

There were blind children weeping in their mothers' arms, and lepers with the flesh rotting and falling from their bones, and still others in the coma of sleeping sickness or some other terrible tropical affliction. Their whines and moans of agony blended with the chanting of the monks, and with the distant clamour of the Nile as it cascaded into the cauldron.

They came at last to the entrance to the cavern cathedral of St Frumentius. It was a circular opening like the mouth of a fish, but the surrounds of the portals were painted with a dense border of stars and crosses, and of saintly heads. The portraits were primitive, and rendered in ochre and soft earthy tones that were all the more appealing for their childlike simplicity. The eyes of the saints were huge and outlined in charcoal, their expressions tranquil and benign.

A deacon in a grubby green velvet robe guarded the entrance, but when Tessay spoke to him he smiled and nodded and gestured for them to enter. The lintel was low and Nicholas had to duck his head to pass under it, but on the far side he raised it again to look about him in amazement.

The roof of the cavern was so high that it was lost in the gloom. The rock walls were covered with murals, a celestial host of angels and archangels who flickered and wavered in the light of the candles and oil lamps. They were partially obscured by the long tapestry banners that hung down the walls, grimy with incense soot, their fringes frayed and tattered. On one of these St Michael rode a prancing white horse; on another the Virgin knelt at the foot of the cross, while above her the pale body of Christ bled from the wound of the Roman spear in his side.

This was the outer nave of the church. In the far wall the doorway to the middle chamber was guarded by a massive pair of wooden doors that stood open. The three of them crossed the stone floor, picking their way between the kneeling petitioners and pilgrims in their rags and tatters, in their misery and their religious ecstasy. In the feeble light of the lamps and the blue haze of incense smoke they seemed lost souls languishing eternally in the outer darkness of purgatory.

The visitors reached the set of three stone steps that led up to the inner doors, but their way was blocked at the threshold by two robed deacons in tall, flat-topped hats. One of these addressed Tessay sternly.

'They will not even let us enter the *qiddist*, the middle chamber,' Tessay told them regretfully. 'Beyond that lies the *maqdas*, the Holy of Holies.'

They peered past the guards, and in the gloom of the *qiddist* could just make out the door to the inner sanctum.

'Only the ordained priests are allowed to enter the *maqdas*, for it contains the *tabot* and the entrance to the tomb of the saint.'

Disappointed and frustrated, they made their way out of the cavern and back along the terrace.

They ate their dinner under a sky full of stars. The air was still stiflingly hot, and clouds of mosquitoes hovered just out of range of the repellents with which they had all smeared their exposed skin.

'And so, English, I have got you where you wanted to be. Now, how are you going to find this animal that you have come so far to hunt?' The vodka was making Boris belligerent again.

'At first light I want you to send out your trackers to work the country downstream from here,' Nicholas told him. 'Dik-dik are usually active in the early morning, and again late in the afternoon.'

'You are teaching your grandpapa to skin a cat,' said Boris, mangling the metaphor. He poured himself another vodka.

'Tell them to check for spoor.' Nicholas deliberately laboured his point. 'I imagine that the tracks of the striped variety will look very similar to those of the common dik-dik. If they find indications, then they must sit quietly along the edge of the thickest patches of bush and watch for any movement of the animals. Dik-dik are very territorial. They won't stray far from their own turf.'

'*Da! Da!* I will tell them. But what will you do? Will you spend the day in camp with the ladies, English?' He grinned slyly. 'If you are lucky, you may soon not need separate huts?' He guffawed at his own wit, and Tessay looked distressed and stood up with the excuse that she was going to the kitchen hut to supervise the chef.

Nicholas ignored the boorish pleasantry. 'Royan and I will work the riverine bush along the banks of the Dandera river. It looked very promising habitat for dik-dik. Warn your people to keep clear of the river. I don't want the game disturbed.'

They left camp the next morning in the glimmer of the dawn. Nicholas carried the Rigby rifle and a light day pack, and led Royan along the bank of the Dandera. They moved slowly, stopping every dozen paces to look and listen. The thickets were alive with the sounds and movements of the small mammals and birds.

'The Ethiopians do not have a hunting tradition, and I imagine the monks never disturb the wildlife here in the gorge.' He pointed to the tracks of a small antelope in the moist earth of the bank. 'Bushbuck,' he told her. 'Menelik's bushbuck. Unique to this part of the world. A much sought-after trophy.'

'Do you really expect to find your great-grandfather's dik-dik?' she asked. 'You seemed so determined when you discussed it with Boris.'

'Of course not,' he grinned. 'I think the old man made it up. It should rather have been named Harper's chimera. It probably was the skin of a striped mongoose that he used after all. We Harpers didn't get on in the world by always sticking to the literal truth.'

They paused to watch a Tacazze sunbird fluttering over a bunch of yellow blossoms on a creeper high above them in the canopy of the riverine forest. The tiny bird's plumage sparkled like a tiara of emeralds.

'Still, it gives us a wonderful excuse to fossick about in the bushes.' He glanced back to make certain that they were well clear of the camp, and then gestured for her to sit beside him on a fallen treetrunk. 'So, let's get it clear in our minds what we are looking for. You tell me.'

'We are looking for the remains of a funerary temple, or the ruins of the necropolis where the workers lived while they were excavating Pharaoh Mamose's tomb.'

'Any sort of masonry or stonework,' he agreed, 'especially some sort of column or monument.'

'Taita's stone testament,' she nodded. 'It should be engraved or chiselled with hieroglyphics. Probably badly weathered, fallen over, covered with vegetation – I don't know. Anything at all. We are fishing blind in dark waters.'

'Well, why are we still sitting here? Let's start fishing.'

In the middle of the morning Nicholas found the tracks of a dik-dik along the river bank. They took up a position against the bole of one of the big trees and sat quietly for a while in the shadows of the forest, until at last they were rewarded by a glimpse of one of the tiny creatures. It passed close to where they sat, wriggling its trunklike proboscis, stepping daintily on elfin hooves, nipping a leaf from a low-hanging branch, and munching it busily. However, its coat was a uniform drab grey, unrelieved by stripes of any kind.

When it disappeared into the undergrowth, Nicholas stood up. 'No luck. Common variety,' he whispered. 'Let's get on.'

A little after noon they reached the spot where the river issued from between the pink flesh-coloured cliffs of the chasm. They explored these as far as they were able before their way was blocked by the cliffs. The rock fell straight into the flood, and there was no foothold at the water's edge that would allow them to penetrate further.

They retreated downstream, and crossed to the far bank over a primitive suspension bridge of lianas and hairy flax rope that Nicholas guessed had been built by the monks from the monastery. Once again they tried to push on into the chasm. Nicholas even attempted to wade around the first buttress of pink rock that barred the way, but the current was too strong and threatened to sweep him off his feet. He was forced to abandon the attempt.

'If we can't get through there, then it's highly unlikely that Taita and his workmen would have done so.'

They went back as far as the hanging bridge and found a shady place close to the water to eat the lunch that Tessay had packed for them. The heat in the middle of the day was stupefying. Royan wet her cotton neckerchief in the river and dabbed at her face as she lay beside him.

Nicholas lay on his back and studied every inch of the pink cliffs through his binoculars. He was looking for any cleft or opening in their smooth polished surfaces.

He spoke without lowering the binoculars. 'Reading *River God*, it looks as if Taita actually enlisted help to switch the bodies of Tanus, Great Lion of Egypt, and the Pharaoh himself.' He lowered the glasses and looked at Royan. 'I find that puzzling, for it would have been an outrageous thing to do in terms of his period and belief. Is that a fair translation of the scrolls? Did Taita truly switch the bodies?'

She laughed and rolled over to face him. 'Your old chum Wilbur has an overheated imagination. The only basis for that whole bit of story-telling is a single line in the scrolls. *"To me he was more a king than ever Pharaoh had been."'* She rolled on to her back again. 'That is a good example of my objection to the book. He mixes fact and fantasy into an inextricable stew. As far as I know and believe, Tanus rests in his own tomb and the Pharaoh in his.'

'Pity!' Nicholas sighed and stuffed the book back in his pack. 'It was a romantic little touch that I enjoyed.' He glanced at his wrist-watch and stood up. 'Come on, I want to do a recce down the other spur of the valley. I spotted some interesting ground up there whilst we were on the approach march yesterday.'

It was late afternoon when they arrived back at the camp, and Tessay hurried out of her kitchen hut to greet them.

'I have been waiting for you to return. We have had an interesting invitation from Jali Hora, the abbot. He has invited us to a banquet in the monastery to celebrate Katera, the eve of Timkat. The servants have set up your shower, and the water is hot. There is just time for you to change before we go down to the monastery.'

The abbot sent a party of young acolytes to escort them to the banqueting hall. These young men arrived in the short African twilight, carrying torches to light the way.

Royan recognized one of these as Tamre, the epileptic boy. When she singled him out for her warmest smile, he came forward shyly and offered her a bouquet of wild flowers that he had picked from beside the river. She was unprepared for this courtesy, and without thinking she thanked him in Arabic.

'Shukran.'

'Taffadali,' the boy replied immediately, using the correct gender of the response, and in an accent that told her instantly that he was fluent in her language.

'How do you speak Arabic so well?' she asked, intrigued.

The boy hung his head with embarrassment and mumbled, 'My mother is from Massawa, on the Red Sea. It is the language of my childhood.'

When they set off for the monastery, the boy monk followed Royan like a puppy.

Once more they descended the stairway down the cliff and came out on to the torchlit terrace. The narrow cloisters were packed with humanity, and as they made their way through the press, with the honour guard of acolytes clearing a way for them, black faces called Amharic greetings and black hands reached out to touch them.

They stooped through the low entrance to the outer nave of the cathedral. The chamber was lit with oil lamps and torches, so that the murals of saints and angels danced in the uncertain light. The stone floor was covered with a carpet of freshly cut reeds and rushes, their sweet herbal perfume leavening the heavy, smoky air. It seemed that the entire brotherhood of monks were seated cross-legged on this spongy carpet. They greeted the entrance of the little party of *ferengi* with cries of welcome and shouts of benediction. Beside each seated figure stood a flask of *tej*, the honey mead of the country. It was clear from the happy, sweaty faces that the flasks had already done good service.

The visitors were led forward to a spot that had been left clear for them directly in front of the wooden doors to the *qiddist*, the middle chamber. Their escort urged them to sit and make themselves comfortable in this space. As soon as they were settled, another party of acolytes came in from the terrace bearing flasks of *tej*, and knelt to place a separate pottery flask in front of each of them.

Tessay leaned across to whisper, 'Better you let me sample this *tej* before you try it. The strength and colour and taste vary in every place that it is served, and some of it is ferocious.' She raised her flask and drank directly from the elongated neck. When she lowered the flask she smiled, 'This is a good brew. If you are careful, you will be all right with it.'

The monks seated around them were urging them to drink, and Nicholas raised his flask. The monks clapped and laughed as he tasted the liquor. It was light and pleasant, with a strong bouquet of wild honey. 'Not bad!' he gave his opinion, but Tessay warned him, 'Later they will almost certainly offer you *katikala*. Be very careful of that! It is distilled from fermented grain and it will take your head off at the shoulders.'

The monks were concentrating their hospitality on Royan now. The fact that she was a Coptic Christian, a true believer, had impressed them. It was obvious also that her beauty had not gone entirely unremarked by this company of holy and celibate men.

Nicholas leaned close to her, and whispered, 'You will have to fake it for their benefit. Hold it up to your lips and pretend to swallow, or they will not leave you in peace.'

As she lifted the flask the monks hooted with delight and saluted her with their own upraised flasks. She lowered the flask again, and whispered to Nicholas.

'It's delicious. It tastes of honey.'

'You broke your vow of abstinence!' he chided her laughing. 'Did you?'

'Just a drop,' she admitted, 'and anyway I never made any vows.'

The acolytes knelt in turn in front of each guest, offering them a bowl of hot water in which to wash their right hands in preparation for the feast.

Suddenly there was the sound of music and drums, and a band of musicians filed through the open doors of the *qiddist*. They took up their positions along the side walls of the chamber, while the congregation craned expectantly to peer into its dim interior.

At last Jali Hora, the ancient abbot, appeared at the head of the steps. He wore a full-length robe of crimson satin, with a gold thread-embroidered stole around his shoulders. On his head was a massive crown. Though it glittered like gold, Nicholas knew that it was gilt brass, and the multi-coloured stones with which it was set were just as certainly glass and paste.

Jali Hora raised his crook, which was surmounted by

161

an ornate silver cross, and a weighty silence fell upon the company.

'Now he will say the grace,' Tessay told them, and bowed her head.

Jali Hora's grace was fervent and lengthy, his reedy falsetto punctuated by devout responses from the monks. When at last he came to the end, two splendidly robed *debteras* helped Jali Hora down the stairs and seated him on his carved *jimmera* stool at the head of the circle of senior deacons and priests.

The religious mood of the monks changed to one of festive bonhomie as a procession of acolytes entered from the terrace, each of them bearing upon his head a flat woven reed basket the size of a wagon wheel. They placed one of these in the centre of each circle of guests.

Then at a signal from Jali Hora, acting in unison they whipped the lid off each basket. A jovial cheer went up from the monks, for each basket contained a shallow brass bowl that was filled from rim to rim with round sheets of the flat grey unleavened *injera* bread.

Two acolytes staggered in from the terrace, barely able to carry between them a steaming brass pot filled with gallons of *wat*, a spicy stew of fat mutton. Over each of the bowls of *injera* bread they tipped the great pot and slopped gouts of the runny red-brown *wat*, the surface glistening with hot grease.

The assembly fell on the food voraciously. They tore off wads of *injera* and scooped up the mess of *wat* with it, and then stuffed the parcel into their open mouths, which remained open as they chewed. They washed it down with long swallows from the *tej* flasks, before wrapping themselves another parcel of running *wat*. Soon every one of them was greasy to the elbow and their chins were smeared thickly, as they chewed and drank and shouted with laughter.

The serving acolytes dumped thick cakes of another

type of *injera* beside each guest. These were stiffer and less yeasty in taste, friable and crumbling, unlike the latex rubber consistency of the thin grey sheets of the first kind.

Nicholas and Royan tried to show their appreciation of the food without coating themselves with layers of it as the others were doing. Despite its appearance the *wat* was really rather tasty, and the dry yellow *injera* helped to cut the grease.

The communal brass bowls were emptied in remarkably short order. Only the churned up mess of bread and grease remained when the acolytes came tottering in under the weight of another set of pots, this time filled to overflowing with curried chicken *wat*. This was splashed into the bowls on top of the remains of the mutton, and again the monks had at it.

While they gobbled up the chicken, the *tej* flasks were replenished and the monks became more raucous.

'I don't think I can take much more of this,' Royan told Nicholas queasily.

'Close your eyes and think of England,' he advised her. 'You are the star of the evening. They aren't going to let you escape.'

As soon as the chicken was eaten, the servers were back with fresh pots, this time brimming with fiery beef *wat*. They dumped this on the remnants of both the mutton and the chicken.

The monk in the circle opposite Royan emptied his flask, and when an acolyte tried to refill it, he waved the lad away with a shout of, '*Katikala!*'

The cry was taken up by the other monks. '*Katikala! Katikala!*'

The acolytes hurried out and returned with dozens of bottles of the gin-clear liquor and brass bowls the size of tea cups.

'This is the stuff to be careful of,' Tessay told them. Surreptitiously both Nicholas and Royan were able to dribble the contents of their bowls into the mat of reeds on which they were sitting, but the monks guzzled theirs down greedily.

'Boris is getting his share,' Nicholas remarked to Royan. The Russian was red-faced and sweating, grinning like an idiot as he downed another bowlful.

Enlivened by the *katikala* the monks started playing a game. One of them would wrap a packet of beef *wat* with a sheet of *injera*, and then, as it dripped fat from his poised right hand, he would turn to the monk beside. The victim would open his mouth until his jaws were at full stretch, and the packet would be stuffed into it by his considerate neighbour. The morsel was, of course, as large as a human gape could possibly accommodate, and in order to engulf it the victim had to risk death by asphyxiation.

The rules of the game seemed to be that he was not allowed to use his hands to get it into his own mouth, neither should he dribble down the front of his robe, nor splutter gravy over those seated near to him. His contortions, together with his gulping and choking and gasping for air, were the source of uncontrollable hilarity. When at last he succeeded in getting it down, a brass bowl of *katikala* was held to his lips as a reward. He was expected to send the contents in the same direction as the parcel of *injera*.

Jali Hora, by now warmed with *tej* and *katikala*, lurched to his feet. In his right hand he held aloft a streaming parcel of *injera*. As he began an unsteady progress across the chamber, with his shiny crown awry, they did not at first realize his intentions. The entire company watched him with interest.

Then suddenly Royan stiffened and whispered with horror, 'No! Please, no. Save me, Nicky. Don't let this happen to me.'

'This is the price you pay for being the leading lady,' he told her. Jali Hora was making his rather erratic way towards where she sat. The gravy from the morsel he carried for her was trickling down his forearm and dripping from his elbow.

The band standing along the side wall struck up a lively air. As the abbot came to a halt in front of Royan, rocking on his suspension like an ancient carriage, they fiddled and fifed and the drummers broke out in a frenzy.

The abbot presented his gift, and with one last despairing glance at Nicholas Royan faced the inevitable. She closed her eyes and opened her mouth.

To roars of encouragement and the urgings of fife and drum, she struggled and chewed. Her face turned rosy and her eyes watered. At one point Nicholas thought she would have to admit defeat and spit it out on to the reed-covered floor. But slowly and courageously, a bit at a time, she forced it down and then fell back exhausted.

Her audience, clapping and hooting, loved every moment of it. The abbot sank stiffly to his knees in front of her and embraced her, almost losing his crown in the process. Then without relinquishing his embrace, he made himself a place beside her.

'It looks as though you have made another conquest,' Nicholas told her dryly. 'I think he will be on your lap at any moment, if you don't duck and run.'

Royan reacted swiftly. She reached across and grabbed a bottle of *katikala*, and a bowl which she filled to the brim.

'Drink it up, Pops!' she told him, and held the bowl to his lips. Jali Hora accepted the challenge, but he had to release her to drink from her hand.

Suddenly Royan started so violently that she spilled what was left in the bowl down the old man's robe. The blood drained from her face and she began to tremble as though in a high fever as she stared at Jali Hora's crown, which had slipped forward over his eyes.

'What is it?' Nicholas demanded quietly but urgently,

and he reached across to steady her with a hand on her arm. Nobody else in the chamber had noticed her distress, but he was fully attuned to her moods by now.

Still staring ashen-faced at the crown, she dropped the bowl and reached down and grasped his wrist. He was startled by her strength. Her grip was painful, and he saw that she had driven her nails into his flesh so hard that she had broken the skin.

'Look at his crown! The jewel! The blue jewel!' she gasped.

He saw it then, amongst the gaudy shards of glass and pebbles of semi-precious garnets and rock crystal. The size of a silver dollar, it was a seal of blue ceramic, perfectly round, and baked to a hard, impervious finish. In the centre of the disc was an etching of an Egyptian war chariot, and above it the distinctive and unmistakable outline of the hawk with the broken wing. Around the circumference was a legend engraved in hieroglyphics. It took him only a few moments to read it to himself:

I COMMAND TEN THOUSAND CHARIOTS.
I AM TAITA, MASTER OF THE ROYAL HORSE.

Royan desperately wanted to escape from the oppressive atmosphere of the cavern. The parcel of *wat* that the abbot had forced upon her had mixed heavily with the few mouthfuls of *tej* she had swallowed, and this feeling in turn was aggravated by the smell of the dirty food bowls thick with congealing grease and the fumes of raw *katikala*. Already some of the monks were puking drunk, and the smell of vomit added to the cloying miasma of incense smoke within the chamber.

However, she was still the centre of the abbot's attention. He sat beside her stroking her bare arm and reciting garbled extracts from the Amharic scriptures; Tessay had long ago given up translating for her. Royan looked hopefully at Nicholas but he was withdrawn and silent, seeming oblivious of his surroundings. She knew that he was thinking about the ceramic seal in the abbot's crown, for his eyes kept returning thoughtfully to it.

She wanted to be alone with him to discuss this extraordinary discovery. Her excitement outweighed the distress of her overloaded stomach. She felt her cheeks flushed with it. Every time she looked up at the old man's crown her heart fluttered, and she had to make an effort to stop herself reaching up, seizing the shiny blue seal and ripping it from its setting to examine it more closely.

She knew how unwise it was to draw attention to the scrap of ceramic, but when she glanced across the circle she saw that Boris was far past noticing anything other than the bowl of *katikala* in his hand. In the end it was Boris who gave her the excuse for which she had been seeking. He tried to get to his feet, but his legs collapsed under him. He sagged forward quite gracefully, and his face dropped into the bowl of grease-sodden *injera* bread. He lay there snoring noisily, and Tessay appealed to Nicholas.

'Alto Nicholas, what am I to do?'

Nicholas considered the unlovely spectacle of the prostrate hunter. There were scraps of bread and beef stew sticking like confetti in his cropped ginger hair.

'I rather suspect Prince Charming has had enough for one night,' he murmured.

He stood up, stooped over Boris and gripped one wrist. With a sudden jerk he lifted him into a sitting position, and then heaved him upright and over his shoulder in a fireman's lift.

'Good night, all!' he told the assembled monks, very few of whom were in any condition to respond. Then he carried Boris away, draped over his shoulders with head and feet dangling. The two women had to hurry to keep up with Nicholas as he strode down the terrace and then up the stone stairway without a pause.

167

'I did not realize Alto Nicholas was so strong,' Tessay panted, for the stairs were steep and the pace was hard.

'I didn't either,' Royan admitted. She experienced a ridiculous proprietary pride in his feat, and smiled at herself in the darkness as they approached the camp.

'Don't be silly,' she admonished herself. 'He isn't yours to boast about.'

Nicholas threw his burden down on Boris's own bed in the thatched hut and stood back panting heavily, the sweat trickling down his cheeks.

'That's a pretty good recipe for a heart attack,' he gasped.

Boris groaned, rolled over and vomited copiously over his pillows and bedlinen.

'On that pleasant note I will bid you all goodnight and sweet dreams,' Nicholas told Tessay, stepping out of the hut into the warm African night.

He breathed in the smell of the forest and the river with relief, and then turned to Royan as she gripped his arm.

'Did you see—' she burst out excitedly, but he laid his fingers on her lips to silence her, and with a cautionary frown in the direction of Boris's hut led her away to her own hut.

'Did you see it?' she demanded, unable to contain herself longer. 'Could you read it?'

'"*I command ten thousand chariots*,"' he recited.

'"*I am Taita, master of the royal horse*,"' she completed it for him. 'He was here. Oh, Nicky! He was here. Taita was here. That's the proof we wanted. Now we know that we are not wasting our time.'

She flopped down on her camp bed and hugged herself ecstatically. 'Do you think the abbot will let us examine the seal?'

He shook his head, 'My guess is no. The crown is one of the monastery treasures. Even for you, his favourite lady,

I don't think he would do it. Anyway, it would not be wise to show any great interest in it. Jali Hora obviously does not have any idea of its significance. Apart from that, we don't want to alert Boris.'

'I suppose you are right.' She moved over on the bed to make room for him. 'Sit down.'

He sat down beside her, and she asked, 'Where do you suppose the seal came from? Who found it? Where, and when?'

'Steady on, dear girl. That's four questions in one, and I don't have an answer to any of them.'

'Guess!' she invited him. 'Speculate! Throw some ideas around!'

'Very well,' he agreed. 'The seal was manufactured in Hong Kong. There is a little factory there that turns them out by the thousands. Jali Hora bought it from a souvenir store in Luxor when he was on holiday in Egypt last month.'

She punched his arm, hard. 'Be serious,' she ordered.

'Let's hear if you can do better,' he invited her, rubbing his arm.

'Okay, here I go. Taita dropped the seal here in the gorge while he was working on the construction of Pharaoh's tomb. Three thousand years later an old monk, one of the very first to live here at the monastery, picked it up. Of course, he could not read the hieroglyphics. He took it to the abbot, who declared it to be a relic of St Frumentius, and had it set in the crown.'

'And they all lived happily ever after,' Nicholas agreed. 'Not a bad shot.'

'Can you find any holes?' she demanded, and he shook his head. 'Then you agree that this proves that Taita really was here, and that it proves our theories are correct?'

'"Proves" is too strong a word. Let's just say that it points in that direction,' he demurred.

She wriggled around on the bed to face him squarely.

'Oh, Nicky, I am so excited. I swear I will not be able to sleep a wink tonight. I just can't wait for tomorrow, to get out there and start searching again.'

Her eyes were bright, and her cheeks flushed a warm rosy brown. Her lips were parted, and he could see the pink tip of her tongue between them. This time he could not stop himself. He leaned very slowly towards her, treating her gently, giving her every opportunity to pull away if she wished to avoid him. She did not move, but her shining expression turned slowly to one of apprehension. She stared into his eyes, as if seeking something, some reassurance. When their lips were an inch apart, Nicholas stopped, and it was she who made the last movement. She brought their mouths together.

At first it was soft, just a light mingling of their breath, and then it became harsher, more urgent. For a long, heart-stopping moment they devoured each other, and her mouth tasted soft and sweet as ripe fruit. Then suddenly she whimpered, and with a huge effort of will tore herself out of his arms. They stared at each other, both of them shaken and confused.

'No,' she whispered. 'Please, Nicky, not yet. I am not ready yet.'

He picked up her hand and turned it between his palms. Then lightly he kissed the tips of her fingers, savouring the smell and the taste of her skin.

'I'll see you in the morning.' He dropped her hand and stood up. 'Early. Be ready!' he said, and stooped out through the doorway of the hut.

As he was dressing the next morning he heard her moving around in her hut, and when he whistled softly at her door she stepped out to meet him, dressed and eager to start.

'Boris is not awake yet,' Tessay told them as she served their breakfast.

'Now that is a great surprise to me,' Nicholas said, without looking up from his plate. He and Royan were still slightly awkward in each other's presence, remembering the circumstances in which they had parted the previous evening. However, as Nicholas slung the rifle and the pack over his shoulder and they set off up the valley, their mood changed to one of anticipation.

They had been going for an hour when Nicholas glanced over his shoulder and then cautioned her with a frown. 'We are being followed.'

Taking her wrist, he drew her behind a slab of sandstone. He flattened himself against the rock and gestured at her to do the same. Then he poised himself, and suddenly leaped forward to seize the lanky figure in a dirty white *shamma* who was sneaking up the valley behind them. With a howl the creature fell to his knees, and began gibbering with terror.

Nicholas hauled him to his feet. 'Tamre! What are you doing following us? Who sent you?' he demanded in Arabic.

The boy rolled his eyes towards Royan. 'No, please, *effendi*, do not hurt me. I meant no harm.'

'Leave the child, Nicky. You will precipitate another fit,' Royan intervened. Tamre scurried behind her and clung to her hand for protection, peering out around her shoulder at Nicholas as though his life were in danger.

'Peace, Tamre,' Nicholas soothed him. 'I will not hurt you, unless you lie to me. If you do, then I will thrash you until there is no skin on your back. Who sent you to follow us?'

'I came alone. Nobody sent me,' blubbered the boy. 'I came to show you where I saw the holy animal with the fingermarks of the Baptist on his skin.'

Nicholas stared at him for a moment, before he began

171

to laugh softly. 'I'll be damned if the boy doesn't really believe he saw great-grandfather's dik-dik.' Then he scowled ferociously. 'Remember what will happen to you, if you are lying.'

'It is true, *effendi*,' Tamre sobbed, and Royan came to his defence.

'Don't badger him. He is harmless. Leave the poor child.'

'All right, Tamre. I will give you a chance. Take us to where you saw the holy animal.'

Tamre would not relinquish his grip on Royan's hand. He clung to it as he danced beside her, leading her along, and within a hundred yards his terror had faded and he was smiling and giggling at her shyly.

For an hour he led them away from the Dandera river and up over the high ground above the valley, into an area of thick scrub and up-thrust ridges of weathered limestone. The thorny branches of the bush were densely intertwined, and grew so close to the ground that there seemed to be no way through them. However, Tamre led them on to a narrow twisting path, just wide enough for them to avoid the red-tipped hook thorns on each side of them. Then abruptly he stopped and pulled Royan to a halt beside him. He pointed down, almost at his own toes.

'The river!' he announced importantly. Nicholas came up beside them and whistled softly with surprise. Tamre had led them around in a wide circle to the west, and then brought them back to the Dandera river at a point where it still ran in the bed of the deep ravine.

Now they stood on the very edge of the chasm. He saw at once that, although the top of the rocky ravine was less than a hundred feet wide, the chasm opened out below the rim. From the surface of the water far below, the rock wall belled out in the shape of one of the pottery *tej* flasks. It narrowed again as it neared the top where they stood.

'I saw the holy thing over there.' Tamre pointed to the

far side of the chasm where a small feeder spring meandered out of the thorny bush. Streamers of bright green moss, nourished by the spring, hung from the lip of the concave rock wall, and the water trickled down them and dripped from the tips into the river two hundred feet below.

'If you saw it there, why did you bring us to this side of the river?' Nicholas demanded.

Tamre looked as though he were on the point of tears. 'This side is easier. There is no path through the bush on the other side. The thorns would hurt Woizero Royan.'

'Don't be a bully,' Royan told him, and put her arm around the boy's shoulder.

Nicholas shrugged, 'It looks like the two of you are ganging up on me. Well, seeing that we are here, we might as well sit a while and see if great-grandpa's dik-dik puts in an appearance.'

He picked out a spot in the shade of one of the stunted trees that hung on the lip of the chasm, and with his hat swept the ground clear of fallen thorns until there was a place for them to sit. He placed his back against the trunk of the thorn tree and laid the Rigby rifle across his lap.

By this time it was past noon, and the heat was stifling. He passed the water bottle to Royan and, while she drank, glanced at Tamre and suggested to her in English, 'This might be a good time to find out what, if anything, the lad knows about the Taita ceramic in the crown. He is besotted with you. He will tell you anything you want to know. Question him.'

She began gently, chatting softly to the boy. Occasionally she stroked his head and petted him as though he were a puppy. She spoke to him of the previous night's banquet, the beauty of the underground church, and the antiquity of the murals and the tapestries, and then at last mentioned the abbot's crown.

'Yes. Yes. That is the stone of the saint,' he agreed readily. 'The blue stone of St Frumentius.'

'Where did it come from?' she asked. 'Do you know?'

The boy looked embarrassed, 'I do not know. It is very old, perhaps as old as Christ the Saviour. That is what the priests say.'

'You do not know where it was found?'

He shook his head, but then, eager to please her, he suggested, 'Perhaps it fell from heaven.'

'Perhaps.' Royan glanced at Nicholas, who rolled his eyes upwards and then pushed his hat forward to cover his face.

'Perhaps St Frumentius gave it to the first abbot when he died.' Tamre warmed to the subject. 'Or perhaps it was in his coffin with him when he was placed in his tomb.'

'All these things are possible, Tamre,' Royan agreed. 'Have you seen the tomb of St Frumentius?'

He looked around him guiltily. 'Only the ordained priests are allowed into the *maqdas*, the Holy of Holies,' he hung his head and whispered.

'You have seen it, Tamre,' she accused him gently, stroking his head. She was intrigued by the boy's guilt. 'You can tell me. I will not tell the priests.'

'Only once,' he admitted. 'The other boys. They sent me to touch the *tabot* stone. They would have beaten me if I had not. All the new acolytes are made to do this.' He began to babble with the horror of the memory of his initiation ordeal. 'I was alone. I was very afraid. It was after midnight when the priests were asleep. Dark. The *maqdas* is haunted by the ghost of the saint. They told me that if I was unworthy the saint would strike me down with lightning.'

Nicholas removed the hat from his face and straightened up slowly. 'My word, the child is telling the truth,' he said softly. 'He *has* been into the Holy of Holies.' Then he looked across at Royan, 'Keep questioning him. He may just give us something useful. Ask him about the tomb of St Frumentius.'

'Did you see the tomb of the saint?' she asked, and the boy nodded vigorously. 'Did you go into the tomb?' This time he shook his head.

'No. There are bars across the entrance. Only the abbot is allowed into the tomb, on the birthday of the saint.'

'Did you look through the bars?'

'Yes, but it is very dark. I saw the coffin of the saint. It is wood and there is painting on it, the face of the saint.'

'Is he a black man?'

'No – a white man with a red beard. The painting is very old. The picture is faded, and the wood of the coffin is rotting and crumbling.'

'Is it lying on the floor of the tomb?'

Tamre screwed up his face in thought, then after careful consideration shook his head. 'No, it is on a shelf of stone in the wall.'

'Is there anything else you remember about the tomb of the saint?' Royan tried to prod his memory, but Tamre shook his head.

'It was very dark, and the opening in the bars is small,' he apologized.

'It does not matter. Is the tomb in the back wall of the *maqdas*?'

'Yes, it is behind the altar and the *tabot* stone.'

'What is the altar made of – stone?'

'No. It is wood, cedarwood. There are candles, and a big cross, and the many crowns of the abbot, and the chalice and staff.'

'Is it painted?'

'No, it is carved with pictures. But they are different from the pictures inside the tomb of the saint.'

'What is different? Tell me, Tamre.'

'I don't know. The faces are funny. They wear different clothes. There are horses.' He looked puzzled. 'They are different.'

Royan tried for a while to get a clearer description from him, but he became more and more confused and contradictory when she pushed him, so she changed tack.

'Tell me about the *tabot*,' she suggested, but Nicholas forestalled her.

'No, you tell me about the *tabot*,' he demanded of her. 'Is it similar to the Jewish Tabernacle?'

She turned to him, 'Yes, at least in the Egyptian Church it is. It is usually kept in a jewelled box and wrapped in an embroidered cloth of gold. The only difference is that the Jewish Tabernacle is carved with the ten commandments, but in our Church it is carved with the words of dedication of the particular church that houses it. It is the living heart of the Church.'

'What is the *tabot* stone?' Nicholas frowned with concentration.

'I don't know,' she admitted. 'Our Church does not have a *tabot* stone.'

'Ask him!'

'Tell me about the *tabot* stone, Tamre.'

'It is so high, and so square.' He indicated a height of a little above his own shoulder, and the width of his spread hands.

'And the *tabot* stands on top of this stone?' Royan guessed.

Tamre nodded.

'Why did they send you to touch the stone and not the *tabot* itself?' Nicholas demanded, but Royan shook her head to silence him.

'Let me do the talking. You are too harsh with him.' She turned back to the boy. 'Why the stone, rather than the Ark of the *tabot* that stands on top of it?'

Tamre shrugged helplessly. 'I don't know. They just did.'

'What does the stone look like? Are there paintings on it also?'

'I don't know.' He looked distraught at not being able to satisfy her. He wanted desperately to please her. 'I don't know. The stone is wrapped with cloth.'

Nicholas and Royan exchanged startled glances, and then Royan turned back to the boy.

'Covered?' Royan leaned closer to him. 'The stone is covered?'

'They say that it is only uncovered by the abbot on the birthday of St Frumentius.'

Again Nicholas and Royan stared at each other, and then he smiled thoughtfully. 'I would rather like to have a look at the tomb of the saint, and the *tabot* stone – in its uncovered state.'

'You'd have to wait for the saint's birthday,' she said, 'and have yourself ordained. Only the priests—' she broke off and stared at him again. 'You aren't thinking of – no, you wouldn't, would you?'

'Who, me?' he grinned. 'Perish the thought.'

'If they caught you in the *maqdas*, they would tear you to little pieces.'

'The answer, then, would be not to let them catch me.'

'If you go, I am going with you. How are we going to manage it?'

'Throttle back, dear girl. The thought only occurred to me ten seconds ago. Even on my good days, I need at least ten minutes to come up with a brilliant plan of action.'

They both stared out across the chasm in silence, until Royan whispered softly, 'The covered stone. Taita's stone testament?'

'Don't say it aloud,' he pleaded, and made the sign against the evil eye. 'Don't even think it aloud. The Devil is listening.'

They were silent again, both of them thinking furiously. Then Royan started, 'Nicky, what if—' she broke off. 'No, that won't work.' She relapsed into frowning silence again.

Tamre broke the quiet with a sudden squeak of excitement, 'There it is. Look!'

They were both startled by the interruption. 'What is it?' Royan turned to him.

Tamre seized her arm and shook it. He was trembling with emotion. 'There it is. I told you.' With his other hand he was pointing out across the river, 'There at the edge of the thorn bushes. Can't you see it?'

'What is it? What can you see?'

'The animal of John the Baptist. The holy marked creature.'

Following the direction of his outflung arm, she picked out a soft, brownish blur of movement at the edge of the thicket on the far bank. 'I don't know. It is too far—'

Nicholas scrabbled in his pack and brought out his binoculars. He lifted and focused them, and then he began to chuckle.

'Hallelujah! Great-grandpa's reputation is safe at last.' He passed the binoculars to Royan. She focused them and found the little creature in the field. It was three hundred yards away, but through the ten-power lens she could make it out in detail.

It was almost half as large again as the common dik-dik that they had seen the previous day, and instead of drab grey its coat was a rich red brown. Its most striking feature, however, was the distinct dark bars of chocolate colour across its shoulders and back – five evenly spaced markings that did indeed look like the imprint of fingers and thumb.

'*Madoqua harperii*, no less,' Nicholas whispered to her. 'Sorry, great-grandfather, for doubting you.'

The dik-dik stood half in shadow, wriggling its nose as it snuffled the air. Its head was held high, suspicious and alert. The soft breeze was quartering between them and the animal, but every so often a wayward eddy gave it the faint whiff of humanity that had alarmed it.

Royan heard the snick of the rifle action as Nicholas worked the bolt and chambered a round. Hurriedly she lowered the glasses, and glanced at him. 'You aren't going to shoot it?' she demanded.

'No, not at that range. Over three hundred yards, and a small target. I'll wait for it to get closer.'

'How can you bring yourself to do it?'

'How can I not? That's what I came here to do, amongst other things.'

'But it's so beautiful.'

'I take it, then, that it would be perfectly all right to whack it if it were ugly?'

She said nothing, but raised the binoculars again. The eddy of the wind must have changed, for the dik-dik lowered its head to nibble at a tuft of coarse brown grass. Then lifted its head again and came on down the clearing in the thorn scrub, stepping daintily, pausing every few paces to feed again.

'Go back!' She tried to will it into safety, but it kept on coming, meandering towards the edge of the chasm.

Nicholas rolled on to his stomach and settled himself behind the root of the tree. He screwed up his hat into a soft pad on which to rest the rifle.

'Two hundred yards,' he muttered to himself. 'That's a fair shot. No further.' Resting the cushioned rifle on the twisted root, he aimed through the telescopic sight. Then he lifted his head, waiting to let it come within certain range.

Abruptly the dik-dik lifted its head again and came to a halt, quivering with tension.

'Something he doesn't like. Dammit all, wind must have changed again,' Nicholas growled. At that moment the little antelope bolted. It streaked across the clearing, back the way it had come, and disappeared into the thorn scrub.

'Go, dik-dik, go!' said Royan smugly, and Nicholas sat up and grunted with disgust.

'I can't make out what frightened him.' Then his expression changed and he cocked his head. There was an alien sound on the air, growing each second – a harsh, rising clatter and a shrill, whining whistle.

'Chopper! What the hell!' Nicholas recognized the sound immediately. He took the binoculars from Royan's hand and turned them to the sky, sweeping the cloudless blue emptiness above the crenellated tops of the escarpment.

'There it is,' he said grimly, adding, 'Bell Jet Ranger,' as he recognized the profile. 'Coming this way, by the looks of it. No point in drawing attention to ourselves. Let's get under cover.'

He shepherded Royan and the boy under the spread branches of the thorn tree. 'Sit tight,' he told her. 'No chance they will spot us under here.'

He watched the approaching helicopter through the binoculars. 'Probably Ethiopian air force,' he said softly. 'Anti-*shufta* patrol, most likely. Both Boris and Colonel Nogo warned us that there are a lot of rebels and bandits operating down here in the gorge—' he broke off abruptly. 'No. Hold on. That's not military. Green and red fuselage, and the red horse emblem. None other than your old friends from Pegasus Exploration.'

The sound of the rotors crescendoed, and now with her naked eye Royan could make out the flying horse on the fuselage of the helicopter as it flew low across their front, half a mile out, headed down towards the Nile.

Neither of them paid any attention to Tamre as he crouched behind Royan, trying to hide behind her body.

His teeth were chattering with terror and his eyes rolled until the whites showed.

'It looks as if our friend Jake Helm has got himself some fancy transport. If Pegasus is in any way connected with Duraid's murder and the other attempts on your life, then we can expect them to be breathing heavily down our necks from now on. They are now in a position to overlook us at will.' Nicholas was still watching the aircraft through the binoculars.

'When your enemy is up in the air, it gives you a helpless feeling.' Royan edged instinctively closer to him, staring up.

The green and scarlet machine disappeared over the hump of the sub-gorge, down towards the monastery.

'Unless he's just on a joy-ride, he's probably looking for our camp,' Nicholas guessed. 'Under orders from the main man to keep tabs on us.'

'He will have no trouble finding it. Boris made no attempt to conceal the huts,' Royan said uneasily. 'Let's get out of here, then.' She stood up.

'Good plan.' Nicholas was about to follow her, when suddenly he caught her hand and drew her down again. 'Hold it. They are coming back this way.'

The engine beat was rising again. Then they caught a glimpse of the helicopter through the canopy of leaves and thorn branches overhead.

'Now he is following the river. Still searching for something, by the looks of it.'

'Us?' Royan asked nervously.

'If they are under orders from the head man, could be,' Nicholas agreed. The machine was very close now, and the shrill whine of the engine was deafening.

At that moment Tamre's nerve broke. He let out a wail of terror, 'It is the Devil, come to take me. Save me, Jesus Christ the Saviour, save me!'

Nicholas put out a hand to restrain him, but he was not quick enough. Tamre broke free and leaped to his feet. Still howling with fear of the pit and the flames of hell, he darted away down the path into the thorn scrub, the skirts of his *shamma* swirling about his skinny legs and his shiny black face swivelled back over his shoulder to watch the approaching machine.

The pilot spotted him immediately, and the nose of the helicopter sank in their direction. It came directly towards them, slowing as it approached the lip of the chasm. They could make out the heads of the two occupants behind the windscreen of the forward cabin. Still decelerating, the aircraft hung suspended over the river, pivoting on the spinning disc of its rotor, while Royan and Nicholas crouched down in the scrub, trying to avoid detection.

'That's the American from the prospecting camp.' Royan recognized Jake Helm, despite the bulky radio earphones and the mirrored dark glasses. He and the black pilot were craning their necks to search the river banks.

'They haven't spotted us—' But even as Nicholas said it, Jake Helm looked directly at them across the open void. Although his expression did not change, he tapped the pilot's shoulder and pointed down at them.

The pilot let the helicopter sink lower until it hovered in the opening of the chasm, almost on the same level as they were. Only a hundred feet separated them now. No longer making any attempt at concealment, Nicholas leaned back against the bole of the thorn tree. He tipped his panama hat forward over one eye and gave Jake Helm a laconic wave.

The foreman made no response to the greeting. He regarded Nicholas with a flat, baleful stare, then struck a match and held the flame to the tip of the half-smoked cigar between his lips. He flipped the dead match away and blew a feather of smoke in Nicholas's direction. Still without change of expression, he said something to the pilot out of the corner of his mouth.

Immediately the helicopter rose vertically and banked away to the north, heading back directly towards the wall of the escarpment and the base camp on its summit.

'Mission accomplished. He found what he was looking for.' Royan sat up. 'Us!'

'And he must have spotted the camp. He knows where to find us again,' Nicholas agreed.

Royan shivered and hugged herself briefly. 'He gives me the creeps, that one. He looks like a toad.'

'Oh, come on!' Nicholas chided her. 'What have you got against toads?' He stood up. 'I don't think we are going to see great-grandfather's dik-dik again today. He has been thoroughly shaken up by the chopper. I'll come back for another try tomorrow.'

'We should go and look for Tamre. He has probably had another fit, the poor little fellow.'

She was wrong. They found the boy beside the path. He was still shivering and weeping, but had not suffered another seizure. He calmed down quickly when Royan soothed him, and followed them back towards the camp. However, when they neared the grove he slipped away in the direction of the monastery.

That evening, while it was still light, Nicholas took Royan back to the monastery.

'I believe that the criminal fraternity refer to a reconnaissance of this nature as "casing the joint",' he remarked, as they stooped through the entrance of the rock cathedral and joined the throng of worshippers in the outer chamber.

'From what Tamre says, it sounds as though the novices wait until they know that the priests on duty are ones that will nod off during their watch,' Royan told him softly, as they paused to gaze through the doors into the middle chamber.

'We don't have that sort of insider knowledge,' Nicholas pointed out.

There were priests passing backwards and forwards through the doors as they watched.

'There doesn't seem to be any sort of procedure,' Nicholas noted. 'No password or ritual to allow them through.'

'On the other hand, they greeted the guards at the door by name. It's a small community. They must all know each other intimately.'

'There doesn't seem any chance at all that I could dress up like a monk and brazen my way through,' Nicholas agreed. 'I wonder what they do to intruders in the sacred areas?'

'Throw them off the terrace to the crocodiles in the cauldron of the Nile?' she suggested maliciously. 'Anyway, you are not going in there without me.'

This was not the time to argue, he decided, and instead he tried to see as much as possible through the open doors of the *qiddist*. The middle chamber seemed much smaller than the outer chamber in which they stood. He could just make out the shadowy murals that covered the portions of the inner walls that he could see. In the facing wall was another doorway. From Tamre's description, he realized that this must be the entrance to the *maqdas*. The opening was barred by a heavy grille gate of dark wooden beams, the joints of the cross-pieces reinforced with gussets of hand-hammered native iron.

On each side of the doorway, from rock ceiling to floor, hung long embroidered tapestries depicting scenes from the life of St Frumentius. In one he was preaching to a kneeling congregation, with the Bible in one hand and his right hand raised in benediction. In the other tapestry he was baptizing an emperor. The king wore a high golden crown like that of Jali Hora, and the saint's head was surrounded by a halo. The saint's face was white, while the emperor's was black.

'Politically correct?' Nicholas asked himself, with a smile.

'What is amusing you?' Royan asked. 'Have you thought of a way of getting in there?'

'No, I was thinking of dinner. Let's go!'

At dinner Boris showed no ill effects from the previous night's debauch. During the day he had taken out his shotgun and shot a bunch of green pigeons. Tessay had marinated these and barbecued them over the coals.

'Tell me, English, how was the hunting today? Did you get attacked by the deadly striped dik-dik? Hey? Hey?' He bellowed with laughter.

'Did your trackers have any success?' Nicholas asked mildly.

'Da! Da! They found kudu and bushbuck and buffalo. They even found dik-dik, but no stripes. Sorry, no stripes.'

Royan leaned forward and opened her mouth to intervene, but Nicholas cautioned her with a shake of the head. She shut her mouth again and looked down at her plate, slicing a morsel from the breast of a pigeon.

'We don't really need company tomorrow,' Nicholas explained mildly in Arabic. 'If he knew, he would insist on coming with us.'

'Did your Mummy never teach you no manners, English? It's rude to talk in a language that others can't understand. Have a vodka.'

'You have my share,' Nicholas invited him. 'I know when I am outclassed.'

During the rest of the meal Tessay replied only in low monosyllables when Royan tried to draw her into the conversation. She looked tragic and defeated. She never looked at her husband, even when he was at his loudest and most overbearing. When the meal ended, they left her sitting with Boris at the fire. Boris had a fresh bottle of vodka on the table beside him.

'The way he is pumping the liquor, it looks as if I might be called out on another midnight rescue mission,' Nicholas remarked as they made their way to their own huts.

'Tessay has been in camp all day with him. There has been more trouble between them. She told me that as soon as they get back to Addis Ababa she is going to leave him. She can't take any more of this.'

'The only thing I find surprising is that she ever got mixed up with an animal like Boris in the first place. She is a lovely woman. She could pick and choose.'

'Some women are drawn to animals,' Royan shrugged. 'I suppose it must be the thrill of danger. Anyway, Tessay has asked me if she can come with us tomorrow. She cannot stand another day in camp with Boris on her own. I think she is really afraid of him now. She says that she has never seen him drink like this before.'

'Tell her to come along,' Nicholas said resignedly. 'The more of us the merrier. Perhaps we will be able to frighten the dik-dik to death by sheer weight of numbers. Save me wasting ammunition.'

It was still dark when the three of them left camp the next morning. There was no sign of Boris and, when Nicholas asked about him, Tessay said simply, 'After you went to bed last night he finished the bottle. He won't be out of his hut before noon. He won't miss me.'

Carrying the Rigby, Nicholas led them up into the weathered limestone hills, retracing the path along which Tamre had taken them the previous day. As they walked, Nicholas heard the two women talking behind him. Royan was explaining to Tessay how they had sighted the striped dik-dik, and what they planned.

The sun was well up by the time they again reached

the spot under the thorn tree on the lip of the chasm, and settled down to wait in ambush.

'How will you retrieve the carcass, if you do manage to shoot the poor little creature?' Royan asked.

'I made certain of that before we left camp,' he explained. 'I spoke to the head tracker. If he hears a shot he will bring up the ropes and help me get across to the other side.'

'I wouldn't like to make the journey across there.' Tessay eyed the drop below them.

'They teach you some useful things in the army, along with all the rubbish,' Nicholas replied. He made himself comfortable against the thorn tree, the rifle ready in his lap.

The women lay close by him, talking together softly. It was unlikely that the sound of their low voices would carry across the ravine, Nicholas decided, so he did not try to hush them.

He expected that if it came at all, the dik-dik would show itself early. But he was wrong. By noon there was still no sign of it. The valley sweltered in the midday sun. The distant wall of the escarpment, veiled in the blue heat haze, looked like jagged blue glass, and the mirage danced across the rocky ridges and shimmered like the waters of a silver lake above the tops of the thorn thickets.

The women had long ago given up talking, and they lay somnolent in the heat. The whole world was silent and heat-struck. Only a bush dove broke the silence with its mournful lament, 'My wife is dead, my children are dead, Oh, me! Oh, my! Oh, me!' Nicholas found his own eyelids becoming leaden. His head nodded involuntarily, and he jerked it up only to have it flop forward again. On the very edge of sleep he heard a sound, close by in the thorn scrub behind him.

It was a tiny sound, but one that he knew so well. A

sound that whiplashed across his nerve endings and jerked him back to full consciousness, with his pulse racing and the coppery taste of fear in the back of his throat. It was the metallic sound of the safety-catch on an AK-47 assault rifle being slipped forward into the 'Fire' position.

In one fluid movement he lifted the rifle out of his lap and rolled twice, twisting his body to cover the two women who lay beside him. At the same time he brought the Rigby into his shoulder, aimed into the scrub behind him from where the sound had come.

'Down!' he hissed at his companions. 'Keep your heads down!'

His finger was on the trigger and, even though it was a puny weapon with which to take on a Kalashnikov, he was ready to return fire. He picked up his target immediately, and swung on to it.

There was a man crouched twenty paces away, the assault rifle he carried aimed into Nicholas's face. He was black, dressed in worn and tattered camouflage fatigues and a soft cap of the same material. His webbing held a bushknife and grenades, water bottle and all the other accoutrements of a guerrilla fighter.

'Shufta!' thought Nicholas. 'A real pro. Don't take chances with this one.' Yet at the same time he realized that if the intention had been to kill him, then he would be dead already.

He aimed the Rigby an inch over the muzzle of the assault rifle, into the bloodshot right eye of the *shufta* behind it. The man acknowledged the stand-off with a narrowing of his eyes, and then gave an order in Arabic.

'Salim, cover the women. Shoot them if he moves.'

Nicholas heard movement on his flank and glanced in that direction, still keeping the *shufta* in his peripheral vision.

Another guerrilla stepped out of the scrub. He was

similarly dressed, but he carried a Soviet RPD light machine gun on his hip. The barrel was sawn off short to make the weapon more handy for bush fighting, and there was a loop of ammunition belt draped around his neck. He came forward carefully, the RPD aimed point-blank at the two women. Nicholas knew that, with a touch on the trigger, he could chop them both to mincemeat.

There were other stealthy rustling sounds in the bush all around them. These two were not the only ones, Nicholas realized. This was a large war party. He might be able to get off one shot with the Rigby, but by then Royan and Tessay would be dead. And he would not be far behind them.

Very slowly and deliberately he lowered the muzzle of the rifle until it was pointing at the ground. Then he laid the weapon down and raised his hands.

'Get your hands up,' he told the women. 'Do exactly what they tell you.'

The guerrilla leader acknowledged his surrender by coming to his full height and speaking rapidly to his men, still in Arabic.

'Get the rifle and his pack.'

'We are British subjects,' Nicholas told him loudly, and the guerrilla looked surprised by his use of Arabic. 'We are simple tourists. We are not military. We are not government people.'

'Be quiet. Shut your face!' he ordered, as the rest of the guerrilla patrol emerged from cover. Nicholas counted five of them all told, though he knew there were probably others who had not come forward. They were very professional as they rounded up their prisoners. They never blocked each other's field of fire, nor offered an opportunity of escape. Quickly they searched them for weapons, then closed in around them and hustled them on to the path.

'Where are you taking us?' Nicholas demanded.

'No questions!' The butt of an AK-47 smashed between his shoulder blades and almost knocked him off his feet.

'Steady on, chaps,' he murmured mildly in English. 'That wasn't really called for.'

They were forced to keep marching through the heat of the afternoon. Nicholas kept a check on the position of the sun and the distant glimpses of the escarpment wall. He realized that they were heading westwards, following the course of the Nile towards the Sudanese border. It was late afternoon, and Nicholas estimated that they had covered some ten miles, before they came upon a side shoot of the main valley. The slopes were heavily wooded, and the three prisoners were herded into a patch of this forest.

They were actually within the perimeter of the guerrilla camp before they were aware of its existence. Cunningly camouflaged, it consisted merely of a few crude lean-to shelters and a ring of weapons emplacements. The sentries were well placed, and all the light machine guns in the foxholes were manned.

They were led to one of the shelters in the centre of the camp, where three men were squatting around a map spread on a low camp table. These were obviously officers, and there was no mistaking which of the three was the commander. The leader of the patrol which had captured them went to this man, saluted him deferentially and then spoke to him urgently, pointing at his captives.

The guerrilla commander straightened up from the table, and came out into the sunlight. He was of medium height, but was imbued with such an air of authority that he seemed taller. His shoulders were broad and his body square and chunky, with the beginning of a dignified spread around the waist. He wore a short curly beard which contained a few strands of grey, and his features were refined and handsome. His skin tones were amber and copper. His dark eyes were intelligent, his gaze quick and restless.

'My men tell me that you speak Arabic,' he said to Nicholas.

'Better than you do, Mek Nimmur,' Nicholas told him. 'So now you are the leader of a bunch of bandits and kidnappers? I always told you that you would never get to heaven, you old reprobate.'

Mek Nimmur stared at him in astonishment, and then began to smile. 'Nicholas! I did not recognize you. You are older. Look at the grey on your head!'

He opened his arms wide and folded Nicholas into a bear hug.

'Nicholas! Nicholas!' He kissed him once on each cheek. Then he held him at arm's length and looked at the two women, who were standing amazed.

'He saved my life,' he explained to them.

'You make me blush, Mek.'

Mek kissed him again, 'He saved my life twice.'

'Once,' Nicholas contradicted him. 'The second time was a mistake. I should have let them shoot you.'

Mek laughed delightedly. 'How long ago was it, Nicholas?'

'It doesn't bear thinking about.'

'Fifteen years ago at least,' Mek said. 'Are you still in the British army? What is your rank? You must be a general by now!'

'Reserves only,' Nicholas shook his head. 'I have been back in civvy street a long time now.'

Still hugging Nicholas, Mek Nimmur looked at the women with interest. 'Nicholas taught me most of what I know about soldiering,' he told them. His eyes flicked from Royan to Tessay, and then stayed on the Ethiopian girl's dark and lovely face.

'I know you,' he said. 'I saw you in Addis, years ago.

You were a young girl then. Your father was Alto Zemen, a great and good man. He was murdered by the tyrant Mengistu.'

'I know you also, Alto Mek. My father held you in high esteem. There are many of us who believe that you should be the president of this Ethiopia of ours, in place of that other one.' She dropped him a graceful little curtsey, hanging her head in a shy but appealing gesture of respect.

'I am flattered by your opinion of me.' He took her hand and lifted her to her full height. Then he turned back to Nicholas, 'I am sorry for the rough welcome. Some of my men are over-enthusiastic. I knew that there were *ferengi* asking questions at the monastery. But enough, you are with friends here. I bid you welcome.'

Mek Nimmur led them to his shelter, where one of his men brought a soot-blackened kettle from the fire and poured viscous black coffee into mugs for them.

He and Nicholas plunged into reminiscences of the days prior to the Falklands war when they had fought side by side, Nicholas as a covert military adviser, and Mek as a young freedom fighter opposing the tyranny of Mengistu.

'But the war is over now, Mek,' Nicholas remonstrated at last. 'The battle is won. Why are you still out in the bush with your men? Why aren't you getting rich and fat in Addis, like all the others?'

'In the interim government in Addis there are enemies of mine, men like Mengistu. When we have got rid of them, then I will come out of the bush.'

He and Nicholas embarked into a spirited discussion of African politics, so deep and complicated that Royan knew very few of the personalities whom they were discussing. Nor could she follow the nuances and the subtlety of religious and tribal prejudices and intolerance that had persisted for a thousand years. She was, however, impressed by Nicholas's knowledge and understanding of the situation, and the way in which a man like Mek Nimmur asked his opinion and listened to his advice.

In the end Nicholas asked him, 'So now you have carried the war beyond the borders of Ethiopia itself? You are operating in Sudan, as well?'

'The war in the Sudan has been raging for twenty years,' Mek confirmed. 'The Christians in the south fighting against the persecution of the Moslem north—'

'I am well aware of that, Mek. But that is not Ethiopia. It's not your war.'

'They are Christians, and they suffer injustice. I am a soldier and a Christian. Of course it is my war.' Tessay had been listening avidly to every word that Mek spoke, and now she nodded her head in agreement, her eyes dark and solemn with hero worship.

'Alto Mek is a crusader for Christ and the rights of the common man,' Tessay told Nicholas in awed tones.

'And he dearly loves a good fight,' Nicholas laughed, punching his shoulder affectionately. It was a familiar gesture which could easily have given offence, but Mek accepted it readily and laughed back at him.

'What are you doing here yourself, Nicholas, if you are no longer a soldier? There was a time when you also loved a good fight.'

'I am completely reformed. No more fighting. I have come to the Abbay gorge to hunt dik-dik.'

'Dik-dik?' Mek Nimmur stared at him with disbelief, and then he roared with laughter. 'I don't believe it. Not you. Not dik-dik. You are up to something.'

'It is the truth.'

'You are lying, Nicholas. You never could lie to me. I know you too well. You are up to something. You will tell me about it when you need my help.'

'And you will still give me your help?'

'Of course. You saved my life twice.'

'Once,' said Nicholas.

'Even once is enough,' said Mek Nimmur.

W hile they talked, the sun slanted down the sky.

'You are my guests for tonight,' Mek Nimmur told them formally. 'In the morning I will escort you back to your camp at the monastery of St Frumentius. That is also my destination. My men and I are going to the monastery to celebrate the festival of Timkat. The abbot, Jali Hora, is a friend and an ally.'

'And the monastery is probably your deep cover base. You use it and the monks for resupply and intelligence. Am I right?'

'You know me too well, Nicholas.' Mek Nimmur shook his head ruefully. 'You taught me much of what I know, so why should you not be able to guess my strategy? The monastery makes a perfect base of operations. It's close enough to the border—' he broke off, smiling. 'But there is no need to explain it to you, of all people.'

Mek had his men build a night shelter for Nicholas and Royan,' and cut a mattress of grass to cushion their sleep. They lay close together under the flimsy roof. The night was sultry, and they did not miss their blankets. Nicholas had a tube of insect repellent in his pack to keep the mosquitoes at bay.

After they had settled down on the grass mattress, their heads were close enough together to allow them to converse in quiet tones. When he turned his head Nicholas could see the dark silhouettes of Mek Nimmur and Tessay still sitting close together by the fire.

'Ethiopian girls are different from the Arabs, and from most other African women.' Royan too was watching the other couple. 'No Arab girl would dare be alone with a man like that. Especially if she were a married woman.'

'Any way you cut it, they make a damned fine pair,' he gave his opinion. 'Good luck to them. Tessay hasn't had much of that lately – she is overdue.'

He turned his head and looked into her face, 'What about you, Royan, what are you? Are you a decorous, submissive Arab, or an independent, assertive Western girl?'

'It's both a little early and much too late for intimate questions of that nature,' she told him, and turned over, presenting him with her back.

'Ah, we are standing on ceremony this evening! Goodnight, Woizero Royan.'

'Goodnight, Alto Nicholas,' she replied, keeping her face turned away from him so that he could not see her smile.

T he guerrilla column moved out before dawn the next morning. They marched in full battle order, with scouts moving ahead and flankers covering each side of the path.

'The army come down here into the gorge very seldom, but we are always ready for them when they do come,' Mek Nimmur explained. 'We try to give them a hearty welcome.'

Tessay was watching Mek Nimmur as he spoke; indeed, she had seldom taken her eyes off him that morning. Now she murmured to Royan, 'He is a truly great man, a man who could unite our land, perhaps for the first time in a thousand years. I feel humble in his presence, and yet I also feel like a young girl again, filled with joy and hope.'

The march back to the monastery took the entire morning. When they came in sight of the Dandera river, Mek Nimmur drew his men back off the path into thick bush, while sending only one scout forward. After an hour's wait, a party of acolytes came up from the monastery, each carrying a large bundle balanced upon his head.

They greeted Mek with deep reverence, and handed over their bundles to his men before returning down the pathway into the gorge of the Abbay.

The bundles contained priestly *shammas*, headcloths and sandals. Mek's men changed out of their camouflage fatigues into these garments, all of which were well worn and unwashed for the sake of authenticity. They wore only their sidearms under the robes. All their other weapons and equipment they cached in one of the caves in the limestone cliffs, and left a detachment to guard them.

Now as a party of monks they covered the last few miles to the monastery, to be welcomed joyously by the community there. Here Nicholas and the women left Mek, and climbed the steep path up into the grove of wild fig trees. Boris was waiting for them, pacing about the camp, angry and frustrated.

'Where the hell have you been, woman?' he snarled at Tessay. 'Been whoring around all night, have you?'

'We lost our way yesterday evening.' Nicholas fed him the cover story that they had agreed with Mek Nimmur, to maintain his security. Boris was hardly the man to trust. 'And we were picked up by a party of monks from the monastery this morning. They brought us back.'

'You are the big hunter and tracker, are you?' Boris sneered at him. 'You didn't need me to guide you, hey? You got yourself lost, did you, English? I see now why you want only to shoot dik-dik.' He guffawed without humour, and looked at Tessay with those pale dead eyes. 'I will talk to you later, woman. Go and see to the food.'

Despite the heat, both Nicholas and Royan were hungry. In short order, Tessay was able to serve a tasty cold lunch under the shady branches of the fig trees. Nicholas refused the wine that Boris offered him.

'I want to go out hunting again this afternoon. I have lost almost a whole day.'

'You want me to hold your hand this time, English? Make sure you don't lose yourself again?'

'Thanks, old chap, but I think I can manage without you.'

While they ate Nicholas nudged Royan and told her, 'Your admirer has arrived.'

He jerked his head at the lanky, ungainly figure of Tamre, who had sneaked up quietly and was now sitting near the kitchen hut. As soon as Royan looked at him his face split into a doting idiotic grin, and he bobbed his head and squirmed with ecstatic shyness.

'I will not come with you this afternoon,' Royan told Nicholas quietly, when Boris was not listening. 'I think there is going to be trouble between him and Tessay. I want to stay here with her. Take Tamre with you.'

'My word, what an attractive alternative. All my life I have waited for this moment.' But when he had picked up his rifle and pack, he beckoned the boy to follow him. Tamre looked around eagerly for Royan, but she was in her hut. At last, dragging his feet, he followed Nicholas up the valley.

'Take me to the other side of the river,' he told the boy. 'Show me how to reach the side where the holy creature lives.' Tamre perked up at the prospect, and broke into a shambling trot as he led Nicholas over the suspension bridge below the pink cliffs.

For an hour they followed the path, but gradually it petered out until it ended in bad and broken ground amongst the erosion-carved hills. Undeterred, Tamre plunged into the thorny scrub, and for another two hours they scrambled over rocky ridges and through thorn-choked valleys.

'I can see why you didn't want to bring Royan this way

round,' Nicholas grunted. His bare arms were scored by thorn, and the legs of his trousers were ripped in half a dozen places. However, he was memorizing the route and knew that he could find his way back again without difficulty.

At last they topped another ridge and Tamre stopped and pointed down over the far side. Below them Nicholas could make out the cleft of the chasm, and the small open glade from which the dik-dik spring issued. He could even recognize the thorn tree on the far bank of the Dandera river under which they had been sitting when Mek's men had surprised them.

He rested a few minutes and swallowed a few mouthfuls from the water bottle before passing it to Tamre. 'He's a monk, for goodness' sake,' he consoled himself. 'The little devil is not going to have AIDS, now, is he?' But he wiped the mouth of the bottle carefully when Tamre handed it back to him.

Before starting down the slope he checked the Rigby rifle again, blowing dust off the lens of the scope. Then he sighted through it at a dik-dik-sized rock at the foot of the slope, whilst he twisted the ring on the telescope down to its lowest magnification. He was now ready for a quick shot at close range in thick bush. Satisfied at last, he chambered a round, set the safety-catch and stood up.

'Keep behind me,' he told the boy. 'And do what I do.'

He drifted down the slope, pausing after every few slow steps to check the thorn scrub ahead and on both sides. When he reached the spring head, the earth was damp and soft. A number of animals and birds had been drinking here. He recognized the spoor of both kudu and bushbuck, but amongst these were the tiny, heart-shaped prints of his quarry.

He moved on quietly and at the edge of the scrub he found a midden, a boundary post which the dik-dik had used to mark out its chosen territory. The pile of buckshot-sized pellets of dung would be added to each time the little antelope returned to defecate at this spot.

By now Nicholas was totally absorbed in the hunt. His earlier failures had merely served to pique his fascination. He brought as much concentration to bear as if it had been a man-eating lion he was following. He crept forward a pace at a time, checking the ground before he let his foot fall on a dry twig or patch of rustling leaves, his eyes moving more swiftly than his feet, picking out any movement or touch of colour in the thorny palisade.

It was a flicker of an ear that gave the creature away. It was standing half in shadow, its ruddy coat blending into the backdrop of dried branches, still as if carved from mahogany. Only that small movement betrayed it. It was so close that Nicholas could see the reflection of light from one eye bright as polished onyx, and then the elongated nose wriggled with agitation. It was aware of danger, but uncertain from what quarter it was to come.

Achingly slowly, Nicholas lifted the Rigby to his shoulder. Through the lens he could make out every hair in the tuft between the pricked ears and the little black needle horns. He moved the cross hairs down on to the junction between neck and head. He wanted to restrict the damage to the pelt, so as to make the mounting and taxidermy easier.

'It is the holy creature. Praise God and St John the Baptist!' cried Tamre in a loud voice at his elbow, and he fell to his knees with his hands clasped in front of his eyes.

The dik-dik dissolved like a puff of brown smoke out of the field of the lens, and there was only a soft rustle in the scrub as it fled. Nicholas lowered the rifle slowly and looked down at the boy. He was still on his knees, gabbling out praises and prayers.

'Nice work. I think Woizero Royan must have you in her pay,' he said in English. He reached down, hauled the boy to his feet and switched into Arabic. 'You will stay here. You will not move. You will not speak. You will even breathe very, very quietly, until I come back to fetch you. If you utter even one little prayer before I return, I will personally start you on your journey to meet St Peter at the gates of heaven. Do you understand me?'

He went forward alone, but the little antelope was thoroughly alarmed by now. Nicholas saw it twice more, but he only had fleeting glimpses of ruddy brown movement almost entirely screened by bush. He stood directing bitter imprecations towards the boy monk and listening to the tick of small hooves on dry earth as it raced away, deeper into the thickets. In the end he was forced to give up the hunt for that day.

It was after dark when he and Tamre got back to camp. As soon as Nicholas stepped into the circle of firelight, Royan came to meet him.

'What happened?' she asked. 'Did you see the dik-dik again?'

'Don't ask me. Ask your accomplice. He scared it off. It is probably still running.'

'Tamre, you are a fine young man, and I am very proud of you,' she told him. The boy wriggled like a puppy, giggling and hugging himself with the joy of her approval as he scurried away down the path to the monastery.

Royan was so pleased with the outcome of the hunt that she poured Nicholas a whisky with her own hand and brought it to him as he sagged wearily by the fire.

He tasted it and shuddered, 'Never let a teetotaller pour for you. With a heavy hand like that you should take up tossing the caber or blacksmithing.' Despite the complaint, he took another tentative sip.

She sat close to him, fidgeting with excitement, but it was a while before he became aware of her agitation.

'What is it? Something is eating you alive.'

She threw a cautionary glance in the direction of where Boris sat on the opposite side of the fire, and then dropped her voice, leaned close to him and spoke in Arabic.

'Tessay and I went down to the monastery this afternoon to see Mek Nimmur. Tessay asked me to go with her, just in case Boris – well, you know what I mean.'

'I have a vague idea. You were playing chaperone.' Nicholas took another sip of the whisky and gasped. He exhaled sharply and his voice was husky. 'Go on,' he invited her.

'At one stage, before I left them alone together, we were discussing the festival of Timkat. On the fifth day the abbot takes the *tabot* down to the Abbay. Mek tells us there is a path down the cliff to the water's edge.'

'Yes, we know that.'

'This is the interesting part – this you didn't know. Everybody joins the procession down to the river. Everybody. The abbot, all the priests, the acolytes, every true believer, even Mek and all his men, they all go down to the river and stay there overnight. For one whole day and night the monastery is deserted. Empty. Nobody there at all.'

He stared at her over the rim of his glass, and then slowly he began to smile, 'Now that is very interesting indeed,' he admitted.

'Don't forget, I am coming with you,' she told him severely. 'Don't you dare to even think of leaving me behind.'

Nicholas went to her hut again that evening after dinner. This was the only place in camp where they could be sure of privacy, and where they were safe from eavesdropping. However, this time he did not make the mistake of sitting on her bed. While she perched on the end of it, he took the stool opposite her.

'Before we start planning this thing, let me ask you one question. Have you considered the possible consequences?'

'You mean, what happens if the monks catch us at it?' Royan asked.

'At the very least we can expect them to run us out of the valley. The abbot has a tremendous amount of power. At the worst we can be physically attacked,' Nicholas told her. 'This is one of the most sacred sites in their religion, and don't underestimate that fact. There is a great deal of danger involved. It could go as far as a knife between the ribs, or something nasty in our food.'

'We would also alienate Tessay. She is a deeply religious woman,' Royan added.

'Even more importantly, we would probably outrage Mek Nimmur as well.' Nicholas looked distressed at the thought. 'I don't know what he would do, but I don't think our friendship would stand the test.'

They were both quiet for a while, considering the cost that they might have to pay. Nicholas broke the silence.

'Then again, have you considered your own position? After all, it is your own Church that we will be desecrating. You are a committed Christian. Can you justify this to yourself?'

'I have thought about it,' she admitted. 'And I am not altogether happy about it, but it isn't really my Church. It's a different branch of the Coptic Church.'

'Splitting hairs, aren't we?'

'The Egyptian Church does not deny anyone access to even the most sacred precincts of its church building. I do not feel myself bound by the abbot's prohibition. I feel that as a believing Christian I have the right to enter any part of the cathedral that I wish.'

He whistled softly, 'And you are the one who once said that I should have been a lawyer.'

'Please don't, Nicky. It's not something you should

joke about. All I know is that, no matter what, I have to go in there. Even if I give offence to Tessay and Mek and all the priesthood, I have to do it.'

'You could let me do it for you,' he suggested. 'After all, I am an old heathen. It would not spoil my chances of salvation. I don't have any.'

'No.' She shook her head firmly. 'If there is an inscription or something of that nature, I need to see it. You read hieroglyphics quite well, but not as well as I do, and you don't know the hieratic script. I am the expert – you are just a gifted amateur. You need me. I am going in there with you.'

'All right. That is settled, then,' he said with finality. 'Let's start planning. We had better draw up a list of equipment that we may need. Flashlight, knife, Polaroid camera, spare film—'

'Art paper and soft pencils to lift an impression of any inscriptions,' she added to the list.

'Hell!' He snapped his fingers with chagrin. 'I didn't think to bring any.'

'See what I mean? Amateur. I did.'

They talked on until late, and at last Nicholas glanced at his wrist-watch and stood up.

'Long after midnight. I am scheduled to turn into a pumpkin at any moment. Goodnight.'

'There are still two days of the festival before the *tabot* is taken down to the river. Nothing we can do until then. What are your plans?'

'Tomorrow I am going back after that damned little Bambi. It has made a fool of me twice already.'

'I am coming with you,' she said firmly, and that simple declaration gave him a disproportionate amount of pleasure.

'Just as long as you leave Tamre at home,' he warned her as he stooped out through the door.

The tiny antelope stepped out from the deep shadow of the thorn thicket, and the early morning sunlight gleamed on the silky pelt. It kept walking steadily across the narrow clearing.

Nicholas's breathing quickened with excitement as he followed it with the telescopic sight. It was ridiculous that he should feel so wrought up with the hunting of such a humble little animal, but his previous failures had sharpened his anticipation. Added to that was the peculiar passion that drives the true collector. Since he had lost Rosalind and the girls, he had thrown all his energy into the building up of the collection at Quenton Park. Now, suddenly, procuring this specimen for it had become a matter of supreme importance to him.

His forefinger rested lightly on the side of the trigger guard. He would not fire until the dik-dik came to a standstill. Even that walking pace would make the shot uncertain. He had to place his bullet precisely, to kill swiftly but at the same time to inflict the least possible damage to the skin.

To this end he had loaded the Rigby with full metal jacket bullets – ones that would not expand on impact and open a wide wound channel, nor rip out a gaping hole in the coat as they exited. These solid bullets would punch a tiny hole the size of a pencil that the taxidermist at the museum would be able to repair invisibly.

He felt his nerves screwing up as he realized that the dik-dik was not going to stop in the open. It made steadily for the thick scrub on the far side of the clearing. This might be his last chance. He fought the temptation to take the shot at the moving target, and it required an effort of will to lift his finger off the trigger again.

The antelope reached the wall of thorn scrub and, the moment before it disappeared, stopped abruptly and thrust its tiny head into the depths of one of the low bushes.

Standing broadside to Nicholas, it began to nibble at the pale green tufts of new leaves. The head was screened, so he had to abandon his intention of going for that shot. However, the shoulder was exposed. He could make out the clear outline of the blade beneath the glossy red-brown skin. The dik-dik was angled slightly away from him, in the perfect position for the heart shot, tucked in low behind the shoulder.

Unhurriedly he settled the reticule of the scope on the precise spot, and squeezed the trigger.

The shot whip-cracked in the heavy heated air and the tiny antelope bounded high, coming down to touch the earth already at a full run. Like a rapier rather than a cutlass, the solid bullet had not struck with sufficient shock to knock the dik-dik over. Head down, the dik-dik dashed away in the typical frantic reaction to a bullet through the heart. It was dead already, running only on the last dregs of oxygen in its bloodstream.

'Oh, no! Not that way,' Nicholas cried as he jumped to his feet. The tiny creature was racing straight towards the lip of the cliff. Blindly it leaped out into empty space and flipped into a somersault as it fell, dropping from their sight, down almost two hundred feet into the chasm of the Dandera river.

'That was a filthy bit of luck.' Nicholas jumped over the bush that had hidden them and ran to the rim of the chasm. Royan followed him and the two of them stood peering down into the giddy void.

'There it is!' She pointed, and he nodded. 'Yes, I can see it.'

The carcass lay directly below them, caught on an islet of rock in the middle of the stream.

'What are you going to do?' she asked.

'I'll have to go down and get it.' He straightened up and stepped back from the brink. 'Fortunately it's still early.

We have plenty of time to get the job done before dark. I'll have to go back to camp to fetch the rope and to get some help.'

It was afternoon before they returned, accompanied by Boris, both his trackers and two of the skinners. They brought with them four coils of nylon rope.

Nicholas leaned out over the cliff and grunted with relief. 'Well, the carcass is still down there. I had visions of it being washed away.' He supervised the trackers as they uncoiled the rope and laid it out down the length of the clearing.

'We will need two coils of it to get down to the bottom,' he estimated and joined them, painstakingly tying and checking the knot himself. Then he plumbed the drop, lowering the end of the rope down the cliff until it touched the surface of the water, and then hauling it back and measuring it between the spread of his arms.

'Thirty fathoms. One hundred and eighty feet. I won't be able to climb back that high,' he told Boris. 'You and your gang will have to haul me back up.'

He anchored the rope end with a bowline to the bole of one of the wiry thorn trees. Then he again tested it meticulously, getting all four of the trackers and skinners to heave on it with their combined weight.

'That should do it,' he gave his opinion as he stripped to his shirt and khaki shorts and pulled off his chukka boots. On the lip of the cliff he leaned out backwards with the rope draped over his shoulder and the tail brought back between his legs in the classic abseil style.

'Coming in on a wing and a prayer!' he said, and jumped out backwards into the chasm. He controlled his fall by allowing the rope to pay out over his shoulder, braking with the turn over his thigh, swinging like a pendulum and kicking himself off the rock wall with both feet. He went down swiftly until his feet dangled into the rush of water, and the current pushed him into a spin on the end of the rope. He was a few yards short of the spur of rock on which the dead dik-dik lay, and he was forced to let himself drop into the river. With the end of the rope held between his teeth he swam the last short distance with a furious overarm crawl, just beating the current's attempt to sweep him away downstream.

He dragged himself up on to the island and took a few moments to catch his breath, before he could admire the beautiful little creature he had killed. He felt the familiar melancholy and guilt as he stroked the glossy hide and examined the perfect head with the extraordinary proboscis. However, there was no time now for regrets, nor for the searching of his hunter's conscience.

He trussed up the dik-dik, tying all four of its legs together securely, then he stepped back and looked up. He could see Boris's face peering down at him.

'Haul it up!' he shouted, and gave three yanks on the rope as the agreed signal. The trackers were hidden from his view, but the slack in the rope was taken up and then the dik-dik lifted clear of the island and rose jerkily up the wall of the chasm. Nicholas watched it anxiously. There was a moment when the rope seemed to snag when the carcass was two-thirds of the way to the top, but then it freed itself and snaked on up the cliff.

Eventually the dik-dik disappeared from his sight, and there was a long delay until the rope end dropped back over the lip. Boris had been sensible enough to weight it with a round stone the size of a man's head, and he was hanging over the top of the cliff, watching its progress and signalling to his men to control the descent.

When the end of the weighted line touched the surface of the water it was just out of Nicholas's reach. From the top of the cliff Boris began to swing the line until the end of it pendulumed close enough for Nicholas to grab it. With a bowline knot Nicholas tied a loop in the end of the line and slipped it under his armpits. Then he looked up at Boris.

'Heave away!' he yelled, and tugged the dangling rope three times. The slack tightened and then he was lifted off his feet. He began to ascend in a series of spiralling jerks and heaves. As he rose, the belled wall of the chasm arched in to meet him, until he could fend off from the rock with his bare feet and stop himself spiralling at the end of the rope. He was fifty feet from the top of the cliff when suddenly he stopped abruptly, dangling helplessly against the rock face.

'What's going on?' he shouted up at Boris.

'Bloody rope has jammed,' Boris yelled back. 'Can you see where it is stuck?'

Nicholas peered up and realized that the rope had rolled into a vertical crack in the face, probably the same one that had almost stopped the dik-dik reaching the top. However, his own weight was almost five times that of the little antelope, and had forced the rope much more deeply into the crack.

He was suspended high in the air, with a drop of almost a hundred feet under him.

'Try and swing yourself loose!' Boris shouted down at him. Obediently, Nicholas kicked himself back and twisted on the rope to try and roll it clear. He worked until the sweat streamed down into his eyes and the rope had rubbed him raw under the arms.

'No use,' he shouted back at Boris. 'Try to haul it out with brute force!'

There was a pause, and then he saw the rope above the crack tighten like a bar of iron as five strong men hauled on the top end with all their strength. He could hear the trackers chanting their working chorus as they threw all their combined weight on the line.

His end of the line did not budge. It was a solid jam, and he knew then that they were not going to clear it. He looked down. The surface of the water seemed much further than a hundred feet below.

'The terminal velocity of the human body is one hundred and fifty miles an hour,' he reminded himself. At that speed the water would be like concrete. 'I won't be going that fast when I hit, will I?' he tried to reassure himself.

He looked up again. The men on the top of the cliff were still hauling with all their weight and strength. At that moment one of the strands of the nylon rope sheared against the cutting edge of the rock crack, and began to uncurl like a long green worm.

'Stop pulling!' Nicholas screamed. 'Vast heaving!' But Boris was no longer in sight. He was helping his trackers, adding his weight to the pull.

The second strand of the rope parted and unravelled. There was only a single strand holding him now.

It was going to go at any moment, he realized. 'Boris, you ham-fisted bastard, stop pulling!' But his voice never reached the Russian, and with a pop like a champagne cork the third and final strand of the rope parted.

He plunged downwards, with the loose end of the severed rope fluttering above his head. Flinging both arms straight upwards over his head to stabilize his flight, he straightened his legs, arrowing his body to hit feet first.

He thought about the island under him. Would he miss its red rock fangs or would he smash into it and shatter every bone in his lower body? He dared not look down to judge it in case he destabilized his fall and tumbled in mid-air. If he hit the water flat it would crush his ribs or snap his spine.

His guts seemed to be forced into his throat by the speed of his fall, and he drew one last breath as he hit the surface feet first. The force of it was stunning. It was transmitted up his spine into the back of his skull, so that his teeth cracked against each other and bright lights starred his vision. The river swallowed him under. He went down deep, but he was still moving so fast when he hit the rocky bottom that his legs were jarred to the hips. He felt his knees buckle under the strain, and he thought that both his legs had been broken.

The impact drove the air out of his lungs, and it was only when he kicked off the bottom, desperate for air, that he realized with a rush of relief that both his legs were still intact. He broke out through the surface, wheezing and coughing, and realized that he must have missed the island by only the length of his body. However, by now the current had carried him well clear of it.

He trod water on the racing stream, shook the water from his eyes and looked around him swiftly. The walls of the chasm were streaming past him, and he estimated his speed at around ten knots – fast enough to break bone if he hit a rock. As he thought it, another small island flashed past him almost close enough to touch. He rolled on to his back and thrust both feet out ahead of him, ready to fend off should he be thrown on to another outcrop.

'You are in for the whole ride,' he told himself grimly. 'There is only one way out, and that is to ride it to the bottom.'

He was trying to calculate how far he was above the point where the river debouched from the chasm through the pink stone archway, how far he still had to swim.

'Three or four miles, at the least, and the river falls almost a thousand feet. There are bound to be rapids and probably waterfalls ahead,' he decided. 'From here it does not look good. I'd say the betting is three to one against getting through without leaving some skin and meat on the rocks behind you.'

He looked up. The walls canted in from each side, so that at places they almost met directly over his head. There was only a narrow strip of blue sky showing, and the depths were gloomy and dank. Over the ages the river had scoured the rock as it cut its way through.

'Damned lucky this is the dry season. What is it like down in here in the rainy season?' he wondered. He looked up at the high-water mark etched on the rock fifteen or twenty feet above his head.

Shuddering at the image he looked down again, concentrating on the river ahead. He had his breath back by now, and he checked his body for any damage. With relief he decided that, apart from some bruising and what felt like a sprained knee, he was unhurt. All his limbs were responding, and when he swam a few strokes to one side to avoid another spur of rock, even the sore knee worked well enough to get him out of trouble.

Gradually he became aware of a new sound in the canyon. It was a dull roar, growing stronger as he sped onwards. The walls of the chasm converged upon each other, the gut of rock narrowed and the flood seemed to accelerate as it was squeezed in and confined. The sound of water built up rapidly into a thunder that reverberated in the canyon.

Nicholas rolled over and swam with all his strength across the current until he reached the nearest rock wall. He tried to find a handhold, a place where he could anchor himself, but the rock was polished smooth by the river. It slipped past under his desperately grasping hands, and the river bellowed in his head. He saw the surface around him flatten out and smooth like solid glass. Like a horse laying back its ears as it gathers itself for a jump, the river had sensed what lay ahead.

Nicholas pushed himself away from the rock wall to try and give himself room in which to manoeuvre, and pointed his feet once more downriver. Abruptly the air opened under him and he was launched out into space. All around him white spuming water filled the air, and he was swirled off balance and tossed like a leaf in the torrent. The drop seemed to last for ever, and his stomach swooped against his ribs. Then once more he struck with all his weight and was driven far below the surface.

He fought his way up and abruptly burst out through the surface with his breathing whistling up his throat. Through streaming eyes he saw that he was caught up in the bowl of swirling water below the falls. The waters revolved and eddied, turning in a stately minuet upon themselves.

As he turned, he saw first the high sheet of white water of the falls down which he had tumbled, and then, still turning, the narrow exit from the basin through which the river resumed its mad career downstream. But for the moment he was safe and quiet here in the back-eddy below the falls. The current pushed him against the side of the basin, close in beneath the chute of the falls. He reached out and found a handhold on a clump of mossy fern growing out of a crack in the wall.

Here, at last, he had a chance to rest and consider his position. It did not take him long, however, to realize that his only way out of the chasm was to follow the course of the river and to take his chances with whatever lay downstream. He could expect rapids, if not another set of falls like this one that thundered away close beside him.

If only there were some way up the wall! He looked up, but his spirits quailed as he considered the overhang that formed a cathedral roof high above him.

While he still stared upwards, something caught his eye. Something too regular and regimented to be natural. There was a double row of dark marks running vertically up the wall of rock, beginning at the surface of the water and climbing up the wall to the rim almost two hundred feet overhead. He relinquished his hold on the clump of fern and dog-paddled slowly down to where these marks reached the water.

As he reached them he realized that they were niches, cut about four inches square into the wall. The two rows were twice the spread of his arms apart, and the niche in one row lined up in the horizontal plane exactly with its neighbour in the second row.

Thrusting his hand into the nearest opening, he found that it was deep enough to accommodate his arm to the elbow. This opening, being below the flood level of the waters, was smoothed and worn, but when he looked to those higher up the wall, above the water mark, he saw that they had retained their shape much more clearly. The edges were sharp and square.

'My word, how old are they to have been worn like that?' he marvelled. 'And how the hell did anybody get down here to cut them?'

He hung on to the niche nearest him and studied the pattern in the cliff face. 'Why would anybody go to all that amount of trouble?' He could think of no reason nor purpose. 'Who did this work? What would they want down here?' It was an intriguing mystery.

Then suddenly something else caught his eye. It was a circular indentation in the rock, precisely between the two rows of niches and above the high-water mark. From so far below it looked to be perfectly round – another shape that was not natural.

He paddled further around, trying to reach a position from which he would have a clearer view of it. It seemed to be some sort of rock engraving, a plaque that reminded him strongly of those marks in the black boulders that flank the Nile below the first cataract at Aswan, placed there in antiquity to measure the flood levels of the river waters. But the light was too poor and the angle too acute for him to be certain that it was man-made, let alone to recognize or read any script or lettering that might have been incorporated in the design.

Hoping to devise some way of climbing closer, he tried

to use the stone niches as aids. With a great deal of effort, using them as foot- and hand-holds, he managed to lift himself out of the water. But the distances between holds were too great and he fell back with a splash, swallowing more water.

'Take it easy, my lad – you still have to swim out of here. No profit in exhausting yourself. You will just have to come back another day to get a closer look at whatever it is up there.'

Only then did he realize how close he was to total exhaustion. This water coming down from the Choke mountains was still cold with the memories of the high snows. He was shivering until his teeth chattered.

'Not far from hypothermia. Have to get out of here now, while you still have the strength.'

Reluctantly he pushed himself away from the wall of rock and paddled towards the narrow opening through which the Dandera river resumed the headlong rush to join her mother Nile. He felt the current pick him up and bear him forward, and he stopped swimming and let it take him.

'The Devil's roller-coaster!' he told himself. 'Down and down she goes, and where she stops nobody knows.'

The first set of rapids battered him. They seemed endless, but at last he was spewed out into the run of slower water below them. He floated on his back, taking full advantage of this respite, and looked upwards. There was very little light showing above him, for the rock almost met overhead. The air was dank and dark and stank of bats. However, there was little time to examine his surroundings, for once again the river began to roar ahead of him. He braced himself mentally for the assault of turbulent waters, and went cascading down the next steep slide.

After a while he lost track of how far he had been carried, and how many cataracts he had survived. It was a constant battle against the cold and the pain of sodden lungs and strained muscle and overtaxed sinew. The river mauled him.

Suddenly the light changed. After the gloom at the bottom of the high cliffs it was as though a searchlight had been shone directly into his eyes, and he felt the force and ferocity of the river abating. He squinted up into bright sunlight, and then looked back and saw that he had passed out below the archway of pink rock into that familiar part of the river which he had explored with Royan. Coming up ahead of him was the rope suspension bridge, and he had just sufficient strength remaining to paddle feebly towards the small beach of white sand below it.

One of the hairy tattered ropes dangled to the surface of the water, and he managed to catch hold of it as he drifted past and swing himself in towards the beach. He tried to crawl fully ashore, but he collapsed with his face in the sand and vomited out the water he had swallowed. It felt so good just to be able to lie without effort and rest. His lower body still hung into the river, but he had neither the strength nor the inclination to drag himself fully ashore.

'I am alive,' he marvelled, and fell into a state halfway between sleep and unconsciousness.

H e never knew how long he had been lying like that, but when he felt a hand shaking his shoulder, and a voice calling softly to him, he was annoyed that his rest had been disturbed.

'*Effendi*, wake up! They seek you. The beautiful Woizero seeks you.'

With a huge effort Nicholas roused himself and sat up slowly. Tamre knelt over him, grinning and waggling his head.

'Please, *effendi*, come with me. The Woizero is searching

the river bank on the far side. She is weeping and calling your name,' Tamre told him. He was the only person Nicholas had ever met who contrived to look worried and to grin at the same time. Nicholas looked beyond him and saw that it must be late afternoon, for the sun sat fat and red on the lip of the escarpment.

While still sitting in the sand Nicholas checked his body, making an inventory of his injuries. He ached in every muscle, and his legs and arms were scraped and bruised, but he could detect no broken bones. And although there was a tender lump on the side of his head where he had glanced off a rock, his mind was clear.

'Help me up!' he ordered Tamre. The boy put his shoulder under Nicholas's armpit, where the rope had burnt him, and hoisted him to his feet. The two of them struggled up to the bank and on to the path, and then hobbled slowly across the swinging bridge.

He had hardly reached the other bank when there was a joyous shout from close at hand.

'Nicky! Oh, dear God! You are safe.' Royan ran down the path and threw her arms around him. 'I have been frantic. I thought that—' she broke off, and held him at arm's length to look at him. 'Are you all right? I was expecting to find your broken body—'

'You know me,' he grinned at her and tried not to limp. 'Ten feet tall and bullet-proof. You don't get rid of me that easily. I only did it just to get a hug from you.'

She released him hurriedly. 'Don't read anything into that. I am kind to all beaten puppies, and other dumb animals.' But her smile belied the words. 'Nevertheless, it's good to have you back in one piece, Nicky.'

'Where is Boris?' he asked.

'He and the trackers are searching the banks lower down the river. I think he is looking forward to finding your corpse.'

'What has he done with my dik-dik?'

'There is certainly nothing too much the matter with you if you can worry about that. The skinners have taken it down to the camp.'

'Damn it to hell! I must supervise the skinning and preparation of the trophy myself. They will ruin it!' He put his arm around Tamre's shoulder. 'Come on, my lad! Let's see if I can break into a trot.'

Nicholas knew that in this heat the carcass of the little antelope would decompose swiftly, and the hair would slough from the hide if it were not treated immediately. It was imperative to skin it out immediately. Already it had been left too long, and the preparation of a hide for a full body mount was a skilled and painstaking procedure.

It was already dark as they limped into the camp. Nicholas shouted for the skinners in Arabic.

'Ya, Kif! Ya, Salin!' and when they came running from their living huts he asked anxiously, 'Have you begun?'

'Not yet, *effendi*. We were having our dinner first.'

'For once gluttony is a virtue. Do not touch the creature until I come. While you are waiting for me, fetch one of the gas lights!' He limped to his own hut as fast as his aches would allow. There he stripped and anointed all his visible scrapes and abrasions with mercurochrome, flung on fresh dry clothes, rummaged in his bag until he found the canvas roll which contained his knives, and hurried down to the skinning hut.

By the brilliant white glare of the butane gas lantern he had only just completed the initial skin incisions down the inside of the dik-dik's legs and belly when Boris pushed open the door of the hut.

'Did you have a good swim, English?'

'Bracing, thank you.' Nicholas smiled. 'I don't expect you want to eat your words about my striped dik-dik, do you?' he asked mildly. 'No such bloody animal, I think you said.'

'It is like a rat. A true hunter would not bother himself with such rubbish,' Boris replied haughtily. 'Now that you have your rat, perhaps we can go back to Addis, English?'

'I paid you for three weeks. It is my safari. We go when I say so,' Nicholas told him. Boris grunted and backed out of the hut.

Nicholas worked swiftly. His knives were of a special design to facilitate the fine work, and he stropped them at regular intervals on a ceramic sharpening rod until he could shave the hairs from his forearm with just the lightest touch.

The legs had to be skinned out with the tiny hooves still attached. Before he had completed this part of the work, another figure stooped into the hut. He was dressed in a priest's *shamma* and headcloth, and until he spoke Nicholas did not recognize Mek Nimmur.

'I hear that you have been looking for trouble again, Nicholas. I came to make sure that you were still alive. There was a rumour at the monastery that you had drowned yourself, though I knew it was not possible. You will not die so easily.'

'I hope you are right, Mek,' Nicholas laughed at him.

Mek squatted opposite him. 'Give me one of your knives and I will finish the hooves. It will go quicker if I help you.'

Without comment Nicholas passed him one of the knives. He knew that Mek could skin out the hooves, for years before he had taught him the art. With two of them working on the pelt, it would go that much faster. The sooner the skin was off, the less chance there would be of deterioration.

He turned his attention to the head. This was the most delicate part of the process. The skin had to be peeled off like a glove, and the eyelids and lips and nostrils must be worked from the inside. The ears were perhaps the most difficult to lift away from the gristle in one piece. They worked in companionable silence for a while, which Mek broke at last.

'How well do you know your Russian, Boris Brusilov?' he asked.

'I met him for the first time when I stepped off the plane. He was recommended by a friend.'

'Not a very good friend.' Mek looked up at him and his expression was grim. 'I came to warn you about him, Nicholas.'

'I am listening,' said Nicholas quietly.

'In '85 I was captured by Mengistu's thugs. They kept me in the Karl Marx prison camp near Addis. Brusilov was one of the interrogators there. He was KGB in those days. His favourite trick was to stick the pressure hose from a compressor up the anus of the man or woman he was questioning and turn on the tap. They blew up like a balloon, until the gut burst.' He stopped speaking while he moved around to work on the other hoof of the antelope. 'I escaped before he got around to questioning me. He retired when Mengistu fled, and went hunting. I don't know how he persuaded Woizero Tessay to marry him, but knowing what I do of the man, I expect she did not have much choice in the matter.'

'Of course, I had my suspicions about him,' Nicholas admitted.

They were quiet after that until Mek whispered, 'I came to tell you that I may have to kill him.'

Neither of them spoke again until Mek had finished working on all four hooves. Then he stood up. 'These days, life is uncertain, Nicholas. If I have to leave here in a hurry, and I do not have a chance to say goodbye to you, then there is somebody in Addis who will pass a message to me if you ever need me. His name is Colonel Maryam

Kidane in the Ministry of Defence. He is a friend. My code name is the Swallow. He will know who you are talking about.'

They embraced briefly. 'Go with God!' said Mek, and left the hut quietly. The night swallowed his robed figure and Nicholas stood for a long time at the door, until at last he turned back to finish the work.

It was late by the time he had rubbed every inch of the skin with a mixture of rock salt and Kabra dip to cure it and protect it from the ravages of the bacon beetle and other insects and bacteria. At last he laid it out on the floor of the hut with the wet side uppermost and packed more rock salt on the raw areas.

The walls of the hut were reinforced with mesh netting to keep out hyenas. One of these foul creatures could gobble down the pelt in a few seconds. He made certain the door was wired shut before he carried the lantern up to the dining hut. The others had all eaten and gone to bed hours earlier, but Tessay had left his dinner in the charge of the Ethiopian chef. He had not realized how hungry he was until he smelt it.

The next morning Nicholas was so stiff that he hobbled down to the skinning hut like an old man. First he checked the pelt and poured fresh salt over it, then he ordered Kif and Salin to bury the skull of the dik-dik in an ant heap to allow the insects to remove the surplus flesh and scour the brain pan. He preferred this method to boiling the skull.

Satisfied that the trophy was in good condition, he went on down to the dining hut, where Boris greeted him jovially.

'And so, English. We leave for Addis now, da? Nothing more to do here.'

'We will stay to photograph the ceremony of Timkat

220

at the monastery,' Nicholas told him. 'And after that I may want to hunt a Menelik's bushbuck. Who knows? I've told you before. We go when I say so.'

Boris looked disgruntled. 'You are crazy, English. Why do you want to stay in this heat to watch these people and their mumbo-jumbo?'

'Today I will go fishing, and tomorrow we will watch Timkat.'

'You do not have a fishing rod,' Boris protested, but Nicholas opened the small canvas roll no larger than a woman's handbag and showed him the four-piece Hardy Smuggler rod nestling in it.

He looked across the table at Royan, 'Are you coming along to ghillie for me?' he asked.

They went upstream to the suspension bridge where Nicholas set up the rod and tied a fly on to his leader.

'Royal Coachman.' He held it up for her appraisal. 'Fish love them anywhere in the world, from Patagonia to Alaska. We shall soon find out if they are as popular here in Ethiopia, as well.'

She watched from the top of the bank as he shot out line, rolling it upon itself in flight, sailing the weightless fly out to midstream, and then laying it gently on the surface of the water so that it floated lightly on the ripples. On his second cast there was a swirl under the fly. The rod tip arced over sharply, the reel whined and Nicholas let out a whoop.

'Gotcha, my beauty!'

She watched him indulgently from the top of the bank. In his excitement and enthusiasm he was like a small boy. She smiled when she noticed how his injuries had miraculously healed themselves, and how he no longer limped as he ran back and forth along the water's edge, playing the fish. Ten minutes later he slid it, gleaming like a bar of freshly minted gold as long as his arm, flopping and flapping up on to the beach.

'Yellow fish,' he told her triumphantly. 'Scrumptious. Breakfast for tomorrow morning.'

He came up the bank and dropped down in the grass beside her. 'The fishing was really just an excuse to get away from Boris. I brought you here to tell you about what I found up there yesterday.' He pointed up through the archway of pink stone above the bridge. She came up on her elbow and watched him with her full attention.

'Of course, I have no way of telling if it has anything to do with our search, but somebody has been working in there.' He described the niches that he had found carved into the canyon wall. 'They reach from the lip right down to the water's edge. Those below the high-water mark have been severely eroded by the floods. I could not reach those higher up, but from what I could see they have been protected from wind and rain by the dished shape of the cliff; it has formed a veranda roof over them. They appear to be in pristine condition, very much in contrast to those lower down.'

'What do we deduce from that?' she asked.

'That they are very old,' he answered. 'Certainly the basalt is pretty hard. It has taken a long, long time for water to wear it down the way it has.'

'What do you think was the purpose of those holes?'

'I am not sure,' he admitted.

'Could it be that they were the anchor points for some sort of scaffolding?' she asked, and he looked impressed.

'Good thinking. They could be,' he agreed.

'What other ideas occur to you?'

'Ritual designs,' he suggested. 'A religious motif.' He smiled as he saw her expression of doubt. 'Not very convincing, I agree.'

'All right, let's consider the idea of scaffolding. Why would anybody want to erect scaffolding in a place like that?' She lay back in the grass and picked a straw which she nibbled reflectively.

He shrugged. 'To anchor a ladder or a gantry, to gain access to the bottom of the chasm?'

'What other reason?'

'I can't think of any other.'

After a while she shook her head. 'Nor can I.' She spat out the piece of grass. 'If that is the motive, then they were fairly committed to the project. From your description it must have been a substantial structure, designed to support the weight of a lot of men or heavy material.'

'In North America the Red Indians built fishing platforms over waterfalls like that from which they netted the salmon.'

'Have there ever been great runs of fish through these waters?' she asked, and he shrugged again.

'Nobody can answer that. Perhaps long ago – who knows.'

'Was that all you saw down there?'

'High up the wall, aligned with mathematical precision between the two lines of stone niches, there was something that looked like a bas-relief carving.'

She sat up with a jerk and stared at him avidly. 'Could you see it clearly? Was it script, or was it a design? What was the style of the carving?'

'No such luck. It was too high, and the light is very poor down there. I am not even certain that it wasn't a natural flaw in the rock.'

Her disappointment was palpable, but after a pause she asked, 'Was there anything else?'

'Yes,' he grinned. 'Lots and lots of water moving very very fast.'

'What are we going to do about this putative bas-relief of yours?' she asked.

'I don't like the idea in the least, but I will have to go back in there and have another look.'

'When?'

'Timkat tomorrow. Our one chance to get into the

maqdas of the cathedral. After that we will make a plan to explore the gorge.'

'We are running out of time, Nicky, just when things are getting really interesting.'

'You can say that again!' he murmured. She felt his breath on her lips, for their faces were as close together as those of conspirators or of lovers, and she realized the double meaning of her own words. She jumped to her feet and slapped the dust and loose straw from her jodhpurs.

'You only have one fish to feed the multitude. Either you have a very high opinion of yourself, or you had better get fishing.'

Two *debteras* who had been detailed by the bishop to escort them tried to force a way for them through the crowds. However, they had not reached the foot of the staircase before the escort itself was swallowed up and lost. Nicholas and Royan became separated from the other couple.

'Keep close,' Nicholas told Royan, and maintained a firm grip on her upper arm as he used his shoulder to open a path for them. He drew her along with him. Naturally, he had deliberately contrived to lose Boris and Tessay in the crush, and it had worked out nicely the way he had planned it.

At last they reached a position where Nicholas could set his back firmly against one of the stone columns of the terrace, to prevent the crowd jostling him. He also had a good view of the entrance to the cavern cathedral. Royan was not tall enough to see over the heads of the men in front of her, so Nicholas lifted her up on to the balustrade of the staircase and anchored her firmly against the column. She clung to his shoulder for support, for the drop into the Nile opened behind her.

The worshippers kept up a low monotonous chant,

while a dozen separate bands of musicians tapped their drums and rattled their sistrums. Each band surrounded its own patron, a chieftain in splendid robes, sheltering under a huge gaudy umbrella.

There was an air of excitement and expectation almost as fierce as the heat and the stink. It built up steadily and, as the singing increased in pitch and volume, the crowd began to sway and undulate like a single organism, some grotesque amoeba, pulsing with life.

Suddenly from within the precincts of the cathedral there came the chiming of brass bells, and immediately a hundred horns and trumpets answered. From the head of the stairway there was a fusillade of gunfire as the body-guards of the chieftains fired their weapons in the air.

Some of them were armed with automatic rifles, and the clatter of AK-47 fire blended with the thunder of ancient black powder muzzle-loaders. Clouds of blue gun-smoke blew over the congregation, and bullets ricocheted from the cliff and sang away over the gorge. Women shrieked and ululated, an eerie, blood-chilling sound. The men's faces were alight with the fires of religious fervour. They fell to their knees and lifted their hands high in adoration, chanting and crying out to God for blessing. The women held their infants aloft, and tears of religious frenzy streaked their dark cheeks.

From the gateway of the underground church emerged a procession of priests and monks. First came the *debteras* in long white robes, and then the acolytes who were to be baptized at the riverside. Royan recognized Tamre, his long gangling frame standing a head above the boys around him. She waved over the crowd and he saw her and grinned shyly before he followed the *debteras* on to the pathway to the river.

By this time night was falling. The depths of the cauldron were obscured by shadows, and hanging over it the sky was a purple canopy pricked by the first bright stars.

At the head of the pathway burned a brass brazier. As each of the priests passed it he thrust his unlit torch into the flames and, as soon as it flared, he held it aloft.

Like a stream of molten lava the torchlit procession began to uncoil down the cliff face, the priests chanting dolefully and the drums booming and echoing from the cliffs across the river.

Following the baptism candidates through the stone gateway came the ordained priests in their tawdry robes, bearing the processional crosses of silver and glittering brass, and the banners of embroidered silk, with their depictions of the saints in the agony of martyrdom and the ecstasy of adoration. They clanged their bells and blew their fifes, and sweated and chanted until their eyes rolled white in dark faces.

Behind them, borne by two priests in the most sumptuous robes and tall, jewel-encrusted head-dresses, came the *tabot*. The Ark of the Tabernacle was covered with a crimson cloth that hung to the ground, for it was too holy to be desecrated by the gaze of the profane.

The worshippers threw themselves down upon the ground in fresh paroxysms of adoration. Even the chiefs prostrated themselves upon the soiled pavement of the terrace, and some of them wept with the fervour of their belief.

Last in the procession came Jali Hora, wearing not the crown with the blue stone, but another even more splendid creation, the Epiphany crown, a mass of gleaming metal and flashing *faux* jewels which seemed too heavy for his ancient scrawny neck to support. Two *debteras* held his elbows and guided his uncertain footsteps on to the stairway that led down to the Nile.

As the procession descended, so those worshippers nearest to the head of the stairs rose to their feet, lit their torches at the brazier and followed the abbot down. There was a general movement along the terrace to join the flow, and as it began to empty, Nicholas lifted Royan down from her perch on the balustrade.

'We must get into the church while there are still enough people around to cover us,' he whispered. Leading her by the hand, with his other hand hanging on to the strap of his camera bag, he joined the movement down the terrace. He allowed them to be carried forward, but all the time he was edging across the stream of humanity towards the entrance to the church. He saw Boris and Tessay in the crush ahead of him, but they had not seen him, and he crouched lower so as to screen himself from them.

As he and Royan reached the gateway to the outer chamber of the church, he eased them out of the throng of humanity and drew her gently through the low entrance into the dim, deserted interior. With a quick glance he made certain that they were alone, and that the guards were no longer at their stations beside the inner gates. Then he moved quickly along the side wall, to where one of the soot-grimed tapestries hung from the ceiling to the stone floor. He lifted the folds of heavy woven wool and drew Royan behind them, letting them fall back into place, concealing them both.

They were only just in time, for hardly had they flattened their backs against the wall and let the tapestry settle when they heard footsteps approaching from the *qiddist*. Nicholas peeked around the corner of the tapestry and saw four white-robed priests cross the outer chamber and swing the main doors closed as they left the church. There was a weighty thud from outside as they dropped the locking beam into place, and then a profound silence pervaded the cavern.

'I didn't reckon on that,' Nicholas whispered. 'They have locked us in for the night.'

'At least it means that we won't be disturbed,' Royan replied briskly. 'We can get to work right away.'

Stealthily they emerged from their hiding-place, and

moved across the outer chamber to the doorway of the *qiddist*. Here Nicholas paused and cautioned her with a hand on her arm. 'From here on we are in forbidden territory. Better let me go ahead and scout the lie of the land.'

She shook her head firmly. 'You are not leaving me here. I am coming with you all the way.' He knew better than to argue.

'Come on, then.' He led her up the steps and into the middle chamber.

It was smaller and lower than the room they had left. The wall hangings were richer and in a better state of repair. The floor was bare, except for a pyramid-shaped framework of hand-hewn native timber upon which stood rows of brass lamps, each with the wick floating in a puddle of melted oil. The meagre light they provided was all that there was, and it left the ceiling and the recesses of the chamber in shadow.

As they crossed the floor towards the gates that closed off the *maqdas*, Nicholas took two electric torches from his camera bag and handed one to her. 'New batteries,' he told her, 'but don't waste them. We may be here all night.'

They stopped in front of the doors to the Holy of Holies. Quickly Nicholas examined them. There were engravings of St Frumentius on each panel, his head enclosed in a nimbus of celestial radiance and his right hand lifted in the act of benediction.

'Primitive lock,' he murmured, 'must be hundreds of years old. You could throw your hat through the gap between the hasp and the tongue.' He slipped his hand into the bag and brought out a Leatherman tool.

'Clever little job, this is. With it you do anything from digging the stones out of a horse's hoof, to opening the lock on a chastity belt.'

He knelt in front of the massive iron lock and unfolded one of the multiple blades of the tool. She watched anxiously as he worked, and then gave a little start as with a satisfying clunk the tongue of the lock slid back.

'Mis-spent youth?' she asked. 'Burglary amongst your many talents?'

'You don't really want to know.' He stood up and put his shoulder to one leaf of the door. It gave with a groan of unlubricated hinges, and he pushed it open only just wide enough for them to squeeze through, then immediately shut it behind them.

They stood side by side on the threshold of the *maqdas* and gazed about them in silent awe.

The Holy of Holies was a small chamber, much smaller than either of them had expected. Nicholas could have crossed it in a dozen strides. The vaulted roof was so low that by standing on tiptoe he could have touched it with his outstretched fingertips.

From the floor upwards the walls were lined with shelves upon which stood the gifts and offerings of the faithful, icons of the Trinity and the Virgin rendered in Byzantine style, framed in ornate silver. There were ranks of statuettes of saints and emperors, medallions and wreaths made of polished metal, pots and bowls and jewelled boxes, candelabra with many branches, on each of which the votive candles burned providing an uncertain wavering light. It was an extraordinary collection of junk and treasures, of objects of virtue and garish bric-à-brac, offered as articles of faith by the emperors and chieftains of Ethiopia over the centuries.

In the centre of the floor stood the altar of cedarwood, the panels carved with visionary scenes of revelation and creation, of the temptation and the fall from Eden, and of the Last Judgement. The altar cloth was crocheted raw silk, and the cross and the chalice were in massive worked silver. The abbot's crown gleamed in the candlelight, with the blue ceramic seal of Taita in the centre of its brow.

Royan crossed the floor and knelt in front of the altar.

She bowed her head in prayer. Nicholas waited respectfully at the threshold until she rose to her feet again, and then he went to join her.

'The *tabot* stone!' He pointed beyond the altar, and they went forward side by side. At the back of the *maqdas* stood an object covered with a heavy damask cloth encrusted with embroidered thread of silver and gold. From the outline beneath the covering they could see that it was of elegant and pleasing proportions, as tall as a man, but slender with a pedestal topping.

They both circled it, studying the cloaked shape avidly, but reluctant to touch it or to uncover it, fearful that their expectations might prove unwarranted, and that their hopes would be dashed like the turbulent river waters plunging into the cauldron of the Nile. Nicholas broke the tension that gripped them by turning away from the *tabot* stone to the barred gate in the back wall of the sanctuary.

'The tomb of St Frumentius!' he said, and went to the grille. She came to his side, and together they peered through the square openings in the woodwork that was black with age. The interior was in darkness. Nicholas prodded his torch through one of the openings and pressed the switch.

The tomb lit up in a rainbow of colour so bright in the beam of the torch that their eyes took a few moments to adjust and then Royan gasped aloud.

'Oh, sweet heaven!' She began to tremble as if in high fever, and her face went creamy pale as all the blood drained from it.

The coffin was set into a stone shelf in the rear wall of the cell-like tomb. On the exterior was painted the likeness of the man within. Although it was badly faded and most of the paint had flaked away, the pale face and reddish beard of the dead man were still discernible.

This was not the only reason for Royan's amazement. She was staring at the walls above and on either side of the shelf on which the coffin lay. They were a riot of colour, every inch of them covered with the most intricate and elaborate paintings that had miraculously weathered the passage of the millennia.

Nicholas played his torchbeam over them in awestruck silence, and Royan clung to his arm as if to save herself from falling. She dug her sharp nails into his flesh, but he was heedless of the pain.

There were scenes of great battles, fighting galleys locked in terrible combat upon the blue eternal waters of the river. There were scenes of the hunt, the pursuit of the river horse and of great elephants with long tusks of gleaming ivory. There were battle scenes of regiments plumed and armoured, raging in their fury and blood lust. Squadrons of chariots wheeled and charged each other across these narrow walls, half obscured by the dust of their own mad career.

The foreground of each mural was dominated by the same tall heroic figure. In one scene he drew the bow to full stretch, in another he swung high the blade of bronze. His enemies quailed before him, he trod them underfoot or gathered together their severed heads like a bouquet of flowers.

Nicholas played the beam over all this splendid array of art, and brought it to a stop upon the central panel that covered the entire main wall above the shelf on which the rotting coffin lay. Here the same godlike figure rode the footplate of his chariot. In one hand he held the bow and in the other a bundle of javelins. His head was bare of any helmet, and his hair flowed out behind him in the wind of his passage, a thick golden braid like the tail of a lion. His features were noble and proud, his gaze direct and indomitable.

Below him was a legend in classical Egyptian hiero-glyphics. In a sepulchral whisper Royan translated them aloud:

Great Lion of Egypt.
Best of One Hundred Thousand
Holder of the Gold of Valour
Pharaoh's Sole Companion
Warrior of all the Gods
May you live for ever!

Her hand shook upon his arm, and her voice choked and died away, stifled with emotion. She gave a little sob, and then shook herself as she brought herself back under control.

'I know this artist,' she said softly. 'I have spent five years studying his work. I would know it anywhere.' She drew a breath. 'I know with utter certainty that nearly four thousand years ago Taita the slave decorated these walls and designed this tomb.'

She pointed to the name of the dead man carved into the stone above the shelf on which his coffin lay.

'This is not the tomb of a Christian saint. Centuries ago some old priest must have stumbled upon it and, in his ignorance, usurped it for his own religion.' She drew another shaky breath. 'Look there! That is the seal of Tanus, Lord Harreb, the commander of all the armies of Egypt, lover of Queen Lostris and the natural father of Prince Memnon, who became the Pharaoh Tamose.'

They were both silent then, lost in the wonder of their discovery. Nicholas broke the silence at last.

'It's all true, then. The secrets of the seventh scroll are all here for us, if we can find the key to them.'

'Yes,' she said softly. 'The key. Taita's stone testament.' She turned back towards the *tabot* stone and approached it slowly, almost fearfully.

'I can't bring myself to look, Nicky. I am terrified that it's not what we hope it is. You do it!'

He went directly to the column, and with a magician's flourish jerked away the damask cloth that covered it. They stared at the pillar of pink mottled granite that he had revealed. It was about six feet high and a foot square at the base, tapering up to half that width at the flat pedestal of the summit. The granite had been polished, and then engraved.

Royan stepped forward and touched the cold stone, running her fingers lingeringly over the hieroglyphic script in the way a blind man reads Braille.

'Taita's letter to us,' she whispered, picking out the symbol of the hawk with a broken wing from the mass of close-chiselled script, tracing the outline with a long, slim forefinger that trembled softly. 'Written almost four thousand years ago, waiting all these ages for us to read and understand it. See how he has signed it.' Slowly she circled the granite pillar, studying each of the four sides in turn, smiling and nodding, frowning and shaking her head, then smiling again as if it were a love letter.

'Read it to me,' Nicholas invited. 'It's too complicated for me – I understand the characters, but I cannot follow the sense or the meaning. Explain it to me.'

'It's pure Taita.' She laughed, her awe and wonder at last giving way to excitement. 'He is being his usual obscure and capricious self.' It was as though she were talking of a beloved but infuriating old friend. 'It's all in verse and is probably some esoteric code of his own.' She picked out a line of hieroglyphics, and followed them with her finger as she read aloud, '*"The vulture rises on mighty pinions to greet the sun. The jackal howls and turns upon his tail. The river flows towards the earth. Beware, you violators of the sacred places, lest the wrath of all the gods descend upon you!"*'

'It's nonsense jargon. It does not make sense,' he protested.

'Oh, yes, it makes sense all right. Taita always makes sense, once you follow the way his oblique mind is working.' She turned to face him squarely. 'Don't look so glum, Nicky. You can't expect to read Taita like an editorial in *The Times*. He has set us a riddle that may take weeks and months of work to unravel.'

'Well, one thing is certain. We can't stay here in the *maqdas* for weeks and months while we puzzle it out. Let's get to work.'

'Photographs first.' She became brisk and businesslike. 'Then we can lift impressions from the stone.'

He set down the camera bag and knelt over it to open the flap. 'I will shoot two rolls of colour first, and then use the Polaroid. That will give us something to work on until we can have the colour developed.'

She stood out of his way as he circled the pillar on his knees, keeping the angle correct so as not to distort the perspective. He took a series of shots of each of the four sides, using different shutter speeds and exposures.

'Don't use up all your film,' she warned him. 'We need some shots of the walls of the tomb itself.'

Obediently he went to the grille gates and studied the locking system. 'This is a bit more complicated than the outer gate. If I try to get in here, I might do some damage. I don't think it will be worth the risk of being discovered.'

'All right,' she agreed. 'Work through the openings in the grille.'

He filmed as best he was able, extending the camera through the openings at the full stretch of his arms, and estimating his focus.

'That's the lot,' he told her at last. 'Now for the Polaroids.' He changed cameras and repeated the entire process, but this time Royan held a small tape measure against the pillar to give the scale.

As he exposed each plate he handed it to her to check the development. Once or twice when the flash setting on the camera had either overexposed or rendered the subject too dull, or for some other reason she was not satisfied, she asked him to repeat the shot.

After almost two hours' work they had a complete set of Polaroids, and Nicholas packed his cameras away and brought out the roll of art paper. Working together, they stretched it over one face of the pillar and secured it in place with masking tape. Then he started at the top and she at the bottom. Each with a black art crayon, they rubbed the precise shape and form of the engravings on to the sheet of blank paper.

'I have learned how important this is when dealing with Taita. If you are not able to work with the original, then you must have an exact copy. Sometimes the most minute detail of the engraving may change the entire sense and meaning of the script. He layers everything with hidden depths. You have read in *River God* how he considers himself to be the riddler and punster *par excellence* and the greatest exponent of the game of bao that ever lived. Well, that much of the book is accurate. Wherever he is now, he knows the game is on and he is revelling in every move we make. I can just imagine him giggling and rubbing his hands together with glee.'

'Bit fanciful, dear girl.' He settled back to work. 'But I know what you mean.'

The task of transferring the outline of the designs on to the blank sheets of art paper was painstaking and monotonous, and the hours passed as they laboured on hands and knees or crouched over the granite pillar. At last Nicholas stepped back and massaged his aching back.

'That does it, then. All finished.'

She stood up beside him. 'What time is it?' she asked, and he checked his wrist-watch.

'Four in the morning. We had better tidy up in here. Make certain we leave no sign of our visit.'

'One last thing,' Royan said, tearing a corner off one of the sheets of art paper. With it she went to the altar where the abbot's crown lay. Quickly she taped the scrap of paper over the blue ceramic seal in the centre of the crown, and filled it with a rubbing of the design of the hawk with a broken wing.

'Just for luck,' she explained to him, as she came back to help him fold the long sheets of paper and pack them back in the bag. Then they gathered up the shreds of discarded masking tape and the empty film wrappers that he had strewn on the stone slabs.

Before they covered the granite stele with the damask cloth, Royan caressed the stone panels of script as if to take leave of them for ever. Then she nodded at Nicholas.

He spread the cloth over the pillar and they adjusted the folds to hang as they had found them. From the threshold of the brass-bound door they surveyed the *maqdas* for the last time, then he opened the door a crack.

'Let's go!' She squeezed through and he followed her out into the *qiddist* of the church. It took him only a few minutes to slide the tongue of the lock back into place.

'How will we get out through the main doors?' she asked.

'I don't think that will be necessary. The priests obviously have another entrance from their quarters directly into the *qiddist*. You very seldom see them using the main gates.' He stood in the centre of the floor, and looked around carefully. 'It must be on this side if it leads directly into the monks' living quarters—' he broke off with a grunt of satisfaction. 'Aha! You can see where all their feet have actually worn a pathway over the centuries.' He pointed out a smooth area of dished and worn stone near the side wall. 'And look at the marks of grubby fingers on the tapestry over there.' He crossed quickly to the hanging and drew a fold aside. 'I thought as much.' There was a narrow doorway concealed behind the hanging. 'Follow me.'

They found themselves in a dark passageway through the living rock. Nicholas flashed his torch down its length, but he masked the bulb with his hand to show only as much light as they needed. 'This way.'

The passage turned at right-angles and ahead they could make out a dull illumination. Nicholas switched off the torch and led her on.

Now there was the smell of stale food and humanity, and they passed the doorless entrance to a monk's rock cell. Nicholas flashed his torch into it. It was deserted and bare. A wooden cross hung on the wall with a truckle bed below it. There were no other furnishings. They went on past a dozen others which were almost identical.

At the next turning of the passage Nicholas paused. He felt a tiny draught on his cheek, and the taste of fresh air on his tongue. 'This way,' he whispered.

They hurried on, until suddenly Royan grabbed his shoulder from behind and forced him to stop.

'What—' he began, but she squeezed his shoulder to silence him. He heard it then, the sound of a human voice, echoing eerily through the labyrinth of passageways.

Then came a weird haunting cry, that of a soul in agony, wailing and sobbing. They crept forward, trying to make their escape before they were discovered, but the sounds grew stronger as they went on.

'Dead ahead,' Nicholas warned her in a whisper. 'We are going to have to sneak past.'

Now they saw soft yellow lamplight spilling from the doorway of one of the cells into the passage. There came another heart-rending female cry that echoed down the passage and froze them in their tracks.

'That's a woman's voice. What is happening?' Royan breathed, but he shook his head for silence and led her on.

They had to pass the open door of the lit cell. Nicholas edged towards it with his back flattened to the opposite wall. She followed him, keeping close and clinging to his arm for comfort.

As they looked into the cell the woman cried out

again, but this time her voice blended with that of a man. It was a duet without words, but racked with all the feral agony of a passion too fierce to be borne in silence.

In their full view a couple lay naked upon the truckle bed. The woman lay spread-eagled, holding the man's hips between her uplifted knees. Her arms wound hard around his back, upon which each separate muscle stood out proudly and gleamed with sweat. He thrust down into her savagely, his buttocks bunching and pounding with the force of a great black battering ram.

She rolled her head from side to side as another incoherent cry was torn from her straining throat. It seemed too much for the man above her to bear, and he reared back like a flaring cobra, his pelvis still locked to hers, but his back arched like a war bow. Spasm after spasm gripped him. The sinews in the back of his legs were stretched to snapping point, and the muscles in his back fluttered and jumped like separate living creatures.

The woman opened her eyes and looked directly at them as they stood transfixed in the doorway, but she was blinded with the strength of her passion. Her eyes were sightless, as she cried aloud to the man above her.

Nicholas drew Royan away, and they slipped down the passageway and out on to the deserted terrace. They stopped at the foot of the staircase, and breathed the sweet cool night air that was perfumed by the waters of the Nile.

'Tessay has gone to him,' Royan whispered softly.

'For tonight at least,' Nicholas agreed.

'No,' Royan denied. 'You saw her face, Nicky. She belongs to Mek Nimmur now.'

The dawn was flushing the serrated crests of the escarpment to the colours of port wine and roses when they reached camp and separated at the door to Royan's hut.

'I am bushed,' she told Nicholas. 'The excitement has been too much for me. You won't see me again before noon.'

'Good thinking! Sleep as long as you wish. I want you scintillating and perceptive when we start going over the material which we gathered last night.'

It was long before noon, however, when Nicholas was woken from a deep sleep by the harsh and intrusive bellows of Boris as he stormed into the hut.

'English, wake up! I must talk to you. Wake up, man, wake up.'

Nicholas rolled over and thrust one arm out from under the mosquito net as he groped for his wrist-watch. 'Damn you, Brusilov! What the hell do you want?'

'My wife! Have you seen my wife?'

'Now what has your wife got to do with me?'

'She has gone! I have not seen her since last night.'

'The way you treat her, that comes as no stunning surprise. Now go away and leave me to sleep.'

'The whore has run off with that black bastard, Mek Nimmur. I know all about them. Don't try and protect her, English. I know everything that goes on around here. You are trying to cover for her – admit it!'

'Get out of here, Boris. Don't try and involve me in your sordid private life.'

'I saw you and that *shufta* bastard talking in the skinning hut the other night. Don't try to deny it, English. You are in this thing with them.'

Nicholas flung back the mosquito net and jumped out of his bed. 'Kindly moderate your language when you talk to me, you great oaf.'

Boris backed off towards the door. 'I know that she has run away with him. I searched for them all last night at the river. They have gone, and most of his men with them.'

'Good for Tessay. She is showing some taste in men for a change.'

239

'You think I will let the whore get away with this? You are wrong, very wrong. I am going to follow them and kill them both. I know which way they are headed. You think I am a fool. I know all about Mek Nimmur. I was head of intelligence—' He broke off as he realized what he had said. 'I will shoot him in the belly and let that whore Tessay watch him die.'

'If you are going after Mek Nimmur, then my bet is that you won't be coming back.'

'You don't know me, English. You beat me up one night when I had a bottle of vodka in my belly, so you think I am easy, *da*? Well, Mek Nimmur will see now how easy I am.'

Boris flung out of the hut. Nicholas pulled on a shirt over his shorts and followed him.

Back in his own hut, Boris had flung a few essential items into a light pack. Now he was stuffing cartridges into the magazine of his 30/06 hunting rifle.

'Let them go, Boris,' Nicholas advised him in a more reasonable tone of voice. 'Mek is a tough lad – they don't come tougher – and he has a war party of fifty men with him. You are old enough to know that you can never hold on to a woman by force. Let her go!'

'I do not want to hold on to her. I want to kill her. The safari is over, English.' He flung a pair of keys on a leather tag on the floor at Nicholas's feet. 'There are the keys of the Land Cruiser. You can make your own way back to Addis from here. I will leave four of my best men to look after you, and hold your hand. Leave the big truck for me to use. When you get to Addis, leave the keys of the Land Cruiser with my tracker, Aly. I will know where to find him later. I will send you the money I owe you for cancellation. Don't worry – I am a man of principles.'

'How could I ever doubt it?' Nicholas smiled. 'Goodbye, old chum. I wish you luck. You'll need plenty of that if you are going up against Mek Nimmur.'

Boris was several hours behind his quarry, and as soon as he had left the camp he broke into a jog trot that carried him down the pathway to join the main track to the west, towards the Sudanese border. He ran like a scout, with an easy swinging gait that ate up the ground.

'Looks as though he is still in good shape, even with the vodka.' Despite himself Nicholas was impressed as he watched him go. 'But I wonder how long he will be able to keep up that pace?'

He turned back to his own quarters to get a little more sleep, but as he passed her hut Royan popped her head out. 'What was all the shouting about? I thought that you and Boris were having another little difference of opinion.'

'Tessay has done a bunk. Boris has guessed that she has gone off with Mek, and he is chasing after them.'

'Oh, Nicky! Can't we warn them?'

'No chance of that, but unless Mek has gone soft he will be expecting Boris to come after him. In fact, now that I come to think of it, he is probably hoping for just that chance to even the score. No, Mek doesn't need any more help from us. Go back to sleep!'

'I can't possibly sleep now. I am so worked up. I have been looking at the Polaroids that we took last night. Taita has given us an overflowing cup. Come and have a look at this.'

'Just one hour's sleep more?' He made a mock plea.

'Immediately, if not sooner.' She laughed at him.

In her hut she had the Polaroids and the rubbings spread out on the camp table, and she beckoned him to take the seat beside her.

'While you were snoring your head off, I made some progress.' She laid four Polaroids side by side, and placed her large magnifying glass over them. It was a professional land surveyor's model on folding legs, and under it every detail of the photographs was revealed. 'Taita has headed each of the sides of the stele with the name of one of the seasons of the year – spring, summer, autumn and winter. What do you think he was getting at?'

'Page numbers?'

'Exactly my own thought,' she agreed. 'The Egyptians considered spring as the beginning of all new life. He is telling us in which order to read the panels. This one is spring.' She selected one of the photographs.

'It starts with four standard quotations from the *Book of the Dead*.' She quoted the first few lines of the opening section: '"*I am the first breeze blowing softly over the dark ocean of eternity. I am the first sunrise. The first glimmer of light. A white feather blowing in the dawn wind. I am Ra. I am the beginning of all things. I will live for ever. I shall never perish.*"' Still holding the glass poised, she looked up at him. 'As far as I can see, they do not differ substantially from the original. My instinct is to set these aside for the time being. We can always come back to them later.'

'Let's go with your instinct,' he suggested. 'Read the next section.'

She held the glass to the Polaroid. 'I am not going to look at you while I read this. Taita can be as earthy as Rabelais when he is in the mood. Anyway, here goes. "*The daughter of the goddess pines for her dam. She roars like a lioness as she hurries to meet her. She leaps from the mountain, and her fangs are white. She is the harlot of all the world. Her vagina pisseth out great torrents. Her vagina has swallowed an army of men. Her sex eateth up the masons and the workers of stone. Her vagina is an octopus that has swallowed up a king.*"'

'Whoa there!' Nicholas chuckled. 'Pretty fruity stuff, don't you think?' He leaned forward to study her face, for it was still turned away from him. 'Och, lassie, you have roses in your bonny cheeks. Not a blush, surely not?'

'Your Scots accent is not in the least convincing,' she told him coldly, still not looking at him. 'When you have finished being clever at my expense, what do you think of what I have just read?'

'Apart from the obvious, I haven't any idea.'

'I want to show you something.' She stood up and packed the photographs and the rolls of art paper back into the haversack. 'You'll need to get your boots on. I am taking you on a little walk.'

An hour later they stood in the centre of the suspension bridge, swaying gently high above the swift waters of the Dandera river.

'Hapi is the goddess of the Nile. Is this river not then her daughter, pining to meet her, leaping from the mountain top, roaring like a lioness, her fangs white with spume?' she asked him.

They stared in silence at the archway of pink stone through which the river poured, and suddenly Nicholas grinned lasciviously. 'I think that I know what you are going to say next. That's what I first thought of when I looked at that cleft. You said it was like a gargoyle's mouth, but I had another image.'

'All I can say is that you must have some extraordinary lady friends,' she said, and then covered her mouth. 'Ooops! I didn't mean to say that. I am being as disgusting as either you or Taita.'

'The workmen swallowed up in there!' His voice became more excited. 'The masons and the workers in stone!'

'Pharaoh Mamose was a god. The river has swallowed up a god with her – with her stone archway.' She was equally excited. 'I must admit that I would not have made the association if you hadn't explored the interior of the cavern, and found those niches in the wall.' She shook his arm. 'Nicky, we have to get in there again. We have to get a clearer look at that bas-relief you found on the cavern wall.'

'It will take some preparation,' he said dubiously. 'I will have to splice the ropes and make some sort of pulley system, and I will have to drill Aly and the other men to avoid a repetition of my last little fiasco. We won't be ready to make the attempt until tomorrow morning at the very earliest.'

'You get on with it. I will have plenty to keep me occupied with the translation of the stele.' Then she stopped and looked up at the sky. 'Listen!' she whispered.

He cocked his head and above the sound of the river, heard the whining flutter of rotors in the air.

'Dammit!' he snapped. 'I thought we had lost the Pegasus presence. Come on!' He grabbed her arm and hustled her off the bridge. When they reached the land he jumped down on to the beach, and she followed him. The two of them crept under the hanging eaves of the bridge.

They sat quietly on the white sandy beach and listened to the Jet Ranger helicopter approaching swiftly, and then circling back over the hills beyond the pink cliffs. This time the pilot had not spotted them, for he turned away and began to patrol up and down the line of the chasm. Suddenly the engine-beat changed dramatically as the pitch altered and the pilot pulled up the collective.

'Sounds as if he is going in for a landing up there in the hills,' Nicholas said as he crawled out from under the bridge. 'I would feel a lot easier without them snooping around.'

'I don't think we have too much to worry about,' Royan disagreed. 'Even if they are connected with Duraid's killers, we are still way out ahead of them. Obviously they have not tumbled to the importance of the monastery, and the stele.'

'I hope you are right. Let's get back to camp. We must not let them see us in the vicinity of the chasm again. It will be too much of a coincidence for them to find us hanging around here every time they come this way.'

While Royan went to her hut and pored over her photographs and etchings, Nicholas worked with the trackers and skinners. He spliced the unravelled end of the nylon rope to the second hank, to make a single length five hundred feet long. Then he cannibalized the canvas fly of the cooking hut, cutting it up and whipping the raw edges to make a sling seat. He fashioned the ends of the rope into a harness which he spliced into the four corners of the canvas seat.

He had no block and tackle, so he put together a crude gantry of poles which could be extended out over the cliff edge to keep the rope clear of the rock. The rope would run through the groove that he drilled in the end of the central beam with a red-hot iron. He lubricated it with cooking lard.

It was the middle of the afternoon by the time he had completed his preparations. Then, leaving Royan in camp, he led his men, burdened with the coils of rope and the pole sections of the gantry, back up the pathway to the spot where he had abseiled down into the ravine to retrieve the carcass of the dik-dik. From there they worked their way downstream, following the rim of the cliff. It was heavy going for thorn scrub grew right up to the edge, and in many places they were forced to use their machetes to hack their way through.

The sound of the waterfall guided him. As they moved downriver it grew louder, until the rock seemed to quiver under his feet with the roar of falling waters. Finally, by leaning out over the edge and peering downwards, Nicholas could make out the flash of spray in the depths below.

'This is the spot.' He grunted with satisfaction, and explained to Aly in Arabic what he wanted done.

In order to determine the exact position in which to set up the gantry, Nicholas climbed into the canvas sling seat and had them lower him twenty feet down the cliff face, just as far as the beginning of the overhang. Up to that point he was able to keep the nylon rope from abrading on the rock, but he was also able to see around the bulge of the face.

Hanging backwards over the falls and the rocky bowl of the river one hundred and fifty feet below him, he was able at last to see the double row of niches in the rock face. However, the bas-relief engraving was still hidden from view by the tumblehome of the cliff. He gave Aly the signal and they hauled him up.

'We must set up the gantry a little further down,' he told him, and directed them as they hacked away the dense shrubbery that choked the rim. Then suddenly he exclaimed, 'I'll be damned!' He went down on one knee to examine the rim rock that the thorns had concealed. 'There are more excavations here.'

Exposed to the elements, unlike those works further down that had been protected by the overhang, these were badly eroded. There were just vague traces remaining in the rim rock, but he was certain that these indentations were the upper anchor points for the ancient scaffolding. They set up their own gantry on the same levelled area, and extended the long pole out over the drop. Then they rigged and secured it with a crude cantilever system of ropes and lighter poles.

When they were finished, Nicholas crawled out to the end to test the structure and to run the end of the rope through the slot he had prepared for it. The whole structure seemed solid and firm. Nevertheless, it was with relief that he crawled back to solid ground.

He stood up and looked over the tops of the thorn scrub to where the lowering sun was fuming red and angry on the horizon.

'Enough for one day,' he decided. 'The rest can wait for tomorrow.'

The next morning Nicholas and Royan were both up and drinking coffee at the campfire while it was still dark. Aly and his men were squatting at their own fire near by, talking quietly and coughing over the first cigarettes of the day. The project seemed to have caught their imagination. They had no inkling of the reason for this second descent into the chasm, but the enthusiasm of the two *ferengi* was infectious.

As soon as it was light enough to see the path, Nicholas led them back up into the hills. The men chatted cheerfully amongst themselves in Amharic as they hurried through the thorn scrub, and they came out on the rim rock just as the sun broke out over the eastern escarpment of the valley. Nicholas had drilled the men the previous day, and he and Royan had sat half the night going over the plans, so each of them knew their part and they lost little time in setting themselves up for the descent.

Nicholas had stripped to shorts and tennis shoes, but this time he had brought along an old Barbarians rugby jersey for warmth. While he pulled this over his head he pointed out to Royan the platform that had been dug out from the solid rock.

She examined it carefully. 'It's very hard to be sure, but I think you are right. This probably is man-made.'

'When you get further down you will have no doubts. There is very little weathering of the face under the overhang, and the niches are almost perfectly preserved – until they reach the high-water mark, that is,' he told her, as he took his seat in the sling and swung out over the cliff. Dangling from the end of the gantry he gave Aly the sign, and the men lowered him down into the gorge. The rope ran smoothly through the lubricated slot.

He saw at once that he had judged it correctly, and that he was descending in line with the double row of niches. He came level with the enigmatic circle on the cliff face, but it was fifty feet from him, and a growth of gaudy-coloured lichens had streaked and discoloured the rock, partially obscuring the details, so that he still could not be certain that it was not a natural flaw. He passed it and went on down as Aly and his team paid out the rope from above.

When he reached the surface of the water he slipped out of the sling and dropped in. The water was very cold. He trod water, gasping, until his body became acclimatized. Then he gave Aly three tugs on the signal rope. While the canvas seat was hauled up he swam to the side of the pool and held on to one of the carved stone niches for support. He had forgotten how gloomy and cold and lonely it was here in the bottom of the chasm.

After a long delay he craned his head backwards and watched Royan come into sight around the bulge of the overhang, dangling in the sling seat and revolving slowly at the end of the nylon rope. She looked down and waved at him cheerfully.

'Full marks to that girl,' he grinned. 'Not much puts the wind up her.' He wanted to shout encouragement, but he knew it was futile because the thunder of the falls smothered all other sound. So he contented himself with returning her wave.

Halfway down he saw her tugging frantically on the signal rope. Aly had been warned to expect this, and her descent was halted immediately. Then she leaned back in the sling, hanging on with only her left hand, as she groped for Nicholas's binoculars which hung from their strap on to her chest. She was twisted at an awkward angle as she held the glasses to her eyes and tried to manipulate the focus wheel with one hand. He saw that she was obviously having difficulty picking up the round mark on the wall and keeping it in the field of the lens, for the sling was swinging from side to side and at the same time revolving slowly.

She struggled at the end of the rope for what seemed

to Nicholas a very long time, but probably was no more than a few minutes. Then abruptly she dropped the binoculars on to her chest, threw back her head and let out a scream that, despite the roar of falling water, carried clearly to Nicholas a hundred feet beneath her. She was kicking her legs joyfully and waving her free hand at him, wild with excitement, as Aly began paying out the rope once more. Still screaming incoherently, she was looking down at him with a face that seemed to light up the cathedral gloom of the gorge.

'I can't hear you,' he yelled back, but the falls defeated both their efforts to communicate.

Royan was wriggling about in her seat, shouting and gesticulating wildly, and now she let go the harness with her other hand and leaned further out to keep him in sight as the sling revolved. She was still twenty feet above the water when she almost lost her balance entirely, and very nearly toppled backwards out of the sling.

'Careful there,' he yelled up at her. 'Those glasses are Zeiss. Two thousand quid at the Zurich duty-free!'

This time his voice must have carried, for she stuck her tongue out at him in a schoolgirlish gesture. But her movements became more circumspect. When her feet were almost touching the water she signalled on the rope to stop her descent and hung there, fifty feet across the pool from him.

'What did you find?' he shouted across.

'You were right, you wonderful man!'

'Is it man-made? Is it an inscription? Could you read it?'

'Yes, yes and yes to all three of your questions!' She grinned triumphantly as she teased him.

'Don't be infuriating. Tell me.'

'Taita's ego got the better of him once again. He couldn't resist signing his work.' She laughed. 'He has left us his autograph – the hawk with a broken wing!'

'Marvellous! Plain bloody marvellous!' he exalted.

'Proof that Taita was here, Nicky. To carve that cartouche, he must have been standing on a scaffolding. Our first guess was right. That niche you are holding on to is part of his ladder to the bottom of the gorge.'

'Yes, but why, Royan?' he yelled back at her. 'Why was Taita down here? There is no evidence of any excavation or building work.'

They both looked around the gloomy cavern. Apart from the tiny rows of niches, the walls were unbroken, smooth and inscrutable until they plunged into the dark water.

'Under the falls?' she shouted across. 'Is there a cutback in the rock? Can you get across there?'

He pushed off from the cliff, and swam towards the thundering chute of water. Halfway across, the current caught him and he had to swim with all his strength to make any headway against it. Thrashing the water with flailing arms and kicking out strongly, he managed to reach a spur of polished, algae-slick rock at the nearest end of the falls.

The water crashed over his head, but he edged his way along under the rock step into the heart of the cascade. Halfway across, the water overwhelmed him. It tore him off his precarious perch, hurled him back into the basin below and swirled him end over end. He surfaced in the middle of the pool, and once again had to swim with all his strength to break free of the grip of the current and to reach the slack water below the wall again. He clung to his handhold in the stone niche, and panted like a bellows.

'Nothing?' she called.

He shook his head, unable to answer until he had finally regained his breath. Finally he managed: 'Nothing. It's a solid rock wall behind the falls.' He gasped another breath, and then invited sarcastically, 'Next bright idea, madam?'

She was silent and he was glad of the respite. Then she called again, 'Nicky, how far do those niches go down?'

'You can see,' he told her, 'right to the one I am holding on to.'

'What about below the surface?'

'Don't be silly, woman.' He was getting cold and irritable. 'How the hell could there be cuttings below the surface?'

'Try!' she yelled almost as irritably. He shook his head pityingly, and drew a deep breath. Still clinging to his handhold, he extended his limbs and body to their full stretch. Then his head went under the dark surface as he groped down as far as he could reach with his toes.

Suddenly he shot back, snorting for air with a startled look on his face. 'By Jove!' he shouted. 'You are right! There is another niche down there!'

'I hate to say I told you so.' Even at that range he could see the smug expression on her face.

'What are you? Some kind of witch?' Then he broke off and rolled his eyes heavenward in despair. 'I know what you are going to ask me to do next.'

'How far do the niches go down?' she called in honeyed tones. 'Will you dive down for me, dear Nicky?'

'That's it,' he said. 'I knew it. I am going to speak to my shop steward. This is slave labour. From now onwards I am on strike.'

'Please, Nicky!'

He hung in the water, pumping air in and out of his lungs, hyper-ventilating, flushing his bloodstream with oxygen to increase his underwater endurance to its limits. In the end he expelled the contents of his lungs completely, squeezing out the last breath until his chest ached with the effort, and then he sucked in again, filling his lungs to their capacity with fresh air. Finally, with his chest fully expanded, he duck-dived, standing on his head with his legs high out of the water and letting their weight drive him under.

Sliding head-first down the submerged wall, he reached down, groping for the next niche below the surface. He found it, and used it to accelerate his dive, pulling himself on downwards.

He found the second niche below that, and pulled himself on downwards. The niches were about six feet apart – a nautical fathom. Using them as a measure, he was able to calculate his progress accurately.

Swimming on downwards, he found another niche, then another. Four rows of niches, twenty-four feet below the surface. His ears were popping and squeaking as the pressure squeezed the air out of his Eustachian tubes.

He kept on downwards and found the fifth row of niches. Now the air in his lungs was compressing to almost half its surface volume, and as his buoyancy decreased so his descent became easier and more rapid.

His eyes were wide open, but the waters below him were dark and turbid. He could make out only the surface of the wall directly in front of his face. He saw the sixth niche appear ahead of him and he grasped it, then hesitated.

'Thirty-six feet of depth already, and no sign yet of bottom,' he thought. There had been a time, when he was spearfishing competitively with the army team, that he could free-dive to sixty feet and stay at that depth for a full minute. But he had been younger then and in peak physical condition.

'Just one more niche,' he promised himself, 'and then back up to the surface.' His chest was beginning to throb and burn with the need to breathe, but he pulled hard on his handhold and shot down. He saw the vague shape of the seventh niche appear out of the murk below him.

'They go right to the bottom,' he realized with amazement. 'How on earth did Taita do it? They had no diving equipment.' He grasped the niche and hovered there for a moment, undecided if he should risk going further. He knew he was almost at his physical limit. Already he was hunting for air, his chest beginning to convulse involuntarily.

'What about one more for the hell of it!' He was beginning to feel light-headed, and a strange glow of euphoria came over him. He recognized the danger signs, and looked down at his own body. Through the murk he saw that his skin was wrinkled and folded by the pressure of water. There were over two atmospheres' weight bearing down upon him, crushing in his chest. His brain was becoming starved of oxygen, and he felt reckless and invulnerable.

'Once more into the breach, dear friends,' he thought drunkenly, and went on down.

'Number eight, and the doctor's at the gate.' He felt the eighth niche under his fingers. He was thinking in gibberish now: 'Number eight, and I'll have her on a plate.'

He turned to go up again, and his feet touched bottom. 'Fifty feet deep,' he realized even through his fuddled state. 'I have left it too late. Got to get back. Got to breathe.'

He was bracing himself to push off from the bottom when something grabbed his legs and dragged him hard against the rock wall.

'Octopus!' he thought, remembering the line from Taita's stele, '*Her vagina is an octopus that has swallowed up a king.*'

He tried to kick out, but his legs were bound as if by the arms of a sea monster; some cold, insidious embrace held him captive. 'Taita's octopus. My oath! He meant it literally. It's got me.'

He was pinned against the wall, crushed, helpless. Terror seized him, and the rush of it through his blood flushed away the hallucinations of his oxygen-impoverished brain. He realized what had happened to him.

'No octopus. This is water pressure.' He had experienced the same phenomenon once before. On an army training exercise, while diving near the inlet to the turbines of the generators in Loch Arran, his buddy diver who was roped to him had drifted into their terrible suction. His companion had been sucked against the grille of the intake and his body had been crushed so that the splinters of his ribs had been driven through the flesh of his chest and had come out through the black neoprene rubber of his suit like daggers.

Nicholas had narrowly escaped the same fate. The fact that he was a few feet to one side of his buddy had meant that he escaped the full brunt of the rush of water into the turbine intake. Nevertheless, one of his legs was broken, and it had taken the strength of two other army divers to prise him out of the grip of the current.

This time he was at the limit of his air, and there was no other diver to assist him. He was being sucked into a narrow opening in the rock, the mouth of an underwater tunnel, a subaqueous shaft that bored into the rock wall.

His upper body was free of the baleful influence of the rushing flood, but his legs were being drawn inexorably into it. He was aware that the surrounds of the opening were sharply demarcated, as straight and as square as a lintel hewn by a mason. He was being dragged over and around this lintel. Spreading out his arms, he resisted with all his strength, but his hooked fingers slid over the polished, slimy surface of the rock.

'This is the big one,' he thought. 'This is the one punch that you can't duck.' He hooked his fingers, and felt his nails tear and break as they rasped against the rock. Then suddenly they locked into the last niche in the wall above the sink-hole which was sucking him under.

Now at least he had an anchor point. With both hands he clung to the niche, and fought the pull of the water. He fought it with all his remaining strength and all his heart, but he was near the end of his store of both. He strained until he felt the muscles in both arms popping, until the sinews in his neck stood out in steely cords and he felt something in his head must burst. But he had halted the insidious slide of his body into the sink-hole.

'One more,' he thought. 'Just one more try.' And he knew that was all he had left within him. His air was all used up, and so were his courage and his resolve. His mind swirled, and dark shapes clouded his vision.

From somewhere deep inside himself he drew out the last reserves, and pulled until the darkness in his head exploded in sheets of bright colours, shooting stars and Catherine wheels that dazzled him. But he kept on pulling. He felt his legs coming out of it, the grip of the waters weakening, and he pulled once more with strength that he had never realized he possessed.

Then suddenly he was free and shooting towards the surface, but it was too late. The darkness filled his head and in his ears was a sound like the roaring of the waterfall in the abyss. He was drowning. He was all used up. He had no knowledge of where he was, how much further he had to go to the surface, but he knew only that he was not going to make it. He was finished.

When he came out through the surface, he did not know that he had done so, and he did not have enough strength left to lift his face out of the water and to breathe. He wallowed there like a waterlogged carcass, face down and dying. Then he felt Royan's fingers lock into the hair in the back of his head, and the cold air on his face as she lifted it clear.

'Nicky!' she screamed at him. 'Breathe, Nicky, breathe!'

He opened his mouth and let out a spray of water and saliva and stale air, and then gagged and gasped.

'You're still alive! Oh, thank God. You were down for so long. I thought you had drowned.'

As he coughed and fought for air and his senses returned, he realized in a vague way that she must have dropped out of the sling seat and come to his aid.

'You were under for so long. I could not believe it.' She held his head up, clinging with her free hand to the niche in the wall. 'You are going to be all right now. I have got you. Just take it easy for a while. It's going to be all right.'

It was amazing how much her voice encouraged him. The air tasted good and sweet and he felt his strength slowly returning.

'We have to get you up,' she told him. 'A few minutes more to get yourself together, and then I will help you into the sling.'

She swam with him across to the dangling sling and signalled to the men at the top of the cliff to lower it into the water. Then she held the folds of canvas open so that he could slip his legs into them.

'Are you all right, Nicky?' she demanded anxiously. 'Hang on until you get to the top.' She placed his hands on the side ropes of the harness. 'Hold tight!'

'Can't leave you down here,' he blurted groggily.

'I'll be fine,' she assured him. 'Just have Aly send the seat down again for me.'

When he was halfway up he looked down and saw her head bobbing in the dark waters. She looked very small and lonely, and her face pale and pathetic.

'Guts!' His voice was so weak and hoarse that he did not recognize it. 'You've got real guts.' But already he was too high for the words to carry down to her.

Once they had got Royan safely up out of the ravine, Nicholas ordered Aly to dismantle the gantry and hide the sections in the thorn scrub. From the helicopter it would be highly visible and he did not wish to stir Jake Helm's curiosity.

He was in no shape to give the men a hand, but lay in the shade of one of the thorn trees with Royan tending to him. He was dismayed to find how much his near-drowning had taken out of him. He had a blinding headache, caused by oxygen starvation. His chest was very painful and stabbed him every time he breathed: in his struggles he must have torn or sprained something.

He was impressed with Royan's forbearance. She made no attempt to question him about his discoveries in the bottom of the gorge, and seemed genuinely more concerned with his wellbeing than with the progress of their exploration.

When she helped him to his feet and they started back towards camp, he moved like an old man, lame and stiff. Every muscle and sinew in his body ached. He knew that the lactic acid and nitrogen that had built up in his tissues would take some time to be reabsorbed and dispersed.

Once they reached camp Royan led him to his hut and fussed over him as she settled him under the mosquito net. By this time he was feeling a lot better, but he neglected to inform her of this fact. It was pleasant to have a woman caring for him again. She brought him a couple of aspirin tablets and a steaming mug of tea, stiff with sugar. He was putting it on a little when he asked weakly for a second mugful.

Sitting beside his bed, she solicitously watched him drink it. 'Better?' she asked, when he had finished.

'The odds are two to one that I will survive,' he told her, and she smiled.

'I can see that you are better. Your cheek is showing again. You gave me an awful scare, you know.'

'Anything to get your attention.'

'Now that we have decided that you will live, tell me what happened. What sort of trouble did you run into down there in the pool?'

'What you really want to know is what I found down there. Am I correct?'

'That too,' she admitted.

Then he told her everything that he had discovered and how he had been caught in the inflow of the underwater sink-hole. She listened without interruption, and even when he had finished speaking she said nothing for a while, but frowned with concentrated thought.

At last she looked up at him. 'You mean that Taita was able to take those stone niches right down to the very bottom of the pool, fifty feet below the surface?' and when he nodded, she was silent again. Then she said, 'How on earth did he accomplish that? What are your thoughts on the subject?'

'Four thousand years ago the water level may have been lower. There may have been a drought year when the river dried up, and enabled him to get in there. How am I doing?'

'Not a bad try,' she admitted, 'but then why go to all the trouble of building a scaffold? Why not just use the dry river bed as an access? Then again, surely the attraction of the spot for Taita was the river. If it was dry, then it would be just like a thousand other places in this gorge. No, I have a feeling that the fact that it was so inaccessible was the main, if not the only, reason he chose to work there.'

'I suspect that you are correct,' he agreed.

'So if the river was running, even at its lowest level as it is now, how on earth did he manage to carve those niches below the surface? And what would be the point in having scaffolding under water?'

'Beats me. I have no idea,' he admitted.

'All right, let's leave that for the moment. Now let's go over your description of the sink-hole that almost sucked you in. Did you form any estimate of the size of the opening?'

He shook his head. 'It is almost totally dark down there. I could not see more than two or three feet in front of me.'

'Was the entrance directly between the two rows of niches?'

'No, not directly,' he said thoughtfully. 'It was slightly to one side. I hit the bottom of the pool with my feet, and was just about to push off when it grabbed me.'

'So it must be at the very bottom of the pool, and slightly downstream from the scaffolding. You say that the entrance seemed to have a square coping?'

'I am not absolutely sure of that – remember that I could see very little. But that was the impression I received.'

'It may have been another man-made structure, then – perhaps some type of adit shaft driven into the side of the pool?'

'It's possible,' he agreed reluctantly. 'But on the other hand it could just as easily be a natural fault in the strata that the river is draining into.'

She stood up to leave, and he demanded, 'Where are you going?'

'I won't be long. I am going to my hut to fetch my notes, and the material from the stele. Back in a moment.'

When she returned she sat on the floor beside his bed, with her legs drawn up under her in that double-jointed feminine fashion. As she spread her papers around her, he pulled up the edge of the mosquito net and looked down at what she was doing.

'Yesterday, while you were busy building the gantry, I was able to decipher most of the rest of the "spring" face of the stele.' She moved her notebook so that he was able to overlook the pages she had opened. 'These are my preliminary notes. You will see where I have inserted a number of question marks – here and here, for instance. That is where I am uncertain of the translation, or where Taita has used a new and strange symbol. I will have to give more time and consideration to those later.'

'I follow you,' he said, and she went on.

'These sections that I have highlighted with green are quotations from the standard version of the *Book of the Dead*. Take this one here: "*The universe is drawn in circles, the disc of the sun god, Ra. The life of man is a circle that begins in the womb and ends in the tomb. The circle of the chariot wheel foreshadows the death of the serpent that it crushes beneath its rim.*"'

'Yes, I recognize the quotation,' he said.

'On the other hand, these parts of the text that I have highlighted in yellow are original Taita writings, or at least are not quotations from the *Book of the Dead* or any other source that I am aware of. This paragraph here in particular is the one that I wanted to bring to your attention.'

She traced a section with her forefinger as she read it aloud, '"*The daughter of the goddess has conceived. She has been impregnated by the one who is without seed. She has begotten her own twin sister. The foetus lies for ever coiled in her own womb. Her twin shall never be born. She will never see the light of Ra. She will live for ever in the darkness. In the womb of the sister her bridegroom claims her in eternal marriage. The unborn twin becomes the bride of the god, who was a man. Their destinies are intertwined. They shall live for ever. They shall not perish.*"'

She looked up from the notebook. 'When I first read it, I was satisfied that the daughter of the goddess was the Dandera river, as we had already agreed. I was also pretty sure that the god that was once a man must be Pharaoh. Mamose was only deified on his ascension to the throne of Egypt. Before that he was a man.'

Nicholas nodded. 'The seedless one is obviously Taita himself. He makes repeated references to the fact that he was a eunuch. But now,' he suggested, 'if you have some new ideas about the mysterious twin sister, let's hear them.'

'The twin of the river would most likely be a branch, or a fork of the stream, wouldn't it?'

'Ah, I see what you are driving at. You are suggesting that the sink-hole is the twin. Down there in the gorge it will never see the light of Ra. Taita, the seedless one, claims paternity, so he is telling us that he is the architect.'

'Exactly, and he has married the twin of the river to Pharaoh Mamose for all eternity. Putting that all together, I have come to the conclusion that we will never find the location of Pharaoh Mamose's tomb until we explore thoroughly that sink-hole that nearly drowned you.'

'How do you suggest we do that?' he asked, and she shrugged.

'I am not the engineer, Nicky. I leave that to you to arrange. All I know is that Taita devised some way of doing it – not only of getting there but of working down there. If our interpretation of the stele is correct, then he carried out extensive mining operations at the bottom of the pool. If he could do it, then there is no reason why you can't do it also.'

'Ah!' he demurred. 'Taita was a genius. He says so repeatedly. I am just an old plodder.'

'I have got all my bets on you, Nicky. You won't let me down, will you?'

There was no call for intensive bushcraft to follow this spoor. His quarry had taken very few anti-tracking precautions. Quite openly they were following the main trail down the Abbay gorge, heading directly westwards towards the Sudanese border. Mek Nimmur was on his way back to his own stronghold.

Boris estimated that he had between fifteen and twenty

men with him. It was difficult to be certain, for the tracks on the pathway overlapped each other, and of course he would have scouts on the point ahead of him and sweeping his flanks. There would also be a rearguard dragging the trail behind him.

They were making good time, but such a large party would not be able to outpace a single pursuer. He was sure he was gaining on them. He reckoned that he had started four hours behind them, but judging by recent signs he was now less than two hours adrift.

Without breaking his trot, he stooped to pick something up from the path. As he ran on he examined it. It was a twig, the soft tip shoot of a kusagga-sagga plant that grew beside the track. One of the men ahead of him had brushed against it as he passed, and snapped it off the main branch. It gave Boris a fairly accurate gauge of how far he was behind. Even in the heat of the gorge, the tender shoot had barely begun to wilt. He was even closer than he had estimated.

He slowed down a little as he considered his next move. He knew this part of the valley fairly well. The previous year he had hunted over much of this terrain with an American client, who had been looking for a trophy Walia ibex. They had spent almost a month combing these same gullies and wooded ravines before they had brought down a huge old ram, black with age and carrying a pair of curled, back-sweeping horns that ranked as the tenth largest ever in the *Rowland Ward* record book.

He knew that two or three miles ahead the Nile began another oxbow loop out to the south, and that it then doubled back upon itself. The main trail followed the river, because a series of sheer and formidable cliffs guarded the high ground in the centre of the loop of the river. It was, however, possible to cut the corner. Boris had done it before, while following the wounded ibex.

The American hunter had not killed cleanly – his

bullet had struck the ram too far back, missing the heart-lung cavity and piercing the gut. The stricken wild goat had taken to the high ground, following one of its secret paths up amongst the crags. Boris and the American had followed it up and over the mountain. Boris remembered how dangerous and treacherous the path had been, but when it descended the far side of the mountain it had cut off nearly ten miles.

If he could find the beginning of the goat path again, there was every chance that he would be able to get ahead of Mek Nimmur and be lying in wait for him on the far side. That would give him an enormous advantage. The guerrilla leader would be expecting pursuit, not ambush. He would be covering his back trail, and it was highly unlikely that Boris would be able to slip past the rearguard without alerting his intended victims. On the other hand, once he was ahead of them he would be in control. Then he could choose his own killing ground.

As the trail and the main flow of the Nile started to turn away towards the south, he kept watching the high ground above it, seeking a familiar landmark. He had not gone another half-mile before he found it. Here there was a break in the line of dark cliffs, a heavily forested re-entrant, that cut into the wall of basalt.

He stopped and mopped the sweat from his face and neck. 'Too much vodka,' he grunted, 'you are getting soft.' His shirt was as sodden as though he had plunged in the river.

He changed the sling of the rifle to his other shoulder, lifted his binoculars and swept the sides of the wooded gully. They appeared sheer and unscalable, but then he picked out the stunted shape of a small tree that grew out of a narrow crack in the face. It looked like a Japanese bonsai, with a twisted, malformed trunk and tortured branches.

The Walia ibex had been standing on the ledge just

above that tree when the American had fired. In his mind's eye Boris could still see the way in which the wild goat had hunched its back as the bullet struck, and then spun around and raced away up the cliff. He panned the glasses upwards gently, and could just make out the inclination of the narrow ledge as it angled up the face.

'*Da, da.* This is the spot.' He was thinking in his mother tongue again. It was a relief after these last days of having to struggle in French and English.

Before he began the climb, he left the trail and scrambled down the boulder-strewn slope to the river. He knelt at the edge of the Nile and splashed double handfuls over himself, soaking his cropped head and sluicing the sweat from his face and neck. He drained and refilled his water bottle, then drank until his belly was painfully full. Then he rinsed out the bottle and refilled it. There was no water on the mountain. Finally he dipped his bush hat in the river and placed it back on his head, sodden and streaming water down his neck and face.

He climbed back to the main trail and followed it for another hundred paces, moving slowly and studying the ground. At one place there was a rock boulder almost blocking the path. The men ahead of him had been forced to step over this obstruction, on to a patch of talcum-fine dust beyond it. They had left perfect impressions of their footprints for him to read.

Most of the men were wearing Israeli-style para boots with a zigzag-patterned sole, and those coming up from behind had overtrodden the spoor of the leaders. He had to go down on one knee to examine the signs minutely before he could pick out the imprint of a much smaller and more delicately formed foot, a lighter, unmistakably feminine tread. It was partially obliterated by other larger masculine footprints, but the outline of the toe was clear, and the pattern was that of a smooth rubber-soled Bata tennis shoe. He would have recognized it from ten thousand others.

He was relieved to find that Tessay was still with the group, and that she and her lover had not left and taken another path. Mek Nimmur was a sly one, and cunning. He had escaped from Boris's clutches once before. But not this time! The Russian shook his head vehemently: not this time.

He gave his full attention to the female footprint once again. It gave him a pang to look at it. His anger returned in full force. He did not consider his feelings for the woman. Love and desire did not enter into the equation. She was his chattel, and she had been stolen from him. It was only the insult that had significance for him. She had rejected and humiliated him, and for that she was going to die.

He felt the old thrill run through his blood at the thought of the kill. Killing had always been his trade and his vocation, but no matter how often he exercised his craft the thrill was never blunted, the pleasure never satiated. Perhaps it was the only true pleasure left to him, pure and unjaded – not even the vodka could weaken and dilute it as it had the physical act of copulation. He would enjoy killing her even more than he had once enjoyed coupling with her.

These past few years he had hunted only the lower animals, but he had never forgotten what it was like to hunt down and to kill a human being, more especially a woman. He wanted Mek Nimmur, but he wanted the woman more.

In the days of President Mengistu, when he had been the head of counter-intelligence, his men had known his tastes and had picked the pretty ones for him. He had only one regret now, and that was that this time he would have to do it swiftly. There could be no question of drawing it out and savouring the pleasure. Not like some of the other experiences, which had lasted for hours, sometimes for days.

'Bitch,' he mouthed, and kicked at the dust, stamping on the faint outline of her footprint, obliterating it just as he would do to her. 'Black fornicating bitch.'

He ran now with fresh strength and determination as he left the trail and climbed up towards the deformed tree and the beginning of the goat track up the cliff.

Exactly where he expected it, he found the start of the track and followed it upwards. The higher he climbed, the steeper it became. Often he had to use both hands to haul himself up a gradient, or to work his way along a narrow traverse.

The first time he had climbed this mountain he had been following the blood spoor of the wounded ibex, but now he did not have those splattered droplets to guide him, and twice he missed the path and found himself in a dead end on the cliff face. He was forced to edge back from the drop and retrace his footsteps until he found the correct turning. Each time he did so he was aware that he was losing time, and that Mek Nimmur might pass before he was able to intercept him.

Once he startled a small troop of wild goats which were lying on a ledge halfway up the cliff. They went bounding away up the rock face, more like birds than animals bound by the laws of gravity. They were led by a huge male with a streaming beard and long spiral horns, which in its flight showed Boris a direct route to the top of the cliff.

He tore the skin off his fingertips dragging himself up the last steep pitch, but finally he reached the top and wormed his way over the skyline, never lifting his head. A human form silhouetted against the clear, eggshell-blue sky would be visible from miles around. He moved along behind the crest until he found a small clump of sanseveria to give him cover, and used the erect, spiny leaves to break up the outline of his head as he surveyed the valley a thousand feet below through the binoculars.

From this height the Nile was a broad, glittering serpent uncoiling into the first bend of the oxbow, its surface ruffled by rapids and rocky reefs. The high ground on either bank formed standing waves of upthrust basalt, turbulent and chopped into confusion like a storm sea in a tropical typhoon. The whole danced and shimmered in the heat and the sun beat down with the blows of an executioner's axe, pounding this universe of red rock into heat-exhausted submission.

Though the air danced and trembled with the mirage in the lenses of his binoculars, Boris traced out the rough trail beside the river, and followed it down the valley to the point where it was hidden by the bend. It was deserted, with no sign of human presence, and he knew that his quarry had moved on out of sight. He had no way of telling how far down the trail they had travelled – he knew only that he must hurry on if he were to cut them off on the far side of the mountain.

For the first time since he had left the river, he drank sparingly from the water bottle. He realized how the heat and the exertion of the climb had dehydrated him. In these conditions a man without water might be dead in hours. It was not in the least surprising that there was so little permanent human habitation down here in the gorge.

When he backed off the skyline he felt rejuvenated, and set out to cross the saddle of the mountain. It was less than a mile across, and without warning he came out on the top of the cliffs on the far side. One more unwary pace and he would have stepped off into space and plunged down a thousand feet. Once again he moved along the crest until he found a concealed vantage point from which to spy the terrain below.

The river was the same – a wide and confused expanse

of white-ruffled rapids, running back towards him as it turned through the leg of the oxbow. The trail followed the near bank, except where it was forced to detour inland by the rugged bluffs and stone needles which rose out of the Nile waters.

In the great desolation of the gorge he could pick out no movement other than the run of wild waters and the ceaseless dance of the heat mirage. He knew it was not possible that Mek Nimmur had moved fast enough to have passed completely ahead of him; therefore he must still be coming around the bend of the oxbow.

Boris drank again, and rested for almost half an hour. At the end of that time he felt strong and fully recovered. He debated with himself whether to descend immediately and stake out an ambush on the trail, but in the end decided to keep to the high ground until he had his quarry in sight.

He checked his rifle carefully, making sure that the telescopic sight had not been bumped out of alignment during the climb, and then emptied the magazine and examined the five cartridges. The brass case of one of them was dented and discoloured, so he discarded it and reloaded with another from his belt. He chambered a round and set the safety-catch.

He set the weapon aside while he changed his sweat-dampened socks with a fresh dry pair from his pack and retied his bootlaces with care. Only a novice would risk blistered feet in these conditions, for within hours they would be infected and festering.

He drank once more, and then stood up and slung the 30/06 on his shoulder. Ready now for anything that the goddess of the chase could send his way, he moved off along the crest to intercept the war party.

From every vantage point along the rim he glassed the valley below, each time without spying his quarry, and the afternoon passed swiftly. He was just beginning to worry that Mek Nimmur had somehow managed to slip past him unseen, that he had crossed the river at some secret ford or taken another path through a hidden valley, when there came a plaintive and querulous cry on the heat-hushed air. He looked up. A pair of kites were circling over one particular clump of thorn scrub on the river bank.

The yellow-billed kite is one of the most ubiquitous scavengers in Africa. It exists in close symbiotic association with man, feeding off his rubbish, picking up his leavings, soaring and circling over his villages or his temporary campsites, watching for his scraps or waiting patiently for him to squat in the bushes and then dropping down immediately he has finished his private business, acting as a universal sewage disposal agent.

Boris studied this pair of birds through his binoculars as they sailed idly in the heated air, always circling directly over that same patch of riverine bush. They had a distinctive manner of steering with their long bifurcated tails, twisting them from side to side as they flirted with the breeze. Their bright yellow beaks showed clearly as they turned their heads to look down at something in the scrub.

He smiled coldly to himself. '*Da!* Nimmur has gone into camp early. Perhaps the heat and the pace are too fierce for his new woman, or perhaps he has stopped to play with her a little.'

He moved on along the rim until he could look down directly into the patch of bush. He studied it through the binoculars, but without picking out any signs of human presence. After almost two hours he was becoming uncertain of his original assumption. The only thing that retained his attention was the pair of kites, which had settled in a treetop overlooking the patch of scrub. He had to trust that they were watching the men hidden in the scrub.

He glanced at the sun anxiously. It was sliding down towards the horizon at last and losing its furious heat. Then he looked down into the valley again.

Directly below the patch of bush was an indentation in the river bank that formed a backwater, almost a small lagoon. When the river was in flood it would be inundated, but now there was a small strip of gravel bank exposed. On this bank stood a number of boulders that had tumbled down from the cliff above. Some of them were lying on the beach, while others had rolled into the river and were half-submerged. The largest was the size of a cottage, a great round mass of dark rock.

As he watched, a man emerged unexpectedly from the scrub. Boris's pulse quickened as he watched him scramble down on to one of the smaller boulders and jump from there on to the gravel bank. He knelt at the water's edge and filled a canvas bucket with water, then climbed back and disappeared into the bush again.

'Ah! The heat is too much even for them. They must drink, and that gives them away. If it had not been for the birds I would never have known that they were there.' He clucked softly with reluctant admiration. 'Nimmur is a careful man. No wonder he has survived so long. He keeps tight control. But even he must have water.'

Boris kept watching through the glasses as he tried to guess what Mek Nimmur would do next. 'He has lost much time here by sheltering from the heat. He will march again as soon as it is cooler. He will make a night march,' he decided, as he looked at the sun again. 'Three hours until dark. I must make my move before then. Once it is dark it will be difficult to pick my targets.'

Before he stood up he wriggled back from the skyline. He retraced his steps back along the mountainside until a bluff shielded him from the eyes of Mek Nimmur's sentries. Then he started down. There was no goat track here and he had to make his own going, but after a few false starts he discovered an inclined rock shelf that afforded him a fairly easy path down the face. When he reached the bottom of the gorge, he took careful stock of the lie and run of the stratum so as to be able to find it again in an emergency. It was a good escape route, and he knew that he might soon be under pursuit and duress.

It had taken him over an hour to negotiate the descent, and he knew that he was running out of time. He reached the trail at the water's edge, and started back along it towards Mek Nimmur's camp. He was in a hurry now, but even then he was careful to take anti-tracking precautions. He walked on the edge of the trail, stepping only on the stony ground, careful to leave no sign of his passing. But despite his caution, he nearly walked right into them.

He had not covered the first two hundred metres when in the back of his mind he registered the low, mournful whistle of a pale-winged starling, and almost ignored it until alarm bells sounded in his mind. The timing was all wrong. The starling only gave that particular call at dawn when it left its nesting site high up in the cliffs. This was late afternoon down in the heated depths of the gorge. He guessed that it was a signal from one of the scouts coming up the trail towards him. Mek Nimmur's party was on the move.

Boris reacted instantly. He slipped off the trail, and ran back the way he had come until he reached the beginning of the pathway along which he had descended the cliff. He climbed just high enough to be able to overlook the trail. However, he realized that he had lost much of the advantage that he had built up by cutting across the mountain. This was not the ideal ambush position, and his escape route was exposed to enemy fire from below – he would be lucky to make it to the top. But the idea of abandoning his vengeance never occurred to him. As soon as his targets were in his sights, he would shoot from this stance.

However, he acknowledged to himself that Mek Nimmur had taken him by surprise. Boris had not anticipated that he would move before the sun had set. He had expected to be able to take up a position above the camp in the thorn patch and to be able to get off two careful, well-aimed shots before he was forced to run.

It was also part of his calculations that, once he had dropped Mek Nimmur, his men would not be eager to follow up with too much despatch. Boris planned to make a running retreat, stopping at every defensible strong point to fire a few shots, knock down one or two of them, and keep the pursuit circumspect and cautious until they eventually lost their taste for the game and let him go.

However, all that had now changed. He would have to take the first opportunity that presented itself – almost certainly a moving target – and as soon as he had fired he would be exposed on the path up the cliff face. His one advantage here was that his hunting rifle was a superbly accurate piece, whereas Mek Nimmur's men were all armed with AK-47 assault rifles, rapid-firing but notoriously wild at longer range, and more especially in the hands of these *shufta*. With proper training, the fighting tribesmen of Africa made some of the finest troops in the world. They possessed all the necessary skills, with one exception – they were notoriously poor marksmen.

He lay flat on the ledge, and the rock under him was so hot from the direct sunlight that it burned painfully even through his clothing. He pulled the pack from his back and set it up in front of him, settling the forestock of the rifle over it to give himself a dead rest. He peered through the telescope, wriggling into a comfortable position, sighting on a small rock beside the main trail and then swinging the barrel from side to side to make certain that he had a clear arc of fire.

Satisfied that this was the best stance he could find in the short time left to him, he set the rifle aside and picked up a handful of dirt. He rubbed this gently into his face, and the sweat turned it to mud that coated his pale skin and dulled the shine that an alert scout might pick out at long range. His last concern was to check the angle of the sun, and to satisfy himself that it was not reflecting off the lens of his scope or off any of the metal parts of the rifle. He reached over and pulled at the branch of the shrub beside him so that it cast its shadow over the weapon.

At last he settled down behind the rifle and cuddled the butt into his shoulder, regulating his breathing to a deep slow rhythm, dropping his pulse rate and steadying his hands. He did not have long to wait. He heard the bird-call again, but this time much nearer at hand. It was answered immediately from the far side of the trail, down closer to the river bank.

'The flankers will be having difficulty maintaining station over this terrain.' He grinned without humour, a death's-head grimace. 'They will be bunching and straggling.' As he thought it, a man came into view around the bend of the trail, about five hundred metres dead ahead.

Boris picked him up in the magnified field of the lens. He was a typical African guerrilla, a *shufta* dressed in a tattered and faded motley of camouflage and civilian clothing, festooned with pack and water bottle, ammunition and grenades, carrying his AK at high port. He halted the moment he came through the turn, and crouched into cover behind a boulder at the side of the trail.

For a long minute he surveyed the lie of the land ahead of him, his head turning slowly from side to side. At one point he seemed to be staring directly at Boris, who held his breath and lay as still as the rock beside him. But finally the *shufta* straightened up and gave a hand signal to those out of sight behind him. Then he came on down the trail at a trot. When he had covered fifty metres the rest of the party began to appear, keeping their intervals as precisely as beads on a string. It would not be possible to enfilade this line even with an RPD from a prepared position.

'Good!' Boris approved. 'These are crack troops. Mek must have hand-picked them.' He watched them through the lens, examining the features of each man as he came into view, searching for Mek Nimmur. There were seven of them spread out down the trail now, but still no sign of their leader. The man on the point drew level with Boris's position and then went on past him. A pair of flankers passed directly beneath where he lay, rustling softly by in the scrub not more than a dozen paces from him. He lay like a stone and let them go. The rest of them passed his position, well spaced and moving swiftly. For some minutes after the last of them had gone, the gorge seemed deserted and devoid of all human presence. Then there was another stealthy movement out there.

'The rearguard,' Boris grunted softly. 'Mek is keeping the woman at the rear. His new plaything. He is taking great care of her.'

He slipped the safety-catch on the rifle gently, making certain that no alien metallic sound fell on the heated and hushed air.

'Now let them come,' he breathed. 'I will take Mek first. Nothing fancy, no head shots. Squarely in the centre of the chest. The woman will freeze when he goes down. She does not have the reflexes of a warrior. She will give me a second unhurried shot. At this range there will be no question of a miss. Right between those pretty little black tits of hers.' He became sexually charged by the image of blood and violent death set opposite Tessay's loveliness and grace. 'I might even have a chance to get one of the others. But I can't bank on that. These men are good. More likely that they will dive into cover before I have even had time to kill the woman.'

He watched the faces of the rearguard as, one at a

time, carefully spaced, they came into view. Each time he felt his heart trip with disappointment. In the end there were three of them on the path, moving past him at a steady, businesslike jog-trot. But no sign of Mek and the woman. The rearguard disappeared down the path, and the small sounds of their progress dwindled into silence. Boris lay alone on the ledge, his heart thumping and the sour taste of disappointment in the back of his throat.

'Where are they?' he thought bitterly. 'Where the hell is Mek?' And the obvious answer to his own question occurred to him immediately. They had taken a different trail. Mek had used this patrol as a decoy to lure him away.

He lay quietly for a measured five minutes by his wristwatch, just in case there might be more men coming up the trail. His mind was racing. His last definite placing of Tessay had been the glimpse of her footprint on the trail at the far bend of the oxbow.

That was several hours ago, and if she and Mek had given him the slip they could be anywhere by now. Mek might have won himself a start of a full day or more – it might take Boris that long to work the spoor through. Feeling waves of anger overwhelm him, he had to close his eyes and fight it off in order to keep his sense of reason from being swamped. He had to think clearly now, not go rushing at the problem like a wounded buffalo. He knew that this was one of his weaknesses: he had to keep tight control of himself.

When he opened his eyes again, his anger had become cold and functional. He knew precisely what he had to do and the order in which he must do it. The very first task was to sweep and check the back trail. He had to establish the point at which Mek had left the main detachment of *shufta*.

He slipped down off the ledge and through the scrub to the open trail. Still anti-tracking, but moving swiftly, he made his way upstream, back towards the patch of thorn scrub where the party of *shufta* had lain up in the heat of the day. The first thing he noticed was that the pair of kites had gone. But he did not take this as proof that the bush was deserted, and began to circle it carefully. First he worked the incoming trail on the far side of the patch of bush. Although several hours old now, it was still clear enough to read.

Suddenly he stopped in the centre of the trail and felt the hair rise on his forearms and down the back of his neck as he stared at the sign in the dust of the path. He realized that he had walked into Mek's trap. There lay the distinctive imprint of a Bata tennis shoe.

Mek and the woman had gone into the patch of scrub and had not come out again. They were still in there, and Boris was seized by the strong premonition that Mek was watching him even at that moment, over the open sights of his AK. While he was out in the open like this, stooped over the spoor, Boris was completely vulnerable.

Hurling himself sideways off the path, he landed like a cat in the wire grass beside it, with the rifle at the ready. It took many minutes for his heartbeats to return to normal, and then he rose again into a stealthy crouch and began circling the patch of scrub very cautiously. His nerves were as taut as guitar strings, and his pale eyes darted from side to side. His finger lay upon the trigger of the 30/06 and he kept the muzzle weaving slowly, like the head of a cobra ready to strike in any direction.

He moved down towards the bank of the river, where the noise of the rapids would mask any sound he might make. But when he had almost reached the shelter of the house-sized boulder that he had noticed from the mountain crest he froze again. He had heard a sound that carried over the sound of Nile waters – a sound so incongruous in this place and at this time that for a moment he doubted his own hearing. It was the sound of a woman's laughter, sweet and clear as the tinkle of a crystal chandelier swinging in the breeze.

The sound came from below him, from the river bank beyond the tumbled boulder. He crept towards the boulder, determined to use it for cover and as a vantage point from which he could cover the bank beyond it. But before he reached it he heard the splash of some heavy object striking the surface of the river, and an excited female squeal, both playful and provocative.

Reaching the side of the boulder, and keeping close in under its protective bulk, he stole towards the corner, from which he could overlook the gravel bank beyond. Then, peeping cautiously around the angle of the boulder, he stared in amazement. He could barely believe what he was seeing. He could not credit this kind of stupidity from a man like Mek Nimmur. This was the hard man, the seasoned warrior and survivor of twenty years of bloody bush war acting like a love-sick teenage booby.

Mek Nimmur had sent his men away so that he could be alone to frolic with his new paramour. Boris took time to make absolutely certain that this was not some elaborate trap that had been set for him. It seemed too fortuitous, too heaven-sent to be really true. He searched every inch of the bank in both directions for hidden gunmen before he smiled his cold little smile.

'Of course they are alone. Mek would never let one of his men see Tessay naked like this.' His smile grew broader as he recognized the full extent of his luck. 'He must have gone crazy. Did he not realize that I would follow him? Did he think he was far enough ahead to be able to indulge himself like this? Is there anything in this world as stupid and as short-sighted as a standing prick?' Boris was gloating delightedly now.

The couple had stripped off their clothes and left them in a pile on the beach of grey basalt gravel in the shade of the tall boulder. They were splashing together in the slack water of the river at the edge of the main current. Both of them were stark mother-naked. Mek Nimmur was broad-shouldered, with a heavily muscled back and hard, tight buttocks. Beside him Tessay was slim as a river reed, her waist tiny and her hips narrow. Her skin was the colour of wild honey. They were completely absorbed in each other, without eyes or ears for anything else in this world.

'He must have left men guarding his back trail.' Boris gave Mek the benefit of some sense. 'He never expected me to be ahead of him on the trail. He thinks they are completely secure. Look at the fool,' he gloated, as Mek chased the girl and she let herself be caught. They fell into the shallow water locked in each other's embrace, mouths seeking each other as they surfaced again, laughing as the water streamed down their darkly beautiful faces, the epitome of handsome masculinity and lovely womanhood, the image of an African Adam and Eve captured for a moment in their own little carefree paradise.

Boris tore his eyes from them, and looked to where their clothing had been abandoned on the gravel bar. Mek's AK rifle lay carelessly on top of his camouflage jacket, within a few paces of where Boris stood. He crossed the open gravel bar with a few quick strides, picked up the AK, unclipped the curved magazine and dropped it into his pocket, ejected the round from the chamber and let it fly away into the gravel, replaced the unloaded rifle on the jacket, and rapidly returned to the lee of the boulder. Both Mek and Tessay remained utterly oblivious to what had happened.

Boris stood there quietly in the shadow of the rock, watching them at play in the river. They were almost childlike in their love and their complete preoccupation with each other.

Tessay at last broke from Mek's embrace and left the water. She came up the gravel bar, running long-legged and coltish, her wet silken breasts swinging and jostling each other at each stride as she looked back at him over her shoulder in open invitation. Mek followed her out, the water glistening in the dense curls of his barrel chest, his genitals weighty and puissant.

He caught her before she could reach her clothing and she struggled playfully for a while in his arms, until his mouth clamped down over hers. Then she gave herself up to him completely. While he kissed her his hands ran down her back and over her wet glistening buttocks. Pressing herself against him she moved her feet apart and spread her thighs, inviting him to explore the secrets of her body. She groaned with desire as his hand cupped her sex gently.

Boris felt his anger mingle with the perverse voyeuristic thrill of watching his own wife being taken by another man. A devil's brew of emotions bubbled up inside him. He felt his loins engorging and stiffening almost painfully with excitement, but at the same time his rage shook him like the branch of a tree in a gale of wind.

The lovers sank down on to their knees. Still locked together, Tessay fell backwards and pulled him over on top of herself.

Boris called out loudly, 'By God, Mek Nimmur, you will never know how ridiculous you look with your bare backside in the air like that.'

Mek reacted as swiftly as a leopard surprised on his kill. With a blur of movement he flipped over and reached for the AK-47. Although Boris was ready for him, covering him with the 30/06, aiming at the back of his neck when he shouted to him, Mek was so quick that he had swept up the AK from where it lay and had it pointed at Boris's belly before he could move. Mek pressed the trigger in the same instant as the muzzle came to bear.

The firing pin fell on the empty chamber with a futile click, and the two men stared at each other across the gravel beach, both with their weapons levelled. Tessay was curled naked where Mek had left her, her dark eyes liquid with pain and horror as she watched her husband and realized that Mek was about to die.

Boris chuckled softly, throatily. 'Where do you want it, Mek? How about I shoot the head off that filthy black tool of yours, while it is still standing up in the air like that?'

Mek Nimmur's eyes darted away from his adversary's face, back towards the mountain, and Boris realized that his guess had been correct. Mek had some of his men up there, but they were keeping out of view of the beach while their commander indulged himself.

'Don't worry about them. You will both be dead long before your chimps can get down here to save you.' Boris chuckled again. 'I am enjoying this. You and I had an appointment once before, but you broke it. Never mind – this is going to be even more fun.' He knew that it was not wise to delay with a man like this. Mek had made one mistake, and it was highly unlikely that he would make another. He should blow his head off now, and that would give him a few minutes more to deal with Tessay. But the temptation to gloat over him was too strong.

'I have good news for you, Mek. You will live a few seconds longer. I am going to kill the whore first, and I am going to let you watch. I hope you enjoy it as much as I am going to.' He sidled away from the shelter of the boulder, edging towards where Tessay lay curled on the gravel beach. She was turned half away from him, trying to cover her breasts and her pubic area with hands too small and delicate for the job. Even as he approached the woman, Boris was watching Mek with his full attention. Mek was the danger, and he never took his eyes off him. It was a mistake. He had underestimated the woman.

While pretending to turn away from him modestly, Tessay had reached down between her thighs and found a round, water-worn stone that fitted neatly into her small fist. Suddenly she uncoiled her lithe body and used all the strength of it to hurl the stone at his head. Boris caught the movement from the corner of his eye and flung up his arm to shield his head.

The stone, flying with surprising force at close range, never struck its target. Instead it caught the point of Boris's upraised elbow. His sleeves were rolled up high around his biceps, and there was no padding to cushion the impact of the stone; his arm was bent and flexed, the thin covering of skin drawn tightly over the bone of the joint. The head of the ulna cracked like glass, and Boris howled at the excruciating agony. His hand opened involuntarily, and his forefinger jerked away from the trigger without the strength to fire the shot he was aiming at Mek's belly.

Mek rolled to his feet, and before Boris could change the rifle to his other hand he disappeared behind the angle of the giant boulder.

With his left hand Boris swung the butt of the rifle at Tessay's head, knocking her backwards into the sand. Then he thrust the muzzle into her throat, pinning her there while he shouted angrily. 'I am going to kill her, you black bastard! If you want your whore, you'd better come fetch her!' The pain of the shattered elbow rendered his voice hoarse and brutish.

From somewhere behind the boulder Mek Nimmur's voice rang out strongly and clearly, calling a single word in Amharic that echoed along the cliffs. Then he spoke in English, 'My men will be here in a moment. Leave the woman and I will spare you. Harm her and I will make you plead for death.'

Boris stooped over Tessay and dragged her to her feet with his good arm locked around her throat. He held the rifle in the same hand, pointing it over her shoulder. The hand of his injured arm had recovered sufficiently from the first shock to be able to hold the pistol grip and to manipulate the trigger.

'She will be dead long before your men get here,' he shouted back as he started to drag her away from the boulder. 'Come and get her yourself, Mek. She is here if you want her.'

He tightened his lock around her throat, choking her until she struggled and gasped, tearing at his arm with her nails and leaving long red welts across the tanned skin.

'Listen to her! I am crushing this pretty neck. Listen to her choking.' He tightened his grip, forcing the sounds of distress out of her.

Boris was watching the corner of the boulder where Mek had disappeared. At the same time he was backing away from it, giving himself space in which to work. His mind was racing, for he knew that he could not escape. His right arm was barely usable, and there were too many of Mek's *shufta* companions. He had the woman, but he wanted the man as well. That was the best trade that he could hope for – both of them, he had to have both of them.

He heard a shout, a strange voice from higher up the slope. Mek's men were on their way. He was desperate now. Mek was not going to be drawn; he had not heard him speak or move for almost two minutes. He had lost him – by this time he could be anywhere.

'Too late,' Boris realized. 'I am not going to get him. Only the woman. But I must do it now.' He forced her to her knees and stooped over her, shifting the lock of his arm around her throat.

'Goodbye, Tessay,' he grated in her ear. He tightened his arm muscles and felt the vertebrae in her neck arched to breaking point. It needed only an ounce more pressure.

'It's all over for you,' he whispered, and began the final pressure. He knew from long experience the sound that the vertebrae would make as they gave, and he tensed himself for it, poised for that crackle like the breaking of a green branch, and the slack weight of her corpse in his grip.

Then something crashed into his back with a force that seemed to drive in his backbone and crush his ribs. Both the strength and the direction were entirely unexpected. It did not seem possible that Mek Nimmur could have moved so far and so swiftly. He must have left the shelter of the boulder and circled out through the scrub. Now he had come at Boris from behind.

His attack was so savage that the arm that Boris had wound around Tessay's neck opened. She drew in a wheezing, strangled breath and twisted out of his grip. Boris tried to turn and swing the rifle around, but Mek was on him again, seizing the rifle and trying to wrest it from Boris's hands.

The Russian's finger was still on the trigger, and a shot went off while the muzzle was level with Mek's face. The detonation stunned him for an instant, and he released the rifle and staggered backwards with his ears ringing.

Boris backed away from him, struggling with the weapon, trying to open the bolt and crank another cartridge into the chamber, but his crippled right arm made his movements clumsy and awkward. Mek gathered himself and charged head down across the gravel beach. He drove into Boris with all his weight, and the rifle flew out of the Russian's hands. Locked chest to chest the two of them spun around in a macabre waltz, trying to throw each other, wrestling for the advantage, until they tripped and went over backwards into the river.

They came to the surface still grappling and rolling over each other, first one on top and then the other, a fearful parody of the lovemaking which Boris had watched a few minutes earlier. Punching and straining and tripping each other, they struggled in the shallows. But every time they fell back into the water the slope of the bank beneath their feet forced them further out, until, when they were waist-deep, the main current of the Nile suddenly picked them up and swept them away downstream. They were still locked together, their heads bobbing in the tumble of waters, their arms thrashing the water white around them, bellowing at each other in primeval rage.

Tessay heard the men that Mek had called coming down through the scrub at the run. She snatched up her *shamma* and pulled it over her head as she ran to meet them. As the first of them burst on to the gravel bar with his AK cocked, she shouted to him in Amharic.

'There! Mek is in the water. He is fighting the Russian. Help him!' She ran with them along the bank. As they drew level with the two men in midstream one of the men stopped and levelled his AK, but Tessay rushed at him and struck up the barrel.

'You fool!' she shouted angrily. 'You will hit Mek.'

Jumping to the top of one of the riverside boulders, she shaded her eyes against the dazzling reflection of the low sun off the water. With a sick feeling in the pit of her stomach she saw that Boris had managed to get behind Mek and had a half nelson hold around his throat. He was forcing Mek's head under the surface. Mek was struggling like a hooked salmon in his grip as they were swept into a long chute of white water.

Tessay jumped down from the rock and ran on down the bank to the next point, from which she could only watch helplessly.

Boris was still holding Mek's head under water as they were borne together into the head of the chute. Fangs of black rock flashed by them on each side as they gathered speed. Mek was a powerful man and Boris had to exert every last ounce of his own strength to hold him, and he knew he could not do so much longer. Suddenly Mek reared back, and for a moment his head came out. He sucked a quick breath of air before Boris could force him under again, but that breath seemed to have renewed his strength.

Desperately Boris looked ahead to the tail of the chute

as they sped towards it. There were more rocks there. Boris picked out one great black slab over which the waters poured in a standing wave three feet high. He steered for it, kicking and hauling Mek's body around with the last of his strength.

They flew down the slope of racing water with the rock slab waiting for them at the end like a lurking sea-monster. Boris continued to wrestle with Mek, until he had turned him into a position ahead of him. He planned to steer him into a head-on collision with the rock and use Mek's body to cushion his own impact.

At the very last moment before they struck Mek dragged his head out from the surface, and as he grabbed a precious lungful of air he saw the rock and realized the danger. With a single violent effort he ducked forward below the surface again and rolled over head-first. It was so powerful and unexpected that Boris was unable to resist. Instinctively he maintained his lock around Mek's neck and was carried forward over his back until their positions were reversed. Now Mek had managed to interpose Boris between himself and the rock, so that when they slammed into it it was the Russian who bore the full brunt of the impact.

Boris's right shoulder crunched like a walnut in the jaws of a steel cracker. Although his head was still under water he screamed at the brutal agony of it, and his lungs filled with water. He relinquished his grip and was flung clear of Mek. When he came to the surface he was floundering like a drowned insect, his right arm shattered in two places, his good arm flailing weakly, and his sodden lungs wheezing and pumping.

Mek exploded through the surface only a few yards behind him. Looking around quickly as he strained for air, he spotted Boris's bobbing head almost immediately and with a few powerful overarm strokes came up behind him.

Boris was so far gone that he was not aware of Mek's

intentions until he seized his shirt collar from behind and twisted it like a strangler's garotte. With his other hand, below the surface, Mek secured a grip on the back of Boris's wide leather belt and used it like the helm of a rudder to steer him towards the next reef of rocks that was boiling the water ahead of them.

Through his waterlogged lungs Boris was trying to shout invective at him. 'Bastard! Black swine! Filthy—' But his voice was barely audible above the rush of the waters and the growl of the rocky spur that lay across their path. Mek rode him head-first into the rock and he felt the impact transferred through Boris's skull to jolt the straining muscles of his forearms. Instantly Boris went slack in his grip, his head lolled and his limbs became as limp and soft as strands of kelp washing in the surf.

As they tumbled into the next run of open water, Mek used his grip on the back of Boris's collar to lift the Russian's face above the surface. For a moment even he was struck with horror at the injury that he had inflicted. Boris's forehead was staved in. The skin was unbroken, but there was a deep indentation in his skull into which Mek could have thrust his thumb. And Boris's eyes bulged, pushed out of their sockets like those of a battered doll.

Mek swung the inert carcass around in the water, and stared at the broken head from a distance of only a few inches. He reached up and touched the depressed area of the skull with his fingertips, and felt the shards of splintered bone grate and give beneath the skin.

Once again he thrust the shattered head below the surface and held it there, while he crabbed sideways across the current towards the bank. There was no resistance from Boris, but Mek kept his head submerged for the rest of that long tortuous swim across the Nile.

'How do you kill a monster?' he thought grimly. 'I should bury him at a crossroads with a stake through his heart.' But instead he drowned him fifty times over, and at the next bend of the river they were washed into the bank.

Mek's men were waiting for him there. They supported him when his legs sagged under him, and they helped him up the bank. When they started to drag Boris's corpse out of the river, Mek stopped them abruptly.

'Leave him for the crocodiles. After what he has done to our country and our people, he deserves nothing better.' But even in his anger and his hatred he did not want Tessay to have to look at that mutilated head. She had been unable to keep pace with the men, but she was coming along the bank towards him now.

One of his men pushed Boris's corpse back into the current, and as it floated away he unslung his AK rifle from his shoulder and let off a burst of automatic fire. The bullets chopped up the surface around Boris's head, and socked heavily into his back. They tore holes in his wet shirt and kicked out lumps of raw flesh. The other men on the bank shouted with laughter and joined in the fusillade, emptying their magazines into the lifeless body. Mek did not attempt to prevent them. Some of their close relatives had died most horribly under the Russian's care. The corpse rolled over in a pink cloud of its own blood, and for a moment Boris's pale bulging eyes stared at the sky. Then he sank away beneath the surface.

Mek stood up slowly and went to meet Tessay. He took her in his arms, and as he held her to his chest he whispered to her softly.

'It's all right. He won't ever hurt you again. It's all over. You are my woman now – for ever!'

287

ince Boris and Tessay had left the camp there was no longer any reason to maintain security, and Nicholas and Royan were no longer obliged to skulk in Royan's hut when they discussed their search for the tomb.

Nicholas transferred their headquarters into the dining hut, and had the camp staff build another large table on which they could spread the satellite photographs and all the other maps and material that they had accumulated. The chef sent a steady supply of coffee from the kitchen, while they pored over the papers and discussed their discoveries in Taita's pool and every theory that either of them dreamed up, no matter how far-fetched.

'We will never be certain if that shaft was made by Taita, or whether it was a natural sink-hole, until we can get back in there with the right equipment.'

'What type of equipment are you talking about?' she wanted to know.

'Scuba, not oxygen rebreathers. Although the navy rebreathing outfits are much lighter and more compact, you cannot use them below a depth of thirty-three feet, the equivalent of one atmosphere of water. After that pure oxygen becomes lethal. Have you ever used an aqualung?'

She nodded. 'When Duraid and I were on honeymoon at a resort on the Red Sea. I had a few lessons and made three or four open-water dives, but let me hasten to add that I am no expert.'

'I promise not to send you down there,' he smiled, 'but I think we can safely say that we have found enough evidence both in Tanus's tomb and Taita's pool to make it imperative that we mount the second phase of this operation.'

She nodded agreement. 'We will have to return with a much more extensive range of equipment, and some expert help. But you are not going to be able to pose as a tourist sportsman next time around. What possible excuse are we going to find for returning that will not set off all the alarm bells in the minds of Ethiopian bureaucracy?'

'You are speaking to the man who has paid unofficial and uninvited visits to both those charming lads Gadaffi and Saddam. Ethiopia should be a Sunday-school picnic in comparison.'

'When do the big rains start up in the mountains?' she asked suddenly.

'Yes!' His expression became serious. 'That is the jackpot question. You only have to look at the high-water mark on the walls of Taita's pool to have some idea what it must be like in there when the river is in full flood.' He flipped over the pages of his pocket diary. 'Luckily, we still have a bit of time – not a great deal, but enough. We will need to move pretty smartly. We have to get back home before I can start work on planning phase two.'

'We should pack up right away, then.'

'Yes, we should. But it seems a damned shame not to take full advantage of every moment we are here, having come all this way. I think we can spare just a few more days to sound out some ideas that I have about Taita's pool and the sink-hole, to try to arrive at some sort of informed guess about what we will need when we return.'

'You are the boss.'

'My word, how pleasant to hear a lady say that.'

She smiled sweetly. 'Enjoy the moment,' she counselled him, 'it may never happen again.' And then she became serious again. 'What are these ideas that you have?'

'What goes up must come down, what goes in must come out,' he said mysteriously. 'The water going into the sink-hole under such pressure must be going somewhere. Unless it joins a subterranean water system and makes its way into the Nile that way, then it should come to the surface where we can find it.'

'Go on,' she invited.

'One thing is certain. Nobody is going to get into the

sink-hole from the pool. The pressure is lethal. But if we can find the outlet, we may be able to explore it from the other end.'

'That's a fascinating possibility.' She looked impressed, and turned to the satellite photograph. Nicholas had identified the monastery and ringed it on the photograph. He had marked in the approximate course of the river through the chasm, although the gorge itself was too narrow and covered with bush to show up on the small-scale picture, even under the high-powered magnifying lens.

'Here is the point where the river enters the chasm.' She pointed it out to him. 'And here is the side valley down which the trail detours. Okay?'

'Okay,' he nodded. 'What are you driving at?'

'On our approach march, we remarked that this valley might at one time have been the original course of the Dandera river, and that it seemed to have cut a new bed for itself through the chasm.'

'That's right,' Nicholas agreed. 'I am still listening.'

'The fall of the land towards the Nile is very steep at this point, isn't it? Well, do you recall we crossed another smaller, but still pretty substantial, stream on our way down the dry valley? That stream seemed to emerge from some-where on the eastern side of the valley.'

'All right, I am with you now. You are suggesting that this may be the overflow from the sink-hole. Clever little devil, aren't you?'

'Just capitalizing on your genius.' She cast down her eyes modestly, and looked up at him from under her lashes. She was clowning, but her lashes were long and dense and curling, and her eyes were the colour of burnt honey with tiny golden highlights in their depths. At this close range he found them disturbing.

He stood up and suggested, 'Why don't we go and take a look?'

Nicholas went to fetch his camera bag and the light day-pack from his hut, and when he returned he found Royan ready to go. But she was not alone.

'I see that you are bringing your chaperon with you,' he remarked with resignation.

'Unless you are tough enough to send him away.' Royan smiled encouragement at Tamre who stood at her side, grinning and bobbing and hugging his shoulders in the ecstasy of being in the presence of his idol.

'Oh, very well.' Nicholas gave in without a struggle. 'Let the little devil come along.'

Tamre lolloped away up the path ahead of them, his grubby *shamma* flapping around his long skinny legs, chanting the repetitive chorus of an Amharic psalm, and every few minutes looking back to make certain that Royan was still following him. It was a hard pull up the valley, and the noonday heat was debilitating. Although Tamre seemed totally unaffected, the other two were both sweating in dark patches through their shirts by the time they reached the point where the stream debouched into the valley. Gratefully, they sought the shade of a patch of acacia trees, and while they rested Nicholas glassed the side of the valley through his binoculars.

'How are they after the dunking I gave them?' she asked.

'Waterproof,' he grunted, 'full marks to Herr Zeiss.'

'What do you see up there?'

'Not much. The bush is too thick. We will have to foot-slog up the side. Sorry.'

They left the shade and made their way up the side of the valley in the direct burning sunlight. The stream tumbled down a series of cascades, each with a pool at its foot. The bush crowded the banks, lush and green where the roots had been able to reach the water. Clouds of black and yellow butterflies danced over the pools, and a black and white wagtail patrolled the moss-green rocks along the edge, its long tail gyrating back and forth like the needle of a metronome.

Halfway up the slope they paused beside one of the pools to rest, and Nicholas used his hat like a fly-swatter to stun a brown and yellow grasshopper. He tossed the insect on to the surface of the pool, and as it kicked weakly and floated towards the exit a long dark shadow rose from the bottom. There was a swirl and a mirrorlike flash of a scaly silver belly, and the grasshopper disappeared.

'Ten-pounder,' Nicholas lamented. 'Why didn't I bring my rod?'

Tamre was crouched near Nicholas on the pool bank, and suddenly he lifted his hand and held it out. Almost at once one of the circling butterflies settled upon his finger. It perched there with its velvety black and yellow wings fanning gently. They stared at him in astonishment, for it was as though the insect had come to his bidding. Tamre giggled and offered the butterfly to Royan. When she held out her hand, he gently transferred the gorgeous insect to her palm.

'Thank you, Tamre. That is a wonderful gift. Now my gift to you is to set it free again.' She pursed her lips and blew it softly into flight. They watched the butterfly climb high above the pool, and Tamre clapped his hands and laughed with delight.

'Strange,' Nicholas murmured. 'He seems to have a special empathy with all the creatures of the wilderness. I think that Jali Hora, the abbot, does not try to control him, but lets him do very much as his simple fancy dictates. Special treatment for a fey soul, one that hears a different tune and dances to it. I must admit that, despite myself, I am becoming quite fond of the lad.'

It was only another fifty feet higher that they came to the source. There was a low cliff of red sandstone, from a grotto at whose foot the stream gushed. The entrance was screened by a heavy growth of ferns, and Nicholas went down on his knees to pull them aside and peer into the low opening.

'What can you see?' Royan demanded behind him.

'Not much. It's dark in there, but it seems to go in for quite some way.'

'You are too big to get in there. You had better let me go in.'

'Good place for water cobra,' he remarked. 'Lots of frogs for them to eat. Are you sure you want to go?'

'I never said that I wanted to.' She sat on the bank while she unlaced her shoes, then lowered herself into the stream. It came halfway up her thighs, and she waded forward against the flow with difficulty.

She was forced to bend almost double to creep under the overhanging roof of the grotto. As she moved deeper in, her voice came back to him.

'The roof gets lower.'

'Be careful, dear girl. Don't take any chances.'

'I do wish you wouldn't call me "dear girl".' Her voice resonated strangely from the cave entrance.

'Well, you are both those things, a girl and dear. How about if I call you "young lady"?'

'Not that either. My name is Royan.' There was silence for a while, then she called again. 'This is as far as I can go. It all narrows down into a shaft of some sort.'

'A shaft?' he demanded.

'Well, at least a roughly rectangular opening.'

'Do you think it is the work of humans?'

'Impossible to tell. The water is coming out of it like the spout of a bath tap. A solid jet.'

'No evidence of any excavation? No marks of tools on the rock?'

'Nothing. It's slick and water-worn, covered with moss and algae.'

'Could a man get into the opening, I mean if it were not for the water pressure?'

'If he was a pygmy or a dwarf.'

'Or a child?' he suggested.

'Or a child,' she agreed. 'But who would send a child in there?'

'The ancients often used child-slaves. Taita might have done the same.'

'Don't suggest it. You are destroying my high opinion of Taita,' she told him as she backed out of the entrance of the grotto. There were pieces of fern and moss in her hair, and she was soaked from the waist downwards. He gave her a hand and boosted her back on to the bank. The curve of her bottom was clearly visible through her wet trousers. He forced himself not to dwell upon the view.

'So we have to conclude that the shaft is a natural flaw in the limestone, and not a man-made tunnel?'

'I didn't say that. No. I said that I couldn't be sure. You might be correct. Children might have been used to dig it. After all, they were used in the coalmines during the industrial revolution.'

'But there is no way that we would be able to explore the tunnel from this end?'

'Impossible.' She was vehement. 'The water is pouring out under enormous pressure. I tried to push my arm up the shaft, but I did not have the strength.'

'Pity! I was hoping for some more irrefutable evidence, or at least another lead.' He sat down beside her on the bank, and ferreted in his pack. She looked at him quizzically when he brought out a small black anodized instrument and opened the lid.

'Aneroid barometer,' he explained. 'Every good navigator should have one.' He studied it for a moment and then made a note of the reading.

'Explain,' she invited.

'I want to know if this spring is below the level of the

entrance to the sink-hole in Taita's pool. If it is not, then we can cross it off our list of possibilities.'

He stood up. 'If you are ready, we can move on.'

'Where to?'

'Why, Taita's pool, of course. We need a reading up there to establish the difference in altitude between the two points.'

Once Tamre knew where they were headed he showed them a short-cut, so it took them just under two hours from the fountain head to the top of the cliff face above Taita's pool.

While they rested, Royan remarked, 'Tamre seems to spend most of his days wandering around in the bush. He knows every path and game trail. He is an excellent guide.'

'Better than Boris, at least,' Nicholas agreed, as he fished out his barometer and took another reading.

'You look particularly pleased with yourself.' Royan watched his face as he studied the instrument.

'Every reason to be,' he told her. 'Allowing one hundred and eighty feet for the height of the cliff below us, and another fifty feet for the depth of the pool, the entrance to the sink-hole is still over a hundred feet higher than your outlet through the fern grotto on the other side of the ridge.'

'Which means?'

'Which means that there is a distinct possibility that the streams are one and the same. The inflow is here in Taita's pool and the outflow is from your grotto.'

'How on earth did Taita do it?' she puzzled. 'How did he get to the bottom of the pool? You are the engineering marvel. Tell me how you would do it.'

He shrugged, but she persisted. 'I mean, there must be some established way of doing things like that, of working under water. How do they build the piers of a bridge, or the foundations of a dam, or – or – or how did Taita himself build the shaft below the level of the Nile to measure the flow of the river? You remember the description that he gives of his hydrograph in *River God?*'

'The accepted technique is to build a coffer dam,' Nicholas said casually, and then broke off and stared at her. 'My oath, you really are a corker. A dam! What if that old ruffian, Taita, dammed the whole flipping river!'

'Would that have been possible?'

'I am beginning to believe that with Taita anything is possible. He certainly had unlimited manpower at his disposal, and if he could build the hydrograph on the Nile at Aswan, then he understood very clearly the principles of hydrodynamics. After all, the old Egyptians' lives were completely bound up with the seasonal inundations of the river and the management of the floods. From what we have gathered about the old man, it certainly seems possible.'

'How could we prove it?'

'By finding the remains of his dam. It had to be a hell of a work to hold the Dandera river. There is a good chance that some evidence of it remains.'

'Where would he have built the dam?' she asked excitedly. 'Or let me put it another way, where would you site the dam if you had to do it?'

'There is one natural place for it,' he answered promptly. 'The spot where the trail leaves the river and detours down the valley, and the river falls into the chasm.' They both turned their heads in unison and looked upstream.

'What are we waiting for?' she asked, and sprang to her feet. 'Let's go look-see!'

Their excitement was infectious, and Tamre giggled and danced ahead of them along the trail through the thorns and then up the valley to the point where it rejoined the river. The sun had lost the worst of its heat by the time they stood once again above the falls where the Dandera river plunged into the mouth of the chasm, and began its last lap in the race to join the Nile.

'If Taita had thrown a dam across here – ' Nicholas made a sweep of his arms across the mouth of the gorge, ' – he could have diverted the river down the side valley here.'

'It looks possible,' she laughed. Tamre giggled in sympathy, not understanding a word of what they were saying, but enjoying himself immensely.

'I would need a dumpy level to take some shots of the actual fall of the land. It can be very deceptive, but with the naked eye it does look possible, as you say.' He shaded his eyes and looked up the bluffs on each side of the waterfall. They formed two craggy portals of limestone, between which the river roared as it plunged over the lip.

'I would like to climb up there to get a clearer picture of the layout of the terrain. Are you game?'

'Try and stop me,' she challenged him, and led the climb. It was a heavy scramble, and in some places the limestone was rotten and crumbling dangerously. However, when they came out on the summit of the eastern portal they were rewarded with a splendid overall view of the ground below.

Directly to the north, the escarpment rose like a sheer wall with its battlements crenellated and serrated. Above and beyond it there was a dream of further mountains, the high peaks of the Choke, blue as a heron's plumage against the clearer distant blue of the African sky.

All around them were the badlands of the gorge, a vast confusion of ridges and spines and reefs of rock of fifty different hues, some ash-grey and white, others black as the hide of a bull buffalo, or red as his heart blood. The riverine bush was green, the poisonous vivid green of the mamba in the treetop, while further from the water the scrub was grey and sear, and along the spines of the broken kopjes stood the stark outlines of ancient drought-struck trees, their tortured limbs twisted and black against the sky.

'The picture of devastation,' Royan whispered as she looked around her, 'untamed and untamable. No wonder Taita chose this place. It repels all intruders.'

They were both silent for a while, awed by the wild grandeur of the scene, but as soon as they had recovered from the exertion of the climb their enthusiasm resurfaced.

'Now you can get a good picture of it.' Nicholas pointed down into the valley below them. 'There is a clear divide at the fork of the valley. You can see the natural fall of the ground. There, from that side of the gorge to that point below us, is the narrowest part. It is a neck where the river squeezes through – the natural site for a dam.' He swivelled and pointed down to the left of where they sat. 'It would not take much to spill the river into the valley. Once he had finished whatever he was up to in the chasm, it would taken even less to break down the wall of the dam and let the river resume its natural course again.'

Tamre watched their faces eagerly, turning his head to each speaker in turn, uncomprehending, but aping Royan's expression like a mirror. If she nodded he nodded, when she frowned he did the same, and when she smiled he giggled happily.

'It's a big river.' Royan shook her head, while Tamre wagged his from side to side in sympathy and looked wise. 'What method would he have used? An earthen dam? Surely not?'

'The Egyptians used earthen canals and dams for a great many of their irrigation works,' Nicholas mused. 'On the other hand, when they had rock available to work with they used it extensively. They were expert masons. You have stood in the quarries at Aswan.'

'Not much topsoil here in the gorge,' she pointed out.

'But on the other hand, there is plenty of rock. It's like a geological museum. Every type of rock that you could wish for.'

'I agree,' he said. 'Rather than an earthen wall, Taita would most probably have used a masonry and rock fill. That is the type of dam the ancients built in Egypt, long before his time. If that is the case, there is a chance that traces of it have survived.'

'Okay. Let's work on that hypothesis. Taita built a dam of rock slabs, and then he breached it again. Where would we find the remains of it?'

'We would have to start searching on the actual site,' he answered. 'There at the neck of the gorge. Then we would have to search downstream from there.'

They scrambled down the slope again, with Tamre picking out the easiest route for Royan, stopping to beckon her whenever she faltered or paused for breath. They came out in the neck of the valley and stood on the rocky bank of the river, looking about them.

'How high would the wall have been?' Royan asked.

'Not too high. Again, I can't give you a precise answer until I have shot the levels.' He climbed a little way up the side of the wall. There he squatted and turned his head back and forth, looking first down the length of the valley and then towards the lip of the waterfall that dropped into the mouth of the chasm.

Three times he changed his position, on each occasion moving a few paces higher up the slope. The cliff became steeper the higher he climbed. In the end he was clinging precariously to the side of it, but he seemed satisfied. Then he called down to her.

'I would say this is about it, where I am now. This would be the height of the dam wall. It looks about fifteen feet high to me.'

Royan was still standing on the bank, and now she

turned and stared across at the far bank of the river, estimating the distance to the limestone cliff rising above it.

'Roughly a hundred feet across,' she shouted up to him.

'About that,' he agreed. 'A lot of work, but not impossible.'

'Taita was never one to be daunted by size or difficulty.' She cupped her hands around her mouth to shout up to him. 'While you are up there, can you see any sign of works? Taita would have had to pin the dam wall into the cliff.'

He scrambled along the cliff, keeping to the same level, until he was almost directly above the falls and could go no further. Then he slid down to where Royan and Tamre waited.

'Nothing?' she anticipated, and he shook his head.

'No, but you can't really expect that there would be anything left after nearly four thousand years. These cliffs have been exposed to wind and weather for all that time. I think our best bet will be to look for any surviving blocks from the dam wall that might have been carried away when Taita breached it to flood the chasm again.'

They started down the valley, where Royan came upon a chunk of stone that seemed to be of a different type from the surrounding country rock. It was the size of an old-fashioned cabin trunk. Although it was half-covered by undergrowth, the uppermost end – the one that was exposed – had a definite right-angled corner to it. She called Nicholas across to her.

'Look at that.' Royan patted it proudly. 'What do you think of that?'

He climbed down beside her and ran his hands over the exposed surface of the slab. 'Possible,' he repeated. 'But to be certain we would have to find the chisel marks where the old masons started the fracture. As you know, they chiselled a hole into the stone, and then wedged it open until it split.'

Both of them went over the exposed surface carefully, and although Royan found an indentation that she declared was a weathered chisel mark, Nicholas gave her only four out of ten on the scale of probability.

'We are running out of time,' he said, enticing her away from her find, 'and we still have a lot of ground to cover.'

They searched the valley floor for half a kilometre further, and then Nicholas called it off. 'Even in the heaviest flood it is unlikely that any blocks would have been carried down this far. Let's go back and see if anything was washed over the falls into the mouth of the chasm.'

They returned to the bank of the Dandera and worked their way down as far as the falls. Nicholas peered over.

'It's not as deep here as it is further down,' he estimated. 'I would guess that it is less than a hundred feet.'

'Do you think you could get down there?' she asked dubiously. Spray blew back out of the depths into their faces, and they had to shout at each other to make themselves heard over the thunder of the waters.

'Not without a rope, and some muscle men to haul me back out of there.' He perched himself on the brink and focused the binoculars down into the bowl. There was a jumble of loose rock down there – small, rounded boulders, and one or two very much larger. Some of them were angular, and some with a little imagination could be called rectangular. However, their surfaces had been smoothed by the rushing waters, and were gleaming wet. All of them seemed partially submerged or obscured by spray.

'I don't think we can decide anything from up here, and to tell the truth I don't fancy going down there – not this evening anyway.'

Royan sat down beside him and hugged her knees to

301

her chest. She was dispirited. 'So there is nothing we can be certain about. Did Taita dam the river, or didn't he?'

Quite naturally he placed his arm around her shoulders to console her, and after a moment she relaxed and leaned against him. They stared down into the chasm in silence. At last she drew back from him gently, and stood up.

'I suppose we should start back to camp. How long will it take us?'

'At least three hours.' He stood up beside her. 'You are right. It will be dark before we get back, and there is no moon tonight.'

'Funny how tired you feel after a disappointment,' she said, and stretched. 'I could lie down and sleep right here on one of Taita's stone blocks.' She broke off and stared at him. 'Nicky, where did he get them?'

'Where did he get what?' He looked puzzled.

'Don't you see! We are going at it from the wrong end. We have been trying to find out what happened to the blocks. This morning you mentioned the quarries at Aswan. Shouldn't we consider where Taita found the blocks for his dam, rather than what happened to them afterwards?'

'The quarry!' Nicholas exclaimed. 'My word, you are right. The beginning, not the end. We should be looking for the quarry, not the remnants of the dam wall.'

'Where do we start?'

'I hoped you were going to tell me.' He laughed out loud, and immediately Tamre bubbled with sympathetic laughter. They both looked at the boy.

'I think we should start with Tamre, our faithful guide,' she said, and took his hand. 'Listen to me, Tamre. Listen very carefully!' Obediently he cocked his head and stared at her face, summoning all his errant concentration.

'We are looking for a place where the square stones come from.' He looked mystified, so she tried again. 'Long

302

ago there were men who cut the rock from the mountains. Somewhere near here, they left a big hole. Perhaps there are still square blocks of stone lying in the hole?'

Suddenly the boy's face cleared and split into a beatific smile. 'The Jesus stone!' he cried happily.

He sprang to his feet without relinquishing his grip on her hand. 'I show you my Jesus stone.' He dragged her after him as he bounded away down the valley.

'Wait, Tamre!' she pleaded. 'Not so fast.' But in vain. Tamre kept up the pace and burst into an Amharic hymn as he ran. Nicholas followed at a more sedate pace, and caught up with them a quarter of a mile down the valley.

There he found Tamre on his knees, pressing his forehead against the rock wall of the valley, his eyes shut tightly as he prayed. He had dragged Royan down beside him.

'What on earth are you doing?' Nicholas demanded, as he came up.

'We are praying,' she told him primly. 'Tamre's instructions. We have to pray before we can go to the Jesus stone.'

She turned away from Nicholas, closed her eyes and clasped her hands in front of her eyes, then began to pray softly.

Nicholas found a seat on a boulder a little way from them. 'I don't suppose it can do any harm,' he consoled himself, as he settled down to wait.

Abruptly Tamre sprang to his feet and performed a giddy little dance, flapping his arms and whirling around until he raised the dust. Then he stopped and chanted. 'It is done. We can go in to the Jesus stone.'

Once again he seized Royan's hand and led her to the rock wall. In front of Nicholas's eyes the two of them seemed to vanish, and he stood up in mild alarm.

'Royan!' he called. 'Where are you? What's going on?'

'This way, Nicky. Come this way!'

He went to the wall and exclaimed with astonishment, 'My oath! We would never have found this in a year of searching.'

The cliff face was folded back upon itself, forming a concealed entrance. He walked through the opening, gazing up the vertical sides, and within thirty paces came out into an open amphitheatre that was at least a hundred yards across and open to the sky. The walls were of solid rock, and he could see at a glance that it was the same micaceous schist as the block which Royan had found lying on the floor of the valley.

It was apparent that the bowl had been quarried out of the living rock, leaving tiers rising up to the top of the walls. The recesses from which the blocks had been hacked were still plain to see and had left deep steps with right-angled profiles. Some scrub and undergrowth had found a precarious foothold in the cracks, but the open quarry was not choked with this growth and Nicholas could see that a stockpile of finished granite blocks remained scattered about the bottom of the excavation. He was so awed by the discovery that he could find no words to express himself. He stood just inside the entrance, his head slowly turning from side to side as he tried to take it all in.

Tamre had led Royan to the centre of the quarry where one large slab lay on its own. It was obvious that the ancients had been on the point of removing it and transporting it up the valley, for it was finished and dressed into a perfect rectangle.

'The Jesus stone!' Tamre chanted, kneeling before the slab and pulling Royan down beside him. 'Jesus led me here. The first time I came here I saw him standing on the stone. He had a long white beard and eyes that were kind and sad.' He crossed himself and began to recite one of the psalms, swaying and bobbing to the rhythm.

As Nicholas moved up quietly behind them he saw the evidence that Tamre had visited this sacred place of his regularly. The Jesus stone was his own private altar, and his pathetic little offerings were lying where he had laid them. There were old *tej* flasks and baked clay pots, most of them cracked and broken. In them stood bunches of wild flowers that had long ago wilted and dried out. There were other treasures that he had gathered and placed upon his altar – tortoise shells and porcupine quills, a cross that had been hand-carved from wood and decorated with scraps of coloured cloth, necklaces of lucky beans, and models of animals and birds moulded from blue river clay.

Nicholas stood and watched the two of them kneeling and praying together in front of the primitive altar. He felt deeply moved by this evidence of the boy's faith, and by his childlike trust in bringing them to this place.

At last Royan stood up and came to join him. Together she and Nicholas began to make a slow circuit of the quarry floor. They spoke little, and then only in whispers as though they were in a cathedral or some holy place. She touched his arm and pointed. A number of the square blocks still lay in their original positions in the quarry walls. They had not been completely freed from the mother rock, like a foetus attached by an umbilical cord which had never been severed by the ancient masons.

It was a perfect illustration of the quarrying methods used by the ancients. Work could be seen in progress in all the various stages, from the marking out of the blocks by the master craftsman, the drilling of the tap holes, the wedging of the cleavage lines, right up to the finished product lifted out of the wall and ready for transport to the dam site.

The sun had set and it was almost dark by the time they came round to the entrance of the quarry again. They sat together on one of the finished blocks, with Tamre sitting at their feet like a puppy, looking up at Royan's face.

'If he had a tail he would wag it,' Nicholas smiled.

'We can never betray his trust, and desecrate this place in any way. He has made it his own temple. I don't think he has ever brought another living soul here. Will you promise me that we will always respect it, no matter what?'

'That is the very least I can do,' he agreed. Then, turning to Tamre, he said, 'You have done a very good thing by bringing us here to your Jesus stone. I am very pleased with you. The lady is very pleased with you.'

'We should start back to camp now,' Royan suggested, looking up at the patch of sky above them. Already it was purple and indigo, shot through with the last rays of the sunset.

'I don't think that would be very wise,' he disagreed. 'Because it is a moonless night one of us could very easily break a leg in the dark. That is something not to be recommended out here. It might take a week to get back to any adequate medical attention.'

'You plan to sleep here?' she asked, with surprise.

'Why not? I can whip up a fire in no time and I also have a pack of survival rations for dinner – I have done this kind of thing before, you know! And you have your chaperon with you, so your honour is safe. So why not?'

'Why not, indeed?' she laughed. 'We will be able to make a more detailed inspection of the quarry tomorrow early.'

He stood up to start gathering firewood, but then stopped and looked up at the sky. She heard it too, that now familiar fluttering whistle in the air.

'The Pegasus helicopter once again,' he said unnecessarily. 'I wonder what the hell they are up to at this time of day?'

They both stared up into the gathering darkness and watched the navigational lights of the aircraft pass a thousand feet overhead, flashing red and green and white as it headed southwards in the direction of the monastery.

Nicholas built a small fire in the corner of the quarry nearest the entrance, and as they sat around it he divided the pack of dry survival rations into three parts. They nibbled them, and washed down the sweet and sticky concentrated tablets with water from his bottle.

The fire threw ghostly reflections up the side of the quarry wall, and enhanced the moving shadows. When a nightjar uttered its warbling cry from a niche high up the wall, it was so eerie and evocative that Royan shivered and moved a little closer to Nicholas.

'I wonder if somewhere on the other side Taita is aware of our progress,' she said. 'I get the feeling that we have him a little worried by now. We have untangled the first part of the conundrum that he set for us, and I'll bet he never expected anybody to do that well.'

'The next step will be to get to the bottom of his pool. That will be really one up on the old devil. What do you hope we might find down there?'

'I hesitate to put it into words,' she replied. 'I might talk it away, and put a jinx on us.'

'I am not superstitious. Well, not much anyway. Shall I say it for you?' he offered, and she laughed and nodded. He went on, 'We hope to find the entrance to the tomb of Pharaoh Mamose. No more hints and riddles and red herrings. The veritable tomb.'

She crossed her fingers. 'From your lips to God's ear!' Then she grew serious. 'What do you think of our chances? I mean of finding the tomb intact?'

He shrugged. 'I will answer that once we get to the bottom of the pool.'

'How are we going to do that? You have ruled out the use of an aqualung.'

'I don't know,' he confessed. 'At this stage I just don't know. Perhaps we might be able to get in there with full-helmeted diving suits.'

She was silent as she considered the seeming impossibility of the task ahead.

'Cheer up!' He put his arm around her shoulders, and she made no move to pull away from him. 'There is one consolation. If Taita has made it so tough for us, he has also made it tough for anyone else to have got in there ahead of us. I think that if the tomb is really down there, no other grave robbers have beaten us to it.'

'If the entrance to the tomb is at the bottom of the pool, then his descriptions in the scrolls are deliberately misleading. The information that has come down to us has been garbled by Taita, then by Duraid, and finally by Wilbur Smith. We are faced with the task of finding our way through this labyrinth of deliberate misinformation.'

They were silent again for a while and then Royan smiled in the firelight, her face lighting up with anticipation.

'Oh, Nicky! It is such an exciting challenge.' Then her voice descended an octave. 'But is there a way? Is it possible to get in there?'

'We will find out.'

'When?'

'In due course. I haven't thought it out fully as yet. All I am certain of is that it is going to take a prodigious amount of planning and hard work.'

'You are still committed, then?' She wanted his assurance. She knew that she could never do it alone. 'You aren't daunted by the project?'

Nicholas chuckled. 'I will admit that I never expected Taita to lead us on such a merry chase. I imagined simply breaking open a stone gateway and finding it all waiting for us there, like Howard Carter walking into the tomb of Tutankhamen. However, to answer your question, yes, I am daunted by what it's going to involve – but hell, nothing could stop me now! I have the smell of glory in my nostrils and the gleam of gold in my eye.'

While they talked, Tamre curled up in the dust on the other side of the fire, and pulled his *shamma* over his head. His rest must have been interrupted by dreams and fantasies, for he burbled and squeaked and giggled in his sleep.

'I wonder what goes on in that poor demented head, and what visions he sees,' Royan whispered. 'He says he saw Jesus here in the quarry, and I am sure that he really believes that he did.'

Their voices became softer and drowsier as the fire burned down, and Royan murmured, just before she fell asleep on Nicholas's shoulder, 'If the tomb of Pharaoh Mamose is below the level of the river, then surely the contents will be water-damaged?'

'I can't believe that Taita would have built his dam and spent fifteen years working on the tomb, as he says that he did in the scrolls, only to flood it deliberately and despoil the mummy of his king and ruin his treasure,' Nicholas murmured, with her hair tickling his cheek. 'No, that would have precluded Pharaoh's resurrection in the other world, and brought all his work to nothing. I think Taita has taken all that into his calculations.'

She snuggled closer, and sighed with satisfaction.

A little while later he said softly, 'Goodnight, Royan,' but she did not reply and her breathing was deep and even. He smiled to himself, and gently kissed the top of her head.

Nicholas was not certain what had woken him. He took a few moments to place himself, and then he realized that he was still in the quarry. There was no moon but the stars hung down close to the earth, as big and fat as bunches of ripe grapes. By their light he saw that Royan had slipped down and was lying flat on the ground beside him.

He stood up carefully, so as not to disturb her, and moved well away from the dead fire to empty his bladder. The night was deathly quiet. No night bird called, nor was there the sound of any of the other nocturnal creatures. The rocks around him still radiated the heat of the previous day's sunlight.

Suddenly the sound that had woken him was repeated. It was a faint and distant susurration that echoed along the cliffs, so that he could form no judgement as to the direction from which it came. But he was in no doubt what the sound was. He had heard it so often before. It was the sound of faraway automatic gunfire, almost certainly an AK-47 assault rifle firing, not long ragged bursts, but short taps of three rounds, an art that took expertise and practice. He was sure that the person doing the shooting was a trained professional.

He tilted his wrist so that the luminescent dial of his watch caught the starlight, and he saw that it was a few minutes after three o'clock in the morning.

He stood listening for a long time, but the firing was not repeated. At last he returned to where Royan lay and settled down beside her again. However, he slept only shallowly and intermittently, and kept starting awake listening for more gunfire in the night.

Royan began to stir at the first lemon and orange flush of dawn in the eastern sky, and while they ate the remains of the survival rations for their breakfast he told her about the noise that had woken him during the night.

'Do you think it could have been Boris?' she asked. 'He may have caught up with Mek and Tessay.'

'I doubt that very much. Boris has already been gone several days. He should be well out of earshot by now, even beyond the sound range of the heaviest weapons.'

'Who do you suppose it was, then?'

'I have no idea. But I don't like it. We should start back to camp as soon as we have had another look around the quarry. After that there is nothing further that we can do at this stage. We should make tracks for home and mother.'

As soon as the light was strong enough, Nicholas shot a spool of film to make a record of the quarry. For comparison of scale, Royan posed beside the wall in which the embryonic blocks still lay. As she warmed to her role as a model she started to clown for him. She climbed on to the biggest of the slabs and hammed it up for the camera, pouting with one hand behind her head in the style of Marilyn Monroe.

When, finally, they went off down the valley towards the monastery they were both exultant and garrulous after their success. Their discussion was animated as they bounced ideas back and forth, and laid their plans for the further exploitation of these wonderful discoveries. By the time they reached the pink cliffs at the lower end of the chasm it was late morning. There they met a small party of monks from the monastery coming up the trail.

Even from a distance it was obvious that something dreadful had happened during their absence: the sorrowful ululations of the monks sent chills down Royan's spine. It was the universal African sound of mourning, the harbinger of death and disaster. As they approached they saw that the monks were picking up handfuls of dust from the track and pouring it over their heads as they wailed and lamented.

'What is it, Tamre?' Royan asked the boy. 'Go and find out for us!' Tamre ran ahead to meet his brother monks. They stopped in the middle of the path and fell into a high-pitched discussion, weeping and gesticulating. Then Tamre ran back to them.

'Your people at the camp. Something terrible has happened. Bad men came in the might. Many of the servants are dead,' he screamed.

Nicholas grabbed Royan's hand. 'Come on!' he snapped, 'let's find out what is going on here.'

They ran the last mile to the camp, and arrived to find another circle of monks gathered around something in front of the kitchen hut. Nicholas pushed them aside and elbowed his way to the front. There he stopped and stared with a sinking feeling in his gut, and the sweat on his face turned cold with horror. Under a buzzing blue pall of flies lay the blood-splattered corpse of the cook and three other camp servants. Their hands had been bound behind their backs, and then they had been forced to kneel before being shot in the back of the head at close range.

'Don't look!' Nicholas warned Royan as she came up. 'It's not very pretty.'

But she ignored his advice and came to stand beside him. 'Oh, sweet heavens. They have been slaughtered like cattle in an abattoir.' She gagged.

'This explains the sound of gunfire that I heard last night,' he answered grimly. He went forward to identify the dead men. 'Aly and Kif are not here. Where are they?' He raised his voice and called in Arabic, turning to face the crowd. 'Aly, where are you?'

The tracker pushed his way forward. 'I am here, *effendi*.' His voice was shaky and his face was haggard. There was blood on the front of his shirt.

'How did this happen?' Nicholas seized his arm and steadied him.

'Men came in the night with the guns. *Shufta*. They shot into the huts where we were sleeping. They gave us no warning. They just started shooting.'

'How many of them? Who were they?' Nicholas demanded.

'I do not know how many of them there were. It was

dark. I was asleep. I ran away when the shooting began. They were *shufta*, bandits, killers. They were hyenas and jackals – there was no reason for what they have done. These men were my brothers, my friends.' He began to sob, and the tears streamed down his face.

Royan turned away, sickened and horrified. She went to her hut and stopped in the doorway. It had been ransacked. Her bags had been turned out on to the floor. Her bedding had been stripped, and the mattress thrown into the corner. As though she were a sleep-walker in a nightmare, she crossed the floor and picked up the canvas folder in which she kept her papers. She turned it upside down and shook it. It was empty. The satellite photographs and the maps, all her rubbings of the stele, the Polaroids that Nicholas had taken in Tanus's tomb – everything was gone.

Royan picked up the bed and set it the right way up. She sat down on it, and tried to gather her thoughts. She felt confused and shaken. The image of those bloody, bullet-ripped corpses laid out in front of the kitchen haunted her, and she found it difficult to concentrate and to think clearly.

Nicholas burst into her hut and looked around quickly. 'They did the same thing to me. Ransacked the place. My rifle has gone, and all my papers. But at least I had the passports and travellers' cheques in my day-pack—' He broke off as he saw the empty canvas folder lying at her feet. 'Have they taken the—'

'Yes!' she forestalled his question. 'They have cleaned out all our research material, even the Polaroids. Thank God you had the undeveloped rolls of film with you. It's the same as happened to Duraid and me all over again. We aren't safe from them, even here, even out in the remotest part of the bush.' There was the edge of hysteria in her voice. She jumped up from the bed and ran to him.

'Oh, Nicky, what would have happened if we had been

in camp last night?' She threw her arms around him, and clung to him. 'We would be lying out there in the sun now, all bloody and covered with flies.'

'Steady on, my dear. Let's not jump to any conclusions. This could just be a chance raid by bandits.'

'Then why did they steal our papers? What value would ordinary *shufta* place on rubbings and Polaroids? Where was the Pegasus helicopter heading just before the raid? They were after us, Nicky. I feel it so strongly. They wanted to kill us just as they did Duraid. They could return at any time, and now we are unarmed and helpless.'

'All right, I agree with you that we are pretty vulnerable here. It would be wise to get out as soon as possible. There isn't any point in staying on here anyway. There's nothing more we can do at this stage.' He hugged her and shook her gently. 'Brace up! We will salvage what we can from this mess, and then get moving back to the vehicles right away.'

'What about the dead men?' She stood back, and with an effort forced back her tears and brought herself under control. 'How many of our people survived?'

'Aly, Salin and Kif escaped. They dived out of their huts and ran off into the darkness as soon as the shooting started. I have told them to get ready to leave right away. I have spoken to one of the senior priests. They will take care of the burial of the dead, and will report to the authorities as soon as they are able. But they agree that the attack was aimed at us, and that we are still in danger, and that we should get away as soon as possible.'

Within the hour they were ready to start. Nicholas had decided to leave all the camping equipment and Boris's personal gear in the charge of Jali Hora. The mules were lightly loaded, and he planned to make a forced march out of the gorge.

The abbot had given them an escort of monks to accompany them to the top of the escarpment. 'Only a truly Godless man would attack you while you are under the protection of the cross,' he explained.

Nicholas found the dried hide and head of the striped dik-dik still in the skinning shed. He rolled it into a bundle and strapped it on to the load atop one of the mules, and then gave the order for the attenuated caravan to move out.

Tamre had insinuated himself into the group of monks who were escorting the party. He kept close behind Royan as they set off up the trail, with the lamentations and farewells of the monastic community following them for the first mile.

It was hot in this brutal midday. There was no movement of air to bring relief, and the stone walls of the valley sucked up the heat of that awful sun and spewed it back over them as they toiled up the steep gradients. It dried their sweat even as it oozed through their pores, leaving patterns of white salt crystals on their skins and clothing. The muleteers, spurred on by fear, set a killing pace, trotting behind their beasts and prodding their testicles with a sharpened stick to keep them moving at their best pace.

By mid-afternoon they had retraced the morning's travel and once more reached the putative site of Taita's dam wall. Nicholas and Royan took a few minutes' breather to dip their heads in the river and sluice the salt and sweat from their faces and necks. Then they stood together above the falls and took a brief farewell of the chasm in which lay all their hopes and dreams.

'How long until we return?' she asked.

'We cannot afford to leave it too long,' he told her. 'Big rains are due soon, and the hyenas have got the scent and are crowding in. From now on every day will be precious, and every hour we lose may be crucial.'

She stared down into the chasm and said softly, 'You haven't won yet, Taita. The game is still afoot.'

They turned away together and followed the mules up the trail towards the escarpment wall. That evening they did not stop at the traditional campsite beside the river, but pressed on several miles further until darkness forced a halt. There was no attempt to build a comfortable camp. They dined on cakes of *injera* bread dipped in the *wat* pot that the monks had carried with them. Then Nicholas and Royan spread their bedrolls side by side on the stony earth and, using the mule packs as pillows, fell into exhausted, dreamless sleep.

The next morning, while the mules were being loaded in the pre-dawn darkness, they drank a bowl of strong bitter black Ethiopian coffee. Then they started out along the trail again.

As the rising sun lit the sheer walls of the escarpment ahead of them they seemed close enough to touch, and Nicholas remarked to Royan, as she swung along long-legged beside him, 'At this pace we should reach the foot of the escarpment this afternoon, and there is a good chance that we might sleep tonight in the cavern behind the waterfall.'

'That means we could cut a couple of days off the journey and reach the trucks some time tomorrow.'

'Possibly,' he said. 'I'll be glad to get out of here.'

'It feels like a trap,' Royan agreed, looking at the rocky, broken ground that rose on either hand, hemming them into the narrow bottom of the Dandera river. 'I have been doing a bit of thinking, Nicky.'

'Let's hear your conclusions.'

'No conclusions, only some disturbing thoughts. Suppose somebody at Pegasus who can understand them is now in possession of our rubbings and Polaroids. What will their reaction be if they know how much progress we have made in the search?'

'Not very happy thoughts,' he agreed. 'But on the other hand there is not much we can do about any of that until we get back to civilization, except keep our eyes wide open and our wits about us. Hell, I haven't even got the little Rigby rifle. We are a flock of sitting ducks.'

Aly, the muleteers and the monks seemed to be of the same opinion, for they never slackened the pace. It was midday before they called the first brief halt to brew coffee and to water the mules. While the men lit fires, Nicholas took his binoculars from the mule pack and began to climb the rock slope. He had not covered much ground before he glanced back and saw Royan climbing after him. He waited for her to catch up.

'You should have taken the chance to rest,' he told her severely. 'Heat exhaustion is a real danger.'

'I don't trust you going off on your own. I want to know what you are up to.'

'Just a little recce. We should have scouts out ahead, not just go charging blindly along the trail like this. If I remember correctly from the inward march, some of the worst ground lies just ahead of us. Lord knows what we may run into.'

They went on upwards, but it was not possible to reach the crest for a sheet of unscalable vertical cliff barred their way. Nicholas chose the best vantage point below this barrier, and glassed both slopes of the valley ahead of them. The terrain was as he had remembered it. They were approaching the foot of the escarpment wall and the ground was becoming more rugged and severe, like the swell of the open ocean sensing the land and rising up in alarm before breaking in confusion upon the shore. The trail followed the river closely. The cliffs hung over the narrow aisle of ground that made up the bank, sculpted by wind and weather into strange, menacing shapes, like the battlements of a wicked witch's castle in an old Disney cartoon. At one point a buttress of red sandstone overhung the trail, forcing the river to detour around it, and the trail was reduced so much that it would be difficult for a laden mule to negotiate without being pushed off the bank into the river.

Nicholas studied the bottom of the valley carefully through the lens. He could pick out nothing that seemed suspicious or untoward, so he raised his head and swept the cliffs and their tops.

At that moment Aly's voice came up from the valley below, echoing along the slope as he shouted, 'Hurry, *effendi*! The mules are ready to go on!'

Nicholas waved down to him, but then lifted the binoculars for one more sweep of the ground ahead. A wink of bright light caught his eye – a brief ephemeral stab of brilliance like the signal of a heliograph. He switched his whole attention to the spot on the cliff from which it had emanated.

'What is it? What have you seen?' Royan demanded.

'I am not sure. Probably nothing,' he replied, without lowering the binoculars. It may have been a reflection from a polished metal surface, or from the lens of another pair of binoculars, or from the barrel of a sniper's rifle, he thought. On the other hand, a chip of mica or a pebble of rock crystal could reflect sunlight the same way, and even some of the aloes and other succulent plants have shiny leaves. He watched the spot carefully for a few more minutes, and then Aly's voice floated up to them again.

'Hurry, *effendi*. The mule-drivers will not wait!'

He stood up. 'All right. Nothing. Let's go.' He took Royan's arm to help her over the rough footing, and they started down. At that moment he heard the rattle of stones from further up the slope, and he stopped her and held her arm to keep her quiet. They waited, watching the skyline.

Abruptly a pair of long curling horns appeared over the crest, and under them the head of an old kudu bull, his trumpet-shaped ears pricked forward and the fringe of his dewlap blowing in the hot, light breeze. He stopped on the edge of the cliff just above where they crouched, but he had not seen them. The kudu turned his head and stared back in the direction from which he had come. The sunlight glinted in his nearest eye, and the set of his head and the alert, tense stance made it clear that something had disturbed him.

For a long moment he stood poised like that, and then, still without being aware of the presence of Nicholas and Royan, he snorted and abruptly leaped away in full flight. He vanished from their sight behind the ridge and the sound of his run dwindled into silence.

'Something scared the living daylights out of him.'

'What?' enquired Royan.

'Could have been anything – a leopard, perhaps,' he replied, and he hesitated as he looked down the slope. The caravan of mules and monks had set off already and was following the trail up along the river bank.

'What should we do?' Royan asked.

'We should reconnoitre the ground ahead – that is if we had the time, which we haven't.' The caravan was pulling away swiftly. Unless they went down immediately they would be left behind alone, unarmed. He had nothing concrete to act upon, and yet he had to make an immediate decision.

'Come on!' He took her hand again, and they slid and scrambled down the slope. Once they reached the trail they had to break into a run to catch up with the tail of the caravan.

Now that they were again part of the column, Nicholas could turn his attention to searching the skyline above them more thoroughly. The cliffs loomed over them, blocking out half the sky. The river on their left hand washed out any other sounds with its noisy, burbling current.

Nicholas was not really alarmed. He prided himself on

being able to sense trouble in advance, a sixth sense that had saved his life more than once before. He thought of it as his early-warning system, but now it was sending no messages. There were any number of possible explanations for the reflection he had picked up from the crest of the cliff, and for the behaviour of the bull kudu.

However, he was still a little on edge, and he was giving the high ground above them all his attention. He saw a speck flick over the top of the cliff, twisting and falling – a dead leaf on the warm, wayward breeze. It was too small and insignificant to be of any danger, but nevertheless he followed the movement with his eye, his interest idle.

The brown leaf spiralled and looped, and finally touched lightly against his cheek. He lifted his hand as a reflex, and caught it. He rubbed the brown scrap between his fingers, expecting it to crackle and crumble. Instead it was soft and supple, with a fine, almost greasy texture.

He opened his hand and studied it more closely. It was no leaf, he saw at once, but a torn scrap of greased paper, brown and translucent. Suddenly all his early-warning bells jangled. It was not just the incongruity of manufactured paper suddenly materializing in this remote setting. He recognized the quality and texture of that particular type of paper. He lifted it to his nose and sniffed it. The sharp, nitrous odour prickled the back of his throat.

'Gelly!' he exclaimed aloud. He knew the smell instantly.

Blasting gelignite was seldom employed for military purposes in this age of Semtex and plastic explosives, but was still widely used in the mining industry and in mineral exploration. Usually the sticks of nitrogelatine in a wood pulp and sodium nitrate base was wrapped in that distinctive brown greased paper. Before the detonator was placed in the head of the stick, it was common practice to tear off the corner of the paper wrapper to expose the treacle-brown explosive beneath. He had used it often enough in the old days never to forget the odour of it.

His mind was racing now. If somebody was expecting them and had mined the cliff with gelignite, then the reflection he had picked up could have been from the coils of copper wiring strung between the explosive in the rock, or it could have been from some other item of equipment. If that was so, then the operator might even at this moment be lying concealed up there, ready to press the plunger on the circuit box. The kudu bull might have been fleeing from the concealed human presence.

'Aly!' he bellowed down to the head of the caravan, 'Stop them! Turn them back!'

He started to run forward towards the head of the caravan, but in his heart he knew it was already too late. If there was somebody up there on the cliff, he was watching every move that Nicholas made. Nicholas could never hope to reach the head of the column and turn the mules around on the narrow trail, and get them back to safety before ... He came up short and looked back at Royan. Her safety was his main concern. He turned and ran back to grab her arm.

'Come on! We have to get off the track.'

'What is it, Nicky? What are you doing?' She was resisting him, pulling back against his grip on her arm.

'I'll explain later,' he snapped at her brusquely. 'Just trust me now.' He dragged her a couple of paces before she gave in and began to run with him, back in the direction from which they had come.

They had not covered fifty yards before the cliff face blew. A vast disruption of air swept over them with a force that made them stagger. It clapped painfully in their skulls and threatened to implode the delicate membranes of their eardrums. Then the main force of the blast swept over them, not a single blast but a long, rolling detonation like thunder breaking directly overhead. It stunned and battered them so that they reeled into each other and lost the direction of their flight.

Nicholas seized her in a steadying embrace, and looked back. He saw a series of explosions leap from the crest of the cliff. Tall, dancing fountains of dirt and dust and rubble, pirouetting one after the other in strict choreography, like a chorus-line of hellish ballerinas.

Even in the terror of the moment he could appreciate the expertise with which the gelignite had been laid. This was a master bomber at work. The leaping columns of rubble subsided upon themselves, leaving the fine, tawny mist of dust drifting and spiralling against the clear blue of the sky, and for a moment longer it seemed that the destruction was complete. Then the silhouette of the cliff began to alter.

Slowly at first the wall of rock started to lean outwards. He saw great cracks appear in the face, opening like leering mouths. Sheets of rock collapsed and in slow motion slithered down upon themselves like the silken skirts of a curtseying giantess. The rock groaned and crackled and rumbled as the entire cliff began to fall into the river far below.

Nicholas was mesmerized by the awful sight, and his brain seemed to have been numbed by the explosion. It took a huge effort to force himself to think and to act. He saw that the centre of the explosion had occurred further down the trail, near the head of the mule caravan. Tamre was up there, beside Aly. He and Royan were at the tail of the caravan. The bomber up on the cliff had obviously been waiting for them to come directly into the epicentre of his explosive trap, but had been forced to trigger it when he saw them running back down the trail and realized that they had been alerted and were about to escape.

Yet they were not clear – they were about to catch the peripheral force of the landslide that was developing above

322

them. Still holding Royan, Nicholas stared up the falling cliff face and made a desperate calculation.

He watched in petrified fascination as the vast tide of falling rock swept over the trail ahead of him, picking up men and mules and carrying them with it over the edge and down into the river bed. It swallowed them, lapping them up like the tongue of some fearsome monster and chewing them to pulp with razor fangs of red rock. Even above the rumbling roar of the rock tide he heard the terrified screams of men and animals as they were ploughed under.

The wave of destruction spread towards where he and Royan stood upon the trail. If they had been directly under the explosion they would have stood as little chance as those others, but as it ran down the cliff its destructive momentum was dissipating. On the other hand, Nicholas realized that there was no hope that they would be able to outrun it, and what was about to fall upon them would still be devastating.

There was no time to explain to Royan what they had to do – he had only seconds left in which to act. Sweeping her up in his arms, he leaped over the bank towards the river. He lost his footing almost immediately and they went down together, rolling end over end, but thirty feet down there was a spur of rock the size of a house. As they came up against the upper side of it, it broke their fall.

They were half-stunned, but Nicholas dragged Royan to her feet and guided her into the lee of the rock wall. There was a cut-back here, and they crept into it and crouched flat. Pressing themselves hard against the wall, they both held their breath as the first chunk of cliff came bounding and bouncing down towards them like a gigantic rubber ball, picking up speed with gravity, until it smashed into their shelter with a force that made the solid rock against which they were cringing vibrate and resound like a cathedral bell, and the hurtling missile leaped high over their heads, spinning massively in flight before it dropped into the river. It raised a tidal wave from the surface that broke like storm surf on both banks.

This was merely the forerunner of the maelstrom that now poured over them. It seemed that half the mountain was falling upon them. As each slab crashed into their shelter daggers and splinters burst from its leading edges, filling the air they breathed with fine white dust and the sulphurous stink of sparking flint. This immense cascade flew over their heads or piled up in front of their shelter, and loose chips and pebbles rained down upon them.

Nicholas crawled over the top of Royan, and covered her with his body. A stone struck the side of his head a glancing blow that made his ears ring, but he gritted his teeth and fought the impulse to lift his head and look up. He felt something warm and ticklish snaking through the short hairs behind his right ear. It crept down his cheek like a living thing, and it was only when it reached the corner of his mouth and he tasted the metallic salt that he realized it was a trickle of blood.

The fine talcum dust powdered them and irritated their throats, so that they coughed and choked in the uproar. The dust seeped into their eyes, and they were forced to clench their lids and keep them tightly shut.

One mass of rock the size of a wagon sprang high in the air and then fell back close beside where they lay. The impact made the earth jump so violently that Royan, with Nicholas's weight on top of her, was struck in the belly and diaphragm with a force that drove the wind from her lungs, and she thought that her ribs had been crushed.

Then gradually the downpouring of earth and rock began to subside. The breath-stopping impact of great boulders into their shelter became less frequent. The fine dust they were breathing began to settle. The rumbling and roaring let up gradually, until the only sound was the slip and slide of settling earth and rock and the burble of the river below them.

Warily, Nicholas at last lifted his head and tried to blink the dust off his eyelashes. Royan stirred under him, and he crawled back to let her sit up. They stared at each other. Their faces were caked into kabuki masks with the antimony-white dust, and their hair was powdered like the wigs of eighteenth-century French aristocrats.

'You are bleeding,' Royan whispered, her voice husky with dust and terror.

Nicholas lifted his hand to his face and it came away covered with a paste of dust and blood. 'It's just a nick,' he said. 'How are you?'

'I think I may have twisted my knee. I felt something give when we fell. I don't think it's serious. There is very little pain.'

'Then we have both been ridiculously lucky,' he told her. 'Nobody deserved to survive that.'

She made an effort to stand, but he restrained her with a hand on her shoulder. 'Wait! The entire slope above us is broken and unstable. Give it time. There will be loose rocks coming down for a while yet.' He untied the Paisley bandana from around his throat and handed it to her. 'Besides which, we don't want—' But he changed his mind and did not finish his sentence.

While she wiped her face she asked shakily, 'You were going to say, besides which—?'

'Besides which, we don't want to give those bastards up there any idea that we have survived their little party. Otherwise we will have them down here finishing the job, cutting throats. Much better they believe that we snuffed it, as intended.'

She stared at him. 'Do you think they are still up there, watching us?'

'Count on it,' he answered grimly. 'They must be pretty chuffed with the fact that they have at last succeeded in getting rid of you. We don't want to pop our heads up right now and spoil it for them.'

'How did you know what was going to happen?' she asked. 'If you hadn't grabbed me—' Her voice petered out.

In a few words he explained about the scrap of gelignite wrapping. 'Simplest thing in the world to pick one of the narrowest sections of the trail and mine the cliff—' He broke off as, faintly but unmistakably, there came the sound of an aircraft engine and the flutter of rotors in fully fine pitch for take-off.

'Quickly,' he snapped at her. 'Get in as close as you can to the overhang.' He pushed her back against the sheltering boulder. 'Lie flat!' When she obeyed without question, he lay beside her and piled loose rubble over them both.

'Lie still. Don't move, whatever you do.'

They lay and listened to the sound of the helicopter approaching, and circling overhead. It moved up and down the valley, flying a few feet above the surface of the river. At one point it was directly above the ledge on which they lay, and they were buffeted by the down-draught of the rotors.

'Looking for survivors,' said Nicholas grimly. 'Don't move. They haven't spotted us yet.'

'If they were watching us before the blast, they should have been able to come directly to where we are,' she whispered. 'They seem confused.'

'They must have lost us in the dust of the avalanche and the break-up of the cliff face. They aren't sure where we are lying.' The sound of the helicopter moved off slowly along the river, and Nicholas told her, 'I am going to risk a peep, to make sure it's the Pegasus job – not that there can be many other choppers in this area. Keep your head down!'

He lifted his head slowly and cautiously, and one glance was sufficient to confirm all his speculations. Half a mile upstream, the Pegasus Jet Ranger hovered over the river. It was moving slowly away from him, so that from this angle Nicholas was unable to see through the windscreen into the cockpit. But at that moment the engine beat changed as the pilot changed pitch and pulled on the collective.

As the aircraft rose vertically and turned northwards, Nicholas caught a glimpse of the passengers. Jake Helm sat in the front seat beside the pilot, and Colonel Nogo was in the seat behind him. They were both staring down into the river valley, but in seconds the helicopter lifted them away and the machine disappeared beyond the ridge, flying in the direction of the escarpment, and the sound of its engines dwindled into silence. Nicholas crawled out from beneath the boulder and pulled Royan to her feet.

'No more doubts. We know who we are dealing with now. That was Helm and Nogo in the chopper. Helm almost certainly laid the gelly, and Nogo probably led the men who hit our camp last night. Each of them doing the job he does best,' Nicholas told her. 'So that confirms it. Whoever owns Pegasus is the ugly behind all this. Helm and Nogo are merely the stooges.'

'But Nogo is an officer in the Ethiopian army,' she protested.

'Welcome to Africa.' He did not smile as he said it. 'Here everything is for sale at a price, including government officials and army officers.' Now he scowled so that the caked dust on his face was dislodged and filtered down in a fine powdering. 'Now, however, our main concern is to get out of the gorge and back to civilization.'

He looked up the slope. The trail above them had been obliterated beneath the rock fall. 'We can't get back that way,' he told her, and took her hand. But when he lifted her to her feet she gasped and quickly shifted her weight to her right leg.

'My knee!' Then she smiled bravely. 'It will be all right.'

However, she was limping heavily as they scrambled down to the river, terrified that their movements would set off another rock slide. They ended up waist-deep in the water under the bank.

Royan stood behind Nicholas and washed the blood and dust from the wound in his scalp. 'Not too bad,' she told him. 'Doesn't need a stitch.'

'I have a tube of Betadyne in my pack,' he said. He fished it out, and she smeared the wound with the yellow-brown ointment before binding it up with the Paisley bandana.

'That will do.' She patted his shoulder.

'Thank the Lord for my bum-bag,' Nicholas remarked as he zipped it closed. 'At least we have a few essentials with us. Now our next job is to look for any other survivors.'

'Tamre!' she exclaimed.

They floundered along the bank. The river was clogged with loose rock and earth that had fallen from the cliff. In the deeper places they were forced in up to their armpits, and Nicholas carried his pack at arm's length above his head. The loose rock was treacherous, and gave way under them when they tried to scramble out of the water to search for the other members of the caravan.

They found the bodies of two of the monks, both of them crushed and half-buried. They did not even attempt to dig them free. One of the mules lay with one leg in the air and the rest of its body completely covered with broken rock. The pack that it had carried had burst open and the contents were scattered about. The rolled skin and trophies of the dik-dik had been churned into the muck. Nicholas rescued them and strapped them on to his bum-bag.

'More to carry,' Royan warned him.

'Only a pound or two, but worth it,' he replied.

They made their way towards the point below the trail where they had last seen Tamre and Aly. But though they searched for almost an hour they found no sign of either of them. The slope above them was devastated: raw ravaged earth, great rocks shattered, bushes and trees uprooted and smashed to kindling.

Royan climbed as high as her injured leg enabled her, then cupped her hands around her mouth and shouted, 'Tamre! Tamre! Tamre!' The echoes took her cry and flung it from wall to valley wall.

'I think he is done for. The poor little devil has been buried,' Nicholas called up to her. 'We have been at it an hour now. We cannot afford more time, if we are to get out ourselves. We will have to leave him.'

She ignored him and worked her way along the rock-slide, loose scree rolling under her feet, and he could see that the knee was giving her pain.

'Tamre! Answer me,' she called in Arabic. 'Tamre! Where are you?'

'Royan! That's enough. You are going to damage that knee even more. You are putting both of us at risk now. Give it up!'

At that moment they both heard a soft groan from higher up the slope. Royan scrambled up towards the sound, slipping and sliding back almost as far as she climbed, but at last she gave a cry of horror. Nicholas dumped his pack and went up after her. When he reached her side, he too dropped to his knees.

Tamre was pinned down in the rubble. His face was barely recognizable. It was torn and lacerated, with half the skin ripped off. Royan had lifted his head into her lap, and was using her sleeve to wipe the filth out of his nostrils to allow him to breathe more freely. Blood was oozing from the corner of his mouth, and when he groaned again it welled up in a fresh flood. Royan dabbed at it, smearing it across his chin.

His lower body was buried, and Nicholas tried to clear the broken rock; but almost immediately he realized the futility of it. A lump of raw rock the size of a billiard table lay across him. It weighed many tons, and must certainly have crushed his spine and pelvis. No single man would be able to move that massive weight unaided. Even if it were possible, the grinding action of any movement would inevitably aggravate the terrible injuries that Tamre had already sustained.

'Do something, Nicky,' Royan whispered. 'We have to do something for him.'

Nicholas looked at her and shook his head. Royan's eyes flooded with tears, and they broke over her lower lids and scattered like raindrops into Tamre's upturned face, diluting the blood to the pink of rosé wine.

'We can't just sit here and let him die,' she protested, and at the sound of her voice Tamre opened his eyes and looked into her face.

He smiled through the blood, and that smile lit his dusty, broken face. 'Ummee!' he whispered. 'You are my mother. You are so kind. I love you, my mother.'

The words were bitten off and a spasm stiffened his body. His face contorted with agony and he gave a soft, strangled cry, and then slumped. The rigidity went out of his shoulders and his head rolled to one side.

Royan sat for long time holding his head and weeping softly, but bitterly, until Nicholas touched her hand and said gently, 'He is dead, Royan.'

She nodded. 'I know. He held on just long enough to say goodbye to me.'

He let her mourn a little longer, and then he told her softly, 'We must go, my dear.'

'You are right. But it is so hard to leave him here. He never had anybody. He was so alone. He called me mother. I think he truly loved me.'

'I know he did,' Nicholas assured her, lifting the boy's

dead head from her lap and helping her to her feet. 'Go down and wait for me. I will cover him the best I can.'

Nicholas crossed Tamre's hands upon his chest, and folded his fingers around the silver crucifix that hung around his neck. Then he piled loose rock carefully over him, covering his head so that the crows and vultures could not reach him.

He slid down to where she waited in the water, and slung his pack over one shoulder.

'We must go on,' he told Royan.

She wiped away the tears with the back of her hand and nodded. 'I am ready now.'

They waded upstream, pushing hard against the current. The rock-slide had blocked half the river bed and the waters squeezed through the gap that was left. When at last they reached the point on the bank above the avalanche, they climbed out of the river and picked their way up the steep bank until at last they could crawl out on to the intact section of the pathway.

They took a moment to recover and looked back. The river below the rock-slide was running red-brown with mud. Even if the monks at the monastery downstream had not heard the explosions, they would be alarmed by that flood of discoloured water and would come to investigate. They would find the bodies and take them down for decent burial. That thought comforted Royan a little as they struck out along the trail, with two days' hard travel still ahead of them.

Royan was limping heavily now, but each time Nicholas tried to help her she brushed his hand away. 'I am all right. It's just a bit stiff.' She would not allow him to inspect the knee, but kept on stubbornly along the trail ahead of him.

They marched mostly in silence for the rest of that day. Nicholas respected her grief and was grateful for her reticence. This ability to be quiet and yet not give out a sense of alienation and withdrawal to those around her was one of the qualities he admired in her. They spoke briefly late that afternoon while they paused to rest beside the path.

'The only consolation is that now Pegasus will believe that we are safely buried under the rock-slide and they won't bother to come looking for us again. We can push on without wasting time scouting the trail ahead,' Nicholas told her.

They camped that night below the escarpment, just before the path began the climb up the vertical wall. Nicholas led her well off the path, into a heavily wooded gully, and built a small screened fire that could not be seen from the trail.

Here at last she relented and allowed him to examine her knee. It was bruised and swollen, and hot to the touch. 'You shouldn't be walking on this,' he told her.

'Do I have any option?' she asked, and he had no reply. He wetted his bandana from the water bottle and bound up her leg as tightly as he dared without cutting off the circulation. Then he found a phial of Brufen in his bum-bag and made her take two of these anti-inflammatories.

'It feels better already,' she told him.

They shared the last bar of survival rations from his pack, sitting hunched up over the fire and talking quietly, still subdued and shaken by their experiences.

'What will happen when we reach the top?' Royan asked. 'Will the trucks still be parked where we left them? Will the men that Boris left to guard them still be there? What will happen if we run into the men from Pegasus again?'

'I can't give you any answers. We will just have to face each problem as it comes up.'

'One thing I am looking forward to when we reach Addis Ababa – reporting the massacre of Tamre and the others to the Ethiopian police. I want Helm and his gang to pay for what they have done.'

He was quiet for a while before he replied. 'I don't know if that is the wisest thing to do,' he ventured at last.

'What do you mean? We were witnesses to murder. We cannot let them get away with it.'

'Just remember that we want to return to Ethiopia. If we make a huge fuss now, we will have the entire valley swarming with troops and police. It may put an end to our further attempts to solve Taita's riddle, and to trace the tomb of Mamose.'

'I hadn't thought of that,' she said thoughtfully. 'But still, it was murder, and Tamre—'

'I know, I know,' he soothed her. 'But there are more certain ways of wreaking vengeance on Pegasus than trying to turn them over to Ethiopian justice. Consider for the moment the fact that Nogo is working with Helm. We saw him in the helicopter. If Pegasus have an army colonel in their pay, who else is working for them? The police? The head of the army? Members of the cabinet? We just don't know at this stage.'

'I hadn't thought about that either,' she admitted.

'Let's begin to think African from here on, and take a leaf out of Taita's scrolls. Like him we must be devious and cunning. We don't go rushing in shouting accusations. If we could just sneak out of the country, leaving everybody to believe that we are buried under the avalanche, that might be ideal. It would make our return to the gorge that much easier. Unfortunately I don't think we will be able to get away with that. But from now on, we should be as cagey and careful as circumstances permit.'

She stared into the dancing flames for a long while, then sighed and asked, 'You said there is a better vengeance to be had on Pegasus. What did you have in mind?'

'Why, simply whisking Mamose's treasure out from under their noses.'

She laughed for the first time that long cruel day. 'You are right, of course. Whoever owns Pegasus wants it desperately enough to kill for it. We must hope that depriving him of it will hurt him almost as badly as he has hurt us.'

Both of them were so tired that it was already half-light when they woke the next morning. As soon as Royan tried to stand she groaned and sank back. He went to her immediately, and she made no protest when he placed her bare leg across his lap.

He unwrapped the bandana, and frowned as he saw the knee. It was nearly twice its normal girth, and the bruising was plum and ripe grape. He wet the bandana again, and rewrapped the knee. He made her take the last two Brufen from the phial, and then helped her to her feet.

'How does it feel?' he asked anxiously, and she hobbled a few paces and smiled at him bravely.

'It will be all right as soon as I walk the stiffness out of it, I'm sure.'

He looked up the escarpment. So close in under the wall, the height was foreshortened, but he recalled every tortuous step of the way. It had taken them a full day to come down.

'Of course it will.' He smiled encouragement at her, and took her arm. 'Lean on me. It'll be a stroll in the park.'

They toiled upwards all that morning. The trail seemed to rise more steeply with every pace they took. She never complained, but she was ashen pale and sweating with the pain. By midday they had not yet reached the waterfall, and Nicholas made her stop to rest. They had nothing to eat, but she drank thirstily from the water bottle. He did not try to ration her, but limited himself to a single mouthful.

When she tried to rise, and go on, she gasped and staggered so violently that she might have fallen if he had not steadied her.

'Damn! Damn! Damn!' she swore bitterly. 'It's stiffened up on me.'

'Never mind,' he said cheerfully, and stripped his bumbag of all but the most crucial items of equipment. He kept the dik-dik skin, however, rolling it into a tight ball and stuffing it into the bag. Then he rebuckled it around his waist, and grinned at her cheerfully. 'Skinny little thing like you. Hop on my back.'

'You can't carry me up there.' She looked up the trail, steep as a ladderway, and was aghast.

'It's the only train leaving from this station,' he told her, and offered her his back. She crawled up on to it.

'Don't you think you should dump the dik-dik skin?' she asked.

'Perish the thought!' he said, and started up.

It was slow and heavy-going. After a while he had nothing left over for talking, and he trudged upwards in dogged silence. Sweat drenched his shirt, but she found neither the wet warmth of it that permeated her blouse on to her own skin, nor the strong masculine odour of it offensive. Instead, it was comforting and reassuring.

Every half-hour he stopped and lowered her to the ground, and lay quietly with his eyes closed until his breathing became regular and even again. Then he opened his eyes and grinned at her.

'Hi ho, Silver!' He pushed himself to his feet, and bowed his back for her to scramble aboard.

As the day wore on, his jokes became more forced and feeble. By late afternoon the pace was down to an exhausted plod, and at the more difficult places he had to pause and gather himself before stepping up. She tried to help him by climbing down from his back, and supporting herself on his shoulder as they struggled over the more arduous pitches, but even with this respite she knew that he was burning up the very last of his strength.

Neither of them could truly credit their achievement when they reeled around another corner of the track and saw before them the waterfall, spilling down like a white lacy curtain across the trail. Nicholas staggered into the cavern behind the sheet of falling water and lowered her to the floor. Then he collapsed and lay like a dead man.

It was dark when he had at last recovered sufficiently to open his eyes and sit up. While he was resting Royan had gathered some wood from the monks' stockpile and managed to get a small fire going.

'Good girl,' he told her. 'If ever you want a job as a housekeeper—'

'Don't tempt me.' She hobbled over to him, and examined the cut in his scalp. 'Nice healthy scab,' she told him, and then suddenly and impulsively she hugged his head to her bosom and stroked his dusty, sweat-stiff hair off his forehead.

'Oh, Nicky! How can I ever repay you for what you did for me today?'

A flippant reply rose to his lips, but even in his weakened state he had the good sense to bite it back. He was in no state to attempt any further intimacy. So he lay in her embrace, enjoying the feel of her body against his, but not taking the risk of scaring her off with a move of his own.

At last she released him gently, and sat back. 'I very much regret, sir, that the housekeeper cannot offer you smoked salmon and champagne for your dinner. How about a mug of mountain water, pure and nourishing?'

'I think we can do better than that.' He took the dry-cell torch from his bum-bag, and by its beam selected a round, fist-sized stone from the floor of the cavern. With this in his right hand he turned the light upwards, and played it over the cavern roof. Immediately there was a rustling of wings and the alarmed cooing of the rock pigeons that were roosting on the ledges. Nicholas manoeuvred into position below them, dazzling them with the torchbeam.

With his first throw he brought down a brace of them, fluttering and squawking to the cavern floor, while the rest of the flock exploded out into the night in a great clattering uproar of frantic wings. Nicholas pounced on the downed birds and with a practised flick of the wrist wrung their necks.

'How do you fancy a juicy slice of roast pigeon?' he asked her.

She lay propped on one elbow, and he sat cross-legged facing her, each of them plucking the vinous-maroon and grey feathers from one of the pigeon carcasses. Even when it came to drawing the bird, she was not squeamish, as many other women might have been faced with the same task. This, together with her stoical performance during the day's struggle up the mountain, enhanced his opinion of her. She had repeatedly proved to him how game and plucky she was. His feelings towards her were strengthening and maturing every day.

Concentrating on removing the fine bristles from the puckered breast skin of the bird, she said, 'It is beyond all doubt now that the material stolen in the raid on our camp is in Pegasus hands.'

'I was thinking the same thing,' Nicholas nodded, 'and we know from the antennae at their base camp above the falls that they have satellite communications. We can place a pretty certain bet that Jake Helm has already telefaxed it through to the big man, whoever he may be.'

'So he has all the details of the stele in Tanus's tomb. We know that he already has the seventh scroll in his possession. If he isn't an expert Egyptologist himself, he must have somebody in his pay who is. Wouldn't you agree with that?'

'I would guess that he can read hieroglyphics himself. I would think that he must be an avid collector. I know the type. It is an obsession with them.'

'I know the type as well.' She smiled at him. 'There is one sitting not a thousand miles away from me at this very moment.'

'*Touché!*' he laughed, and held up his hands in surrender. 'But I have only been lightly bitten by the bug, compared to others I could name. Those other two on Duraid's list, for instance.'

'Peter Walsh and Gotthold von Schiller,' she reeled off the names.

'Those two are homicidal collectors,' he confirmed. 'I am sure neither of them would hesitate to kill for the chance of having Pharaoh Mamose's treasure to themselves.'

'But from what I know about them, both of them are billionaires, at least in dollar terms.'

'Money has nothing to do with it, don't you see. If they laid hands upon it, they would never ever dream of selling a single artefact from the hoard. They would lock it all away in some deep vault, and not let another living soul lay eyes upon it. They would gloat on it in private – it's a bizarre, masturbatory passion.'

'What an odd word to describe it,' she protested.

'But accurate, I assure you. It's a sexual thing, a compulsion, like that of a serial killer.'

'I love all things Egyptian, but I don't think I can even imagine a craving that intense.'

'You must remember that these are not ordinary men whom we are considering. Their wealth allows them to pander to any appetite. All the normal, natural human appetites soon become jaded and satiated. They can have anything they want. Any man or any woman. Any thing, any perversion, whether legal or not. In the end they have to find something that no one else can ever have. It's the only thing that can still give them the old thrill.'

'So in whoever is behind Pegasus we are dealing with a madman?' she asked softly.

'Much more than that,' he corrected her. 'We are dealing with an enormously wealthy and powerful maniac, who in his disease will stop at nothing.'

They picked the cold carcasses of the roasted pigeons for their breakfast. Then, while the other one tactfully went to the back of the cavern and averted his or her gaze, they took turns to strip naked and bathe under the waterfall.

After the heat of the gorge the water was icy cold. It battered them with the force of a fire hose. Royan hopped on her good leg, gasping and whimpering under the torrent, and emerged covered in goose-pimples and shuddering blue with cold. However, it refreshed her, and even in her filthy, sweat-stinking clothes it gave her heart to start out on the last bitter climb to the summit.

Before leaving the cavern they examined each other's injuries again. Nicholas's scalp wound was healing cleanly, but Royan's knee was no better than the previous day. The bruises were starting to turn a virulent puce, the colour of decomposing liver, and the swelling was unabated. There was very little he could do for it, other than strapping it again with the bandana.

At last Nicholas admitted defeat, and abandoned his bum-bag and the roll of dik-dik skin. He knew that he was reaching the limit of his physical reserves, and he realized that, light as these items were, every extra pound that he carried today might mean the difference between reaching the summit or breaking down on the trail. He retained only the three rolls of undeveloped film, each in its plastic capsule. These were their only record of the hieroglyphics on the stele in Tanus's tomb. He dared not risk losing them, so he buttoned them into the breast pocket of his khaki shirt. He tucked both the bag and the skin into a crack in the wall at the back of the cavern, determined to retrieve them at some later date.

And so they started out on the last but most onerous leg of the trail. To begin with Royan was on her own two feet, but leaning heavily on his shoulder. However, before the first hour was over her knee could no longer take the strain, and she subsided on to a rock on the edge of the pathway.

'I am being an awful nuisance, aren't I?'

'Come on board, lady. Always room for a small one.'

With Royan perched on Nicholas's back, her injured leg sticking out stiffly in front of her, they toiled upwards, but their progress was even slower than it had been the day before. Nicholas was forced to pause and rest at shorter and shorter intervals. On the easier pitches she dismounted and hopped along on one leg beside him, steadying herself with one hand on his shoulder. Then she would collapse, and he had to lift her to her feet and pull her up on to his back once again.

The journey descended into nightmare, and both of them lost all sense of the passage of time. Hours blended with hours into a single unremitting agony. At one stage they lay beside each other on the path, sick and nauseated with thirst and exhaustion and pain. They had emptied the water bottle an hour ago, and there was no more on this section of the path – nothing to drink until they reached the summit and were reunited with the Dandera river.

'Go on and leave me here,' she whispered hoarsely.

He sat up immediately and stared at her aghast. 'Don't be silly. I need you for ballast.'

'It can't be much further to the top,' she insisted. 'You can come back with some of Boris's men to help carry me.'

'If they are still there, and if Pegasus doesn't find you first.' He stood up a little unsteadily. 'Forget it. You are coming along on this ride, all the way.' And he hoisted her to her feet.

He made her count aloud every step he took, and at every hundredth he paused and rested. Then he started the next hundred, with her counting softly in his ear, clinging with both arms around his neck. The whole universe seemed to shrink in upon them to the ground directly at his feet. They no longer saw the rock cliff on one side nor the deep void of space on the other. When he lurched or jolted her and the pain shot through her knee, she closed her eyes and tried not to let her voice betray it to him as she kept counting.

When he rested, he had to lean against the cliff face, not trusting his legs to get him up again if he lay down. He dared not lower her to the ground. The effort of lifting her again would be too much. He no longer had the strength for it.

'It's almost dark,' she whispered in his ear. 'You must stop here for the night. It's enough for one day. You are killing yourself, Nicky.'

'Another hundred,' he mumbled.

'No, Nicky. Put me down!'

For answer he pushed off from the rock wall with his shoulder and staggered on upwards.

'Count!' he ordered.

'Fifty-one, fifty-two,' she obeyed. Suddenly the gradient altered so sharply under his feet that he almost fell. The path had levelled out, and like a drunkard he reached up for a step that wasn't there.

He staggered and then caught his balance. He stood teetering on the brink of the precipice and peered into the dusk ahead of him, at first unable to credit what he was seeing. There were lights in the gloom, and he thought that he had begun to hallucinate. Then he heard men's voices, and he shook his head to clear it and bring himself back to reality.

'Oh, dear God. You have made it. We are at the top, Nicky. There are the vehicles. You did it, Nicky. You did it!'

He tried to speak, but his throat had closed up and no words came. He reeled forward towards the lights, and Royan cried out weakly on his back.

'Help us here. Please help us.' First in English and then in Arabic. 'Please help us.'

There were startled cries and the sounds of running men. Nicholas sank down slowly into the fine highland grass and let Royan slide off his back. Dark figures gathered around them, chattering in Amharic, and friendly hands seized them and half-carried, half-dragged them towards the lights. Then a torch was shone into Nicholas's face and a very English voice said, 'Hello, Nicky. Nice surprise. I came down from Addis to look for your corpse. Heard you were dead. Bit premature, what?'

'Hello, Geoffrey. Good of you to take the trouble.'

'I dare say you could use a cup of tea. You look a bit done in,' said Geoffrey Tennant. 'Never realized that your beard had ginger and grey bits in it. Designer stubble. Fashionable. Suits you actually.'

Nicholas realized what a picture he must present, ragged and unshaven, filthy and haggard with exhaustion.

'You remember Dr Al Simma? She has a bit of a dicky knee. Wonder if you would mind taking care of her?'

Then his legs gave way under him, and Geoffrey Tennant caught him before he fell.

'Steady on, old boy.' He led him to a canvas-backed camp chair, and seated him solicitously. Another chair was brought for Royan.

'*Letta chai hapa!*' Geoffrey gave the universal call of an Englishman in Africa, and minutes later thrust mugs of steaming over-sweetened tea into their hands.

Nicholas saluted Royan with his mug. 'Here's to us. There's none like us!'

They both drank deeply, scalding their tongues, but the caffeine and sugar hit their bloodstreams like a charge of electricity.

'Now I know I am going to live,' Nicholas sighed.

'Don't want to be pushy, Nicky, but do you mind telling me what the hell is going on here?' Geoffrey asked.

'Why don't you tell me?' Nicholas countered. He needed time to evaluate the situation. What did Geoffrey know and who had told him? Geoffrey obliged immediately.

'First thing we heard was that white hunter chappie of yours, Brusilov, had been fished out of the river near the Sudanese border, absolutely riddled with bullet holes. The crocs and catfish had snacked on his face, so the border police identified him by the documents in his money belt.'

Nicholas glanced across at Royan and cautioned her with a frown.

'Last time we saw him, he went off on a scouting expedition on his own,' Nicholas explained. 'He probably ran into the same bunch of *shufta* who raided our camp four nights ago.'

'Yes, we heard about that too. Colonel Nogo here radioed in a report to Addis.'

Neither of them had recognized Nogo in the crowd of men. It was only when he stepped forward into the light of the camp lanterns that Royan stiffened, and such an expression of loathing flashed across her face that Nicholas reached across surreptitiously and took her hand to restrain her from any indiscretion. After a moment she relaxed and composed her features.

'I am very relieved to see you, Sir Quenton-Harper. You have given us all a very worrying few days,' said Nogo.

'I do apologize,' said Nicholas smoothly.

'Please, sir, I meant no offence. It is just that we had a report from the Pegasus Exploration Company that you and Dr Al Simma had been caught up in a blasting accident. I was present when Mr Helm of the exploration company warned you that they were conducting blasting in the gorge.'

'But you—' Royan flared bitterly, and Nicholas squeezed her hand hard to stop her going on.

'It was probably our own carelessness, as you suggest. Nevertheless, Dr Al Simma has been injured and we are both badly shaken up by the accident. More important than that, however, is the fact that a number of other people, camp staff and monks from the monastery, have been killed in the *shufta* raid and in the blasting accident. As soon as we get back to Addis I will make a full statement to the authorities.'

'I do hope that you don't think any blame attaches—' Nogo started, but Nicholas cut him short.

'Of course not. Not your fault at all. You warned us about the danger of *shufta* in the gorge. You were not present, so what could you have done to prevent any of this? I would say that you have done your duty in the most exemplary fashion.'

Nogo looked relieved. 'You are most gracious to say so, Sir Quenton-Harper.'

Nicholas studied him for a moment longer. He seemed the most amiable of young men behind the metal-rimmed spectacles, so concerned and eager to please. For a moment Nicholas almost believed that he had been mistaken, and that it had been somebody else that he had seen in the Jet Ranger, hovering over the avalanche site like a vulture, searching for their dead bodies.

Nicholas forced himself to smile in his most friendly manner. 'I would be most grateful if you could do me a favour, Colonel.'

'Of course,' Nogo agreed readily. 'Anything at all.'

'I left a bag and one of my hunting trophies in the cavern under the Dandera waterfall. The bag contains our passports and travellers' cheques. Very grateful if you could send one of your men down to bring it up for me.'

While giving Nogo directions on how to find his possessions, he derived a perverse enjoyment from sending his would-be assassin on such a trivial errand. Then he turned back to his friend so that Nogo would not pick up the vindictive glint in his eyes. 'How did you get here, Geoffrey?'

'Light plane to Debra Maryam. There is an emergency landing field there. Colonel Nogo met us, and brought us the rest of the way by army jeep,' Geoffrey explained. 'The pilot and the aircraft are waiting for us at Debra Maryam.'

Geoffrey broke off and spoke to the camp staff in execrable Amharic, before turning back to Nicholas. 'I have just arranged a hot bath for you and Dr Al Simma. After that, a meal and a good night's sleep should work wonders. Tomorrow we can fly back to Addis. No reason why we shouldn't be there by tomorrow evening at the latest.'

He patted Royan's shoulder, disguising his carnal interest in her behind a benign avuncular smile. 'I must say I am rather pleased not to have to go traipsing down into the Abbay gorge looking for the pair of you. I hear that it's a pretty beastly part of the world.'

'Do you mind, Dr Al Simma, if I sit in front? Terribly rude of me, but I am inclined to suffer from mal de air. Ha ha!' Geoffrey explained to Royan as they waited for three small boys to chase the goats off the emergency airfield at Debra Maryam. In the meantime Nicholas was stuffing the roll of dik-dik skin under the rear passenger seat. One of Nogo's sergeants had made a night descent of the escarpment, and had delivered both his bag and the skin while they were breakfasting that morning.

Nogo gave them a smart salute as they taxied out in a cloud of dust. Nicholas waved and smiled at him through the side window, murmuring, 'Screw you, Nogo, screw you very much indeed.'

When at last the pilot lifted the little Cessna 260 off the rough grass strip, the horizon over the Abbay gorge resembled a field of cosmic mushrooms, vast thunderheads reaching up into the stratosphere. The air beneath them was turbulent as a storm sea and they were thrown about mercilessly in the rear seats. Up in front Geoffrey seemed to be faring no better. He was very quiet and took no interest in their conversation.

There had been no opportunity for them to talk privately the previous evening, what with either Geoffrey or Nogo hovering within earshot at all times. Now with their heads close together, the engine beat covering their voices and Geoffrey occupied with his own queasy thoughts, they were able to concoct their story.

Geoffrey had made it clear that the British Ambassador in Addis was less than delighted with the inconvenience they had caused him. Apparently there had been a string of faxes from Whitehall since they had been reported missing. Added to that, the Ethiopian Commissioner of Police was anxious to question them. They had to make sure that they did not implicate Mek Nimmur in the killing of Boris Brusilov, and at the same time they must not alert or alarm Pegasus in any way. They realized that the reaction from that quarter would be swift and probably lethal if they gave the least suspicion that they knew who the other players were in Taita's game.

Most of all they must avoid antagonizing the Ethiopian authorities, or give them any cause to cancel their visas and declare them to be undesirable immigrants. They agreed to feign ignorance and play the role of innocents caught up in affairs which they had not precipitated and which they did not understand.

By the time that they landed at Addis Ababa they had prepared their story and rehearsed it thoroughly. As soon as the Cessna pulled on to the hardstand in front of the airport buildings and the pilot cut the engine, Geoffrey came back to life again, only a little green around the gills, and handed Royan down the aircraft steps with a flourish.

'Of course, you will stay at the residence,' he told them. 'The hotels in town are too dreadful to contemplate, and HE has a half-decent chef and a passable wine cellar. I will rustle up some togs for both of you. My missus is about the same size as you, Dr Al Simma, and Nicky will fit into my gear at a pinch. Thank God, I have a spare dinner jacket. HE is a bit of a stickler for form.'

The British Ambassador's residence had been built during the reign of the old Emperor, Haile Selassie, before Mussolini's invasion in the 1930s. Set on the outskirts of the town, it was an example of the better colonial architecture, with a thatched roof and wide verandas. The lawns, tended by a host of gardeners, were wide and green, contrasting with the brilliant crimson of the poinsettia. The mansion had survived both the revolution and the war of liberation that followed.

At the front entrance Geoffrey handed them over to an Ethiopian butler in a long, spotlessly white *shamma*, who showed them to adjoining bedrooms on the second floor. Nicholas heard the bathwater running in Royan's suite next door as he lay in his own brimming bath, sipping a whisky and soda and twiddling the taps with his big toe. Then there was the murmur of the doctor's voice from next door as he attended to Royan's knee.

Geoffrey's dinner jacket was loose round his waist and too short in the arms and legs, and his shoes pinched, added to which Nicholas was in need of a haircut, he realized, as he surveyed himself in the mirror.

'No help for it, now,' he decided with resignation, and went to knock on Royan's door.

'I say!' he exclaimed as she opened it. Sylvia Tennant had loaned her a lime-green cocktail dress that set off Royan's olive skin marvellously well. Royan had washed her hair and left it loose on her shoulders. He felt his pulse accelerate like a teenager on his first date, and laughed at himself.

'You look absolutely scrumptious,' he told her, and meant it.

'Thank you, sir,' she laughed back at him, 'and you look very dashing yourself. May I take your arm?'

'I was hoping to carry you. Addictive activity.'

'Those days are over,' she told him, and brandished the carved ebony walking-stick with which the butler had provided her. She used it on her bad side. As they started down the long corridor, she asked in a whisper, 'What is the name of our host?'

'Her Britannic Majesty's Ambassador, Sir Oliver Bradford KCMG.'

'Which stands for Knight Commander of St Michael and St George, right?' she asked.

'No,' he corrected her, 'it stands for Kindly Call Me God.'

'You are impossible!' She giggled, and then became serious. 'Did you manage to send the fax to Mrs Street?'

'It went through at the first attempt and she acknowledged. Sends you her salaams, and promises to have some information about Pegasus double pronto.'

It was a mild evening and Sir Oliver was waiting to greet them on the veranda. Geoffrey hurried forward to make the introductions. The Ambassador had a bush of white hair and a red face. Geoffrey had warned them about him and his view on troublesome tourists, but his hostile frown started to fade as soon as he laid eyes on Royan.

There were a dozen other guests for dinner apart from Geoffrey and Sylvia Tennant, and Sir Oliver took Royan's arm and led her around the group introducing her. Nicholas trailed along behind them, resigned by now to the fact that Royan had that effect on most men.

'May I present General Obeid, the Commissioner of Police,' Sir Oliver said. The head of the Ethiopian police force was tall and very dark-complexioned, suave and elegant in his blue mess uniform. He bowed over Royan's hand.

'I believe that we have an appointment to meet tomorrow morning. I look forward to that with the keenest pleasure.'

Royan glanced at Sir Oliver uncertainly. She had been told nothing of this.

'General Obeid wants to know from you and Sir Nicholas a little more about this business in the Abbay gorge,' Sir Oliver explained. 'I took the liberty of having my secretary make the appointment.'

'Just a routine interview, I assure you both, Dr Al Simma and Sir Nicholas. I will take up very little of your time, I promise you that.'

'Of course we will do everything that we can to assist you,' Nicholas told him politely. 'What time are we coming to see you?'

'I believe we are meeting at eleven in the morning, if that suits you.'

'A most civilized hour,' Nicholas agreed.

'My driver will pick you up at ten-thirty, and take you down to police headquarters,' Sir Oliver promised.

At the dinner table Royan was seated between Sir Oliver and General Obeid. She was pretty and charming, and both men were attentive. Nicholas realized that he would have to become accustomed to sharing her company with other men; he had had her to himself for much too long.

For his own part, Nicholas found Lady Bradford at the other end of the table rather heavy-going. She was a second wife, thirty years younger than her husband, with a pronounced London accent and an even more pronounced common streak, with a mane of dyed blonde hair and an improbable bust which overflowed her sequined *décolletage*. An old man's folly, Nicholas concluded. It appeared that she had made herself an expert on the genealogy of the English aristocracy – in other words she was an arrant snob. She questioned him closely on his antecedents, insisting on going back several generations.

In the end she called to her husband down the table, 'Sir Nicholas owns Quenton Park. Did you know that, dear?' And then she turned back to Nicholas. 'My husband is a very keen shot.'

Sir Oliver looked suitably impressed by his wife's intelligence. 'Quenton Park, hey? I read an article in the *Shooting Times* the other day. You have a drive there called the "High Beeches". Is that right?'

'The "High Larches",' Nicholas corrected him.

'Some of the best birds in Britain. That's what they said,' Sir Oliver enthused, looking eager and expectant.

'I don't know about that,' Nicholas protested modestly. 'But we are rather proud of them. You must come and have a shot at them next time you are home – as my guest, of course.'

From that moment Sir Oliver's attitude towards Nicholas altered dramatically. He became affable and solicitous, even going so far as to send the butler to fetch a bottle of the 1954 Lafite.

'You have made a good impression,' Geoffrey murmured wryly. 'HE doesn't waste the 1954 on anybody but the chosen few.'

It was after midnight when Nicholas was at last able to escape from his hostess and rescue Royan from Sir Oliver and General Obeid. He led her away, supporting her as she limped along fetchingly at his side, avoiding Geoffrey Tennant's knowing and speculative gaze until they had negotiated the first landing of the staircase.

'Well, you were definitely the star of the evening,' he told her.

'You had Lady Bradford purring like a cat,' she counter-attacked, and he was delighted to hear the faint tone of possessive jealousy in her voice. He had not been the only one.

At her door she solved any problems by offering him her cheek, and he kissed it chastely.

'Those bosoms!' she murmured. 'Don't have nightmares about them.' And she closed the door behind her.

He felt quite jaunty as he went to his own room, but as he opened the door he saw the envelope lying at the threshold. During dinner, one of the servants must have pushed it under the door. Quickly he tore open the flap of the envelope and unfolded the pages that it contained. His expression changed as he scanned through them, and he left the bedroom and went back to tap on Royan's door.

After a moment she opened it a crack, and peeped out at him. He saw the confusion in her eyes, and he hurried to allay her suspicions.

'Reply to my fax.' He showed her the sheaf of papers. 'Are you decent?'

'One moment.' She closed the door, and opened it again only seconds later. 'Come in,' she said.

She indicated the decanter on the cabinet. 'Would you like a nightcap?'

'I think I need one. We know who runs Pegasus now.'

'Tell me!' she ordered, but he took his time pouring a Scotch, and then smiled at her over his shoulder. 'How about a soda water for you?'

'Damn you, Nicholas Quenton-Harper.' She stamped her stockinged foot. 'Don't you dare torment me. Who is it?'

'When I first met you, you were a dutiful little Arab girl. One who realized the superiority of the male species. Listen to you now. I think I have spoiled you.'

'I think I should warn you that you are flirting with disaster.' She tried to suppress her smile. 'Tell me, please, Nicky.'

'Sit down,' he ordered, and took the armchair facing her. He unfolded the fax and then looked up at her. 'Mrs Street has worked fast. In my fax, I suggested that she rang my stockbroker in the city. We are three hours ahead of Greenwich Mean Time, so it seems that she must have caught him before he left his office. Anyway, she has all the information I asked for.'

'Stop it, Nicky, or I will tear my bodice and scream and cause a scandal. Tell me!'

He rustled the pages, and then read. 'Pegasus Exploration is registered on the Sydney Stock Exchange in Australia with a share capital of twenty million—'

'Don't go through all the details,' she pleaded. 'Just name the man.'

'Sixty-five per cent of the shares in Pegasus are owned by Valhalla Mining Company,' he continued imperturbably, 'and the remaining thirty-five per cent are owned by Anaconda Metals of Austria.'

She had given up pleading with him and sat forward in her chair, watching him with a fixed gaze.

'Both Valhalla and Anaconda are fully-owned subsidiaries of HMI, Hamburg Manufacturing Industries. All the shares in HMI are owned by the von Schiller family trust, the sole trustees of which are Gotthold Ernst von Schiller and his wife, Ingemar.'

'Von Schiller,' she repeated softly, still staring at him. 'Duraid had him on his list of possible sponsors. He must have read the Wilbur Smith book – I know it has been translated into German. He probably contacted Duraid just the way that you did. But he was not put off as easily as you were by Duraid's denials.'

'That's the way I read it also,' Nicholas nodded. 'It would have been easy to sniff around the Cairo museum, and find that Duraid and you were working on something big. The rest of it we know only too well.'

'But how did he move Pegasus into Ethiopia so quickly?' she demanded.

'That must have been a stroke of luck on von Schiller's side – the luck of the devil. Geoffrey tells me that Pegasus obtained a concession to prospect for copper from President Mengistu five years ago, just before he was ousted. Von Schiller was already in place, even before he heard about the scrolls. All it involved was moving the base camp down from the north where they were working and relocating it on the escarpment of the Abbay gorge, to be ready to take advantage of any fresh developments. We will probably find that Jake Helm is one of his heavies, his dirty tricks specialist that he sends to any of his trouble spots around the world. It's apparent that he has Nogo in his pocket. We waltzed right into their arms.'

Royan looked thoughtful. 'It all makes sense. As soon as Helm reported our arrival to his master, von Schiller must have ordered him to set up the *shufta* raid on our camp. Oh, sweet heaven, I hate him. I have never laid eyes on him, but I hate him more than I thought I was capable of hating anything or anybody.'

'Well, at least we know now who we are dealing with.'

'Not altogether,' she demurred. 'Von Schiller must have had a man in Cairo. Somebody on the inside there.'

'What is the name of your minister?' Nicholas wanted to know.

'No,' she denied it instantly. 'Not Atalan Abou Sin. I have known him all my life. He is a tower of integrity.'

'It's amazing what effect a bribe of a hundred thousand dollars or so can have on the foundations of even the best-constructed tower,' Nicholas observed quietly, and she looked stricken.

They were the only two at breakfast. Sir Oliver had left for his office an hour earlier, and Lady Bradford had not yet risen to greet the clear, cool highland morning.

'I hardly slept last night, thinking about Atalan. Oh, Nicky, I can't bear even the suspicion that he might be involved in Duraid's murder.'

'Sorry if I gave you a rough night, but we have to consider all the angles,' he tried to soothe her, and then changed the subject. 'We have wasted enough time here. Pegasus have got a clear run of the field at the moment. I want to get back home, and start putting together our own expeditionary force for the return.'

'Would you like me to get on to the airline and make our reservations?' She stood up immediately. 'I will go off and find a phone.'

'Finish your breakfast first.'

'I have had all I want.' She made for the door, and he called after her.

'No wonder you are so skinny. They tell me anorexia nervosa is a rotten way to go.' And he helped himself to another slice of toast and marmalade.

She was back within fifteen minutes. 'Tomorrow afternoon at three-thirty. Kenya Airways to Nairobi, connecting the same evening with British Airways to Heathrow.'

'Well done.' He wiped his mouth on his napkin, and stood up. 'Our car is waiting to take us down to police headquarters to speak to your new admirer, General Obeid. Let's go.'

There was a police officer waiting to meet them and

usher them into the headquarters building, through the private entrance. He introduced himself as Inspector Galla and treated them with the greatest deference as he led them through to the Commissioner's suite.

General Obeid rose to his feet as soon as they entered his office, and came around his desk to greet them. He was charming and affable, fussing over Royan as he led them through to his private sitting room. Once they were seated, Inspector Galla poured the inevitable tiny bowls of bitter black coffee.

After a polite interval of small talk the general came directly to the business in hand. 'As I promised, I won't detain you longer than is absolutely necessary. Inspector Galla here will be recording your statements. Firstly I would like to deal with the disappearance and death of Major Brusilov. I presume you are aware that he was formerly an officer in the Russian KGB?'

The interview lasted much longer than they had expected. General Obeid was thorough, but unfailingly polite. Finally he had their statements typed out by a police stenographer, and after they had read and signed them, the general walked with them as far as the entrance where their car was waiting. Nicholas recognized this as a mark of special favour.

'If there is anything I can do for you, anything that you need, please do not hesitate to call upon me. It has been a great pleasure meeting you, Dr Al Simma. You must come back to Ethiopia and visit us again soon.'

'Despite our little misadventure, I have thoroughly enjoyed your beautiful country,' she told him sweetly. 'You may see us again sooner than you expect.'

'What a charming man,' she remarked, as they settled into the back seat of Sir Oliver's Rolls. 'I really like him.'

'It would seem to be mutual,' said Nicholas.

oyan's words were prophetic. There were identical envelopes addressed to each of them lying at their places on the dining-room table the next morning when they came down to breakfast.

Nicholas opened his as he ordered coffee from the waiter in his ankle-length *shamma*, and his expression changed as he read the note.

'Hello!' he exclaimed. 'We made an even bigger impression on the boys in blue than we realized. General Obeid wants to see me again.' He read aloud from the note, '"You are ordered to present yourself at police headquarters at or before noon."' Nicholas whistled softly. 'Strong language. No please or thank you.'

'Mine is identical.' Royan glanced at the note on an official police letterhead. 'What on earth do you suppose it means?'

'We will find out soon enough,' Nicholas promised her. 'But it sounds a little ominous. Methinks the love affair is over.'

This morning, when they arrived at police headquarters, there was no reception committee to welcome them. The guard at the private entrance sent them around to the general charge office, where they were involved in a long, confused discussion with the desk officer, who had only a rudimentary knowledge of English. From previous experience in Africa Nicholas knew better than to lose his temper, or even to let his irritation show. Finally the desk officer held a long whispered telephone conversation with some unknown person, at the end of which he waved them airily towards a hard wooden bench against the far wall.

'You wait. Man come soon.'

For the next forty minutes they shared their seat with a colourful selection of other supplicants, applicants, complainants and petty criminals. One or two of them were bleeding copiously from assault by persons unknown, and yet others were in manacles.

'It seems our star is on the wane,' Nicholas remarked as he held a handkerchief to his nose. It was obvious that some of his neighbours had not had a close acquaintance with soap and water for some time. 'No more VIP treatment.'

At the end of forty minutes Inspector Galla, he who had treated them so deferentially the day before, looked over the partition and beckoned to them in a high-handed fashion.

He ignored Nicholas's outstretched right hand and led them through to one of the back rooms. There he did not offer them a seat but addressed Nicholas coldly. 'You are responsible for the loss of a firearm that was in your possession.'

'That is correct. As I explained to you in my statement yesterday—'

Inspector Galla cut him off. 'The loss of a firearm due to negligence is a very serious offence,' he said severely.

'There was no negligence on my part,' Nicholas denied.

'You left the firearm unguarded. You made no attempt to lock it in a steel safe. That is negligence.'

'With respect, Inspector, there is a notable dearth of steel safes in the Abbay gorge.'

'Negligence,' Galla repeated. 'Criminal negligence. How are we to know that the weapon has not fallen into the hands of elements opposed to the government?'

'You mean some unknown person may overthrow the government with a 275 Rigby?' Nicholas smiled.

Inspector Galla ignored the sally, and produced two documents from the drawer of his desk. 'It is my duty to serve these deportation orders on both you and Dr Al Simma. You have twenty-four hours to leave Ethiopia, and thereafter you will be considered to be prohibited immigrants, both of you.'

'Dr Al Simma has not lost any weapons,' Nicholas pointed out mildly. 'In fact as far as I am aware, she has never been even mildly negligent in her entire life.' And again his comment was ignored.

'Please sign here to acknowledge that you have received and understood the orders.'

'I would like to speak to General Obeid, the Commissioner of Police,' said Nicholas.

'General Obeid left this morning for an inspection tour of the northern frontier districts. He will not return to Addis Ababa for some weeks.'

'By which time we will be safely back in England?'

'Exactly.' Inspector Galla smiled for the first time, a thin, wintry smirk. 'Please sign here, and here.'

'What happened?' Royan demanded, as the driver opened the door of the Rolls for her and she settled into the seat beside Nicholas. 'It was all so sudden and unexpected. One moment everybody loved us, and the next we are being booted down the stairs.'

'Do you want my guess?' Nicholas asked, and then went on without waiting for her reply. 'Nogo is not the only one in Pegasus's back pocket. Overnight Obeid has been in contact with von Schiller, and received his orders.'

'Do you realize what this means, Nicky? It means that we will not be able to return to Ethiopia. That puts the tomb of Mamose beyond our grasp.' She stared at him with large dark eyes full of dismay.

'When Duraid and I visited Iraq and Libya, neither of us had letters of invitation from either Saddam or Gadaffi, as I recall.'

'You look delighted at the prospect of breaking the law,' she accused. 'You are smirking all over your face.'

'After all, it is only Ethiopian law,' he pointed out virtuously. 'Not to be taken too seriously.'

'And it will be an Ethiopian prison they toss you into. That you can take seriously.'

'You too,' he grinned, 'if they catch us.'

'Y ou can be certain that HE has already registered a formal complaint with the President's office,' Geoffrey told them as he drove them to the airport the next day. 'He is most upset at the whole business, I can tell you. Deportation orders and all that rot. Never heard the likes.'

'Don't fuss yourself, old boy,' Nicholas told him. 'As it is, neither of us intends coming back here again. No harm done.'

'It's the principle of the thing. Prominent British subject being treated like a common criminal. No respect shown.' He sighed. 'Sometimes I wish I had been born a hundred years ago. We wouldn't have to put up with this sort of nonsense. Just send a gunboat.'

'Quite so, Geoffrey, but please don't let it upset you.'

Geoffrey hovered around them like a cat with kittens while they checked in at the Kenya Airways counter. They had only their hand luggage, two small cheap nylon holdalls that they had bought that morning at a street market. Nicholas had rolled his dik-dik skin into a ball and wrapped it in an embroidered *shamma* that he had purchased in the same market.

Geoffrey waited with them until their flight was called and waved to them after they passed through the barrier, aiming this affectionate display more at Royan than Nicholas.

They had been allocated seats behind the wing, and Royan was beside the window. The Kenya Airways plane started its engines and began to taxi slowly past the airport buildings. Nicholas was arguing with a stewardess who wanted him to stow his precious dik-dik skin in its purple nylon bag in the overhead locker, while Royan peered out of the porthole beside her for her last glimpse of Addis during take-off.

Suddenly Royan stiffened in her seat, and while still gazing out of the window reached across and seized Nicholas's arm.

'Look!' she hissed with such venom in her tone that he leaned across her to see what had excited her.

'Pegasus!' she exclaimed, and pointed to the Falcon executive jet that had just taxied in and parked at the far end of the airport buildings. The small, sleek aircraft was painted green and on its tall tail fin the scarlet horse reared on its hind legs in that stylized pose. While they watched through the window, the door in the fuselage of the green Falcon was lowered, and a small reception committee waiting on the tarmac pressed forward expectantly to greet the passengers as they appeared in the doorway of the jet.

The first of these was a small man, neatly dressed in a cream tropical suit and a white panama straw hat. Despite his size he exuded an air of confidence and command, that special aura of power. His face was pale, as though he had come from a northern winter, and it looked incongruous in this setting. His jaw was firm and stubborn, his nose prominent and his gaze beneath dark beetling eyebrows penetrating.

Nicholas recognized him immediately. He had seen him often enough on the auction floors at Sotheby's and Christie's. This man was not the type of person whom anyone would forget in a hurry.

'Von Schiller!' he exclaimed, as the German surveyed with an imperial gaze the men who waited on the tarmac below him.

'He looks like a bantam rooster,' Royan murmured, 'or a standing cobra.'

Von Schiller raised his panama hat and ran down the

steps of the Falcon with a light, athletic tread, and Nicholas said quietly, 'You wouldn't think that he is almost seventy.'

'He moves like a man of forty,' Royan agreed. 'He must dye his hair and eyebrows – see how dark they are.'

'My oath!' Nicholas was startled. 'Look who is here to greet him.'

There was the glint of sunlight on decorations and regimental insignia. A tall figure in blue uniform detached itself from the welcoming group and touched the shiny patent-leather brim of his cap in a respectful salute, before taking von Schiller's hand and shaking it cordially.

'Your erstwhile admirer, General Obeid. No wonder he could not meet us yesterday. He was much too busy.'

'Look, Nicky,' Royan gasped. She was no longer watching the pair at the foot of the steps, who were still clasping hands as they chatted with animation. Her whole attention was focused on the top of the steps of the Falcon jet, where another, younger, man had appeared. He was bare-headed, and Nicholas had the impression of sallow skin and dense, dark, wavy hair.

'Never seen him in my life before. Who is he?' Nicholas asked her.

'Nahoot Guddabi. Duraid's assistant from the museum. The man who now has his job.'

As Nahoot started down the steps of the Falcon their own aircraft trundled on down the tarmac, then swung out on to the main taxi-way and blocked any further view of the gathering beside the Pegasus jet. Both of them fell back in their seats and stared at each other for a long moment. Nicholas recovered his voice first.

'A witches' sabbath. A convocation of the ugly ones. We were lucky to witness it. There are no more secrets now. We know very clearly who the opposition is.'

'Von Schiller is the puppet-master,' she agreed, breathless with anger and horror. 'But Nahoot Guddabi is his hunting dog. Nahoot must be the one who hired the killers in Cairo and turned them loose on us. Oh God, Nicky, you should have heard him at the funeral, going on about how much he admired and respected Duraid. The filthy, murderous hypocrite!'

They were both silent until the aircraft had taken off and climbed to cruise altitude, then Royan said quietly, 'Of course, you were right about Obeid. He is deep in von Schiller's pocket also.'

'He may simply have been acting as the representative of the Ethiopian government, paying respect to a major foreign concession-holder, somebody who they hope is going to discover fabulous copper deposits in their poverty-stricken country and make them all rich.'

She shook her head firmly. 'If it was as simple as that, it would be one of the cabinet ministers meeting him, not the chief of police. No, Obeid has the stink of treachery on him, just the same as Nahoot.'

Seeing her husband's killers in the flesh had reopened the half-healed wounds of Royan's grief and mourning. These bitter emotions were a flame that was burning her up, like the bushfire in the trunk of a hollow forest tree, consuming her from within. Nicholas knew that he could not quench that flame, that he could only hope to distract her for a while. He talked to her quietly, turning her dark thoughts away from death and vengeance to the challenge of Taita's game and the riddle of the lost tomb.

By the time that they had changed planes at Nairobi and landed at Heathrow the following morning, the two of them had sketched out a plan of action for their return to the Nile gorge and the exploration of Taita's pool in the chasm. But although now Royan appeared on the surface to be her usual calm and cheerful self once again, Nicholas knew that the pain of her loss was still there beneath the surface.

They landed at Heathrow so early that they walked through the immigration gates without running into a queue, and since they had no bags in the hold they did not have to play the customary game of roulette at the luggage carousel – will they arrive or won't they?

Carrying the dik-dik skin in the nylon bag under his arm, and with Royan limping on her cane on his other arm, Nicholas sauntered through the green channel of HM Customs, as innocent as a cherub from the roof of the Sistine Chapel.

'You are so brazen,' she whispered to him once they were through and clear. 'If you can lie so convincingly to Customs, how can I ever trust you again?'

Their luck held. There was no queue at the taxi rank, and in a little over an hour after touch-down the taxi deposited them on the pavement outside Nicholas's town house in Knightsbridge. It was only eight-thirty on a Monday morning.

While Royan showered, Nicholas went down to the corner shop under an umbrella to fetch some groceries. Then they shared the task of cooking breakfast, Royan taking care of the toast while Nicholas whipped up his speciality, a herb omelette.

'Surely you're going to need expert help when we go back to the Abbay gorge?' Royan observed, as she let the butter melt into the hot toast.

'I already have the right man in mind. I have worked with him before,' he told her. 'Ex-Royal Engineers. Expert in diving and underwater construction. Retired and living in a little cottage in Devon. I suspect he is a little short of the ready, and bored out of his considerable mind. I expect him to jump at any opportunity to alleviate either condition.'

As soon as they had finished breakfast, Nicholas told her, 'I will do the dishes. You take the films of the stele to be developed. There is a one-hour service at the branch of Boots opposite Harrods.'

'That's what I call a fair distribution of labour,' she remarked with a long-suffering air. 'You have a dishwasher, and it's raining again outside.'

'All right,' he laughed. 'To sweeten the pill, I'll lend you my raincoat. While you are waiting for the films to be developed you can go shopping to replace the togs you lost in the rock-fall. I have some crucial phone calls to make.'

As soon as she had left, Nicholas settled at his desk with a notepad at one hand and the telephone at the other. His first call was to Quenton Park, where Mrs Street tried not to show how delighted she was to have him home.

'Your desk is about two feet deep with mail awaiting your return. It's mostly bills.'

'Cheerful, aren't we?'

'The lawyers have been pestering me, and Mr Markham from Lloyd's has been ringing every day.'

'Don't tell any of them that I am back, there's a good girl.' Nicholas knew exactly what they wanted from him – the same thing that persistent callers always wanted: money. In this case it was not simply five hundred guineas for an overdue tailor's bill, but two and a half million pounds. 'It's probably better if I stay in York, rather than at Quenton,' he told Mrs Street. 'They won't be able to find me at the flat.'

He pushed his debts to the back of his mind, and concentrated on the task at hand. 'Have you got your pencil and notepad ready? All right, here's what I want you to do.'

It took him ten minutes to finish his dictation, and then Mrs Street read it back to him. 'Okay. Get on with it, will you. We'll be back this evening. Dr Al Simma will be staying indefinitely. Ask the housekeeper to prepare the second bedroom for her at the flat.'

Next he rang the number in Devon, and while the

phone rang he imagined the converted coastguard's cottage on top of the cliffs overlooking a grey, storm-whipped winter sea. Daniel Webb was probably in his workshop in the back garden, either tinkering with his 1935 Jaguar, the great love of his life, or tying salmon flies. Fishing was his other passion, the one that had originally brought them together.

'Hello?' Daniel's voice was guarded and suspicious. Nicholas could imagine him, his bald head freckled like a plover's egg, gripping the telephone with a hairy, work-scarred fist.

'Sapper, I have a job for you. Are you a starter?'

'Where are we headed, Major?' Although it had been three years, he recognized Nicholas's voice instantly.

'Sunny climes and dancing girls. Same pay as the last time.'

'I'm a starter. Where do we meet?'

'At the flat. You remember it from last time. Tomorrow. Bring your slide rule.' Nicholas knew that Danny put no store by these new-fangled pocket computers.

'The Jag is still in good nick. I'll leave early and be there for lunch tomorrow.'

Nicholas hung up, and then made two more calls: one to his Jersey bank, and the other to the Cayman Islands. The funds in both his emergency accounts were running low. His budget for the expedition that he had worked out with Royan on the flight was two hundred and thirty thousand. Like all budgets, he knew that it was optimistic.

'Always add fifty per cent,' he warned himself. 'Which means that the cupboard will be bare by the time we are finished. Let's hope and pray that you are not pulling our legs, Taita.'

He gave the passwords to the respective bank accountants and instructed them to make transfers into his holding accounts, ready to draw on immediately.

There were two more calls he had to make before they

left for York. The fate of all their plans hung on them, and the contacts that he had for both of them were at the best tenuous, and at the worst chimerical.

The first number was engaged. He rang it five times more, and on each occasion got the irritating high-pitched busy tone in his ear. He tried one last time and was answered by a reassuring west country accent.

'Good afternoon. British Embassy. How may I help you?' Nicholas glanced at his wrist-watch. There was a three-hour time difference. Of course, it would be afternoon in Addis.

'This is Sir Nicholas Quenton-Harper calling from the UK. Is Mr Geoffrey Tennant, your military attaché, available, please?'

Geoffrey came on the line almost immediately. 'My dear boy. So you made it all the way home. Lucky you.'

'Just thought I would set your mind at rest. Knew you would be losing sleep.'

'How is the charming Dr Al Simma?'

'She sends her love.'

'I wish I could believe you.' Geoffrey sighed dramatically.

'Big favour, Geoff. Do you know a Colonel Maryam Kidane at the Ministry of Defence?'

'First-rate chap,' Geoffrey affirmed immediately. 'Know him well. Played tennis with him last Saturday, actually. Demon back-hand.'

'Please ask him to contact me urgently.' He gave Geoffrey the telephone number of the flat in York. 'Tell him it's in connection with a rare breed of Ethiopian swallow for the museum collection.'

'Up to your shenanigans again, Nicky. Not enough that you get slung out of Ethiopia on your ear. Now you are trading in rare birds. Probably CITES Schedule One. Endangered species.'

'Will you do it for me, Geoff?'

'Of course. Serve to Lead, old boy. Always the sucker.'

'I owe you one.'

'More than one. Half a dozen, more like it.'

He had less success with his next call. International Enquiries gave him a number in Malta. On his first attempt he received an encouraging ringing tone.

'Pick it up, Jannie,' he pleaded in a whisper, but on the sixth ring an answering machine cut in.

'You have reached the head office of Africair Services. There is nobody available to take your call at the moment. Please leave your name and number and a short message after the tone. We will get back to you as soon as possible. Thank you.' Jannie Badenhorst's rich South African accent was unmistakable.

'Jannie. This is Nicholas Quenton-Harper. Is that broken-down old Herc of yours still airworthy? This job should be a lark. What's more, the money is good. Call me at the flat in the UK. No hurry. Yesterday, or the day before, will do just fine.'

Royan rang the doorbell a minute after he finished the last call, and he ran down the stairs.

'Your timing is impeccable,' he told her as she came in with the end of her nose pink with cold, shaking the raindrops off the coat he had lent her. 'Did you get the films developed?'

She pulled the yellow packet out of the coat pocket and brandished it triumphantly.

'You are a master photographer,' she told him. 'They have turned out perfectly. I can read every character on the stele with the naked eye. We are back in Taita's game again.'

They spread the glossy photographs across his desktop and gloated over them.

'You have had duplicates made? A set for each of us.

Excellent,' Nicholas approved. 'The negatives will go into the safe deposit box at my bank. We won't take a chance on losing them the second time around.'

Using his large magnifying glass, Royan studied each of the prints in turn, and she picked out the clearest shot of each of the four sides of the stele.

'These will be our working copies. I don't think we are really going to miss the rubbings that we lifted from the stone. These should suffice.' She read aloud a snippet from one of the blocks of hieroglyphics. '"*The cobra uncoils and lifts his jewelled hood. The stars of morning shine within his eyes. Three times his black and slippery tongue kisses the air.*"' She was flushed with excitement. 'I wonder what Taita is telling us with that verse. Oh, Nicky, it's so exciting to be unravelling the mysteries again!'

'Leave it alone now,' he ordered sternly. 'I know you. Once you start, we'll be here all night. Let's get the Range Rover packed up. It's a long, hard haul up to York, and there is an AA warning of black ice on the motorway. A bit of a change from the weather in the Abbay gorge.'

She straightened up and shuffled the prints into a neat pile. 'You are right. Sometimes I do tend to get carried away.' She stood up. 'Before we go, may I make a phone call home?'

'By home, I take it that you mean Cairo?'

'Sorry. Yes, to Cairo. Duraid's family—'

'Please! No need to explain. There is the phone. Help yourself. I'll be waiting downstairs in the kitchen when you are finished. We both need a cup of tea before we get going.'

She came down into the kitchen half an hour later looking guilty, and told him directly, 'I am afraid that I am going to be a nuisance again. I have a confession to make.'

'Spit it out,' he invited.

'I have to go back home – to Cairo,' she said, and he looked at her startled. 'Just for a few days,' she qualified hurriedly. 'I was speaking to Duraid's brother. There are some of Duraid's affairs that I have to see to.'

'I don't like you going back there on your own,' he shook his head, 'after your last experiences.'

'If our theory is correct, and Nahoot Guddabi was the danger, then he is in Ethiopia now. I should be quite safe.'

'Still, I don't like it. You are the key to Taita's game.'

'Thank you kindly, sir,' she said with mock outrage. 'Is that the only reason you don't want me bumped off?'

'If forced into a corner, I may admit that I have also grown rather partial to having you around.'

'I'll be back before you know I've even gone. Besides which, you will have plenty to keep you busy while I am away.'

'I don't suppose that I can stop you,' he grumbled. 'When do you plan to leave?'

'There's a flight at eight this evening.'

'A bit sudden. I mean, we have only just arrived.' He made one last feeble protest, then capitulated. 'I will run you out to the airport.'

'No, Nicky. Heathrow is out of your way. I can catch the train.'

'I insist.'

On a Monday evening the traffic was reasonably light and, once they had cleared the main built-up area, they made good time. The journey was further lightened by their animated discussion as he related the contents of the phone calls he had made in her absence.

'Through Maryam Kidane, I hope to be in contact with Mek Nimmur again pretty soon. Mek is the kingpin of the whole plan. Without him we can't even make the first move on Taita's bao board.'

He dropped her off at the departures entrance at Heathrow. 'Phone me tomorrow morning from Cairo to let me know you are all right, and when you are coming back. I'll be at the flat.'

'Reversed charges,' she warned him as she offered him her cheek to kiss. Then she slid across the seat and slammed the door behind her.

He watched her waiflike figure in the rear-view mirror as he pulled away, and he was filled with melancholy and a sense of loss. Then quite suddenly he was aware of a new sensation of disquiet. His early-warning bells were jangling. Something unpleasant was afoot. Something nasty was about to happen when she reached Egypt. Another dangerous beast had escaped from its cage and was prowling the darkness waiting its opportunity to pounce, but it was still too early for him to discern its colour or shape.

'Please don't let anything happen to her,' he spoke aloud, but he did not know to whom his plea was addressed. He thought of turning back and making her stay with him, but he had no rights in the matter, and he knew she would not obey him. Short of physical force, there was no way he could impose his will upon her. He had to let her go.

'But I don't like it one little bit,' he reaffirmed.

His private secretary, and the other men who worked for him, knew exactly what he expected of them. Everything was as he required it. Gotthold von Schiller looked around the interior of the Quonset hut with approval. Helm had done well in the time that he had been given to prepare the base for his boss's arrival.

His own private quarters occupied half the long portable building. They were spartan, but sterilely clean and neat. His clothes hung in the cupboard and his cosmetics and medicines were set out in the bathroom cabinet. His private kitchen was fully equipped and stocked with provisions. His own Chinese chef had flown out in the Falcon with him, bringing everything with him that he needed to provide the meals that his master demanded.

Von Schiller was a vegetarian, a non-smoker and a teetotaller. Twenty years ago he had been a famous trencherman who loved the hearty food of the Black Forest, the wines of the Rhine valley and the rich dark tobaccos of Cuba. In those days he had been obese, with rolls of chin sagging over his collar. Now, despite his age, he was as lean and fit and vital as a racing greyhound.

In the autumn of his life, the pleasures were of the mind and the emotions, more than of the physical senses. He placed a higher value on inanimate objects than on living creatures, either human or animal. A piece of stone carved by masons who had been dead for thousands of years could excite him more than the soft warm body of the most lovely young woman. He loved order and control. Power over men and events sustained him more than did the taste of food. Power and the possession of beautiful and unique objects were his passions, now that his body was running down and his animal appetites were losing their zest.

Every item of all that vast and priceless collection of ancient treasures that he had already assembled had been discovered by other men. This was his chance, his very last chance to make his own discovery, to break the seals on the door of a Pharaoh's tomb and be the first man in four thousand years to gaze upon the contents. Perhaps that was his real hope for immortality, and there was no price in gold and human life he was not fully prepared to pay for it. Already men had died in this passion of his, and he cared not that there would be other sacrifices. No price was too high.

He checked his image in the full-length mirror that hung on the wall opposite his bed. He smoothed the thick, coarse, dark hair. Of course it was dyed, but that was one of his few remaining conceits. Then he crossed the uncarpeted wooden floor of his own quarters, and opened the door into the long conference room which would be his headquarters over the days to come.

The persons seated there rose to their feet immediately, their attitudes servile and their expressions obsequious. Von Schiller strode to the head of the long table and stepped up on to the block of wood covered with carpeting that his private secretary had placed there for him. This block went everywhere with him. It was nine inches high. From this elevation von Schiller looked down upon the men and one woman who waited for him. He looked them over unhurriedly, letting them stand a while. From the vantage point of his block, he was taller than any of them.

First he looked at Helm. The Texan had worked for him for over a decade. Completely reliable, he was strong both physically and mentally and would follow orders without question or qualms. Von Schiller had come to rely on him. He could send him anywhere in the world, from Zaïre to Queensland, from the Arctic Circle to the steaming equatorial forests, and Helm would get the job done with the minimum of fuss and with very few unpleasant consequences. He was ruthless but discreet, and like a good hunting dog he knew his master.

From Helm he looked at the woman. Utte Kemper was his private secretary. She ordered and directed the details of his life, from his food to his block, from his medicine to his social calendar, No man or woman was ever received into his presence without her prior arrangement. She was also his communications expert. The mass of electronic equipment that occupied one wall of the hut was her preserve. Utte was able to find her way through the ether with the infallible instinct of a homing pigeon. From the archaic art of the keyboard and Morse code to burst transmissions and random switching he had never known another person, male or female, who could match her wizardry. She was at that perfect age for a woman, forty, slim and blonde, with slanting green eyes over high cheekbones, resembling the young Dietrich.

Von Schiller's own wife, Ingemar, had been an invalid for the last twenty years, and Utte Kemper had stepped into the void she had left in his life. Yet she was more than either secretary or wife to him.

When he had first met Utte, she had been holding a very senior position in the technical section of the German national telecommunications network, and moonlighting as a pornographic actress – not for the money but for love of the job. Copies of the videos she had made at that time were amongst von Schiller's most precious possessions, after his collection of Egyptian antiquities. Like Helm, she had no qualms. There was nothing she would not do to him, or allow him to do to her, to fulfil his most bizarre fantasies. When he watched her videos and she did some of these things to him, she was the only woman who could still bring him to orgasm. Yet even this happened less frequently with every month that passed, and each time the spasms of sexual release she could evoke from his aging body were less intense.

Utte had her recording equipment set up before her on the table. It was part of her multifarious duties to keep accurate and complete records of every meeting and conversation. Then von Schiller looked past these two trusted employees to the two other men standing at the table.

Colonel Nogo he had met for the first time that morning, as he stepped down from the Jet Ranger helicopter that had flown them down from Addis Ababa to the base camp here on the summit of the escarpment of the Nile gorge. He knew very little about him, except that Helm had selected him, and was so far satisfied with his performance. Von Schiller himself was not equally impressed. There had already been some bungling. Nogo had allowed Quenton-Harper and the Egyptian woman to slip through his clutches. After a lifetime of operating in Africa, von Schiller placed little trust or store in blacks and preferred to work with Europeans. However, he realized that for the time being Nogo's services were indispensable. He was, after all, the military commander of the southern Gojam. No doubt once he had served his purpose he could be taken care of. Helm would see to that. He would not have to bother himself with the details.

Von Schiller looked now at the last man at the table. Here was another who was indispensable for the time being. Nahoot Guddabi was the one who had brought the existence of the seventh scroll to his attention. Apparently some English author had written a fictionalized version of the scrolls, but von Schiller never read fiction of any sort, either in German or in any of the four foreign languages in which he was fluent. Without Nahoot bringing the existence of the Taita scrolls to his notice, he might have overlooked this opportunity of his lifetime.

The Egyptian had come to him as soon as the original translation of the scrolls had been completed by Duraid Al Simma, and the existence of an unrecorded Pharaoh and his tomb had been mooted. Since then they had been in constant contact, and when the time came that Al Simma and his wife had started to make too much headway with their investigations, von Schiller had employed Nahoot to get rid of them and to bring the seventh scroll to him.

The scroll was now the shining star of his collection, safely housed with his other ancient treasures in the steel and concrete vaults below the Schloss in the mountains that was his private retreat, his Eagle's Nest.

Despite this, the choice of Nahoot to undertake the more sensitive work of ridding him of Al Simma and his wife had proved to be a mistake. He should have sent a professional to take care of them, but Nahoot had argued that he was capable of seeing it through, and he had been well paid for the work that he had mismanaged so ineptly.

He too would be disposable in time, but right now von Schiller still needed him.

There was no question that Nahoot's understanding of Egyptology and hieroglyphics was far in advance of von Schiller's own. After all, Nahoot had spent most of his life studying them, while von Schiller was an amateur and only a comparatively recent enthusiast. Nahoot was able to read the scrolls and this new material that they had acquired as though they were letters from a friend, whereas von Schiller was obliged to puzzle over each symbol and resort frequently to his reference books. Even then, he was not capable of picking up the finer nuances of meaning in the text. Without Nahoot's assistance he could not hope to solve the riddles which confronted him in the search for Mamose's tomb.

This was the team who were now assembled beneath him, waiting for him to start the proceedings. 'Sit down, please, Fräulein Kemper,' he said at last. 'You too, gentlemen. Let us get started.'

Von Schiller remained standing on his block at the head of the table. He enjoyed the feeling of superior height. His short stature had been a source of humiliation ever since his school-days when he had been nicknamed 'Pippa' by his peers.

'Fräulein Kemper will be recording everything which is said here this afternoon. She will also issue each of you with a folder of documents which she will collect from you again at the end of this meeting. I want to make it very clear that none of this material will ever leave this room. It is of the most confidential nature, and belongs to me alone. I will take a most stringent view of any breach of this instruction.'

As Utte handed out the folders, von Schiller looked at each recipient in turn. His expression made it clear what the penalty would be for any contravention of his instructions.

Then von Schiller opened the dossier that lay on the tabletop in front of him. He stood over it, leaning forward on his bunched fists.

'In your folders you will find copies of the Polaroid photographs that were recovered from Quenton-Harper's camp. Please look at these now.'

Each of them opened their own folder.

'Since our arrival Dr Nahoot has had an opportunity to study these, and he is of the opinion that they are genuine, and that the stele in the photographs is an authentic artefect of ancient Egyptian origin, almost certainly dating from the Second Intermediate Period, circa 1790 BC. Is there anything you wish to add to that, Doctor?'

'Thank you, Herr von Schiller.' Nahoot smiled oleaginously, but his dark eyes were nervous. There was something cold and dispassionate about the old German that terrified him. He had displayed no emotion whatsoever as he ordered Nahoot to arrange the death of Duraid Al Simma and his wife. Nahoot knew that he would be equally unmoved if he were to order Nahoot's own murder. He realized that he was riding the tiger's back. 'I would just like to qualify that statement. I said that the stele pictured in these prints *appeared* to be genuine. Of course, I would not be able to give you a definite opinion until I was able to examine the actual stone at first hand.'

'I note your qualification,' von Schiller nodded, 'and we are assembled here to find the means to obtain the stele for your examination and verdict.' He picked up the glossy print that Utte had made from the original that morning in the laboratory darkroom in the adjoining hut. Photography was not the least of her many talents and skills, and she had done a very competent job. The copies of the Polaroids that Helm had transmitted to him in Hamburg had been blurred and distorted, but still they had been sufficient to bring him rushing across the continents in all this haste. Now he held these clear likenesses in full colour, and his excitement threatened to suffocate him.

While they were all silent, he caressed the print as lovingly as if it had been the actual object that it portrayed. If this were genuine, as he knew instinctively that it was, then it alone would be well worth the considerable cost in time and money and human life that he had already paid. It was a marvellous treasure, to match even the original seventh scroll which was already in his collection. The condition and state of preservation of the stele after four thousand years seemed to be extraordinary. He lusted for it as he had for few things in his long life. It required an effort to set aside this pervasive longing, and to apply his mind to the task ahead of him.

'If, however, the stele is genuine, Doctor, can you tell us, or rather, can you suggest to us where it may be situated, and where we should direct our search?'

'I believe that we should not consider the stele in isolation, Herr von Schiller. We should look at the other Polaroids that Colonel Nogo was able to recover for us, and which Fräulein Kemper has so ingeniously copied.' Nahoot set aside the one print, and selected another from the pile in the folder in front of him. 'This one, for example.'

The others riffled through their own folders and selected the same print as he was displaying.

'If you study the background of this copy, you will see that in the shadows behind the stele there appears to be the wall of some type of cave or cavern.' He looked up at von Schiller, who nodded encouragement. 'There also appears to be some type of barred doorway.' Nahoot set the print aside and selected another. 'Now, see here. This is a photograph taken of another subject. It is, I believe, of a mural decoration painted upon either a plastered wall or the bare rock of a cave, possibly an excavated tomb. It seems to have been taken through the grille of the gate which I pointed out to you in the first photograph of the stele. This mural is almost certainly Egyptian in style and influence. In fact it very strongly reminds me of those murals that decorated the tomb of Queen Lostris in Upper Egypt in which the original Taita scrolls were uncovered.'

'Yes. Yes. Go on!' von Schiller encouraged him.

'Very well, then. Using the barred gate as the connecting factor, there is every reason to believe that both stele and murals are located in the same cave or tomb.'

'If that is so, what indications do we have as to where Quenton-Harper photographed these Polaroids?' Von Schiller was still frowning angrily as he looked at each of them in turn. They all tried to avoid his blue, penetrating scrutiny.

'Colonel Nogo,' von Schiller singled him out, 'this is your country. You know the terrain intimately. Let's hear your thoughts on the subject.'

Colonel Nogo shook his head. 'This man, this Egyptian—' he used the epithet disparagingly, 'is mistaken. This is not an Egyptian tomb in the photographs.'

'Why do you say that?' Nahoot challenged him angrily. 'What do you know about Egyptology? I have spent twenty-five years—'

'Wait,' von Schiller silenced him peremptorily. 'Let him finish.' He looked at Nogo. 'Go on, colonel.'

'I agree that I don't know anything about Egyptian tombs, but these photographs were taken in a Christian church.'

'What makes you so sure?' Nahoot demanded bitterly, his authority challenged.

'Let me explain to you that I was ordained as a priest fifteen years ago. Later, I became disillusioned with Christianity and all other religions, and left the Church to become a soldier. I tell you this so that you may believe that I know what I am talking about.' He smiled with supercilious malice at Nahoot, before going on. 'Look at this first print again, and you will be able to make out on the wall in the background, near the corner of the grille gate, the outline of a human hand and the stylized picture of a fish. Those are symbols of the Coptic Church. You can see them reproduced in any church or cathedral in the land.'

Each of them peered at their own copy of the same print, but none of them ventured an opinion until von Schiller had given his.

'You are right,' von Schiller said softly. 'There is, as you say, the hand and the fish.'

'But I assure you the hieroglyphics on the stele and the murals and the wooden coffin are all Egyptian,' Nahoot defended himself stoutly. 'I would stake my life on it.'

Nogo shook his head, and began to argue. 'I know what I am saying—'

Von Schiller held up his hand to silence them both while he considered the problem. At last he came to some decision.

'Colonel Nogo, show me on the satellite photograph the site of Quenton-Harper's camp where you obtained these Polaroids.'

Nogo stood up, and came around the table to stand beside von Schiller. He leaned over the satellite photograph and prodded his forefinger at the spot near where the Dandera river joined the Nile. The photograph had once been in the possession of Quenton-Harper, and had been captured in the raid on his camp. There were numerous markings in coloured marker pen on the copy, which Nogo presumed had been placed there by the Englishman.

'It was here, sir. You can see that Quenton-Harper has marked the spot with a green circle.'

'Now show me where the nearest Coptic church is situated.'

'Why, Herr von Schiller, it's right here. Again

Quenton-Harper has marked it with red ink. It is situated only a mile from the campsite. The monastery of St Frumentius.'

'There is your answer, then.' Von Schiller was still frowning. 'Coptic and Egyptian symbols together. The monastery.'

They stared at him, none of them daring to question his conclusion.

'I want that monastery searched,' he said softly. 'I want every room and every inch of every wall examined.' He turned back to Nogo. 'Can you get your men in there?'

'Of course, Herr von Schiller. I already have one of my reliable men in the monastery – one of the monks is in my pay. Added to that, there is still martial law in force here in Gojam. I am the military commander. I am fully empowered to search for rebels and dissidents and bandits wherever I suspect they may be sheltering.'

'Will your men enter a church to perform their duty?' Helm wanted to know. 'Do you personally have any religious scruples? It may be necessary to – how can I put it – desecrate hallowed premises.'

'I have already explained to you that I have renounced religion for other more worldly beliefs. I would take pleasure in destroying such superstitious and dangerous symbols as will certainly be found in the monastery of St Frumentius. As for my men, I will select only Moslems or Animists who are hostile to the cross, and all it stands for. I will lead them personally. I assure you that there will be no difficulty in that respect.'

'How will you explain this to your superiors in Addis Ababa? I do not want to be associated in any way with your actions at the monastery,' von Schiller said.

'I have been ordered by the high command in Addis to take all possible steps against the dissident rebels that are operating in the Abbay gorge. I will be completely able to justify any search of the monastery.'

'I want that stele. I want it at any cost. Do you understand me, colonel?'

'I understand you perfectly, Herr von Schiller.'

'As you already know, I am a generous man to those who serve me well. Bring it to me in good condition and you will be well rewarded. You may call on Mr Helm for any assistance that he can give you, including the use of Pegasus equipment and personnel.'

'If we are able to use your helicopter, it will save a great deal of time. I can take my men down there tomorrow, and if the stone is in the monastery I will be able to deliver it to you by tomorrow evening.'

'Excellent. You will take Dr Guddabi with you. He must search the area for other valuables and translate any inscriptions or engravings that you find in the monastery. Please provide him with military uniform. He must appear to be one of your troopers. I do not want to become involved in recriminations at a later date.'

'We will leave as soon as it is light enough to take off tomorrow morning. I will commence the arrangements immediately.' Tuma Nogo saluted von Schiller and strode eagerly from the hut.

Although Colonel Nogo had never entered either the *qiddist* or the *maqdas*, he had often visited the monastery of St Frumentius. He was therefore fully aware of the magnitude of the task ahead of him, and the likely reaction of the monks and the congregation to his forced entry to their premises. In addition, he was familiar with numerous similar rock cathedrals in other parts of the country. In fact he had been ordained in the famous cathedral of Lalibelela, so he knew just how labyrinthine one of these subterranean warrens could be.

He estimated that he would need at least twenty men

to secure and search the monastery, and to fend off the outraged retaliation of the abbot and his monks. He selected his best men personally. None of them was squeamish.

Two hours before dawn he paraded them within the security of the Pegasus compound, under the glare of the floodlights, and briefed them carefully. At the end of the briefing he made each man step from the ranks in turn and recite his orders to ensure there was no misunderstanding. Then he inspected their arms and equipment meticulously.

Tuma Nogo was painfully conscious of his own culpability in allowing the Englishman and the Egyptian woman to escape, and he could sense the danger in Herr von Schiller's attitude towards him. He had few illusions about the consequences if he were to fail again. In the short time since he had made the acquaintance of Gotthold von Schiller, Nogo had come to fear him as he had never feared God or the Devil in the days of his priesthood. He realized that this raid was an opportunity to reinstate himself with the formidable little German.

The Jet Ranger was standing by, the pilot at the controls, the engines running and the rotors turning lazily, but it could not carry such a large number of fully equipped men. It would need four round trips to ferry them all down to the assembly point in the gorge. Nogo flew with the first flight, and took Nahoot Guddabi with him. The helicopter dropped them three miles from the monastery, in a clearing on the banks of the Dandera river, the same drop area as they had used for the raid on Quenton-Harper's camp.

The drop area was just far enough from the monastery for the engine noise of the Jet Ranger not to alarm the monks. Even if they did hear it, Nogo was banking on the probability that they were by this time thoroughly conditioned to the frequent sorties of the machine, and would not associate it with any threat to themselves.

The men waited in the darkness, warned to silence

and not even allowed by Nogo to smoke, while the Jet Ranger ferried in the remaining troopers. When the last flight came in Nogo ordered his detachment to fall in, and led them in single file down the path beside the river. They were all trained bush fighters in top physical condition, and they moved swiftly and purposefully through the night. Only Nahoot was a soft urbanite, and within half a mile he was wheezing and whining for a chance to rest. Nogo smiled vindictively to himself as he listened to Nahoot's pathetic whispered pleas for mercy as he was prodded along by the men behind him.

Nogo had timed his arrival at the monastery to coincide with the hour of matins and lauds, the break of day. He led his contingent down the cliff staircase at a trot. Their weapons were at high port, all the equipment was carefully muted so as not to clatter or creak, and their rubber-soled paratrooper boots made little noise on the stone paving as they hurried along the deserted cloisters to the entrance of the underground cathedral.

From the interior echoed the monotonous chanting and drumming of the ceremony, punctuated at intervals by the higher treble descant of the abbot leading the service. Colonel Nogo paused outside the doors, and his men drew up in double ranks behind him. There was no need for orders, for his briefing had covered every aspect of the raid. He looked the men over for a moment, then nodded at his lieutenant.

The outer chamber of the church was empty, as the monks were gathered in the middle chamber, the *qiddist*. Nogo crossed the outer nave swiftly, with his detachment moving up close behind him. Then he ran up the steps to the wooden doors of the *qiddist*, which stood open. As he entered, his men fanned out in two files behind him and swiftly took up their positions along the side walls of the *qiddist*, their assault rifles cocked and locked, and with bayonets fixed, covering the kneeling congregation.

It was done so silently and swiftly that it was some minutes before the monks gradually became aware of this alien presence in their holy place. The chanting and drumming died away, and the dark faces turned apprehensively towards the ranks of armed men. Only Jali Hora, the ancient abbot, was unaware of anything untoward happening. Completely absorbed in his devotions, he continued kneeling before the doors of the *maqdas*, the Holy of Holies, his quavering voice the lonely cry of a lost soul.

In the silence Colonel Nogo marched down the centre of the nave, kicking the kneeling monks out of his way. When he came up behind Jali Hora he seized him by his skinny black shoulder and threw him roughly to the ground. The tinsel crown flew from his silvered pate and rolled across the slabs with a brassy clatter.

Nogo left him sprawling and turned to face the rows of monks in their white *shammas*, addressing them imperiously in Amharic.

'I am here to search this church and the other buildings of this monastery, on suspicion that there are dissident rebels and other bandits harboured here.' He paused and surveyed the cowering holy men haughtily and threateningly. 'I must warn you that any attempt to prevent my men performing their duties will be regarded as an act of banditry and provocation. It will be met with force.'

Jali Hora crawled to his knees and then, using one of the embroidered hangings for support, slowly hoisted himself to his feet. Still clinging to the tapestry of the Virgin and child, he gathered himself with an effort.

'These are hallowed precincts,' he cried, in a surprisingly clear and strong voice. 'We are dedicated to the service and worship of almighty God, the Father, the Son and the Holy Ghost.'

'Silence!' Nogo bellowed at him. He unbuckled the flap of the webbing holster on his hip and placed his hand threateningly on the grip of the Tokarev pistol it contained.

Jali Hora ignored the threat. 'We are holy men in a place of God. There are no *shufta* here. There are no law-breakers amongst us. In the name of God the most high, I call upon you to be gone, to leave us to our prayers and our worship, and not to desecrate—'

Nogo drew the pistol and in the same movement swung the black steel barrel into the abbot's face with a vicious back-handed blow. Jali Hora's mouth burst open like the rind of a ripe pomegranate; the red juice burst from his crushed lips and flooded down the front of his tattered velvet vestments. A low moan of horror went up from the ranks of squatting monks.

Still clinging to the tapestry, Jali Hora kept his feet, but he was swaying and teetering wildly. He opened his shattered mouth to speak again, but the only sound that came from it was a high-pitched cawing, like that of a dying crow, and the blood splattered in bright droplets from his lips.

Nogo laughed and kicked his legs from under him. Jali Hora collapsed like a heap of dirty laundry and lay on the paving, groaning in his own blood and spittle.

'Where is your God now, you old baboon? Bleat to him as loud as you will, and he will never answer you,' Nogo chuckled.

With the pistol he gestured to his lieutenant across the church. He left six of his men guarding the monks, four at the doorway and one at each side wall. The others bunched up and followed him to the entrance to the *maqdas*.

The doors were locked. Nogo rattled the ancient padlock impatiently. 'Open this immediately, you old crow!' he shouted at Jali Hora who still lay in a bundle, moaning and sobbing.

'He is too far gone in senility,' the lieutenant shook his head. 'His mind has gone, colonel. He does not understand the command.'

'Break it open, then,' Nogo ordered. 'No, don't waste any more time. Shoot the lock away. The wood is rotten.'

Obediently the lieutenant stepped up to the door, and gestured his men to stand well clear. He aimed his AK-47 into the wood of the door lintel and fired a long, continuous burst.

Dust and chips of wood and stone flew in a cloud, and fresh yellow splinters splattered the paving. The noise of gunfire and the whine of ricochets was deafening in the echoing hall of the *qiddist*, and the monks wailed and howled and covered their ears and their eyes where they knelt. The lieutenant stepped back from the shattered door. The black wrought-iron hasp and staple hung at an angle, the supporting woodwork almost shot through.

'Break it down now!' Nogo ordered, and five of his men ran forward and put their shoulders to the sagging door. At their combined thrust there was a crackling, rending sound, and now the monks were screaming. Some of them had covered their heads with the skirts of their *shammas* so as not to have to witness this sacrilege; others were tearing at their faces with their fingernails, leaving long bloody gouges down their own cheeks.

'Again!' roared Nogo, and his men rushed the door once more, using their shoulders in unison. The lock was ripped away from its fastenings, and they pushed the massive door fully open and peered into the dim recesses of the *maqdas* beyond. The chamber was lit only by a few smoky oil lamps.

Now suddenly even these non-Christians were reluctant to cross that threshold into the holy place. They all hung back, even Tuma Nogo, despite his defiant protestations of non-belief.

'Nahoot!' He looked back over his shoulder at the

bedraggled and still sweating Egyptian. 'This is your job now. Herr von Schiller has ordered you to find the things we want. Come here.'

As Nahoot came forward, Nogo seized his arm and thrust him through the doorway. 'Get in there, oh follower of the Prophet. The Trinity of Christian gods cannot harm you.'

He stepped into the *maqdas* immediately after Nahoot and shone his torch around the low chamber. The beam of light danced over the shelves of votive offerings, sparkling on the glass and precious stones, on the brass and gold and silver. It stopped on the high cedarwood altar, lighting the Epiphany crown and the chalices, reflected from the communion plate and the tall silver Coptic cross.

'Beyond the altar,' Nahoot cried out with excitement. 'The barred gateway! This is the place where the Polaroids were taken.'

He broke away from the group in the doorway and ran wildly across the chamber. Gripping the bars of the gate in his clenched fists, he peered between them like a prisoner sentenced to life imprisonment.

'This is the tomb. Bring the light!' His voice was a high-pitched and frantic scream.

Nogo ran to join him, brushing past the damask-covered *tabot* stone. He shone the torch through the bars of the gate.

'By the sweet compassion of God, and the eternal breath of his Prophet,' Nahoot's voice sank from a scream to a whisper, 'these are the murals of the ancient scribe. This is the work of the slave Taita.' As Royan had done, he recognized the style and the execution immediately. Taita's brush was so distinctive, and his talent had outlasted the ages.

'Open this gate!' Nahoot's tone rose again, becoming strident and impatient.

'Here, you men!' Nogo responded, and they crowded

387

around the ancient structure, trying at first to rip it from the cavern wall by main strength. Almost at once it became apparent that this was a futile effort, and Nogo stopped them.

'Search the monks' quarters!' he ordered his lieutenant. 'Find me tools to do the job.'

The junior officer hurried from the chamber, taking most of the troopers with him. Nogo turned from the gate and studied the rest of the interior of the *maqdas*.

'The stele!' he rasped. 'Herr von Schiller wants the stone above everything else.' He played the torchbeam around the chamber. 'From what angle was the Polaroid taken—'

He broke off abruptly, and held the light on the damask-covered *tabot* stone, on which the velvet-cloaked tabernacle stood.

'Yes,' cried Nahoot at his shoulder. 'That is it.'

Tuma Nogo crossed to the pillar with half a dozen strides and seized the gold-tasselled border of the tabernacle cloth. He pulled it away. The tabernacle was a simple chest carved from olive wood, glowing with the patina that priestly hands had imparted to the wood over the centuries.

'Primitive superstitions,' Nogo muttered contemptuously and, picking it up in both hands, hurled it against the cavern wall. The wood splintered and the lid of the chest burst open. A stack of inscribed clay tablets spilled out on to the cavern paving slabs, but neither Nogo nor Nahoot took any notice of these sacred items.

'Uncover it,' Nahoot encouraged him. 'Uncover the stone.'

Nogo tugged at the corner of the damask cloth, but it caught on the angle of the pillar beneath it. Impatiently he heaved at it with all his strength, and the old and rotten material tore with a soft ripping sound.

Taita's stone testament, the carved stele, was revealed.

Even Nogo was impressed by the discovery. He backed away from it with the torn covering cloth in his hand.

'It is the stone in the photograph,' he whispered. 'This is what Herr von Schiller ordered us to find. We are rich men.'

His words of avarice broke the spell. Nahoot ran forward, and threw himself on his knees in front of the stele. He clasped it with both arms, like a lover too long deprived. He sobbed softly, and with amazement Nogo saw tears streaming unashamedly down his cheeks. Nogo himself had considered only the value of the reward that it would bring. He had never thought that any man could long so deeply for an inanimate object, especially something so mundane as this pillar of ordinary stone.

They were still posed like this, Nahoot kneeling at the stele like a worshipper and Nogo standing silently behind him, when the lieutenant ran back into the cavern. Somewhere he had found a rusty mattock with a raw timber handle.

His arrival roused both men from their trance, and Nogo ordered him, 'Break open the gate!'

Although the gate was antique and the wood brittle, it took the efforts of several men working in relays to rip the stanchions out of their foundations in the rock of the cavern wall.

At last, however, the heavy gate sagged forward. As the workers jumped aside it fell with a shattering crash to the slabs, raising a mist of red dust that dimmed the light of the lamps and the electric torch.

Nahoot was the first one into the tomb. He ran through the veil of swirling dust and once again threw himself to his knees beside the ancient crumbling wooden coffin.

'Bring the light,' he shouted impatiently. Nogo stepped up behind him and shone the torchlight on the coffin.

The portraits of the man were three dimensional, not only on the sides, but on the lid too. Clearly the artist was the same as the one who had executed the murals. The upper portrait was in excellent condition. It depicted a man in the prime of life with a strong, proud face, that of a farmer or a soldier with a calm and unruffled gaze. He was a handsome man, with thick blond tresses, skilfully painted as if by someone who had known him well and loved him. The artist seemed to have captured his character, and then eulogized his salient virtues.

Nahoot looked up from the portrait to the inscription on the wall of the tomb above it. He read it aloud, and then, with tears still backing up behind his eyelids, he looked down again at the coffin and read the cartouche that was painted below the portrait of the blond general.

'Tanus, Lord Harrab.' His voice choked up with emotion, and he swallowed noisily and cleared his throat. 'This follows exactly the description in the seventh scroll. We have the stele and the coffin. They are great and priceless treasures. Herr von Schiller will be delighted.'

'I wish I could believe what you say,' Nogo told him dubiously. 'Herr von Schiller is a dangerous man.'

'You have done well so far,' Nahoot assured him. 'It remains only for you to move the stele and the coffin out of this monastery to where the helicopter can fly them to the Pegasus camp. If you can do that, you will be a very rich man. Richer than you ever believed was possible.'

This spur was enough for Nogo. He stood over his men as they laboured around the base of the stele, digging in clouds of dust, levering the paving slabs out of their mooring. Finally they freed the foundation of the stele and between them lifted the stone out of the position in which it had stood for nearly four thousand years.

Only once it was free did they realize the weight of the stone. Although slender, it was a solid half-ton weight. Nahoot went back into the *qiddist* and, ignoring the rows of squatting monks, pulled down a dozen of the thick woollen tapestries from the walls and had the troopers carry them back into the *maqdas*.

He wrapped both the stele and the coffin in the heavy folds of coarse-spun wool. It was tough as canvas, and afforded the men who were to carry it a secure handhold. Ten of the burly troopers were able to lift and carry the stele, while three men were able to handle the wooden coffin and its desiccated contents. This left seven armed men free to provide an escort. Then the heavily burdened procession moved out through the ruined doorway of the Holy of Holies into the crowded central *qiddist*.

As soon as the assembled monks realized what they were carrying away with them, a shocked babble of voices, of lamentations and exhortations, rose from the squatting ranks of holy men.

'Quiet!' Nogo roared. 'Silence! Keep these fools quiet.'

The guards waded forward into the mass of humanity, clearing a passage for the treasures they were plundering, laying about them with boot and rifle butt, shouting at the monks to give way and to let the staggering porters through. The hubbub rose louder, the monks encouraging each other with their howls of protest, whipping themselves into a frenzy of religious outrage. Some of them leaped to their feet, defying the commands bellowed at them to remain seated. They crowded closer and closer to the armed troopers, clutching at their uniforms, chanting and whirling about them in a challenging display of mounting hostility.

In the midst of this uproar, suddenly the spectral figure of Jali Hora reappeared. His beard and robes were stained with blood, his eyes were crazy, bloodshot and staring. From his battered lips and ruined mouth issued a long, sustained shriek. The ranks of dancing monks opened to let him through, and he rushed like an animated scarecrow with his skirts flapping around his thin legs straight at Colonel Nogo.

'Get back, you old maniac!' Nogo warned him, and lifted the muzzle of his assault rifle to fend him away.

Jali Hora was far past any earthly restraint. He did not even check, but ran straight on to the point of the bayonet that Nogo was aiming at his belly.

The needle-pointed steel stabbed through his gaudy robes and ran into the flesh beneath them as easily as a gaff into the body of a struggling fish. The point of the bayonet emerged from the middle of his back, pricking through the velvet cloak, all pinkly smeared with the old man's blood. Spitted upon the steel, Jali Hora wriggled and contorted, a dreadful squeal bursting from his bloody lips.

Nogo tried to pull the bayonet free, but the wet clinging suction of the abbot's guts held the steel fast, and when Nogo jerked harder, Jali Hora was tossed about like a puppet, his arms flapping and his legs kicking and dancing comically.

There was only one way to free the blade of a bayonet that was trapped like this. Nogo slipped the rate-of-fire selector on the AK-47 to 'Single Shot'. He fired once.

The detonation of the shot was muffled by Jali Hora's body, but was yet so thunderous that for a moment it stilled the outcry of the monks. The high-velocity bullet tore down the entry track of the blade. It was moving at three times the speed of sound, creating a wave of hydrostatic shock behind it that turned the old man's bowels to jelly and liquidized his flesh. The suction that had held the bayonet was broken, and the blast of shot hurled Jali Hora's carcass off the point of the blade, flinging it into the arms of the monks who were crowding close behind him.

For a moment longer the strained, unnatural silence persisted, and then it was shattered by a higher, more angry chorus of horror from the monks. It was as though they were compelled by a single mind, a single instinct. Like a flock of white birds they flew at the band of armed men in their midst and descended upon them, intent on retribution for murder. They counted no cost to themselves, but with their bare hands they tore at them, hooked fingers clawing for their eyes, seizing the barrels of the levelled rifles. Some of them even grasped the blades of the bayonets with their naked hands, and the razor steel sliced through flesh and tendons.

For a short while it seemed that the soldiers would be overwhelmed and smothered by the sheer weight of numbers, but then those troopers carrying the stele and the coffin dropped their loads and unslung their weapons.

The monks crowded them too closely for them to swing the rifles, and they were forced to hack and stab with the bayonets to clear a space around them in which to do their work. They did not need much room, for the AK-47 has a short barrel and compact action. Their first burst of fully automatic fire, aimed into the monks at belly height and point-blank range, scythed a windrow through them. Every bullet told, and the full metal jacket ball whipped through one man's torso with almost no check, going on to kill the man behind him.

By now all the troopers were firing from the hip, traversing back and forth, spraying the packed ranks of monks like gardeners hosing a bed of white pansies. As one magazine of twenty-eight rounds emptied they snapped it off and replaced it with another, fully loaded.

Nahoot cowered behind the fallen pillar, using it as a shield. The roar of gunfire deafened and confused him. He stared around him and could not credit the carnage he was witnessing. At such close range the 7.62 round is a terrible missile, which can blow off an arm or a leg as efficiently as an axe-stroke, but more messily. Taken in the belly, it can gut a man like a fish.

Nahoot saw one of the monks hit in the forehead. His skull erupted in a cloud of blood and brain tissue, and the gunman who had shot him laughed as he fired. They were all caught up in the madness of the moment. Like a pack of wild dogs that had run down their prey, they kept on firing and reloading and firing again.

The monks in the front rows turned to flee and ran into those behind. They struggled together, howling with agony and terror, until the storm of bullets swept over them, killing and maiming, and they fell upon the heaps of dead and dying. The floor of the chamber was carpeted with the dead and the wounded. Trying to escape the hail of bullets the monks blocked the doorway, plugging it tight with their struggling white-clad bodies, and now the troopers standing clear in the centre of the *qiddist* turned their guns upon this trapped mass of humanity. The bullets socked into them and they heaved and tossed like the trees of the forest in a gale of wind. Now there was very little screaming; the guns were the only voices that still clamoured.

It was some minutes before the guns stuttered into silence, and then the only sound was the groans and the weeping of the wounded. The chamber was filled with a blue mist of gunsmoke and the stink of burned powder. Even the laughter of the soldiers was silenced as they stared around them, and realized the enormity of the slaughter. The entire floor was carpeted with bodies, their *shammas* splashed and speckled with gouts of scarlet, and the stone paving beneath them was awash with sheets of fresh blood in which the empty brass cartridge cases sparkled like jewels.

'Cease firing!' Nogo gave the belated order. 'Shoulder arms! Pick up the load! Forward march!'

His voice roused them, and they slung their weapons and stooped to lift their heavy, tapestry-wrapped burdens. Then they staggered forward, their boots squelching in the blood, tripping over the corpses, stepping on bodies that either convulsed or lay inert. Gagging in the stench of gunsmoke and blood, of bowels and guts ripped wide open by the bullets, they crossed the chamber.

When they reached the doorway and staggered down the steps into the deserted outer chamber of the church, Nahoot saw the relief on the faces of even these battle-hardened veterans as they escaped from the reeking charnel-house. For Nahoot it was too much. Never in his worst nightmares had he seen sights such as these.

He tottered to the side wall of the chamber and clung to one of the woollen hangings for support; then, heaving and retching, he brought up a mouthful of bitter bile. When he looked around him again, he was alone except for a wounded monk who was dragging himself across the flags towards him, his spine shot through and his paralysed legs slithering behind him, leaving a slimy snail's trail of blood across the stone floor.

Nahoot screamed and backed away from the wounded monk, then whirled and fled from the church, along the cloisters above the gorge of the Nile, following the group of soldiers as they carried their burdens up the stone staircase. He was so wild with horror that he did not even hear the approach of the helicopter until it was hovering directly overhead on the glistening silver disc of its spinning rotor.

Gotthold von Schiller stood outside the front door of the Quonset hut, with Utte Kemper waiting a pace behind him. The pilot had radioed ahead while the Jet Ranger was in flight, so all was in readiness to receive the precious cargo it was carrying. The helicopter raised a cloud of pale dust from the landing circle as it sank down to the earth. The long tapestry-covered load it carried had not been able to fit into the cabin, and was strapped across the landing skids of the aircraft. The instant that the skids kissed the ground and the pilot cut back the throttle, Jake Helm led out a team of a dozen men to loosen the nylon retaining straps and lift the heavy bundle down. Between them the gang of overall-clad workers carried the stele to the hut and eased it through the door. Helm hovered close at hand, issuing terse orders.

A space had been cleared in the centre of the conference room, the long table pushed back against the wall. With extreme care the stele was laid there, and minutes later the coffin of Tanus, the Great Lion of Egypt, was laid beside it.

Brusquely Helm dismissed the gang and closed and bolted the door behind them as they left. Only the four of them remained in the room. Nahoot and Helm crouched beside the stele, ready to unwrap the woollen tapestry. Von Schiller stood at the head of it, with Utte at his side.

'Shall we begin?' Helm asked softly, watching von Schiller's face the way a faithful dog watches its master.

'Carefully,' von Schiller warned him in strangled tones. 'Do not damage anything.' He was sweating in a sheen across his forehead, and his face was very pale. Utte edged protectively closer to him, but he did not glance in her direction. He was staring fixedly at the treasure that lay at his feet.

Helm opened his clasp-knife and cut away the tasselled cords that secured the covering. As he watched, von Schiller's breathing became louder. It rasped in his throat like a man in the terminal stages of emphysema.

'Yes,' he whispered hoarsely, 'that's the way to do it.' Utte Kemper watched his face. He was always like this when he made another significant addition to his collection of antiquities. He seemed on the verge of a seizure, of a massive heart attack, but she knew he had the heart of an ox.

Helm came to the top end of the pillar and carefully opened a small slit in the cloth. He eased the point of the blade into this opening, and then ran it slowly down towards the base, like a zip fastener. The blade was razor-sharp and the cloth fell away to reveal the inscribed stone beneath it.

The sweat burst out like a heavy dew on von Schiller's skin. It dripped from his chin on to the front of his khaki bush jacket. He made a small moaning sound as he saw the carved hieroglyphics. Utte watched him, her own excitement mounting. She knew what to expect of him, when he was caught up in this paroxysm of emotion.

'See here, Herr von Schiller.' Nahoot knelt beside the obelisk and traced the outline of a broken-winged hawk with his finger. 'This is the signature of the slave, Taita.'

'Is it genuine?' Von Schiller's voice was that of a very sick man, wheezing and gusty.

'It is genuine. I will guarantee it with my life.'

'It may come to that,' von Schiller warned him. His eyes were glittering with the hard brilliance of pale sapphires.

'This column was carved nearly four thousand years ago,' Nahoot repeated stoutly. 'This is the veritable seal of the scribe.' He translated glibly and easily from the blocks of figures, his face shining with an almost religious rapture: '"*Anubis, the jackal-headed, the god of the cemeteries, holds in his paws the blood and the viscera, the bones and the lungs and the heart that are my separate parts. He moves them like the stones of the bao board, my limbs serve him as counters, my head is the great bull of the long board*"—'

'Enough!' von Schiller commanded. 'There will be time for more later. Go now. Leave me alone. Do not return until I send for you.'

Nahoot looked startled and scrambled to his feet uncertainly. He had not expected to be dismissed so abruptly in the moment of his triumph. Helm beckoned him, and the two of them went quickly to the door of the hut.

'Helm,' von Schiller called thickly after him, 'make certain that nobody disturbs me.'

'Of course, Herr von Schiller.' He glanced enquiringly at Utte Kemper.

'No,' said von Schiller. 'She stays.'

The two men left the room, and Helm shut the door carefully behind them. Utte crossed the room and turned the key. Then she faced von Schiller with her hands behind her and her back pressed to the door.

Her breasts were thrust forward, firm and pointed. The nipples showed clearly through the thin cotton blouse, hard as marbles.

'The costume?' she asked. 'Do you want the costume?' Her own voice was tight and strained. She enjoyed this game almost as much as he did.

'Yes, the costume,' he whispered.

She crossed the room and disappeared through the door into his private quarters. As soon as she was gone von Schiller began to undress. When he stood mother-naked in the centre of the room, he threw his clothing in a heap into one corner and turned to face the door through which she would return.

Suddenly she stood in the doorway, and he gasped at the transformation. She wore the wig of tight Egyptian braids and over it the *uraeus*, the golden circlet with the hooded cobra standing erect above her forehead. The crown was genuine, as old as the ages – von Schiller had paid five million Deutschmarks for it.

'I am the reincarnation of the ancient Egyptian Queen Lostris,' she purred. 'My soul is immortal. My flesh is incorruptible.' She wore golden sandals from the tomb of a princess, and bracelets and finger rings and earrings from the same tomb. All were authentic royal relics.

'Yes.' His voice was choking, his face as pale as death.

'Nothing can destroy me. I will live for ever,' she said. Her skirt was diaphanous yellow silk, belted with gold and precious stones.

'For ever,' he repeated.

She was naked above the waist. Her breasts were big and white as milk. She cupped them in her own hands.

'These have been young and smooth for four thousand years,' she purred. 'I offer them to you.'

She stepped out of the open golden sandals and her feet were slim and neat. She parted the frontal split in the yellow skirts and held it so that her lower body was exposed. All her movements were slow and calculated. She was a clever actress.

'This is the promise of eternal life.' She placed her right hand on her dense honey-coloured pubic bush. 'I offer it to you.'

He groaned softly and blinked the streaming sweat out of his eyes, watching her avidly.

She undulated her hips, slowly and lewdly as an uncoiling cobra. She moved her feet apart and opened her thighs. With her fingers she spread the lips of her vulva.

'This is the gateway to eternity. I open it for you.'

Von Schiller groaned aloud. No matter how often repeated, the ritual never failed. Like a man in a trance he moved towards her. His body was thin, dried out like a thousand-year-old mummy. His chest hair was a silver fuzz, the skin of his sunken belly was folded and wrinkled, but his pubic hair was dark and thick as the hair on his head. His penis was huge, out of all proportion to the skinny old frame from which it dangled. As she moved slowly to meet him it filled out and hung at a different angle, and of its own accord the wizened foreskin peeled back to reveal the massive purple head beneath it.

'On the stele,' he grunted. 'Quickly! On the stone.'

She turned her back to him and knelt upon the stone, watching him over her shoulder as he came up behind her. Her buttocks were round and white as a pair of ostrich eggs.

Helm and his men worked late that night in the Pegasus workshop, making the wooden crates to house both the stele and the coffin securely. At dawn the next day they were loaded on to one of the heavy trucks, cushioned with thick rubber matting and strapped down on to specially fitted cradles.

At his own suggestion Nahoot rode in the back of the truck, which would take just over thirty hours to cover the long and arduous journey to Addis Ababa. The Pegasus Falcon was standing on the airport tarmac when the dusty truck trundled out through the security gates and parked beside it.

Von Schiller and Utte Kemper had made the journey in the company helicopter. General Obeid was with them. He had come to wish them *au revoir* and Godspeed.

While the wooden crates were loaded into the jet, Obeid spoke to the waiting Customs officer. He stamped the documents clearing the two cases of 'Geological Samples' for export, and then discreetly retired.

'Loaded and ready to start engines, Herr von Schiller,' said the uniformed Pegasus chief pilot, saluting.

Von Schiller shook hands with Obeid and clambered up the boarding ladder. Utte and Nahoot Guddabi followed him. The rings under Nahoot's eyes were even darker and deeper than usual. The journey had come close to exhausting him entirely, but he would not let the wooden cases out of his sight.

The Falcon climbed up into a bright clear sky over the mountains and headed northwards. A few moments after the pilot extinguished the Seat Belt panel, Utte Kemper thrust her lovely blonde head through the cockpit door and asked the chief pilot, 'Herr von Schiller would like to know our ETA.'

'I expect to touch down at Frankfurt at 2100 hours. Please inform Herr von Schiller that I have already radioed head office to give instructions for transport to be awaiting our arrival at the airport.'

The Falcon landed a few minutes ahead of schedule and taxied to the private hangar. The senior Customs and Immigration officials who were waiting for them were old acquaintances who were always on hand when the Falcon carried a special cargo. After they had completed the formalities they drank a schnapps with Gotthold von Schiller at the Falcon's tiny fitted bar, and discreetly pocketed the envelopes that lay on the bar counter beside each crystal glass.

The drive up into the mountains took most of the rest of the night. Von Schiller's chauffeur followed the covered Pegasus truck along the icy winding mountain road, never letting it and its cargo out of sight. At five in the morning they drove through the stone gate of the Schloss, where the snow lay half a metre deep in the deer park. The castle itself, with its dark stone battlements and arrow-slit windows, looked like something from Bram Stoker's novel. However, even at this hour the butler and all his staff were on hand to welcome the master.

Herr Reeper, the custodian of von Schiller's collection, and his most trusted assistants were also waiting, ready to move the two wooden cases down into the vault. Reverently they loaded them on to the forklift and rode down with them in the specially installed elevator.

While they unpacked the crates, von Schiller returned to his suite in the north tower. He bathed and ate a light breakfast, prepared by the Chinese chef. When he had eaten, he went to his wife's bedroom. She was even frailer than she had been when last he had seen her. Her hair was now completely white, her face pinched and waxy. He sent the nurse away, and kissed his wife's forehead tenderly. The cancer was eating her away slowly, but she was the mother of his two sons, and in his own peculiar way he still loved her.

He spent an hour with her, and then went to his own bedroom and slept for four hours. At his age he never needed more sleep than that, no matter how tired he might be. He worked until mid-afternoon with Utte and two other secretaries, and then the custodian called on the house intercom to tell him that they were ready for him in the vault.

Von Schiller and Utte rode down together in the elevator, and when the door slid open both Herr Reeper and Nahoot were waiting for them. One look at their faces told von Schiller that they were beside themselves with excitement, bubbling over with news for him.

'Are the X-rays completed?' von Schiller demanded as they hurried after him down the subterranean passageway to the vault.

'The technicians have completed their work,' Reeper told him. 'They have done a fine job. The plates are wonderful. *Ja, wunderbar!*'

Von Schiller had endowed the clinic, so any request of his was treated as a royal command. The director had sent down his most modern portable X-ray equipment and two technicians to photograph the mummy of Lord Harrab, and a senior radiologist to interpret the plates.

Reeper inserted his plastic pass card into the lock of the steel vault door, and with a soft pneumatic hiss it slid open. They all stood aside for von Schiller to enter first. He paused in the doorway, and looked around the great vault. The pleasure never palled. On the contrary, it seemed to grow more intense every time he entered this place.

The walls were enclosed in two metres of steel and concrete, and were guarded by every electronic device that genius could devise. But this was not apparent when he viewed the softly lit and elegantly appointed main display room. It had been planned and decorated by one of Europe's foremost interior designers. The theme colour was blue. Each item of the collection was housed in its own case, and each of these was cunningly arranged to show it to its best advantage.

Everywhere was the soft glimmer of gold and precious gems nestling on midnight-blue velvet cushions. Artfully concealed spotlights illuminated the lustre of lovingly polished alabaster and stone, the glow of ivory and obsidian. There were marvellous statues. The pantheon of the old gods were here assembled: Thoth and Anubis, Hapi and Seth, and the glorious trinity of Osiris and Isis and Horus, the son. They gazed out with those inscrutable eyes which had looked upon the procession of the ages.

On its temporary plinth in the centre of the room, in pride of place, stood the latest addition to this extraordinary hoard, the tall, graceful stone testament of Taita. Von Schiller stopped beside it to caress the polished stone before he passed on into the second room.

Here the coffin of Tanus, Lord Harrab, lay across a pair of trestles. A white-coated radiologist hovered over her back-lit display board on which the X-ray plates were clipped. Von Schiller went directly to the display and peered at the shadowy pictures upon it. Within the outline of the wooden coffin, the reclining human shape with hands crossed over its chest was very clear. It reminded him of a carved effigy atop the sarcophagus of an old knight in the precincts of a medieval cathedral.

'What can you tell me about this body?' he asked the radiologist without looking at her.

'Male,' she said crisply. 'Late middle age. Over fifty and under sixty-five at death. Short stature.' All the listeners winced and glanced at von Schiller. He seemed not to have noticed this solecism. 'Five teeth missing. One front upper, one eye tooth and three molars. Wisdom teeth impacted. Extensive caries in most surviving teeth. Evidence of chronic bilharzia infection. Possible poliomyelitis in infancy, withering in left leg.' She recited her findings for five minutes, and then ended, 'Probable cause of death was a puncture wound in upper right thorax. Lance or arrow. Extrapolating from the entry angle, the head of the lance or arrow would have transfixed the right lung.'

'Anything else?' von Schiller asked when she fell silent. The radiologist hesitated, and then went on.

'Herr von Schiller, you will recall that I have examined several mummies for you. In this instance, the incisions through which the viscera were removed appear to have been made with more skill and finesse than those of the other cadavers. The operator seems to have been a trained physician.'

'Thank you.' Von Schiller turned from her to Nahoot. 'Do you have any comments, at this stage?'

'Only that these descriptions do not fit those given in the seventh scroll for Tanus, Lord Harrab, at the time of his death.'

'In what way?'

'Tanus was a tall man. Much younger. See the portraits on the coffin lid.'

'Go on,' von Schiller invited.

Nahoot stepped up to the display of X-ray plates and pointed out several solid dark objects, all of them with clean outlines, that adorned the body.

'Jewellery,' he said. 'Amulets. Bracelets. Pectorals. Several necklaces. Rings and earrings. But, most significant,' Nahoot touched the dark circle around the dead brow, 'the *uraeus* crown. The outline of the sacred serpent is quite unmistakable, beneath the bandages.'

'What does that indicate?' Von Schiller was puzzled.

'This was not the body of a commoner, or even of a noble. The extent of ornamentation is too extensive. But most significant, the *uraeus* crown. The sacred cobra. That was only worn by royalty. I believe that what we have here is a royal mummy.'

'Impossible,' snapped von Schiller. 'Look at the

inscription on the coffin. Those that were painted on the walls of the tomb. Clearly this is the mummy of an Egyptian general.'

'With respect, Herr von Schiller. There is a possible explanation. In the book written by the Englishman, *River God*, there is an interesting suggestion that the slave Taita swopped the two mummies, that of Pharaoh Mamose and his good friend, Tanus.'

'For what earthly reason would he do that?' Von Schiller looked incredulous.

'Not for any earthly reason, but for a spiritual and supernatural reason. Taita wished his friend to have the use and ownership of all Pharaoh's treasure in the after-world. It was his last gift to a friend.'

'Do you believe that?'

'I do not disbelieve it. There is one other fact that tends to support this theory. It is quite obvious from the X-rays that the coffin is too large for the body within. To me, it seems obvious that it was designed to accommodate a larger man. Yes, Herr von Schiller, I do believe that there is an excellent chance that this is a royal mummy.'

Von Schiller had gone ashen pale as he listened. Sweat beaded upon his forehead, and his voice was hoarse and chesty as he asked,

'A royal mummy?'

'It may very well be so.'

Slowly von Schiller moved closer to the sealed coffin on its trestle, until he was staring down at the portrait of the dead man upon its lid.

'The golden *uraeus* of Mamose. The personal jewellery of a pharaoh.' His hand was shaking as he laid it on the coffin lid. 'If that is so, then this find exceeds our most extravagant hopes.'

Von Schiller drew a deep steadying breath. 'Open the coffin. Unwrap the mummy of the Pharaoh Mamose.'

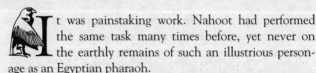It was painstaking work. Nahoot had performed the same task many times before, yet never on the earthly remains of such an illustrious personage as an Egyptian pharaoh.

Nahoot first had to establish where the joint of the lid lay beneath the paint. Once he had done this, he could whittle away at the ancient varnish and glues that secured the lid in place. Great care had to be taken to inflict as little damage as possible: the fragile coffin in itself was a priceless treasure. This work took the greater part of two days.

When the lid was free and ready to be lifted, Nahoot sent a message to von Schiller, who was in an executive meeting with his sons and the other directors of his company in the library upstairs. Von Schiller had refused to go into the city for this meeting: he could not bear to be separated from his latest treasure. Immediately he heard from Nahoot he adjourned the meeting until the following Monday, and dismissed his directors and his offspring unceremoniously. Then, without waiting to see them into their waiting limousines, he hurried down to the vaults.

Nahoot and Reeper had rigged a light scaffold over the coffin, from which hung two sets of block and tackle. As soon as von Schiller entered the vault, Reeper sent away his assistants. Only the three of them would be present to witness the opening of the coffin.

Reeper brought him the carpet-covered block for him to stand on and positioned it at the head of the coffin, so that von Schiller would be able to see inside as they worked. From this eminence the old man nodded to them to proceed. The ratchets of the two blocks clicked, one pawl at a time, as both Reeper and Nahoot gently put pressure on the tackle. There was a faint crackling and tearing sound, at which von Schiller winced.

'It is only the last shreds of glue holding the lid,' Nahoot reassured him.

'Go on!' von Schiller ordered, and they lifted the lid another six inches until it hung suspended over the body of the coffin. The scaffolding was on nylon castors which rolled smoothly over the tiled floor. They wheeled away the entire structure, with the coffin lid still suspended from it.

Von Schiller peered into the open coffin. His expression changed to one of astonishment. He had expected to see the neatly swathed human form lying serenely in the traditional funereal pose. Instead, the interior of the coffin was stuffed untidily with loose linen bandages that entirely hid the body from view.

'What on earth—' von Schiller exclaimed with astonishment. He reached out to take a handful of the old discoloured wrappings, but Nahoot stopped him.

'No! Don't touch it,' he cried out excitedly, and then was immediately apologetic. 'Forgive me, Herr von Schiller, but this is fascinating. It strongly supports the theory of an exchange of bodies. I think we should study it, before we proceed with the unwrapping. With your permission of course, Herr von Schiller.'

Von Schiller hesitated. He was anxious to discover what lay beneath this rat's nest of old rags, but he realized the virtue of caution and prudence now. A hasty move might do irreparable damage. He straightened up and stepped down from his block.

'Very well,' he grunted. He pulled a handkerchief from the breast pocket of his dark blue double-breasted suit jacket, and mopped the heavy sweat from his face. His voice was shaky as he asked, 'Is it possible? Could this be Mamose himself?'

Stuffing the handkerchief back into his trouser pocket, he discovered with mild surprise that he had a painful erection. With his hand in his pocket he rearranged it to lie flat against his stomach. 'Remove the loose wrappings.'

'With your permission, Herr von Schiller, we should take the photographs first,' Reeper suggested tactfully.

'Of course,' von Schiller agreed at once. 'We are scientists, archaeologists, not common looters. Take the photographs.'

They worked slowly, and von Schiller found the delay tantalizing. There was no sense of the passage of time down here in the vault, but at one stage von Schiller, now in his shirtsleeves, glanced at his gold wrist-watch and was surprised to see that it was past nine o'clock at night. He unknotted his necktie, threw it on the bench where his jacket already lay, and reapplied himself to the task.

Gradually the shape of a human body emerged from under the compacted mass of ancient bindings, but it was after midnight when at last Nahoot teased away the last untidy clump of old cloth from the mummy's torso. They blinked at the glimpse of gold just visible through the neat layers of bandages laid upon the corpse by the meticulous and skilful hands of the embalmers.

'Originally, of course, there would have been several massive outer coffins. These are missing, as are the masks. Those must still be in Pharaoh's original sarcophagus, covering the body of Tanus in the royal tomb that still awaits discovery. What we have left here is only the inner dressing of the royal mummy.'

With long forceps he peeled away the top layer of bandage as von Schiller, perched on his block, grunted and shuffled his feet.

'The pectoral medallion of the royal house of Mamose,' Nahoot whispered reverently. The great jewel blazed under the arc light. Resplendent in blue lapis lazuli and red carnelian and gold, it covered the entire chest of the mummy. The central motif was of a vulture in flight, soaring on wide pinions, and in its talons it clutched the golden cartouche of the king. The craftsmanship was marvellous, the design splendid.

'There is no doubt now,' von Schiller whispered. 'The cartouche proves the identity of the body.'

Next they unwrapped the king's hands, clasped over the great medallion. The fingers were long and sensitive, each of them loaded with circle after circle of magnificent rings. Clasped in his dead hands were the flail and sceptre of majesty, and Nahoot exulted when they saw them.

'The symbols of kingship. Proof on proof that this is Mamose the Eighth, ruler of the Upper and Lower Kingdoms of ancient Egypt.'

He moved up to the king's still veiled head, but von Schiller stopped him. 'Leave that until last!' he ordered. 'I am not yet ready to look upon the face of Pharaoh.'

So Nahoot and Reeper transferred their attention to the king's lower body. As they lifted away each layer of linen, so were revealed scores of amulets that the embalmers had placed beneath the bandages as charms to protect the dead man. They were of gold and carved jewels and ceramic in glowing colours and marvellous shapes – all the birds of the air and the creatures of the land and the fish of the Nile waters. They photographed each amulet *in situ* before working it free and placing it into a numbered slot in the trays that had been set out upon the workbench.

Pharaoh's feet were as small and delicate as his hands, and each toe was laden with precious rings. Only his head was still covered, and both men looked enquiringly at von Schiller. 'It is very late, Herr von Schiller,' Reeper said, 'if you wish to rest—'

'Continue!' he ordered brusquely. So they moved up on each side of the mummy's head, while von Schiller remained on his stand between them.

Gradually the king's face was exposed to the light, for the first time in nearly four thousand years. His hair was thin and wispy, still red with the henna dye he had used in his lifetime. His skin had been cured with aromatic resins until it was hard as polished amber. His nose was thin and beaked. His lips were drawn back in a soft, almost dreamy smile which exposed the gap in his front teeth.

The resin coated his eyelashes, so that they seemed wet with tears and the lids only half-shut. Life seemed to gleam there still, and only when von Schiller leaned closer did he realize that the light in those ancient sockets was the reflection from the white porcelain discs that the undertakers had placed in the empty sockets during the embalming.

On his brow the Pharaoh wore the sacred *uraeus* crown. Every detail of the cobra head was still perfect. There was no wearing or abrading of the soft metal. The serpent's fangs were sharp and recurved, and the long forked tongue curled between them. The eyes were of shining blue glass. On the band of gold beneath the hooded asp was engraved the royal cartouche of Mamose.

'I want that crown.' Von Schiller's voice was choking with passion. 'Remove it, so that I can hold it in my own hands.'

'We may not be able to lift it without damaging the head of the royal mummy,' Nahoot protested.

'Do not argue with me. Do as I tell you.'

'Immediately, Herr von Schiller,' Nahoot capitulated. 'But it will take time to free it. If Herr von Schiller wishes to rest now, we will inform you when we have loosened the crown and have it ready for you.'

The circle of gold had adhered to the resin-soaked skin of the king's forehead. In order to remove it Nahoot and Reeper first had to lift the complete body out of the coffin and lay it on the stainless steel mortuary stretcher which already waited to receive it. Then the resin had to be softened and removed with specially prepared solvents. The whole process took as long as Nahoot had predicted, but finally it was completed.

They laid the golden *uraeus* upon a blue velvet cushion, as if for a coronation ceremony. They dimmed all the other lights in the main chamber of the vault, and arranged a single spot to fall upon the crown. Then they both went upstairs to inform von Schiller.

He would not let the two archaeologists accompany him when he returned to the vaults to view the crown. Only Utte Kemper was with him when he keyed the lock to the armoured door of the vault, and the heavy door slid open.

The first thing that caught von Schiller's eye as he entered the vault was the glittering crown in its velvet nest.

Immediately he began to wheeze for air like an asthmatic, and he seized her hand and squeezed until her knuckles crackled with the pressure and she whimpered with pain. But the pain excited her. Von Schiller undressed her, placed the golden crown upon her head and laid her naked in the open coffin.

'I am the promise of life,' she whispered from the ancient coffin. 'Mine is the shining face of immortality.'

He did not touch her. Naked, he stood over the coffin with his inflamed and swollen rod thrusting from the base of his belly like a creature with separate life.

She ran her hands slowly down her own body, and as they reached her mons Veneris, she intoned gravely, 'May you live for ever!'

The wondrous efficacy of the crown of Mamose was proven beyond any doubt. Nothing before had produced this effect upon Gotthold von Schiller. For at her words, the purple head of his penis erupted of its own accord and glistening silver strings of his semen dribbled down and splattered upon her soft white belly.

In the open coffin Utte Kemper arched her back, and writhed in her own consuming orgasm.

It seemed to Royan that she had been away from Egypt for years instead of weeks. She realized just how much she had missed the crowded and bustling streets of the city, the wondrous smells of spices and food and perfume in the bazaars, and the wailing voice of the muezzin calling the faithful to prayer from the turrets of the mosques.

That very first morning she left her flat in Giza while it was still dark, and since her injured knee was still swollen and painful she used her stick as she limped along the banks of the Nile. She watched the dawn cobble the river waters with a pathway of gold and copper and set the triangular sails of the feluccas ablaze.

This was a different Nile from the one she had encountered in Ethiopia. This was not the Abbay, but the true Nile. It was broader and slower, and the muddy stink of it was familiar and well beloved. This was her river and her land. She found that her resolve to do what she had come home to do was reinforced. Her doubts were set at rest, her conscience soothed. As she turned away from it she felt strong and sure of herself and the course that she must take.

She visited Duraid's family. She had to make amends to them for her sudden departure and her long, unexplained absence. At first her brother-in-law was cool and stiff towards her; but after his wife had wept and embraced Royan and the children had clambered all over her – she was always their favourite *ammah* – he warmed to her and relented sufficiently to offer to drive her out to the oasis. When she explained that she wanted to be alone when she visited the cemetery, he unbent so far as to lend her his beloved Citroën.

As she stood beside Duraid's grave the smell of the desert filled her nostrils and the hot breeze fidgeted with her hair. Duraid had loved the desert. She was glad for him that from now onwards he would always be close to it. The headstone was simple and traditional: just his name and dates under the outline of the cross. She knelt beside it and tidied the grave, renewing the wilted and dried bouquets of flowers with those that she had brought with her from Cairo.

Then she sat quietly beside him for a long while. She made no rehearsed speeches, but simply ran over in her mind so many of the good quiet times they had passed together. She remembered his kindness and his understanding, and the security and warmth of his love for her. She regretted that she had never been able to return it in the same measure, but she knew that he had accepted and understood that.

She hoped that he also understood why she had come back now. This was a leave-taking. She had come to say goodbye. She had mourned him and, although she would always remember him and he would always be a part of her, it was time for her to move on. It was time for him to let her go. When at last she left the cemetery, she walked away without looking back.

She took the long road around the south side of the lake to avoid having to pass the burnt-out villa; she did not wish to be reminded of that night of horror on which Duraid had died there. It was therefore after dark when she returned to the city, and the family were relieved to see her. Her brother-in-law walked three times around the Citroën, checking for damage to the paintwork, before ushering her into the house where his wife had set a feast for them.

Atalan Abou Sin, the minister whom Royan had come specifically to see, was out of Cairo on an official visit to Paris. She had three days to wait for his return, and because she knew that Nahoot Guddabi was no longer in Cairo, she felt safe and able to spend much of that time at the museum. She had many friends there, and they were delighted to see her and to bring her up to date with all that had happened during the time that she had been away.

The rest of the time she spent in the museum reading room, going over the microfilm of the Taita scrolls, searching for any clues that she might have missed in her previous readings. There was a section of the second scroll which she read carefully and from which she made extensive notes. Now that the prospect of finding the tomb of Pharaoh Mamose intact had become real and credible, her interest in what that tomb might contain had been stimulated.

The section of the scroll upon which she concentrated was a description that the scribe, Taita, had given of a royal visit by the Pharaoh to the workshops of the necropolis, where his funerary treasure was being manufactured and assembled within the walls of the great temple that he had built for his own embalming. According to Taita they had visited the separate workshops, first the armoury with its collection of accoutrements of the battlefield and the chase, and then the furniture workshop, home of exquisite workmanship. In the studio of the sculptors, Taita described the work on the statues of the gods and the life-sized images of the king in every different activity of his life that would line the long causeway from the necropolis to the tomb in the Valley of the Kings. In this workshop the masons were also hard at work on the massive granite sarcophagus which would house the king's mummy over the ages. However, according to Taita's later account history had cheated Pharaoh Mamose of this part of his treasure, and all these heavy and unwieldy items of stone had been abandoned and left behind in the Valley of the Kings when the Egyptians fled south along the Nile to the land they called Cush, to escape the Hyksos invasion that overwhelmed their homeland.

As Royan turned with more attention to the scribe's description of the studio of the goldsmiths, the phrase which he used to describe the golden death-mask of the Pharaoh struck her forcibly. '*This was the peak and the zenith. All the unborn ages might one day marvel at its splendour.*' Royan looked up dreamily from the microfilm and wondered if those words of the ancient scribe were not prophetic. Was she destined to be one of those who would marvel at the splendour of the golden death-mask? Might she be the first to do so in almost four thousand years? Might she touch this wonder, take it up in her hands and at last do with it as her conscience dictated?

Reading Taita's account left Royan with a sense of ancient suffering, and a feeling of compassion for the people of those times. They were, after all – no matter how far removed in time – her own people. As a Coptic Egyptian, she was one of their direct descendants. Perhaps this empathy was the main reason why, even as a child, she had originally determined to make her life's work a study of these people and the old ways.

However, she had much else to think of during those days of waiting for the return of Atalan Abou Sin. Not least of these were her feelings for Nicholas Quenton-Harper. Since she had visited the little cemetery at the oasis and made her peace with Duraid's memory, her thoughts of Nicholas had taken on a new poignancy. There was so much she was still uncertain of, and there were so many difficult choices to make. It was not possible to fulfil all her plans and desires without sacrificing others almost equally demanding.

When at last the hour of her appointment to see Atalan came around, she had difficulty bringing herself to go to him. Like somebody in a trance she limped through the bazaars, using her stick to protect her injured knee, hardly hearing the merchants calling their wares to her.

From her skin tone and European clothing they presumed she must be a tourist.

She hesitated so long over taking this irrevocable step that she was almost an hour late for the appointment. Fortunately this was Egypt, and Atalan was an Arab to whom time did not have the same significance as it did to the Western part of Royan's make-up.

He was his usual urbane and charming self. Today, in the privacy of his own office, he was comfortably dressed in a white *dishdasha* and a headcloth. He shook hands with her warmly. If this had been London he might have kissed her cheek, but not here in the East where a man never kissed any woman but his wife and then only in the privacy of their home.

He led her through to his private sitting room, where his male secretary served them small cups of tar-thick coffee and lingered to preserve the propriety of this meeting. After an exchange of compliments and the obligatory interval of polite small-talk, Royan could come obliquely to the main reason for her visit.

'I have spent much of the last few days at the museum, working in the reading room. I managed to see many of my old colleagues there, and I was surprised to hear that Nahoot had withdrawn his application for the post of director.'

Atalan sighed, 'My nephew is a headstrong boy at times. The job was his, but at the very last moment he came to tell me that he had been offered another in Germany. I tried to dissuade him. I told him that he would not enjoy the northern climate after being brought up in the Nile valley. I told him that there are many things in life such as country and family that no amount of money can recompense. But—' Atalan spread his hands in an eloquent gesture.

'So who have you chosen to fill the post of director?' she asked with an innocence that did not deceive him.

'We have not yet made any permanent appointment. Nobody automatically comes to mind, now that Nahoot has withdrawn. Perhaps we will be forced to advertise internationally. I for one would be very sad to see it go to a foreigner, no matter how well qualified.'

'Your excellency, may I speak to you in private?' Royan asked, and glanced significantly at the male secretary hovering at the doorway. Atalan hesitated only a moment.

'Of course.' He gestured to the secretary to leave the room, and when he had withdrawn and closed the door behind him Atalan leaned towards her and dropped his voice slightly. 'What is it that you wish to discuss, my dear lady?'

It was an hour later that Royan left him. He walked with her as far as the lift outside his suite of offices.

As he shook hands his voice was low and mellifluous, 'We will meet again soon, inshallah.'

When the Egyptair flight landed at Heathrow and Royan left the airport arrivals hall for a place in the queue at the taxi rank outside, it seemed that the temperature difference from Cairo was at least fifteen degrees. Her train arrived at York in the damp misty cold of late afternoon. From the railway station she phoned the number that Nicholas had given her.

'You silly girl,' he scolded her. 'Why didn't you let me know you were on your way? I would have met you at the airport.'

She was surprised at how pleased she was to see him, and at how much she had missed him, as she watched him step out of the Range Rover and come striding towards her on those long legs. He was bare-headed and obviously had not subjected himself to a haircut since she had last seen him. His dark hair was rumpled and wind-tossed and the silver wings fluffed over his ears.

'How's the knee?' he greeted her. 'Do you still need to be carried?'

'Almost better now. Nearly time to throw away the stick.' She felt a sudden urge to throw her arms around his neck, but at the last moment she prevented herself from making a display and merely offered him a cold, rosy brown cheek to kiss. He smelt good – of leather and some spicy aftershave, and of clean virile manhood.

In the driver's seat he delayed starting the engine for a moment, and studied her face in the street light that streamed in through the side window.

'You look mighty pleased with yourself, madam. Cat been at the cream?'

'Just pleased to see old friends,' she smiled, 'but I must admit Cairo is always a tonic.'

'No supper laid on. Thought we would stop at a pub. Do you fancy steak and kidney pud?'

'I want to see my mother. I feel so guilty. I don't even know how her leg is mending.'

'Popped in to see her day before yesterday. She's doing fine. Loving the new puppy. Named it Taita, would you believe?'

'You are really a very kind person – I mean, taking the trouble to visit her.'

'I like her. One of the good old ones. They don't build them like that any more. I suggest we have a bite to eat, and then I will pick up a bottle of Laphroaig and we will go and see her.'

It was after midnight when they left Georgina's cottage. She had dispensed rough frontier justice to the malt whisky that Nicholas had brought and now she waved them off, standing in the kitchen doorway, clutching her new puppy to her ample bosom and teetering slightly on her plaster-cast leg.

'You are a bad influence on my mother,' Royan told him.

'Who's a bad influence on whom?' he protested. 'Some of those jokes of hers turned the Stilton a richer shade of blue.'

'You should have let me stay with her.'

'She has Taita to keep her company now. Besides, I need you close at hand. Plenty of work to do. I can't wait to show you what I have been up to since you went swanning off to Egypt.'

The Quenton Park housekeeper had prepared her a bedroom in the flat in the lanes behind York Minster.

As Nicholas carried her bags up the stairs rip-saw snoring came from behind the door of the bedroom on the second landing, and she looked at Nicholas enquiringly.

'Sapper Webb,' he told her. 'Latest addition to the team. Our own engineer. You will meet him tomorrow, and I think you will like him. He is a fisherman.'

'What's that got to do with me liking him?'

'All the best people are fishermen.'

'Present company excluded,' she laughed. 'Are you staying at Quenton Park?'

'Giving the house a wide berth, for the time being.' He shook his head. 'Don't want it bruited about that I am back in England. There are some fellows from Lloyd's that I would rather not speak to at the moment. I will be in the small bedroom on the top floor. Call if you need me.'

When she was alone she looked around the tiny chintzy room with its own doll's house bathroom, and the double bed that took up most of the floor area. She remembered his remark about calling if she needed him, and she looked up at the ceiling just as she heard him drop one of his shoes on the floor.

'Don't tempt me,' she whispered. The smell of him lingered in her nostrils, and she remembered the feel of his lean hard body, moist with sweat, pressed against hers as he had carried her up out of the Abbay gorge. Hunger and need were two words she had not thought of for many years. They were starting to loom too large in her existence.

'Enough of that, my girl,' she chided herself, and went to run a bath.

Nicholas pounded on her door the next morning on his way downstairs.

'Come along, Royan. Life is real. Life is urgent.'

It was still pitch dark outside, and she groaned softly and asked, 'What time is it?' But he was gone, and faintly she could hear him whistling 'The Big Rock Candy Mountain' somewhere downstairs.

She checked her watch and groaned again. 'Whistling at six-thirty, after what he and Mummy did to the Laphroaig last night. I don't believe it. The man is truly a monster.'

Twenty minutes later she found him in a dark blue fisherman's sweater and jeans and a butcher's apron, working in the kitchen.

'Slice toast for three, there's a love.' He gestured towards the brown loaf that lay beside the electric toaster. 'Omelettes coming up in five minutes.'

She looked at the other man in the room. He was middle-aged, with wide shoulders and sleeves rolled up high around muscular biceps, and he was as bald as a cannonball.

'Hello,' she said, 'I am Royan Al Simma.'

'Sorry.' Nicholas waved the egg-whisk. 'This is Danny – Daniel Webb, known as Sapper to his friends.'

Danny stood up with a cup of coffee in his big competent-looking fist. 'Pleased to meet you, Miss Al Simma. May I pour you a cup of coffee?' The top of his head was freckled, and she noticed how blue his eyes were.

'Dr Al Simma,' Nicholas corrected him.

'But please call me Royan,' she cut in quickly, 'and yes, I'd love a cup.'

There was no mention of Ethiopia or Taita's game during breakfast, and Royan ate her omelette and listened respectfully to a passionate dissertation on how to catch sail fish on a fly rod from Sapper, while Nicholas heckled him mercilessly, calling into question almost every statement he made. Very obviously they had a good relationship, and she supposed she would become accustomed to all the angling jargon.

As soon as breakfast was over, Nicholas stood up with the coffee pot in one hand. 'Bring your mugs, and follow me.'

He led Royan to the front sitting room. 'I have a surprise for you. My people up at the museum worked round the clock to get it ready for you.'

He threw open the door of the sitting room, with an imitation of a trumpet flourish, 'Tarantara!'

On the centre table stood a fully mounted model of the striped dik-dik, crowned with the pricked horns and clad in the skin that Nicholas had smuggled back from Africa. It was so realistic that for a moment she expected it to leap off the table and dash away as she walked towards it.

'Oh, Nicky. It's beautifully done!' She circled it appraisingly. 'The artist has captured it exactly.'

The model brought back to her vividly the heat and smell of the bush in the gorge, and she felt a twinge of nostalgia and sadness for the delicate, beautiful creature. Its glass eyes were deceptively lifelike and bright, and the end of its proboscis looked wet and gleaming as though it was about to wiggle it and sniff the air.

'I think it's splendid. Glad you agree with me.' He stroked the soft, smooth hide. She felt this was not the moment to spoil his boyish pleasure. 'As soon as we have sorted out Taita's puzzle, I intend writing a paper on it for the Natural History Museum, the same lads that called Great-grandpapa a liar. Restore the family honour.' He laughed and spread a dust-sheet over the model. Carefully he lifted it down from the table and placed it safely in a corner of the room where it was out of harm's way.

'That was the first surprise I had saved up for you. But now for the big one.' He pointed to a sofa against one wall. 'Take a seat. I don't want you to be bowled over by this.'

She smiled at his nonsense, but went obediently to the furthest end of the sofa and curled her legs under her as she settled there. Sapper Webb came to sit awkwardly at the other end, obviously uncomfortable at being so close to her.

'Let's talk about how we are going to get into the chasm on the Dandera river,' Nicholas suggested. 'Sapper and I have talked about nothing else the whole time that you have been away.'

'That and catching fish, I'll warrant.' She grinned at him, and he looked guilty.

'Well, both subjects involve water. That is my justification.' His expression became serious. 'You recall that we discussed the idea of exploring the depths of Taita's pool with scuba gear, and I explained the difficulties.'

'I remember,' she agreed. 'You said the pressure into the underwater opening was too great, and that we would have to find another method of getting in there.'

'Correct.' Nicholas smiled mysteriously. 'Well, Sapper here has already earned the exorbitant fee that I have promised him – promised, I emphasize, not yet paid. He has come up with the alternative method.'

Now she too became serious and unfolded her legs. She placed both feet on the floor and leaned forward attentively, with her elbows on her knees and her chin cupped in her hands.

'It must have been all those brains of his that pushed

out his hair. I mean, it's very neat thinking. Although it was staring us both in the face, neither you nor I thought of it.'

'Stop it, Nicky,' she told him ominously, 'you are doing it again.'

'I am going to give you a clue.' He ignored the warning and went on teasing her blithely. 'Sometimes the old ways are the best. That's the clue.'

'If you are so clever, how come you aren't famous?' she began, and then broke off as the solution occurred to her. 'The old ways? You mean, the same way as Taita did it? The same way he reached the bottom of the pool without the benefit of diving equipment?'

'By George! I think she's got it!' Nicholas put on a convincing Rex Harrison imitation.

'A dam.' Royan clapped her hands. 'You propose to redam the river at the same place where Taita built his dam four thousand years ago.'

'She's got it!' Nicholas laughed. 'No flies on our girl! Show her your drawings, Sapper.'

Sapper Webb made no attempt to disguise his self-satisfaction as he went to the board that stood against the facing wall. Royan had noticed it, but had paid no attention to it, until now he pulled away the cover and proudly displayed the illustrations that were pegged to it.

She recognized immediately the enlargements of the photographs that Nicholas had taken at the putative site of Taita's dam on the Dandera river, and others that he had taken in the ancient quarry that Tamre had shown them. These had been liberally adorned with calculations and lines in thick black marker pen.

'The major has provided me with estimates of the dimensions of the river bed at this point, and he has also calculated the height that we will have to raise the wall to induce a flow down the former course. I have, of course, allowed for errors in these calculations. Even if these errors

423

are in the region of thirty per cent, I believe that the project is still feasible with the very limited equipment we will have available to us.'

'If the ancient Egyptians could do it, it will be a breeze for you, Sapper.'

'Kind of you to say so, major, but "breeze" is not the word I would have chosen.'

He turned to the drawings pegged beside the photographs on the board, and Royan saw that they were plans and elevations of the project based upon the photographs and Nicholas's estimates.

'There are a number of different methods of dam construction, but these days most of them presuppose the availability of reinforced concrete and heavy earth-moving equipment. I understand that we will not have the benefit of these modern aids.'

'Remember Taita,' Nicholas exhorted him. 'He did it without bulldozers.'

'On the other hand, the Egyptians probably had unlimited numbers of slaves at their disposal.'

'Slaves I can promise you. Or the modern equivalent thereof. Unlimited numbers? Well, perhaps not.'

'The more labour you can provide, the sooner I can divert the flow of the river for you. We are agreed that this has to be done before the onset of the rainy season.'

'We have two months at the most.' Nicholas dropped his flippant attitude. 'As regards the provision of labour, I will be relying on enlisting the aid of the monastic community at St Frumentius. I am still working out a sound theological reason that might convince them to take part in the building of the dam. I don't think they will fall for the idea that we have discovered the site of the Holy Sepulchre in Ethiopia and not in Jerusalem.'

'You find me the labour, and I will build your dam,' Sapper grunted. 'As you said earlier, the old ways are the best. It is almost certain that the ancients would have used a system of gabions and coffer dams to lay the foundations of the original dam.'

'Sorry,' Royan interrupted. 'Gabions? I don't have an engineering degree.'

'I am the one who must apologize.' Sapper made a clumsy attempt at chivalry. 'Let me show you my drawings.' He turned to the board. 'What this fellow Taita probably did was to weave huge bamboo baskets, which he placed in the river and filled with rock and stone. These are what we call gabions.' He indicated the plans on the board. 'After that he would have used rough-cut timber to build circular walls between the gabions – the coffer dams. These he would also have filled with stone and earth.'

'I get the general idea,' Royan said, sounding dubious, 'but then it is not really necessary for me to understand all the details.'

'Right you are!' Sapper agreed heartily. 'Although the major assures me that there is all the timber we will need on the site, I plan to use wire mesh for the construction of the gabions and human labour for the filling of the mesh nets with stone and aggregate.'

'Wire mesh?' Royan demanded. 'Where do you hope to find that in the Abbay valley?'

Sapper began to reply, but Nicholas forestalled him. 'I will come to that in a moment. Let Sapper finish his lecture. Don't spoil his fun. Tell Royan about the stone from the quarry. She will enjoy that.'

'Although I have designed the dam as a temporary structure, we have to make certain that it is capable of holding back the river long enough to enable the members of our team to enter the underwater tunnel in the down-stream pool safely—'

'We call it Taita's pool,' Nicholas told him, and Sapper nodded.

'We have to make sure that the dam does not burst while people are in there. You can imagine the consequences, should that happen.'

He was silent for a moment while he let them dwell upon the possibility. Royan shuddered slightly and hugged her own arms.

'Not very pleasant,' Nicholas agreed. 'So you plan to use the blocks?' he prompted Sapper.

'That's right. I have studied the photographs taken in the quarry. I have picked out over a hundred and fifty granite blocks lying there completed or almost completed, and I calculate that if we use these in combination with the steel mesh gabions and the timber coffer walls, this would give us a firm foundation for the main dam wall.'

'Those blocks must weigh many tons each,' Royan pointed out. 'How will you move them?' Then, as Sapper opened his mouth to explain, she changed her mind. 'No! don't tell me. If you say it's possible, I will take your word for it.'

'It's possible,' Sapper assured her.

'Taita did it,' Nicholas said. 'We will be doing it all his way. That should please you. After all, he is a relative of yours.'

'You know, you are right. In a strange sort of way, it does give me pleasure.' She smiled at him. 'I think it's a good omen. When does all this happen?'

'It's happening already,' Nicholas told her. 'Sapper and I have already ordered all the stores and equipment that we will be taking with us. Even the mesh for the gabions has been precut to size by a small engineering firm near here. Thanks to the recession, they had machines standing idle.'

'I have been down there at their workshop every day, supervising the cutting and packing,' Sapper butted in. 'Half the shipment is already on its way. The rest of it will follow before the weekend.'

'Sapper is leaving this afternoon to take charge and get it all loaded. You and I have some last-minute arrangements to see to, and then we will follow him at the end of the week. You must remember I was not expecting you back from Cairo so soon,' Nicholas said. 'If I had known, I could have arranged for us all to fly down to Valletta together.'

'Valletta?' Royan looked mystified. 'As in Malta? I thought we were going to Ethiopia.'

'Malta is where Jannie Badenhorst has his base.'

'Jannie who?'

'Badenhorst. Africair.'

'Now you have really lost me.'

'Africair is an air transport company that owns one old ex-RAF Hercules, flown by Jannie and his son Fred. They use Malta as their base. It's a stable and pragmatic little country – no African politics, no corruption – and yet it is the door to most of the destinations in the Middle East and in the northern half of Africa where Jannie and Fred do most of their work. His main employment is smuggling booze into the Islamic countries, where of course it is prohibited. He's the Al Capone of the Mediterranean. Bootlegging is big business in that part of the world, but he does take on other work. Duraid and I flew into Libya from there with Jannie on our little jaunt to the Tibesti Massif. Jannie will be taking us down to the Abbay.'

'Nicky, I don't want to be a killjoy, but you and I are now undesirable immigrants to Ethiopia. Had you overlooked that little fact? How do you propose to get back in there?'

'Through the back door,' Nicholas grinned, 'and my old pal Mek Nimmur is the gatekeeper.'

'You have been in contact with Mek?'

'With Tessay. It seems that she is now his go-between. I imagine it's very convenient for Mek to have her on board. She has all the right connections, and she can slip in and out of Khartoum or Addis or places where it might be awkward or even dangerous for him to be seen.'

'Well, well!' Royan looked impressed. 'You have been busy.'

'Not all of us can afford a holiday in Cairo whenever the fancy takes us,' he told her tartly.

'One more little question.' She ignored the jibe, although she realized that despite his easy smile her absence must have irked him. 'Does Mek know about Taita's game?'

'Not in detail.' Nicholas shook his head. 'But he has some suspicions, and anyway I know I can rely on him.' He hesitated, and then went on. 'Tessay was very cagey when I spoke to her on the phone, but it seems that there has been some sort of attack on St Frumentius monastery. Jali Hora and thirty or forty of his monks were massacred, and most of the sacred relics from the church were stolen.'

'Oh, dear God, no!' Royan looked stricken. 'Who would do a thing like that?'

'The same people who murdered Duraid, and made three attempts to wipe you out.'

'Pegasus.'

'Von Schiller,' he agreed.

'Then we are directly responsible,' Royan whispered. 'We led them to the monastery. The Polaroids they captured from us when they raided our camp would have shown them the stele and the tomb of Tanus. Von Schiller wouldn't have to be a clairvoyant to guess where we had taken them. Now there is more blood on our hands.'

'Hell, Royan, how can you take responsibility for von Schiller's madness? I am not going to let you punish yourself for that.' Nicholas's tone was sharp and angry.

'We started this whole thing.'

'I don't agree with that, but I admit that von Schiller is the one who must have cleaned out the *maqdas* of St Frumentius and that the stele and the coffin are now almost certainly part of his collection.'

'Oh, Nicky, I feel so guilty. I never realized what a danger we were to those simple devout Christians.'

'Do you want to call off the whole thing?' he asked cruelly.

She thought about it seriously for a while, then shook her head.

'No. Perhaps when we go back we will be able to compensate the monks for their losses with what we find in the bottom of Taita's pool.'

'I hope so,' he agreed fervently. 'I do hope so.'

The giant Hercules C-Mk1 four-engined turbo-prop aircraft was painted a dusty nondescript brown, and the identification lettering on the fuselage was faded and indistinct. There was no Africair legend displayed anywhere on the machine, and it had a tired and scruffy appearance that spoke eloquently of the fact that it was almost forty years old and had flown well over half a million hours even before it had fallen into Jannie Badenhorst's hands.

'Does that thing still fly?' Royan asked, as she looked at it standing forlornly in a back corner of the Valletta airfield. Its drooping belly gave it the air of a sad old street-walker who had been put out of business by an unexpected and unlooked-for pregnancy.

'Jannie keeps it looking that way deliberately,' Nicholas assured her. 'The places that he flies to, it's best not to draw envious eyes.'

'He certainly succeeds.'

'But both Jannie and Fred are first-rate aero-engineers. Between them they keep Big Dolly perfect under her engine cowlings.'

'Big Dolly?'

'Dolly Parton. Jannie is an avid fan.' The taxi dropped them and their meagre luggage outside the side door of the hangar, and Nicholas paid the driver while Royan thrust her hands into the pockets of her anorak and shivered in the cold wind off the Mediterranean.

'There's Jannie now.' Nicholas pointed to the bulky figure in greasy brown overalls coming down the loading ramp of the Hercules. He saw them and jumped down off the ramp.

'Hello, man! I was beginning to give up on you,' he said as he came shambling across the tarmac. He looked like a rugby player, as he had been in his youth, and the slight limp was from an old playing-field injury.

'We were late leaving Heathrow. Strike by French air traffic control. The joys of international travel,' Nicholas told him, and then introduced Royan.

'Come and meet my new secretary,' Jannie invited. 'She may even give you a cup of coffee.'

He led them through a wicket in the main hangar door and into the cavernous interior. There was a small office cubicle beside the entrance with a sign over the door saying 'Africair' and the company logo of a winged battleaxe. Mara, Jannie's new secretary, was a Maltese lady only a few years younger than himself. What she lacked in youth and beauty she fully made up for across the chest.

'Jannie likes them mature and with plenty of top hamper,' Nicholas murmured to Royan from the side of his mouth.

Mara gave them coffee, while Jannie went over his flight plan with Nicholas.

'It's a little complicated,' he apologized. 'As you can imagine, we will have to do a bit of ducking and diving. Muammar Gadaffi is not wallowing in affection for me at the moment, so I'd rather not overfly any of his territory. We will be going in through Egypt, but without landing there.' He pointed out their flight path on the maps spread over his desk.

'Bit of a problem over the Sudan. They are having a

little civil war there.' He winked at Nicholas. 'However, the northern government are not equipped with the most up-to-date radar in the world. Lot of old Russian reject stuff. It's an enormous bit of country, and Fred and I have worked out their blank spots. We will be keeping well clear of their main military installations.'

'What's our flying time?' Nicholas wanted to know.

Jannie pulled a face. 'Big Dolly is no sprinter, and as I have just told you we will not be taking any short-cuts.'

'How long?' Nicholas insisted.

'Fred and I have rigged up bunks and a kitchen, so that during the flight you will have all the comforts of home.' He lifted his cap and scratched his head before he admitted, 'Fifteen hours.'

'Has Big Dolly got that sort of endurance?' Nicholas wanted to know.

'Extra tanks. Seventy-one thousand kilos of fuel. Even with the load you have given us, we can get there and back without refuelling.' He was interrupted by the huge hangar doors rolling open, and a heavy truck being driven through. 'That will be Fred and Sapper now.' Jannie swigged the last of his coffee and hugged Mara. She giggled, and her bosom quivered like a snowfield on the point of an avalanche.

The truck parked at the far end of the hangar, where an array of equipment and stores was already neatly stacked, ready for loading. When Fred climbed down from the cab, Jannie introduced him to Royan. He was a younger version of the father, already beginning to spread around the waist, and with an open bucolic face, more like a Karroo sheep farmer than a commercial pilot.

'That's the last truckload.' Sapper came around the front of the truck and shook Nicholas's hand. 'All set to begin loading.'

'I want to take off before four o'clock tomorrow morning. That will get us into our rendezvous at the

431

optimum time tomorrow evening,' Jannie cut in. 'We have a bit of work to do, if we are going to get some sleep before we leave.' He gestured to the pallets waiting to be loaded. 'I wanted to get some of the local lads to give a hand with the loading, but Sapper wouldn't hear of it.'

'Quite right,' Nicholas agreed. 'The fewer who are in on this, the merrier. Let's get cracking.'

The cargo had been prepacked on the steel pallets, secured with heavy nylon strapping and covered with cargo netting. There were thirty-six loaded pallets, and the canvas packs containing the parachutes formed an integral part of each load. This huge cargo would require two separate flights to ferry it all across to Africa.

Royan called out the contents of each pallet from the typed manifest, while Nicholas checked it against the actual load. Nicholas and Sapper had worked out the loads carefully to ensure that the items that would be required first were on the initial flight. Only when he was certain that each pallet was complete in every detail did he signal to Fred, who was operating the forklift. Fred ran the arms into the slots of the pallet and lifted it, then he drove it out of the hangar and up the ramp of the Hercules.

In the hold of the enormous aircraft, Jannie and Sapper helped Fred to position each pallet precisely on the rollers and then strap it down securely. The last part of the cargo to go aboard was the small front-end-loading tractor. Sapper had found this in a secondhand yard in York, and after testing it exhaustively declared it to be a 'steal'. Now he drove this up the ramp under its own power, and lovingly strapped it down to the rollers.

The tractor made up almost a third of the total weight of the entire shipment, but it was the one item that Sapper considered essential if they were to complete the earth-works for the dam in the time that Nicholas had stipulated. He had calculated that it would require a cluster of five cargo parachutes to get the heavy tractor back to earth without damage. Fuel for it would of course present a problem, and the bulk of the second cargo would be made up of dieseline in special nylon tanks that could withstand the impact of an airdrop.

It was after midnight before the aircraft was loaded with the first shipment. The remaining pallets were still stacked against the hangar wall awaiting Big Dolly's return for the second flight. Now they could turn their full attention to the farewell banquet of island specialities that Mara had laid out for them in the tiny Africair office.

'Yes,' Jannie assured them, 'she's also a good cook,' and gave Mara a loving squeeze as she rested her bosom on his shoulder, leaning over him to refill his plate with calamari.

'Happy landings!' Nicholas gave them the toast in red Chianti.

'Eight hours between the throttle and the bottle,' Jannie apologized, as he drank the toast in Coca-Cola.

They lay down in their clothes to get a few hours' sleep on the bunks bolted to the bulkhead behind the flight deck, but it seemed to Royan that she was woken only a few minutes later by the quiet voices of the two pilots completing their pre-take-off checks, and the whine of the starters on the huge turbo-prop engines. As Jannie spoke on the radio to the control tower, and Fred taxied out to the holding point, the three passengers climbed out of their bunks and strapped themselves into the folding seats down the side of the main cabin. Big Dolly climbed into the night sky and the lights of the island dwindled and were swiftly lost behind them. Then there was only the dark sea below and the bright pricking of the stars above. Royan turned her head to smile at Nicholas in the dim overhead lights of the cabin.

'Well, Taita, we are back on court for the final set.' Her voice was tight with excitement.

'The one good thing about being forced to sneak about like this is that Pegasus may take a while to find out that we are back in the Abbay gorge.' Nicholas looked complacent.

'Let's hope that you are right.' Royan held up her right hand and crossed her fingers. 'We will have enough to worry about with what Taita has in store for us, without Pegasus muscling in on us again just yet.'

'T'hey are on their way back to Ethiopia,' said von Schiller with utter certainty.

'How can we be certain of that, Herr von Schiller?' Nahoot asked.

Von Schiller glared at him. The Egyptian irritated him intensely, and he was beginning to regret having employed him. Nahoot had made very little headway in deciphering the meaning of the engravings on the stele that they had taken from the monastery.

The actual translation had offered no insurmountable problems. Von Schiller was convinced that he could have done this work himself, without Nahoot's assistance, given time and the use of his extensive library of reference works. It comprised, for the most part, nonsensical rhymes and extraneous couplets out of place and context. One face of the stele was almost completely covered by columns of letters and figures that bore no relation whatsoever to the text on the other three faces of the column.

But although Nahoot would not admit it, it was clear that the underlying meaning behind most of this had eluded him. Von Schiller's patience was almost exhausted. He was tired of listening to Nahoot's excuses, and to promises that were never fulfilled. Everything about him, from his oily ingratiating tone of voice to his sad eyes in their deep lined sockets, had begun to annoy him. But especially he had come to detest his exasperating habit of questioning the statements that he, Gotthold von Schiller, made.

'General Obeid was able to inform me of their exact flight arrangements when they left Addis Ababa. It was very simple to have my security men at the airport when they arrived in England. Neither Harper nor the woman are the kind of people that are easily overlooked, even in a crowd. My men followed the woman to Cairo—'

'Excuse me, Herr von Schiller, but why did you not have her taken care of if you were aware of her movements?'

'*Dummkopf!*' von Schiller snapped at him. 'Because it now seems that she is much more likely to lead me to the tomb than you are.'

'But, sir, I have done—' Nahoot protested.

'You have done nothing but make up excuses for your own failure. Thanks to you, the stele is still an enigma,' von Schiller interrupted him contemptuously.

'It is very difficult—'

'Of course it is difficult. That's why I am paying you a great deal of money. If it were easy I would have done it myself. If it is indeed the instruction to find the tomb of Mamose, then the scribe Taita meant it to be difficult.'

'If I am allowed a little more time, I think I am very near to establishing the key—'

'You have no more time. Did you not hear what I have just told you? Harper is on his way back to the Abbay gorge. They flew from Malta last night in a chartered aircraft that was heavily loaded with cargo. My men were not able to establish the nature of that cargo, except that it included some earth-moving equipment, a front-end-loading tractor. To me, this can mean only one thing. They have located the tomb, and they are returning to begin excavating it.'

'You will be able to get rid of them as soon as they reach the monastery.' Nahoot relished the thought. 'Colonel Nogo will—'

'Why do I have to keep repeating myself?' Von Schiller's voice turned shrill and he slapped his hand down on the tabletop. 'They are now our best chance of finding the tomb of Mamose. The very last thing that I want to happen is that any harm should come to them.' He glared at Nahoot. 'I am sending you back to Ethiopia immediately. Perhaps you will be of some use to me there. You are certainly no use here.'

Nahoot looked disgruntled, but he had better sense than to argue again. He sat sullenly as von Schiller went on, 'You will go to the base camp and place yourself under the command of Helm. You will take your orders from him. Treat them as if they come directly from me. Do you understand?'

'Yes, Herr von Schiller,' Nahoot muttered sulkily.

'Do not interfere in any way with Harper and the woman. They must not even know that you are at the base camp. The Pegasus geological team will carry on its normal duties.' He paused and smiled bleakly, then went on, 'It is most fortunate that Helm has actually discovered very promising evidence of large deposits of galena, which as you may know is the ore from which lead is obtained. He will continue the exploratory work on these deposits, and if they bear out their promise they will make the entire operation highly profitable.'

'What exactly will be my duties?' Nahoot wanted to know.

'You will be playing the waiting game. I want you there ready to take advantage of any progress that Harper makes. However, you are to give him plenty of elbow room. You will not alert him by any overflights with the helicopter, or by approaching his camp. No more midnight raids. Every move that you make must be cleared with me before, I repeat before, you take any action.'

'If I am to operate under these restrictions, how will I know if Harper and the woman have made any progress?'

'Colonel Nogo already has a reliable man, a spy, in the monastery. He will inform us of every move that Harper makes.'

'But what about me? What will be my work?'

'You will evaluate the intelligence that Nogo collects. You are familiar with archaeological methods. You will be able to judge what Harper is trying to achieve, and you will be able to tell what success he is enjoying.'

'I see,' Nahoot muttered.

'If it were possible I would have gone back to the Abbay gorge myself. However, this is not possible. It may take time, months perhaps, before Harper makes any important progress. You know as well as anybody that these things take time.'

'Howard Carter worked for ten years at Thebes before he found the tomb of Tutankhamen,' Nahoot pointed out maliciously.

'I hope that it will not take that long,' said von Schiller coldly. 'If it does, it is very unlikely that you will still be involved with the search. As for myself, I have a series of very important negotiations coming up here in Germany, as well as the annual general meeting of the company. These I cannot miss.'

'You will not be coming back to Ethiopia at all, then?' Nahoot perked up at the prospect of escaping from von Schiller's malignant influence.

'I will come as soon as there is something for me there. I will be relying on you to decide when my presence is needed.'

'What about the stele? I should—'

'You will continue to work on the translation.' Von Schiller forestalled his objections. 'You will take a full set of photographs with you to Ethiopia, and you will continue your work while you are there. I shall expect you to report to me by satellite, at least once a week, on your progress.'

'When do you want me to leave?'

'Immediately. Today if that is possible. Speak to Fräulein Kemper. She will make your travel arrangements.'

For the first time during the interview Nahoot looked happy.

Big Dolly droned on steadily south-eastwards, and there was very little to relieve the boredom of the flight. The dawn was just breaking when they crossed the African coast at a remote and lonely desert beach that Jannie had chosen for just this reason. Once they were over the land there was as little of interest to see as there had been over the sea. The desert stretched away, bleak and brown and featureless in every direction.

At irregular intervals they heard Jannie in the cockpit speaking to air traffic control, but as they were able to hear only half the conversation they had no idea as to the identity or the nationality of the station. Occasionally Jannie dropped the heavily accented English he was affecting and broke into Arabic. Royan was surprised by Jannie's fluency in the language, but then as an Afrikaner the guttural sounds came naturally to him. He was even able to mimic the different accents and dialects of Libyan and Egyptian convincingly as he lied his way across the desert.

For the first few hours Sapper pored over his dam drawings; then, unable to proceed further until he had the exact measurements of the site, he curled up on his bunk with a paperback novel. The unfortunate author was unable to hold his attention for long. The open book sagged down over his face, and the pages fluttered every time he emitted a long grinding snore.

Nicholas and Royan huddled on her bunk with the chessboard between them, until hunger overtook them and they moved to the makeshift galley. Here Royan took the subservient role of bread-slicer and coffee-maker, while

Nicholas demonstrated his artistry in creating a range of Dagwood sandwiches. They shared the food with Jannie and Fred, perched up behind the pilots' seats in the cockpit.

'Are we still over Egyptian territory?' Royan asked.

With his mouth full, Jannie pointed out over the port wingtip of Big Dolly. 'Fifty nautical miles out there is Wadi Halfia. My father was killed there in 1943. He was with the Sixth South African Division. They called it Wadi Hellfire.' He took another monstrous bite of sandwich. 'I never knew the old man. Fred and I landed there once. Tried to find his grave.' He shrugged eloquently. 'It's a hell of a big piece of country. Lots of graves. Very few of them marked.'

Nobody spoke for a while. They chewed their sandwiches, thinking their own thoughts. Nicholas's father had also fought in the desert against Rommel. He had been more fortunate than Jannie's father.

Nicholas glanced across at Royan. She was staring out of the window at her homeland, and there was something so passionate and fraught in her gaze that Nicholas was startled. The temptation to think of her as an English girl, like her mother, was at most times irresistible. It was only in odd moments such as these that he became intensely aware of the other facets of her being.

She seemed unaware of his scrutiny. Her preoccupation was total. He wondered what she was thinking – what dark and mysterious thoughts were smouldering there. He remembered how she had seized the very first opportunity on their return from Ethiopia to hurry back to Cairo, and once again a feeling of disquiet came over him. He wondered if other emotional ties of which he was unaware might not transcend those loyalties which he had taken for granted. He realized with something of a shock that they had been together for only a few short weeks, and despite the strong attraction that she exerted over him he knew very little about her.

At that moment she started and looked round at him quickly. Crowded as they were at the portside window, they stared into each other's eyes from a distance of only a foot or so. It was only for a few seconds but what he saw in her eyes, the dark shadows of guilt or some other emotion, did nothing to allay his misgivings.

She turned back to Jannie, leaning over his shoulder to ask, 'When will we cross the Nile?'

'On the other side of the border. The Sudanese government concentrate all their attentions on the rebels in the far south. There are some stretches of the river here in the north that are completely deserted. Pretty soon now we will be going down right on the deck, to get under the radar pings from the Sudanese stations around Khartoum. We will slip through one of the gaps.'

Jannie lifted the aeronautical map on its clipboard from his lap, and held it so she could see it. With one thick, stubby finger he showed Royan their intended route. It was drawn in with blue wax pencil, 'Big Dolly has taken this route so often that she could fly it without my hands on the stick, couldn't you, old girl?' He patted the instrument panel affectionately.

Two hours later, when Nicholas and Royan were back at the chess board in the main cabin, Jannie called them on the PA, 'Okay, folks. No need to panic. We are going to lose some altitude now. Come up front and watch the show.'

Strapped into fold-down seats in the back of the flight deck, they were treated to a superb exhibition of low flying by Fred. The descent was so rapid that Royan felt they were about to fall out of the sky, and that she had left her stomach back there somewhere at thirty thousand feet. Fred levelled Big Dolly out only feet above the desert floor, so low that it was like riding in a high-speed bus rather than flying. Fred lifted her delicately over each undulation of the tawny, sun-scorched terrain, skimming the black rock ridges and standing on a wingtip to swerve around the occasional wind-blasted hill.

'Nile crossing in seven and a half minutes.' Jannie punched the stopwatch fixed to the control wheel in front of him. 'And unless my navigation has gone all to hell there should be an island shaped like a shark directly under us as we cross.'

As the needle of the stopwatch came up to the mark, the broad, glittering expanse of the river flashed beneath them. Royan caught a brief glimpse of a green island with a few thatched huts on the tip, and a dozen dugout canoes lying on the narrow beach.

'Well, the old man hasn't lost his touch yet,' Fred remarked. 'Still good for a few thousand miles before we trade him in.'

'Not so much of the old man stuff, you little squirt. I have some tricks up my sleeve that I haven't even used yet.'

'Ask Mara.' Fred grinned affectionately at his father as he banked on to a new southwesterly heading, and with his wingtip so close to the ground that he scattered a herd of camels feeding in the sparse thorn scrub. They lumbered away across the plain, each trailing a wisp of white dust like a wedding train.

'Another three hours' flying time to the rendezvous.' Jannie looked up from the map. 'Spot on! We should land forty minutes before sunset. Couldn't be better.'

'I'd better go and change into my hiking gear, then.' Royan went back into the main cabin, pulled her bag from under the bunk and disappeared into the lavatory. When she emerged twenty minutes later she wore khaki culottes and a cotton top.

'These boots were made for walking.' She stamped them on the deck.

'That's fine.' Nicholas watched her from the bunk. 'But how about that knee?'

'It will get me there,' she said, defensively.

'You mean I am to be deprived of the pleasure of back-packing you again?'

The Ethiopian mountains came up so subtly on the eastern horizon that Royan was not aware of them until Nicholas pointed out to her the faint blue outline against the brighter blue of the African sky.

'Almost there.' He glanced at his wrist-watch. 'Let's go up to the flight deck.'

Looking forward through the windshield there was no landmark ahead of them – just the vast brown savannah, speckled with the black dots of acacia trees.

'Ten minutes to go,' Jannie intoned. 'Anyone see anything?' There was no reply, and they all stared ahead.

'Five minutes.'

'Over there!' Nicholas pointed over his shoulder. 'That's the course of the Blue Nile.' A denser grove of thorn trees formed a dark line far ahead. 'And there is the smokestack of the derelict sugar-mill on the river bank. Mek Nimmur says that the airstrip is about three miles from the mill.'

'Well, if it is, it's not shown on the chart,' Jannie grumbled. 'One minute before we are on the coordinates.' The minute ticked off slowly on the stopwatch.

'Still nothing—' Fred broke off as a red flare shot up from the earth directly ahead and flashed past Big Dolly's nose. Everyone in the cockpit smiled and relaxed with relief.

'Right on the nose.' Nicholas patted Jannie's shoulder in congratulations. 'Couldn't have done better myself.'

Fred climbed a few hundred feet and came round in a one-eighty turn. Now there were two signal fires burning out there on the plain – one with black smoke, the other sending a column of white straight up into the still evening sky. It was only when they were a kilometre out that they were able to make out the faint outline of the overgrown and long-disused landing strip. Roseires airstrip had been built twenty years before by a company that tried to grow sugar cane under irrigation from the Blue Nile. But Africa had won again and the company had passed into oblivion, leaving this feeble scrape mark on the plain as its epitaph. Mek Nimmur had chosen this remote and deserted place for the rendezvous.

'No sign of a reception committee,' Jannie grunted. 'What do you want me to do?'

'Continue your approach,' Nicholas told him. 'There should be another flare – ah, there it is!' The ball of fire shot up from a clump of thorn trees at the far end of the runway, and for the first time they were able to make out human figures in the bleak landscape. They had stayed hidden until the very last moment.

'That's Mek, all right! Go ahead and land.'

As Big Dolly finished her roll-out and the end of the rough and pitted runway came up ahead, a figure in camouflage fatigues popped up ahead of them. With a pair of paddles it signalled them to taxi into the space between two of the tallest thorn trees.

Jannie cut the engines and grinned at them over his shoulder. 'Well, boys and girls, looks like we pulled off another lucky one!'

Even from the height of Big Dolly's cockpit there was no mistaking the commanding figure of Mek Nimmur as he emerged from the cover of the clump of acacia trees. Only now did they realize that the trees had been shrouded with camouflage netting; this was why they had not been able to spot any sign of human presence from the air. As soon as the loading ramp was lowered, Mek Nimmur came striding up it.

'Nicholas!' They embraced and, after Mek had kissed him noisily on each cheek, he held Nicholas at arm's length and studied his face, delighted to see him again. 'So I was right! You are up to your old tricks. Not simply a dik-dik shoot, was it?'

'How can I lie to an old friend?' Nicholas shrugged.

'It always came easy to you,' Mek laughed, 'but I am glad we are going to have some fun together. Life has been very boring recently.'

'I bet!' Nicholas punched his shoulder affectionately.

A slim, graceful figure followed Mek up the ramp. In the olive-green fatigues Nicholas hardly recognized Tessay until she spoke. She wore canvas para boots and a cloth cap that made her look like a boy.

'Nicholas! Royan! Welcome back!' Tessay cried. The two women embraced as enthusiastically as the men had done.

'Come on, you Ous!' Jannie protested. 'This isn't Woodstock. I have to get back to Malta tonight. I want to take off before dark.'

Swiftly Mek took charge of the offloading. His men swarmed aboard and manhandled the pallets forward on the rollers, while Sapper started up his beloved front-end loader and used it to run the cargo down the ramp and stack it in the acacia grove under the camouflage netting. With so many hands to help it went swiftly, and Big Dolly's hold was emptied just as the sun settled wearily on to the horizon, and the short African twilight bled all colour from the landscape.

Jannie and Nicholas had one last hurried discussion in the cockpit while Fred completed his flight checks. They went over the plans and radio procedures one last time.

'Four days from today,' Jannie agreed, as they shook hands briefly.

'Let the man go, Nicholas,' Mek bellowed from below. 'We must get across the border before dawn.'

They watched Big Dolly taxi down to the end of the strip and swing around. The engine beat crescendoed as she came tearing back in a long rolling shroud of dust and lifted off over their heads. Jannie waggled his wings in farewell and, without navigation lights showing, the great aircraft blended like a black bat into the darkening sky and disappeared almost immediately.

'Come here.' Nicholas led Royan to a seat under the acacia. 'I don't want that knee to play up again.' He pushed her culottes halfway up her thigh and strapped the knee with an elastic bandage, trying not to make his pleasure in this task too apparent. He was pleased to see that the bruising had almost faded and there was no longer any swelling.

He palpated it gently. Her skin was velvety and the flesh beneath it firm and warm to the touch. He looked up, and from the expression on her face realized that she was enjoying this intimacy as much as he was. As he caught her eye she flushed slightly, and quickly smoothed down her culottes.

She jumped up and said, 'Tessay and I have a lot of catching up to do,' and hurried across to join her.

'I am leaving a full combat platoon to guard your stores here,' Mek explained to Nicholas as Tessay led Royan away. 'We will travel in a very small party as far as the border. I don't expect any trouble. There is very little enemy activity in this sector at the moment. Lots of fighting in the south, but we are quiet here. That is why I chose this rendezvous.'

'How far to the Ethiopian border?' Nicholas wanted to know.

'Five hours' march,' Mek told him. 'We will slip through one of our pipelines after the moon has set. The rest of my men are waiting in the entrance to the Abbay gorge. We should rendezvous with them before dawn tomorrow.'

'And from there to the monastery?'

'Another two days' march,' Mek replied. 'We will be

there just in time to receive the drop from your fat friend in the fat plane.'

He turned away and gave his last orders to the platoon commander who would remain at Roseires to guard the stores. Then he assembled the party of six men who would form their escort across the border. Mek divided up the loads between them. The most important single item was the radio, a modern military lightweight model which Nicholas carried himself.

'Those bags of yours are too difficult to carry. You will have to repack them,' Mek told Nicholas and Royan. So they emptied their bags and stuffed the contents into the two canvas haversacks that Mek had ready for them. Two of his men slung the haversacks over their shoulders and disappeared into the darkness.

'He is not taking that!' Mek stared aghast at the bulky legs of the theodolite that Sapper had retrieved from one of the pallets. Sapper spoke no Arabic, so Nicholas had to translate.

'Sapper says that it is a delicate instrument. He cannot allow it to be dropped from the aircraft. He says that if it is damaged he will not be able to do the work he was hired for.'

'Who is going to carry it?' Mek demanded. 'My men will mutiny if I try to make them do it.'

'Tell the cantankerous bugger that I will carry it myself.' Sapper drew himself up with dignity. 'I wouldn't let one of his great clumsy oafs lay a finger on it.' He picked up the bundle, placed it over his shoulder and stalked away with a stiff back.

Mek let the advance guard have a five-minute start, and then he nodded. 'We can go now.'

Thirty minutes after Big Dolly had taken off, they left the airfield and set out across the dark and silent plain, headed into the east. Mek set a hard pace. He and Nicholas seemed to have the eyes of a pair of cats, Royan thought,

446

as she followed close behind them. They could see in the darkness, and only a whispered warning from one of them prevented her falling into a hole or tripping over a pile of rocks in the darkness. When she did stumble, Nicholas seemed always to be there, reaching back to steady her with a strong, firm grip.

They marched in complete and disciplined silence. It was only every hour, when they rested for five minutes, that Nicholas and Mek sat close together, and from the few quiet words she picked up Royan realized that Nicholas was explaining to him the full reasons for their return to the Abbay gorge. She heard Nicholas repeat the names 'Mamose' and 'Taita' often, and Mek's deep voice questioning him at length. Then they would be up again and moving forward in the night.

After a while she lost all sense of the distance they had travelled. Only the hourly rest periods orientated her to the passage of time. Fatigue crept over her slowly, until it required an effort to lift her foot for each pace. Despite her boast, her knee was beginning to ache. Now and then she felt Nicholas touch her arm, guiding her over the rough places. At other times they would stop abruptly at some whispered warning from up front. Then they would stand quietly waiting in the darkness, nerves tensed, until at another whisper they would move on again at the same pressing pace. Once she smelt the cool muddy effluvium of the river on the dry warm night air, and she knew that they must be very close to the Nile. Without a word being spoken she sensed the nervous tension in the men ahead of her, and was aware of the alertness in the way they carried themselves and their weapons.

'Crossing the border now,' Nicholas breathed close to her face, and the tension was infectious. She forgot her tiredness, and heard her pulse beating in her own ears.

This time they did not stop for the usual rest break,

447

but continued for another hour until slowly she felt the mood of the men changing. Someone laughed softly, and there was a lightness in their pace as they swung on towards the luminescence in the eastern sky. Abruptly the moon thrust its crescent horns above the dark silhouette of far-off mountain ranges.

'All clear. We are through,' Nicholas told her in his normal voice. 'Welcome back to Ethiopia. How are you feeling?'

'I'm okay.'

'I am tired too.' He grinned at her in the moonlight. 'Pretty soon we will camp and rest. Not much further.'

He was lying, of course: the march went on and on until she wanted to weep. And then suddenly she heard the sound of the river again, the soft rushing flow of the Nile in the dawn. Up ahead she heard Mek talking to the men who were waiting for them, and then Nicholas guided her off the path and made her sit while he knelt in front of her and unlaced her boots.

'You did well. I am proud of you,' he told her, as he stripped off her socks and examined her feet for blisters. Then he unbandaged the knee. It was slightly swollen, and he massaged it with a skilled and tender touch.

She sighed softly, 'Don't stop. That feels good.'

'I'll give you a Brufen for the inflammation.' He dug the pills out of his pack and then spread his padded jacket for her to lie on. 'Sorry, the sleeping bags are with our other gear. Have to rough it until Jannie makes his air drop.'

He passed her the water bottle, and while she swallowed the pill he pulled the tab on a pack of emergency rations. 'Not exactly gourmet fare.' He sniffed the contents. 'In the army we call them rat packs.' She fell asleep with her mouth still half-filled with tasteless meat loaf and plastic cheese.

When Nicholas woke her with a mug of hot sweet tea,

she saw it was already late afternoon. He sat beside her and sipped at his own mug, noisily blowing away the steam between each mouthful.

'You will be pleased to know that Mek is now fully in the picture. He has agreed to help us.'

'What have you told him?'

'Just enough to keep him interested.' Nicholas grinned. 'The theory of progressive disclosure. Never tell everything all at once, feed it to them a little at a time. He knows what we are looking for, and that we are going to dam a river.'

'What about men to work on the dam?'

'The monks at St Frumentius will do whatever he tells them. He is a great hero.'

'What have you promised him in return?'

'We haven't got round to that yet. I told him that we have no idea what we are going to find, and he laughed and said he would trust me.'

'Silly boy, isn't he?'

'Not exactly how I would describe Mek Nimmur,' he murmured. 'I think when the time is ripe he will let us know what the price of his cooperation is.' He looked up at that moment. 'We were just talking about you, Mek.'

Mek strode up to them, and then squatted on his haunches beside Nicholas.

'What were you saying about me?'

'Royan says you are a hard bastard, pushing her on a forced march all night.'

'Nicholas is spoiling you. I have been watching him fussing over you,' he chuckled. 'What I say is, treat them rough. Women love it.' Then he grew serious. 'I am sorry, Royan. The border is always a bad place. You will find me less of a monster now we are on home ground.'

'We are very grateful for all you are doing.'

He inclined his head gravely, 'Nicholas is an old friend, and I hope that you are a new friend.'

'I have been terribly distressed. Tessay told me last night that there had been trouble at the monastery.'

Mek scowled and tugged at his short beard, pulling a tuft of hair from his own chin with the force of his anger. 'Nogo and his killers. This is just a sample of what we are fighting against. We have been rescued from the tyranny of Mengistu, only to be plunged into fresh horror.'

'What happened, Mek?'

Speaking tersely but vividly, he described the massacre and the plunder of the monastery's treasures. 'There was no doubt it was Nogo. Every one of the monks that escaped knows him well.'

His anger was too fierce for him to contain, and he stood up abruptly. 'The monastery means much to all the people of the Gojam. I was christened there, by Jali Hora himself. The murder of the abbot and the desecration of the church is a terrible outrage.' He jammed his cap down on his head. 'And now we must get on. The road ahead is steep and difficult.'

Now that they were clear of the border, it was safe to move in daylight. The second day's march carried them into the depths of the gorge. There were no foothills: it was like entering through the keep of a vast castle. The walls of the great central massif rose up almost four thousand feet on either hand, and the river snaked along in the depths, its entire length churned by rapids and breaking white water. At noon Mek broke the march to rest in a grove of trees beside the river. There was a beach below them, sheltered by massive boulders which must have rolled down from the cliffs that hung like a rampart above them.

The five of them sat a little apart from each other. Sapper was still smarting from his altercation over the theodolite with Mek, and keeping himself aloof. He placed the heavy instrument in a conspicuous position and sat ostentatiously close to it. Mek and Tessay seemed strangely quiet and withdrawn, until suddenly Tessay reached out and grasped Mek's hand.

'I want to tell them,' she blurted out impulsively.

Mek looked away at the river for a moment before he nodded. 'Why not?' he shrugged at last.

'I want them to know,' Tessay insisted. 'They knew Boris. They will understand.'

'Do you want me to tell them?' Mek asked softly, and he was still holding her hand.

'Yes,' she nodded, 'it is best that it comes from you.'

Mek was silent for a while, gathering his words, and then he started in that low rumbling voice, not looking at them, but watching Tessay's face. 'The very first moment I looked upon this woman, I knew that she was the one that God had sent my way.'

Tessay moved closer to him.

'Tessay and I said our vows together on the night of Timkat and asked for God's forgiveness, and then I took her away as my woman.'

She laid her head upon his great muscular shoulder.

'The Russian followed us. He found us here, on this very spot. He tried to kill us both.'

Tessay looked down at the beach upon which she and Mek had so nearly died, and she shuddered at the memory.

'We fought,' he said simply, 'and when he was dead, I sent his body floating away down the river.'

'We knew he was dead,' Royan told them. 'We heard from the people at the embassy that the police found his body downstream, near the border. We didn't know how it had happened.'

They were all quiet for a while, and then Nicholas broke the silence, 'I wish I had been there to watch. It must have been one hell of a fight.' He shook his head in awe.

'The Russian was good. I am glad I don't have to fight him again,' Mek admitted, and stood up. 'We can reach the monastery before dark, if we start now.'

Mai Metemma, the newly elected abbot of St Frumentius, met them on the terrace of the monastery overlooking the river. He was only a little younger than Jali Hora had been, tall and with a dignified silver head, and today he was wearing the blue crown in honour of such a distinguished guest as Mek Nimmur.

After the visitors had bathed and rested for an hour in the cells that had been set aside for them, the monks came to lead them to the welcome feast that had been prepared. When the *tej* flasks had been refilled for the third time, and the mood of the abbot and of his monks had mellowed, Mek began to whisper into the old man's ear.

'You recall the history of St Frumentius – how God cast him up on our shore from the storm-tossed sea, so that he might bring the true faith to us?'

The abbot's eyes filled with tears. 'His holy body was entombed here, in our *maqdas*. The barbarians came and stole the relic away from us. We are children without a father. The reason for the building of this church and monastery has been taken away,' he lamented. 'No longer will the pilgrims come from every corner of Ethiopia to pray at his shrine. We will be forgotten by the Church. We are undone. Our monastery will perish and our monks will be blown away like dead leaves on the wind.'

'When St Frumentius came to Ethiopia he was not alone. Another Christian came with him from the High Church in Byzantium,' Mek reminded him in a soft, soothing rumble.

'St Antonia.' The abbot reached for his *tej* flask to allay the intensity of his sorrow.

'St Antonia,' Mek agreed. 'He died before St Frumentius, but he was no less holy than his brother.'

'St Antonia was also a great and holy man, deserving of our love and veneration.' The abbot took a long swallow from the flask.

'The ways of God are mysterious, are they not?' Mek shook his head at the wonder of the workings of the universe.

'His ways are deep and not for us to question or understand.'

'And yet he is compassionate, and he rewards the devout.'

'He is all-compassionate.' The abbot's tears overflowed and ran down his cheeks.

'You and your monastery have suffered a grievous loss. The sacred relic of St Frumentius has been taken from you – alas, never to be recovered. But what if God were to send you another? What if he were to send you the sacred body of St Antonia?'

The abbot looked up through his tears, his expression suddenly calculating. 'That would be a miracle indeed.'

Mek Nimmur placed his arm around the old man's shoulders and whispered quietly in his ear, and Mai Metemma stopped weeping and listened intently.

'I have obtained your workers for you,' Mek told Nicholas as they began the march up the valley the next morning. 'Mai Metemma has promised to give us a hundred men within two days and another five hundred to follow them within the next week. He is handing out indulgences to all those who volunteer to work on the dam. They will be spared the fires of purgatory if they take part in such a glorious project as the recovery of the holy relic of St Antonia.'

Both the women stopped in their tracks and stared at him.

'What did you promise the poor old man?' Tessay demanded.

'A body to replace the one that Nogo plundered from the church. If we do discover the tomb, then the monastery's share will be the mummy of Mamose.'

'That's a mean thing to do,' Royan exploded. 'You will cheat him into helping us.'

'It is not a cheat.' Mek's dark eyes flashed at the accusation. 'The relic that they lost was not the veritable body of St Frumentius, and yet for hundreds of years it served the purpose of uniting the community of monks and drawing Christians from all over this land. Now that it is gone, the very existence of the monastery is threatened. They have lost their reason for continuing.'

'So you are tempting them with a false promise!' Royan was still angry.

'The body of Mamose is every bit as authentic as the one they lost. What does it matter if it is the body of an ancient Egyptian rather than that of an ancient Christian, just as long as it serves as a focus for the faith and if it is the means by which the monastery might survive for another five hundred years?'

'I think Mek is making sense.' Nicholas gave his opinion.

'Since when have you been an expert in Christianity? You are an atheist,' Royan flashed at him, and he held up his hands as if to ward off a blow.

'You are right. What do I know about it anyway? You argue it out with Mek. I am going to discuss the theory of dam-building with Sapper Webb.' He sauntered up to the head of the file of men and fell in beside his engineer.

From time to time he heard heated voices raised behind him, and he grinned. He knew Mek, but he was also beginning to understand the lady. It would be fascinating to see who would win this argument.

They reached the head of the chasm in the middle of the afternoon, and while Mek searched out a campsite Nicholas took Sapper immediately to the narrow neck of the river just above where it plunged over the waterfall. While Sapper set up the theodolite, Nicholas took the graduated levelling staff. Sapper ordered him up and down the face of the cliff with peremptory hand signals, all the while peering into the lens of the theodolite, while Nicholas teetered on insecure footing and tried to keep the staff upright for Sapper to take his sightings.

'Okay!' Sapper bellowed, after taking his twentieth shot. 'Now I want you on the other side of the river.'

'Fine!' Nicholas bellowed back. 'Do you want me to fly or swim?'

Nicholas hiked three miles upstream to the ford where the trail crossed the Dandera river, and then fought his way back through the tangled riverine undergrowth to the point on the bank opposite which Sapper lay in the shade smoking a soothing cigarette.

'Don't rupture yourself, will you?' Nicholas yelled across the water at him.

It was almost dark before Sapper had made all the shots he wanted, and Nicholas was still faced with the long return trip over the ford. He covered the last mile in almost total darkness, guided only by the flicker of the campfires. Wearily he stumbled into the camp and flung down the levelling staff.

'You had better tell me that it was worth it,' he growled at Sapper, who did not look up from his slide rule. He was working over his revised drawings by the glaring light of a small butane lantern.

'You weren't too far out in your estimates,' he congratulated Nicholas. 'The river is forty-one yards wide at the critical point above the falls, where I want to site the structure.'

'All I want to know is if you will be able to throw a dam across it.'

Sapper grinned and laid his finger down the side of his nose, 'You get me my ruddy front-ender, and I'll dam the bleeding Nile itself.'

After they had eaten their dinner – another of the rat packs – Royan glanced across the fire at Nicholas. When she caught his eye she inclined her head in invitation. Then she stood up and casually drifted out of camp, looking back once to make sure he was following her. Nicholas lighted the path with his torch as they picked their way back to the dam site and found a boulder overlooking the water on which to sit.

He switched off the torch and they were silent for a while as their eyes adjusted to the starlight, and then Royan whispered, 'There were times that I thought we would never return here – that it was all a dream, and that Taita's pool never existed.'

'For us perhaps it never will, without the help of the monks from the monastery.' There was a note of enquiry in his voice.

'You and Mek Nimmur win,' she chuckled softly. 'Of course we have to accept their help. Mek's arguments were very convincing.'

'So you agree that their reward should be the mummy of Mamose?'

'I agree that they may take whatever mummy we discover, if we discover one at all,' she qualified. 'For all we know, the true mummy of Mamose may be the one that Nogo stole.'

Quite naturally he slipped his arm around her shoulders, and after a moment she relaxed against him.

'Oh, Nicky, I am afraid and excited. Afraid that all our hopes are vain, and excited that we might have found the key to Taita's game.' She turned her face to his, and he felt her breath on his lips.

He kissed her, tenderly. Then he drew back with the warmth of her lingering on his lips and studied her face in the starlight. She made no movement to pull away from him. Instead she swayed towards him, and kissed him back. At first it was a staid sisterly kiss, with her mouth tightly closed. He brought his right hand up behind her head and weaved his fingers into her hair, holding her face to his. He opened his mouth over hers, and she made a little sound of dissent through her closed lips.

Slowly, voluptuously, he worked her lips apart, and her protests died away as he probed her mouth deeply with his tongue. She was making a contented little mewling sound now, like a kitten nursing on the teat, and her arms went around him. She kneaded his back with strong supple fingers, her mouth wide open to his kiss, her tongue sinuous and slippery as it twined around his.

He slid his other hand up between their bodies and unhooked the buttons of her shirt down as low as her belt. She leaned back slightly in his embrace to make it easier for him. With a delicious shock he discovered that her breasts were naked under the thin cotton shirt. He cupped one of them in his hand: it was small and firm, only just filling his hand. When he pinched the nipple gently, it stiffened between his fingers like a tiny ripe strawberry.

He broke off the kiss and bowed his head to her bosom. She moaned softly, and with one hand guided him down. When he sucked her nipple into his mouth she gasped and hooked the nails of her other hand into his back, like a cat responding to a caress. Her whole body undulated in his embrace, and after a while she pulled his mouth away. He thought for a moment that she was rejecting him, but then she moved his head across and placed her other nipple in his mouth. Once again she gasped as he sucked it in.

Her movements became more abandoned, keeping pace with his own arousal. He could restrain himself no longer and he reached up under her khaki culottes and laid his hand on the plump mound of her sex. Then with one swift lithe movement she broke away and sprang to her feet. She stood back from him, smoothing down her culottes and buttoning her shirt with fingers that trembled.

'I am so sorry, Nicky. I want to, oh God, you will never know how much I want to. But—' she shook her head and she was panting wildly, 'not yet. Please, Nicky, forgive me. I am caught between two worlds. One half of me wants this so very much, but the other half will not allow me—'

He stood up and kissed her chastely. 'There is no hurry. Good things are worth waiting for,' he told her with his mouth just touching hers. 'Come! I will take you home now.'

While it was still dark the next morning, the first levy of priests that Mai Metemma had promised came filing up the valley. Their chanting awoke the camp, and everyone came sleepily out of their thatched lean-to shelters to welcome the long column of holy men.

'Sweet heavens,' Nicholas yawned, 'it looks as though we have started another crusade. They must have left the monastery in the middle of the night to get here at this hour.' He went to find Tessay, and when he did he told her, 'You are hereby appointed official translator. Sapper speaks not a word of either Arabic or Amharic. Stick close to him.'

As soon as it was fully light, Mek and Nicholas left

camp to reconnoitre a drop site. By noon they had agreed that there was only one possibility: they would have to use the valley itself. Compared to the rocky ridges that surrounded them, the floor of the valley was level and fairly free of obstructions. It was imperative that the drop should take place as close to the dam site as possible, for every mile that the stores must be manhandled would add immeasurably to the time and effort needed for the work.

'Time is the major factor,' Nicholas told Mek as they stood in the chosen drop zone the following morning. 'Every day counts from now until the rains break.'

Mek looked up at the sky. 'Pray God for late rains.'

They marked out their drop site a mile down from the river, along the stretch where the valley was widest and there was a clear approach through a gap in the hills. Jannie would need to fly straight and level for five miles under full flap and with the loading ramp down.

'Cutting it fine,' Mek remarked, as they surveyed the rugged slopes and frowning peaks that surrounded them. 'Can your fat friend fly?'

'Fly? He is half-bird,' Nicholas told him.

They moved down the valley to check the placement of the flares and the markers. The markers consisted of crosses of quartz stones laid out down the centre of the valley floor, and they would be highly visible from the air. Sapper was up at the head of the valley. They could see him there on the skyline as he moved around, setting out his smoke flares to mark the approach to the drop zone.

When Nicholas turned around and looked in the opposite direction, he could see the two women sitting on a rock together at the far end of the valley. Sapper had already helped them to set up their flares. These would mark the far limit of the zone, and give Jannie a mark for his climb out of the valley.

Nicholas then turned his attention back to Mek's men as they finished laying out the stark white quartz markers.

Once these were all in place, Mek ordered the area to be cleared. Then, lugging the radio, they climbed up to join Sapper on the high ground at the head of the valley. Mek helped Nicholas string out the aerial. Then Nicholas switched on and adjusted the gain carefully before he thumbed the microphone.

'Big Dolly. Come in, Big Dolly!' Nicholas invited, but the static hummed and whined.

'They must be running late.' Nicholas tried not to let his disquiet show. 'Jannie will be coming straight in from Malta on this run. After the first drop he will go back to your base at Roseires and pick up the second load. With luck, both loads should all be dropped before noon tomorrow.'

'If the fat man comes at all,' Mek remarked.

'Jannie is a pro,' Nicholas grunted. 'He will come.' He held the microphone to his lips, 'Big Dolly. Do you read? Over.'

Every ten minutes he called out into the empty echoing silence. Each time his call went unanswered he had visions of Sudanese MiG interceptors racing in with their missiles cocked and locked, and the old Hercules plunging earthwards in flames.

'Come in, Big Dolly!' he pleaded, and at last a thin, scratchy voice floated into his headset. 'Pharaoh. This is Big Dolly. ETA forty-five minutes. Standing by.' Jannie's transmission was terse. He was too much of an old hand at the smuggling game to give a hostile listener time to fix his position.

'Big Dolly. Understand four five. Pharaoh standing by.' Nicholas grinned at Mek. 'Looks like we are in business after all.'

Mek heard it first. His ear was battle-tuned. In this land, if you wanted to go on living it paid to pick up any aircraft long before it arrived. Nicholas was out of training, so it was almost five minutes later that he picked up the distinctive drone of the multi-props echoing weirdly off the cliffs of the gorge. It was impossible to be certain of the direction, but they shaded their eyes and stared into the west.

'There she is.' Nicholas redeemed himself as he spotted the tiny dark speck, so low as almost to blend into the background of the escarpment wall. He nodded at Sapper.

Sapper ran out to his flares and fussed over them briefly. When he backed away they bloomed into clouds of dense marigold-yellow smoke that drifted out sluggishly on the light breeze. The smoke would give Jannie the strength and direction of the wind, as well as his orientation for the drop zone.

Nicholas lifted his binoculars and gazed towards the other end of the narrow valley. He saw that Royan and Tessay were busy with their flares. Suddenly crimson smoke billowed from them, and the women ran back to their original position and stood staring up at the sky.

Nicholas called softly into the microphone. 'Big Dolly. Smoke is up. Do you have it visual?'

'Affirmative. You are visual. For what you are about to receive may you be truly thankful.' Jannie's South African accent was unmistakable as he uttered the cheerful blasphemy.

They watched the aircraft grow in size until its wings seemed to fill half the sky, and then its profile altered as the great wing flaps dropped and the ramp below its belly drooped open. Big Dolly slowed her flight so dramatically that she seemed to hang suspended on an invisible thread from the high African sun. Slowly she came around, banking steeply as Jannie lined her up on the smoke flares, dropping lower and still lower, headed directly at where they stood.

With a savage roar that made all three of them duck, she passed so low over their heads that it seemed she would wipe them off the crest. Nicholas had a glimpse of Jannie

461

peering down at him from the cockpit, a fat smile on his face and one hand raised in a laconic wave, and then he was past.

Nicholas straightened up and watched Big Dolly sweep majestically down the centre of the valley. The first pallet dropped out of her and plunged earthwards, until at the last moment its parachutes burst open like a bride's bouquet. The fall of the heavy container was arrested abruptly. It dangled and swung, and seconds later struck the floor of the valley in a cloud of yellow dust and with a crash they could hear up on the ridge. Then two more loads dropped from her, and they too hung for a moment on their chutes before they slammed in.

Big Dolly's engines howled under full throttle and her nose lifted as she bored for height while she passed over the crimson smoke clouds, and then climbed out of the deadly trap of the valley. She came round in another wide turn and lined up for the second run. Once again the pallets dropped out of her as she roared over the quartz markers and then climbed out over the end wall of the valley, skimming the rocky spikes that would have clawed her down.

Six times Jannie repeated the dangerous manoeuvre, and each time he dropped three of the heavy rectangular loads. They lay strewn down the length of the valley, shrouded by the tumbled white silk of their own parachutes.

As Jannie climbed away from the last pass, his voice echoed in Nicholas's earphones. 'Don't go away, Pharaoh! I will be back.' Then Big Dolly lifted her belly ramp like an old lady hoisting her knickers and headed away westwards.

Nicholas and Mek ran down into the valley, where the monks were already jabbering and laughing around the pallets. Quickly the two of them took control, sorting the men into gangs and directing them as they broke down the loads and carried them away.

Nicholas and Sapper had planned that the pallets should be dropped in the order that their contents would be needed. The first pallet contained canned and dried food, all their personal effects and camping equipment, along with those other little creature comforts that Nicholas had allowed, including mosquito nets and a case of malt whisky. He was relieved to see that there was no leakage from the precious case: not one of the bottles had been broken in the drop.

Sapper took charge of the building material and heavy equipment. With Tessay relaying his orders, it was dragged and manhandled away to the ancient quarry where it would be packed and stored until needed on site. Darkness fell with more than half the pallets still not unpacked, lying where they had fallen. Mek placed an armed guard over them, and they all traipsed wearily back up the valley to the camp.

That night, with a dram of whisky and a decent meal warming his belly, a mosquito net over his head and a thick foam mattress under him, Nicholas drifted off to sleep with a smile on his face. They were off to a good start.

The chanting of the monks at their matins woke him, 'We won't need an alarm clock here,' he groaned, and staggered down to the river to wash and shave.

As the sun gilded the battlements of the escarpment, he and Mek were already at their post on the heights, searching the western sky. The plan had been for Jannie to spend the night at Roseires, while Mek's men assisted him with the loading of the cargo they had stored there on their first flight out from Malta. This was one of the vulnerable stages of the operation. Although Mek had assured them that there was little military presence in the area at the moment, it needed only a stray Sudanese government patrol to stumble on Big Dolly while she was on the ground to plunge them all into disaster. So it was with a leap of the heart that they heard the familiar drone of the turbo-props reverberating off the cliffs.

Big Dolly lined up again for her first pass down the valley, and as she flew over the quartz crosses the huge yellow front-end loader tumbled out of her hold. Instinctively Nicholas held his breath as he watched it come hurtling down and then jerk up short on the parachute shrouds. It swayed wildly all over the sky, yoyoing on the nylon ropes, and the monks howled with amazement and excitement as they watched it drop in. It struck in a cloud of dust.

Sapper was standing next to Nicholas, groaning and covering his eyes so that he did not have to watch the cloud of dust rising into the air. 'Shit!' he said in a hollow voice.

'Is that a command, or merely a request?' Nicholas asked, but he wasn't really amused.

As the last pallet dropped, and the aircraft climbed away under full power, Nicholas called Jannie on the radio.

'Many thanks, Big Dolly. Safe flight home.'

'Inshallah! If God wills!' Jannie called back.

'I will call you when I need a lift back.'

'I'll be waiting.' Big Dolly trundled away. 'Break a leg!'

'Well now.' Nicholas slapped Sapper's back. 'Let's go down and see if you still have a front-ender.'

The battered yellow machine lay on its side with oil pouring out of her, like blood from a heart-shot dinosaur.

'You can push off. Just leave me a dozen of these black guys to help me,' Sapper told them as sorrowfully as if he was standing at the graveside of his beloved.

Sapper did not return to camp for dinner, so Tessay sent a bowl of *wat* and some *injera* bread down to him to eat while he worked. Nicholas considered going down to offer his help with repairing the damaged tractor, but thought better of it. From bitter experience he knew that at certain times Sapper wanted to be left alone, and that this was one of those times.

In the small dark hours of the morning the camp was lit up by the blaze of headlights and the hills reverberated to the roar of a diesel engine. With even his bald head covered with grease and dust, hollow-eyed but triumphant, Sapper drove the yellow tractor into the camp and shouted at them from the high driver's seat.

'Okay, knaves and nymphs! Drop your cocks and grab your socks. Let's go build a dam.'

It took them another two full days to gather in all the pallets that lay strewn down the valley and to carry the stores into the ancient quarry. There they stacked them carefully in accordance with the manifest that Nicholas and Sapper had drawn up in England. It was essential that they knew where every item was stored, and that they had immediate access to it when needed. In the meantime Sapper was at work on the dam site, laying out his foundations, driving numbered wooden pegs into the banks of the river, and taking his final measurements with the long steel surveyor's tape.

During this preliminary work Nicholas was watching the performance of the monks, and getting to know them individually. He was able to pick out the natural leaders and the most intelligent and willing men amongst them. He was also able to identify those who spoke Arabic or a little English. The most promising of these was a monk named Hansith Sherif, whom Nicholas made his personal assistant and interpreter.

Once they were settled into the camp, and had worked out a relationship with the monks, Mek Nimmur took Nicholas aside out of earshot of the two women.

'From now on, my work will be the security of the site.

We will have to be ready to prevent another raid like the one on your camp, and the slaughter at St Frumentius. Nogo and his thugs are still out there. It won't take long for him to hear that you are back in the gorge. When he comes, I will be waiting for him.'

'You are better with an AK-47 than with a pickaxe,' Nicholas agreed. 'Just leave Tessay here with me. I need her.'

'So do I.' Mek smiled and shook his head ruefully. 'I am only just learning how much. Look after her for me. I will be back every night to check on her.'

Mek took his men into the bush and deployed them in defensive positions along the trail and around the camp. When Nicholas looked up from his own work he could often make out the figure of one of Mek's sentries on the high ground above the camp. It was reassuring to know that they were there.

However, as he had promised, Mek was back in camp most evenings, and often in the night Nicholas heard, coming from the shelter he shared with Tessay, his deep rumbling laughter blending with her sweet silvery tones. Then Nicholas lay awake and thought about Royan in the hut so close, but yet so far away from where he lay.

On the fifth day the second draft of three hundred labourers that Mai Metemma had conscripted for them arrived, and Nicholas was astonished. Things seldom worked that way in Africa. Nothing ever happened ahead of the promised time. He wondered what exactly Mek had told the abbot, but then decided that he didn't really want to know, for now the main construction work could begin.

These men were not monks, for St Frumentius had already given its all to the sacred labour, but villagers who lived up on the highlands of the escarpment. Mai

466

Metemma had coerced them with promises of religious indulgences and threats of hellfire.

Nicholas and Sapper divided this workforce into gangs of thirty men each, and set one of the picked monks as foreman over each gang. They were careful to grade the men by their physical appearance, so that the big strapping specimens were all grouped together as the project storm-troopers, while the smaller, more wiry men could be reserved for the tasks in which brute strength was not a necessity.

Nicholas dreamed up a name for each gang – the Buffaloes, the Lions, the Axes and so on. It taxed his powers of invention, but he wanted to inspire in them a sense of pride and, to his own particular advantage, to encourage the gangs to compete with one another. He paraded them in the quarry, each group headed by its newly appointed ecclesiastical foreman. Using one of the ancient stone blocks as a platform, and with Tessay interpreting for him, he harangued them heartily and then told them that they would be paid in silver Maria Theresa dollars. He set their wages at three times the going rate.

Up to this stage the men had listened to him with a sullen air of resignation, but now a remarkable transformation came over them. None of them had expected to be paid for the work, and most of them were wondering how soon they could desert and go home. Now Nicholas was promising them not only money, but silver dollars. In Ethiopia for the past two hundred years the Maria Theresa dollar had been regarded as the only true coinage. For this reason they were still minted with the original date of 1780 and the portrait of the old Empress, with her double chin and her *décolletage* exposing half her great bust. One of these coins was more prized than a sackful of the worthless paper birr issued by the regime in Addis. To pay his labour bills, Nicholas had included a chest of these silver coins in the first pallet load that Jannie had dropped.

Celestial grins bloomed as they listened, and white teeth sparkled in their ebony faces. Someone began to sing, and they all stamped and danced and cheered Nicholas as they trooped off to queue for their tools. With mattocks and shovels at the slope they filed off up the valley to the dam site, still singing and prancing.

'St Nicholas,' Tessay laughed. 'Father Christmas. They will never forget you now.'

'They may even enshrine you and build a monastery over you,' Royan suggested sweetly.

'What they don't know is that they are going to earn every single dollar, the hard way.'

From then onwards the work began as soon as it was light enough to see, and stopped only when it was too dark to continue. The men came back to their temporary compound each night by the light of grass torches, too weary to sing. However, Nicholas had contracted with the headmen from the highland villages to supply a slaughter beast every day. Each morning the women came down the trail driving the animal before them, and with huge pots of *tej* balanced on their heads.

Over the days that followed, there were no deserters from Nicholas's little army of workers.

Mounted on the high seat of the front-ender, Sapper lifted the first filled mesh gabion in the hydraulic arms. The mesh-bound parcel of boulders weighed several tons, and all work on the site came to a halt as the men crowded the banks of the Dandera river to watch. A hum of astonishment went up as Sapper eased the yellow tractor down the steep bank and, with the gabion held high, drove the vehicle into the water. The current, affronted by this invasion, swirled angrily around the high rear wheels, but Sapper pushed in deeper.

The crowds lining the bank began to chant and clap encouragement as the water reached as high as the belly of the machine, and clouds of steam hissed from the hot steel of the sump. Sapper locked the brakes, and then lowered the heavy gabion into the flood before reversing back up the bank. The men cheered him wildly, even though the first gabion was instantly submerged and only a whirlpool on the river's surface marked its position. Another filled gabion lay ready. The front-ender waddled up to it, lowered its steel arms and picked it up as tenderly as a mother gathering up her infant.

Nicholas shouted at the foremen to get their gangs back to work. The long lines of men came up the valley, naked except for their brief white loincloths. Sweating heavily in the heat of the gorge, their skin glistened like anthracite freshly cut from the coal face. Each of them carried on his head a basket of stone aggregate, which he dumped into the mouth of the waiting gabion. Then he returned with his empty basket down the hill to the quarry. As each gabion was filled, another team fitted the mesh lid and laced it closed with heavy eight-gauge wire.

'Twenty dollars bonus to the team with the most baskets filled today!' Nicholas bellowed. They shouted with glee and redoubled their efforts, but they were unable to keep up with Sapper on the front-ender. He laid his stone piers artfully, working out from the shallow water alongside the bank so that each gabion lay against its neighbour, keying into the wall to give mutual support.

At first there was little evident progress, but as a solid reef was built up beneath the surface the river began to react savagely. The voice of the water changed from a low rustle to a dull roar as it tore at Sapper's wall.

Soon the top of the wall of gabions thrust its head above the surface, and the river was constricted to half its former width. Now its mood was truculent. It poured through the gap in a solid green torrent, and crept almost imperceptibly up the banks as it was forced to back up behind the barrier. The river worried the foundations of the dam, clawing at it to find its weak spots, and the progress of the work slowed down as the waters rose higher.

Up in the riverine forests along the banks the axemen were at work, and Nicholas winced each time one of the great trees toppled, groaning and shrieking like a living creature. He liked to think of himself as a conservationist, and some of these trees had taken centuries to reach this girth.

'Do you want your bleeding dam, or your pretty trees?' Sapper demanded ferociously, when Nicholas lamented in his hearing. Nicholas turned away without replying.

They were all becoming tired with the unremitting labour. Their nerves were stretching towards snapping point, and tempers were mercurial. Already there had been a number of murderous fights amongst the workmen, and each time Nicholas had been forced to duck in under the swinging steel mattocks to break it up and separate the combatants.

Slowly they squeezed the river in its bed as the pier crept out from the bank, and the time came when they had to transfer their efforts to the far bank. It required the combined efforts of their entire labour force to build a new road along the bank as far as the ford. There they manhandled the front-ender into the water, and, with a hundred men hauling on the tow ropes and her tall lugged rear wheels spinning and churning the surface to a froth, they dragged her across.

Then they had to build another road back along the far bank to reach the dam site. They cut out the treetrunks that obstructed them and levered the boulders out of the way to get the tractor through. Once they had her back at

470

the dam site they could begin the same process of laying out gabions from the far bank.

Gradually, a few metres each day, the two walls crept closer to each other, and as the gap between them narrowed the water rose higher and became more raucous, making the work more difficult.

In the meanwhile, two hundred metres upstream of the dam site, the Falcons and the Scorpions were at work. These two teams were building the raft of treetrunks that they had hacked from the forest. The timbers were lashed together to form a grating. Over this was laid heavy PVC sheeting to make it waterproof; then a second grating of treetrunks went over this to form a gigantic sandwich. It was all lashed together with heavy baling wire. Finally, one end of the grating was ballasted with boulders.

Sapper arranged the ballast of boulders to make the raft one-side heavy, so that it would float almost vertically in the water, with one end of it scraping the bottom of the river and the other sticking up above the surface. The dimensions of the completed raft were carefully related to the gap between the two buttresses of the dam. And while the work on the raft and the wall continued Sapper built up a stockpile of filled gabions, which he stacked on both banks below the dam.

Three other full work teams, the Elephants, the Buffaloes and the Rhinos, comprising the biggest and strongest men in the force, laboured at the head of the valley. They were digging out a deep canal into which the river could be diverted.

'Your hot-shot engineer, Taita, never thought of that little refinement,' Sapper gloated to Royan as they stood on the lip of the trench. 'What it means is that we only have to raise the level of the river another six feet before it will start flowing down the canal and into the valley. Without it we would have had to lift the water almost twenty feet to divert it.'

'Perhaps the river levels were different four thousand years ago.' Royan felt a strange loyalty to the long-dead Egyptian, and she defended him. 'Or perhaps he dug a canal but all traces of it have been obliterated.'

'Not bleeding likely,' Sapper grunted. 'The little perisher just plain didn't think of it.' His expression was smug and self-satisfied. 'One up on Mr Taita, I think.'

Royan smiled to herself. It was strange how even the practical and down-to-earth Sapper felt that this was a direct personal challenge from down the ages. He too had been caught up in Taita's game.

By dint of neither threat nor heavenly reward could the monks be inveigled into working on Sundays. Each Saturday evening they knocked off an hour earlier and trooped away down the valley on the trail to the monastery, so as to be in time for Holy Communion the next day. Although Nicholas grumbled and scowled at their desertion, secretly he was as relieved as any of them for the chance to rest. They were all exhausted, and for once there would be no chanting of matins to wake them at four o'clock the next morning.

So on Saturday night they all swore to each other that they would sleep late the next morning, but from force of habit Nicholas found himself awake and fully alert at that same iniquitous hour. He could not stay in his camp bed, and when he came back from his ablutions at the riverside he found that Royan was also awake and dressed.

'Coffee?' She lifted the pot off the fire and poured a mugful for him.

'I slept terribly badly last night,' she admitted. 'I had the most ridiculous dreams. I found myself in Mamose's tomb, lost in a labyrinth of passages. I was searching for the burial chamber, opening doors, but there were always people in the rooms that I looked into. Duraid was working

472

in one room and he looked up and said, "Remember the protocol of the four bulls. Start at the beginning." He was so real and alive. I wanted to go to him but the door closed in my face, and I knew I would never see him again.' Tears filled her eyes and glistened in the light of the campfire.

Nicholas sought to distract her from the painful memory. 'Who were in the other rooms?' he asked.

'In the next room was Nahoot Guddabi. He laughed spitefully and said, "The jackal chases the sun," and his head changed into the head of Anubis, the jackal god of the cemetery, and he yelped and barked. I was so frightened that I ran.'

She sipped her coffee. 'It was all meaningless and silly, but von Schiller was in the next room, and he rose in the air and flapped his wings and said, "The vulture rises, and the stone falls." I hated him so much I wanted to strike him, but then he was gone.'

'And then you woke up?' Nicholas suggested.

'No. There was one other room.'

'Who was in it?'

She dropped her eyes, and her voice was small, 'You were,' she said.

'Me? What did I say?' He smiled.

'You didn't say anything,' she whispered, and blushed so suddenly and fiercely that he was instantly intrigued.

'What did I do then?' He was still smiling.

'Nothing. I mean, I can't tell you.' The dream returned to her, vivid and real as life, every detail of his naked body, even the smell and the feel of him. She forced herself to stop thinking about it. She felt vulnerable as she had been in the dream.

'Tell me about it,' he insisted.

'No!' She stood up quickly, confused and still blushing, trying to thrust the images from her.

Last night had been the first time in her life that she

473

had ever dreamed of a man in that way, the first time she had ever experienced a full orgasm in her sleep. This morning, when she awoke, she found that she had soaked right through her pyjamas bottoms.

'We have a full day ahead of us with no work to do,' she blurted – the first thought that came into her mind.

'On the contrary.' He stood up with her. 'We still have to make the arrangements for getting out of here. When the time comes, we will probably be in something of a hurry.'

'Mind if I tag along?' she asked.

Two teams, the Buffaloes and the Elephants, with only their foremen missing, were waiting for them at the quarry. They comprised sixty of the strongest men in the labour force. Nicholas unpacked the inflatable Avon rafts from one of the pallets. Each raft was deflated and folded into a neat pack, with the paddles strapped along the sides. These craft had been specifically designed for river-running in turbulent water, and each was capable of carrying sixteen crew and a ton of cargo.

Nicholas directed them to strap the heavy packs on to the carrying poles that they had cut for that purpose. Five men on each end of the long poles, with the bundle of the boat slung in the centre, made light of the load. They set off at a cracking pace down the trail, and as soon as one team tired the next was ready to take over. They made the exchange without even stopping, the new porters slipping their shoulders under the pole on the run while the exhausted team dropped out.

Nicholas carried the radio in its shockproof and waterproof fibreglass case. He would not trust such a precious instrument to one of the porters. He and Royan trotted along behind the caravan, joining in the chorus of the work chant that the porters sang as they carried their loads down to the monastery.

Mai Metemma was waiting on the terrace outside the church of St Frumentius to welcome them. He led them down the staircase hewn out of the rock of the cliff, two hundred feet to the very water's edge. There was a narrow rocky ledge against which the Nile waters dashed, and the spray from the high waterfalls drifted over them like a perpetual drizzle of rain. After the heat and the bright sunlight above, it was cold and gloomy and dank down here in the depths of the gorge. The black cliffs ran with water, and the ledge on which they stood was wet and slippery underfoot.

Royan shivered as she watched the river racing by, forming a great spinning vortex as it swirled around the deep rock bowl and then raced out through the narrow throat of the gorge on its long hectic journey towards Egypt and the north.

'If only I had known that this was the road you were planning on taking home—' she eyed the river dubiously.

'If you would prefer to walk, it's okay by me,' Nicholas told her. 'With luck we will be carrying some extra baggage. The river is the logical escape route.'

'I suppose it makes sense, but still it's not terribly inviting.' She broke off a piece of driftwood from a stranded tangle that lay trapped upon the ledge and tossed it into the river. It was whipped away, and raced over the standing wave where some submerged obstacle forced the surface to bulge up.

'What speed is that current?' she asked in a subdued voice as the splinter of driftwood was sucked below the surface.

'Oh, not much more than eight or nine knots,' he told her offhandedly, 'but that's nothing. The river is still very low. Just wait until it starts raining up in the mountains, then you will really see some water passing through here.

It will be great fun. Lots of people would pay good money for the chance to run a river like this. You are going to love it.'

'Thanks,' she said drily. 'I can't wait.'

Fifty feet above the ledge, out of reach of the Nile's highest water level, was a small cavern – the Epiphany shrine. Long ago the monks had cut this passage deeply into the rock face, and it ended in a spacious, candle-lit chamber that housed a life-sized statue of the Virgin, dressed in faded velvet robes, with the infant in her arms. Mai Metemma gave them his sanction to store the rafts in the shrine, and they stacked them against a side wall. When the porters had left, Nicholas showed Royan how to operate the quick-release handles on the packs, and the CO_2 cylinders which would inflate the rafts within minutes. He wrapped the radio case and his small emergency pack in a sheet of plastic and stowed them in one of the boat packs, where he could lay his hands on them again in a hurry.

'You do intend coming along on this joy ride?' she asked anxiously. 'You aren't planning on sending me down on my ownsome?'

'It is best that you know how it all works,' he told her. 'If things start to get a little hairy when the time comes to leave here, I may need your help in launching the rafts.'

When they climbed back up the staircase into the warmth and the sunlight, Royan's uncertain mood had changed. 'It's not yet noon, and we have the rest of the day to ourselves. Let's go back to Taita's pool again,' she suggested, and he shrugged indulgently.

The Buffaloes and the Elephants accompanied them as far as the branch in the trail. Here the teams headed back towards the dam, and shouted and hallooed their farewells after Nicholas and Royan.

Even in the short time since their last visit, the path through the undergrowth had become overgrown. Nicholas was forced to use his machete to hack a way through, and they ducked under the trailing thorn branches. It was mid-afternoon when they eventually crossed the high ridge and stood once again on the cliff directly above Taita's pool.

'It looks as though we were the last ones here.' Nicholas's tone was relieved. 'No signs of any other visitors since us.'

'Were you expecting any?'

'You never know. Von Schiller is a formidable character, and he has some charming lads working for him. Helm is one that worries me, and I had a nasty feeling that he might have been snooping around here. I am going to take a closer look.'

He worked quickly around the entire area, casting widely for any sign of intruders. Then came back to where she sat on the lip of the abyss and dropped down beside her.

'Nothing,' he admitted. 'We have still got the running to ourselves.'

'Once Sapper stops the river upstream, this is going to be our main area of operations, isn't it?' she asked.

'Yes, but even before Sapper closes the dam I want to open a fly camp here, and move all the gear and equipment we will need from the quarry to have it handy when we start the exploration of the pool.'

'How are we going to get down into the pool? Down the river bed, once it is dry?'

'I suppose we could use the dry river bed as a road, and come down it from below the dam or up from the monastery end, through the pink cliffs.'

'But that is not the way you are planning to get in, is it?' she guessed.

'Even with no water in it, the river bed will be a long way round. It's a three- or four-mile haul from either end of the abyss, added to which it will be a pretty rough road to travel.' He grinned ruefully. 'You are speaking to an expert on the subject. I went down it the hard way, and I wouldn't want to do it again. There are at least five chutes and rock jams that I can remember being thrown over.'

'What is your better idea, then?' she asked.

'It's not my idea,' he contradicted her. 'It's Taita's idea really.'

She peered over the edge. 'You mean to build a scaffold down the cliff, just the way he did it?'

'What's good enough for Taita is good enough for me,' he acknowledged. 'The old boy probably had a good look at the alternative of using the river bed as an access road, and abandoned the idea.'

'When will you start work on the scaffold, then?'

'One of our teams is already cutting bamboo poles higher up the gorge. Tomorrow we will begin carrying them up here, and stacking them. We can't waste a day. Once the dam is closed, we have to get into the dry pool as soon as possible.'

As if to add weight to his words there came a far-off mutter of thunder, and they both craned their heads to peer up with trepidation at the escarpment. Probably a hundred miles to the north, faintly washed as a sepia print superimposed upon the razor-edged blue silhouette of the escarpment wall, rose high tumbled towers of cumulo-nimbus clouds. Neither of them spoke about it, but both were aware of how ominously the storm clouds were settling on the distant mountains.

Nicholas glanced at his wrist-watch and stood up. 'Time to start back if we are to get into camp before dark.'

He gave her his hand and lifted her to her feet. She dusted off her clothes and then stepped right to the very lip of the canyon.

'Wake up, Taita. We are hot on your tracks,' she called down into the shadows.

'Don't challenge him.' Nicholas took her arm and drew

her back. 'The old ruffian has given us enough trouble already.'

The axemen had left the stumps of several great trees standing on the banks of the Dandera upstream from the dam. Sapper used these as anchor points for the heavy cables that he strung across the river. Through the cables he had rigged a cunning series of pulley blocks. The main cable was run back and connected to the tow hitch on the front-ender. Two other cables were laid out, one to each bank, where the Buffaloes and the Elephants stood ready to handle them. One team was under the direction of Nicholas, and the other under Mek Nimmur. For this crucial part of the construction, Mek had come down from the hills to lend a hand.

The grating of massive treetrunks lay on the river verge, already half in the water. Heavily weighted with boulders, it was an unwieldy structure that would require all their combined efforts to manoeuvre into position. Sapper slitted his eyes as he studied the layout, and then looked downstream to the partially completed dam. The two walls of gabions stretched out from either bank, but the gap in the middle of the river was twenty feet across and the whole volume of the river roared through it.

'The one thing we don't want is to let the bleeding plug run away from us and slam into the ruddy wall,' he warned Nicholas and Mek. 'Otherwise we are going to lose a big chunk of what we have done so far. I want to cuddle her in there, nice and softly, and let her sit snug in the gap. Any questions? This is your last chance to ask. You all know the signals.'

Sapper took one last drag on his cigarette, and flicked the stub into the river. Then, looking lugubrious, he said, 'Okay, gents. The last one in the water is a sissy.'

Compared to their men, Nicholas and Mek were overdressed in their khaki shorts. The others were all stark naked. When the order was given they trooped waist-deep into the river and took up their stations along the cables.

Before he followed them into the river, Nicholas took one last look round. At breakfast that morning Royan had innocently asked to borrow his binoculars. Now he knew why. She and Tessay were perched up on top of the slope high above the gorge. Even as Nicholas watched, he saw Royan pass the binoculars to Tessay. They were not missing a moment of this fateful operation.

Nicholas looked back from the ridge to the rows of big naked men, pulled a face and muttered, 'My oath, there are some prize specimens around here. I just hope that Royan isn't making comparisons.'

Sapper climbed up on to the yellow tractor, and with a roar and a cloud of diesel smoke the engine burst into life. He raised one hand above his head with the fist clenched, and Nicholas relayed the order to his team: 'Take the strain.'

The foremen repeated it in Amharic, and the men leaned back against the cables. Sapper threw the tractor into extra low, and eased her forward. The belly straightened in the lines, the sheave wheels squealed, and the timber grating slid ponderously down the bank into the river. The weighted end of the grating sank immediately and bumped along the bottom, while the lighter end floated high. Slowly they hauled it out into midstream, until it was hanging vertically in the water.

The current seized it and began to bear it away, straight at the wall of gabions. It picked up speed alarmingly. The tractor bellowed and blew out clouds of black smoke as Sapper threw her into reverse and backed up on the cables. The teams of naked black men heaved and chanted – some of them had already been dragged in neck-deep as they hauled on the lines.

The grating steadied across the current, and they let it fall away at a more sedate pace, down towards the open gap in the wall. As it began to slew towards one bank, Sapper lifted his right arm and windmilled it. Obediently, Mek's team on the far bank paid out rope and Nicholas's team on the near bank picked it up. Once again the grating was lined up on the gap.

'Rock and roll. Close the hole,' bellowed Sapper, and now the full current was too powerful to resist. It dragged both teams into the river until some of them were in over their heads, losing their hold on the lines and floundering and swimming. However, those men who still had their footing managed to slow the rush of the grating just enough to prevent it smashing out of control into the dam. It settled firmly across the gap, like a mammoth plug in the outlet of a giant's bathtub, and instantly the current was cut off.

While the men in the water struggled ashore, their bodies wet and gleaming in the sunlight, Sapper threw off the cables from his tow hitch and roared along the bank with the front-ender in its highest gear. As it passed him, Nicholas grabbed a handhold and swung himself up on to the footplate behind Sapper's seat.

'Got to shore up now, before the grating bursts,' Sapper yelled.

From his vantage point, clinging to the rear of the tall machine, Nicholas had a moment to assess the position. The dam was holding, but only just. Numerous jets of water spurted through every gap between the grating and the gabions. The pressure of water against the sheets of PVC in the grating was enormous. It was taking the full thrust of the river, flexing and bowing before it like a castle portcullis attacked with a battering ram.

Sapper picked up one of the gabions that were standing ready on the bank and drove down into the river bed below the dam. The flow of the water had shrivelled to a mere knee-deep trickle. Jets of water squirted through every chink in the wall, and the gabions were not impermeable; water was finding its way through the tightly packed stones.

As the front-ender churned and lurched over the rough bed at the back of the wall, Nicholas and Sapper were drenched by the jets spurting over them. It was like working under a cold shower. Sapper drove in close behind the straining grating and placed the heavy gabion against it. He threw the tractor into reverse and climbed up the bank to pick up another gabion. Slowly he built up a retaining wall behind the grating, placing the gabions in sloping ranks, until this revetment was as strong as the side piers.

Nicholas jumped down from the tractor and left Sapper to it while he ran back upstream to the canal that the teams had dug at the head of the valley. Most of the workers had gathered along the banks of this cutting already, and Nicholas saw both Royan and Tessay in the front row of the excited crowd.

Nicholas pushed his way through to Royan's side, and she grabbed his hand. 'It's working, Nicky. The dam wall is holding.'

Even as they watched they could see the level of the trapped waters rising up the wall of grating and gabions. While the men chattered and laughed and urged it on, the river lapped at the entrance of the canal.

Fifty men seized their tools and jumped down into the bottom of the canal. Dust flew in clouds as they shovelled the broken earth aside to lead the first trickle of water into the mouth of the canal. The men on the banks above them whooped and chanted to encourage them, and a thin snake of river water found its way into the mouth of the canal. The men with the mattocks and shovels ran ahead of it, enticing it on down the cutting. Every time it met any obstruction and faltered, they fell upon the blockage and tore it away.

At last the thin trickle of water felt the gradient fall

away as the valley opened before it. The trickle increased to a freshet, and then to a torrent. With its new strength it gouged out the canal and burst through with the full flow of the river behind it.

The men in the bottom of the cutting yelled with fright at the suddenness and ferocity of it, and scrambled up the sides of the canal. But some of them were not quick enough and were swept away, struggling and screaming for help. The men on the banks ran alongside them, throwing ropes and dragging them sodden and muddy from the flood.

Now the river roared through the canal and tore on down the valley, rediscovering the ancient course that it had not followed for thousands of years. For almost an hour they stood upon the bank watching it, for it exercised over them the particular spell that turbulent waters always have over men. They were forced to retreat step by step as the river cut the banks out from under their feet.

At last Nicholas roused himself, and went back to where Sapper was still shoring up the dam wall. By now he had erected a sloping revetment on the downstream side of the dam wall, with four rows of gabions on the bottom course gradually narrowing as it reached the top of the retaining wall. For the time being the dam was secure, the vulnerable grating had been shored up with the heavy, stone-filled mesh baskets, and the overflow through the canal into the valley had relieved much of the pressure upon it.

'Do you think it will hold?' Royan eyed the structure with suspicion.

'Until the rains come, we hope.' Nicholas drew her away. 'We don't want to waste any more time here. Time to go on downstream to begin work at Taita's pool.'

They followed the banks of the new river that they had created, down the length of the long valley. At places they were forced to detour higher up the slope because the overflow from the dam had cut away and submerged the old trail. Eventually they reached the confluence of the stream that had as its source the butterfly fountain that they had explored with Tamre. They paused on the bank, and Nicholas and Royan looked at each other wordlessly. The stream had dried up.

Turning aside, they followed the empty stream bed up the hills and at last scrambled out on to the ledge from which the butterfly fountain had poured. The cave was still surrounded by lush green ferns, but it was like the eye socket in a skull, dark and empty.

'The spring has dried up!' Royan whispered. 'The dam has shrivelled it. That's the proof that the fountain was fed from Taita's pool. Now we have diverted the river we have killed the fountain.' Her eyes were bright and sparkling with excitement. 'Come on. Let's waste no more time here. Let's get on up to Taita's pool.'

Nicholas was the first one down into Taita's pool. This time he had a bosun's chair to sit in and a properly rigged block and tackle to lower him over the cliff. As he swung down around the overhang of the cliff, the chair swung awkwardly against the rock and the thumb of his right hand was trapped between the wooden seat of the chair and the wall. He exclaimed with the pain and, when he wrenched it free, he found that the skin had been torn from the knuckle and that blood was oozing up and dripping down his legs. It was painful but not serious, and he sucked the wound clean. It was still weeping drops of blood, but he had no time to attend to the injury now.

He was around the overhang, and the abyss opened

under him, sombre and repellent. His eye was drawn irresistibly to the engraving on the wall, etched between the vertical rows of niches. Now that he knew what to look for, he could make out the outline of the maimed hawk. It cheered and encouraged him. Since their flight from the gorge over a month previously he had often been haunted by the feeling that they had imagined it all, that the cartouche of Taita was a hallucination, and that when they returned they would find the cliff wall smooth and unblemished. But there it was, the signpost and the promise.

He peered down past his own feet to the bottom of the gorge, and saw at once that the waterfall above the pool had been reduced to a trickle. The water still coming down the smooth black chute of polished rock was that which was filtering through the gaps and chinks in the dam wall upstream and the last drainage from the sandbanks and the pools higher up the gorge.

The level of the great pool under him had fallen drastically. He could make out the high-water level by the wet markings on the rock cliff. Fifty feet of the wall that had previously been submerged was now exposed. Another eight pairs of chiselled niches were visible in the face. Where once he had been forced to swim down to them, they were now high and dry.

However, the pool was not completely drained. It was dished below the level of the downstream outlet, so that it was unable to empty itself by gravitational flow. There was still a puddle of black water trapped in the centre, with a narrow ledge surrounding it. Nicholas landed on this ledge and stepped out of the bosun's chair. It was strange to stand on firm rock down here where last he had struggled for his life and very nearly been sucked under and drowned.

He looked up to where beams of sunlight penetrated the upper levels of the chasm. It was like being in the bottom of a mineshaft, and he shuddered at the feel of the clammy air on his bare arms and the eerie sensation in the pit of his stomach. He tugged on the line to send the rope chair back to the surface, and then edged his way along the slippery rock ledge towards the cliff face where the rows of dark niches stood out clearly against the lighter stone.

Now he could make out the shape of the opening in the wall that had so nearly sucked him down into its dark and slimy throat. It was almost completely submerged in a deeper corner where the pool flowed back against the cliff. All that was visible above the surface was the top arch of an irregular entrance at the foot of the descending rows of niches. The rest of it was still submerged.

The ledge narrowed as he worked his way along the foot of the cliff until he had his back to the rock and was moving sideways with his toes in the water. Eventually he could go no further without actually stepping down into the water. He had no way of judging the depth of the waters, which were turbid and uninviting.

Still trying to keep his feet dry, he squatted down on the narrow ledge and leaned out so far that his balance was threatened. He steadied himself with one hand against the wall, and with the other reached out towards the partially submerged opening.

The lip of the hole was smooth, as he had remembered it, and once again it seemed to him that it was too square and straight to be anything other than man-made. As he rolled up his sleeve he noticed that his injured thumb was still bleeding, but he ignored it and thrust his arm down below the surface of the pool. He groped downwards, trying to trace the sill of the opening. He felt what seemed to be blocks of roughly dressed masonry, and reached down further until the water reached halfway up his biceps.

Suddenly some living creature, swift and weighty, swirled in the dark waters right in front of his face, and as an immediate reflex he jerked his arm out of the water. The thing followed his arm up to the surface, slashing at his bare flesh with long, needle-sharp fangs, and he had a glimpse of a head as evil and villainous as that of a barracuda. He realized instinctively that it must have been attracted by the smell of the blood from his injured thumb.

He leaped to his feet and teetered on the narrow ledge, clutching his arm. Only one of the creature's frontal fangs had touched him, but it had opened the skin like a razor cut, a long shallow wound across the back of his right hand from which fresh blood dribbled and splattered into the pool at his feet.

Instantly the black waters seemed to come alive, roiling and seething with frenzied writhing aquatic shapes. Nicholas, his back flattened against the rock wall, stared down at them with loathing and horror. He could vaguely make out the shape of them, sinuous and ribbonlike, some of them as thick as his calf, black and gleaming.

One of them thrust its head out on to the ledge and snapped its jaws. Its eyes were huge and glistening and its snout was elongated, the long jaws lined with fangs that overlapped its thin lips. The body behind the head was six feet long, and lashed like a whip as it drove itself high up on to the ledge, reaching out for Nicholas's bare legs. He shouted with revulsion and leaped back, stumbling and splashing on to safer footing. Clutching his bleeding hand, he stared back. The evil head had disappeared, but the surface of the pool was still agitated by the lithe ophidian shapes.

'Eels!' he realized. 'Giant tropical eels.'

Of course the blood had excited them. The fall in the water-level had trapped them in the pool, congregated them in such numbers that they had probably already devoured the fish that they depended upon for food. Now they were ravenous. Probably all the pools of water that remained in the abyss were infested with these fearsome creatures. He was thankful that during his last swim in this pool he had not bled into the water.

He unwound the cotton kerchief from his neck and wrapped it round his wounded hand. The eels were a deadly threat to any attempt to explore the opening in the cliff. But already he was considering ways of ridding the pool of them and of gaining access to the underwater opening.

Slowly the frenzy in the pool quietened and its surface grew still again. Nicholas looked up to see the bosun's chair descending, with Royan's slim, shapely legs dangling below the wooden seat.

'What have you found?' she called down to him excitedly. 'Is there a tunnel—' then she broke off suddenly as she saw the blood on his clothing, and the bandage swathing his hand.

'Oh dear God,' she exclaimed. 'What have you done? You are hurt. How badly?' Her feet touched the ledge beside him and she slid from the chair and took his injured hand gently. 'What have you done to yourself?'

'It's not as bad as it looks,' he assured her. 'Lots of blood but not deep.'

'How did you do it?' she insisted.

For an answer he tore a corner off the bloodstained kerchief. 'Watch!' he instructed her, wadding it into a ball and tossing it out into the pool.

Royan screamed with horror as the waters boiled with the long fleeting shapes. One of them wriggled half its monstrous length out on to the ledge, before flopping back. It left a shining trail of silver slime across the black stones.

'Taita has left his guard dogs to see us off,' Nicholas remarked. 'We are going to have to take care of those beauties before we can explore the entrance below the surface.'

The bamboo scaffolding that Sapper and Nicholas had built down the cliff was anchored in the niches that had been cut into the rock nearly four thousand years before. Taita had probably lashed his framework together with bark rope, but Sapper had used heavy-gauge galvanized wire, and the structure was strong enough to bear the weight of many men. The Buffaloes formed a living chain and passed all the material and equipment down the scaffolding from hand to hand.

The very first piece of equipment to reach the floor of the cavern was the portable Honda EM500 generator. Sapper connected it up to the lights that he had rigged along the foot of the cliff. The small petrol engine ran smoothly and quietly, but the amount of power it put out was impressive. The floodlights chased the shadows from the furthest corners of the cavern, and lit the deep rock bowl like a stage.

Immediately the mood changed. Everybody became more cheerful and confident. There was laughter and excited chatter from the chain of men on the scaffolding as Royan climbed down to join Sapper and Nicholas at the side of the pool.

'Now that we know that they are working, switch off those lights,' Nicholas ordered.

'It's so dark and gloomy without them,' Royan protested.

'Saving fuel,' Nicholas explained. 'No filling station on the corner. We only have two hundred litres in reserve, and although the little Honda is pretty economical we have to be careful. We don't know how long we are going to need it in the tunnel.'

Royan shrugged with resignation, and when Sapper cut the generator the cavern was plunged once more into gloom and shadow. She looked at the dark pool and pulled a face.

'What are you going to do about those horrid pets of yours?' she demanded, glancing at Nicholas's bandaged right hand.

'Sapper and I have worked out a plan. We thought of trying to empty the pool completely, using a bucket chain. But the amount of water still coming down the river bed makes that a poor choice.'

'We would be lucky to hold our own against that flow, even working around the clock with buckets,' Sapper grunted. 'If only the major had thought to bring along a high-speed water pump—'

'Even I can't think of everything, Sapper. What we are going to do is to build a small coffer dam around the underwater opening, and bale that out with buckets.'

Royan stood back and watched the preparations. Half a dozen of the empty mesh gabions were carried down the scaffolding and placed at the edge of the pool. Here they were partially filled with boulders that the men gathered up from the river bed. However, the gabions were not filled so full that they became too heavy to handle. There was no front-ender down here to move them around, and they would be forced to rely on old-fashioned manpower. There was just sufficient of the yellow PVC sheeting left over to wrap around each gabion and render it waterproof.

'What about your eels?' Royan was fascinated by these loathsome creatures, and she hung well back from the edge of the pool. 'You can't send any of your men in there!'

'Watch and learn.' Nicholas grinned at her. 'I have a little treat in store for your favourite fish.'

Once all the preparations for the construction of the coffer were complete, Nicholas cleared the cavern, sending Royan and Sapper and all of the men up the scaffolding. He alone remained at the edge of the pool, with the bag of fragmentation grenades that he had begged from Mek Nimmur slung over his shoulder.

With a grenade in each hand, he hesitated. 'Seven-second delay,' he reminded himself. 'Quenton-Harper dry flies. More effective than the Royal Coachman!'

He pulled the pins from each of the grenades and then lobbed them out into the middle of the pool. Quickly he turned away and hurried to the furthest corner of the cavern. He knelt with his face to the rock wall and covered his ears with both hands.

Squeezing his eyes shut, he braced himself. The rock floor jumped under him and the double shock waves from the explosions swept over him in quick succession, with a savage power that drove in his chest and stopped his breath. In the confines of the chasm the detonations were thunderous, but his ears were protected and the deep water of the pool absorbed much of the blast. A twin fountain of water shot high into the air and splashed against the cliff above his head. It poured down in a sheet over him, soaking his clothing.

As the echoes died away, he stood up. His hearing had not been adversely affected, and he had suffered no injury other than the shower of cold water. Back at the edge of the pool the water shimmered with movement. Scores of the great eels flopped and writhed on the surface, flashing their white bellies as they twisted. Many of them were dead, their bellies burst open, floating inert, while others were merely stunned by the blast. Knowing how tenaciously they clung to life he suspected that they would soon recover, but for the time being they were no longer a danger.

He bellowed up toward the top of the cliff. 'All clear, Sapper. Send them down.'

The men came swarming down the scaffolding, amazed by the carnage that the grenades had wreaked in the pool. They lined the bank and began to fish out the bodies of the dead eels.

'You eat them?' Nicholas demanded of one of the monks.

'Very good!' The monk rubbed his belly in anticipation.

'Enough of that, you greedy perishers.' Sapper drove them back to work. 'Let's get those gabions in place before they wake up and start eating you.'

With a bamboo pole Nicholas sounded the depth of the water that covered the entrance to the shaft, and found that it was well over the height of a man's head. They were forced to roll the gabions down into it, and complete the filling once they were in position. It was difficult and taxing work, and took almost two days to complete, but at last they had built a half-moon-shaped weir around the underwater entrance, walling it off from the main body of water in the pool.

Using leather buckets and clay *tej* pots the Buffaloes began to bale out the coffer and scoop the water over the wall into the main pool. Nicholas and Royan watched with silent trepidation as the level in the coffer fell and the opening in the cliff was gradually revealed.

Very soon they were able to see that it was almost rectangular, about three metres wide by two metres high. The sides and the roof had been eroded by the rush of water through the opening, but as the level fell lower they could see the remains of shaped stone blocks that had probably once sealed the opening. Four courses of them still stood where the ancient masons had placed them across the threshold of the opening, but the others had been torn out by thousands of years of flood seasons and thrown into the tunnel behind, partially blocking it.

Eagerly Nicholas climbed down into the coffer. It was not yet empty, but he could not control his impatience. The water was knee-deep as he crawled forward into the opening, and with his bare hands tried to shift some of the rock debris that choked it.

'It's definitely some sort of shaft,' he shouted back, and Royan could not restrain herself either. She came slithering and sloshing down into the coffer, and pushed into the opening beside him.

'There's an obstruction,' she cried in disappointment. 'Did Taita do that deliberately?'

'Might have,' Nicholas gave his opinion. 'Hard to tell. A lot of this rubble and flotsam has been sucked in from the main flow of the river, but he might have filled the tunnel behind him as he pulled out.'

'It's going to take a tremendous amount of work just to clear it enough to find out where this passage leads to.' Royan's voice had lost its ring of excitement.

'I am afraid it is,' Nicholas agreed. 'We are going to have to clear every bit of this rubbish by hand, and there won't be time for the niceties of formal archaeological excavation. We are just going to rip it out.' He clambered back out of the coffer, and reached back to hand her up the bank. 'Well, at least we have the floodlights,' he added. 'We can keep the men working in shifts, night and day, until we get through.'

'They have dammed the Dandera river,' said Nahoot Guddabi, and Gotthold von Schiller stared at him in astonishment.

'Dammed the river? Are you certain?' he demanded.

'Yes, Herr von Schiller. We have a report from our spy in Harper's camp. He has over three hundred men working in the gorge. That is not all. He has air-dropped huge amounts of equipment and supplies. It is like a military operation. Our spy tells us that he even has an earth-moving machine, some sort of tractor, which he has brought in.'

Von Schiller looked across the table at Jake Helm for confirmation, and Helm nodded. 'Yes, Herr von Schiller. That is true. Harper must have spent a large amount of money. The air charter alone could have cost him fifty grand.'

Von Schiller felt the first stirrings of real passion since the urgent satellite message had summoned him from Frankfurt. He had flown directly to Addis Ababa, where the Jet Ranger had been waiting to carry him to the Pegasus base camp on the escarpment above the Abbay gorge.

If this was true, and he did not doubt Helm's word, then Harper was on to something of enormous importance. He looked out of the window of the Quonset hut to where the Dandera flowed down the valley below the base camp. It was a large river. To dam that volume of water would be an expensive and difficult project in this remote and primitive situation – not a project to be taken on lightly without the prospect of substantial reward.

He felt a reluctant admiration for the Englishman's achievement. 'Show me where he has placed his dam!' he ordered, and Helm came around the table to stand beside him. Von Schiller was standing on his block, and their eyes were on the same level.

Helm bent over the satellite photograph and carefully marked in the site of the dam. They both studied it for a minute, and then von Schiller asked, 'What do you make of it, Helm?'

Helm shook his head, hunching it down on his bull-like shoulders. 'I can only guess.'

'Guess then,' said von Schiller, but still Helm hesitated.

'Go on!'

'Either he wants to move the water to another area downstream, to use it for washing out a deposit, gold nuggets or artefacts made of precious metals, perhaps even to use it for hosing the overburden off the site of the tomb—'

'Highly unlikely!' von Schiller interjected. 'That would be an inefficient and expensive manner of excavation.'

'I agree that it is far-fetched.' Nahoot obsequiously followed von Schiller's lead, but no one even looked at him.

'What is your other supposition?' Von Schiller glared at Helm.

'The only other reason for damming the river, that I can think of, would be to reach something that has been covered by the water. Something lying in the bed of the river.'

'That is more logical,' von Schiller mused, and turned his attention back to the photograph. 'What is there below this dam site?'

'The river enters a deep and narrow ravine here.' Helm pointed at the spot. 'Just below his dam. The ravine stretches about eight miles, down to this point, just above the monastery. I have flown over it in the helicopter, and it seems to be impassable, and yet—' he broke off.

'Yes, go on! And yet – what?'

'On one flight over the area, we found Harper and the woman on the high ground above the ravine. They were at this spot here.' He touched the photograph, and von Schiller leaned forward to peer at it.

'What were they doing there?' he demanded, without looking up.

'Nothing. They were merely sitting on the top of the cliff above the ravine.'

'But they were aware of your presence?'

'Of course. We were in the helicopter. They heard our approach. They were watching us, and Harper even waved.'

'And so they would have ceased whatever activity they were engaged in when they became aware of your approach?'

Von Schiller was silent for so long that they began to fidget uncomfortably and exchange glances. When he spoke it was so unexpected that Nahoot started.

'Harper obviously has reason to believe that the tomb lies in the gorge below the dam. When and how do you make contact with your spy that you have in Harper's camp?'

'Harper is receiving some of his supplies from the villages here on the escarpment. The women are driving down slaughter cattle to feed his men, and carrying down pots of *tej*. Our man sends back his reports with the women when they return.'

'Very well. Very well!' Von Schiller waved him to silence. 'I don't need to know his life history. All I want to know is if Harper is working in the ravine below his dam. How soon can you find this out?'

'By the day after tomorrow at the latest,' Helm promised him.

Von Schiller turned to Colonel Nogo at the far end of the conference table. So far he had not spoken, but had watched and listened quietly to the others.

'How many men have you deployed in this area?' von Schiller asked.

'Three full companies, over three hundred men. All well trained. Many are battle-hardened veterans.'

'Where are they? Show me on the map.'

The colonel came to stand beside him. 'One company here, another billeted at the village of Debra Maryam, and the third company at the foot of the escarpment, ready to move forward and attack Harper's camp.'

'I think you should attack them now. Wipe them out, before they can uncover the tomb—' Nahoot came in again.

'Shut your mouth,' von Schiller snapped without looking up at Nahoot. 'I will ask for your opinion when I need it.'

496

He considered the map for a while longer, then asked Nogo, 'How many men has this guerrilla commander, what is his name, the one who has allied himself to Harper?'

'Mek Nimmur is not a guerrilla. He is a bandit, and notorious *shufta* terrorist,' Nogo corrected him hotly.

'One man's freedom fighter is the next man's terrorist,' von Schiller remarked drily. 'How many men has he under his command?'

'Not many. Fewer than a hundred, perhaps no more than fifty. He has them all guarding Harper's camp, and the dam.'

Von Schiller nodded to himself, plucking at the lobe of his ear. 'How did Harper and his gang return to Ethiopia?' he mused. 'I know he flew from Malta, but it is not possible that the aircraft could have landed down there in the gorge.'

He hopped down off his block and strutted to the window of the hut through which he had a panoramic view spread below him. He stared down into the depths of the gorge, a vista of cliffs and broken hilltops and wild tablelands, smoked blue with distance.

'How did they get in without being discovered by the authorities? Did he parachute in, the same way as he dropped his supplies?'

'No,' said Nogo. 'My informer tells us that he marched in with Mek Nimmur, some days before the supplies were dropped to him.'

'So from where did he march?' von Schiller pondered. 'Where is the nearest airfield where a heavy aircraft could land?'

'If he came in with Mek Nimmur, then they almost certainly came in from the Sudan. That is where Nimmur operates from. There are many old abandoned airfields near the border. The war,' Nogo shrugged expressively, 'the armies are always on the move, that war has been going on for twenty years.'

'From the Sudan?' Von Schiller picked out the border on the map. 'So they must have trekked in along the river.'

'Almost certainly,' Nogo agreed.

'Then just as certainly Harper plans to escape the same way. I want you to move the company of men that you have at Debra Maryam and deploy them here and here. On both banks of the river, below the monastery. They must be in a position to prevent Harper reaching the Sudanese border, if he should try to make a run for it.'

'Yes. Good! I understand. That is good tactics,' Nogo nodded gloatingly, his eyes bright behind the lenses of his spectacles.

'Then I want your remaining men moved down to the foot of the escarpment. Tell them to avoid contact with Mek Nimmur's men, but to be in a position to move forward very quickly and seize the dam area, and to block off the ravine below the dam as soon as I give you the word.'

'When will that be?' Nogo asked.

'We will continue to watch him carefully. If he makes a discovery, he will start moving the artefacts out. Many of them will be too large to conceal. Your informer will know about it. That is when we will move in on him.'

'You should move in now, Herr von Schiller,' Nahoot advised him, 'before he gets a chance to open the tomb.'

'Don't be an idiot,' von Schiller snarled at him. 'If we strike too soon, we might never discover what he obviously has learned about the whereabouts of the tomb.'

'We could force him—'

'If I have learned anything in my life, it is that you cannot force a man like Harper. There is a certain type of Englishman – I remember during the last war with them—' He broke off and frowned. 'No. They are very difficult people. We must not rush it now. When Harper makes a discovery in the ravine, that will be the time to pounce.'

The frown faded and he smiled a small, cold smile. 'The waiting game. In the meantime, we play the waiting game.'

The debris that filled the shaft was not so tightly packed that it completely blocked the flow of water through it. If it had done so, Nicholas would never have been sucked in by the current, as he had been on his first dive into the pool. There were still gaps in the blockage where the larger boulders had lodged or where a treetrunk had been sucked in and jammed sideways across the width of the tunnel. Through these sections the water had found the weak spots and kept them open.

Nevertheless, the debris had taken centuries to wedge itself in, and it required back-breaking effort to prise it apart. The clearing operation was further hampered by the lack of working space in the shaft. Only three or four of the big men from the Buffaloes were able to work in the shaft at any one time. The rest of the team were employed in passing back the rubble as it was levered out.

Nicholas changed the shifts every hour. They had more labour than they needed, and changing them often meant that the men at the face were always rested and strong, and eager to earn the bonus of silver dollars that Nicholas promised them for their progress along the shaft. At each change of shift, Nicholas disappeared into the mouth of the tunnel with Sapper's steel tape and measured the advance.

'One hundred and twenty feet! Well done, the Buffaloes,' he told Hansith Sherif, the foreman monk, and then watched the water trickling past his feet. The floor of the tunnel was still sloping downwards at a constant angle. He looked back along it towards the pool, and now in the floodlights the rectangular shape of the walls was very clear to see. It was obvious that the tunnel had been designed and surveyed by an engineer.

He transferred his attention back to the floor of the tunnel and watched the run of water, trying to judge how deep they were below the original river level.

'Eighty or ninety feet,' he estimated. 'No wonder the pressure in the mouth of the tunnel almost crushed me—' he broke off as an unusually shaped fragment in the muck at his feet caught his eye. He stooped and picked it up. Then took it to one of the floodlamps and by its light examined it closely. As he rubbed it clean between finger and thumb, he began to grin.

Sloshing back along the tunnel, he yelled, 'Royan!' Triumphantly brandishing the fragment, he demanded, 'What do you make of that, then?'

She was sitting on the wall of the coffer, and reached down and snatched the object out of his grasp.

'Oh, sweet Mary! Where did you find this, Nicky?'

'Lying in the mud. Right there in the adit, where it's been for the last four thousand years. Where one of Taita's workmen dropped and broke it, probably while he was sneaking a sup of wine behind the slave driver's back.'

Eagerly Royan held the broken shard of pottery up to the lamplight. 'You are right, Nicky,' she exclaimed. 'It's part of a wine vessel. Look at the flared neck and belled lip. But if there was any doubt, which there isn't, the black firing around the rim dates it perfectly in our period. No older than 2000 BC.'

Still clutching the fragment of broken pottery, she jumped down into the mud and slush of the coffer and flung both arms around his neck.

'Further proof, Nicky. We are on Taita's tracks. Can't you get them to clear any faster? We are breathing down the back of the old rogue's neck.'

Halfway through the next shift an excited yelling

echoed out of the mouth of the tunnel, and Nicholas hurried back down to the face.

'What is it, Hansith?' he demanded in Arabic of the foreman monk. 'What are you shouting about?'

'We have broken through, *effendi*.' Hansith Sherif grinned at him, his teeth gleaming in his black and mud-smeared face. Nicholas eagerly pushed his way through the workmen. They had levered a huge round boulder out of the pack, and beyond it lay an opening. He shone his electric torch through this window in the wall, but could make out very little except empty black space.

Stepping back, he slapped the monk on the back. 'Well done, Hansith. A dollar bonus for every man in the team. But keep them working! Clear away all this rubbish.' But it was not as easily done as he had ordered. The shifts changed twice more before the shaft was cleared completely of the last of the extraneous rubble and broken rock. Only then could Nicholas and Royan stand in the threshold of the cavern beyond the tunnel.

'What has happened here? What has caused this?' Royan's voice was puzzled as Nicholas played his torch out into the void.

'I think this is a cave-in area. There was probably a fault in the rock strata running through here and here.' He picked out the cracks in the roof of the cavern.

'You think the flow of the water through the shaft has scoured it out?' she asked.

'I would say so, yes.' Nicholas turned the beam of light downwards. 'The floor has fallen out of the shaft also.'

The rock had subsided in front of them, leaving a deep hole. Ten feet below where they stood the hole was filled with water, forming a large circular pool with vertical rock sides. Overhead the roof had fallen in and was now a high dome of irregular rock, and the far side of the pool was shrouded in shadows a hundred feet or more in front of them.

There was no apparent way around this obstacle without entering the water. Nicholas shouted to Hansith to bring one of the long bamboo poles that they had used for the scaffolding. The pole was thirty feet long and they had to manoeuvre its length down the tunnel. Nicholas sounded the pool with the bamboo, probing it down into the turbid water as deeply as he could reach.

'No bottom.' He shook his head. 'Do you know what I think?' He retrieved the pole and passed it back to Hansith.

'Tell me,' Royan invited.

'I think that this is the natural fault that leads the water away to the other side of the hills, and comes to the surface again at the butterfly fountain. The river has carved its own path.'

'Why hasn't it drained, then?' Royan looked down dubiously in the pool below them.

'A U-bend in the shaft, probably. Water still trapped in the top of the shaft like the bowl of a lavatory.'

He probed the waters of the pool with the beam of his torch, and Royan exclaimed with horror and disgust as one of the giant eels came racing to the surface, attracted by the light.

'The filthy creatures!' She stepped back involuntarily. 'The whole river must be infested with them.'

The long dark shape circled the pool swiftly and then disappeared back into the depths as suddenly as it had appeared.

'If you are right, and a section of Taita's adit has collapsed, then the continuation of his tunnel should be on the far side of this.' She pointed across the pool, and Nicholas lifted the beam of the torch and shone it in the direction she indicated.

'Look, Nicky!' she cried. 'There it is.'

The dark rectangular opening yawned at them from across the pool.

'How do we get across there?' Royan asked, disconsolate.

'The answer to that is, not very easily. Dammit to hell!' Nicholas swore heartily. 'This is going to cost us another couple of days that we can ill afford. We are going to have to build some sort of bridge across it.'

'What kind of bridge?'

'Get Sapper down here. This is his department.'

Sapper stood at the brink of the sink-hole and glared across at the far bank.

'Pontoons,' he grunted. 'How many of those inflatable rafts have you got squirrelled away?'

'Forget it, Sapper!' Nicholas shook his head. 'You are not getting those dirty great paws of yours on my rafts.'

'Suit yourself.' Sapper spread his hands in resignation. 'It would be the easiest and quickest way of doing it. Anchor a raft in the middle and build a catwalk over the top of it. I need something that floats high—'

'Baobab.' Nicholas snapped his fingers. 'That should do the trick very nicely. When it's dried out, baobab wood is as light as balsa. Floats just as well as one of my inflatable rafts.'

'Plenty of baobabs growing along the hills,' Sapper agreed. 'Every second tree in this valley seems to be a ruddy baobab.'

T hree hundred yards from the top of the cliff grew a massive specimen of *Adansonia digitata*. Its smooth bark resembled the skin of one of the great reptiles from the age of the dinosaurs. Its girth was tremendous – twenty men with outstretched arms could not have encircled it. The upper branches were bare and twisted, and it looked as though it had been dead for a hundred years. Only the heavy velvet-covered pods proved that it still lived; they hung thickly from the high branches, bursting open to spill the black seeds which were coated thickly with white cream of tartar.

'The Zulus say that the Nkulu Kulu, the Great Spirit, planted the baobab upside down with its roots in the air to punish it,' Nicholas told Royan as they looked up at the enormous spread of its branches.

'Why would he want to do that?' she wanted to know. 'What did the poor old baobab do that was so bad?'

'It boasted that it was the tallest and thickest tree of the forest, and so the Nkulu Kulu decided to teach it a little lesson in humility.'

One of the gigantic branches had snapped off under its own weight, and lay on the rocky ground beneath the trunk. The wood was white and fibrous, light as cork. Under Nicholas's direction the axemen cut it into manageable lengths. Once they had been carried down the adit shaft to the sink-hole, Sapper stapled the logs together and floated them across the pool to form a causeway. He anchored this to the rock face at either end, and then over it he laid a catwalk of bamboo poles. The bridge of baobab logs floated high, and although it bobbed and swayed, it could easily support the weight of a dozen men at a time.

Nicholas was the first one across the sink-hole. He placed a roughly made ladder against the high vertical bank, and scrambled up into the mouth of the adit on the far side of the pool. Royan was close behind him.

The two of them stood in the entrance to this continuation of the shaft, and as soon as Nicholas shone his torch into it they realized that the nature of the construction had changed. This section had not been so heavily scoured out and eroded by the rush of river water through it. The main flow must have drained away through the sink-hole. The dimensions were the same, three metres wide by two high, but the rectangular shape was more precise and although the walls and roof were rough, like those of a mine, the marks of the tools that had shaped it were now clearly visible. The footing of the tunnel was roughly paved with slabs of crudely dressed stone.

This whole length of the tunnel had also been submerged, for it lay below the natural level of the river before it had been dammed. The paving under their feet was wet and covered with a slime that had not yet had time to dry out since it had been exposed by the receding waters. The roof and walls of the tunnel ran with moisture, and the air was dank and cold and smelled of mud and rot.

They waited for Sapper to string the cables for the lights across the causeway. He set up the lamps and switched them on. At once they were aware that ahead of them the shaft had begun to rise at an angle of about twenty degrees.

'You can see what the old devil Taita was up to here. He has taken us down well below water level to flood the tunnel to a length and depth that nobody would be able to swim along. Now he is angling up again,' Nicholas pointed out to Royan. They started forward, moving slowly up the ascending shaft, and Nicholas counted aloud each pace he took.

'One hundred and eight, one hundred and nine, one hundred and ten—' suddenly they came to the recent low river level. It was clearly marked as a dry line on the walls of the tunnel. The paving under their feet was also dry and free of the slippery coating of slime. Fifty paces further on they passed the high flood level of the river, which was just as clearly etched on the rock floor and the walls. Beyond that the tunnel had never been immersed, and the walls were in the same condition as the Egyptian slave workmen had left them four thousand years earlier. The marks of the bronze chisels were as pristine as if they had been inflicted just days before.

Only ten feet beyond the highest point that the river waters had ever reached, they came out upon a stone landing. Here the floor levelled out, and then the tunnel turned sharply back upon itself.

'Let's spare a minute just to think about this as a feat of engineering.' Nicholas took Royan's arm and pointed back down the tunnel. 'Taita has placed this landing on which we are standing precisely above the high-water mark of the river. How did he work it out so exactly? He had no dumpy level, and only the crudest measuring equipment. And yet he calculated it as accurately as this. It's a hell of a piece of work.'

'Well, he tells us repeatedly in the scrolls that he is a genius. I suppose we will have to believe him now.' She pulled against his grip. 'Let's go on. I must see what lies around this corner,' she urged.

Side by side they turned through the one hundred and eighty degree corner and Nicholas held the hand lamp high, with the electrical cable trailing back down the shaft behind him. As he lit the way ahead, Royan exclaimed aloud and seized Nicholas's free hand. Both of them froze with astonishment.

Taita had designed the turning of the ascending ramp for dramatic effect. The lower section of the shaft through which they had passed was crudely constructed, the walls irregular and undressed, the roof lumpy and cracked. Taita had calculated his levels so finely that he had known that the lower levels of the shaft would be submerged and damaged by the water. He had wasted no effort on beautifying them.

Now before them rose a wide stairway. The angle of its ascent was such that, from where they stood on the landing, the top of it was hidden from their view. Each step stretched the full width of the tunnel, and rose a hand's breadth. The treads were cut from slabs of mottled gneiss, polished and fitted to each other so precisely that the joints between them were barely visible. The roof of the tunnel was three times as high as it had been in the lower reaches

of the tunnel, perfectly domed and proportioned. The walls
and the curved roof were of beautifully dressed blue granite
blocks, keyed into each other with marvellous precision
and symmetry. The whole was a masterpiece of the mason's
art, majestic and portentous. There was both a promise and
a menace in this vestibule to the unknown. Its simplicity
and lack of ornamentation made it even more impressive.

Royan tugged softly at Nicholas's hand and together
they stepped on to the first tread of the stairway. It was
carpeted with a fine layer of dust, soft and white as talcum
powder. The dust rose in soft eddies and wisps around their
knees and then subsided as they passed on upwards. It
muted the harsh glare of the electric lamp that Nicholas
carried high in his right hand.

Gradually, as they went on upwards, the top of the
staircase came into view ahead of them. Royan dug her
fingernails into the palm of Nicholas's hand as she saw
what lay ahead. The staircase ended on another level
landing, across which a rectangular doorway faced them.
They stepped up on to the landing and stood before the
doorway. Neither of them had words to express this
supreme moment: they stood in silence for what seemed
like an eternity, holding each other's hand with a fierce
and possessive grip.

Finally Nicholas tore his eyes off the gateway, and
looked down at Royan. He saw his own feelings mirrored
in her face, her eyes shone as though lit from within by an
incandescent passion. There was no other person alive
with whom he would wish to share this moment. He
wanted it to last for ever.

She turned her head and looked at him. They stared
deeply and solemnly into each other's eyes. Both of them
were aware that this was a high tide in their lives, one that
could never be repeated. She tightened her grip on his
hand, and looked back to the doorway facing them. It had
been plastered over with white river clay, a surface that

had mellowed to the shade of ivory. There was no crack or blemish in its smooth expanse, like the flawless skin of a beautiful virgin.

Their eyes fastened avidly on the two embossed seals in the centre of the expanse of white clay. The upper one was in the shape of the royal cartouche, the rectangular knot surmounted by the scarab, the horned beetle that signified the great circle of eternity.

Royan's lips formed the words as she read them from the hieroglyphics, but she uttered no sound. '"*The Almighty. The Divine. Ruler of the Upper and Lower Kingdoms of Egypt. Familiar of the god, Horus. Beloved of Osiris and of Isis. Mamose, may he live for ever!*"'

Below this magnificent royal seal was a smaller, simpler design in the shape of a hawk, with one broken wing drooping across its barred breast, and the legend: '*I, Taita the slave, have obeyed your command, divine Pharaoh.*' Underneath the maimed hawk was a single column of hieroglyphics that spelled out the stern warning: '*Stranger! The gods are watching. Disturb the king's eternal rest at your peril!*'

Breaking the seals on the doorway was a momentous act, and despite the fact that the time before the onset of the rains was fast running out, neither of them was prepared to undertake it lightly. They had to make every effort to keep permanent records of everything they discovered, and to inflict as little damage as possible while gaining access.

They spent one of their precious remaining days preparing for the break-in to the tomb. Naturally, Nicholas's first concern was the security of the tomb area. He asked Mek Nimmur to place an armed guard on the causeway over the sink-hole in the approach tunnel, and access beyond this point was restricted. Only Nicholas,

Royan, Sapper, Mek, Tessay and four of the monks whom Nicholas had selected were allowed across the bridge.

Hansith Sherif had proved himself repeatedly during the clearing of the lower tunnel. Physically strong, willing and intelligent, he had become Nicholas's principal assistant. It was Hansith who carried the tripod and spare camera equipment while Nicholas photographed the approach tunnel and the sealed doorway. He shot three rolls of high-speed film to make certain that they had a complete record of the unbroken seals and the doorway surrounds. Only when the filming was completed would Nicholas allow Hansith and the other three monks to bring up the tools needed for the break-in.

Sapper moved the Honda generator up as far as the sink-hole, to reduce the voltage drop over the distance that the current had to travel down the cable. Then he set up the floodlights on the upper landing of the staircase and focused them on the white expanse of the plastered doorway.

When they assembled at the threshold they were all in a sober mood. Despite the fact that the tomb was thousands of years old, it was still an act of desecration that they were about to perpetrate. Royan had translated the hieroglyphic warning on the sealed doorway to Sapper, Mek and Tessay, and none of them was prepared to take it lightly.

Nicholas marked out the square opening he intended cutting through the plaster covering. This was large enough to afford access, but it also enclosed the royal cartouche and Tatia's maimed hawk seal. He intended lifting these out in one piece, and preserving them intact. In his imagination, he could already see them displayed in a prominent position in the museum at Quenton Park.

Nicholas began on the right-hand upper corner of the opening. First he used a long, needle-sharp awl as a probe. He pressed and twisted the needle point through the dried clay in an attempt to determine exactly what lay beneath the surface. Very soon he found out that the plaster had been laid over laths of finely interwoven reeds.

'That makes it a lot easier,' he told Royan. 'The reed mat will help to hold the plaster together and prevent it cracking and breaking up.'

He kept working the point of the awl deeper, until suddenly the resistance gave way and the blade ran in its full length.

'Six inches,' he said, measuring the thickness of the door off the blade. 'Taita never skimps, does he? It's a heavy bit of work.'

Still using the awl, Nicholas drilled all four corners of the square opening he intended cutting. Then he stepped back and gestured for Hansith to bring up the heavy four-inch gimlet to enlarge them. This was the type of drill that fishermen use for cutting through lake ice in winter.

As soon as the gimlet broke through, Nicholas impatiently pulled Hansith aside and peered into the hole. Beyond the opening all was completely dark, but he caught a whiff of the faint breath of ancient air that washed through the opening. The odour was dry and dead and austere, the smell of the ages long past.

'What do you see?' Royan demanded at his elbow.

'The light! Give me the light!' he ordered, and when Sapper handed it to him, he held it to the opening.

'Tell me!' Royan was dancing beside him with impatience. 'What do you see now?'

'Colours!' he whispered. 'The most marvellous, indescribable colours.' He stepped back and, lifting her around the waist, held her so that she could look into the aperture.

'Beautiful!' she cried. 'It's so beautiful.'

apper rigged up the heavy-duty electric blower fan which would circulate the air in the shaft, while Nicholas prepared the chain-saw. When he was ready, Nicholas handed Royan a pair of goggles and a dust mask and helped her to adjust them. Then he made her fit a pair of wax ear plugs.

Before he started the chain-saw, he sent the rest of them back down the tunnel as far as the causeway over the sink-hole. In the confined space the exhaust fumes from the chain-saw and the dust, together with the noise of the petrol engine, would be overpowering, but apart from that he wanted only Royan with him at the moment of the break-in.

When they were alone, Nicholas switched the blower fan to its highest speed, then donned his own mask and goggles and plugged his ears. He pulled the starter cord of the chain-saw motor and it burst into life in a cloud of blue exhaust smoke.

Nicholas braced himself and pressed the spinning chain blade into the gimlet hole in the plastered doorway. It cut through the thick white plaster and the laths beneath it like a knife through the icing on a wedding cake. Carefully he ran the cutting edge down the line he had marked out.

A cloud of flying white plaster dust filled the air. Within seconds they could see only a few feet in front of their eyes. Doggedly Nicholas kept the cut going, down the right-hand side, across the bottom, then up the left side. Finally he made the last cut across the top, and when the square trapdoor began to sag forward under its own weight he killed the engine of the chain-saw and set it aside.

Royan jumped forwards to help him, and together in the eddies of dust and smoke they steadied the square of plaster and prevented it from crashing to the paving and shattering into a thousand pieces. Gently they lifted it out of the opening and, with the seals still intact, laid it against the side wall of the landing.

The open hatchway they had cut through the plaster was a dark square. Nicholas adjusted the floodlight to shine through it, but the dust was still too dense for them to be able to see much of the interior. Nicholas climbed through the hatch into the space beyond. All was obscured by a dense fog of dust that not even the lamps could penetrate.

He did not attempt to explore further, but immediately turned back to help Royan through the opening after him. He recognized her right to share every moment of this discovery. Beyond the wall they stood quietly together, waiting for the blower fan to clear the air. Slowly the dust fog began to dissipate, and the first thing they became aware of was the floor beneath their feet.

No longer made of stone slabs, it was covered with tiles of yellow agate that had been polished to a gloss and fitted together so cunningly that no joints were visible. It was like a single sheet of lovely opaque glass, dulled only by the film of fine talcum dust that had settled upon it. Where their feet had disturbed the layer of dust the agate sparkled through it, catching the light of the floodlamp.

Then the fog of dust that surrounded them thinned, and gradually a miraculous blaze of colours and shapes began to appear through the murk. Royan lifted the dust mask from her face and let it drop to the agate floor. Nicholas followed her example, and took a breath of the stagnant air. No draught had disturbed it for thousands of years and it had the odour of great antiquity, the musty smell of the linen bandages of an embalmed corpse.

Now the miasma of dust faded away and before them opened a long straight passageway, the end of which was hidden in shadow and darkness. Nicholas turned back to the opening in the sealed door behind them, and reached through it to bring in the floodlight on its stand. Quickly he arranged it to illuminate the full length of the passage-way ahead of them.

As they started forward, the images of the old gods hovered around them. They glowered at the intruders from the walls and hung over them, watching them with huge and hostile eyes from the ceiling high overhead. Nicholas and Royan passed on slowly. Their footfalls on the agate tiles were muted by the thin carpet of dust, and the dust that still hung in the air reflected the light and cast over them a luminous net that had an ethereal, dreamlike quality.

Inscriptions covered every inch of space upon the walls and the high roof. There were long quotations from all the mystical writings, from the *Book of Breathings*, the *Book of the Pylons* and the *Book of Wisdom*. Other blocks of hieroglyphics recited the history of Pharaoh Mamose's existence on this earth, and extolled those virtues that made the gods love him.

Further along they came to the first of eight shrines set into the walls of the long funeral gallery. This one was the shrine of Osiris. It was a circular chamber, the curved wall decorated with texts in praise of the god, and in its niche a small statue of Osiris in his tall feathered head-dress, with eyes of onyx and rock crystal which stared at them so implacably that Royan shivered. Nicholas reached out and touched the foot of the god.

He said one word, 'Gold!'

Then he looked up at the towering mural that covered the wall and half the domed ceiling above and around the shrine. It was another gigantic figure of the father Osiris, god of the Underworld, with his green face and false beard, his arms crossed upon his chest, holding the flail and the crook, wearing his tall feathered head-dress and with the erect cobra on his brow. They gazed up at him with a sense of awe. As the lamplight wavered in the shifting dust cloud the god seemed to become imbued with life, and to move and sway before their eyes.

They did not linger at the first shrine, for beyond it the gallery ran on, straight as the flight of an arrow to its target. They followed it. The next shrine set into the wall was dedicated to the goddess. The golden figure of Isis sat in her niche, upon the throne that was her symbol. The infant Horus suckled at her breast. Her eyes were ivory and blue lapis lazuli.

Her murals covered the walls around her niche. There she was, the mother with great kohl-lined eyes as black as night, wearing the sun disc and the horns of the sacred cow upon her head. All around her, hieroglyphic symbols covered the wall, so bright that they glowed like a cloud of fireflies; for she possessed a hundred diverse names. Amongst these were Ast and Net and Bast. She was also Ptah and Seker and Mersekert and Rennut. Each of these names was a word of power, for her sanctity and her benevolent aura had lived on where most of the old gods had withered away for lack of worshippers to repeat and keep alive these mystic names.

In ancient Byzantium and later in Christian Egypt they had bestowed the old goddess's virtues and attributes upon the Virgin Mary. The image of her suckling the infant Horus had been perpetuated in the icons of the Madonna and child. Thus Royan responded to the goddess in all her entities, the mingled blood of Royan's forefathers in her veins acknowledging both Isis and Mary, heresy and truth mingling inextricably in her heart, so that she felt at once both guilt and religious elation.

In the next shrine was a golden figure of Horus, the falcon-headed, the last of the holy trinity. In his right hand he held the war-bow and in his left the *ankh*, for life and death were his to dispense. His eyes were red carnelians.

Portraits of his other entities surrounded the statue: Horus the infant, suckling at the breast of Isis, Horus as the divine youth Harpocrates, proud and lithe and beautiful, one finger touching his chin in the ritual gesture, striding out on sandalled feet under his short, stiff kilt. Then Horus the falcon-headed, sometimes with the body of a lion and then with the body of a young warrior, wearing the great crown of the south and the north united. Beneath him was the inscription: '*Great God and Lord of Heaven, of manifest power, Mighty one amongst all the gods, whose strength has vanquished the foes of his divine father, Osiris.*'

In the fourth shrine stood Seth, the arch-fiend, the god of violence and discord. His body was gold, but his head was the head of a black hyena.

In the fifth shrine stood the god of the dead and of the cemeteries, Anubis the jackal-headed. It was he who officiated at the embalming, and whose duty it was to examine the tongue of the great balance when the heart of the deceased was weighed. If the beam of the scales were exactly horizontal, then the dead man was declared worthy, but if the balance tipped against him Anubis threw the heart to the crocodile monster and it was devoured.

The sixth shrine was dedicated to the god of writing, Thoth. He had the head of a sacred ibis and his stylus was in his hand. In the seventh shrine the sacred cow Hathor stood squarely on all four hooves, her piebald body spotted black and white, her face benignly human but with huge, trumpet-shaped ears. The eighth shrine was the largest and most splendid of all, for it belonged to Amon-Ra, father of all creation. He was the sun, an enormous golden disc from which the slanting golden rays emanated.

Nicholas paused here and looked back down the long gallery. Those eight sacred statues comprised a treasure that matched anything that Howard Carter and Lord Carnarvon had discovered in the tomb of Tutankhamen. He felt in his heart that it was crass even to consider their monetary value. However, the simple truth was that even one of these extraordinary works of art would be sufficient to pay off all his debts many times over. But he thrust the thought aside and turned once more to face the commodious chamber at the far end of the gallery.

'The burial chamber,' Royan murmured with awe. 'The tomb.'

As they walked towards it the shadows retreated before them, like the ghost of the long-dead pharaoh scurrying back to its final resting place. Now they could see into the tomb. Its walls were aflame with still more magnificent murals. Though they had gazed upon so many of these already, their eyes and their senses were not yet jaded or wearied by such profusion.

A single elongated figure rose up the far wall, and then stooped across the ceiling. It was the supple, sinuous body of the goddess Nut, giving birth to the sun. The golden rays poured forth from her open womb, suffusing the sarcophagus of the pharaoh and endowing the dead king with new life.

The royal sarcophagus stood in the centre of the chamber, a massive coffin hewn from a solid granite block. How many slaves must have laboured to bring this mass of stone along the subterranean passages, Nicholas wondered. He could imagine their sweating bodies gleaming in the lamplight, and hear the grating squeal of the wooden rollers under the immense weight of the coffin.

Then Nicholas looked down into the coffin, and felt the plunge of his spirits as he realized that the sarcophagus was empty. The massive granite lid had been lifted from its seat, and flung aside with such violence that it had cracked across its width and now lay in two pieces on the floor beside the coffin.

They moved forward slowly, the bitter taste of disappointment mingling with the dust upon their tongues, until they could look down into the open sarcophagus. It contained only the shattered fragments of the four canopic jars. These vessels had been carved from alabaster to contain the entrails, liver and other internal organs of the king. The broken lids were decorated with the heads of gods and fabulous creatures from beyond the grave.

'Empty!' whispered Royan. 'The body of the king has gone.'

Over the following days, while they photographed the murals and packed the statues of the eight gods and goddesses from the funeral gallery, Royan and Nicholas discussed and argued the disappearance of the royal mummy from its sarcophagus.

'The seals on the gate of the tomb were intact,' Royan pointed out repeatedly.

'There is probably an explanation for that,' Nicholas told her. 'Taita himself might have removed the treasure and the body. Many times in the writing of the seventh scroll he laments the waste of such treasure. He points out that it could have been much better spent in protecting and nurturing the nation and its people.'

'No, it does not make sense,' Royan argued, 'to go to such lengths as to dam the river and tunnel under the pool, to build this elaborate tomb, and then to remove and destroy the king's mummy. Taita was always a logical person. In his own way he revered the gods of Egypt. It shows in all his writings. He would never have flouted the religious traditions in which he believed so strongly. Something about this tomb does not ring true for me – the mysterious and almost offhanded disappearance of the body, even the paintings and the inscriptions upon the walls.'

'I agree with you about the missing corpse, but what do you find illogical about the decorations?' Nicholas wanted to know.

'Well, the paintings first.' She indicated the image of

Isis with a wave of her hand. 'They are lovely, and they are the work of a competent classical artist, but they are hackneyed and stylized in form and choice of colour. The figures are stiff and wooden – they do not move and dance. They lack that spark of genius that we were shown in the tomb of Queen Lostris where the original scrolls in their alabaster jars were hidden.'

Nicholas considered the murals thoughtfully. 'I see what you mean. Even the murals in the tomb of Tanus at the monastery are in a different class from these.'

'Exactly!' she said forcefully. 'Those were the paintings of Taita himself. These are not. They were done by one of his hacks.'

'What else is there about the inscriptions that you don't like?'

'Have you ever heard of another tomb that did not have the text of the *Book of the Dead* inscribed upon its walls, or that did not depict the dead person's journey through the seven pylons to reach the paradise beyond?'

Nicholas looked startled; he had never considered that fact. Without replying he left her and went back down the long gallery, ostensibly to supervise the packing of the sacred statues, but in reality to give himself more time to consider what she had said.

Before leaving England Nicholas had seen to it that all of the more vulnerable and breakable equipment that they had air-freighted into the gorge had been packed in sturdy metal ammunition crates. All these crates had waterproof rubber seals and strong lever fastenings. The original contents had been padded and protected with polystyrene packing. When they left Ethiopia the equipment would be abandoned, but the crates, together with the packing material, had been carefully preserved for transporting the treasures that they might find in the tomb.

While six of the sacred statues fitted neatly into the crates, the images of Hathor the cow and satanic Seth were too large. However, Nicholas discovered that these had been carved in separate parts. The heads were detachable, and the hoofed legs of Hathor were held into the body by wooden pins that were rotted to dust. Broken down into their separate parts, even these two larger statues could also be packed into the metal cases.

Nicholas watched Hansith packing Seth's ferocious head of ebony and black resin into one of the crates. Then after a while he went back to where Royan was working on the inscriptions on the wall above the empty sarcophagus.

'Very well. I agree. You are right about the lack of inscriptions from the *Book of the Dead*. It does seem strange. But what can we do about it, other than accepting it as a mystery which we can never unravel?'

'Nicky, there is something more here. This is not everything. I feel it in every fibre of my being. We are missing something.'

'Who am I, a mere male, to question the veracity of a woman's instincts.'

'Stop being superior,' she snapped. 'How long do I have to work over the inscriptions from the stele?'

'A week or two at the most. I have to set up an RV with Jannie. We have to be there at Roseires airstrip when he comes in to pick us up. That's one date we dare not break.'

'Good Lord. I thought you would have arranged that long ago. How will you contact Jannie from here?'

'Quite simple really.' Nicholas smiled. 'There is a public telephone at the post office in Debra Maryam. Tessay can move freely anywhere in the Gojam. She will go up the escarpment with an escort of monks and telephone Geoffrey Tennant at the British Embassy in Addis. I have already arranged it with Geoffrey. He will relay a message on to Jannie.'

'Will Tessay do it for you?'

He nodded. 'She has agreed to go up to Debra Maryam

tomorrow. Jannie must have as much notice as possible to get himself prepared for the flight out from Malta. It's going to need some fine timing for all of us to arrive at the airstrip simultaneously. It will be asking for trouble for one party to sit around waiting at Roseires for the others to arrive.'

'Dawn on the first of April,' Nicholas gave Tessay the message. 'Tell Jannie we will be there on April Fools' Day! A nice easy one to remember.'

They watched Tessay set off along the trail with her escort of monks and Royan asked Mek Nimmur quietly, 'Don't you worry about her going off like this on her own?'

'She is a very competent person, and she is well known and liked throughout the Gojam. She is as safe as any person can be in a dangerous land.' Mek watched Tessay's slim figure in *shamma* and jodhpur pants becoming smaller with distance. 'I wish I could go with her, but—' Mek shrugged.

Suddenly Royan exclaimed, 'There is something that I forgot to ask her.' She left Nicholas and Mek standing, and ran down the trail calling after the other woman. Her voice floated back to where Nicholas stood watching her.

'Tessay! Wait! Come back!'

Tessay turned and waited for Royan to catch up with her. While the two women stood talking together, Nicholas lost interest and turned to study the distant silhouette of the escarpment. With a sinking feeling in the pit of his stomach he saw that the thunderheads on the mountain tops were denser and more ominous than they had been only days before. The rains were building up swiftly now. He wondered if they really had as long as they hoped before the dam was threatened and they were driven out of the gorge by the rising waters.

He looked back down the path just in time to see Royan pass something to Tessay, who nodded and pushed it into the pocket of her jodhpurs. Then at last the two women embraced warmly, and Tessay turned away. Royan stood in the middle of the trail, watching until a bend in the valley hid Tessay from her. Then she walked slowly back to where Nicholas waited.

'What was all that about?' he wanted to know, and she smiled mysteriously.

'Girls' secrets. There are some things that it's best you brutish males don't know about.' But when Nicholas raised an eyebrow at her, she relented and told him, 'Tessay will ask Geoffrey Tennant to send a message to Mummy, just to let her know that I am all right. I don't want her to worry about me.'

As they climbed back down the scaffolding to where the fly camp had been set up on the rock ledge beside Taita's pool, Nicholas thought how fortuitous it was that Royan had her mother's phone number already written down to hand to Tessay, and he wondered at this sudden urge of Royan's to report her whereabouts to her mother. 'I wonder what she is really up to?' he mused. 'I will try and wheedle it out of Tessay when she returns.'

Royan would have preferred to camp in the tomb itself, so as to be in the midst of the inscriptions on which she was working, but Nicholas had insisted that they sleep in the open air, and the ledge was as close as they could get to their workplace. 'The musty air in the tomb is very probably unhealthy,' he told her. 'Cave disease is a real danger in these old enclosed places. They say that is what killed some of Howard Carter's people working in the tomb of Tutankhamen.'

'The fungus spores that cause cave disease breed in bat dung,' she pointed out. 'There are no bats in Mamose's tomb. Taita sealed it up too tightly.'

'Humour me,' he begged. 'You cannot work in there

for days on end. I want you at least to get out of the tomb for a few hours each day.'

She shrugged. 'Only as a special favour to you,' she agreed, but as they reached the foot of the scaffolding she gave her new sleeping quarters only a perfunctory glance and then headed for the coffer dam and the entrance to the approach tunnel.

They had converted the landing at the top of the staircase, outside the plaster-sealed entrance to the tomb, into their workshop. Royan spread her drawings and photographs and reference books on the rough table of hand-hewn planks that Hansith made for her. Sapper had placed one of the floodlamps above this crude desk so that she had good light to work by. Against one wall of the landing they had stacked the ammunition crates which contained the eight sacred statues. Nicholas had insisted on storing all their discoveries where he could safeguard them adequately. Mek's armed men still kept a twenty-four-hour guard on the causeway over the sink-hole.

While Nicholas completed his photographic record of the walls of the long gallery and the empty burial chamber, Royan sat at her table and pored over her papers for hours at a time, scribbling notes and calculations from them into her notebooks. Now and then she would jump up from her desk and dart through the hatch in the white plaster doorway into the long gallery to study a detail on the decorated walls.

Whenever this happened, Nicholas straightened up from his camera tripod and watched her with a fond and indulgent expression. So intent was she that she seemed completely oblivious of him and everybody else about her. Nicholas had never seen her in this mood, and the depth of her powers of concentration impressed him.

When she had worked for fifteen hours without a break he went out on to the landing to rescue her and to lead her, protesting, back down the tunnel to the pool where there was a hot meal waiting for them. After she had eaten he led her to her hut and insisted that she lie down on her inflatable mattress.

'You are going to sleep now, Royan,' he ordered.

He woke to hear her creeping stealthily out of the hut next door to his, back along the ledge to the entrance to the tomb. He checked his watch and grunted with disbelief when he realized that they had slept for only three and a half hours. He shaved quickly and bolted back a slab of toasted *injera* bread and a cup of tea before following her into the tomb.

He found her standing in the long gallery before the empty niche in the shrine where the statuette of Osiris had stood. She was so preoccupied that she did not hear him come up behind her, and she started violently when he touched her arm.

'You startled me,' she scolded him.

'What are you staring at?' he asked. 'What have you discovered?'

'Nothing,' she denied swiftly, and then after a moment, 'I don't know. It's just an idea.'

'Come on! What are you up to?'

'It's easier for me to show you.' She led him back to her table on the stone landing, and rearranged her notebooks carefully before she spoke again.

'What I have been doing these last few days is going through the material on the stele of Tanus's tomb, picking out all the quotations that I recognize from the classical books of mystery, the *Book of Breathings*, the *Book of the Pylons* and the *Book of Thoth*, and setting those on one side.' She showed him fifteen pages in her neat small script. 'All this is ancient material, none of it original compositions by Taita. I have discarded it for the time being.'

She set the first notebook aside and picked up the next. 'All this is from the fourth face of the stele. It's nothing that I recognize, but seems to be only long lists of numbers and figures. Some sort of code, perhaps? I am not sure, but I do have some ideas on it that I will come to later.

'Now this here,' she showed him the next book, 'this is all fresh material that I don't remember reading in any of the ancient classics. Much of it, if not all of it, must be original Taita writings. If he has left any more clues for us, I believe they will be here, in these sections.'

He grinned, 'Like that marvellous quotation describing the pink and private parts of the goddess. Is that what you are referring to?'

'Trust you not to forget that.' She flushed lightly and refused to look up from her notebook. 'Look at this quotation from the head of the third face of the stele, the side Taita has headed "*autumn*". It's the very first one that caught my attention.'

Nicholas leaned forward and read the hieroglyphics aloud: '"*The great god Osiris makes the opening coup with deference to the protocol of the four bulls. At the first pylon he bears full testimony to the immutable law of the board.*"' He looked up at her. 'Yes, I remember that quotation. Taita is referring to bao, the game that the old devil loved so passionately.'

'That's right.' Royan looked slightly embarrassed. 'But do you also remember that I told you about a dream that I had in which I saw Duraid again in one of the chambers of the tomb?'

'I remember.' He chuckled at her discomfort. 'He said something to you about the protocol of the four bulls. Now we are going into the realm of divination by dreams, are we?'

She looked annoyed by his levity. 'All I am suggesting is that my subconscious had been digesting the quotation and come up with an answer, which it put into the mouth of Duraid in the dream. Can't you be serious just for one moment?'

524

'Sorry.' He was contrite. 'Remind me what you heard Duraid say.'

'In the dream he told me, "*Remember the protocol of the four bulls – Start at the beginning.*"'

'I am no expert on the game of bao. What did he mean?'

'The rules and subtleties of the game have been lost in the mists of antiquity. But as you know, we have found examples of the bao board amongst the grave goods in the tombs of the eleventh to the seventeenth dynasties, and we can only guess that it was an early form of chess.' She began to sketch for him on one of the blank pages at the back of her notebook.

'The wooden board was laid out like a chessboard, eight rows of cups wide and eight rows deep. Like this.' She drew it in with quick, deft strokes of her ballpoint pen. 'The pieces were coloured stones that moved in a prescribed fashion. I won't go into all the details, but the protocol of the four bulls was an opening gambit in the game favoured by grand masters of Taita's calibre. It consisted of making sacrifices to mass the highest-ranking stones in the first cup from where they could dominate the important central files of the board.'

'I am not sure where we are going, but lead on. I am listening.' Nicholas tried not to look too mystified.

'The first cup of the board.' She indicated it on her sketch, as though instructing a backward child. 'The beginning. Duraid said, "*Start at the beginning.*" Taita said, "*The great god Osiris makes the opening coup.*"'

'I still don't follow you.' Nicholas shook his head.

'Come with me.' Carrying the notebooks, she led him through the hatch in the white plaster doorway and stood beside him at the shrine of Osiris. 'The opening coup. The beginning.'

She turned and faced down the gallery. 'This is the first shrine. How many shrines are there altogether?'

'Three for the trinity, then Seth, Thoth, Anubis, Hathor and Ra,' he listed. 'Eight altogether.'

'Glory be!' She laughed. 'The lad can count! How many cups in the files of the bao board?'

'Eight across, and eight down—' he broke off and stared at her. 'You think—?'

She did not answer, but opened the notebook. 'All of these numbers and extraneous symbols – they spell no coherent words. They do not relate to each other in any way, except that no number in the list is greater than eight.'

'I thought I had caught up with you, but I just lost you again.'

'If somebody were to read the notations of a game of chess four thousand years from now, what would he make of it?' she asked. 'Wouldn't it just be lists of numbers and extraneous symbols to him? You really are being extremely dense, aren't you? This is like pulling teeth.'

'Oh, Lordy, Lordy!' His face cleared. 'You clever lady! Taita is playing the game of bao with us.'

'And this is the first pylon, where it starts.' She gestured to the shrine. 'This is where the great god Osiris makes the opening coup. This is where we must start at the beginning of the sacred bao board. This is where we counter his opening move.'

They both looked around the shrine for a while, studying the curved walls and the high domed roof, and then Nicholas broke the silence. 'At the risk of being called extremely dense and having my teeth pulled, may I ask a question? How the hell do we play a game when we don't even know the rules?'

Colonel Nogo exuded confidence and self-importance as he swaggered into the conference room to answer von Schiller's summons. Nahoot Guddabi bustled along behind him, determined not to be excluded from any of the proceedings. He too tried to look confident and important, but in truth he felt his position was very insecure and that he needed to justify himself to his master.

Von Schiller was dictating correspondence to Utte Kemper, but as soon as they entered the room he stood up quickly and stepped on to the carpeted block.

'You promised that you would have a report for me yesterday,' he snapped at Nogo, ignoring Nahoot. 'Have you not heard anything from this informer of yours in the gorge?'

'I apologize for keeping you waiting like this, Herr von Schiller.' Nogo was immediately deflated by this sharp attack, and he became restless and uneasy. The German frightened him. 'The women were a day late returning from Harper's camp. They are very unreliable, these country people. Time means very little to them.'

'Yes, yes.' Von Schiller was impatient. 'I know the failings of your black brethren, and I might add you are not completely innocent of these yourself, Nogo. But tell me what news you have for me.'

'Harper finished work on the dam seven days ago, and immediately he moved his camp downstream, to a new place on the hills above the ravine. He then built some sort of bamboo ladder down into the ravine. My informer tells me that they are clearing a hole at the bottom of the empty pool—'

'A hole? What kind of hole?' Von Schiller turned pale as he listened, and began sweating in a light sheen across his forehead.

'Are you all right, Herr von Schiller?' Nogo was alarmed. The German looked very ill, as if he were about to collapse.

'I am perfectly well,' von Schiller shouted at him. 'What hole was this? Describe it to me.'

'The woman bringing the message is a stupid peasant.' Nogo was uncomfortable, squirming under von Schiller's grilling. 'She says only that when the river water fell, there was a hole in the bottom that was filled with rock and rubbish and that they have cleared this out.'

'A tunnel!' Nahoot could contain himself no longer. 'It must be the entrance tunnel to the tomb.'

'Be quiet!' Von Schiller turned on him furiously. 'You have no facts to back up that supposition. Let Nogo finish.' He turned back to the colonel. 'Go on. Give me the rest of it.'

'The woman says that there is a cave at the end of the hole. Like a rock shrine, with pictures on the walls—'

'Pictures? What pictures?'

'The woman said they were pictures of the saints.' Nogo made a deprecating gesture. 'She is a very uneducated woman. Stupid—'

'Christian saints?' von Schiller demanded.

Nahoot interjected, 'That is not possible, Herr von Schiller. I tell you that Harper has discovered the tomb of Mamose. You must act swiftly now.'

'I will not warn you again, you miserable little man,' von Schiller snarled at him. 'Keep quiet.'

He turned back to Nogo. 'Was there anything else in the cavern? Tell me everything the woman said.'

'Pictures and statues of the saints.' Nogo spread his hands. 'I am sorry, Herr von Schiller, that's what she said. I know this is all nonsense, but that is what the woman told me.'

'I will judge what is and what is not nonsense,' von Schiller told him. 'What did she say happened to these statues of the saints?'

'Harper has packed them in boxes.'

'Has he removed them from the shrine?'

'I do not know, Herr von Schiller. The woman did not say.'

Von Schiller stepped down from his block. He began to pace up and down the length of the hut, muttering to himself distractedly.

'Herr von Schiller—' Nahoot began, but the German waved him to silence. At last he stopped in front of Nogo and stared up at him.

'Did they find a mummy, a body, in the shrine?' he demanded.

'I do not know, Herr von Schiller. The woman did not say.'

'Where is she?' Von Schiller was so agitated that he clutched the front of Nogo's uniform jacket and stood on tiptoe to thrust his face up close to his. 'Where is this woman? Have you let her go?' Tiny droplets of spittle flew into Nogo's face and he blinked and tried to duck, but von Schiller had him in a death grip.

'No, sir. She is still here. I did not want to bring her to you—'

'You fool. All you are telling me is secondhand. Bring her in here immediately. I want to question her face to face.' He shoved Nogo away from him. 'Go and fetch her.'

Nogo returned minutes later dragging the woman into the room by one arm. She was young, and despite the blue tattoos across her cheeks and chin she was pretty. She wore the long black robes and head-covering of a married woman, and carried an infant on her hip.

As soon as Nogo released her arm she sank to the floor and whimpered with terror. The child she carried whined in sympathy. Its nostrils were plugged with white crusts of dried snot. The woman opened the top of her robe with a shaking hand, fished out one of her milk-swollen breasts and thrust the nipple into the child's mouth. Infant and mother stared at von Schiller with terrified eyes.

'Ask her if there was a coffin or body of the saint in the shrine,' von Schiller ordered, eyeing the woman with distaste.

Nogo questioned her for a minute and then shook his head. 'She does not know anything about a body. She is very stupid. She does not understand very well.'

'Ask her about the statues of the saints. What has Harper done with them? Where are they now? Has he removed them from the shrine?'

After another long exchange with the woman, Nogo shook his head. 'No. She says that the statues are still in the shrine. The white man has packed them into boxes and the soldiers are guarding them.'

'Soldiers? What soldiers?'

'Soldiers of Mek Nimmur, the *shufta* commander that I told you about. He is still with Harper.'

'How many boxes are there?' In his impatience von Schiller went up to where the woman sat and prodded her with the toe of his boot. 'How many statues are there?'

The woman wailed with terror and shrank away from him. Von Schiller recoiled from her at the same time, with an expression of disgust.

'*Gott im Himmel!*' He pulled a handkerchief from his pocket and patted his mouth and nose with it. 'She stinks like an animal. Ask her how many boxes.'

'Not many,' Nogo translated, 'perhaps five, not more than ten. She is not sure.'

'What size? How big are they?'

When Nogo put the question to her, the woman indicated the length of her arm. Von Schiller's disappointment registered clearly in his face.

'So few pieces, and so insignificant.' He turned away from the woman and went to stare out of the south-facing window of the hut, down over the escarpment rim into the wilderness of the gorge. 'If what this creature says is true, then Harper has not yet discovered the treasure of Mamose. There should be more, much more.'

Nogo was talking rapidly to the woman again, and now he turned back to von Schiller. 'She says that one of Harper's party has left the camp in the gorge, and gone to Debra Maryam.'

Von Schiller spun away from the window and stared at him. 'One of his party? Who? Which one?'

'She is an Ethiopian woman. The concubine of Mek Nimmur. A woman she calls Woizero Tessay. I know of her. She was married to the Russian hunter, before she became Mek Nimmur's whore.'

Von Schiller rushed across the room and seized the woman by the front of her robe. He hauled her to her feet with such violence that the infant was jerked from her grip and fell howling to the floor.

'Ask her where the woman is now,' he instructed Nogo.

The mother pulled free from his grip and grovelled on the floor, trying to pick up and console her screaming infant. Nogo grabbed her and slapped her face resoundingly to get her attention. She clasped her baby to her breast and gabbled out a reply.

'She does not know,' Nogo admitted. 'She thinks she is still at Debra Maryam.'

'Get that filthy bitch out of here!' Von Schiller jerked his head at the woman and her child. Nogo dragged them from the hut.

'What else do you know of this woman of Mek Nimmur's?' he asked in milder tones when Nogo returned.

'She is from one of the noble families in Addis Ababa, a blood relative of Ras Tafari Makonnen, the old Emperor Haile Selassie.'

'If she is Mek Nimmur's woman, and has come directly from Harper's camp, then she will be able to answer the questions that this other creature could not.'

'That is true, Herr von Schiller. But she may not wish to tell us.'

'I want her,' von Schiller said. 'Bring her here. Helm will speak to her. I am sure he will be able to make her see reason.'

'She is an important person. Her family has much influence.' Nogo thought about it for a moment. 'But on the other hand, she has been consorting with a notorious bandit. That is all the reason I need for bringing her in. I will send a detachment of my men, under one of my most trusted officers, to arrest her immediately.' He hesitated. 'If the woman is questioned severely, it would be as well that she were not allowed to return to her friends in Addis. They could make trouble for all of us. Even for you, Herr von Schiller.'

'What do you propose?' von Schiller wanted to know.

'When she has answered your questions, there will have to be a little accident,' Nogo suggested.

'Do what is necessary,' von Schiller ordered. 'I will leave the details to you, but make sure that if it is necessary to dispose of the woman it is done properly. I have had enough bungling.' As he spoke these words he looked across at Nahoot Guddabi, who lowered his gaze and flushed angrily.

They had spent almost two full days at the shrine of Osiris in the long gallery. No ancient worshipper had ever studied the texts upon those walls more avidly than Nicholas and Royan, or examined the flamboyant murals of the great god with more minute attention.

They took it in turn to recite aloud the extracts from the stele of Tanus that Royan had picked out and recorded in her notebooks, repeating them until they knew each quotation by heart. While one read aloud, the other concentrated his or her full attention upon the walls, trying to discover some connecting link.

'"My love is a flask of cold water in the desert. My love is a banner unfurling in the breeze. My love is the first shout of the newborn infant,"' Nicholas read.

Royan looked up at him from where she squatted attentively before the shrine, and smiled. 'At times Taita was really rather cute, wasn't he?' she said. 'Such a romantic.'

'Concentrate, for heaven's sake. This isn't a poetry appreciation class. We are doing serious business here.'

'Barbarian!' she muttered under her breath, but turned back to the wall of inscriptions.

'Try this one again,' Nicholas ordered, and read out, '"We lie in the vale of a thousand joinings, of infant to mother, of man to woman, of friend to friend, of teacher to pupil, of sex to sex."'

'That's the third time you have picked out that particular quotation this morning. What is there about it that appeals to you so strongly?' She did not look up at him, but the back of her neck turned a ruddier shade of brown.

'Sorry! Thought you might find that one as romantic as the other,' he mumbled. 'Let's try this one then. "I have suffered and loved. I have withstood the wind and the storm. The arrow pierced my flesh but did not harm me. I have eschewed the false path that lies straight before me. I have taken the hidden stairway to the seat of the gods."'

Royan rocked back on her heels and glanced down the long gallery. 'Something there perhaps. "The false path that lies straight before me. The hidden stairway"?'

'We are straining a bit now. Snapping at gnats like a hungry trout.'

She stood up and pushed the tendrils of sweaty hair off her forehead. 'Oh, Nicky. It's so discouraging. We don't even know where to begin.'

'Courage, lassie.' He feigned the cheerfulness he did not feel. 'We begin at the beginning like your friend Taita said we must. Let me try you with this one again.' He placed his hand over his heart like a Victorian actor and emoted, '"*The vulture rises on mighty pinions to greet the sun*"—'

She laughed softly at his clowning, and then her eyes wandered from his face and passed over his shoulder. Suddenly she started.

'The vulture!' she blurted, and pointed at the wall behind him.

He spun around and stared in the direction she was indicating.

There was the vulture, a magnificent image of the bird, the fierce eyes glaring and the yellow beak hooked and pointed. Its wings were spread wide, with each feather outlined in jewel-like colours. It stood as tall as Nicholas, but its wing-spread covered half the wall. They stared at it together, and then Royan lifted her eyes to the ceiling high above where they stood. She touched his arm and motioned him to do the same.

'The sun!' she whispered. The golden sun disc of Ra was painted in the highest portion of the roof. Its warmth seemed to illuminate the shadows. Its rays spread out in every direction, but one of these beams followed the curve of the wall and descended to envelop the vulture image in its spreading luminosity.

'"*The vulture rises to greet the sun*",' she repeated. 'Does Taita mean it literally?'

He moved closer to the mural and examined it minutely, running his hands over the wings and down its belly to the cruel curved talons. Beneath the paint the plastered wall was smooth. There was no projection or any irregularity.

'The head, Nicky. Look at the head of the bird!' She jumped up and tried to reach it, but her fingers fell short and she turned to him with a desperate edge to her voice. 'You do it – you are much taller than I am.'

Only then did he see the slight shadow down one side of the bird's head where the floodlamp caught it, and as he touched it he realized that the head was in relief, standing slightly above the level of the surrounding wall. He ran his fingers over the raised head and found that the beak was part of the relief.

'Can you feel any joint in the plaster?' Royan demanded.

He shook his head. 'No. It's smooth. It all seems to be part of the main wall.'

'"*The vulture rises to greet the sun*",' she insisted. 'Can't you detect any movement? Try pushing the head upwards towards the sun painting.'

He placed the heel of his hand under the bulge of the head and pushed upwards. 'Nothing!' he grunted.

'It's been there for almost four thousand years.' She was hopping from one foot to the other with frustration. 'Dammit, Nicky, if there is a moving part, it will be stiff. Harder! Push harder!'

He shifted his feet to get well under it and placed both hands under the projection of the head. Slowly he brought all his strength to bear. The cords in his neck stood out and blood flooded his face, turning it a deep, angry red.

'Harder!' she implored him, but at last he dropped his arms to his sides and stood back.

'No.' His voice was hoarse and strained with the effort. 'It's solid. Won't budge.'

'Lift me up. Let me look.'

'With the greatest of pleasure. Any excuse to lay

lascivious hands on you.' He stepped behind her and placed both arms around her waist, then lifted her until she was able to touch the bird's head.

Quickly she explored it with her fingertips, and then she let out a small cry of triumph.

'Nicky! You have started something. The paint is cracked all around the outline of the head. I can feel it. Lift me higher!'

He grunted with the effort but raised her another foot off the floor.

'Yes, definitely!' she exclaimed. 'Something has moved. There is a hairline crack in the wall above the head, as well. You have a look!'

He fetched one of the empty ammunition crates from the landing outside the entrance and placed it below the vulture image. When he stepped up on to it he was on a level with the vulture's eye.

His expression changed. Quickly he groped in his pocket and brought out his clasp knife. He opened the blade and probed carefully around the outline of the head. Tiny specks of dried paint and plaster filtered down as he worked.

'It does look as though the head is a separate detached piece,' he admitted.

'Look on top of it, higher up the wall. There along the edge of the sunbeam. Can't you see a vertical crack in the plaster?'

'You are right, you know,' he admitted. 'But if I try to open that crack I am going to damage the mural. Do you want me to do that?'

She hesitated only a moment. 'This tomb is going to be reflooded when the river rises, so we are going to lose it again anyway. It's worth the risk. Do it, Nicky!'

He pressed the point of the knife-blade into the fine crack and twisted it gently. A slab of painted plaster the size of his spread hand fell out of the wall and splattered into the dust on the agate tiles of the floor.

He peered into the cavity that it had left in the wall.

'It looks like some kind of slot or groove in the wall,' he said. 'I am going to clear its full length.' Carefully he worked at the cavity he had opened, and more loose plaster rained down.

Royan sneezed in the dust, but would not retreat. Particles of debris lodged in her hair like confetti.

'Yes,' he said at last. 'There is a vertical groove running up here.'

'Chip the plaster away from the crack around the vulture's head,' she ordered, and he wiped the blade against his trouser leg and attacked the wall again.

'It's free,' he said at last. 'It looks as though the head will travel up the groove. Anyway, I am going to try it. Stand back and give me room to work.'

He placed the heels of both hands under the head of the vulture, and heaved upwards against it. Royan bunched her hands into fists and screwed up her face in sympathy with his effort.

There was a soft grating sound, and the head began to move jerkily up the exposed groove in the wall. It reached the top of the slot and Nicholas jumped down from the crate. They both stared expectantly at the disembodied head, now disfigured by the chipped and damaged plaster.

After a long, breathless wait, Royan whispered dejectedly, 'Nothing! It hasn't changed anything.'

'The rest of the quotation from the stele,' he reminded her. 'There was more to it than just the vulture and the sun.'

'You are right.' She looked around the rest of the wall eagerly. '"*The jackal howls and turns upon his tail.*"'

She pointed with a trembling finger at the small, almost insignificant figure of Anubis, the jackal-headed god of the graveyards, on the wall opposite the vulture that they had mutilated. Standing at the foot of the huge, towering painting of Osiris, he was only a little larger in size than the ringed and bejewelled big toe of the husband of Isis and father of Horus.

Royan ran to the wall, and the moment she touched Anubis she felt that his image too was raised. She flung all her strength against the tiny figure, trying to twist it first one way and then the other.

'"*The jackal turns upon his tail*",' she panted as she wrestled with him. 'He must turn!'

'Here, let me do that.' Gently Nicholas pulled her away, and knelt before the black-headed god image. Once again he used the blade of his clasp knife to chip away the plaster and the thick layer of paint from around the outline.

'It seems to be carved in some sort of hard wood and then it's been plastered over,' he told her, as he tested the construction of the figure with the point of the blade.

When at last he had chipped it clear he tried to twist it in a clockwise direction, and grunted with the effort.

'No!' He gave up at last.

'They had no clock dials in ancient Egypt,' she reminded him agitatedly. 'The other way. Turn it the other way.'

When he tried to turn it counter-clockwise, there was another rasping, gritty sound from behind the wall panel. The tiny figure revolved slowly in his hands, until the black head pointed down towards the yellow tiles.

They both stood well back from the wall, looking expectantly at it, but after another long wait even Nicholas was disheartened.

'I don't know what to expect, but whatever it is, it isn't happening,' he grunted with disgust.

'There is still the last part of the quotation,' Royan whispered. '"*The river flows towards the earth. Beware, you violators of the sacred places, lest the wrath of all the gods descend upon you!'"*

'The river?' Nicholas asked. 'As Sapper might say, I don't see no perishing river.'

Royan did not even smile at the cockney accent. Instead she searched the profusion of writing and images that covered all the walls around them. Then she saw it.

'Hapi!' Her voice was shrill with excitement. 'The god of the Nile! The river!'

High up the wall, on a level with the head of the great god Osiris, the god of the river looked down upon them. Hapi was a hermaphrodite, with the breasts of a woman and the genitals of a man protruding from under the pendulous belly. The mouth in his hippopotamus head gaped wide to display the great curved tusks that lined his cavernous jaws.

Standing on a pile of ammunition boxes, Nicholas was able to reach the Hapi image at the full stretch of his arms. As he touched it he exulted, 'This one is raised also.'

'"*The river flows towards the earth*,"' she called up to him. 'It must move downwards. Try it, Nicky.'

'Give me a chance to clear the edges.' He used the point of the blade to chip the outline of the god free, and then he probed the plaster beneath it and found another vertical slot running towards the floor.

'Ready to give it a go now.' He folded the knife and tucked it back into his pocket. 'Hold your breath and say a little prayer for me,' he instructed.

He settled both hands on the image of the god and began to pull steadily downwards. Gradually he brought more pressure to bear upon it, until he was hanging all his weight on it. Nothing moved.

'It's not working,' he grunted.

'Wait!' she ordered. 'I am coming up.'

She scrambled up on to the boxes behind him and

placed both arms around his neck. 'Hang on tight,' she ordered.

'Every little bit helps, I suppose,' he agreed, as she lifted her feet and hung her full weight on his shoulders.

'It's moving!' he shouted. Suddenly the image of Hapi gave way under his hands, and with a sharp grating sound travelled down to the bottom end of the groove in the wall.

Nicholas lost his grip on the smoothly rounded shape as it came up hard against the end of its slot. The stack of boxes under them toppled, and both he and Royan dropped back to the floor of the gallery. She was still hanging around his neck, and he lost his balance as she pulled him over backwards. The two of them sprawled on the agate floor in an untidy tangle of arms and legs. Nicholas scrambled to his feet and pulled her up beside him.

'What has happened?' she gasped, looking up wildly at the damaged Hapi figure and then around the walls of the gallery.

'Nothing,' he said. 'Nothing has moved.'

'Perhaps there is another—' she began, but broke off at a sound from the roof above them. They both stared upwards, startled and filled with sudden trepidation. There was a ponderous movement from above the high plastered ceiling.

'What is that?' Royan whispered. 'There is something up there. It sounds like a living thing.'

A giant was moving, coming awake after slumbering for thousands of years, stretching and turning as he awoke.

'Is it—?' She could not finish the question. She had an image in her mind of the great god himself stirring in a hidden chamber in the rock, opening those baleful, slanted eyes, rising on one elbow to discover who had disturbed him from his eternal sleep.

Then there was another sound, a creaking and rumbling as though the arm of a mighty balance was swinging slowly across, as its equilibrium altered. Softly at first, then louder, the movement gathered momentum, like the beginning of a mountain avalanche. Then there was a report like the shot of a cannon.

A crack appeared in the high ceiling, running the length of the gallery. Dust smoked from the jagged opening, and then, slowly as a nightmare, the roof began to sag down over where they stood. Both of them were paralysed with superstitious horror, unable to tear their gaze from the slow, inexorable collapse of the ceiling upon them. Then a chunk of plaster struck Nicholas's upturned face, slamming into his cheek, tearing the skin and sending him staggering backwards against the wall. The shock and pain aroused him at last.

'The warning!' he blurted. 'Taita's warning. The wrath of the gods.' He sprang to her side and grabbed her hand, 'Run!' He pulled her after him. 'Taita has booby-trapped the roof!'

They raced back along the gallery towards the opening in the sealed entrance. Lumps of stone and plaster began to rain down and dust filled the passageway, half-blinding them. The dull rumble overhead became a rising roar as progressively the roof collapsed. They did not dare to look back as the thunder of falling masonry swept towards them, threatening to overtake and overwhelm them before they were able to reach the entrance.

A jagged piece of rock as large as her head struck Royan a glancing blow on her shoulder, and her legs sagged under her. She would have gone down if he had not flung one arm around her and held her upright, dragging her along the gallery. The dust obscured the passage ahead of them, so that the square opening that offered their only chance of escape receded in the choking fog.

'Keep going!' he yelled at her. 'Almost there.' As he

spoke, a thick sheet of plaster came crashing down and smashed into the tripod stand of the floodlamp. Instantly the gallery was plunged into utter darkness.

Completely unsighted, Nicholas's first instinct was to come up short and try to orientate himself. But all around him the rubble of the roof was falling heavier and faster. He knew that at any second the entire roof would come down on top of them, burying and crushing them. Running on without a check, he dragged Royan along behind him in the darkness. He reached the end wall at full tilt, and the impact knocked the breath out of him. Now, through the swirling dust cloud, he was just able to make out the rectangular opening in the plaster wall in front of him, back-lit by the lamps on the landing at the head of the staircase outside.

As he reeled backwards he seized Royan around the waist and lifted her bodily off her feet. He hurled her through the opening and heard her cry out as she fell heavily on the far side. Another piece of rubble struck him on the back of his head and knocked him to his knees. He felt himself teetering on the very brink of consciousness, but crawled forward, groping frantically until he touched the jagged edge of the opening. With this handhold he was able to drag himself over the sill, just as the full weight of the roof came thundering down along the entire gallery.

Here on the upper landing of the staircase Royan was crouching on her knees. She crawled towards him, guided once more by the lamplight.

'Are you all right?' she panted. A trickle of blood snaked down her cheek from a wound in her scalp line. It cut a dark glistening runnel through the caked white dust that powdered her face.

He did not answer, but dragged himself to his feet and pulled Royan up beside him. 'Can't stay here,' he croaked, just as a thick white breath of dust blew through the mouth of the opening and swept over them, choking them and dimming the floodlamps to a faint glimmer.

'Not safe.' He pulled her away from the opening. 'The whole thing might cave in.' His voice was rough, his throat closing with the dust.

He dragged her to the head of the steps and they staggered down together, stumbling against each other, their feet sliding under them as they came on to the algae-slippery footing. Through the dust mist ahead of them loomed the broad square figure of Sapper.

'What the ruddy hell is going on?' he bellowed with relief as he saw them.

'Give me a hand here,' Nicholas yelled back at him. Sapper lifted Royan in his arms and together they ran back down the tunnel, only stopping to draw breath when they reached the causeway over the sink-hole.

The post office in the village of Debra Maryam was a small building in the dusty street behind the church. Its walls were of unplastered unburnt and unpainted brick, and its galvanized iron roof glared like a mirror in the high mountain sunlight. The public telephone should have been in its booth outside the front door. However, the instrument had long since vanished – stolen, vandalized or, more likely, removed by the military to prevent it being used by political dissidents and rebels.

Tessay had expected this, and hardly glanced into the booth before she strode into the small room which was the main post office. It was filled with a motley crowd of peasants and villagers, queuing to conduct their leisurely business with the elderly postmaster, the only person behind the barred counter. Some of the customers had spread their cloaks on the floor and settled in for a long wait, chatting and smoking while their children romped and crawled around them.

Most of the patient crowd recognized Tessay as soon as she entered the room. Even those who had waited most of the morning in the lines at the counter greeted her respectfully and stood aside to allow her to go to the head of the queue. Despite two decades of African socialism, the feudal instincts of the rural population were still strong. Tessay was a noblewoman and she was entitled to this preference.

'Thank you, my friends.' She smiled at them and shook her head. 'You are kind, but I will wait my turn.'

They were embarrassed by her refusal, and when the old postmaster leaned over his counter top and added his insistence to the others, one of the older women seized Tessay's arm and forcefully propelled her forward.

'Jesus and all the saints bless you, Woizero Tessay.' The postmaster clapped his hands in respectful greeting. 'Welcome back to Debra Maryam. What is it that your ladyship desires?'

The entire clientele of the post office crowded around Tessay so as not to miss a detail of her transaction.

'I want to make a telephone call to Addis,' she told the postmaster and there was a hum of comment and discussion. This was unusual and important business indeed.

'I will take you to the telephone exchange,' the postmaster told her importantly, and donned his official blue cap for the occasion. He came around the counter shouting and hectoring the other customers, pushing them aside to make way for Lady Sun. Then he ushered her through to the back room of the building, where the telephone exchange occupied a cubicle the size of a small lavatory.

Tessay, the postmaster and as many of the other customers who could find standing room pushed their way into the tiny room. The exchange operator was almost overcome by the honour being accorded him by the beautiful Tessay, and he shouted into his headset like a sergeant major commanding a flag party.

'Soon now!' he beamed at Tessay. 'Only small delay. Then you speak to British Embassy in Addis.'

Tessay, who knew well what a small delay constituted, retired to the front veranda of the post office and sent for food and flasks to be brought from the village *tej* shop. She treated her escort of monks, together with half the population of Debra Maryam, to a happy picnic while she waited for her call to be patched through half a dozen antiquated village exchanges to the capital. Thanks to the *tej*, spirits were high amongst her entourage when finally, an hour later, the postmaster rushed out to tell her proudly that they had succeeded and that her party was awaiting her on the line in the back room.

Tessay, the monks and fifty villagers followed the postmaster back into the exchange and crowded, jabbering, into the cubicle. The overflow backed up into the main post hall.

'Geoffrey Tennant speaking.' The upper-class English accent was tinny with distance and static.

'Mr Tennant, this is Woizero Tessay.'

'I was expecting your call.' Geoffrey's voice lightened as he realized that he was talking to a pretty girl. 'How are you, my dear?'

Tessay passed Nicholas's message to him.

'Tell Nicky it's as good as done,' Geoffrey acknowledged, and hung up.

'Now,' Tessay addressed the postmaster, 'I want to place another call to Addis – to the Egyptian Embassy.'

There was a buzz of delight from her audience when they realized that the entertainment was not yet over for the day. Everybody repaired to the veranda for more *tej* and conversation.

The second call took even longer to connect, and it was after five o'clock when Tessay was at last put in contact with the Egyptian cultural attaché. Had she not once met him at one of those ubiquitous cocktail parties on the diplomatic circuit in Addis, and made a profound impression on him then, he would probably not have accepted her call now.

'You are very lucky to have reached me so late,' he told her. 'We usually close at four-thirty, but there is a meeting of the Organization of African Unity on at the moment and I am working late. Anyway, how may I help you, Woizero Tessay?'

As soon as she told him the name and rank of the person in Cairo to whom Royan's message was addressed, his superior and condescending attitude altered dramatically and he became effusive and eager to please. He wrote down everything she said in detail, asking her to repeat and spell the names of people and places. Finally he read his notes back to her for confirmation.

At the end of the long conversation, he dropped his voice to an intimate level and told her. 'I was greatly saddened to hear of your recent bereavement, Lady Sun. Colonel Brusilov was a man I held in high regard. Perhaps when you return to Addis you would do me the honour of dining with me one evening.'

'How kind and thoughtful of you.' Tessay's tones were honeyed. 'I would so much enjoy meeting your charming wife again.' She hung up while he was still making confused noises of assent and denial.

By this time the sun was already setting behind the sky castles of cumulo-nimbus, and there was the smell of rain in the air. It was too late to start the journey back down the escarpment that evening, so Tessay was relieved when the headman of Debra Maryam village sent one of his teenage daughters to invite her to spend the night as a guest in his home.

The headman's house was the finest in the village, not one of the circular *tukuls*, but a square brick building with an iron roof. His wife and daughters had prepared a banquet in Tessay's honour, and all the village notables, including the priests from the church, had been invited. It was therefore after midnight before Tessay was able to escape to the principal bedroom, which the headman and his wife had vacated for her.

Just before Tessay fell asleep she heard the heavy raindrops rattling on the corrugated iron roof over her head. It was a comforting sound, but she thought briefly of the dam further downstream in the gorge, and hoped that this shower was merely the harbinger and not the true onset of the big rains.

When she started awake much later the rain had passed. Beyond her uncurtained window the night was moonless and silent, except for the howling of a pariah-dog down in the village. She wondered what had woken her, and was filled suddenly with a premonition of impending disaster, a legacy from the Mengistu days, when any sound in the night might warn of the arrival of the security police. So strong was this feeling that she could not get to sleep again. Creeping quietly out of her bed, she began dressing in the dark. She had decided to call her monks and start back along the trail in the darkness. Only when she was at Mek Nimmur's side once again would she feel secure.

She had just pulled on her jodhpurs and was searching beneath the bed for her sandals when she heard the sound of a truck engine in the distance. She went to the window and listened. The air had been cooled by the rain and she felt the chill on her naked arms and chest.

The truck sounded as though it was approaching the village from the south, up the track that followed the river bank. It was coming fast, and her sense of unease sharpened. The villagers had spoken to the monks, and it was now common knowledge that she was Mek Nimmur's woman. Mek was a wanted man. Suddenly she felt very vulnerable and alone.

Quickly she pulled the woollen *shamma* over her head and thrust her feet into her sandals. As she crept from the room she heard the headman snoring in the front room where he and his wife had moved to make room for her. She turned down the short passage to the kitchen. The fire in the hearth had burned down, but she could make out the shapes of the sleeping monks on the mud floor. They lay with their *shamma*s pulled over their heads, completely covered, like a row of bodies on mortuary tables. She knelt beside the nearest of them and shook him, but obviously he had enjoyed the *tej* at dinner because he was difficult to rouse.

The sound of the approaching truck was much louder and closer by now, and she felt her uneasiness take on a tinge of panic. Realizing that in an emergency the monks would probably be of little real help to her, she stood up and groped her way quickly towards the back door.

The truck was right outside the front of the house now. The headlights flashed across the front windows and were briefly reflected down the passageway. Abruptly the engine roar sank to a burble as the driver decelerated, and she heard the squeal of brakes and the crunch of tyres in the gravel outside. Then there was shouting and the trampling of many feet as men jumped down from the back of the stationary truck.

Tessay froze halfway across the small kitchen, her head cocked to listen. Suddenly there was a loud banging on the flimsy front door, and chillingly familiar shouts of, 'Open up here! Central Intelligence! Open the door! Nobody leave the house!'

Tessay ran for the back door, but in the darkness she tripped over a low table covered with dirty dishes from the previous evening's meal. She fell heavily and the bowls and *tej* flasks crashed to the floor and shattered. Instantly the men at the front door put their shoulders to it, tearing it off its hinges. They burst into the house, shouting and breaking furniture, torches flashing as they searched the front rooms. There was a confused babble of alarm as the headman and his family struggled awake, and then the sound of heavy blows with club and rifle butt, followed by shrieks of pain and terror.

Tessay reached the back door and struggled to open it. The sound of strange men rampaging through the house made her fingers clumsy. She struggled with the lock. All the while she could hear other men outside running through the yard to surround the house completely. At last she got the door open. It was dark and the area was unfamiliar so she did not know in which direction to run, but she heard the river close by in the night.

'If I can only reach the bank,' she thought, and started across the yard.

As she did so the beam of an electric torch blinded her, and a coarse voice bellowed, 'There she is!'

Any doubt that she was the prey was instantly dispelled, and she fled like a startled hare in the beam of the light. They bayed behind her like a pack of hounds. She reached the bank of the river and spun off to the right, downstream. A pistol cracked out behind her and she ducked as a shot fluted past her head.

'Don't shoot, you baboons!' a voice roared in commanding tones. 'We want her for questioning.'

In the torchbeam her white *shamma* flashed like the wings of a moth flitting around the candle flame.

'Stop her!' shouted the officer behind her. 'Don't let her get away.'

But she was fleet as a gazelle, and her lightly sandalled feet flew across the rough terrain while the heavily equipped soldiers blundered along behind her. Her spirits soared as she realized that she was pulling away from them.

The sound of the pursuit dwindled behind her and she had reached the limit of the effective range of the torch-beam when she ran into a fence of rusty barbed wire. Three wire strands whipped across her lower body, at the level of her knees, her hips and her diaphragm. The top strand drove the breath from her lungs, and the barbs tore through the wool of her clothing and into her flesh. They snagged her like a fish in the mesh of a net, and she hung there struggling helplessly. Rough hands seized her and dragged her off the wire, and she sobbed with despair and with the pain of the sharp wire spurs tearing her skin. One of the soldiers grabbed her wrist and twisted it up between her shoulder-blades, laughing with sadistic relish when she cried out at the pain.

The officer came up panting over the rough ground. He was overweight, and even in the cold night air he was sweating heavily. It greased his fat cheeks and glistened in the light of the torch.

'Do not hurt her, you oaf,' he gasped. 'She is not a criminal. She is a high-bred lady. Bring her to the truck, but treat her with respect.'

With a man on each arm they marched her to the truck, holding her so that her feet barely touched the rough ground, and then shoved her up into the cab on to the seat beside the uniformed driver. The plump officer climbed in heavily after her, and she found herself wedged in firmly between the two men. The soldiers scrambled up into the rear of the truck, and the driver revved the engine and let out the clutch.

Tessay was sobbing softly, and the officer glanced sideways at her. She saw in the reflection of the headlights that his expression was gentle and sympathetic, completely at odds with his actions.

'Where are you taking me?' she asked softly, stifling her sobs. 'What have I done wrong?'

'I have been ordered to take you to Colonel Nogo, the

district commander, for questioning in connection with *shufta* activities in the Gojam,' he told her, as they jolted and bounced down the rough track.

They were both silent for a while, and then the officer said quietly in English, 'The driver speaks only Amharic. I wanted to tell you that I knew your father, Alto Zemen. He was a good man. I am sorry for what is happening here tonight, but I am only a lieutenant. I have to follow my orders.'

'I understand that it is not your choice, or your blame.'

'My name is Hammed. If I can, I will help you. For Alto Zemen's sake.'

'Thank you, Lieutenant Hammed. I need friends now.'

While they waited for the dust of the cave-in to settle, and for any loose hanging rock to fall or stabilize, Nicholas dressed the minor injuries that Royan had sustained. The cut over her temple was not deep, barely more than a scratch. Nicholas saw that it did not require a stitch. He disinfected it and covered it with a Band Aid. However, her shoulder, which the falling rock had struck, was badly bruised. He massaged it with arnica cream.

His own bruises he treated less ceremoniously. Within an hour of the cave-in he was ready to go back up the tunnel. He ordered Royan and Sapper to remain on the causeway over the sink-hole while he returned to the landing at the top of the stairs alone. He carried a bamboo pole and a hand lamp connected to the Honda generator.

Nicholas proceeded with the utmost caution, probing the roof of the tunnel for weakness as he went. When he reached the landing he saw at once that the rock fall had smashed down what remained of the white plaster door that had originally sealed the entrance to the tomb. The ammunition crates, eight of which contained the statues from the shrines, had been knocked about and scattered, and some of them were partially buried under the fallen rubble. He retrieved them and opened each of the packed crates in turn to check the contents. With immense relief he discovered that the stout metal containers had withstood the rough treatment and there was no damage to the precious statues they held. One at a time he carried them back down the tunnel as far as the causeway and handed them into Sapper's care.

When he returned to the landing outside the tomb, Royan insisted on accompanying him. Even his lurid descriptions of the danger of a further rock-fall could not dissuade her. Her dismay when she stood outside the shattered gallery was overwhelming.

'It's totally destroyed,' she whispered. 'All those marvellous works of art. I cannot believe that Taita wanted this to happen.'

'No,' Nicholas agreed ruefully. 'His plan was to give us a big send-off along the road past the seven pylons to the happy hunting grounds. And he damned nigh succeeded.'

'It's going to take a lot of hard work to clear up this mess,' she said.

'What on earth are you talking about?' He turned on her in genuine alarm. 'We have saved the statues, and that's all we can hope for. Now I think it's time to cut our losses and get out of here.'

'Get out of here? Are you crazy?' She rounded on him furiously. 'Are you out of your mind?'

'At least the statues will pay our costs,' he explained, 'and there might even be something left over to divvy up between us, in accordance with our agreement.'

'You aren't dreaming of giving up now, when we are so close?' Her voice rose sharply with agitation.

'The gallery is destroyed—' he began in more reasonable tones, but she stamped her foot with agitation and shouted him down.

'The tomb is still there. Dammit, Nicky, Taita would not have gone to those lengths if it were not. We are getting too close now – that is why he fired that warning shot across our bows. Don't you see? We have him really worried now. We can't give up with the prize almost in sight.'

'Royan, be reasonable.'

'No! No! You be reasonable.' She refused to listen. 'You have to start clearing the gallery right away. I know the entrance is open now. All we have to do is clear this mess, and I am certain that we will find the true entrance to the tomb behind the rubble that Taita deliberately dropped on us.'

'I think that bang on your head has loosened a couple of nuts and bolts.' He threw up his hands in resignation. 'But what's the use arguing with a crazy woman? We will clear just enough of the scree to prove to you that there is nothing more to discover in there.'

'The dust is going to be our big problem.' Sapper eyed the blocked gallery entrance when they told him what they intended. 'As soon as we touch that rubble there is going to be clouds of it – more than our little blower fan can handle.'

'Right,' Nicholas agreed briskly. 'We will have to wet it all down. Two lines of men back down the tunnel to the sink-hole. One chain passing up water buckets, and the other chain passing back the rubble from the cave-in.'

'It's going to take a lot of work.' Sapper sucked his bottom lip lugubriously.

'You signed on to be tough,' Nicholas reminded him. 'No time to start whinging now.'

The monks, still convinced that they were engaged on the Lord's work, accepted this new task cheerfully. They sang as they passed the chunks of broken plaster and rock in one direction and the clay pots of water from the sink-hole in the other. Nicholas worked at the rock-fall with the gang of Buffaloes, led by Hansith. It was hard, messy and dangerous work, for each piece of rubble had to be doused with water before it could be levered out of the pack and passed down the chain. The staircase was soon running with muddy water and the steps were treacherous underfoot. The fallen rock was loose and unstable, and there was always the danger of a secondary collapse.

So many men working in the confined spaces of the gallery and tunnel taxed the ability of the little blower fan to recirculate the air, and it was hot and oppressive. The men stripped to loincloths and their bodies glistened with sweat. The rubble passed back down the tunnel was dumped into the sink-hole. Even that large volume of material made no difference to the level of the black waters. It was simply swallowed up into the depths without trace.

Nicholas found the crowded workings so humid and claustrophobic that at the change of the first shift he had to escape into the open air, if only for a few minutes. Even the dark and forbidding chasm of Taita's pool was a relief after the close confines of the underground workings. Mek Nimmur was waiting for him when he climbed out over the wall of the coffer dam on to the ledge beside the pool.

'Nicholas!' Mek's handsome dark face was grave. 'Has Tessay returned from Debra Maryam yet? She should have been back yesterday.'

'I have not seen her, Mek. I thought she was with you.'

Mek shook his head. 'I wanted to make certain that she had not returned without my men seeing her, before I send a patrol up the trail to search for her.'

'I am sorry, Mek. I did not anticipate any danger in sending her up the escarpment.' Nicholas felt a stab of guilt.

'If I had thought there was any danger, I would not have allowed her to go,' Mek agreed. 'I have sent men to search for her.'

But Tessay's absence was another worry for Nicholas. It lurked at the edge of his mind during the days that followed, as the clearing of the long funeral gallery proceeded too slowly for his satisfaction.

Royan spent as much time at the face as Nicholas did, and both of them were as filthy with mud and dirt as the Buffaloes who were labouring there beside them. She mourned over each fragment of the shattered murals. Before they were carried away to be thrown into the sink-hole, she tried to retrieve those on which significant portions of the paintings were still intact. There was one jagged piece of plaster on which the lovely head of Isis was still in one piece, and another on which the entire figure of Thoth, the god of writing, was preserved. However, most of the paintings were destroyed beyond any hope of ever restoring them, and sadly they were consigned to the pit.

There was no sense of time in the long gallery, and they could not tell night from day. It was always a surprise to leave the precincts of the tomb and find that the stars were shining in the narrow strip of sky that showed above Taita's pool, or to find the bright African sun burning hotly down out of the cloudless blue. They ate and slept only when their bodies demanded it, not according to the passage of the hours.

Re-entering the tomb after a few hours' sleep in their shelters beside the pool, they were crossing the causeway over the sink-hole when a wild cry reverberated down the shaft ahead of them. Immediately there was a hullabaloo of query and answer, and excited shouts from the men working in the upper levels of the tunnel.

'Hansith has found something,' Royan cried. 'Dammit, Nicky, I knew we should have stayed—' She began to run, and he hurried after her.

They came out on the landing in front of the gallery to find it crowded with chattering, gesticulating, half-naked workmen. Nicholas forced his way through them with

Royan on his heels. They realized that Hansith had cleared the gallery as far as where the shrine of Osiris had once stood. The roof above them was jagged and broken, and lying amongst the rubbish on the ruined agate tiles of the floor Nicholas made out the remains of the mechanism which Taita had placed in the roof, and which they had brought crashing down when they had activated the device. The main part of this was an enormous stone wheel, resembling a mill wheel and weighing many tons. Nicholas stopped to give it a cursory examination.

'When you read *River God*, you realize that Taita had an obsession with the wheel,' he told Royan. 'Chariot wheels, water wheels, and now this must have been the balance wheel of his booby-trap. When we moved the levers, we toppled the wedges that held this monstrosity in place. Once it started rolling, it tumbled all the drop-stones that he had stacked above the ceiling of the gallery.' He glanced up at the shattered roof.

'Not now, Nicky!' Royan was hopping with impatience. 'Time for your lectures later. Taita's death-trap is not what has excited Hansith. He has found something else. Come on!'

They pushed their way through the pack of workmen until they reached Hansith's tall figure.

'What is it?' Nicholas shouted over the heads of the others. 'What have you found, Hansith?'

'Here, *effendi*,' Hansith shouted back. 'Come quickly.'

They pushed their way to the face, and stopped beside the monk at the end of the blocked gallery.

'There!' Hansith pointed proudly.

Nicholas went down on one knee in the shattered remains of the shrine. Small pieces of the painted plaster still adhered to the fractured rock wall. Hansith pulled a slab out of the collapsed face, and pointed into the space it had left. Nicholas peered into it and felt his pulse begin to race. There was an opening in the side of the gallery. Even at first glance he realized that it was the mouth of another tunnel leading off at right-angles from the long gallery. It had been concealed behind the plaster-covered image of the great god.

As he stared into it with awe, he felt Royan's hand on his arm and her warm breath on his cheek. 'This is it, Nicky. The entrance to the true tomb of Mamose. This gallery was a bluff. Taita's red herring. This is the veritable tomb.'

'Hansith!' Nicholas called to him in a voice that was hoarse with emotion. 'Get your men to clear this doorway.'

As the workmen moved the rocks Nicholas and Royan hovered close behind them, so that they were able to watch the shape of the doorway as it was fully revealed. It proved to be a dark rectangle, of the same dimensions as the tunnel leading up from the sink-hole, three metres wide by two high. The lintel and the door jambs were of beautifully cut and dressed stone, and when Nicholas shone his lamp into the opening he saw a flight of stone steps rising before him.

They moved the cables and the lights into the gallery and arranged them at the entrance to this new doorway, but when Nicholas set foot on the first step he found Royan at his side.

'I am coming with you,' she told him firmly.

'It's probably booby-trapped,' he warned her. 'Taita is lying in wait for you around the first bend.'

'Don't try that. It just won't work, mister! I am coming.'

They went slowly up the steep steps, pausing on each one to survey the walls and the way ahead. Twenty steps from the bottom they reached another landing. A pair of doorways led off it, one on either side. However, the staircase continued climbing directly ahead of them.

'Which way?' Nicholas asked.

'Keep going up,' Royan urged him. 'We can explore these side passages later.'

Cautiously, they continued climbing. After twenty more steps they came out on an identical landing, with a doorway on each side and the stairway in front of them.

'Keep going up,' Royan ordered, without waiting for him to ask.

Twenty more steps and there was another landing, with the familiar openings on either side and the stairway straight ahead.

'This isn't making sense,' Nicholas protested, but she prodded him in the back.

'We should keep going on upwards,' she told him, and he did not protest further. They passed another landing and then yet another, each of them the exact image of those that they had passed lower down.

'At last!' Nicholas exclaimed when they came out at the top of the staircase, with the expected doorway on each side but now a blank wall in front of them. 'This is as far as it goes.'

'How many landings are there?' she asked. 'How many altogether?'

'Eight,' he answered.

'Eight,' she agreed. 'Isn't that a familiar number by now?'

He turned to stare down at her in the lamplight. 'You mean—'

'I mean the eight shrines in the long gallery, these eight landings, and the eight cups of the bao board.'

They stood silent and undecided on the top landing and looked about them.

'Okay,' he said at last, 'if you are so damned clever, tell me which way to go now.'

'Eeny-meeny-miny-moe,' she recited. 'Let's try the right-hand doorway.'

They followed the right-hand passage only a short distance before they were confronted by a T-junction – a blank wall with identical twin passageways on each side.

'Take the right one again,' she counselled, and they followed it. But when they came to the next T-junction Nicholas stopped and faced her.

'You know what is happening here, don't you?' he demanded. 'This is another one of Taita's tricks. He has led us into a maze. If it were not for the cable, we would be lost already.'

With a bemused expression she looked back the way they had come, and then down the unexplored passages to their right and left.

'When he built this, Taita could not have anticipated the age of electricity. He expected any grave robber to be equipped the same way he was. Imagine being caught in here without the electric cable to follow back the way we have come,' Nicholas said softly. 'Imagine having only an oil lamp for light. Imagine what would happen to you when the oil burnt out and you were lost in here in the utter darkness.'

Royan shivered and gripped his arm. 'It's scaring!' she whispered.

'Taita is beginning to play rough,' Nicholas said softly. 'I was developing rather a soft spot for the old boy. But now I am beginning to change my mind.'

She shuddered again. 'Let's go back,' she whispered, 'We should never have rushed in here like this. We must go back and work it out carefully. We are unprepared. I have the feeling that we are in danger – I mean real danger, the same as we were in the long gallery.'

As they started back through the twists and turns, picking up the electric cable as they retreated down the stone passageways, the temptation to break into a run became stronger with each step. Royan hung tightly to Nicholas's arm. It seemed to both of them that some intelligent and malignant presence lurked behind them in the darkness, following them, watching them and biding its time.

T he army truck carrying Tessay drove back through the village of Debra Maryam, and then turned off on to the track that followed the Dandera river downstream towards the escarpment of the Abbay gorge.

'This is not the way to army headquarters,' Tessay told Lieutenant Hammed, and he shifted awkwardly on the seat beside her.

'Colonel Nogo is not at his headquarters. I have orders to take you to another location.'

'There is only one other place in this direction,' she said. 'The base camp of the foreign prospecting company, Pegasus.'

'Colonel Nogo is using that as a forward base in his campaign against the *shufta* in the valley,' he explained. 'I have orders to take you to him there.'

Neither of them spoke again during the long, bumpy ride over the rough track. It was almost noon when at last they reached the edge of the escarpment and turned off on to the fork that brought them at last to the Pegasus camp. The camouflage-clad guards at the gate saluted when they recognized Hammed. The truck drove through the gates, and parked in front of one of the long Quonset huts within the compound.

'Please wait here.' Hammed got down and went into the hut, but was gone for only a few minutes.

'Please come with me, Lady Sun.' He looked awkward and embarrassed, and could not meet her eyes as he helped her down from the cab. He led her to the door of the hut, and stood aside to let her enter first.

She looked around the sparsely furnished room, and

realized that it must be the company's administration centre. A conference table ran almost the full length of the room, and there were filing cabinets and two desks set against the side walls. A map of the area and a few technical charts were the only decorations on the bare walls. Two men sat at the table, and she recognized both of them immediately.

Colonel Nogo looked up at her, and his eyes were cold behind his metal-framed spectacles. As always, his long, thin body was immaculately uniformed; but his head was bare. His maroon beret lay on the table in front of him. Jake Helm leaned back in his chair with his arms folded. At first glance, his short-cropped hair made him look like a boy. Only when she looked closer did she see how his skin was weathered, and notice the crows' feet at the corners of his eyes. He wore an open-necked shirt and blue jeans that were bleached almost white. His belt buckle was of ornate Indian silver, the shape of a wild mustang's head. The sleeves of his cotton shirt were rolled high around his lumpy biceps. He chewed upon the dead butt of a cheap Dutch cheroot, and the smell of the strong tobacco was rank and offensive.

'Very well, lieutenant,' Nogo dismissed Hammed in Amharic. 'Wait outside. I will call you when I need you.'

Once Hammed had left the room, Tessay demanded, 'Why have I been arrested, Colonel Nogo?'

Neither man acknowledged the question. They both regarded her expressionlessly.

'I demand to know the reason for this high-handed treatment,' she persisted.

'You have been consorting with a band of notorious terrorists,' said Nogo softly. 'Your actions have made you one of them, a *shufta*.'

'That is not true.'

'You have trespassed in a mineral concession in the Abbay valley,' said Helm. 'And you and your accomplices have begun mining operations in the area which belongs to this company.'

'There are no mining operations,' she protested.

'We have other information. We have evidence that you have built a dam across the Dandera river—'

'That is nothing to do with me.'

'So you do not deny that there is a dam?'

'It is nothing to do with me,' she repeated. 'I am not a member of any terrorist group, and I have not taken part in any mining operations.'

They were both silent again. Nogo made an entry in the notebook in front of him. Helm stood up and sauntered across to the window behind her right shoulder. The silence drew out until she could bear it no longer. Even though she knew it was part of the campaign of nerves they were waging against her, she had to break it.

'I have travelled most of the night in an army truck,' she said. 'I am tired, and I need to go to a lavatory.'

'If what you need to do is urgent you can do it where you are standing. Neither Mr Helm nor I will be offended.' Nogo tittered in a surprisingly girlish manner, but did not look up from his book.

She looked over her shoulder at the door, but Helm crossed to it and turned the key in the lock, slipping the key into his pocket. She knew she must show no weakness in front of these two, and, though she was tired and afraid and her bladder ached, she feigned an air of confidence and assurance and crossed to the nearest chair. She pulled it from the table and sat down in it easily.

Nogo looked up at her and frowned. He had not expected her to react this way.

'You know the *shufta* bandit Mek Nimmur,' he accused abruptly.

'No,' she said coldly. 'I know the patriot and democratic leader Mek Nimmur. He is no *shufta*.'

'You are his concubine, his whore. Of course, you will say this.'

She looked away from him with disdain, and his voice rose shrilly. 'Where is Mek Nimmur? How many men does he have with him?' Her composure was beginning to rattle him.

She ignored the question, and Nogo scowled at her furiously. 'If you do not cooperate with us, I will have to use stronger methods to make you answer my questions,' he warned.

She turned in her chair and stared out of the window. In the long silence that followed, Jake Helm crossed the room and went to the door behind Nogo that led through to the rooms at the rear of the hut. He disappeared through it, and closed it behind him. The walls of the hut were thin, and Tessay made out the murmur of voices from the room beyond. The cadence and inflection were neither English nor Amharic. They were using a foreign language in there. She guessed that Helm was receiving instructions from a superior, who did not want her to be able to recognize him at some later date.

After a few minutes Helm re-emerged and closed the door behind him without locking it. He nodded to Nogo, who at once stood up. They both came across to stand in front of Tessay.

'I think that it will be better for all of us if we finish this business as quickly as possible,' said Helm softly. 'Then you can go to the bathroom, and I can go to my breakfast.'

She raised her chin and stared at him defiantly, but did not answer him.

'Colonel Nogo has tried to be reasonable. He is bound by certain niceties of his official position. Fortunately I do not have the same restraints. I am going to ask you the same questions that he did, but this time you will answer them.'

He took the dead cheroot from his mouth and examined the tip. Then he threw the butt into a corner of the room and took a flat tin from his hip pocket. From it he selected a fresh cheroot, long and black, and lit it carefully, holding the match to it until it was drawing evenly. Then, amid a cloud of pungent tobacco smoke, he waved the match to extinction and asked,

'Where is Mek Nimmur?'

She shrugged and looked away, out of the side window of the hut.

Abruptly, without signalling the blow in any way, he hit her open-handed across her face. It was a savage blow, delivered with a force that snapped her head around. Then, before she could recover, he swung back again and slammed his knuckles across her jawline. Her head was thrown back violently in the opposite direction and she was knocked flying from her chair.

Nogo stooped over her and seized her arms, twisting them up behind her back. He lifted her back into the seat and stood behind her. He held her in such a surprisingly powerful grip that she could feel the skin of her upper arms bruising beneath his fingers.

'I have no more time to waste,' Helm said quietly, taking the burning cheroot from his lips to inspect the glowing tip. 'Let us start again. Where is Mek Nimmur?'

Tessay's left eardrum felt as if it had burst with the ferocity of those blows. Her hearing buzzed and sang. Her teeth had been driven halfway through the flesh of her cheek, and her mouth filled slowly with her own blood.

'Where is Mek Nimmur?' Helm repeated, leaning his face closer to hers. 'What are your friends doing with the dam in the Dandera river?'

She gathered the blood and saliva in her mouth, and suddenly and explosively spat it into his face.

He recoiled violently and wiped the bloody mess from his eyes with the palm of his hand.

'Hold her!' he said to Nogo, and seized the front of her blouse. With one heave he ripped it open down to her waist, and Nogo giggled and leaned forward over her shoulder to look at her breasts. He giggled again as Helm took one of them in his hand and squeezed out the nipple between his finger and thumb. It was the dark purple colour of a ripe mulberry.

He held her like that, pinching her flesh with his nails until the skin tore and a droplet of blood welled up and trickled over his thumb. Then with his other hand he took the burning cheroot from his lips and blew on the top until it glowed hotly.

'Where is Mek Nimmur?' he asked, and lowered the cheroot towards her breast. 'What are they doing in the Dandera river?'

She stared down in horror as he brought the burning cheroot closer, and tried to wriggle away from him. But Nogo held her firmly from behind. She screamed once, on an agonized drawn-out note, as the glowing coal touched the tip of her nipple and the delicate skin began to blister.

'Winter,' said Royan, spreading the enlargement of the fourth face of the stele from Tanus's tomb under the bright glare of the floodlamp. 'This is the side that contains Taita's notations, which I am postulating are those of the bao board. I don't understand all of them, but by a process of elimination I have determined that the first symbol denotes one of the four sides, or as he terms them the castles of the board.'

She showed him the pages of her notebook on which she had made her calculations.

'See here, the seated baboon is the north castle, the bee is the south, the bird is the west and the scorpion the east.' She pointed out to him the same symbols on the photograph of the stele. 'Then the second and third figures are numbers – I believe that they designate the file and the cup. With these we can follow the moves of his imaginary red stones. The reds are the highest-ranking colours on the board.'

'What about the verses between each set of notations?' Nicholas asked. 'Such as this one here, about the north wind and the storm?'

'I am not sure about those. Probably merely smoke-screens, if I know Taita. He is never one to make life too easy for us. Perhaps they do have significance, but we can only hope to unravel them as we work through the moves of our stones.'

Nicholas studied her figures a while, then grinned ruefully. 'Just think how remote was the possibility that anybody would ever be able to decipher the clues he left behind. The first requirement is that the searcher must have access to both chronicles, the seventh scroll and the stele of Tanus, before he had any chance of understanding the key to the tomb.'

She laughed – a throaty, well-satisfied sound. 'Yes, he must have believed that he was perfectly safe. Well, we will see now, Master Taita. We will see just how clever you really were.' Then, sober and businesslike once more, she looked up the stone staircase that led to Taita's maze.

'Now we have to see if my figures and theories fit into the hard stones and walls of Taita's architecture. But where do we start?'

'At the beginning,' Nicholas suggested, 'the god plays the first coup. That's what Taita told us. If we start here in the shrine of Osiris, at the foot of the staircase, then perhaps that will give us the alignment of his imaginary bao board.'

'I had the same idea,' she agreed immediately. 'Let's postulate that this is the north castle of Taita's board. Then we work the protocol of the four bulls from here.'

It was slow and painstaking work, trying to work their

way into the mind of the ancient scribe by probing the labyrinth of passages and tunnels that he had built four thousand years previously. This time they moved into the maze with more circumspection. Nicholas had filled his pockets with lumps of dried white river clay, and he used these like a schoolmaster's stick of chalk to write on the stone walls at each branch and fork of the tunnels, setting out the notations from the winter face of the stele and marking a signpost to enable them not only to find their way through the maze but to relate it to the model that Royan was drawing up in her notebook.

They found that their first assumption that the shrine of Osiris was the north castle of the board seemed to be correct, and they happily believed that with this as the key it would be a simple matter to follow the moves of play to their conclusion. But these hopes were soon dashed as they realized that Taita was not thinking in the simple two dimensions of the conventional board. He had added the third dimension to the equation.

The stairway leading up from the shrine of Osiris was not the only link between the eight landings. Each of the passages leading off from it was subtly angled either upwards or downwards. As they followed the twists and turns of one of these tunnels they did not detect the fact that they were changing levels. Then suddenly they re-emerged on to the central staircase, but on a landing higher than the one they had entered from.

They stood there and stared at each other in horrified disbelief.

Royan spoke first. 'I didn't even have the feeling that we were ascending,' she whispered. 'The whole thing is infinitely more complex than I first assumed.'

'It must be constructed like one of those nuclear models of some complicated carbon atom,' Nicholas agreed with awe. 'It interlinks on all eight planes. Quite frankly, it's terrifying.'

'Now I have some inkling what those extraneous symbols signify,' Royan muttered. 'They set out the levels. We are going to have to rethink the entire concept.'

'Three-dimensional bao, played to enigmatic rules. What chance have we got against him?' Nicholas shook his head ruefully. 'What we really need is a computer. Taita wasn't puffing his own virtues without good reason. The old hooligan really was a mathematical genius.' He shone the lamp back down the tunnel from which they had come. 'Even when you know it's there you cannot actually see the fall in the floor level. He designed and built it without even a slide rule or a spirit level in his back pocket. This maze is an extraordinary piece of engineering.'

'You can form your fan club later,' she suggested. 'But right now let's start grinding those numbers again.'

'I am going to move the lights and the desks up here, on to this central landing of the staircase.' Nicholas agreed, 'I think we should work from the centre of the board. It may help us to visualize it. Right now he has got me thoroughly confused.'

The only sound in the room was the soft sobbing of the woman who lay curled on the floor in a puddle of her own blood and urine.

Tuma Nogo sat at the long conference table and lit a cigarette. His hands trembled slightly, and he looked sickened. He was a soldier, and he had lived through the Mengistu terror. He was a hard man and accustomed to violence and cruelty, but he was shaken with what he had just witnessed. He knew now why von Schiller placed such reliance on Helm. The man was barely human.

Across the room Jake Helm was washing his hands in the small basin. He dried them fastidiously and then dabbed at the stains on his clothing with the towel as he came back and stood over Tessay.

'I don't think there is anything else she can tell us,' he said calmly. 'I don't think she held anything back.'

Nogo glanced down at the woman, and saw the livid burns that spotted her chest and her cheeks like the running ulcerations of some dreadful smallpox. Her eyes were closed, and her lashes were frizzled away. She had held out well. It was only when Helm had touched her eyelids with the burning cheroot that she had at last capitulated, and gabbled out the answers to his questions.

Nogo felt queasy, but he was relieved that it had not been necessary to hold her lids open, as Helm had ordered, and to watch as he quenched the flame of the cheroot against her weeping eyeballs.

'Watch her,' Helm ordered, as he rolled down his sleeves. 'She is a tough one. Don't take any chances with her.'

Helm walked past him, and went to the door in the far end of the hut. He left the door open, and Nogo could hear their voices, but they were speaking in German so he could not understand what they were saying. He understood now why von Schiller had chosen not to be present during the questioning. He obviously knew how Helm worked.

Helm came back into the room, and nodded at Nogo. 'Very well. We are finished with her. You know what to do.'

Nogo stood up nervously and placed his hand on the webbing holster at his side.

'Here?' he asked. 'Now?'

'Don't be a bloody fool,' Helm snapped. 'Take her away. Far away. Then get somebody in here to clean up this mess.' Helm turned on his heel and went back into the rear room.

Nogo roused himself and then went to the door of the hut. He walked wide of where Tessay lay, so as not to soil his canvas paratrooper boots.

'Lieutenant Hammed!' he called through the door.

Hammed and Nogo lifted Tessay to her feet. Neither of them spoke and they were subdued, almost chastened, as they helped her into her torn and bloodied clothing. Hammed averted his eyes from her naked body and the burns and other injuries that marred her glossy amber skin. He draped the *shamma* over her shoulders, and led her towards the door. When she stumbled he caught her before she fell and supported her with a hand under her elbow. He led her down the steps to the truck, and she moved slowly, like a very old woman. She sat in the passenger seat with her burned and swollen face in her cupped hands.

Nogo summoned Hammed with a jerk of his head, and led him aside. He spoke quietly to him, and Hammed's expression became stricken as he listened to his orders. At one point he started to protest, but Nogo snarled at him savagely and he chewed his lower lip in silence.

'Remember!' Nogo repeated. 'Well away from any of the villages. Make certain that there are no witnesses. Report back to me immediately.'

Hammed straightened his shoulders and saluted before he marched back to the truck and climbed up into the seat beside Tessay. He gave the driver a curt order and they drove out of the camp, following the track back towards Debra Maryam.

Tessay was so confused and in such pain that she had lost all sense of time. Only half-conscious, she lurched about in the seat when the truck hit a particularly rough stretch of the track, and her head rolled loosely on her shoulders. Her face was so swollen that it required an effort to force her eyelids apart, and when she did she thought that her vision was failing and that she was going blind. Then she realized that the sun had set and darkness had fallen. She must have spent the whole day in the hut with Helm.

She felt a mild lift of relief that the burns on her eyelids had not done more damage. At least she was still able to see. She peered out through the windscreen, and found that in the headlights the road was unfamiliar.

'Where are you taking me?' she mumbled. 'This is not the way back to the village.'

Lieutenant Hammed sat slumped beside her in the seat and would not answer. She relapsed into a daze of pain and exhaustion.

She was jerked awake when the truck braked abruptly and the driver switched off the ignition. Rude hands dragged her out of the cab and into the glare of the headlights. Her hands were jerked behind her back and her wrists were bound together with a raw-hide thong.

'You are hurting me,' she whimpered. 'You are cutting my wrists.' She had used up the last of her strength and courage. She felt beaten and pathetic, with no fight left in her.

One of the soldiers yanked on her bound wrists and shoved her off the road. Two others followed, each carrying trenching tools. There was enough of a moon for her to see a grove of eucalyptus trees about a hundred metres from the side of the road, and they led her there. They pushed her down at the base of one of the trees and the man who had tied her wrists stood over her, holding his rifle casually aimed down at her and smoking a cigarette with his free hand. The others stacked their rifles and began digging. They seemed to take no interest in her at all, but were discussing the All Africa Soccer Championships that were being held in Lusaka, and the Ethiopian team's chances of reaching the finals.

It was only after a while that it began to sink into Tessay's befuddled mind that they were digging a grave for her. The saliva in her injured mouth dried up and she looked around desperately for Lieutenant Hammed. But he had stayed with the truck.

'Please,' she whispered to her guard, but before she could say more he kicked her painfully in the belly.

'Keep quiet!' he used the derogatory term of address only applied to an animal or a person of the lowest order, and as she lay doubled up on the ground she realized the futility of appealing to them. A feeling of weakness and resignation overwhelmed her and she found herself weeping softly and hopelessly in the darkness.

When she looked up again through her swollen lids, there was sufficient moonlight for her to see that the grave was now so deep that the two men still digging in it were out of her line of sight. Spadefuls of dirt flew over the lip of the hole and splattered on to the growing pile. Her guard left her side for a moment and sauntered over to the edge of the hole. He looked down in it and then grunted.

'Good. That is deep enough. Call the lieutenant.'

The two soldiers scrambled up out of the grave, then gathered up their tools and weapons and traipsed off into the darkness of the grove. Chatting amicably amongst themselves they headed back towards where the truck was parked, leaving Tessay and her guard.

She lay there shivering with the cold and with terror, while her guard squatted at the lip of her grave and puffed on his cigarette. She thought that if she could get to her feet she could kick him into the hole and make a run for it, back through the trees. But when she tried to sit up her movements were stiff and slow, and she had no feeling in her hands or feet. She tried to force herself to move, but at that moment she heard Lieutenant Hammed coming from the truck and she slumped back in despair.

Hammed was carrying an electric torch. He flashed it down into the grave.

'Good,' he said loudly. 'That is deep enough.'

He switched off the torch and said to the man guarding her, 'No witnesses. Go back and wait at the truck. When you hear the shots, come back with the others to help me fill the hole.'

The guard slung his rifle over his shoulder and disappeared amongst the trees. Hammed waited until the man was well out of earshot, then he came to Tessay and hoisted her to her feet. He pushed her to the edge of the grave, and then she felt him fumbling with her clothing. She tried to lash out at him, but her arms were still bound behind her.

'I want your *shamma*.' He pulled the white woollen cloak off over her shoulders, and then went with it to the edge of the grave. He jumped down into the hole and she heard him scuffling about in the bottom.

His voice came back to her, speaking softly. 'They must see something here. A body—'

He climbed back beside her, puffing with the exertion, and stepped behind her. She felt the touch of cold metal on the inside of her wrists, and then he was sawing at the leather thong. She felt her bonds fall away, and she gasped at the pain as the blood poured back into her numb hands.

'What are you doing?' she whispered in confusion. She looked down into the grave and saw the pale *shamma* arranged to look like a human body. 'Are you going—'

'Please don't talk,' he instructed her softly, as he took her by the shoulder and led her back amongst the trees.

'Lie here.' He pushed her down and made her lie flat, with her face to the ground. He began piling dead leaves and fallen branches over her.

'Stay here! Do not try to run. Don't move or speak until we are gone.'

He flashed the torch briefly over the mound of dead branches to make certain she was covered, then he left her and hurried back to the graveside, unbuckling the flap of his pistol holster as he went. Two spaced pistol shots cracked out in the night, so loud and unexpectedly that she jumped and her heart raced wildly.

Then she heard Hammed shout, 'Come, you men. Let's get this thing finished.'

They trooped back into the grove, and she heard the

sound of their spades and the thump of earth clods falling into the grave.

'I cannot see what I am doing, lieutenant,' a voice complained. 'Where is your torchlight?'

'You don't need a light to fill a hole,' Hammed snarled. 'Get on with your work. Tramp that loose soil down. I don't want anybody stumbling on this place.'

She lay quietly, trying to stop the wild tremors that shook her body. At last the sound of the shovels let up, and she heard Hammed's voice again.

'That will do. Make certain you leave nothing here. Back to the truck!'

Their footsteps and their voices died away. At a distance she heard the truck engine whirl and fire. The headlights shone through the trees as the truck backed and filled, turning in the direction from which they had come.

Long after the sound of the engine had died away completely, she continued to lie under the pile of dead branches. She was still shaking with the cold and weeping softly and silently with exhaustion and pain and relief. Then slowly she pushed the branches off herself and crawled to the trunk of the nearest tree. She used it to pull herself up to her feet, and then stood there, swaying weakly in the darkness.

It was only then that guilt overwhelmed her. 'I have betrayed Mek,' she thought sickeningly. 'I have told everything to his enemies. I must warn him. I must get back to him and warn him.'

She pushed herself away from the treetrunk and blundered back through the darkness towards the track.

The only means of ascertaining if they had solved Taita's codes correctly was to play out the moves he had listed. They went very carefully through the tunnels of the maze, stepping out the moves that he had noted and marking them on the walls in white chalk figures.

There were eighteen moves set out on the winter face of the stele. Using Royan's first interpretation of the symbols, they were able to advance through twelve of these. Then they found themselves at a dead end, confronted by a blank stone wall and unable to make the next move.

'Damnation!' Nicholas kicked the wall, and when this had no effect he hurled the chunk of white chalk at it. 'I wish I could get my hands on that old devil. Castration would be the least of his worries.'

'Sorry.' Royan scraped the hair back out of her eyes. 'I thought I had it right. It must be the figures in the second column. We will have to invert them.'

'We will have to start again,' Nicholas groaned.

'Right at the very beginning,' she agreed.

'How do we know when we have finally got it right?' he wanted to know.

'If by following the clues we arrive at one of the winning combinations, a bao equivalent of checkmate, on precisely the eighteenth move. There will be no logical move after that, and we can assume we have worked through it correctly.'

'And what will we find if we ever reach that position?'

'I will tell you when we get there.' She smiled at him sweetly. 'Cheer up, Nicky. It's only just starting to hurt.'

Royan inverted the values of the second and third numbers of Taita's notations, taking the first as the cup value and the second as the file value. This time they completed only five moves before they were stymied and could proceed no further.

'Perhaps our assumption about the third symbol being the change of level is incorrect?' Nicholas suggested. 'Let's start again and give that the second value.'

'Nicky, do you realize just how many possible

combinations there are, given the three variables?' She was at last starting to waver. 'Taita has assumed an intimate knowledge of the game. We have only the sketchiest notions of how it was played. It's like a grand master trying to explain to a novice the intricacies of the King's Indian Defence.'

'In Russian!' Nicholas embroidered the simile. 'At this rate we are getting nowhere in a hurry. There must be some other way of approaching it. Let's go over the epigrams Taita stuck in between the notations again.'

'All right. I'll read and you listen.' She hunched over her notes. 'The trouble is that a subtle variation of the translation might change the sense. Taita loved puns, and a pun can rely on a single word for effect. One wrong twist or slant to a word and we have lost it.'

'Try anyway,' Nicholas encouraged her. 'Remember that even Taita had never played bao in three dimensions before. If he left a clue it would have to be at the very beginning of the stele. Concentrate on the first couple of notations and the epigrams that separate them.'

'We'll try it that way,' Royan agreed. 'The first notation is the bee followed by the numbers five and seven and the sistrum.'

Nicholas grinned. 'Okay, I have heard that so often already that I will never forget it. What follows?'

'The first quotation.' She ran her finger over the hieroglyphics. '"*What can be given a name can be known. What is nameless can only be felt. I sail with the tide behind me and the wind in my face. O, my beloved, the taste of you is sweet upon my lips.*"'

'Is that all?' he asked.

'Yes, then the next notation. The scorpion and the number two and three and the sistrum again.'

'Slowly! Slowly! First things first. What can we make out of the "*sailing*" and the "*beloved*"?'

So they riddled and wrestled with the text of the stele,

until their eyes burned and they had lost track of day or night. They were eventually recalled to reality by Sapper's voice echoing up the staircase. Nicholas stood up from the desk and stretched before he looked at his watch.

'Eight o'clock. But I'm not sure if that is morning or evening.'

Then he started as Sapper came up the staircase, and saw that his bald head was shining with moisture and his shirt was soaked.

'What happened to you?' Nicholas demanded. 'Did you fall into the sink-hole?'

Sapper wiped his face with the palm of his hand. 'Didn't anybody tell you? It's pissing with rain outside.'

They both stared at him in horror.

'So soon?' Royan whispered. 'It wasn't supposed to start for weeks yet.'

Sapper shrugged. 'Somebody forgot to tell the weatherman.'

'Has it set in?' Nicholas asked. 'What's the state of the river? Has the level started to rise yet?'

'That's what I came to tell you. I am going up to the dam, taking the Buffaloes with me. I want to keep an eye on it. As soon as it gets unsafe I will send a runner down to you. When I do that, don't stop to argue. Get out of here fast. It will mean that I expect the dam to burst at any moment.'

'Don't take Hansith with you,' Nicholas ordered. 'I need him here.'

When Sapper had gone, taking most of the workers from the tunnel with him, Royan and Nicholas looked at each other seriously.

'We are running out of time fast, and Taita still has us in a tangle,' Nicholas said. 'One thing I must warn you. When the river starts to rise—'

She did not let him finish. 'The river!' she cried. 'Not the sea! I was mistaken in the translation. I read it as "*tide*".

I assumed Taita was referring to the sea, but it should have been "*current*". The Egyptians made no distinction between the two words.'

They both rushed back to the desk and her notebooks. '"*The current behind me and the wind in my face*",' Nicholas changed the quotation.

'On the Nile,' Royan exulted, 'the prevailing wind is always from the north, and the current always from the south. Taita was facing north. The north castle.'

'We assumed the symbol for the north was the baboon,' he reminded her.

'No! I was wrong.' Her face was alight with the fires of inspiration. '"*O, my beloved, the taste of you is sweet upon my lips.*" Honey! The bee! I had the symbols for the north and south inverted.'

'What about east and west? What can we find there?' He turned back to the texts with fresh enthusiasm. '"*My sins are red as carnelians. They bind me like chains of bronze. They prick my heart with fire, and I turn my eyes towards the evening star.*"'

'I don't see—'

'"*Prick*" is the wrong translation,' he stuttered eagerly. 'It should be "*sting*". The scorpion looking towards the evening star. The evening star is always in the west. The scorpion is the western castle, not the eastern castle.'

'We had the board inverted.' She jumped up excitedly. 'Let's play it that way!'

'We still have not determined the levels,' he objected. 'Is the sistrum the upper level, or is it the three swords?'

'Now that we have made this breakthrough, that is the only variable. We are either right or wrong. We will play the sistrum first as the upper level, and if that doesn't work we can play it the other way round.'

It was so much easier now. The intricacies of the maze had become less forbidding with familiarity. There were the large white chalk signs in Nicholas's handwriting on each corner and at each fork and T-junction of the tunnels. They moved swiftly through the complex twists and turns, their excitement rising sharply as they followed each notation and found the way still clear before them.

'The eighteenth move.' Royan's voice trembled. 'Hold both thumbs. If it takes us into one of the open files that threaten the opponent's south castle, then that will be the check coup.' She drew a deep breath and read it aloud to him. 'The bird. The numbers three and five. With the lower level symbol of the three swords.'

They paced it out and passed the five junctions into the lowest level of the maze, reading their position from the chalk marks on the stone blocks of the walls at each fork.

'This is it!' Nicholas told her, and they stood together and looked about them.

'There is nothing outstanding about this spot.' Disappointment was bitter in Royan's tone. 'We have passed over it fifty times before. It is just like any of the other turns.'

'That is exactly what Taita would have wanted. Hell! He wouldn't have put up a signpost saying "X marks the spot", would he now?'

'So what do we do?' She looked at him, for once at a loss.

'Read the last epigram from the stele.'

She had her notebook in her hand. '"*From the black and holy earth of this very Egypt the harvest is abundant. I whip the flanks of my donkey, and the wooden spike of the plough breaks new ground. I plant the seed, and reap the grape and the ears of corn. In time I drink the wine and eat the loaf. I follow the rhythm of the seasons, and tend the earth.*"'

She looked up at him. 'The rhythm of the seasons? Is he referring us to the four faces of the stele? The earth?'

she asked and looked down at the slabs beneath their feet. 'The promise of reward from the earth? Under our feet, perhaps?' she asked.

He stamped his foot on the slabs, but the sound was dull and solid. 'Only one way to find out.' He raised his voice and it echoed weirdly through the labyrinth. 'Hansith! Come down here!'

Sapper sat on the high seat of his yellow front-end loader in the rain and cheerfully cursed his gang of Buffaloes, secure in the knowledge that they understood not a word of his insults. The rain swept over them in intermittent gusts off the high mountains. It was not yet the solid, drenching downpour of the true wet season. However, the river was rising sullenly, turning dirty blue-grey with the mud and sediment that it was bringing down.

He knew that the flood had not yet begun in earnest. The thunder that growled ominously along the mountain peaks like a pride of hunting lions was only the prelude to the vast celestial onslaught which would soon follow. Although the river was lapping the top course of gabions of Sapper's dam, and was roaring through the bypass that he had cut into the side valley, he was still holding it at bay.

His Buffaloes were packing more baskets with aggregate, using up the last of the steel mesh from the stores in the quarry. As soon as each of these was filled and wired closed, Sapper picked it up in the front bucket of the tractor and drove it down the bank of the Dandera. He reinforced all the weak spots in the dam wall, and then he began raising it another course. Sapper was fully aware of the overturning effect that the river would exert once it began to pour over the top of the wall. Nothing would be able to withstand its power once this happened. It would carry away a rock-filled gabion as if it were the branch of a baobab tree. It needed only a single breach in the wall to bring the entire structure tumbling and rolling down. He had no illusions as to just how swiftly the river could do its fatal work.

He knew that he dared not wait for the first breach to develop in the wall before he warned Nicholas and Royan in the chasm downstream. The river could easily outrun any messenger he sent, and once the wall began to go it would already be too late. It would be a matter of fine judgement, and he slitted his eyes against another gust of slanting rain that blew into his face. His instinct was to call them out of the chasm now – there was already less than twelve inches of free-board at the top of the wall.

However, he knew that Nicholas would be furious if he was made to evacuate the workings prematurely, and in so doing aborted all their efforts. Sapper was fully aware of the extreme risks that Nicholas had taken and of the crippling expenditure he had made to reach this stage. Before they had left England, he had hinted to Sapper of the straitened circumstances in which he found himself. Although Sapper did not understand the intricacies or the responsibilities of being a 'Name' at Lloyd's, there had been so much publicity in the British press that he could not but realize that, if their venture here failed, the next stop for Nicholas would be the bankruptcy courts – and Nicholas was his friend.

The squall of rain blew over, and a bright hot sun burst through the low cloud banks. The flow of the river seemed undiminished, but at least the water level on the dam wall was no longer rising.

'I'll give it another hour,' he grunted, engaging the gears of the tractor and easing her down the bank to place another gabion in position.

Nicholas worked shoulder to shoulder with Hansith's gang as they began to strip the paving slabs from the floor of the lowest level of the maze. The joints between the slabs were so tight that, even using crowbars, they had difficulty prising them apart. In order to save time, Nicholas made the hard choice of going into a destructive search. He put four of the strongest men in the team to work with home-made sledgehammers, lumps of ironstone on wooden shafts, to break up the slabs so that they could be more readily levered out of the floor. He felt guilty about the damage they were causing to the site, but the work went ahead very much faster.

The high spirits and enthusiasm of the men were at last beginning to wane. They had worked too long in the oppressive confines of the maze, and every one of them was fully aware of the rising level of the river at the head of the gorge, and of the mortal threat behind those waters. Their expressions were surly and there was little laughter or banter. But more worrying for Nicholas was the fact that at the beginning of this shift Hansith had reported the first desertions. Sixteen of his men had failed to report for duty. They had quietly rolled their blankets during the night, picked up whatever items of value or utility they found lying around the camp, and crept away into the darkness.

Nicholas knew that it was no use sending anyone after them – they had too much of a start, and would be halfway up the escarpment already. This was Africa, and Nicholas was certain that now that the rot had started it would spread very quickly.

He joked and jollied them along, not allowing them to sense his true feelings. He worked shoulder to shoulder and sweated along with them in the excavation in an attempt to hold them. But he knew that, unless they made another discovery under these slabs to keep their interest and expectations alight, he might wake up tomorrow to find that even the monks and the faithful Hansith were gone.

He had started lifting the slabs in the angle of the corner of the maze, and they worked out from there in both directions down the arms of the tunnel. His heart sank as they broke up each paving slab with the hammers only to find beneath it the solid stratum of the country rock with no indication of any joint or opening.

'It doesn't look very hopeful,' he muttered to Royan as he took a short break to drink from one of the water flasks.

She too was looking unhappy as she poured water from the flask into his cupped hands, so that he could wash the sweat and grime from his face.

'I may have got the symbols for the levels wrong,' she suggested. 'It is just the kind of trick Taita would play, to work out combinations which would both give a logical solution.' She hesitated before she appealed to him for guidance. 'Do you think I should start working back the other combination—'

Her question was interrupted by a bellow from Hansith. 'In the name of the Blessed Virgin, *effendi*, come quickly!'

They spun around together. In her haste Royan dropped the flask, which shattered at her feet. She did not seem to notice that it had drenched her legs, but ran back to where Hansith was standing with the hammer poised for another stroke.

'What is it—' she broke off as they both saw that beneath the paving slabs Hansith had uncovered another layer of dressed stone sills.

These were laid neatly across the floor of the tunnel from wall to wall, recessed into the surrounding rock, with knife-edge joints between them. Their sides were smooth and plain, without engravings or markings upon them.

'What is it, Nicky?' Royan demanded.

'Either it's another layer of paving, or it's a cover over

an opening in the floor,' he told her eagerly. 'We won't know until we lift one of them.'

The stone sills were too thick and heavy to be cracked with the primitive hammers, although Hansith tried his best. In the end they were forced to dig around the first of them and lever it free. It took five men to raise the end of it and lift it off its foundation.

'There is an opening under it.' Royan went down on her knees to peer into the space that it had left. 'Some kind of open shaft!'

Once the first sill was removed it was easier to get a purchase on the others that blocked the rectangular opening. When they had cleared them all away, Nicholas shone the lamp down into the dark shaft that was revealed. It stretched from wall to wall of the tunnel, and the head room was sufficient for even Nicholas to stand up to his full height on the steps that led down at a forty-five degree angle.

'Another stairway,' he exulted. 'Surely this must be it. Even Taita must have exhausted all the false leads by now.'

The workmen were crowding up behind them, their sullen mood evaporating at this fresh discovery and the certainty of additional bonuses in silver dollars that they had earned.

'Are we going down?' Royan asked. 'I know we should be careful and check it for traps, but we are running out of time, Nicky.'

'You are right, as always. The time has come when we have to press on regardless.'

'Caution thrown to the winds.' She took his hand, laughing. 'Let's go down together.'

They descended side by side, one cautious step at a time, with the lamp held head high and the shadows retreating before them.

'There is a chamber at the bottom,' Royan exclaimed.

'Looks like a store room – what are all those objects stacked along the walls? There must be hundreds of them. Are they coffins, sarcophaguses?' The dark shapes were almost human, standing shoulder to shoulder, rank after rank, around the walls of the square chamber.

'No, I think those are corn baskets on one side,' she said, recognizing them. 'Those on the other side look like wine amphorae. Probably some sort of offering to the dead.'

'If this is one of the funeral store rooms,' said Nicholas in a voice tight with excitement, 'then we are getting very close to the tomb now.'

'Yes!' she cried. 'Look – there is another doorway on the far side of this store room. Shine the light over there.'

The beam picked out the square opening facing them across this lower chamber. It was inviting, beckoning them almost seductively. They almost ran down the last few steps into the chamber lined with the reed baskets and pottery wine jars. But as they reached the level floor of the store room they ran into an invisible barrier that stopped both of them dead and sent them reeling backwards.

'God!' Nicholas clutched at his throat, his voice a strangled choke. 'Get back. Got to get back.'

Royan was sinking to her knees, also gasping and hunting for breath.

'Nicky!' she tried to scream, but her breath was trapped in her lungs. She felt that a steel noose had encircled her chest and, as it tightened, the breath was being forced out of her.

'Nicky! Help me!' She was strangling, like a fish thrown up on the bank. The strength drained from her limbs, and her vision began to break up and fade. She did not have the strength to stand.

He stooped over her and tried to lift her, but he was almost as weak. He felt his own legs buckling, no longer able to support even his own weight.

'Four minutes,' he thought desperately as he suffocated. 'That's all we have got. Four minutes to brain death and oblivion. We have to get air.'

From behind her, he slipped his arms under her armpits and locked his hands together over her breasts. Again he tried to lift her, but his strength was gone. He began to walk backwards towards the stairs down which they had run so lightly, and every pace required a huge effort. She was already unconscious, lying inert in the circle of his arms. Her limp legs trailed across the stone floor as he dragged her back.

The lowest step caught his heels and he almost toppled over backwards. With an effort he regained his balance and lugged her back up the steps, her feet sliding and bumping loosely over the treads. He wanted to shout to Hansith for help, but he did not have the air in his lungs to utter a sound.

'If you drop her now, she's dead,' he told himself, and he struggled up another five steps, his lungs hunting for precious air and finding none. His strength oozed out of him a drop at a time as his vision slid and wobbled and distorted.

'Let me breathe,' he pleaded. 'Please God, let me breathe.'

Miraculously, like a direct answer to his prayer, he felt the precious oxygen slide down his panting throat and swell his lungs. At once his strength began flooding back and he tightened his grip around Royan's chest and lifted her bodily. He staggered up the remaining steps with her body in his arms and sprawled out of the mouth of the shaft on to the slabs of the tunnel at Hansith's feet.

'What is is, *effendi*? What has happened to you and the lady?'

Nicholas had no breath to answer him. He laid Royan in the position for mouth-to-mouth resuscitation, and slapped her cheeks.

'Come on!' he pleaded with her. 'Speak! Talk to me!'

There was no response, so he knelt over her, covered her open mouth with his own and blew down her throat, until from the corner of his eye he saw her chest swelling and inflating.

He sat back for a count of three. 'Please, my darling, please breathe!' There was no colour in her yellow, corpse-like face.

He bent over her and covered her mouth again, and as he filled her lungs with his own breath he felt her stir under him.

'That's it, my darling,' he told her. 'Breathe! Breathe for me.'

At the next breath she pushed him away and sat up groggily, staring round at the circle of faces that hovered over her anxiously. She picked out Nicholas's pale face amongst the black faces of the men.

'Nicky! What happened?'

'I am not sure – but whatever it was, it almost got both of us. How are you feeling now?'

'It was as though an invisible hand had me by the throat, and was strangling me. I couldn't breathe, and then I passed out.'

'It must be some kind of gas filling the lower levels of the passage. You were only out for less than two minutes,' he reassured her. 'It takes four minutes of oxygen starvation to kill the brain.'

'I have a terrible headache.' She pressed her fingers to her temples. 'I heard your voice calling me back. You called me "my darling".' She dropped her eyes.

'Just a little slip of the tongue.' He lifted her to her feet and for a moment she swayed against him, her breasts soft and warm against his chest.

'Thank you once again, Nicky. I am so deeply in your debt already, I will never be able to repay you.'

'I am sure we will be able to work something out.'

She was suddenly aware of the men's eyes watching her and drew away from him. 'What kind of gas? And how did it get there? Was it another of Taita's tricks, do you think, Nicky?'

'One of the gases of decay, most probably,' was his opinion. 'Because it is trapped in the lower part of the passage, it must be a heavier-than-air type. I would guess that it is probably carbon dioxide, although it could be something like methane. I think methane is heavier than air, isn't it?'

'Did Taita do it deliberately?' The colour was returning to her cheeks, and she was recovering swiftly.

'I don't know, but those baskets and jars are suspicious. I will be able to answer that question when we have had a chance to examine their contents.' He touched her cheek tenderly. 'How are you feeling? How is your headache?'

'Better. What do we do now?'

'Clear the gas from the chamber,' he told her, 'and as soon as possible.'

He used a candle from his emergency pack to test for the gas level in the shaft. With it burning in his right hand he went back down the steps, holding it low to the floor, descending a step at a time. The candle flame burned brightly, dancing to the movement of air as he went down. Then, abruptly on the sixth step above the floor level of the chamber, the flame turned yellow and snuffed out.

He marked the level on the wall in white chalk, and called up to Royan at the head of the shaft, 'Well, at least it's not methane. I am still here. Must be carbon dioxide.'

'Pretty conclusive test,' she laughed. 'If it goes boom, it's methane.'

'Hansith, bring down the blower fan,' Nicholas shouted to the big monk.

Holding his breath as though he were snorkelling

under water, Nicholas carried the fan down the lower steps and set it up on the floor of the chamber. He set the fan speed at 'High' and immediately retreated up the shaft, drawing a huge breath as soon as he was above the chalk mark on the wall.

'How long will it take to clear the gas?' Royan asked anxiously, looking at her wrist-watch.

'I will test with the candle every fifteen minutes.'

It was an hour before the gas had dispersed enough to enable him to reach the floor of the chamber again, and breathe the air down there. Then Nicholas ordered Hansith to bring down a bundle of firewood and build a fire in the centre of the stone floor, to heat and circulate the air more rapidly.

While he was doing this, Nicholas and Royan examined one of the baskets that stood against the wall.

'The crafty old ruffian!' Nicholas muttered half in exasperation and half in admiration. 'It looks like a mixture of manure and grass and dead leaves, the same as a compost heap.'

They crossed the chamber, turned one of the pottery jars on its side, and studied the powder that spilled out of it. Nicholas took up a handful and rubbed it between his fingers, then sniffed it warily.

'Crushed limestone!' he muttered. 'Although it has long ago dried out and lost any odour, Taita probably soaked it with some form of acid. Vinegar, perhaps, or even urine would have done the trick. As it broke down the limestone, it formed carbon dioxide.'

'So it was another deliberate trap,' Royan exclaimed.

'Even so many thousands of years ago, Taita must have understood the processes of decay. He knew what gases those mixtures would produce. Amongst all the other accomplishments he boasts of, he must also have been a nifty chemist.'

'Furthermore, he must have known that without a

draught or any movement of air, these heavy inert gases would hang here in the bottom of the chamber indefinitely,' she agreed. 'I expect that this shaft is designed like a U-trap. I bet that the passage rises again—' she pointed at the mysterious doorway in the far wall, 'in fact I can see the first steps even from here.'

'We will soon find out if you are right,' he told her, 'because that's exactly where we are heading right now – up those steps.'

Sapper had placed cairns of stones at the water's edge to monitor the river level. He watched them the way a stockbroker watches his ticker tape.

It had been six hours since the last rain squall had passed. The clouds over the valley had burned away in the hot, bright sunlight, although they still hung densely over the northern horizon. Their great dun-coloured thunderheads reared to the heavens, menacing and ominous, forming their own mighty ranges that dwarfed the mountains beneath them. At any time the downpour might begin up there in the highlands. Once that happened, Sapper wondered how long it would take the flood waters to reach them here in the Abbay gorge.

He dismounted stiffly from the tractor, and went down the bank to inspect his stone markers. The water level had fallen almost a foot in the past hour. He forced himself not to let his optimism bubble over – after all, it had taken only fifteen minutes for the river to rise the same amount. The final outcome was inevitable. The rains would come. The river would spate. The dam would burst. He looked downstream at the dam wall, and shook his head with resignation.

He had done as much as possible to delay that moment. He had raised the level of the dam wall almost four feet, and packed in another buttress behind the wall to strengthen it. There was nothing further for him to do, and he could only wait.

Climbing up the bank, he leaned wearily against the yellow steel of his machine and looked across at his team of Buffaloes, strewn along the bank like casualties on a battlefield. They had worked for two days to hold back the waters, and now they were exhausted. He knew that he could not call on them for another effort; the next time the river attacked, it would overwhelm them.

He saw some of the men stir and sit up, and their faces turned upstream. He heard their voices faint on the wind. Something was exciting their interest. He climbed up on to the tractor and shaded his eyes. The unmistakable figure of Mek Nimmur was coming down the trail from the direction of the escarpment, stocky and powerful in his camo fatigues, his gait determined. He was accompanied by two of his company commanders.

Mek hailed Sapper from a distance. 'How is your dam holding?' he called in Arabic, which Sapper did not understand. 'Soon it will rain on the mountains. You won't be able to hold out here much longer.' But his gestures towards sky and river were immediately intelligible to Sapper.

Sapper jumped down from the machine to greet him, and they shook hands cordially. They had recognized in each other the qualities of strength and professionalism that they both admired.

Mek seized his company commander, who spoke English, by the arm, and the man fell into his by now familiar role of interpreter.

'It is not only the weather that troubles me,' Mek confided in a low voice, and the interpreter relayed the information to Sapper. 'I have reports that the government troops are moving into position to attack us. My intelligence is that they have a full battalion moving down this way from Debra Maryam, and another force below the monastery at St Frumentius, moving up the Abbay river.'

'Pincer movement, hey?' said Sapper.

Mek listened to the translation and nodded gravely. 'I am heavily outnumbered and I don't know how long I will be able to hold them when they attack. My men are guerrillas. It is not our role to fight set-piece battles. It is the war of the flea for us. Hit and run. I came to warn you to be ready to pull out at short notice.'

'Don't worry too much about me,' Sapper grunted. 'I am a sprinter. Hundred yards dash is my speciality. It's Nicholas and Royan you should be thinking of, them in that ruddy rabbit warren of theirs.'

'I am on my way to them now, but I wanted to arrange a fall-back position. If we get cut off from each other in the fighting, Nicholas has cached the boats at the monastery. That is where we will assemble.'

'Okay, Mek—' Sapper stopped speaking and all three of them looked up the trail, where there was a fresh disturbance amongst the men along the bank. 'What's going on?'

'One of my patrols coming in,' Mek narrowed his eyes. 'There must be some new development.' He stopped speaking as he realized that Sapper could not understand him, and then his expression changed as he recognized the small, slim figure that was being carried on a rough litter by the men of his patrol.

Tessay saw him running towards her and sat up weakly on the litter. The men lowered her to the ground and Mek went down on his knees beside the litter and placed both his arms around her. They held each other in silence for a long moment. Then Mek gently cupped her face in his hands and examined her swollen and scarred features. Some of the burns had become infected, and her eyes were slits beneath the bloated lids.

'Who did this to you?' he asked softly.

She mumbled incoherently through her black-scabbed lips. 'They made me—'

'No! Don't try to talk.' He changed his mind as her lower lip cracked open and a droplet of fresh blood welled up and glistened like a ruby on her skin.

'I have to tell you,' she insisted in a broken whisper. 'They made me tell them everything. The numbers of your men. What you and Nicholas are doing here. Everything. I am sorry, Mek. I betrayed you.'

'Who was it? Who did this to you?'

'Nogo and the American, Helm,' she said, and although he embraced her as gently as a father with his infant in his arms, his eyes were terrible.

The lower chamber of the tunnel was cleared of gas at last. Hansith's fire burned bright and steady in the middle of the floor, the rising hot air wafting away the noxious vapours and dispersing them through the upper levels of the maze, where they mingled with the cleaner oxygen-rich air and lost their toxicity. By this time Royan had fully recovered from the physical effects of the gassing, but her confidence was shaken, and she allowed Nicholas to lead the way up the steps that rose from the far side of the chamber.

'It's the perfect gas trap,' Nicholas pointed out to her as they climbed cautiously. 'No doubt at all that Taita knew exactly what he was doing when he built this section of the tunnel.'

'Surely he must have expected any interloper of his period to have either succumbed to his hellish devices, lost his way in the maze, or given up and turned back by now,' she reasoned.

'Are you trying to convince me that this was Taita's

last line of defence, and that he has no more tricks in store for us? Is that it?' Nicholas asked as he took another step upwards.

'No. Actually I was trying to convince myself, and not having much success. I just don't trust him one little bit any more. I have come to expect the worst from him. I expect the roof to collapse on me at any moment, or the floor to open and drop us into a fiery furnace or something worse.'

They had descended forty steps down into the chamber, and the staircase they were now climbing was a mirror image of that. It rose at the same angle and the tread of each step was the same depth and width. As their heads rose above the fortieth step, Nicholas played the beam of the lamp down the spacious, level arcade that opened before them, and they were dazzled by a riot of colour and pattern, bright and lovely as a field of desert blooms after rain. The paintings covered the walls and ceiling of the arcade, stunning in their profusion, wondrous in their execution.

'Taita!' Royan cried in a voice that quivered and broke. 'These are his paintings. There is no other artist like him, I could never mistake it. I would know his work anywhere.'

They stood on the top step and gazed around in wonder. When compared to these, the murals in the long gallery seemed pale and stilted, the tawdry sham that they really were. This was the work of a great master, a timeless genius, whose art could enchant and enrapture now just as readily as it had four thousand years ago.

They moved forward slowly, almost involuntarily, down the arcade. It was lined on each side with small chambers, like the stalls in an oriental bazaar. The entrance to each was guarded by tall columns that reached up to the roof. Each column was a carved statue of one member of the pantheon of gods. Between them they held the high-vaulted ceiling suspended.

As they drew level with the first two stalls, Nicholas stopped and squeezed her arm.

'The treasure chambers of Pharaoh,' he whispered.

The stalls were packed from floor to ceiling with wonderful and beautiful things.

'The furniture store.' Royan's voice was as reverential as his as she recognized the shapes of chairs and stools and beds and divans. She went to the nearest chamber and touched a royal throne. The arms were twining serpents of bronze and lapis lazuli. The legs were those of lions with claws of gold. The seat and back were chased with scenes of the hunt, and wings of gold surmounted the high back.

Stacked behind the throne was a great profusion of other furniture. They recognized a screened divan, its sides enclosed in an exquisite lacework of ebony and ivory. But there were dozens of other items besides, most of them broken down into their separate parts so that it was not possible to guess what they were. They gleamed with precious metals and coloured stones in such confusion and variety that it was too much to take in in a single glance. Both the alcoves on either side of the arcade were stuffed with these marvellous collections. Royan shook her head in wonder, and Nicholas led her on. The walls that separated the alcoves were decorated with panels illustrating the *Book of the Dead*, and the journey of Pharaoh through the pylons, the dangers and the trials, the demons and the monsters that awaited him along the way.

'These are the paintings that were missing from the mock tomb in the long gallery,' Royan told him. 'But just look upon the face of the king. You can see he was a real person. Those are perfect royal portraits.'

The mural beside them depicted the great god Osiris leading Pharaoh by the hand, protecting him from the monsters that crowded close on either hand, waiting their chance to devour him. It showed the face of the king as he must truly have been, a man with a kind and gentle, if rather weak, face.

'Look at the figures,' Nicholas agreed. 'They are not stiff wooden dolls always stepping forward with the right foot. These are real men and women. They are anatomically correct. The artist understood perspective and had studied the human body.'

They came to the next pair of alcoves, and paused to peer into them.

'Weapons,' said Nicholas. 'Just look at that chariot!'

The panels of the chariot were covered with a skin of gold leaf, so that it dazzled the eye. The harness and traces seemed only to await the horses that would draw it into battle, and the quivers strapped to the side panels behind each tall wheel bulged with arrows and javelins. The cartouche of Mamose was emblazoned on the side panels.

Piled beside this magnificent vehicle were war bows whose stocks were bound with wire of electrum and bronze and gold. There were arrays of daggers with ivory handles and swords with blades of glistening bronze. There were racks of spears and pikes. There were shields of bronze, the targets decorated with scenes of war and the name of the divine Mamose. There were helmets and breastplates made from the skin of the crocodile, and the uniforms and regalia of the famous regiments of Egypt dressed the life-sized wooden statues of the king that stood in rows against the walls of the alcoves.

They walked on down the aisle, between more paintings and murals depicting the life and the death of the king. They saw him playing with his daughters and dandling his infant son. They saw him fishing and hunting and hawking, in council with his ministers and his nomarches, dallying with his wives and concubines, and feasting with the priests of the temple.

'What a chronicle of life in ancient times,' Royan breathed with awe. 'There has never been a discovery remotely like this before.'

Each of the persons in the panels had obviously been drawn from life. They were real breathing living men and women, every face and every expression different, captured with the keen eye, the humour and the great humanity of the artist.

'That must be Taita himself.' Royan pointed out the self-portrait of the eunuch in one of the central panels. 'I wonder if he took poetic licence, or was he truly so noble and beautiful?'

They paused to admire the face of Taita, their adversary, and looked into his searching, intelligent eyes. Such was the skill of the artist that he watched them as keenly as they studied him. A small, enigmatic smile played on Taita's lips. The painting had been varnished, so that it was perfectly preserved, as if it had been painted the day before. Taita's lips seemed moist and his eyes gleamed softly with life.

'His complexion is fair and his eyes are blue!' Royan exclaimed. 'Although that red hair is almost certainly dyed with henna.'

'It is weird to think that, although he lived so long ago, he almost succeeded in killing us,' Nicholas said softly.

'In what land was he born? He never tells us that in the scrolls. Was it Greece or Italy? Was he from one of the Germanic tribes, or was he of Viking stock? We will never know, for he himself probably did not know his own origins.'

'There he is again in the next panel.' Nicholas pointed down the arcade to where the unmistakable face of the eunuch appeared in the throng that knelt in homage before the throne on which sat Pharaoh and his queen. 'Like Hitchcock, he seems to like to appear in his own creations.'

They went on past the treasure stalls in which were

stored plates and goblets and bowls of alabaster and bronze chased with silver and gold, polished bronze mirrors and rolls of precious silk and linen and woollen cloth that had long ago rotted to shaggy black amorphous heaps. On the walls that divided these from the next set of stalls they saw re-enacted the battle with the Hyksos in which Pharaoh had been struck down, the arrow shot by the Hyksos king lodged in his breast. Then in the next panel Taita, the surgeon, bent over him with the surgical instruments in his hands, removing the blood-smeared barb from deep in his flesh.

Now they came to alcoves in which were stacked hundreds of cedarwood chests. The boxes were painted with the royal cartouche of Mamose, and with scenes of the king at his toilet: lining his eyes with kohl, painting his face with white antimony and scarlet rouge, being shaved by his barbers and dressed by his valets.

'Some of those chests will contain the royal cosmetics,' Royan murmured, 'and some of them will be Pharaoh's wardrobes of clothing. There will be costumes in them for every occasion in his after-life. I long to be able to unpack and examine them.'

The next set of wall panels showed the marriage of the king to the young virgin, Taita's mistress. The face of Queen Lostris was rendered with loving detail. The artist gloated on her beauty and exaggerated it, his brush strokes caressing her naked breasts and lingering on all her virtues until they epitomized feminine perfection.

'How much Taita loved her,' Royan murmured, and there was envy in her voice. 'You can see it in every line he drew.'

Nicholas smiled softly and put his arms around her shoulders.

There were hundreds more wooden chests stacked in the next alcoves. Painted on the lids were miniatures of the king decked in all his jewellery: his fingers and toes were thick with rings and his chest was covered with pectoral medallions, while bangles of gold adorned his arms and bracelets his wrists. In one portrait he wore the double crown of the two kingdoms of Egypt united, the red crown and the white with the heads of the vulture and the cobra on his brow. In another he wore the blue war crown, and on a third the Nemes crown with gold and lapis wings that covered his ears.

'If each of those chests contains the treasures depicted on its lid—' Nicholas broke off, unable to continue the thought. The possibility of such riches was daunting, and the imagination balked at the magnitude of it.

'Do you remember what Taita wrote in the scrolls? "*I cannot believe that such a treasure was ever before accumulated in one place at one time*"?' Royan asked him. 'It seems that it is all still here, every single gem and grain of gold. The treasure of Mamose is intact.'

Beyond the treasury there was another alcove lined with shelves on which stood the *ushabti* figures: dolls made of green glazed porcelain or carved from cedarwood. They were an army of tiny figures, men and women from all the trades and professions. There were priests and scribes and lawyers and physicians, gardeners and farmers, bakers and brewers, handmaidens and dancing girls, seamstresses and laundrymaids, soldiers and barbers, and common labourers. Each of them carried the tools and accoutrements of his or her trade. They would accompany the king to the after-world and there would work for Pharaoh, and would go forward in his place if he were ever called upon to perform a service for the other gods.

At last Nicholas and Royan came to the end of this fabulous arcade, and found their way closed off by a series of tall, free-standing screens, tabernacles that had been once fine white linen mesh but were now decayed and rotted into ribbons and streamers, dirty and shabby as old cobwebs. And yet the stars and rosettes of shining gold that decorated these curtains were still hanging in the mesh like fish in a fisherman's net. Through this ethereal web of silken wisps and golden stars they could make out the shape of another gateway beyond.

'That must be the entrance to the actual tomb,' Royan whispered. 'There is only a thin veil between us and the king now.'

They hesitated at the threshold, gripped by a strange reluctance to take the final step.

As an old warrior, Mek Nimmur had seen and treated most of the injuries that a man might sustain on the battlefield. His little guerrilla group did not have a doctor, or even a medical orderly. Mek himself treated most of his casualties, and he always had a medical kit close at hand.

He had the men carry Tessay to one of the huts near the quarry, where, screened by the grass walls, he stripped her of her tattered clothing and treated her injuries. He cleaned her burns and abrasions with disinfectant, and covered the worst of them with clean field dressings. Then he rolled her gently on to her stomach and snapped the glass phial off the needle of the disposable syringe which was preloaded with a broad-spectrum antibiotic.

She winced at the sting of the needle, and he said, 'I am not a very good doctor.'

'I would have no other. Oh, Mek! I thought I would never see you again. I did not fear death as much as I feared that.'

He helped her dress in the spare clothing from his pack, a sweatshirt and fatigues that were many sizes too large for her. He rolled up the cuffs for her, and his touch was gentle. His hands were those of a lover, not a soldier.

'I must look so ugly,' she whispered through her swollen, black-scabbed lips.

'You are beautiful,' he denied it. 'To me you will always be beautiful.' He touched her cheek carefully, so as not to harm the raw burns that covered it.

At that moment they heard the gunfire. It was still faint with distance, borne down from the north on the rain winds.

Mek stood up immediately. 'It has begun. Nogo is attacking at last.'

'It's all my fault. I told him—'

'No,' he told her firmly. 'It is not your fault. You did what you had to do. If you had not, they would have hurt you even worse than this. They would have attacked us, even if you had told them nothing.'

He picked up his webbing belt and strapped it around his waist. From far off they heard the crumping detonation of exploding mortar shells.

'I have to go now,' he told her.

'I know. Do not worry about me.'

'I will always worry about you. These men will carry you down to the monastery. That is the assembly point. Wait for me there. I cannot hope to hold Nogo for long. He is too strong. I will come to you soon.'

'I love you,' she whispered. 'I will wait for you for ever.'

'You are my woman,' he told her in his deep, soft voice, and then he ducked through the doorway of the hut and was gone.

When Nicholas touched the frame of the screen, fragments of the mesh veil tore free with even that tiny movement and fell to the tiles of the floor. The golden rosettes trapped in their folds tinkled on the stones. Now there was an opening in the curtain large enough for them to step through. They found themselves before the inner doorway. It was guarded on one side by a massive statue of the great god Osiris with his hands crossed over his chest, clutching the crook and the flail. Opposite stood his wife Isis, with the lunar crown and horns on her head. Their blank eyes stared out into eternity, and their expressions were serene. Nicholas and Royan passed between these twelve-foot-high statues and found themselves at last in the veritable tomb of Mamose.

The roof was vaulted, and the quality of the murals that covered it and the walls was different – formal and classical. The colours were of a deeper, more sombre hue, and the patterns more intricate. The chamber was smaller than they had anticipated; just large enough to accommodate the huge granite sarcophagus of the divine Pharaoh Mamose.

The sarcophagus stood chest-high. Its side panels were engraved in bas-relief with scenes of Pharaoh and the other gods. The stone lid was in the shape of a full-length effigy of the supine figure of the king. They saw at once that it was still in its original position, and that the clay seals of the priests of Osiris which secured the lid were intact. The tomb had never been violated. The mummy had lain within it undisturbed through the millennia.

But this was not what amazed them. There were two extraneous items within the otherwise classically correct tomb. On the lid of the sarcophagus lay a magnificent war bow. Almost as long as Nicholas was tall, the entire length of its stock was bound with coils of shining electrum wire, that alloy of gold and silver whose formula has been lost in antiquity.

The other item that should never have been placed in a royal tomb stood at the foot of the sarcophagus. It was a small human figure, one of the *ushabti* dolls. A glance confirmed the superior quality of the carving of this effigy, and both of them recognized the features instantly. Only minutes before, they had seen that face painted upon the walls of the arcade, outside the tomb.

The words of Taita, from the scrolls, seemed to reverberate within the confines of the tomb, and hang like fireflies in the air above the sarcophagus:

> *When I stood for the very last time beside the royal sarcophagus, I sent all the workmen away. I would be the very last to leave the tomb, and after me the entrance would be sealed.*
>
> *When I was alone I opened the bundle I carried. From it I took the long bow, Lanata. Tanus had named it after my mistress, for Lanata had been her baby name. I had made the bow for him. It was the last gift from the two of us. I placed it upon the sealed stone lid of his coffin.*
>
> *There was one other item in my bundle. It was the wooden* ushabti *figure that I had carved. I placed it at the foot of the sarcophagus. While I carved it, I had set up three copper mirrors so that I could study my own features from every angle and reproduce them faithfully. The doll was a miniature Taita.*
>
> *Upon the base I had inscribed the words—*

Royan knelt at the foot of the coffin and pick up the *ushabti* figure. Reverently she turned it in her hands and studied the hieroglyphics carved into the base of the figure.

Nicholas knelt beside her. 'Read it to me,' he said.

Softly she obeyed. '"My name is Taita. I am a physician and a poet. I am an architect and a philosopher. I am your friend. I will answer for you."'

'So it's all true,' Nicholas whispered.

Royan replaced the *ushabti* exactly as she had found it and, still on her knees, turned her face to his.

'I have never known another moment like this,' she whispered. 'I want it never to end.'

'It will never end, my darling,' he answered her. 'You and I are only just beginning.'

Mek Nimmur watched them coming, skirting the bottom slope of the hill. It took the trained eye of a bush-fighter to pick them out as they moved through the thick scrub and thorn. As he evaluated them he felt a twinge of dismay. These were crack troops, seasoned during long years of war. He had once fought with them against the Mengistu tyranny, and he had probably trained many of those men down there. Now they were coming against him. Such was the cycle of war and violence in this racked continent, where the endless struggles were fuelled and nurtured by the age-old tribal enmities and the greed and corruption of the new-age politicians and their outmoded ideologies.

But this was not the moment for dialectics, he thought bitterly, and focused his mind on the tactics of the battlefield beneath him. Yes! These men were good. He could see it in the way they advanced, like wraiths through the scrub. For every one of them he picked out, he knew there were a dozen others that remained unseen.

'Company strength,' he thought, and glanced around at his own small force. Fourteen men amongst the rocks, they could only hope to hit their adversary hard while they still had the advantage of surprise, and then pull back before Nogo ranged his mortars in on the hilltop where they lay.

He looked up at the sky and wondered whether Nogo would call in an air strike. Thirty-five minutes' flying time for a stick of those Soviet-built Tupolevs from the air base at Addis, and he could almost smell the sweet stench of napalm on the humid wind, and see the rolling cloud of flame sweeping towards them. That was the only thing his men really feared. But there would be no air strike – not this time, he decided. Nogo and his paymaster, the German von Schiller, wanted the spoils from the tomb that Nicholas Quenton-Harper had discovered in the gorge. They did not want to share any of it with those political fat cats in Addis. They would not want to draw any government attention to themselves and this little private campaign of theirs in the Abbay gorge.

He looked back down the slope. The enemy was moving in nicely, swinging around the hillside to intersect the trail along the Dandera river. Soon they must send a patrol up here to secure their flank before they could sweep on. Yes, there they were. Eight, no, ten men detaching from the main advance, and moving cautiously up the slope beneath him.

'I will let them get in close,' he decided. 'I would like to get them all, but that is too much to hope for. I would settle for four or five of them, and it would be good to leave a few squealers in the scrub.' He grinned cruelly. 'Nothing like a man screaming with a belly wound to take the fire out of his comrades, and make them keep their heads down.'

He looked across the rock-strewn slope, and saw that his RPD light machine gun was perfectly sited to enfilade their advance up the slope. Salim, his machine gunner, was an artist with that weapon. Perhaps, after all, he could hope to put down more than five of them.

'We will see,' thought Mek, 'but I must time it right.'

He saw that there was a gap in the ridge of rock just below him.

'They will not want to expose themselves by crossing the open ridge,' he judged. 'They will tend to bunch up and sneak through the gap. That will be the moment.'

He looked back at the RPD. Salim was watching him, waiting for his signal. Mek looked back down the slope.

'Yes,' he thought. 'Their line is bunching. The big one on the left is already out of position. Those two inside him are angling across towards the gap.'

Nogo's men's camouflage blended perfectly with the scrub, and the barrels of their weapons were wrapped with rags and scraps of camouflage netting so that they threw no sunlight reflections. They were almost invisible in the bush; it was only their movements and the skin tones that betrayed them. They were so close now that Mek caught the occasional gleam of one of their eyeballs but he still could not pick out their machine gunner.

He must silence the gun with his first burst. 'Ah, yes,' he thought with relief. 'There he is. On the right flank. I nearly missed him.'

The man was short and thick-set, with heavy shoulders and long arms, simian, carrying the gun easily on his hip. It was a Soviet-made 7.62mm RPD. The wink of brass from the cartridges in the ammunition belts festooned over those great shoulders had given him away.

Mek eased himself down and inched around the base of the rock that covered him. He slipped the rate-of-fire selector on his AKM to rapid, and laid his cheek on the wooden butt. It was his personal weapon. A gunsmith in Addis had trued the action and lapped the barrel for him, as well as glass-bedding the barrel into the stock. All this had been done to improve the accuracy of this notoriously inaccurate assault rifle. It was still no sniper's weapon, but with these modifications he could expect to place all his shots within a two-inch circle at a hundred metres.

The man carrying the RPD up the slope was now only fifty metres below where he lay. Mek glanced to his right to make sure that the three others were moving into the gap where Salim could take them out with a single burst; then he settled the pip of his foresight in the centre of the RPD machine gunner's belly, using his belt buckle as an aiming mark, and fired a tap of three.

The AKM rode up viciously and the triple detonation stung his eardrums, but Mek saw his bullets strike, stitching a row up the man's torso. One hit low in the belly, the second in the diaphragm and the third at the base of his throat. He spun around, his arms flinging out and jerking, and then crashed over backwards, out of sight in the underbrush.

All around Mek his men were firing. He wondered how many of them Salim had taken with that first burst, but there was no longer anything to see. The enemy were all down in cover. A faint haze of gunsmoke blued the air as they returned fire, and the scrub trembled and shook to the recoil and the muzzle blast of their weapons.

Then, in the uproar of fire, in the whine and wail of ricochets off the rocks, one of them began to scream.

'I am hit. In Allah's name, help me.' His cries rang eerily across the hillside, and the enemy fire slackened perceptibly. Mek clipped a fresh magazine on to the AKM.

'Sing, little bird. Sing!' he muttered grimly.

It required the combined strength of Nicholas, Hansith and eight other men to lift the lid off the stone sarcophagus. Staggering under its weight, they laid it carefully against the wall of the tomb. Then Royan and Nicholas stood on the plinth of the sarcophagus to look down into the interior.

Fitted neatly into the stone receptacle was an enormous wooden coffin. Its lid too was in the form of the reclining Pharaoh. He was in the posture of death with his hands crossed at his breast, clutching the flail and the crook. The coffin was gilded and encrusted with semiprecious stones. The expression on the face of the king's effigy was serene.

They lifted the coffin out of the sarcophagus, and its weight was less than that of the stone lid. Carefully

Nicholas split the golden seals and the layer of hard dried resin that held the lid of the coffin in place. Within it they found another coffin, fitted perfectly, and when they opened that yet another coffin was revealed. It was like a nest of Russian dolls, one within the other, becoming smaller with each revelation.

In the end there were seven coffins, each of them progressively more ornate and richly decorated than the previous one. The seventh coffin was only slightly larger than a man, and it was made of gold. The polished metal caught the light of the lamps like a thousand mirrors and threw bright arrows and darts into every recess of the tomb.

When at last they opened the golden inner coffin they found that it was filled with flowers. The blooms had dried and faded, so their colour was sepia. Their scent had long ago evaporated, so that only the musky aroma of great age wafted up from the coffin. The petals were so dry and papery that they crumbled at the first touch. Beneath the faded blooms was a layer of the finest linen; once it must have been snowy white, but now it was brown with age and the stain of the juices from the flowers. Through the soft folds they saw once again the gleam of gold.

Standing on either side of the coffin, Nicholas and Royan peeled back the linen mesh. It crackled softly and tore like tissue paper under their fingers, but as it came away they both involuntarily gasped with wonder as the death-mask of Pharaoh was revealed. It was only fractionally larger than the head of a man, but it was a perfect image in every detail. Pharaoh's features had been preserved for all eternity in this extraordinary work of art. They stared in silent wonder into the obsidian and rock crystal eyes of Pharaoh, and Pharaoh gazed back at them sadly, almost accusingly.

It was a long time before either of them could summon the courage and presumption to lift it away from the head of the mummy. But when they did so, they found further evidence that in antiquity the body of the king and that of his general, Tanus, had been changed. The mummy that lay before them was obviously too large for the coffin that contained it. It had been partially unwrapped, and cramped into the interior.

'A royal mummy would have had hundreds of charms and amulets placed beneath the wrappings,' Royan whispered. 'This is the plainly dressed corpse of a nobleman and not that of the king.'

Nicholas gently lifted the inner layer of bandage away from the dead head and a thick coil of braided hair was revealed.

'The portraits of Pharaoh Mamose on the walls of the arcade show that his head hair was dyed with henna,' Nicholas murmured. 'Look at this.'

The braid was the colour of the winter grasses of the African savannah, gold and silver.

'There can be no doubt now. This is the body of Tanus. The friend of Taita and the lover of the queen.'

'Yes,' Royan agreed, her eyes soft with tears. 'He is the true father of Lostris's son, who became in his time the Pharaoh Tamose and the forefather of a great line of kings. So this is the man whose blood runs through the history of ancient Egypt.'

'In his way he was as great as any Pharaoh,' Nicholas said quietly.

It was Royan who roused herself first. 'The river!' she cried, with a razor edge to her voice. 'We cannot let all this go again, when the river rises.'

'Neither can we hope to save all of it. There is too much. A great mass of treasure. Our time here has almost run out, so we must pick out the most beautiful and important pieces and pack them into the crates. Lord alone knows if we even have time for that.'

So they worked in a frenzy in the short time that was left to them. They could not even think about saving the statues and the murals, the furniture and the weapons, the banqueting utensils and the wardrobes of costumes. The great golden chariot must stand where it had stood for four thousand years.

They removed the golden death-mask from over Tanus's head, but they left his mummy in the innermost of the golden coffins. Then Nicholas sent for Mai Metemma. The old abbot came with twenty of his monks to receive the holy relic of the ancient saint that he had been promised as his reward. Reverentially, chanting deep and slow, they bore Tanus's coffin away to its new resting place in the *maqdas* of the monastery.

'At least the old hero will be treated with respect,' Royan said softly. Then she looked around the tomb. 'We cannot leave the site like this, with the coffins thrown about and the lids discarded,' Royan protested. 'It looks as though grave-robbers have been at work here.'

'Grave-robbers is exactly what we are.' Nicholas smiled at her.

'No, we are archaeologists,' she denied hotly, 'and we must try to act like it.'

So they replaced the six remaining coffins one within the other, laid them back in the great sarcophagus, and finally replaced the massive stone lid. Only then did Royan allow them to begin selecting and packing the treasures they would take with them.

The death-mask was without any doubt the premier item in the entire tomb. It fitted neatly into one of the crates, with the wooden *ushabti* of Taita laid alongside it, packed with Styrofoam until it was firmly secured. Royan scribbled on the lid in waterproof wax crayon: 'Mask & Taita Ushabti'.

Their final selection was, perforce, hurried and superficial. They could not rip open every one of the cedarwood chests that were piled high in the alcoves of the arcade. The painted and gilded chests themselves were priceless artefacts, and should be treated with respect. So they allowed themselves to be guided by the illustrations on the lid of each. They discovered immediately that these were indeed an accurate inventory and catalogue of the contents. In the chest which showed Pharaoh decked in the blue war crown, they found the actual crown laid on gilded leather pillows that had been moulded to fit it exactly and to protect it.

Even in the short time left to them they became almost surfeited by the magnificence of the items they uncovered as they selected and opened the cedarwood chests. Not only the blue crown, but the red and white crown of the kingdoms united was there, and the splendid Nemes crown, all three in such a miraculous state of preservation that they might have been lifted from Pharaoh's brow that morning.

From the very outset it had to be a prerequisite that any artefact must be small enough to fit into one of the ammunition crates. If it were too large, no matter what its value or historical significance, then it had to be rejected and left in the tomb. Fortunately, many of the cedarwood chests containing the royal jewellery fitted snugly into the metal crates, so that not only the contents but also the chests themselves could be saved. However, the larger items, the crowns and the huge jewelled gold pectoral medallions, had to be repacked.

As the ammunition crates were filled, they carried them down and stacked them on the landing outside the sealed doorway, ready to be carried out. Including the crates that contained the eight statuettes of the gods from the long gallery, they had packed and catalogued forty-eight crates when they heard Sapper's unmistakable accents floating up the staircase.

'Major, where the hell are you? You can't bugger about

in here any longer. Come on, man! Get your hairy arse out of here. The river is in full spate, and the dam is going to burst at any minute.'

Sapper came bounding up the staircase, but even he stopped in wonder and awe as he looked for the first time upon the splendours of the funeral arcade of Pharaoh Mamose. It took some minutes for him to recover from the shock and to revert to his old prosaic self again.

'I mean it, major! It's a matter of minutes, not hours. That ruddy dam is going to go. Apart from that, Mek is fighting in the hills at the head of the chasm. You can hear the gunfire even at the bottom of the cliff in Taita's pool. You and Royan have to get out and fast, I kid you not!'

'Okay, Sapper. We are on our way. Get back to the chamber at the bottom of those stairs. You saw those ammunition crates down there?' Sapper nodded, and Nicholas went on quickly, 'Have the men lug those crates out of here. Get them down to the monastery. I want you to supervise that part of it. We will follow you down the trail with the rest of them.'

'Don't mess around, major. Your life isn't worth a pile of old junk like this. Get moving now.'

'Get on with it, Sapper. But don't let Royan hear you call it a pile of old junk. You could be in really serious trouble.'

Sapper shrugged. 'Don't say I didn't warn you.' He turned and started back down the staircase.

'You know where the boats are stashed,' Nicholas shouted after him. 'If you get there before me, get them inflated and the crates lashed down. We will be right behind you.'

The moment Sapper was gone, Nicholas raced back down the arcade to where Royan was still at work in the treasury.

'That's it!' he shouted at her. 'No more time. Let's get out.'

'Nicky, we can't leave this—'

'Out!' He grabbed her arm. 'We are getting out now. Unless you want to share Tanus's tomb with him on a permanent basis.'

'Can't I just—'

'No, you crazy woman! Now! The dam will go at any moment.'

She broke away from him, snatched up some handfuls of left-over jewellery from the open chest at her feet, and began stuffing them into her pockets.

'I can't leave these.'

He seized her around the waist and swung her over his shoulder. 'I told you I meant it,' he said grimly, and ran with her down the arcade.

'Nicky! Put me down.' She kicked with outrage, but he continued running down into the chamber at the foot of the staircase.

Hansith and his men were carrying the last few packed ammunition crates up the staircase on the far side of the chamber. They balanced the crates easily on their heads and went up the steps with alacrity.

Here Nicholas set Royan down on her own feet again. 'Will you promise to behave now? We aren't playing games. This is deadly serious – I mean deadly, if we get trapped down here.'

'I know.' She looked contrite. 'I just couldn't bear to leave the rest of it.'

'Enough of that. Let's go.' Nicholas grabbed her hand and dragged her after him. After the first few steps she shook her hand free and started to run in earnest, outstripping him and reaching the top of the staircase a few paces ahead of him.

Even under their burdens the porters were making good time. Caught up in the long hurrying column, Nicholas and Royan wound their way back through the maze, grateful for the signposts at each corner, and made it

613

down the central staircase into the ruined long gallery without taking a wrong turning. Sapper was waiting for them at the ruins of the sealed doorway, and grunted with relief when he saw them amongst the porters.

'I thought I told you to go on ahead and get the boats ready,' Nicholas shouted at him.

'Couldn't trust you not to be bloody stupid.' Sapper looked miserable. 'Wanted to make sure you didn't hang about in there.'

'I am touched, Sapper.' Nicholas punched his shoulder, and then they ran down the approach tunnel and clattered over the bridge across the sink-hole.

'Where is Mek?' Nicholas panted at Sapper's back as he jogged in front of him. 'Have you seen Tessay?'

'Tessay is back. She had a nasty experience. She was in a terrible mess. Seems she got badly knocked about.'

'What has happened to her?' Nicholas was appalled. 'Where is she?'

'It looks like she fell into the hands of von Schiller's gorillas and they beat the hell out of her. Mek's men are taking her down to the monastery. She will wait for us at the boats.'

'Thank God for that,' Nicholas muttered, and then louder, 'What about Mek?'

'He is trying to hold off Nogo's attack. I have been hearing rifle fire and grenades and mortar shells all morning. He too is going to fall back and wait for us at the boats.'

They ran the last few yards down the tunnel ankle-deep in slush and water, and at last crawled over the wall of the coffer dam on to the rocky ledge around Taita's pool. Nicholas looked up to see Hansith's porters scrambling up the bamboo scaffolding ladder towards the top of the cliff, each of them hauling up one of the ammunition crates.

At that moment he caught a sound that he recognized

instantly. He cocked his head to listen and then told Royan grimly, 'Gunfire! Mek is fighting it out, but it's pretty darned close.'

'My bag!' Royan started towards her thatched shelter at the foot of the cliff. 'I must get my kit.'

'You won't need your make-up or your pyjamas, and I've got your passport.' He seized her arm and turned her back towards the foot of the ladder. 'In fact the only thing you need now is plenty of space between you and Colonel Nogo. Come along, Royan!'

They swarmed up the bamboo scaffolding and when they reached the cliff top Royan was surprised to discover that, although the earth was wet underfoot from the recent rain squalls, the sun was high and hot. She had lost all sense of time in the cold, gloomy passages of the tomb, and now she held up her face to the sunlight and drank it in gratefully for a moment while Nicholas checked the porters and made certain that they were all out of the chasm.

Sapper set off at the head of the column along the trail through the thorn forest, with the file of porters strung out behind him. Nicholas and Royan waited until all the men were on the pathway before they themselves brought up the rear of the column. The sound of the fighting was frighteningly close now. It seemed to be almost at the brink of the chasm close behind them, less than half a mile away. The crackle of automatic fire gave a spring and a lift to the feet of the porters, and the entire party raced back through the forest to reach the main trail down to the monastery before they were cut off by Nogo's advance.

Before they reached the junction of the paths, they ran into a party of stretcher-bearers carrying a litter. They too were headed down towards the monastery. Nicholas thought the person they were carrying was one of the wounded guerrillas of Mek's force. But even when he caught up with them it took a moment for him to recognize Tessay's swollen and burned face.

'Tessay!' He stooped over her. 'Who did this to you?'

She looked up at him with the huge dark eyes of a wounded child, and told him in halting, broken words.

'Helm!' Nicholas blurted. 'I'd love to get my hands on that bastard.' At that moment Royan caught up with them, and she let out a small cry of horror as she saw Tessay's face. Then immediately she took charge of her.

Nicholas spoke quickly to one of the stretcher-bearers whom he recognized.

'Mezra, what is happening out there?'

'Nogo moved a force in from the east of the gorge. They outflanked us, and we are pulling out. This is not our kind of fighting.'

'I know,' Nicholas remarked grimly. 'Guerrillas must keep moving. Where is Mek Nimmur?'

'He is retreating down the eastern bank of the chasm.' As Mezra replied, they heard a renewed outburst of firing behind them. 'That is him!' Mezra nodded. 'Nogo is pushing him hard.'

'What are your orders?'

'To take Lady Sun to the boats and wait for Mek Nimmur there.'

'Good!' Nicholas told him. 'We will go with you.'

The Jet Ranger was flying low, hugging the contours of the land, never cresting the high ground. Helm knew that Mek Nimmur's *shufta* were armed with RPGs, rocket-launchers. In the hands of a trained man, these were deadly weapons against a slow-flying, unarmoured aircraft such as the Jet Ranger. The pilot's defence was to use the terrain as cover, weaving and twisting up the valleys so as to deny the rocketeers a clear shot.

Although the rain clouds were slumping down the escarpment into the Abbay gorge, the helicopter was keeping well below them. However, the sudden squalls of wind rocked the machine dangerously and splatterings of heavy raindrops rattled against the windshield. The pilot sat forward in the seat, leaning against his shoulder-straps as he concentrated on this dangerous low flying in these unpleasant conditions. Helm sat in the right-hand seat, beside the pilot. Von Schiller and Nahoot Guddabi were together in the rear passenger seat, both of them craning nervously to peer out of the side windows as the heavily wooded slopes of the valley streamed past, seemingly close enough to touch.

Every few minutes the radio crackled into life, and they could hear the terse transmissions of Nogo's men on the ground calling for mortar support or reporting objectives attained. The pilot translated the radio gabble for them, twisting round in his seat to tell von Schiller, 'There is a sharp fire-fight going on along the top of the chasm, but the *shufta* are on the run. Nogo is handling his force well. They have just dislodged a strong force from the hillside to the east of us,' he pointed out of the left-hand port, 'and they are hammering the *shufta* with mortars as they run.'

'Have they reached the spot in the chasm where Quenton-Harper was working?'

'It isn't clear. All a bit confused.' The pilot listened to the next burst of Arabic on the radio. 'I think that was Nogo himself speaking just then.'

'Call him up!' von Schiller ordered Helm, leaning over the back of his seat. 'Ask him if they have secured the tomb site yet.'

Helm reached across and lifted the microphone off its hook below the instrument panel. 'Rose Petal, this is Bismarck. Do you copy?'

There was a pause filled with static, and then Nogo's voice speaking English. 'Go ahead, Bismarck.'

'Have you secured the primary objective? Over.'

'Affirmative, Bismarck. All secured. All opposition suppressed. I am sending men down the ladder to clear the workings.'

Helm swivelled in his seat to look back at von Schiller. 'Nogo has men in the chasm already. We can go in and land.'

'Tell him not to let any of his men into the workings before I arrive,' von Schiller ordered sternly, but his expression was triumphant. 'I must be the first in there. Make him understand that.'

While Helm relayed his orders to Nogo, von Schiller tapped the pilot on the shoulder. 'How long to the objective?'

'About five minutes' flying time, sir.'

'Circle the site when you arrive. Don't land until we are sure Nogo has it under his control.'

The pilot lifted the collective and the sound of the rotors altered as they changed pitch. The helicopter slowed and then hovered in mid-air, while the pilot pointed down.

'What is it?' von Schiller followed his gesture. 'What do you see?'

'The dam,' Helm answered. 'Quenton-Harper's dam. He did a load of work down there.'

The wide body of trapped water gleamed grey and sullen under the rain clouds, tainted with the run-off from the highlands. The water diverted into the side canal boiled white and angrily down into the long valley.

'Deserted!' Helm commented. 'All Harper's men have pulled out.'

'What is that yellow object on the bank?' von Schiller wanted to know.

'That's the earth-moving machine. You remember? My informer told us about it.'

'Don't waste any more time,' von Schiller ordered. 'Nothing more to see here. Let's get on!'

Helm tapped the pilot's shoulder, and gestured downstream.

Sapper was waiting for them to catch up at the junction of the trail, where the diverted river was roaring down the valley in a torrent and had washed out a long section of the original track. The porters, strung out in a long line down the valley, each with an ammunition crate balanced on his head, were picking their way along the higher ground above the water.

Tessay's litter was near the rear of the column, with Royan and Nicholas trotting on each side of it and steadying it over the rough and uneven sections of the path.

'Where is Hansith?' Nicholas shouted at Sapper, shading his eyes to check the men ahead of him, and trying to pick out the big monk's distinctive form from amongst the others in the caravan.

'I thought he was with you,' Sapper shouted back. 'I haven't seen him since we left the chasm.'

Nicholas turned and stared back the way they had come, along the footpath through the thorn forest.

'Damn the man,' he grunted. 'We can't go back to look for him. He will have to make his own way down to the monastery.'

At that moment they heard the faint but familiar flutter of rotors in the hot, humid air below the lowering cloud masses.

'The Pegasus chopper! Sounds as though von Schiller is heading directly for Taita's pool. He must have known all along exactly where we were working,' said Nicholas bitterly. 'Not wasting any time. Like a vulture coming in to a fresh carcass.'

Royan was also looking up at the sound, trying to pick out the shape of the aircraft against the dark clouds. Her face was flushed from the run, the tendrils of sweat-damp hair dangled down her cheeks. 'If those swine are allowed to enter our tomb it will be a dreadful desecration of a sacred place,' she said angrily.

Suddenly Nicholas reached across the litter and took her arm. His expression was stern and determined. 'You are right. Go on down to the monastery with Tessay. I will follow you later.' Before she could protest or question him, he strode across to Sapper.

'I am putting the two women in your care, Sapper. Look after them.'

'Where are you going, Nicky?' Royan had come up behind him, and overheard his orders to Sapper. 'What are you going to do?'

'One little chore. Won't take me long.'

'You aren't going back there?' She was horrified. 'You will get yourself killed or worse. You saw what Helm did to Tessay—'

'Don't fuss yourself, my love,' he laughed, and before she realized what he intended he kissed her full on the lips. While she was still flustered and confused by this display in front of so many men, he pushed her gently away.

'Take care of Tessay. I will meet you at the boats.'

Before she could protest further, he turned and struck out up the valley at a long-legged lope which carried him over the rough terrain so swiftly that she had no further chance to prevent him.

'Nicky!' she screamed after him despairingly, but he pretended not to hear and kept going, following the diverted river upstream, back towards the dam.

The Jet Ranger followed the convoluted course of the river below the dam. At moments they could look directly down into the narrow gap between the high cliffs, into the shaded depths of the chasm, almost dry now, with only the occasional gleam of the shrunken and still pools.

'There they are!' Helm pointed dead ahead. There was a small cluster of men on the brink of the chasm.

'Make sure they aren't *shufta*!' There was fear in von Schiller's voice.

'No!' Helm reassured him loudly. 'I recognize Nogo, and that tall one beside him in the white *shamma* is the monk Hansith Sherif, our informer.' He shouted above the engine beat at the pilot, 'You can go in and land. There! Nogo is waving you in!'

The moment the skids of the helicopter touched the ground, both Nogo and Hansith ran forward. Between them they helped von Schiller down from the passenger cabin and hustled him clear of the spinning rotors.

'My men have secured the area,' Nogo assured him. 'We have driven the *shufta* down the valley towards the river. This man is Hansith Sherif, who has been working beside Harper in the tomb. He knows every inch of the tunnels.'

'Does he speak English?' Von Schiller looked up at the tall monk eagerly.

'A little bit,' Hansith answered for himself.

'Good! Good!' Von Schiller beamed at him. 'Show me the way. I will follow you. Come on, Guddabi, it's about time you did some work for the money I am paying you.'

Hansith led them quickly to the head of the scaffolding, where von Schiller paused and looked down nervously into the gloomy depths of the chasm. The bamboo framework seemed flimsy and rickety, the drop deep and terrifying. Von Schiller was on the point of protesting when Nahoot Guddabi whimpered behind him.

'He does not expect us to climb down there, does he?'

His terror bolstered von Schiller immediately, and he turned on Nahoot with relish. 'It is the only access to the tomb. Follow the man down. I will be close behind you.'

When Nahoot still hesitated, Helm put a calloused hand in the small of his back and shoved him forward.

'Get on with it. You are wasting time.'

Reluctantly Nahoot started down the scaffolding after the monk, and von Schiller followed him. The framework of bamboo shook and swayed under their combined weight and the drop to the rocks below sucked at them, but at last they reached the ledge beside Taita's pool. There they stood in a small group, staring about them in awe and wonder.

'Where is the tunnel?' von Schiller demanded as soon as he had regained his breath, and Hansith beckoned to him to follow him to the wall of the small coffer dam.

Here von Schiller paused and looked around at Helm and Nogo. 'I want you to remain on guard here. I will enter the tomb with Guddabi and this monk. I will send for you when you are needed.'

'I would feel happier to be with you, to protect you, Herr von Schiller—' Helm began, but the old man frowned at him.

'Do as I tell you!' And with Hansith steadying him he climbed stiffly down the wall of the coffer dam into the mouth of the tunnel. Nahoot Guddabi followed him closely.

'The lights? Where does the power come from?' von Schiller wanted to know.

'There is a machine,' Hansith explained, and at that moment they heard the soft burble of the generator ahead of them. None of them spoke again as they moved down the entrance tunnel after Hansith, until they reached the bridge over the dark waters of the sink-hole.

'This is very rough construction,' Nahoot muttered, his uneasiness at last giving way to professional interest. 'It does not remind me of any other Egyptian tomb I have ever inspected. I think we may have been misled. It is probably some native Ethiopian workings.'

'You are making a premature judgement,' von Schiller admonished him. 'Wait until we have seen the rest of what this man has to show us.'

Von Schiller steadied himself with a hand on Hansith's shoulder as they crossed the bobbing pontoons of baobab wood, and he scrambled ashore on the far side with relief. They started up the rising section of the tunnel and passed the high-water mark.

As soon as the construction of the walls changed to packed and dressed stone, Nahoot remarked on it. 'Ah! I was disappointed at first. I thought we had been duped, but now one can see the Egyptian influence.'

They reached the landing outside the ruined gallery on which stood the Honda generator. By now both von Schiller and Nahoot were sweating with exertion and trembling with excitement.

'This looks more and more promising. It may very well be a royal tomb,' Nahoot exulted. Von Schiller pointed to the plaster seals stacked against the side wall where Nicholas and Royan had abandoned them. Nahoot fell to his knees beside them and examined them eagerly, his voice trembling as he cried out.

'The cartouche of Mamose, and the seal of the scribe Taita!' He looked up at von Schiller with shining eyes, 'There can be no doubts now. I have led you to the tomb as I promised you I would.'

For a moment von Schiller stared at him, speechless in the face of such bare-faced arrogance. Then he snorted with disgust and stooped to peer through the open doorway into the long gallery.

'This has been destroyed!' he cried in horror. 'The tomb has been annihilated.'

'No, no!' Hansith assured him. 'Come this way. There is another tunnel beyond.'

As they picked their way through the rubble and wreckage, Hansith told them in halting, broken English how the roof of the gallery had collapsed, and how he, Hansith, had found the true entrance under the ruins.

Nahoot stopped every few paces to examine and exclaim over the scraps of painted plaster that had survived the fall of the roof. 'These must have been magnificent. Classical work of the highest order—'

'There is more to show you. Much more,' Hansith promised them, and von Schiller snarled at Nahoot.

'Leave these damaged sections now. Time is running out on us. We must hurry on directly to the burial chamber.'

Hansith led them up the hidden staircase into the maze of the bao, and then through the twists and turns to the lowest level.

'How did Harper and the woman ever find their way through this?' von Schiller marvelled. 'It's a rabbit warren.'

'Another concealed staircase!' Nahoot was amazed, and stuttered with excitement as they descended into the gas trap where the ranks of amphorae had stood undisturbed for thousands of years, and then climbed the last flight of stairs to the beginning of the funeral arcade.

Now both of them were stunned by the splendour of the murals and the majesty of the great god images that guarded the length of the arcade. They stood side by side unable to move, frozen with awe as they gazed about them.

'I never expected anything like this,' von Schiller whispered. 'This exceeds anything that I ever hoped for.'

'The rooms on each side are filled with treasures.' Hansith pointed down the arcade. 'There are such things as you have never dreamed. Harper was able to take very little with him – a few small boxes. He has left piles of goods, stacks of chests.'

'Where is the coffin? Where is the body that was in the tomb?' von Schiller demanded.

'Harper has given the body, in its golden coffin, to the abbot. They have taken it away to the monastery.'

'Nogo will soon fetch it back for us. You need not worry about that, Herr von Schiller,' Nahoot assured him.

As though the spell that held them was shattered by this promise, they started forward together, slowly at first, and then both of them began to run. Von Schiller tottered into the nearest store room on his old, stiff legs, and giggled like a child on Christmas morning as he gazed upon the piled treasures. 'Incredible!'

He dragged down one of the cedarwood chests from the nearest stack, and ripped off the lid with trembling fingers. When he saw the contents he was struck speechless. He knelt over the chest and began to weep softly with emotion too overwhelming to express in words.

Nicholas was banking on the fact that Nogo's men would be driving along the cliff tops to reach Taita's pool, and that he would have a free run up the course of the diverted stream to the dam site. He took no precautions against running into them, other than to pause every few minutes to listen and peer ahead. He knew that he had little time left to him. He could not expect the rest of the party to wait for him at the boats and endanger themselves for this whimsy of his.

Twice he heard automatic gunfire in the distance, coming from the direction of the chasm, down towards the pool. However, the chance he took paid off, and he reached the dam site without running into any of Nogo's forces. He did not, however, push his luck too far. Before approaching the dam openly, he climbed the hillside above it and surveyed the area. It gave him time to recover from the hard run up the valley, and to check that Nogo had not left men to guard the dam, although he considered this unlikely.

He could see that the yellow front-loader tractor was still parked on the bank high above the wall where Sapper had left it. He could also see no sign of any human presence, no armed Ethiopian army guards. He grunted with relief and wiped the sweat out of his eyes with his shirtsleeve.

Even with his naked eye he could see that the water was lapping the top of the wall and squirting through the gaps and chinks between the gabions. Yet from where he stood the wall still seemed to be holding well, and it would need another foot rise in the level of the backed-up river to overturn it.

'Well done, Sapper,' he thought, grinning. 'You did a hell of a job.'

Nicholas studied the level of the river and the condition of the waters that were being held back by the wall. The flow down from the mountains was much stronger than when he had last been here. The river bed was brimming from bank to bank, and some of the trees and bushes at the edge were already partially submerged, bowing and nodding as the swift current tugged at them. The flood was a sullen grey colour, fast and hostile, swirling into the pond of the dam before finding the outlet into the side channel and tearing down it, growling like a wild animal released from its cage, brimming into spume and white water as it felt the sharp fall into the valley.

Next he looked towards the escarpment of the gorge. It was blotted out by banks of dark, menacing cloud that obscured the northern horizon. At that moment a squall of wind swept over him, cold with the threat of rain. He needed no further urging and started down the slope towards the dam, slipping and sliding in his haste. Before he reached the bottom, the squall of wind had turned to cold rain. It flung needles into his face and plastered his shirt to his body.

He reached the tractor and scrambled up into the driver's seat. There was a moment of panic when he thought that Sapper might have removed the key from its hiding-place under the seat. He scrabbled for it for a few seconds until his fingers closed over it, and then let out a sigh of relief.

'Sapper, for a moment there you were very close to death. I would have broken your neck with my own hands.'

He thrust the key into the ignition lock and turned it to the pre-heat position, waiting for the coil light on the dashboard to turn from red to green.

'Come on!' he muttered impatiently. Those few seconds of delay seemed like a lifetime. Then the green light flashed and he twisted the key to start.

The engine fired at the first turn and Nicholas hooted, 'Full marks, Sapper. All is forgiven.'

He gave the machine time to warm up to optimum operating temperature, slitting his eyes against the rain as he waited and looking around at the hills above him, fearful that the sound of the engine might bring Nogo's gorillas swarming down on him. However, there was no sign of life on the rainswept heights.

He eased the tractor into her lowest gear and turned her down the bank. Below the dam wall the water that was finding its way through the gaps was less than hub-deep. The tractor bounced and ground its way through the boulder-strewn watercourse. Nicholas stopped the machine in the middle of the river bed while he studied the downstream face of the dam wall for its weakest section. Then he lined up below the centre of the wall, at the point where Sapper had shored up the raft of logs with rows of gabions.

'Sorry for all your hard work,' he apologized to Sapper, as he manoeuvred the steel scoop of the tractor to the right height and angle before attacking the wall. He worried the gabion he had selected out of its niche in the row, reversing and thrusting at it until he could get the scoop under it and drag it free. He pulled away and dropped the heavy wire mesh basket over the waterfall, then drove back and renewed the attack.

It was slow work. The pressure of the water had wedged in the gabions, keying them into the wall so it took almost ten minutes to free the second basket. As he dropped that one over the waterfall, he glanced for the first time at the fuel gauge on the dashboard of the tractor and his heart sank. It was registering empty. Sapper must have neglected to refuel it: either he had exhausted the fuel supply or he had not expected ever to use the machine again when he abandoned it.

Even as Nicholas thought about it the engine stuttered as it starved. He reversed it sharply, changing the angle of inclination so that the remaining fuel in the tank could slosh forward. The engine caught and cleared, running smoothly and strongly once again. Quickly he changed gear and ran back at the wall.

'No more time for finesse,' he told himself grimly. 'From here on in it's brute force and muscle.'

By removing two of the gabions he had exposed a corner of the log raft behind them. This was the vulnerable part of the wall. He worked the hydraulic controls and lifted the scoop to its highest travel. Then he lowered it carefully, an inch at a time, until it hooked over the end of the thickest log in the jam. He locked the hydraulics and thrust the tractor into reverse, gradually pouring on full power until the engine was roaring and blowing out a cloud of thick blue diesel smoke.

Nothing gave. The log was jammed solidly and the wall was held together by the keying of the gabions into each other and the enormous pressure of water behind them. Despairingly, Nicholas kept the throttle wide open. The lugged tyres spun and skidded on the boulders under them, throwing a tall shower of spray high into the air and churning out loose rock and gravel.

'Come on!' Nicholas pleaded with the machine. 'Come on! You can do it.'

The engine beat faltered again as she starved for fuel. She spluttered and coughed, and almost stalled.

'Please!' Nicholas begged her aloud. 'One more try.'

Almost as if it had heard him, the engine fired again, ran unevenly for a few moments, and then abruptly bellowed at full power again.

'That's it, my beauty,' Nicholas yelled, as it lurched and hammered against the wall.

With a sound like a cannon shot the log snapped and the top end of it flew out of the wall, leaving a long, deep hole through which the river poured triumphantly, a thick, solid column of dirty grey water.

'Thar she blows!' Nicholas shouted, jumping down from the driver's seat. He knew there was not enough time left for him to drive the tractor out of the river bed. He could move more quickly on his own feet.

The current seized his legs, trying to pull them out from under him. It was like one of those childhood nightmares when monsters were pursuing him and, despite his every effort, his legs would only move in slow motion. He glanced back over his shoulder, and at that instant he saw the central section of the dam wall burst, blowing outward in a violent eruption of furious waters. He struggled on another few paces towards the bank before the deep and turbulent tide picked him up. He was helpless in its grip. It swept him away, over the waterfall and down, down into the hungry maw of the chasm.

'These are the royal crook and sceptre of the Pharaoh,' cried von Schiller in a voice that was gusty and faint with emotion as he lifted them out of the cedarwood chest.

'And this is his false beard and his ceremonial pectoral

emblem.' Nahoot knelt beside him on the floor of the tomb under the great statue of Osiris. All the ill feelings between them were forgotten in the wonder of the moment as they examined the fabulous treasures of Egypt.

'This is the greatest archaeological discovery of all time,' von Schiller whispered, his voice tremulous. He pulled his handkerchief from his pocket and dabbed at the perspiration of excitement that trickled down his cheeks.

'There is years of work here,' Nahoot told him seriously. 'This incredible collection will have to be catalogued and evaluated. It will be known for ever as the von Schiller hoard. Your name will be perpetuated for all time. It is like the Egyptian dream of immortality. You will never be forgotten. You will live for ever.'

A rapturous expression crossed von Schiller's features. He had not considered that possibility. Up until this moment he had not considered sharing this treasure with anybody, except in his particular way with Utte Kemper, but Nahoot's words had awakened in him the old impossible dream of eternity. Perhaps he might make arrangements for it to be made accessible to the public – but only after his own death, naturally.

Then he thrust the temptation aside. He would not debase this treasure by making it available to the common rabble. It had been assembled for the funeral of a pharaoh. Von Schiller saw himself as the modern equivalent of a pharaoh.

'No!' he told Nahoot violently. 'This is mine, all mine. When I die it will go with me, all of it. I have made the arrangements already, in my will. My sons know what to do. This will all be with me in my own grave. My royal grave.'

Nahoot stared at him aghast. He had not realized until that moment that the old man was mad, that his obsessions had driven him over the edge of sanity. But the Egyptian knew that there was no point in arguing with him now –

later he would find a way to save this marvellous treasure from the oblivion of another tomb. So he bowed his head in mock acquiescence.

'You are right, Herr von Schiller. That is the only fitting manner to dispose of it. You deserve that form of burial. However, our main concern now must be to get all of it to safety. Helm has warned us about the danger of the river, of the dam bursting. We must call him and Nogo. Nogo's men must clear out the tomb. We can ferry the treasure in the helicopter up to the Pegasus camp, where I can pack it securely for the journey to Germany.'

'Yes. Yes.' Von Schiller scrambled to his feet, suddenly terrified at the prospect of being deprived of this wondrous hoard by the flooded river. 'Send the monk, what is his name, Hansith, send him to call Helm. He must come at once.'

Nahoot jumped up to his feet. 'Hansith!' he shouted. 'Where are you?'

The monk had been waiting at the entrance to the burial chamber, kneeling in prayer before the empty sarcophagus which had contained the body of the saint. He was torn now between religious conviction and greed. When he heard his name called he genuflected deeply, and then rose and hurried back to join von Schiller and Nahoot.

'You must go back to the pool where we left the others—' Nahoot started to relay the orders, but suddenly a strange, distracted expression crossed Hansith's darkly handsome features and he held up his hand for silence.

'What is it?' Nahoot demanded angrily. 'What is it that you can hear?'

Hansith shook his head. 'Be quiet! Listen! Can't you hear it?'

'There is nothing—' Nahoot began, but then broke off suddenly, and wild terror filled his dark eyes.

There was the softest sound, gentle as the sigh of a summer zephyr, lulling and low.

'What do you hear?' von Schiller demanded. His hearing had long ago deteriorated, and the sound was far beyond the range of his old ears.

'Water!' whispered Nahoot. 'Running water!'

'The river!' shouted Hansith. 'The tunnel is flooding!' He whirled round and went bounding down the funeral arcade with long, lithe strides.

'We will be trapped in here!' screamed Nahoot, and raced after him.

'Wait for me,' von Schiller yelled, and tried to follow. But he soon fell behind the two much younger men.

The monk, however, was far ahead of both of them as he took the flight of stairs up from the gas trap two at a time.

'Hansith! Come back! I order you,' Nahoot cried despairingly in his wake, but he caught only a flash of the monk's white robe as he darted into the first twist of the labyrinth.

'Guddabi, where are you?' von Schiller's voice quavered and echoed through the stone corridors. But Nahoot did not reply as he ran on in the direction which he thought the monk had taken, passing the first turn in the maze without even glancing at the chalk marks on the wall. He thought he heard Hansith's racing footsteps ahead of him, but by the time he had turned the third corner he knew he was lost.

He stopped with his heart racing savagely and the bitter gall of terror in the back of his throat.

'Hansith! Where are you?' he screamed wildly.

Von Schiller's voice came back to him, ringing weirdly down the passageways, 'Guddabi! Guddabi! Don't leave me here.'

'Shut up!' he screamed. 'Keep quiet, you old fool!'

Panting heavily, the blood pounding in his ears, he

tried to listen for the sound of Hansith's feet. But he heard only the sound of the river. The gentle susurration seemed to emanate from the very walls around him.

'No! Don't leave me here,' he screamed, and began to run without direction, panic-stricken, through the maze.

Hansith took each twist and turn unerringly, with the terror of dreadful death driving his feet. But at the head of the central staircase his ankle twisted under him and he fell heavily. He tumbled down the steeply inclined shaft, bumping and rolling the full length, gathering speed as he went until he reached the bottom and lay sprawled on the agate tiles of the long gallery.

He dragged himself to his feet, bruised and shaken by the fall, and tried to run on. But his leg gave way under him again, and he fell in a tangle. His ankle was badly sprained and would not carry his weight. Nevertheless he dragged himself up a second time and hobbled down the gallery, supporting himself with one hand on the shattered wall.

When he reached the doorway and crawled through it on to the landing beside the generator the sound of the water came up the tunnel. It was much louder now – a low, reverberating growl which almost blotted out the soft, discreet hum of the generator.

'Sweet loving Christ and the Virgin, save me!' he pleaded as he staggered and lurched down the tunnel, falling twice more before he reached the lower level.

On his knees he peered ahead, and in the glare of the electric lights strung along the roof of the tunnel he could make out the sink-hole below him. He did not at first recognize it, for it had all changed. The water level was no longer lower than the paved floor on which he sprawled. It was brimming, a great swirling maelstrom, and the water pouring into it was being sucked away through the hidden outlet almost as fast as it entered from the tunnel mouth on the far side. The pontoon bridge was tangled and half-submerged, bobbing and canting and rearing as it fought its retaining cables like an unbroken horse on a tether.

From Taita's pool a roaring river of water was boring down the far branch of the tunnel across the sink-hole. The tunnel was flooding rapidly, the water already reaching halfway up the walls, but he knew that it was the only escape route from the tomb. Every moment he delayed, the flood became stronger.

'I have to get out through there.' He pushed himself to his feet again.

He reached the first pontoon of the bridge, but it was careering about so madly that he dared not attempt to remain upright upon it. He dropped to his hands and knees, crawled out on to the flimsy structure and managed to drag himself forward from one pontoon to the next.

'Please God and St Michael help me. Don't let me die like this,' he prayed aloud. He reached the far side of the sink-hole and groped for a handhold on the roughly hewn walls of the tunnel.

He found a hold with his fingertips and pulled himself into the mouth of the tunnel, but now the full force of the water pouring down the shaft struck his lower body. He hung there for a moment, pinned by the raging waters, unable to move a pace forward. He knew that if his grip failed he would be swept back into the sink-hole and sucked down into those terrible black depths.

The electric bulbs strung along the roof of the tunnel ahead of him still burned brightly, so that he could see almost to the open basin of Taita's pool where the bamboo scaffolding would offer escape to the top of the chasm. It was only two hundred feet ahead of him. He gathered all his strength and pulled himself forward against the raging waters, reaching forward from one precarious handhold to the next. His fingernails tore and the flesh smeared from the tips of his fingers on the jagged rock, but he forced his way onwards.

At last he could see daylight ahead of him, filtering from Taita's pool. Only another forty feet to go, and he realized with a surge of relief and joy that he was going to make it out of the deadly trap of the shaft. Then he heard a fresh sound, a harsher, more brutal roar as the full flood of the burst dam poured down the waterfall into Taita's pool. It found the entrance to the tunnel and came down it in a solid wave, filling the passageway to the roof, ripping out the wiring of the lights and plunging Hansith into darkness.

It struck him with such force that it seemed to be not mere water but the solid rock of an avalanche, and he could not resist it. It tore him from his insecure perch and plucked him away, tossing him backwards, spinning him down the length of the shaft that he had gained with so much effort, and hurling him into the sink-hole beyond. He was swirled end over end by the crazed waters. In the darkness and wild confusion he did not know which direction was up and which down, but it made no difference for he could not swim against its power.

Then the sink-hole seized him full in its grip and sucked him swiftly and deeply down. The pressure of the water began to crush him. One of his eardrums burst, and as he opened his mouth to scream at the agony of it the water spurted down his throat and flooded his lungs. The last thing he ever felt was when he was flung against the side wall of the sink-hole, travelling as fast as the falling waters, and the bones of his right shoulder shattered. He could not scream again through his sodden lungs, but soon the pain faded into oblivion.

As his corpse was drawn swiftly through the subterranean shaft it became mangled and dismembered on the jagged rock sides, and was no longer recognizable as human by the time it was discharged through the butterfly fountain on the far side of the mountain. From there the torn fragments were washed down the diverted Dandera river to join, at last, the wider and more stately waters of the Blue Nile.

The waters pouring through the gap in the dam wall picked up the yellow front-loader and tumbled it over the waterfall into the chasm as though it were a child's toy. Nicholas had a glimpse of it in the air below him. Even as he fell himself, he realized that if he had stayed with the machine he would have been crushed beneath it. The huge machine struck the surface of the pool in a fountain of white spray and disappeared.

Nicholas followed it down, falling free, even managing to keep his head uppermost, feet foremost, as he swooped down the waterfall. The flood that carried him cushioned his fall, so that instead of being dashed against the exposed boulders at the bottom, he bounced and tumbled in the racing torrent. He came to the surface fifty yards downstream, tossed his wet hair out of his eyes and glanced around him quickly.

The tractor was gone, swallowed deep into the pool at the foot of the waterfall, but ahead of him was a small island of rock in the middle of the river. With a dozen overarm strokes he swam to it and clung to a rocky spur. From there he looked up at the sheer walls of the chasm and remembered the last time he had been trapped down here. The elation he had felt at the destruction of the dam and the flooding of Pharaoh's tomb evaporated.

He knew that he would not be able to climb those slick, water-smoothed cliffs that offered no handholds and which belled outwards in an overhang over his head. Instead he weighed the chances of working his way back upstream to the foot of the falls. From here it looked as though there was some sort of funnel or crevice up the east side of the chute which might offer a ladderway to the top, but it would be a hard and dangerous climb.

The volume of water coming over the falls was not as heavy as he had expected, considering the vast body of water that was being held back by the dam. He realized then that the greater part of the wall of gabions must still be in place and that this torrent was only the result of water escaping through the narrow gap he had torn in the centre of the wall. The remaining gabions must still be holding in place under their own weight. However, he realized that they could not hold much longer and that the river must soon plough them aside and burst through in full force. So he abandoned the idea of swimming back to the foot of the falls.

'Have to get out of its way,' he thought desperately, as he imagined being caught up in the terrible flood which would certainly come down at any moment. 'If I can reach the side somewhere, perhaps find a ledge, climb above the flood.' But he knew it was a forlorn hope. He had swum the length of the canyon once before without finding a handhold on the slick walls.

'Swim ahead of it?' he thought. 'A slim chance, but the only one I have.' He kicked off his boots, and gathered himself. He was about to push off from his temporary refuge, when he heard the rest of the dam wall high above him give way.

There was a rumbling roar, the crackle of logs snapping and breaking, the grating and grinding of heavy gabions being thrown around like empty rubbish cans, and then suddenly and terrifyingly a solid wave of grey water burst over the top of the falls, carrying with it a wall of trash and debris.

'Oh mother! Too late. Here comes the big one!'

He shoved off from his rock, turning downstream, and swam with all his strength, kicking and flailing his arms in a wild crawl stroke. He heard the roar of the approaching wave and glanced back over his shoulder. It was overhauling him swiftly, filling the chasm from wall to wall, fifteen feet high and curling at the top. He had a fleeting mental image from his youth, waiting to surf that notorious wave at Cape St Vincent, hanging on the line-up and seeing it humping up behind him, this great wall of water, so mountainous and so overwhelming.

'Ride it!' he told himself, judging the moment. 'Catch it like a slider.'

He clawed through the water, trying to get up speed to ride up the wall. He felt it seize him and lift him so violently that his guts swooped, and then he was on the crest of it. He arched his back and tucked his arms behind him in the classic body-surfer's position, hanging in the face of the wave, slightly head down, the front half of his body thrust clear of the water, steering with his legs. After the first few terrifying seconds he realized that he was riding her high and had some control; his panic abated and he was overcome by a sense of wild exhilaration.

'Twenty knots!' He estimated his speed by the giddy blur of the canyon walls passing him on either side. He steered away from the nearest wall, sliding across the face, taking up station in the centre of the wave. He was carried along by the wave and by the thrilling sensation of speed and danger.

The increased depth of water in the chasm covered the dangerous, knife-sharp rocks, enabling him to ride clear of them. It smoothed out the waterfalls and the chutes, so that instead of dropping down them and plummeting below the surface of the pool beneath he slid down them with a smooth rush, holding his position in the face of the wave with a few quick overarm strokes or a kick of the legs.

'Hell! This is fun!' He laughed aloud. 'People would pay money to do this. Beats the hell out of bungee jumping.'

Within the first mile the wave began to lose its shape and impetus as it spread out down the canyon. Soon it would no longer have the power to hold him up in the surfing position, and he glanced around him swiftly. Floating near by, keeping pace with him in the flotsam of debris from the dam, was one of the treetrunks that had formed part of the raft with which Sapper had plugged the gap in the wall.

He steered across to this ponderous piece of timber. It was thirty feet long and floated low in the flood, its back showing like that of a whale. Its branches had been roughly hacked away by the axemen, and the spikes that remained provided secure handholds. Nicholas pulled himself up on to the treetrunk, lying on his belly, facing downstream, with his legs still dangling in the water. Swiftly he recovered his breath and felt his full strength returning.

Although it had smoothed out and lost its wave formation, the flood was still tearing down the chasm at a tremendous pace. 'Still not much under ten knots,' he estimated. 'When this lot hits Taita's pool, I pity von Schiller and any of his uglies who are in the tomb. They are going to stay in there for the next four thousand years.' He threw back his head and laughed triumphantly. 'It worked! Damn me to hell, if it didn't work just the way I planned it.'

He stopped laughing abruptly as he felt the treetrunk veer across the river towards one of the canyon walls.

'Oh, oh! More trouble.'

He rolled to one side of the treetrunk and kicked out strongly. His ungainly vessel responded, swinging heavily across the current. It was sluggish steering, not enough to avoid contact with the rock wall entirely, but instead of striking full-on it was merely a glancing collision that pushed him back again into the main flow of the current.

He was gaining confidence and expertise every moment, 'I can ride her all the way down to the monastery!'

he exclaimed delightedly. 'At this rate of knots I might even get to the boats before Sapper and Royan.'

Looking ahead, he recognized this stretch of the chasm that he was hurtling through.

'This is the bend above Taita's pool. Be there in another minute or two. I expect the scaffolding has been washed away by now.'

He pulled himself as high on the log as he could without upsetting its balance, and peered ahead, blinking the water out of his eyes. He saw the head of the falls above Taita's pool racing towards him, and he braced himself for the drop.

The long, smooth chute of racing water opened ahead of him, and the moment before he flew down it he had a glimpse into the basin of rock below it. He saw at once that his expectations had been premature. The bamboo scaffolding had not been entirely washed away, although it was badly damaged. The lowest section was gone, but the upper part hung drunkenly down the rock cliff, just touching the surface of the racing waters. It was swaying and swinging loosely as the current snatched at it, and incredulously he realized that there were at least two men trapped on the flimsy structure, clinging desperately to the ladder-way of lurching, clattering poles. Both of them were trying to claw their way up it to the top of the cliff.

In that fraction of a second Nicholas saw a flash of steel-rimmed spectacles under a maroon beret, and realized that the man nearest the top of the cliff was Tuma Nogo. Then Nogo succeeded in reaching the top of the scaffolding and disappeared over the top of the cliff. That one glance was all Nicholas had time for before his log was plunged into the water-chute, gathering speed until it was tearing downwards at a steeply canted angle. The point dug in as it hit the surface of the pool at the bottom, and the log almost pole-vaulted end over end, but Nicholas clung on to his handholds, and gradually it righted itself.

For a few moments the log was stalled in the vortex below the falls, but almost at once the current grabbed it again and it gathered speed, bearing away down the length of Taita's pool as ponderously as a wooden man-o'-war.

Nicholas had a second of respite in which to look around the basin of Taita's pool. He saw at once that the entrance tunnel to the tomb was entirely submerged and, judging by the water level up the cliff wall, it was already fifty feet or more beneath the surface. He felt a leap of triumph. The tomb was once more protected from the depredations of any other grave-robber.

Then he looked up the battered remnants of the bamboo scaffolding skewed down the cliff, torn half away from the ancient niches in the rock, and he saw the other man still clinging to the wreckage. He was twenty feet above the water level, and seemed frozen there like a cat in the high branches of a windswept tree.

At that moment Nicholas realized that his log was swinging in the grip of the river, curling in towards the dangling scaffold. He was about to try to steer it clear, when the man on the framework high above him turned his head and looked down at him. Nicholas saw that he was a white man, his face a pale blob in the gloom of the canyon, and a moment later he recognized him with a stab of hatred through the chest.

'Helm!' he exclaimed. 'Jake Helm.'

He had an image of Tamre, the epileptic boy, crushed beneath the rockfall, and of Tessay's burned and battered face. His outrage and hatred surged. Instead of steering the log away from the scaffold, he reversed his thrust and swung in towards the cliff. There was a breathless interval when Nicholas thought he might miss, but at the last moment the leading end of the log swung sharply and the point of it crashed into the trailing end of the bamboo, hooking on to it.

The log's weight and momentum were irresistible. The

bamboo poles crackled and snapped like dry kindling, and then the whole rickety structure tore loose from the wall and came crashing down over the log. Helm swung out overhead, then released his grip and dropped feet first into the water close alongside the log. He went deep below the surface. While he was under, Nicholas pulled himself up to sit astride the log and grabbed a length of bamboo pole that had broken off the scaffolding and was floating alongside his perch.

The log was trapped in a back eddy of the swollen river, and now it began to spin slowly in the slack water outside the main current. Nicholas was still riding high on the log. He hefted the bamboo, swinging it back and forth like a baseball bat, to get the feel of it. Then he cocked it over his shoulder and waited for Helm to show himself.

A second later the Texan's head broke out, streaming water. His eyes were screwed closed, and he let out a gasp of water and air and tried to suck in a breath. Nicholas aimed the pole at his head and swung with all his strength, but just at that moment Helm opened his eyes and saw the blow coming.

He was as quick as a water snake, rolling his head under the swinging club so that it merely touched the side of his cropped blond head and then glanced away. Nicholas was thrown off balance by his own swing, and before he could recover Helm had drawn a quick breath and ducked below the surface again.

Nicholas poised the club, ready to strike a second time, peering down into the murky water, muttering angrily at himself for having missed the first blow while he still had the advantage of surprise. He had no illusions about what he was in for, now that Helm had been warned.

The seconds drew out with no sign of his adversary reappearing, and Nicholas looked behind him anxiously, trying to anticipate where he would come up again. For a long minute nothing happened. He lowered the club nervously, and changed his grip so as to be ready to stab in any direction with the sharp broken tip.

Suddenly his left ankle was seized in a crushing grip below the water and, before he could grab a handhold to resist, Nicholas was jerked from his seat on the log and went over backwards into the river. As he plunged beneath the water he felt Helm's fingers clawing at his face. He grabbed one of the fingers and wrenched it back, feeling it snap in his grasp as he forced it back towards its own wrist. But Helm was galvanized by the agony of the dislocated joint, and one of his long muscular arms whipped around Nicholas's neck like the tentacles of an octopus.

The two of them came to the surface for a moment, both of them drew one quick, harsh breath, then Helm forced Nicholas's head backwards and water flooded into his open mouth. The lock on his neck tightened, and he felt the tension on his vertebrae. It was a killer grip. If Helm had only had a solid purchase he could have exerted the last ounce of pressure which would have snapped his spine. But Nicholas kept rolling back in the direction of the thrust, giving with it, and preventing Helm from bringing all his strength to bear. As he went over he saw Helm's face in front of his, magnified and distorted through the tainted grey water. He looked monstrous and evil.

As Helm rolled over the top of him Nicholas locked both hands around his waist to hold him firmly, then brought up his right knee between Helm's legs, hard into his crotch, and felt the bone of his kneecap make contact. The bunch of genitals was full and rubbery; Helm contorted and his lock on Nicholas's neck eased. Nicholas used the slack to reach down and grab a handful of Helm's damaged testicles and twist them savagely. He saw the man's face inches in front of his own twist into a rictus of pain and Helm pulled away from him, releasing his lock on Nicholas's throat and reaching down to grab his wrist with both hands.

Again they came to the surface close alongside the floating log, and Nicholas realized that the current had taken hold of them again and was carrying them away through the outlet of Taita's pool into the full stream of the river. Nicholas released his grip on Helm's balls and with his other hand aimed a punch at his face, but they were too close to each other and the blow lacked power. It glanced off Helm's cheek, and Nicholas tried to lock his extended arm around his neck, going for a headlock himself. Helm hunched his head down on his shoulders, slipping under the hold. Then suddenly he reached forward fast as a striking adder and sank his teeth into Nicholas's chin.

The surprise was complete, and the pain was excruciating as his teeth locked into the flesh. Nicholas shouted and clawed at Helm's face, going for his eyes, trying to drive his fingernails through the lids. But Helm squeezed his eyes tight closed and his teeth cut in ever deeper, so that Nicholas's blood welled up and oozed from the corners of Helm's mouth.

The log was still floating beside them, inches from the back of Helm's head. Nicholas seized his ears, one in each hand, and twisted him around in the water. He could see over the top of Helm's head, while Helm's vision was blocked. There was a nub of raw wood sticking out of the tree trunk where an axe had hacked away a side branch. The cut was at an angle, leaving a sharp spike. Through tears of agony Nicholas lined up the spike with the back of Helm's head. He could feel Helm's teeth almost meeting in the flesh of his face. They had cut through the lower lip so that blood was starting to fill Nicholas's mouth. Helm was worrying him like a pit-bull in the arena, wrenching his head from side to side. Soon he would come away with a bloody mouthful of Nicholas's flesh.

With all the strength of pain and desperation, Nicholas hurled himself forward, and, using his upper body and his grip on the sides of Helm's head, drove him on to the sharp wooden spike. The point found the joint between the vertebrae of the spine and the base of Helm's skull, going in like a nail and partially severing the spinal cord. Helm's jaws sprang open as he went into spasm. Nicholas pulled away from him with a flap of loose flesh hanging from his chin, and blood streaming and spurting from the deep ragged wound.

Helm was impaled upon the spike, like a carcass on a butcher's hook. His limbs twitched and the muscles of his face convulsed, his eyelids shivered and jumped like those of an epileptic, and his eyeballs rolled back into his skull so that only the whites showed, flashing grotesquely in the gloom of the chasm.

Nicholas pulled himself up on to the log beside the Texan's body, and hung there panting and bleeding in gouts down his chin on to his chest. Slowly the log revolved under the eccentric weight distribution, and Helm began to slide off the spike. His skin tore with a sound like silk parting, and the vertebrae of his spine grated on wood. Then the corpse, at last quiescent, flopped face down into the water and began to sink.

Nicholas would not let him go so easily. 'Let's make sure of you, dear boy,' he grated through his swollen, bleeding mouth. He spat out a mouthful of blood and saliva as he stretched out and grabbed the back of Helm's collar, holding him face down in the water under the log. They picked up speed rapidly down the last stretch of the canyon, but Nicholas held on doggedly, drowning any last spark of life from Helm's carcass, until at last it was torn from his grip by the current and he watched it sink away into the grey, roiling waters.

'I'll give your love to Tessay,' Nicholas called after him as he disappeared. Then he gave all his concentration to balancing the log and staying aboard for the ride through the tumbling, racing current. At last he was spewed out through the pink rock portals into the bottom reach of the Dandera river. As he was swept beneath the rope suspension bridge he slid off the log and struck out for the western bank, very much aware of the terrible drop into the Nile that lay half a mile downstream.

Sitting on the bank, he tore a strip from the tail of his shirt. Then he bound up his wounded chin as best he could, strapping it around the back of his head. The blood soaked through the thin wet cotton, but he knotted it tighter and it began to staunch the flow.

He stood up unsteadily and pushed his way through the strip of thick riverine bush which bounded the river, until at last he struck the trail that led down to the monastery and hobbled down it on his bare feet. He only stopped once, and that was when he heard the sound of the helicopter taking off from the top of the cliff above the chasm far behind him.

He looked back. 'Sounds as though Tuma Nogo made it out of there, more's the pity. I wonder what happened to von Schiller and the Egyptian,' he muttered grimly, fingering his injured face. 'At least none of them are going to get into the tomb, not unless they dam the river again.' Suddenly a thought occurred to him.

'My God, what if von Schiller was already in there when the river hit?' He began to chuckle, and then shook his head. 'Too much to hope for. Justice is never that neat.' He shook his head again, but the movement started his wound aching brutally. He clutched his bandaged jaw with one hand and started down the trail again, breaking into a trot as he reached the paved causeway that led down to the monastery.

ahoot Guddabi ran full into von Schiller around a corner of the maze, and in a peculiar way the old man's presence, even though he was of no conceivable value in this crisis, steadied him and kept at bay the panic that threatened at any moment to boil over and overwhelm him. Without Hansith the maze was a weird and lonely place. Any human company was a blessing. For a moment the two of them clung together like children lost in the forest.

Von Schiller still carried part of the treasure that they had been examining when Hansith had panicked and run. He had Pharaoh's golden crook in one hand and the ceremonial flail in the other.

'Where is the monk?' he screamed at Guddabi. 'Why did you run off and leave me? We have to find the way out of these tunnels, you idiot. Don't you realize the danger?'

'How do you expect me to know the way—' Nahoot began furiously, and then broke off as he noticed the chalk notations on the wall behind von Schiller's shoulder, and for the first time realized their significance.

'That's it!' he exclaimed with relief. 'Harper or the Al Simma woman have marked it out for us. Come on!' He started down the tunnel, following the signposting. However, by the time they came out on the central staircase almost an hour had passed since Hansith had left them. As they hurried down the staircase into the long gallery the sound of the river rose to a pervading hiss, like the breathing of a sleeping dragon.

Nahoot broke into a run and von Schiller staggered along behind him, his aged legs weakening with fear.

'Wait!' he shouted after Nahoot, who ignored his plea and ducked out through the opening in the plaster-sealed doorway. On the landing the generator was still running smoothly, and Nahoot did not even glance at it as he hurried down the inclined shaft in the bright dazzle of the light bulbs along the roof.

He turned the corner still at a run, and stopped dead as he realized that the tunnel below him was flooded, right back up to the level of the ancient high-water mark on the masonry blocks of the walls. There was no sign of the sink-hole or the pontoon bridge. They were submerged under fifty feet or more of water.

The Dandera river, guardian of the tomb down all the ages, had resumed its duty. Dark and implacable, it sealed the entrance to the tomb as it had done these four thousand years past.

'Allah!' whispered Nahoot. 'Allah have mercy on us.'

Von Schiller came around the corner of the tunnel and stopped beside Nahoot. The two of them stared in horror at the flooded shaft. Then slowly von Schiller sagged against the side wall.

'We are trapped,' he whispered, and at those words Nahoot whimpered softly and sank to his knees. He began to pray in a high, nasal sing-song. The sound infuriated von Schiller.

'That will not help us. Stop it!' He swung the golden flail in his right hand across Nahoot's bowed back. Nahoot cried out at the pain and crawled away from von Schiller.

'We must find a way out of here.' Von Schiller's voice steadied. He was accustomed to command, and now he took charge.

'There must be another way out of here,' he decided. 'We will search. If there is an opening to the outside then we should feel a draught of air.' His voice became firmer and more confident. 'Yes! That's what we will do. Switch off that fan, and we will try to detect any movement of air.'

Nahoot responded eagerly to his tone and authority, and hurried back to switch off the electric fan.

'You have your cigarette lighter,' von Schiller told him. 'We will light tapers from these.' He pointed at the papers and photographs that Royan had left lying on the

648

trestle table by the doorway. 'We will use the smoke to detect any draught.'

For the next two hours they moved through all levels of the tomb, holding aloft the burning tapers, watching the movement of the smoke. At no point could they detect even the faintest movement of air in the tunnels, and in the end they came back to the flooded shaft and stared despairingly at the pool of still black water that blocked it.

'That is the only way out,' von Schiller whispered.

'I wonder if the monk escaped that way,' said Nahoot as he slumped down the wall.

'There is no other way.'

They were silent for a while; it was difficult to judge the passage of time in the tomb. Now that the river had found its own level there was no movement of water in the shaft, and the faint and distant sound of the current running through the sink-hole seemed merely to enhance the silence. In it they could hear their own breathing.

Nahoot spoke at last. 'The fuel in the generator. It must be running low. I did not see any reserves—'

They thought about what would happen when the small fuel tank ran dry. They thought about the darkness to come.

Suddenly von Schiller screamed, 'You have to go out through the shaft to fetch help. I order you to do it.'

Nahoot stared at him in disbelief. 'It's over a hundred yards back through the tunnel to the outside, and the river is in flood.'

Von Schiller sprang to his feet and stood over Nahoot threateningly. 'The monk escaped that way. It's the only way. You must swim through the tunnel and reach Helm and Nogo. Helm will know what to do. He will make a plan to get me out of here.'

'You are mad.' Nahoot backed away from him, but von Schiller followed him.

'I order you to do it!'

'You crazy old man!' Nahoot tried to scramble to his feet, but von Schiller swung the heavy golden flail, a sudden unexpected blow in Nahoot's face that knocked him over backwards, splitting his lips and breaking off two of his front teeth.

'You are mad!' he wailed. 'You can't do this—' but von Schiller swung again and again, lacerating his face and shoulders, the heavy golden tails of the whip cutting through the thin cotton of his shirt.

'I will kill you,' von Schiller screamed, raining blows on him. 'If you don't obey me I will kill you.'

'Stop!' Nahoot whined. 'No, please, stop. I will do it, only stop.'

He crawled away from von Schiller, dragging himself along the floor of the tunnel until he sat waist-deep in the water.

'Give me time to prepare,' he pleaded.

'Go now!' Von Schiller menaced him, lifting the whip high. 'Very likely you will find air trapped in the tunnel. You will find your way through. Go!'

Nahoot scooped a double handful of water and dashed it into his own face, washing away the blood that poured from one of the deep cuts in his cheek.

'I have to take off my clothes, my shoes,' he whimpered, pleading for time, but von Schiller would not allow him to leave the water.

'Do it where you are standing,' he ordered, brandishing the heavy whip. In his other hand he held the heavy golden crook. Nahoot realized that a blow from that weapon could crack his skull.

Standing knee-deep at the water's edge, Nahoot hopped on one foot as he pulled off his shoes. Then, slowly and reluctantly, he stripped to his underpants. His shoulders were deeply scored by the lash of the flail, fresh blood welling up and slithering like scarlet serpents down his back.

He knew that he had to placate this crazy old madman. He would duck under the surface and swim a short way down the tunnel, hold on to the side wall down there for as long as his breath lasted, and then swim back again.

'Go!' von Schiller shouted at him. 'You are wasting time. Don't think that I will let you get out of this.'

Nahoot waded deeper into the shaft until the water covered his chest. He paused there for a few minutes as he drew a series of deep breaths. Then at last he held his breath and ducked below the surface. Von Schiller stood waiting at the edge of the pool, staring down into it but unable to see anything beneath the black and ominous surface. In the lamplight Nahoot's blood stained the surface.

A minute passed slowly, and then suddenly there was a heavy swirl beneath the waters, and a human arm rose through the dark surface, hand and fingers extended as though in supplication. Then slowly it sank out of sight again.

Von Schiller craned forward, 'Guddabi!' he called angrily. 'What are you playing at?'

There was another swirl below the water, and something flashed like a mirror in the depths.

'Guddabi!' von Schiller's voice rose petulantly.

Almost as if in response to the summons, Nahoot's head broke out through the surface. His skin was waxen yellow, drained of all blood, and his mouth gaped open in a dreadful, silent scream. The water around him boiled as though a shoal of great fish were feeding below. As von Schiller stared in incomprehension, a dark tide rose up around Nahoot's head and stained the surface a rose-petal red. For a moment von Schiller did not realize that it was Nahoot's blood.

Then he saw the long, sinuous shapes darting and twisting beneath the surface, surrounding Nahoot, feeding upon his flesh. Nahoot lifted his hand again and extended it towards von Schiller, pleadingly. The arm was half-devoured, mutilated by deep half-moon wounds where the flesh had been bitten away in chunks.

Von Schiller screamed in horror, backing away from the pool. Nahoot's eyes were huge and dark and accusing. He stared at von Schiller and a wild cawing sound that was not human issued from his straining throat.

Even as von Schiller watched, one of the giant tropical eels thrust its head through the surface and its teeth gleamed like broken glass as it gaped wide, and then locked its jaws on to Nahoot's throat. Nahoot made no effort to tear the creature away. He was too far gone. He stared at von Schiller all the while that the eel, twisting and rolling into a gleaming ball of slimy coils, still hung from his throat.

Slowly Nahoot's head sank below the surface again. For long minutes the pool was agitated by the movements in its depth and the occasional gleam of one of the serpentine fish. Then gradually the surface settled as still and serene as a sheet of black glass.

Von Schiller turned and ran, back up the incline shaft, past the landing on which the generator still puttered quietly, blindly trying to get as far away as he could from that dreadful pool. He did not know where he was going, but followed any passageway that opened in front of him. At the foot of the central stairway he ran into the corner of the wall and stunned himself, falling to the agate tiles and lying there blubbering as a large purple lump rose on his forehead.

After a while he dragged himself to his feet and lurched up the stairs. He was confused and disorientated, his mind starting to break up in delirium, driven over the edge of sanity by horror and fear. He fell again, and crawled along the tunnel on his hands and knees to the next corner of the maze. Only then was he able to regain his feet to stagger onwards.

The steep shaft leading down into Taita's gas trap opened under his feet without him seeing it. He fell down the steps, jarring and bruising his legs and chest. Then he was on his feet again, reeling across the store room past the ranks of amphorae, up the far staircase and into the painted arcade that led to the tomb of Pharaoh Mamose.

He had tottered down half the length of it, dishevelled and wild-eyed and demented, when suddenly the lights dimmed for a moment, fading to a yellow glow. Then they brightened again as the generator sucked the last drops of fuel from the bottom of the tank. Von Schiller stopped in the centre of the arcade and looked up at the lights with despair. He knew what was coming. For another few minutes the bulbs burned on, bright and cheerfully, and then again they dimmed and faded.

The darkness settled over him like the heavy velvet folds of a funeral pall. It was so intense and complete that it seemed to have a physical weight and texture. He could taste the darkness in his mouth as it seemed to force its way into his body and suffocate him.

He ran again, wildly and blindly, losing all sense of direction in the blackness. He crashed headlong into stone and fell again, stunned. He could feel the warm tickle of blood running down his face, and he could not breathe. He whimpered and gasped and slowly, lying on his side, he curled himself into a ball like a foetus in the womb.

He wondered how long it would take him to die, and his soul quailed as he knew that it might take days and even weeks. He moved slightly, cuddling in closer to the stone object with which he had collided. In the darkness he had no way of telling that it was the great sarcophagus of Mamose that sheltered him. Thus he lay in the darkness of the tomb, surrounded by the funeral treasures of an emperor, and waited for his own slow but inexorable death.

The monastery of St Frumentius was deserted. The monks had heard the gunfire and the sounds of battle echoing down the gorge, and had gathered up their treasures and fled.

Nicholas ran down the long, empty cloister, pausing to catch his breath at the head of the staircase that led down to the level of the Nile and the Epiphany shrine where he had stored the boats. Panting, he searched the gloom of the deep basin below him into which the sunlight seldom reached, but the moving clouds of silver spray from the twin waterfalls screened the depths. He had no way of telling if Sapper and Royan were down there waiting for him, or if they had run into trouble on the trail.

He adjusted the tattered and bloodstained bandage around his chin, and then started down. Then he heard her voice in the silver mist below him, calling his name, and she came pelting up the slippery, slime-covered stairs towards him.

'Nicholas! Oh, thank God! I thought you weren't coming.' She would have rushed into his embrace, but then she saw his bandaged and blood-smeared face, and she stopped and stared at him, appalled.

'Sweet Mary!' she whispered. 'What happened to you, Nicky?'

'A little tiff with Jake Helm. Just a scratch, but I am not much good at kissing right now,' he mumbled, trying to grin around the bandage. 'You will have to wait for later.'

He put one arm around her shoulders, almost swinging her off her feet, as he turned her to face down the stairs again.

'Where are the others?' He hurried her down.

'They are all here,' she told him. 'Sapper and Mek are pumping the boats and loading.'

'Tessay?'

'She's safe.'

They scrambled down the last flight of steps on to the jetty below the Epiphany shrine. The Nile had risen ten feet since Nicholas had last stood there. The river was full and angry, muddy and swift. He could barely make out the cliffs on the far bank through the drifting clouds of spray.

The five Avon boats were drawn up at the edge. Four of them were already fully inflated, and the last one was billowing and swelling as the air was released into it from the compressed air cylinder. Mek and Sapper were packing the ammunition crates into the ready boats and strapping them down under green nylon cargo nets.

Sapper looked up at Nicholas and a comical expression of astonishment spread over his bluff features, 'What the blue bleeding blazes happened to your face?'

'Tell you about it one day,' Nicholas promised, and turned to embrace Mek.

'Thank you, old friend,' he said sincerely. 'Your men fought well, and you waited for me.' Nicholas glanced at the row of wounded guerrillas that lay against the foot of the cliff. 'How many casualties?'

'Three dead, and these six wounded. It could have been much worse if Nogo's men had pushed us harder.'

'Still, it's too many,' said Nicholas.

'Even one is too many,' Mek agreed gruffly.

'Where are the rest of your men?'

'On the run for the border. Kept just enough of them with me to handle the boats.' Mek stripped the filthy bandage from Nicholas's chin. Royan gasped when she saw the injury, but Mek grinned.

'Looks as though you were chewed by a shark.'

'That's right, I was,' Nicholas agreed.

Mek shrugged. 'It needs at least a dozen stitches.' He shouted for one of his men to bring his pack.

'Sorry, no anaesthetic,' he warned Nicholas as he forced him to sit on the transom of one of the boats and poured antiseptic straight from the bottle.

Nicholas let out a gasp of pain. 'Burns, doesn't it?' Mek agreed complacently. 'But just wait until I start sewing.'

'This kindness will be written down against your name in the golden book,' Nicholas told him, and with an evil leer Mek broke the seal on a suture pack.

As Mek worked on the wound, pulling the edges together and tugging the thread tight, he spoke quietly so that Nicholas alone could hear. 'Nogo has at least a full company of men guarding the river downstream. My scouts tell me that he has placed them to cover the trails on both banks.'

'He doesn't know that we have boats to run the river, does he?' Nicholas asked through gritted teeth.

'I think it is unlikely, but he knows a great deal about our movements. Perhaps he had an informer amongst your workmen.' Mek paused as he pricked the needle into Nicholas's flesh, and then went on, 'And Nogo still has the helicopter. He will spot us on the river as soon as this cloud breaks.'

'The river is our only escape route. Let's pray that the weather stays socked in, like this.'

By the time Mek had tied off the last knot and covered Nicholas's chin with a Steri-Strip plaster, Sapper had finished inflating and loading the last boat.

Four of Mek's men carried Tessay's litter to one of the boats. Mek helped her aboard and settled her on the deck, making sure that she had one of the safety straps close at hand. Then he left her and hurried to where his wounded men lay in order to help them into the boats too. Most of them could walk, but two had to be carried.

After that he came back to Nicholas. 'I see you have

found your radio,' he said, as he glanced at the fibreglass case that Nicholas had slung over his shoulder on its carrying strap.

'Without it we would be in big trouble.' Nicholas patted the case affectionately.

'I will take command of that boat, with Tessay.'

'Good!' Nicholas agreed. 'Royan will go with me in the lead boat.'

'You had better let me lead,' Mek said.

'What do you know about river running?' Nicholas asked him. 'I am the only one of us who has ever shot this river before.'

'That was twenty years ago,' Mek pointed out.

'I am an even better man now than I was then,' Nicholas grinned. 'Don't argue, Mek. You come next, and Sapper in the one behind you. Are there any of your men who know the river to command the other two boats?'

'All my men know the river,' Mek told him, and shouted his orders. Each of them hurried to the Avon he had been allocated. Nicholas gave Royan a boost over the gunwale of their boat, and then helped his men launch her down the rocky bank. As soon as the hull floated free they scrambled aboard and each man grabbed a paddle.

As they bent to their paddles, Nicholas saw at once that every man of his crew was indeed a riverman, as Mek had boasted. They pulled strongly but smoothly, and the light inflatable craft shot out into the main stream of the Nile.

The Avons were designed to accommodate sixteen, and were lightly loaded. The ammunition cases that held the grave goods from the tomb were bulky but weighed little, and there were not more than a dozen people in any one boat. They all floated high and handled well.

'Bad water ahead,' Nicholas told Royan grimly. 'All the way to the Sudanese border.' He stood at the steering sweep in the stern, from where he had a good forward view.

Royan crouched at his feet, clinging to one of the safety straps and trying to keep out of the way of the oarsmen.

They cut across the current that was scouring the great stone basin below the falls, and Nicholas lined up for the narrow heads through which the river was escaping to the west. He looked up at the sky and saw through the spray that the rain clouds were low and purple. They seemed to sag down upon the tops of the tall cliffs.

'Luck starting to run our way,' he told Royan. 'Even with the helicopter they won't be able to find us in this weather.'

He glanced at his Rolex and the spray was beading the glass. 'Couple of hours until nightfall. We should be able to put a few miles of river behind us before we are forced to stop for the night.'

He looked back over his stern and saw the rest of the little flotilla bobbing along behind him. The Avons were reflective yellow in colour and stood out brilliantly even in the mist and murk of the gorge. He lifted his clenched fist high in the signal to advance, and from the following boat Mek repeated the gesture and grinned at him through his beard.

The river grabbed them and they shot through its portals into the narrow, twisted gut of the Nile. The men at the oars stopped paddling, and let the river take them. All they could do now was to help Nicholas to steer her through any desperate moments, and they crouched ready along the gunwales.

The high water in the gorge had covered many of the reefs of rock, but their presence below the surface was clearly marked by the waters that humped up in standing waves or foamed white in the narrows between them. The flood reached up high on either bank, dashing against the cliffs of the sub-gorge. If an Avon overturned, or even if a crew member were thrown overboard, there would be no place on this river to heave-to and pick up survivors.

Nicholas stood high and craned ahead. He had to pick his route well in advance, and once committed he had to steer her through. It all depended on his ability to read the river and judge her moods. He was out of practice, and he had that tight, hard cannonball of fear in the pit of his belly as he put the long sweep over and steered for the first run of fast green water. They went swooping down it, Nicholas holding their bows into it with delicate touches of the sweep, and came out into the bottom of it with all the other boats following them down in sequence.

'Nothing to it!' Royan laughed up at him.

'Don't say it!' Nicholas pleaded with her. 'The bad angel is listening.' And he lined up for the head of the next set of rapids that raced towards them with terrifying speed.

Nicholas steered through the gap between two out-crops of rock and they shot the barrel, gaining speed down the chute. It was only when they were halfway down that he saw the tall standing wave below them over which the river leaped. He put the sweep across and tried to steer round it, but the river had them firmly in its grip.

Like a hunter taking a fence they shot up the front of the standing wave, and then with a sickening lurch plummeted down the far side into the deep trough. The Avon folded across the middle, the bows almost touching the stern as she tried to pull through the hole in the river surface.

The crew were tumbled over each other and Nicholas would have been catapulted overside if it had not been for his body line and his grip on the steering sweep. Royan flung herself flat on the deck and hung on to the safety strap with all her strength as the Avon's buoyancy exerted itself and the boat bounded high in the air, whipping back elastically into its original shape, then hovered a moment and almost capsized before it crashed back, right side up.

One of the crew had been hurled overboard and was

floundering alongside, carried along at the same speed as the flying Avon, so his comrades were able to lean out and haul him back on board. The cargo of ammunition crates had tumbled and shifted, but the nets had prevented any of them from being lost over the side.

'What did you do that for?' Royan yelled at him. 'Just when I was beginning to trust you.'

'Just testing,' he yelled back. 'Wanted to see how tough you really are.'

'I admit it, I am a sissy,' she assured him. 'You really don't need to do it again.'

Looking back, Nicholas saw Mek's boat crash through the trough just as they had, but the following craft had enough warning to steer clear and slip through the sides of the run.

He looked ahead again, and his whole existence became the wild waters of the river. His universe was contained within the tall cliffs of the sub-gorge as he battled to bring the racing Avon through. He did not know whether it was spray or rain that stung his cheeks and his wounded chin, and that flew horizontally into his eyes and half-blinded him. At times it was a mixture of the two.

An hour later Nicholas misjudged the rapids again, and they went in sideways and almost capsized. Two of his crew were hurled overboard. Steering fine and leaning outboard they managed to pull one of them from the river, but the other man struck a rock before they could reach him. He went under and did not rise again. None of them spoke or mourned him, for they were all too busy staying alive themselves.

Once Royan shouted up at Nicholas through the rattling spray and the thunder of the river all around them, 'Helicopter! Can you hear it?'

Half-deafened, he looked up at the lowering grey belly of the clouds that hung at the level of the cliffs, and faintly made out the whistle and flutter of the rotors.

'Above the cloud!' he shouted back, wiping the rain and the spray from his eyes with the back of his hand. 'They will never spot us in this.'

The onset of the African night was sped upon them by the low cloud. In the gathering darkness another hazard leaped upon them with no warning at all. One instant they were running hard and clear down a smooth stretch of the river, and the next the waters opened ahead of them and they were hurled out into space. It seemed that they fell for ever, although it was a drop of not more than thirty feet, before they hit the bottom and found themselves floating in a tangle of men and boats in the pool below the falls. Here the river was stalled for a moment, revolving upon itself while it gathered its strength for the next mad charge down the gorge.

One of the Avons had capsized and was floating belly up – even its highly stable hull had not been able to weather the drop down the falls. The crews of the other boats gathered themselves and then paddled across to drag the survivors from the water and to salvage the oars and other floating equipment. It took the combined efforts of all of them to right the overturned Avon, and then it was almost completely dark by the time they had it back on even keel.

'Count the crates!' Nicholas ordered. 'How many have we lost?'

He could hardly credit his good fortune when Sapper shouted back, 'Eleven still on board. All present and correct.' The cargo nets were holding well. But all of them, men and women, were exhausted and soaked through and shivering with the cold. Any attempt to go on in darkness would be suicidal. Nicholas looked across at Mek in the nearest boat and shook his head.

'There is a bit of slack water in the angle of the cliff.' Mek pointed towards the tail of the pool. 'We might be able to find moorings for the night.'

There was a stunted but tough little tree growing out of the vertical fissure in the rock, and they used this as a bollard and made a line fast to it. Then they lashed all the Avons together in a line down the cliff and settled in for the night. There was no chance of hot food or drink, and they had to make do with some cold tinned rations eaten off the blade of a bayonet, and a few chunks of soggy *injera* bread.

Mek scrambled over from his own boat and huddled down close beside Nicholas with one arm over his shoulder and his lips close to his ear.

'I have made a roll call. Another man missing when we went over the falls. We won't find him now.'

'I am not doing too well,' Nicholas admitted. 'Perhaps you should lead tomorrow.'

'Not your fault.' Mek squeezed his shoulders. 'Nobody could have done better. It was this last waterfall—' he broke off and they listened to it thundering away in the darkness.

'How far have we come?' Nicholas asked. 'And how much further to go?'

'It's almost impossible to tell, but I guess we are halfway to the border. Should reach there some time tomorrow afternoon.'

They were silent for a while, and then Mek asked, 'What is the date today? I have lost count of the days.'

'So have I.' Nicholas tilted his wrist-watch so that he could read the luminous dial in the last of the light. 'Good God! It's the thirtieth already,' he said.

'Your pick-up aircraft is due at Roseires airstrip the day after tomorrow.'

'The first of April,' Nicholas agreed. 'Will we make it?'

'You answer that question for me.' Mek grinned in the night without humour. 'What chances of your fat friend being late?'

'Jannie is a pro. He is never late,' said Nicholas. Again

a silence fell, and then Nicholas asked, 'When we reach Roseires, what do you want me to do with your share of the booty?' Nicholas kicked one of the ammunition crates. 'Do you want to take it with you?'

'After we see you off on the plane with your fat friend, we are going to be doing some hot-footed running from Nogo. I don't want to be carrying any extra luggage. You take my share with you. Sell it for me – I need the money to keep fighting here.'

'You trust me?'

'You are my friend.'

'Friends are the easiest to cheat – they never expect it,' Nicholas told him, and Mek punched his shoulder and chuckled.

'Get some sleep. We will have to do some hard paddling tomorrow.' Mek stood up in the Avon as she pitched and rolled gently to the push of the current. 'Sleep well, old friend,' he said, and climbed across to the boat alongside, where Tessay waited for him.

Nicholas braced his back against the soft pneumatic gunwale of the Avon and took Royan in his arms. She sat between his knees and leaned back against his chest, shivering in her sodden clothes.

After a while her shivering abated, and she murmured, 'You make a very good hot-water bottle.'

'That's one reason for keeping me around on a permanent basis,' he said, and stroked her wet hair. She did not answer him, but snuggled closer, and a short while afterwards her breathing slowed as she fell into an exhausted sleep.

Although he was cold and stiff and his shoulders ached and his palms were blistered from wrestling with the steering oar, he could not find sleep as readily as she had. Now that the prospect of reaching the airstrip at Roseires loomed closer, he was troubled by problems other than those of simply navigating the river and battling his way through Nogo's men. Those were enemies he could recognize and fight; but there was something more than that which he would soon have to face.

Royan stirred in his arms and muttered something he could not catch. She was dreaming and talking in her sleep.

He held her gently and she settled down again. He had started to drift off himself when she spoke again, this time quite clearly. 'I am sorry, Nicky. Don't hate me for it. I couldn't let you—' her words slurred and he could make no sense of the rest of it.

He was fully awake now, her words aggravating his doubts and misgivings. During the rest of that night he slept only intermittently, and his rest was troubled by dreams as distressing as hers must have been to her.

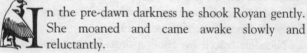

I n the pre-dawn darkness he shook Royan gently. She moaned and came awake slowly and reluctantly.

They bolted down a few mouthfuls of the cold rations that remained from the previous night. Then, as dawn lit the gorge just enough for them to see the surface of the river and the obstacles ahead, they pushed off from their moorings and the yellow boats strung out down the current. The battle against the river began all over again.

The cloud cover was still low and unbroken, and the rain squalls swept over them at intervals. They kept going all that morning, and slowly the mood of the river began to ameliorate. The current was not so swift and treacherous, and the banks not so high and rugged.

It was mid-afternoon and the clouds were still closed in solidly overhead as they entered a stretch where the river threaded itself through a series of bluffs and headlands, and they came upon another set of rapids. Perhaps Nicholas was more expert in his technique by now, for they swept through them without mishap, and it seemed to him that each stretch of white water was progressively less severe than the last.

'I think we are through the worst of it now,' he told Royan as she sat on the deck below him. 'The gradient and the fall of the river are definitely more gentle now. I think it is flattening out as we approach the plains of the Sudan.'

'How much further to Roseires?' she asked.

'I don't know, but the border can't be too far ahead now.'

Nicholas and Mek were keeping the flotilla closed up in line astern, so that orders could be shouted across the gaps between them and all the boats kept under their command.

Nicholas steered for the deeper water on the outside of the next wide bend, and as he came through it he saw that the stretch of river ahead seemed open and altogether free of rapids or shoals. He relaxed and smiled at Royan.

'How about lunch at the Dorchester grill next Sunday? Best roast beef trolley in London.'

He thought he saw a shadow pass across her eyes before she smiled brightly and replied, 'Sounds good to me.'

'And afterwards we can go back home and curl up in front of the telly and watch *Match of the Day*, or play our own little match.'

'You are rude,' she laughed, 'but it does sound tempting.'

He was about to stoop over her, and kiss her for the pleasure of watching her blush again, when he saw the dance of tiny white fountains spurting up from the surface of the river ahead of their bows, coming swiftly towards them. Then, moments later, he heard the crackle of automatic fire, the distinctive sound of a Soviet RPD.

He threw himself down over the top of Royan, covering her with his own body, and heard Mek bellowing from the boat behind them.

'Return fire! Keep their heads down.'

His men threw down their paddles and seized their weapons. They blazed away towards the inner curve of the bank from where the attack was coming.

The attackers were completely concealed amongst the rocks and scrub, and there was no definite target to shoot at. However, in an ambush like this it was essential to lay down as heavy a covering fire as possible, to keep the attackers' heads down and to upset their aim.

A bullet tore through the nylon skin of the Avon close to Royan's head and went on to slam into one of the metal ammunition crates. The sides of their craft offered no protection at all from the heavy fusillade that lashed them. One of their crew was hit in the head. The bullet cut the top off his skull like the shell of a soft-boiled egg, and he was flung over the side. Royan screamed more with horror than with fear, while Nicholas snatched up the assault rifle that the dead man had dropped and emptied the magazine towards the bank, firing short taps of three and raking the scrub that concealed their attackers.

The Avon still raced downstream on the current, spiralling aimlessly as she lost direction without the steering oar. It took them less than a minute to be carried past the ambush and around the next bend of the river.

Nicholas dropped the empty rifle and shouted across at Mek, 'Are you all right?'

'One man hit here,' Mek yelled back. 'Not too bad.'

Each of the boats reported their casualties: a total of one dead and three wounded. None of the wounded was in a serious condition, and although three of the boats had been holed, the hulls were made up of watertight compartments and were all still floating high.

Mek steered his Avon alongside Nicholas's and called across. 'I was beginning to think we had given Nogo the slip.'

'We got off lightly that time,' Nicholas called back.

'We probably took them by surprise. They weren't expecting us to be on the water.'

'Well, no more surprises for him now. You can bet they are on the radio already. Nogo knows exactly where we are and where we are headed.' He looked up at the cloud. 'We can only hope the cloud stays thick and low.'

'How much further to the Sudanese border?'

'Not sure, but it can't be more than another couple of hours.'

'Is the crossing guarded?' Nicholas asked.

'No. Nothing there. Just empty bush on both sides.'

'Let's hope it stays empty,' Nicholas muttered.

Within thirty minutes of the fire-fight, they heard the helicopter again. It was flying above the clouds, and as they listened it passed overhead, but out of sight, and headed on downstream. Twenty minutes later they heard it again, coming back in the opposite direction, and shortly after that it flew downstream again, still above the cloud.

'What the hell is Nogo playing at?' Mek called across to Nicholas. 'Sounds as though he is patrolling the river, but he can't get under the cloud.'

'My guess is that he is ferrying men downstream to cut us off. Now he knows we are using boats, he also knows that we can only head in one direction. Nogo isn't one to worry about international borders. He may even have realized by now that we are heading for Roseires. It's the nearest unmanned airstrip along the river. He could be waiting for us when we try to land.'

Mek steered his Avon closer and passed a line across, tying the two boats together so that they could talk in normal tones.

'I don't like it, Nicholas. We are going to walk right into them again. What do you suggest?'

Nicholas pondered for a long minute. 'Don't you recognize this part of the river? Don't you know precisely where we are yet?'

Mek shook his head. 'I always keep well away from the river when we cross the border, but I will recognize the old sugar-mill at Roseires when we get there. It's about three miles upstream from the airstrip.'

'Deserted?' Nicholas asked.

'Yes. Abandoned ever since the war began twenty years ago.'

'With this cloud cover, it will be dark in an hour,' Nicholas said. 'The river is slower now and not so dangerous. We can take a chance and keep on going after dark. Perhaps Nogo won't expect that. We might be able to give him the slip in the dark.'

'Is that the best you can do?' Mek chuckled. 'As a plan it sounds to me a bit like closing your eyes and hoping for the best.'

'Well, if somebody could tell me where the hell we are, and what time Jannie will arrive tomorrow, I might be able to come up with something a bit more specific.' Nicholas grinned back at him. 'Until that happens, I am flying by the seat of my pants.'

All of them were tense with strung-out nerves as they paddled on into the premature dusk beneath the thick blanket of cloud and rain. Even in the gathering darkness the crew kept their weapons cocked and locked, trained on either bank of the river, ready to return fire instantly.

'We must have crossed the border an hour ago,' Mek called to Nicholas. 'The old sugar mill can't be far ahead.'

'In the dark, how will you find it?'

'There is the remains of an old stone jetty on the bank, from which the riverboats taking the sugar down to Khartoum used to load.'

Night came down upon them abruptly, and Nicholas felt a sense of relief as the river banks receded into the murk and the darkness hid them from hostile eyes ashore. As soon as it was fully dark they lashed the boats together to prevent them becoming separated and then let the river carry them on silently, keeping so close in to the right-hand bank that they ran aground more than once, and some of the men had to slip over the side and push them out into deeper water.

The stone piers of the jetty at Roseires sprang out at them unexpectedly, and Nicholas's leading Avon slammed into them before he could steer clear. However, the crew were ready and they jumped over the side into chest-deep water and dragged the boat to the bank. Immediately Mek leaped ashore and, with twenty of his men, spread out into the overgrown canefields along the bank to secure the area and prevent a surprise attack by Nogo's men.

There was confusion and more noise than Nicholas felt was safe as the rest of the flotilla beached, and they began to bring the wounded ashore and unload the cargo of ammunition cases. Nicholas piggy-backed Royan to the bank and then waded back to fetch Tessay. She was much stronger by now. The enforced rest during the voyage downriver had given her a chance to recover, and she stood up unaided in the Avon and climbed on to Nicholas's shoulders to be brought ashore.

Once on dry ground he let her slide down on to her own feet and asked her quietly, 'How are you feeling?'

'I will be all right now, thank you, Nicholas.'

He supported her for a moment while she recovered her balance and said quickly, 'I did not have a chance to ask earlier. What about Royan's message that she asked you to telephone from Debra Maryam? Did you get it through for her?'

'Yes, of course,' Tessay replied guilelessly. 'I told Royan that I had given her message to Moussad at the Egyptian Embassy. Didn't she tell you?'

Nicholas winced as though he had taken a low punch, but he smiled and kept his tone casual. 'It must have slipped her mind. Not important, anyway. But thanks nevertheless, Tessay.'

At that moment Mek came striding out of the darkness and spoke in a harsh whisper. 'This sounds like a camel market. Nogo will hear us from five miles away.' Quickly he took command and started to organize the shore party.

Once the last of the ammunition crates were unloaded, they dragged the boats into the canefields and unscrewed the valves that deflated the pontoons. Then they piled cane trash over them. Still working in the dark, they distributed the cargo of ammunition crates amongst Mek's men. Sapper took a case under each arm. Nicholas slung the radio over one shoulder and his emergency pack over the other, and balanced on his head the case that contained Pharaoh's golden death-mask and the Taita *ushabti*.

Mek sent his scouts forward to sweep the route out to the airstrip and make certain that they did not run into an ambush. Then he took the point and the rest of them strung out in Indian file along the rough, overgrown track behind him. Before they had covered a mile the clouds suddenly opened overhead, and the crescent moon and the stars showed through and gave them enough light to make out the chimneystack of the ruined mill against the night sky.

But even with this moonlight their progress was slow and broken by long pauses, for the stretcher-bearers carrying the wounded had difficulty keeping up. By the time they reached the airstrip it was after three in the morning and the moon had set. They stacked the ammunition cases in the same grove of acacia trees at the end of the runway where they had cached the pallets of dam-building equipment and the yellow tractor on the inward journey.

Although they were all exhausted by this time, Mek set out his pickets around the camp. The two women tended the wounded, working by the light of a small screened fire as they used up the last of Mek's medical supplies.

Sapper used the one electric torch whose batteries still

held a charge, and he gave Nicholas a discreet screened light while he set up the radio and strung the aerial. Nicholas's relief was intense when he opened the fibreglass case and found that, despite its dunking in the Nile, the rubber gasket that sealed the lid had kept the radio dry. When he switched on the power, the pilot light lit up. He tuned in to the short-wave frequency and picked up the early morning commercial transmission of Radio Nairobi.

Yvonne Chaka Chaka was singing; he liked her voice and her style. But he quickly switched off the set so as to conserve the battery, and settled back against the bole of the acacia tree to try and get a little rest before daylight broke. However, sleep eluded him – his sense of betrayal and anger were too strong.

Tuma Nogo watched the sun push its great fiery head out of the surface of the Nile ahead of them. They were flying only feet above the water to keep under the Sudanese military radar transmissions. He knew there was a radar station at Khartoum that might be able to pick them up, even at this range. Relations with the Sudanese were strained, and he could expect a quick and savage response if they discovered that he had violated their border.

Nogo was a confused and worried man. Since the débâcle in the gorge of the Dandera river everything had run strongly against him. He had lost all his allies. Until they were gone he had not realized how heavily he had come to rely on both Helm and von Schiller. Now he was on his own and he had already made many mistakes.

But despite all this he was determined to pursue the fugitives, and to run them down no matter how far he had to intrude into Sudanese territory. Over the past weeks it had gradually dawned upon Nogo, mostly by eaves- dropping on the conversations of von Schiller and the

Egyptian, that Harper and Mek Nimmur were in possession of treasure of immense value. His imagination could barely grasp the enormity of it, but he had heard others speak of tens of millions of dollars. Even a million dollars was a sum so vast that his mind had difficulty assimilating it, but he had a vague inkling as to what it might mean in earthly terms, of the possessions and women and luxuries it could buy.

Equally slowly it had dawned upon him that, now that von Schiller and Helm were gone, this treasure could be his alone; there was no longer any other person to stand in his way, other than the fleeing *shufta* led by Mek Nimmur and the Englishman. And he had overwhelming force on his side and the helicopter at his command.

If only he could pin the fugitives down, Nogo was certain he could wipe them out. There must be no survivors, no one to carry tales to Addis. After Mek and the Englishman and all their followers were dead it would be a simple matter to spirit his booty out of the country in the helicopter. There was a man in Nairobi and another in Khartoum whom he had dealt with before; they had bought contraband ivory and hashish from him. They would know how to market the booty to best advantage, although they were both devious men. He had already decided that he would not trust it all to one person but would spread the risk, so that even if one of them betrayed and cheated him—

His mind raced off on another tack, and he savoured the thought of great riches and what they could buy for him. He would have fine clothes and motor cars, land and cattle and women – white women and black and brown, all the women he could use, a new one for every day of his life. He broke off his greedy daydreams. First he had to find where the runaways had vanished to.

He had not realized that Harper and Mek Nimmur had inflatable boats hidden somewhere near the monastery.

Hansith had not informed him of that fact. He and Helm had expected them to try to escape on foot, and all the plans to head them off before they could reach the Sudanese border had been based on that assumption. On Helm's orders, he had even set up a reserve fuel dump near the border where they expected Mek Nimmur to cross, from which they could refuel the helicopter. Without those supplies of fuel he would long ago have been forced to give up the chase.

Nogo had placed his men to cover the trails leading along the river bank towards the west, and he had not even considered guarding the river itself. It was quite by chance that one of his patrols had been in a position to spot the flotilla of yellow boats as they came racing downstream. However, there had not been enough warning to enable them to set up an effective ambush, and they had been able to fire on the boats only briefly before they escaped. They had not inflicted serious damage on any of the boats – at least, not enough to stop them getting through.

Immediately the company commander had radioed his report of this contact with Mek Nimmur, Nogo had started ferrying men downstream to the Sudanese border to cut off the flotilla. Unfortunately, the Jet Ranger could carry no more than six fully armed men at a time, and transporting them had been a time-consuming business. He had only succeeded in bringing sixty of his men into position before night had fallen.

During the night he fretted that the flotilla was slipping past him, and with the dawn they were in the air again. Fortunately the cloud had broken up during the night. There was still some high cumulus overhead, but they were now able to fly low along the river and search for any sign of Mek Nimmur's flotilla.

They had first flown back along the river on the Ethiopian side of the border, as far as the point where Mek

Nimmur and Harper had been fired upon. They had picked up no sign of the boats, so Nogo had forced the pilot to turn back, cross the border and search the Sudanese stretch of the Nile. But Nogo had only been able to persuade his pilot to penetrate sixty nautical miles along the Nile into the Sudan before the man had rebelled. Despite the Tokarev pistol that Nogo held to his head, he had banked the Jet Ranger into a 180-degree turn and headed back low along the river.

By now Nogo knew he had been defeated and outwitted. He brooded unhappily in the front seat of the helicopter beside the pilot, trying to fathom out what had happened to his quarry. He saw the tall smokestack of the abandoned sugar-mill at Roseires poking up into the early morning sky, and he glowered at it angrily. They had passed the mill only a short while before on their way downstream.

'Turn in towards the north bank,' he ordered the pilot, and the man hesitated and glanced at him before he obeyed.

They passed directly over the building, flying lower than the chimney. The factory was roofless and the windows were empty rectangles in the broken walls. The boilers and machinery had been removed twenty years previously, and Nogo could look into the empty shell. The pilot hovered the aircraft while Nogo peered down, but there was no place where anyone could hide, and Nogo shook his head.

'Nothing! We have lost them. Head back upstream.'

The pilot lifted the machine's nose and turned away towards the river, obeying the order with alacrity. As the aircraft banked steeply, Nogo was looking down directly into the overgrown canefields verging the river when a flash of bright yellow caught his eye.

'Wait!' he shouted into his mike. 'There is something there. Go back!'

The helicopter hovered over the field, and Nogo gestured urgently downwards. 'Down! Put us down.'

As soon as the skids touched the earth, the stick of six heavily armed troopers dived out of the rear cabin and raced out to take up defensive positions. Nogo clambered out of the front door and ran into the overgrown bed of tall cane. One look was all he needed. The yellow boats had been deflated and folded and hastily covered. The earth around them had been churned up by booted feet. The tracks led away inland. The men who had made them had been heavily laden, for they had trodden deeply into the soft, sandy earth.

Nogo ran back to the helicopter and thrust his head in through the open cabin door. 'Is there an airstrip near here?' he shouted at the pilot, who shook his head.

'There is nothing shown on the chart.'

'There must have been one. The sugar-mill would have had a strip.'

'If there was one, it must have been decommissioned years ago.'

'We will find it,' Nogo declared. 'Mek Nimmur's tracks will lead us to it.' He sobered immediately. 'But I will have to bring up more men. Judging by his spoor, Mek Nimmur has at least fifty of his *shufta* with him.'

He left his men at the sugar-mill and flew back to the border with an empty rear cabin to pick up the first load of reinforcements.

'Big Dolly! Come in, Big Dolly. This is Pharaoh. Do you read?' Nicholas put out his first call an hour before sunrise.

'If I know the way Jannie's mind works, and I should, he would plan to make his approach flight in darkness and arrive here as soon as there is enough light to pick up the strip and land.'

'If the Fat Man comes,' Mek Nimmur qualified.

'He will come,' said Nicholas confidently. 'Jannie has never let me down yet.' He thumbed the microphone and called again: 'Big Dolly! Come in, Big Dolly.'

The static hummed softly, and Nicholas retuned the set carefully. He called again every fifteen minutes as they huddled around the set in the dark under the acacia trees.

Suddenly Royan started to her feet and exclaimed excitedly, 'There he is. I can hear Big Dolly's engines. Listen!'

Nicholas and Mek ran out into the open, and turned their faces upwards, looking into the north.

'That's not the Hercules,' Nicholas exclaimed suddenly. 'That's another machine.' He turned and faced southwards, towards the river. 'Anyway, it's coming from the wrong direction.'

'You are right,' Mek agreed. 'That's a single engine, and it's not a fixed wing. You can hear the rotors.'

'The Pegasus helicopter!' Nicholas exclaimed bitterly. 'They are on to us again.'

As they listened, the sound of the rotors faded. Nicholas looked relieved. 'They missed us. They can't have spotted the Avons.'

They trooped back under the cover of the acacias, and Nicholas called again on the radio, but there was no reply from Jannie.

Twenty minutes later they heard the sound of the Jet Ranger returning, and they monitored it anxiously.

'Gone again,' said Nicholas after a while, but then twenty minutes later they heard it yet again.

'Nogo is up to something out there,' Mek said uneasily.

'What do you think it is?' Nicholas was infected by his mood. When Mek worried, there was usually a damned good reason to worry.

'I don't know,' Mek admitted. 'Perhaps Nogo has spotted the Avons and is bringing up more men before he comes after us.' He went out into the open and listened intently, then came back to where Nicholas crouched over the radio.

'Keep calling,' he said. 'I am going out to the perimeter to make certain my men are ready to hold Nogo off if he comes.'

The helicopter moved up and down the Nile at short intervals during the next three hours, but the lack of any further developments lulled them, and Nicholas barely looked up from the radio each time they heard the distant beat of the rotors. Suddenly the radio crackled, and Nicholas started violently at the shock.

'Pharaoh! This is Big Dolly. Do you read?'

Nicholas's voice bubbled over with relief as he replied, 'This is Pharaoh. Speak sweet words to me, Big Dolly.'

'ETA your position one hour thirty minutes.' Jannie's accent was unmistakable.

'You will be very welcome!' Nicholas promised him fervently.

He hung up the microphone and beamed at the two women, 'Jannie is on his way, and he will—'

He broke off and his smile shrivelled to an expression of dismay. From the direction of the river came the unmistakable rattle of AK-47 rapid fire, followed a few seconds later by the crump of an exploding grenade.

'Oh, dammit to hell!' he groaned. 'I thought it was too good to last. Nogo has arrived.'

He picked up the mike again and spoke into it expressionlessly. 'Big Dolly! The uglies have arrived on the scene. It's going to have to be a hot extraction.'

'Hang on to your crown, Pharaoh!' Jannie's voice floated back. 'I am on my way.'

During the next half-hour the sounds of the fighting along the river intensified until the rattle of small-arms fire was almost continuous, and gradually it crept closer to the far end of the airstrip. It was clear that Mek's men, spread

677

out thinly along the river end of the strip, were falling back before the thrust of Nogo's men. And every twenty minutes or so there was the sound of the returning helicopter, as it ferried another stick of men to increase the pressure on Mek's scanty defence.

Nicholas and Sapper were the only able-bodied men left in the acacia grove, for all the others had gone out to defend the perimeter. The two of them moved the ammunition crates to the edge of the trees, where they could be loaded in haste once the Hercules landed.

Nicholas sorted out the cargo, reading the contents of each crate from the notations on the lids in Royan's handwriting. The crate containing the death-mask and the Taita *ushabti* would be the first to go aboard, followed by the three crowns: the blue war crown, the Nemes crown and the red and white crown of the united kingdoms of upper and lower Egypt. The value of those three crates probably exceeded that of all the rest of the treasure combined.

Once the cargo had been taken care of, Nicholas went down the row of wounded men and spoke to each of them in turn. First, he thanked them for their help and sacrifice, and then offered to take them out on the Hercules to where they could receive proper medical attention. He promised each of them that, if they accepted the offer, he would see to it that once they had recovered from their wounds they could return to Ethiopia.

Seven of them – those who were less seriously wounded and were able to walk – refused to leave Mek Nimmur. Their loyalty was a touching demonstration of the high regard in which Mek was held by his men. The others reluctantly agreed to be evacuated, but only after Tessay had intervened and added her assurances to Nicholas's. Then he and Sapper carried them to the point at the edge of the grove where Jannie would halt Big Dolly for the pick-up.

'What about you?' Nicholas asked Tessay. 'Are you coming out with us? You are still in pretty bad shape.'

Tessay laughed. 'While I can still stand on my two feet, I will never leave Mek Nimmur.'

'I can't understand what you see in that old rogue,' Nicholas laughed with her. 'I have spoken to Mek. He wants me to take his share of the booty with me. He won't be able to carry any extra luggage at the moment.'

'Yes, I know. Mek and I discussed it. We need the money to continue the struggle here.'

She broke off and ducked involuntarily, as a stunning explosion cracked in their eardrums and a tall column of dust leaped into the air close to the edge of the grove. Shrapnel whistled over their heads and twigs and leaves rained down on them.

'Sweet Mary! What was that?' Tessay cried.

'Two-inch mortar,' said Nicholas. He had not moved, nor made any attempt to take cover. 'More bark than bite. Nogo must have brought it in with his last flight.'

'When will the Hercules get here?'

'I'll give Jannie a call, and ask him.'

As Nicholas sauntered over to the radio set Tessay whispered to Royan, 'Are you English always so cool?'

'Don't ask me – I'm mostly Egyptian, and I am terrified.' Royan smiled easily and put her arm around Tessay. 'I am going to miss you, Lady Sun.'

'Perhaps we will meet again in happier times.' Tessay turned her head and kissed her impulsively, and Royan hugged her hard.

'I hope so. I hope so with all my heart.'

Nicholas spoke into the microphone. 'Big Dolly, this is Pharaoh. What is your position now?'

'Pharaoh, we are twenty minutes out, and hurrying. Did you have baked beans for dinner or is that mortar fire I hear in the background?'

'With your wit you should have gone on the stage,'

Nicholas told him. 'The uglies have control of the south end of the strip. Make your approach from the north. The wind is westerly at about five knots. So any way you come in, it will be cross-wind.'

'Roger, Pharaoh. How many passengers and cargo do you have for me?'

'Passengers are six cas-evac plus three. Cargo is fifty-two crates, about a quarter of a ton weight.'

'Hardly worth coming all this way for so little, Pharaoh.'

'Big Dolly. Be advised, there is another aircraft in the circuit. A Jet Ranger helicopter. Colour green and red. It is a hostile, but unarmed.'

'Roger, Pharaoh. I will call again on finals.'

Nicholas went back to where the two women were waiting with the wounded.

'Not long now,' he told them cheerfully. He had to raise his voice to make himself heard above the din of mortar bursts and rapid small-arms fire.

'Just enough time for a cup of tea,' he said. He pushed a few twigs into the embers of the previous night's fire, then rummaged in his small emergency pack for the last of his tea bags while Sapper placed the smoke-blackened billycan back on the burgeoning flames.

They only had one mug between them. 'Girls first,' said Nicholas, passing it to Royan. She took a swallow and scalded her lips.

'Good!' she sighed, and then cocked her head. 'This time it is definitely Big Dolly I can hear.'

Nicholas listened and then nodded. 'I think you are right.' He stood up and went to the radio. 'Big Dolly. You are audible.'

'Five minutes to landing, Pharaoh.'

From where he stood, Nicholas looked down the long strip. Mek's men were retreating, flitting like smoke

680

through the thorn scrub and firing back in the direction of the river. Nogo was pushing them hard now.

'Hurry along, Jannie,' he murmured, and then adjusted his expression as he turned back to the two women. 'Plenty of time to finish your tea. Don't waste it.'

The rumble of Big Dolly's engines was louder than the sound of gunfire now. Then suddenly she was in sight, coming in so low that she seemed to brush the tops of the thorn trees. She was enormous. Her wingspan reached from one side of the narrow overgrown strip to the other. Jannie touched her down short, and she blew out a long rolling cloud of brown dust behind her as he put the engines into reverse thrust.

Big Dolly went barrelling past the clump of acacia, and Jannie waved to them from the high cockpit. The moment he had bled off enough speed, he stood on his footbrakes and rudder bar. Big Dolly spun around in her own length and came roaring back down the strip towards them, her loading ramp beginning to drop open even before she reached them.

Fred was waiting in the open hatchway, and he ran down to help Sapper and Nicholas with the wounded men on the litters. It took only a few minutes to carry them up the ramp, and then they started loading the ammunition crates. Even Royan gave a hand, staggering up the ramp with one of the lighter crates clutched to her chest.

A mortar shell exploded a hundred and fifty yards beyond the parked Hercules, and then half a minute later a second shell fell a hundred yards short.

'Ranging shots,' Nicholas grunted, picking up a crate under each arm and running up the ramp.

'They have us in their sights now,' Fred shouted. 'We have to get out of here. Leave the rest of the cargo. Let's go! Go!'

There were only four crates still lying under the

spreading branches of the acacia, and both Nicholas and Sapper ignored the order and ran back down the ramp. They snatched up a crate under each arm and raced back. The ramp was starting to rise and Big Dolly's engines roared as she began to taxi out. They hurled the crates over the tailboard of the rising ramp and then jumped up to grab a handhold and pull themselves aboard. Nicholas was the first up and reached down to haul Sapper in.

When he looked back, Tessay was a small, lonely figure under the acacias.

'Give Mek my love and thanks,' he bellowed at her.

'You know how to contact us,' she screamed back.

'Goodbye, Tessay.' Royan's voice was lost in the blast of the great engines, and the dust blew back in a sheet over Tessay so that she was forced to cover her face and turn away. The ramp hissed closed on its hydraulic rams, and cut out their last glimpse of her.

Nicholas put an arm around Royan's shoulders and hustled her down the length of the cavernous cargo hold and into one of the jump seats at the entrance to the cockpit.

'Strap yourself in!' he ordered, and ran up the steps to the cockpit.

'Thought you had decided to stay behind,' Jannie greeted him mildly, without looking up from his controls. 'Hold tight! Here we go.'

Nicholas clung on to the back of the pilot's seat as Jannie and Fred between them pushed forward the bank of throttle levers to full power, and Big Dolly built up speed until she was careering down the strip.

Looking over Jannie's shoulder, Nicholas saw the vague shapes of men in camouflage battledress amongst the thorn scrub at the end of the runway. Some of them were firing at the huge aircraft as it raced towards them.

'Those popguns aren't going to hurt her much,' Jannie grunted. 'Big Dolly is a tough old lady.' And he lifted her into the air.

They flashed over the heads of the enemy troops on the ground, and Jannie set her nose high in the climb attitude.

'Welcome aboard, folks, thank you for flying Africair. Next stop Malta,' Jannie drawled, and then his voice rose sharply, 'Oh, oh! Where did this little piss-cat come from?'

Directly ahead of them the Jet Ranger rose out of the thick scrub on the banks of the Nile. The angle of the helicopter's climb meant that the approaching Hercules was hidden from the pilot's view, and he continued to rise directly into their path.

'Only five hundred feet and a hundred and ten knots on the clock,' Fred shouted a warning at his father from the right-hand seat. 'Too low to turn.'

The Jet Ranger was so close that Nicholas could clearly see Tuma Nogo in the front seat, his spectacles reflecting the sunlight like the eyes of a blind man, and his face freezing into a rictus of terror as he suddenly saw the great machine bearing down on them. At the last possible moment the pilot put his aircraft over in a wild dive to try to clear the nose of the approaching Hercules. It seemed impossible to avoid the collision, but he managed to bank the lighter, more manoeuvrable machine over until it rolled almost on to its back. It slipped under the belly of the Hercules, and the men in the cockpit of Jannie's plane barely felt the light kiss of the two fuselages.

However, the helicopter was flung over on to its nose by the impact, until it was pointing straight down at the earth only four hundred feet below. While Big Dolly flew on, climbing away steadily on an even keel, the pilot of the Jet Ranger struggled to control his crazily plummeting machine. Two hundred feet above the earth the turbulence thrown out astern by the massive T56-A-15 turbo-prop engines of the Hercules, each rated at 4900 horsepower, struck the helicopter with the force of an avalanche.

Like a dead leaf in an autumn gale she was swept away, spinning end over end, and when she struck the ground her own engines were still squealing at full power. On impact the fuselage crumpled like a sheet of aluminium cooking foil, and Nogo was dead even before the fuel tanks exploded and a fireball engulfed the Jet Ranger.

As soon as Jannie reached safe manoeuvring altitude he brought Big Dolly around on her northerly heading, and they could look back over the wing at the Roseires airstrip falling away behind them. The column of black smoke from the burning helicopter was tar-thick as it drifted away on the light westerly wind.

'You did say they were the uglies?' Jannie asked. 'So rather them than us, then?'

Once Jannie had settled Big Dolly on her northerly heading, and they were sailing low over the open deserted Sudanese plains, Nicholas went back into the main hold.

'Let's get the wounded settled down comfortably,' he suggested. Sapper and Royan unbuckled their safety belts and went back with him to attend to the men lying where their litters had been dumped during the haste of the getaway from Roseires.

After a while Nicholas left them to it and went forward to the small, well-stocked galley behind the flight deck. He opened some canned soup and sliced hunks of fresh bread from the loaves he found in the refrigerator. While the tea water boiled, he found his small emergency pack, and took from it the nylon wallet which contained his medicines and drugs. From one of the vials he shook five white tablets into the palm of his hand.

In the galley he crushed the tablets to powder, and when he poured tea into two of the mugs he stirred the powder in with it. Royan had enough English blood in her veins never to be able to refuse a mug of hot tea.

After they had served soup and buttered toast to the wounded men, Royan accepted her mug from Nicholas gratefully. While she and Sapper sipped their tea, Nicholas went back to the flight deck and leaned over the back of Jannie's seat.

'What is our flying time to the Egyptian border?' he asked.

'Four hours twenty minutes,' Jannie told him.

'Is there any way that we can avoid flying into Egyptian air space?' Nicholas wanted to know.

Jannie swivelled around in his seat and stared at him with astonishment. 'I suppose we could make a turn out to the west, through Gadaffi-land. Of course, it would mean an extra seven hours' flying time, and we would probably run out of fuel and end up making a forced landing somewhere out there in the Sahara.' He lifted an eyebrow at Nicholas. 'Tell me, my boy, what inspired that stupid question?'

'It was just a rare thought,' Nicholas said.

'Let it be not merely rare, but extinct,' Jannie advised. 'I don't want to hear it asked again, ever.'

Nicholas slapped his shoulder. 'Put it out of your mind.'

When he went back into the main hold, Sapper and Royan were sitting on two of the fold-down bunks that were bolted to the main bulkhead. Royan's empty tea mug stood on the deck at her feet. Nicholas sat down beside her, and she reached up and touched the bloodstained dressing that covered his chin.

'You had better let me see to that.' Her fingers were deft and cool on his hot inflamed skin as she cleaned the stitches with an alcohol swab and then placed a fresh plaster over them. Nicholas felt a strong twinge of guilt as he submitted to her ministrations.

However, it was Sapper who was the first to show the effects of the doped tea. He lay back gently and closed his eyes, then a soft snore vibrated his lips. Minutes later Royan sagged drowsily against Nicholas's shoulder. When she was fast asleep, he let her down gently and lifted her feet up on to the bunk. He spread a rug over her. She did not even stir, and he had a moment's doubt about the strength of the tablets.

Then he kissed her forehead softly. 'How could I ever hate you?' he asked her softly. 'Whatever you did.'

He went into the lavatory and locked the door. He had plenty of time. Sapper and Royan would not wake for hours yet, and Jannie and Fred were happily ensconced on the flight-deck, listening to Dolly Parton tapes on the audio system.

When at last he had finished, Nicholas glanced at his wrist-watch and realized that it had taken him almost two hours. He closed the toilet seat and washed his hands carefully. Then he took one last careful look around the tiny cabin and unlocked the door.

Sapper and Royan were still fast asleep on the fold-down bunks. He went forward to the flight-deck, and Fred pulled his earphones down around his neck and grinned at him.

'Nile water. It's poisonous. You have been locked in the loo for the last couple of hours. Surprised that there is anything left of you.'

Nicholas ignored the jibe and leaned over Jannie's seat back. 'Where are we?'

With a thick forefinger Jannie stabbed the chart that he was balancing on his protruding belly. 'Almost in the clear,' he said complacently. 'Egyptian border in one hour twelve minutes.'

Nicholas remained standing behind his seat until Jannie grunted and lifted the microphone. 'Time to go into my act.'

'Hallo, Abu Simbel Approach!' he said in a Gulf States accent. 'This is Zulu Whiskey Uniform Five Zero Zero.'

There was a long silence from the Egyptian controller. Jannie grunted. 'He probably has a bint in the tower with him. Got to give him time to get his pants back on.'

Abu Simbel Control answered on his fifth call. Jannie launched into his tried and tested routine, feigning ignorance in fluent colloquial Arabic.

After five minutes, Abu Simbel cleared him to continue on northwards, with an instruction to 'call again abeam Aswan'.

They flew on serenely for another hour, but Nicholas's nerves were screwing up tighter every minute.

Suddenly, without the least warning, there was a silvery flash ahead of them as a fighter interceptor, coming from below them, pulled up steeply across their bows. Jannie shouted with surprise and anger as another two warplanes rocketed up from under them, so close that they were buffeted by the turbulence of their jet trails.

They all recognized the type. They were MiG21 'Fishbeds' sporting the Egyptian air force livery, and with air-to-air missiles hanging in menacing pods under their swept-back wings.

'Unidentified aircraft!' Jannie yelled into his mouthpiece. 'You are on collision course. State your call sign!'

They all craned their necks and stared up through the Perspex canopy over the flight-deck. High above them they could see the three MiG fighters in formation circling against the blue of the African sky.

'ZWU 500. This is Red Leader of the Egyptian people's air force. You will conform to my orders.'

Jannie looked back at Nicholas, his expression forlorn.

'Something has gone wrong here. How the hell did they tumble to us?'

'You'd better do what the man says, Dad,' Fred advised miserably, 'otherwise he is going to blow us all over the sky.'

Jannie shrugged helplessly, and then spoke into his microphone mournfully. 'Red Leader. This is ZWU 500. We will cooperate. Please state your intentions.'

'Your new heading is 053. Execute immediately!'

Jannie brought Big Dolly around into the east and then glanced at his chart.

'Aswan!' he said dolefully. 'The Gyppos are taking us to Aswan. What the hell, I might as well warn Aswan tower that we have wounded on board.'

Nicholas went back to Royan's bunk and shook her awake. She was groggy and unsteady on her feet from the effects of the drug as she staggered to the lavatory. However, when she emerged again ten minutes later her hair was combed and she seemed alert and recovered from the mild draught that she had drunk in her tea.

There was the Nile ahead of them once more, and the town of Aswan on both banks, nestling below the first cataract and the impounded waters of the High Dam. Kitchener's Island swam like a green fish in the middle of the stream.

As the voice of the military controller at the Aswan airfield gave Jannie his orders, Big Dolly settled with unruffled dignity and lined up for the straight-in approach to the tarmac runway. The MiG fighters which had shepherded them in from the desert were no longer visible, but their presence high above was betrayed by their terse radio transmissions as they handed over their captive to the ground control.

Big Dolly sailed in over the perimeter fence and

touched down, and the voice of the controller ordered them, 'Turn first taxi-way right.'

Jannie obeyed, and as he turned off the main runway there was a small vehicle with a sign on its roof which read, in both English and Arabic, 'FOLLOW ME'.

The vehicle led them to a row of camouflaged concrete hangars in front of which a ground crew in khaki overalls signalled them with paddles into a parking stand. As soon as Jannie applied his brakes and brought Big Dolly to a halt, a file of four armoured half-tracks raced out and surrounded the huge aircraft, training their turret weapons upon her.

Obedient to the instructions radioed by control, Jannie shut down his engines and lowered the tail ramp of the aircraft. No one on the flight-deck had spoken since they had landed. They stood crowded together, looking unhappy, peering out of the cockpit windows.

Suddenly a white Cadillac with an escort of armed motorcyclists, followed by a military ambulance and a three-ton transport truck, drove through the gate of the perimeter fence and came directly to the foot of the cargo ramp of the Hercules. The chauffeur jumped out and opened the door, and his passenger stepped out into the late afternoon sunshine. He was clearly a person of authority, dignified and composed. He wore a light tropical suit and white shoes, a panama hat and dark glasses. As he came up the ramp to where the five of them waited, he was followed by two male secretaries.

He removed his dark glasses and tucked them into his breast pocket. As he recognized Royan he smiled and lifted his hat, 'Dr Al Simma – Royan! You did it. Congratulations!' He took her hand and shook it warmly, not relinquishing his grip as he looked directly at Nicholas.

'You must be Sir Nicholas Quenton-Harper. I have been looking forward to meeting you immensely. Won't you please introduce us, Royan?'

689

Royan could not meet Nicholas's accusing scrutiny as she said, 'May I present His Excellency, Atalan Abou Sin, Minister of Culture and Tourism in the Egyptian government.'

'You may indeed,' said Nicholas coldly. 'What an unexpected pleasure, Minister.'

'I would like to express the thanks of the President and the people of Egypt for returning to this country these precious relics of our ancient but glorious history.' He made a gesture that encompassed the stack of ammunition crates.

'Please, think nothing of it,' said Nicholas, but he never took his eyes off Royan. She kept her face turned half-away from him.

'On the contrary, we think the world of what you have done, Sir Nicholas.' Abou Sin's smile was charming and urbane. 'We are fully aware of the expense to which you have been put, and we would not want you to be out of pocket in this extraordinarily generous gesture of yours. Dr Al Simma tells me that the expedition to recover these treasures for us has cost you a quarter of a million sterling.' He took an envelope from his inside pocket, and proffered it to Nicholas.

'This is a banker's draft drawn on the Central Bank of Egypt. It is irrevocable, and payable anywhere in the world. It is for the sum of £250,000.'

'Very generous of you, Your Excellency.' Nicholas's voice was heavy with irony as he slipped the envelope into his top pocket. 'I presume this was Dr Al Simma's suggestion?'

'Of course,' beamed Abou Sin. 'Royan holds you in the very highest regard.'

'Does she, now?' Nicholas murmured, still staring at her expressionlessly.

'However, this other small token of our appreciation was the suggestion of the President himself.' The minister snapped his fingers and one of his secretaries stepped forward with a leather-covered medal case, which he opened before he presented it to Abou Sin.

On a bed of red velvet nestled a magnificent decoration, a star encrusted with seed pearls and tiny pavé diamonds. In the centre of the star was a golden lion rampant.

Abou Sin lifted the star from its case and advanced on Nicholas. 'The Order of the Great Lion of Egypt, First Class,' he announced, placing the scarlet ribbon over his head. The star hung resplendent on Nicholas's grubby shirt-front, heavily stained with sweat and dust and Nile mud.

Then the minister stood aside and made a gesture to the army colonel who was standing to attention at the foot of the ramp. Immediately there was an orderly rush of uniformed men up the ramp. The detachment of soldiers obviously had their orders. First they picked up the litters on which the wounded Ethiopians lay.

'I am glad that your pilot had the good sense to radio ahead that you had wounded men on board. Rest assured that they will receive the best care available,' Atalan Abou Sin promised as they were carried down to the waiting ambulance.

Then the soldiers returned and began carrying the ammunition cases down the ramp. They were loaded neatly into the three-tonner. Within ten minutes Big Dolly's hold was bare and empty. A tarpaulin cover was roped down securely over the back of the loaded truck. An escort of heavily armed motorcyclists fell into formation around it, and then, with sirens wailing, the little convoy roared away.

'Well, Sir Nicholas.' Abou Sin held out his hand courteously, and Nicholas took it with an air of resignation. 'I am sorry to have taken you out of your way like this. I know that you will be anxious to continue on your journey, so I will not detain you further. Is there anything I can do for you before you leave? Do you have sufficient fuel?'

Nicholas glanced at Jannie, and he shrugged. 'We have plenty of juice. Thank you, sir.'

Abou Sin turned back to Nicholas, 'We are planning to build a special annexe to the museum at Luxor to house these artefacts of Pharaoh Mamose that you have returned to Egypt. In due course you will be receiving a personal invitation from President Mubarak to attend, as an honoured guest, the opening of that museum. Dr Al Simma, whom I am sure you know has been appointed the new Director of the Department of Antiquities, will be in charge of the museum. I am sure she will be delighted to review the exhibits with you when you come back.'

He bowed to Sapper and the two pilots.

'Go with God,' he said, and went down the ramp. Royan began to follow him, but Nicholas called softly after her.

'Royan!' She froze, and then turned her head slowly and reluctantly to meet his eyes for the first time since they had landed.

'I didn't deserve that,' he said, and then with a stab of emotion he realized that she was weeping softly. Her lips quivered and the tears ran slowly down her cheeks.

'I am sorry, Nicky,' she whispered, 'but you must have known that I am not a thief. It belongs to Egypt, not to us.'

'So everything that I thought there was between us was a lie?' he demanded remorselessly.

'No!' she said. 'I—' and then she broke off without finishing what she was going to say. She ran down the ramp into the sunlight to where the chauffeur was holding the back door of the limousine open for her. She slipped on to the seat beside Abou Sin without looking back, and the Cadillac pulled away and drove through the gate.

'Let's get the hell out of here, before these Gyppos change their minds,' said Jannie.

'What a splendid idea,' said Nicholas bitterly.

Once they were airborne again, Aswan Control cleared them for a direct flight northwards to the Mediterranean coast. The four of them, Jannie and Fred, Sapper and Nicholas, stayed together on the flight-deck and watched the long green snake of the Nile crawl along their right wingtip.

They spoke very little during this long leg of the flight. Once Jannie said quietly, 'So I can kiss my fee goodbye, I suppose?'

'I didn't really come along for the money,' said Sapper, 'but it would have been nice to be paid. Baby needs new shoes.'

'Does anybody want a cup of tea?' Nicholas asked, as though he had not heard.

'That would be nice,' said Jannie. 'Not as nice as the sixty grand that you owe me, but nice anyway.'

They flew over the battlefield of El Alamein, and even from twenty thousand feet they could pick out the twin monuments to the Allied and German dead. Then the blue of the sea stretched ahead of them.

Nicholas waited until the Egyptian coast receded behind them and then he let out a long, soft sigh.

'O, ye of little faith,' he accused them. 'When did I ever let you down? Everybody gets paid in full.'

They all stared at him long and hard, and then Jannie voiced their doubts. 'How?' he asked.

'Give me a hand, Sapper,' Nicholas invited, and started down the staircase. Jannie could not control his curiosity and handed over the controls to Fred. He followed the two Englishmen down to the lavatory on the main deck.

Sapper and Jannie watched from the doorway as Nicholas took the Leatherman tool from his pocket and lifted the cover of the chemical toilet. Jannie grinned as Nicholas started to work on the screws, holding the hidden panel in place. Big Dolly was a smugglers' aircraft, and these little modifications were evidence of the pains that Jannie and Fred had taken to adapt her to that role. There were a number of these hidey-holes cunningly built into the engine housings and other parts of the fuselage.

When they had flown back from Libya, the Hannibal bronzes had reposed in the secret compartment behind this panel. The location of the panel in the back of the toilet made it highly unlikely that any follower of Islam would want to investigate such an unclean area.

'So that's what you were doing in here for so long,' Jannie laughed as Nicholas lifted out the panel. His grin faded as Nicholas reached into the space beyond and carefully drew out an extraordinary object. 'My God, what is that?'

'The blue war crown of ancient Egypt,' said Nicholas. He handed it to Sapper. 'Lay it on the bunk, but treat it carefully.'

He reached into the compartment again, 'And this is the Nemes crown.' He handed it to Jannie.

'And this is the red and white crown of the two kingdoms. And this is the death-mask of Pharaoh Mamose. Last but not least, this is the *ushabti* of the scribe Taita.'

The relics lay on the fold-down bunk, and they stood and stared at them reverently.

'I have helped you bring out stone friezes and little bronze statues,' said Jannie softly. 'But nothing like this before.'

'But,' Sapper shook his head, 'the ammunition crates the Gyppos offloaded at Aswan? What was in them?'

'Five one-gallon bottles of chemical for the toilet,' said

Nicholas, 'plus half a dozen spare oxygen cylinders, just to make up weight.'

'You switched them.' Sapper beamed at him. 'But how the hell did you know that Royan was going to scupper us?'

'She was right when she said I must have known she was no thief. The whole lark was out of character for her. She is,' he searched for the correct description, 'much too upright and honest. Not at all like the present company.'

'Thanks for the compliment,' said Jannie drily, 'but she must have given you more reason than that to make you suspicious.'

'Yes, of course.' Nicholas turned to him. 'The first real inkling I had was when we came back from Ethiopia the first time, and she immediately pushed off to Cairo. I guessed she was up to something. But I was absolutely certain only when I learned that she had passed a message, through Tessay, to the Egyptian Embassy in Addis. It was clear then that she had alerted them to our return flight.'

'The perfidious little bitch,' Jannie guffawed.

'Careful there!' said Nicholas stiffly. 'She is a decent, honest and patriotic young woman, warm-hearted and—'

'Well, well!' Jannie winked at Sapper. 'Please excuse my slip.'

Only two of the great crowns of ancient Egypt were set out on the polished walnut conference table. Nicholas had placed them on the heads of two genuine Roman marble busts that he had borrowed from a dealer with whom he did regular business here in Zurich. He had drawn the blinds over the tenth-storey windows, and arranged the lighting to show the crowns to the best effect. The private conference room that he had hired for the occasion was in the Bank Leu building on Bahnhofstrasse.

While he waited alone for the arrival of his invited guest, he reviewed his preparations and could find no fault with them. He went to the full-length mirror on one wall and tightened the knot of his old Sandhurst tie. The stitches had been removed from his chin. Mek Nimmur had done a first-rate job, and the scar was neat and clean. His suit had been made by his tailor in Savile Row, so it was in a muted chalk stripe and had been worn enough to have acquired just the right degree of casual bagginess. The only shiny items of his dress were the hand-made shoes from Lobb of St James's Street.

The intercom buzzed softly and Nicholas lifted the handset.

'There is a Mr Walsh to see you, Sir Nicholas,' said the receptionist at the desk in the bank lobby downstairs.

'Please ask him to come up.'

Nicholas opened the door at the first ring and Walsh glowered at him from the threshold.

'I hope you are not wasting my time, Harper. I have flown all the way from Fort Worth.' It was only thirty hours since Nicholas had telephoned him at his ranch in Texas. Walsh must have jumped into his executive jet almost immediately to have got here so soon.

'Not Harper. Quenton-Harper,' said Nicholas.

'Okay then, Quenton-Harper. But cut the crap,' Walsh said angrily. 'What have you got for me?'

'I am also delighted to see you again, Mr Walsh.' Nicholas stood aside. 'Do come in.'

Walsh strode into the room. He was tall and round-shouldered, his jowls drooping and wrinkled and his nose beaky. With his hands clasped behind his back he looked like a buzzard on a fence pole. *Forbes* magazine listed his net worth at 1.7 billion dollars.

Two men followed him into the room, and Nicholas recognized both of them. The antiquarian world was very small and incestuous. One of them was the professor of ancient history at Dallas University. Walsh had endowed the chair. The other was one of the most respected and knowledgeable antiques dealers in the United States.

Walsh stopped so suddenly that they both ran into him from behind, but he did not seem to notice.

'Son of a gun!' he said softly, and his eyes lit with the flames of fanaticism. 'Are those fakes?'

'As fake as the Hannibal bronzes and the Hammurabi bas-relief you bought from me,' said Nicholas.

Walsh approached the exhibits as though they were the cathedral communion plate and he the archbishop.

'These must be fresh,' he whispered. 'Otherwise I would have known about them.'

'Fresh out of the ground,' Nicholas confirmed. 'You are the first one to have seen them.'

'Mamose!' Walsh read the cartouche on the *uraeus* of the Nemes crown. 'Then the rumours are true. You have opened a new tomb.'

'If you can call nearly four thousand years old new.'

Walsh and his advisers gathered around the table, pale and speechless with shock.

'Leave us, Harper,' said Walsh. 'I will call you when I am ready to talk to you again.'

'Sir Nicholas,' he prompted the American. Nicholas knew that he had the upper hand now.

'Please leave us, Sir Nicholas,' Walsh pleaded.

An hour later Nicholas sauntered back into the conference room. The three men were seated around the table as though they could not bear to be parted from the two great crowns. Walsh nodded at his minions and they stood up and obediently but reluctantly filed from the room.

As soon as the door closed, Walsh asked brusquely, 'How much?'

'Fifteen million US dollars,' Nicholas replied.

'That's seven and a half mill each.'

'No, that's fifteen mill each. Thirty million the two.'

Walsh reeled in his chair. 'Are you crazy, or something?'

'There are those who think so,' Nicholas smiled.

'Split the difference,' said Walsh. 'Twenty-two and a half.'

Nicholas shook his head. 'Not negotiable.'

'Be reasonable, Harper!'

'Reasonability has never been one of my vices. Sorry.'

Walsh stood up. 'I am sorry too. Perhaps next time, Harper.'

He clasped his hands behind his back and stalked to the door. As he opened it, Nicholas called after him.

'Mr Walsh!'

He turned back eagerly. 'Yes?'

'Next time you may call me Nicholas, and I shall call you Peter, as old friends.'

'Is that all you have to say?'

'Of course. What else is there?' Nicholas looked puzzled.

'Damn you,' said Walsh, and came back to the table. He dropped into his chair. 'Damn you to hell and back!'

He sighed and pursed his lips, and then asked, 'Okay. How do you want it?'

'Two irrevocable bank drafts. Each for fifteen million.'

Walsh picked up the intercom, and spoke into it. 'Please ask Monsieur Montfleuri, your chief accountant, to come up here,' he ordered dolefully.

Nicholas sat at his desk in his study at Quenton Park. He stared at the panelling that covered the wall facing him. Although the panelling had originally come from one of the Catholic abbeys dissolved by Henry VIII in 1536 and had been bought by his grandfather almost a hundred years ago, it was newly installed in this setting.

He reached under the top of his desk and pressed the hidden button of the electronic control. A section of the panelling slid smoothly and silently aside to reveal the armoured plate glass of the display cabinet built into the wall behind it. At the same time the spotlights in the ceiling lit automatically, and their beams fell on the contents of the cabinet. The spots had been placed so that there was no reflection from the glass window to distract the eye, and the beams brought out the full glory of the double crown and the golden death-mask of Mamose.

He poured whisky into a crystal glass, and while he sipped it he savoured the thrill of ownership. But after a while he knew there was something missing. He picked up the Taita *ushabti* from the desk in front of him, and spoke to it as though he were addressing the subject himself.

'You knew the real meaning of loneliness, didn't you?' he asked softly. 'You knew what it was like to love someone you could never have.'

He set down the statuette and picked up the telephone. He dialled an international number and it rang three times before a man answered in Arabic.

'This is the office of the Director of Antiquities. How may I help you?'

'Is Dr Al Simma available?' he asked in the same language.

'Please hold the line. I am putting you through!'

'Dr Al Simma.' Her voice sent an electric thrill down his spine.

'Royan,' he said, and he could sense her shock in the long silence that followed.

'You!' she whispered. 'I did not think I would ever hear from you again.'

'I just rang to congratulate you on your appointment.'

'You cheated me,' she said. 'You switched the contents of three of the crates.'

'As a wise man once said, friends are the easiest to

cheat – they don't expect it. You, of all people, should know the truth of that, Royan.'

'You have sold them, of course. I have heard a rumour that Peter Walsh paid twenty million.'

'Thirty million,' Nicholas corrected her. 'But only for the blue and the Nemes. Even as I speak to you, the red and white crown and the death-mask repose before me.'

'So now you can pay off your Lloyd's insurance losses. You must be very relieved.'

'You won't believe this, but the Lloyd's syndicate on which I am a Name has come up with much better results than were forecast. I wasn't really broke after all.'

'As my mother would say, "Bully for you."'

'Half of it has already gone to Mek Nimmur and Tessay.'

'At least that is a good cause.' Her tone tingled with hostility. 'Is that all you called to tell me?'

'No. There's something else that might amuse you. Your favourite author, Wilbur Smith, has agreed to write the story of our discovery of the tomb. He is calling the book *The Seventh Scroll*. It should be published early next year. I will send you a signed copy.'

'I hope he gets his facts straight this time,' she said drily.

They were both silent for a while, before Royan broke it. 'I have a mountain of work in front of me. If there is nothing else on your mind—'

'As a matter of fact there is.'

'Yes?'

'I would like you to marry me.'

He heard her draw breath sharply, and then after a long pause she asked softly, 'Why would you want anything so unlikely?'

'Because I have come to realize how much I love you.'

She was silent again, and then she said in a small voice, 'All right.'

'What do you mean, "All right"?'

'I mean, all right, I will marry you.'

'Why would you agree to anything so unlikely?' he asked.

'Because I have come to realize, despite everything, how much I love you back.'

'There is an Air Egypt flight from Heathrow at 5.30 this afternoon. If I drive like fury, I may just make it. But it gets me into Cairo rather late.'

'I will be waiting at the airport, no matter how late.'

'I am on my way!' Nicholas hung up, and went to the door, but suddenly he turned back and picked up the the Taita *ushabti* from the desk.

'Come on, you old rogue.' He laughed triumphantly. 'You are going home, as a wedding gift.'

EPILOGUE

They strolled along the corniche in the mauve evening. Below them the Nile ran on eternally green and slow and inscrutable, disposing of the secrets of the ages. At the point on the river bank, below the ruins of the temple of Ramesses at Luxor, where once the great barge of Pharaoh Mamose had docked with Taita and his beloved mistress upon her prow, they paused for a while and leaned upon the coping of the stone retaining wall. They gazed out to the darkening hills across the river.

Time had long since obliterated the funerary temple and the great causeway of Mamose, and other kings had built their own monuments over the foundations. No man had ever discovered the tomb that he had never occupied, but it must have been situated close to the secret opening in the rock through which Duraid Al Simma had entered the tomb of Lostris and discovered there the scrolls of Taita in their alabaster jars.

All four of them were silent in the gathering dusk, the shared silence of firm friendship. They watched a cruise boat pass, coming upriver with the tourists clustered upon her decks, still agog after ten days of voyaging from Cairo on these enigmatic waters, pointing out to each other the great pylons and engraved walls of Ramesses' temple, their excited voices small and inconsequential in the hush of the desert evening.

Then Royan slipped her arm through Tessay's and the two women walked on ahead. They made a lovely pair, slim and young and honey-skinned, their laughter gay and sweet, their dark heads ruffling in the sultry puffs of Saharan air off the desert. Nicholas and Mek Nimmur followed them, each watching his own woman fondly as they bantered.

'So now you are one of the fatcats in Addis, you, the hard man, the bush fighter, you are now a politician. I can hardly believe it, Mek.'

'There is a time to fight and a time to make peace.' Mek was serious for a moment, but Nicholas mocked him lightly.

'I see that now that you are a politician you have to practise your clichés and your platitudes.' Nicholas punched his arm lightly. 'But how did you swing it, Mek? From dirty *shufta* bandit to Minister of Defence in one mighty bound.'

'The money from the sale of the blue crown helped a little. It gave me the clout I needed,' Mek admitted, 'but they knew they could never hold a democratic election without me as a candidate. In the end they were eager to have me on board.'

'The only quibble I have with the deal is that you handed all that lovely hard-won lolly over to them,' Nicholas mourned. 'Hell, Mek, fifteen million iron men don't come along every day.'

'I didn't hand it to them,' Mek corrected him. 'It was paid into the state coffers, where I can keep an eye on what eventually happens to it.'

'Still, fifteen mill is a lot of bread,' Nicholas sighed. 'Try as I might, I cannot approve of such extravagance, but I must admit that I do approve of your choice of running mate in your bid for the Presidency in the coming elections.'

They both looked at Tessay's slim back and bush of springing black curls as she strode along ahead of them on shapely brown legs under the white skirt.

'I may not approve of you as Minister of Defence, but I can see that she makes a very charming Minister of Culture and Tourism in the interim government.'

'She will make an even more impressive Vice-President when we win next August,' Mek predicted easily, and at that moment Royan looked back over her shoulder at them.

'We'll cross the road here,' she called. Nicholas had been so engrossed that he had not realized they had come up opposite to the new annexe to the Luxor Museum of Antiquities. The two women waited for them to catch up and then they separated and each of them took the arm of her own husband.

As they crossed the wide boulevard, threading their way between the slow clip-clopping horse-drawn gharries, Nicholas leaned down and brushed her cheek with his lips. 'You are really quite delectable, Lady Quenton-Harper.'

'You make me blush, Sir Nicky,' she giggled. 'You know that I am still not used to being called that.'

They reached the other side of the thoroughfare and paused before the entrance to the museum annexe. The sloping roof was supported by tall hypostyle columns, miniature copies of those at the temple of Karnak. The walls were made of massive blocks of yellow sandstone, and the lines of the building were clean and simple. It was very impressive.

Royan led them to the entrance doors of the museum, which was not yet open to the public. The President was flying up on Monday for the official opening, and Mek and Tessay were to be the official representatives of the Ethiopian government at the opening ceremony. The guards at the door saluted Royan respectfully and hurried to open the heavy brass-bound doors to let them pass.

The interior was hushed and cool, the air conditioning carefully regulated to preserve the ancient exhibits. The display cases were built into the sandstone walls, and the lighting was subtle and artful. It showed off the wondrous treasures of the Mamose funerary hoard to full advantage. The exhibits, arranged in ascending order of beauty and archaeological importance, sparkled and glowed in their nests of blue satin, the royal blue of the Pharaoh Mamose.

The four visitors were quiet and reverential as they passed, their voices soft and subdued as they asked questions of Royan. Wonder and amazement held them enthralled. They paused at the entrance of the final chamber, the one that housed the most extraordinary and valuable items in this glittering collection.

'To think that this is only a small part of what treasure still remains in Mamose's tomb, sealed by the waters of the Dandera river,' whispered Tessay. 'It's so exciting that I can hardly wait for the adventure to continue.'

'I forgot to tell you!' Mek exclaimed, and it was clear from his triumphant grin that he had not forgotten at all, but had been merely waiting for the appropriate moment to impart his news. 'The Smithsonian have confirmed their grant to redam the Dandera and reopen the tomb. It will be a joint venture between the Institution and the governments of our two countries, Egypt and Ethiopia.'

'That is wonderful news,' Royan exclaimed delightedly. 'The tomb itself will be one of the great archaeological sites of the world, and a huge source of tourist revenue for Ethiopia—'

'Not so fast,' Mek interrupted her. 'There is one condition that they stipulate.'

Royan looked crestfallen. 'What is their condition?'

'They insist that you, Royan, take on the job of director of the project.'

She clapped her hands with delight, and then put on a mock-serious expression. 'However, I have my own condition before I accept,' she said.

'And what is that?' Mek demanded.

'That I am able to appoint my own assistant on the dig.'

Mek let out a roar of laughter. 'We all know who that will be.' And he clapped Nicholas on the back. 'Just make sure that none of the artefacts cling to his sticky little fingers!' he warned.

Royan hugged Nicholas around the waist. 'He has completely reformed, I will now give you final proof of that.' Still clinging to her husband, she led them into the last chamber.

Mek and Tessay stopped in the entrance, silent with awe as they stared at the contents of the free-standing display case of armoured glass in the centre of the room. The red and white crown of the united kingdoms of upper and lower Egypt stood side by side with the glistening golden death-mask of Pharaoh Mamose in the brilliant light of the overhead spotlights.

At last Mek Nimmur recovered from the shock. Advancing slowly to the front panel of the display case, he stooped to read aloud the brass plate fixed to the front of it: "*The permanent loan of Sir Nicholas and Lady Quenton-Harper.*"

He turned back to stare at Nicholas incredulously. 'And you were the one who picked on me for turning over the money from the sale of the blue crown!' he accused him. 'How could you bring yourself to give up your share of the loot, Nicholas?'

'It wasn't easy,' Nicholas admitted with a sigh, 'but I was faced with a delicate ultimatum from a certain party who is not standing a million miles away from us at this very moment.'

'Don't feel too sorry for the poor boy,' Royan laughed. 'He still has a big lump of Peter Walsh's money tucked away in Switzerland, the proceeds of the sale of the Nemes crown. I was unable to talk him into handing everything over.'

'Enough of these public disclosures of my domestic affairs,' said Nicholas firmly. 'The sun is long gone, and it's whisky time. I think I saw a bottle of Laphroaig behind the bar at the hotel. Let's go and find out if I was mistaken.'

He took Royan's arm and led her away, and the other two followed closely, laughing delightedly at his discomfort.

GOLD MINE

This book is for my wife
and the jewel of my life, Mokhiniso,
with all my love and gratitude for
the enchanted years that
I have been married to her

- 1 -

It began in the time when the world was young, in the time before man, in the time before life itself had evolved upon this planet.

The crust of the earth was still thin and soft, distorted and riven by the enormous pressures from within.

What is now the flat, compacted shield of the African continent, stable and unchanging, was a series of alps. It was range upon range of mountains, thrown up and tumbled down by the movements of the magma at great depth. These were mountains such as man has never seen, so massive as to dwarf the Himalayas, mountains of steaming rock from whose clefts and gaping wounds the molten magma trickled.

It came up from the earth's centre along the fissures and weak places in the crust, bubbling and boiling, yet cooling steadily as it neared the surface so that the least volatile minerals were deposited deeper down, but those with a lower melting point were carried to the surface.

At one point in the measureless passage of time, another series of these fissures opened upon one of the nameless mountain ranges, but from them gushed rivers of molten gold. Some natural freak of temperature and chemical change had resulted in a crude but effective process of refinement during the journey to the earth's surface. The gold was in high concentration in the matrix, and it cooled and solidified at the surface.

If the mountains of that time were so massive as to challenge the imagination of man, then the storms of wind and rain that blew around them were of equal magnitude.

It was a hellish landscape in which the gold field was conceived, cruel mountains reaching stark and sheer in the clouds. Cloud banks dark with the sulphurous gases of the belching earth, so thick that the rays of the sun never penetrated them.

The atmosphere was laden with all the moisture that was to become the seas, so heavy with it that it rained in one perpetual wind-lashed storm upon the hot rock of the cooling earth, then the moisture rose in steam to condense and fall again.

As the years passed by their millions, so the wind and the rain whittled away at the nameless mountain range with its coating of gold-rich ore, grinding it loose and carrying it down in freshets and rivers and rushes of mud and rock into the valley between this range and the next.

Now as the country rock cooled, so the waters lay longer upon the earth before evaporating, and they accumulated in this valley to form a lake the size of an inland sea.

Into this lake poured the storm waters from the golden mountains, carrying with them tiny particles of the yellow metal which settled with other sand and quartz gravel upon the lake bed, to be compacted into a solid sheet.

In time all the gold was scoured from the mountains, transported and laid down upon the lake beds.

Then, as happened every ten million years or so, the earth entered another period of intense seismic activity. The earth shuddered and heaved as earthquake after mammoth earthquake convulsed it.

One fearsome paroxysm cracked the bed of the lake from end to end draining it and fracturing the sedimentary beds, scattering fragments haphazardly so that great sheets of rock many miles across tilted and reared on end.

Again and again the earthquakes gripped and shook the

2

earth. The mountains tottered and collapsed, filling the valley where the lake had stood, burying some of the sheets of gold-rich rock, pulverizing others.

That cycle of seismic activity passed, and the ages wheeled on in their majesty. The floods and the great droughts came and receded. The miraculous spark of life was struck and burned up brightly, through the time of the monstrous reptiles, on through countless twists and turns of evolution until near the middle of the Pleistocene age a man-ape – Australopithecus – picked up the thigh bone of a buffalo from beside an outcrop of rock to use it as a weapon, a tool.

Australopithecus stood at the centre of a flat, sun-seared plateau that reached five hundred miles in each direction to the sea, for the mountains and the lake beds had long ago been flattened and buried.

Eight hundred thousand years later, one of the Australopithecus' distant but direct line stood at the same spot with a tool in his hand. The man's name was Harrison and the tool was more sophisticated than that of his ancestor, it was a prospector's pick of wood and metal.

Harrison stooped and chipped at the outcrop of rock that protruded from the dry brown African earth. He freed a piece of the stone and straightened with it in his hand.

He held it to catch the sun and grunted with disgust. It was a most uninteresting piece of stone, conglomerate, marbled black and grey. Without hope he held it to his mouth and licked it, wetting the surface before again holding it to the sun, an old prospectors' trick to highlight the metal in the ore.

His eyes narrowed in surprise as the tiny golden flecks in the rock sparkled back at him.

History remembers only his name, not his age nor his antecedents, not the colour of his eyes nor how he died, for within a month he had sold his claim for £10 and disappeared – in search, perhaps, of a really big strike.

He might have done better to retain his title to those claims.

In the eighty years since then an estimated five hundred million ounces of fine gold have been recovered from the fields of the Transvaal and Orange Free State. This is a fraction of that which remains, and which in time will be taken from the earth. For the men who mine the South African fields are the most patiently persistent, inventive and pig-headed of all Vulcan's brood.

This mass of precious metal is the foundation on which the prosperity of a vigorous young nation of eighteen million souls is based.

Yet the earth yields her treasure reluctantly – men must coax and wrest it from her.

– 2 –

Even with the electric fan blowing up a gale from the corner it was stinking hot in Rod Ironsides' office.

He reached for the silver Thermos of iced water at the edge of his desk, and arrested the movement as the jug began to dance before his finger tips touched it. The metal bottle skittered across the polished wooden surface; the desk itself shuddered, rustling the papers upon it. The walls of the room shook, so that the windows rattled in their frames. Four seconds the tremor lasted, and then it was still again.

'Christ!' said Rod, and snatched up one of the three telephones on his desk.

'This is the Underground Manager. Get me the rock mechanic's lab, honey, and snap it up, please.'

He drummed his fingers on the desk impatiently as he waited to be connected. The interleading door of his office opened and Dimitri put his head around the jamb.

'You feel that one, Rod? That was a bad one.'

'I felt it.' Then the telephone spoke into his ear.

'Dr Wessels here.'

'Peter, it's Rod. Did you read that one?'

'I haven't got a fix on it yet – can you hold on a minute?'

'I'll wait.' Rod curbed his impatience. He knew that Peter Wessels was the only person who could read the mass of complicated electronic equipment that filled the instrument room of the rock mechanic's laboratory. The laboratory was a joint research project by four of the major gold-mining companies; between them they had put up a quarter of a million Rand to finance an authoritative investigation of rock and seismic activity under stress. They had selected the Sonder Ditch Gold Mining Company's lease area as the site for the laboratory. Now Peter Wessels had his microphones sited thousands of feet down in the earth, and his tape recorders and stylus graphs ready to pinpoint any underground disturbance.

Another minute ticked by, and Rod swivelled his chair and stared out of the plate glass window at the monstrous head gear of No. 1 shaft, tall as a ten-storey building.

'Come on, Peter, come on, boy,' he muttered to himself. 'I've got twelve thousand of my boys down there.'

With the telephone still pressed to his ear, he glanced at his watch.

'Two-thirty,' he muttered. 'The worst possible time. They'll still be in the stopes.'

He heard the receiver picked up on the other end, and Peter Wessels' voice was almost apologetic.

'Rod?'

'Yes.'

'I'm sorry, Rod, you've had a force seven pressure burst at 9,500 feet in sector Sugar seven Charlie two.'

'Christ!' said Rod and slammed down the receiver. He was up from his desk in one movement, his face set and angry.

'Dimitri,' he snapped at his assistant still in the doorway.

'We won't wait for them to call us, it's a top sequence emergency. That was a force seven bump, with its source plumb in the middle of our eastern longwall at 95 level.'

'Sweet Mary Mother,' said Dimitri, and darted back into his own office. He bent his glossy black head of curls over the telephone and Rod heard him start his top sequence calls.

'Mine hospital ... emergency team ... Chief Ventilation Officer ... General Manager's office.'

Rod turned away, as the outer door of his office opened and Jimmy Paterson, his electrical engineer, came in.

'I felt it, Rod. How's it look?'

'Bad,' said Rod, then there were the other line managers crowding into his office talking quietly, lighting cigarettes, coughing and shuffling their feet, but all of them watching the white telephone on Rod's desk. The minutes crawled by like crippled insects.

'Dimitri,' Rod called out to break the tension. 'Have you got a cage held at the shaft head?'

'They're holding the Mary Anne for us.'

'I've got five men checking the high tension cable on 95 level,' said Jimmy Paterson, and they ignored him. They were watching the white phone.

'Have you located the boss yet, Dimitri?' Rod asked again; he was pacing in front of his desk. It was only when he stood close to other men that you saw how tall he was.

'He's underground, Rod. He went down at twelve-thirty.'

'Put in an all-stations call for him to contact me here.'

'I've done that already.'

The white phone rang.

Only once, a shrill note that ripped along Rod's nerve ends. Then he had the receiver up to his ear.

'Underground Manager,' he said. There was a long silence and he could hear the man breathing on the other end.

'Speak, man, what is it?'

6

'The whole bloody thing has come down,' said the voice. It was husky, rough with fear and dust.

'Where are you speaking from?' Rod asked.

'They're still in there,' said the voice. 'They're screaming in there. Under the rock. They're screaming.'

'What is your station?' Rod made his voice cold, hard, trying to reach the man through his shock.

'The whole stope fell in on them. The whole bloody thing.'

'God damn you! You stupid bastard!' Rod bellowed into the phone. 'Give me your station!'

There was stunned silence for a moment. Then the man's voice came back, steadier now, angry from the insult.

'95 level main haulage. Section 43. Eastern longwall.'

'We're coming.' Rod hung up, picked up his yellow fibreglass hard helmet and lamp from the desk.

'43 section. The hanging wall has come down,' he said to Dimitri.

'Fatals?' the little Greek asked.

'For sure. They've got squealers under the rock.'

Rod clapped on his hat.

'Take over on surface, Dimitri.'

– 3 –

Rod was still buttoning the front of his white overalls as he reached the shaft head. Automatically he read the sign above the entrance:

STAY ALERT.   STAY ALIVE.
WITH YOUR CO-OPERATION THIS MINE HAS WORKED
16 FATALITY-FREE DAYS.

'We'll have to change the number again,' Rod thought with grim humour.

7

The Mary Anne was waiting. Into its heavily wired confines were crowded the first aid team and emergency squad. The Mary Anne was the small cage used for lowering and hoisting personnel, there were two much larger cages that could carry one 120 men at one trip, while the Mary Anne could handle only forty. But that was sufficient for now.

'Let's go,' said Rod as he stepped into the cage, and the onsetter slammed the steel roller doors closed. The bell rang once, twice, and the floor dropped away from under him as the Mary Anne started down. Rod's belly came up to press against his ribs. They went down in one long continuous rush in the darkness. The cage jarring and racketing, the air changing in smell and taste, becoming chemical and processed, the heat building up rapidly.

Rod stood hunch-shouldered, leaning against the metal screen of the cage. The head room was a mere six foot three, and with his helmet on Rod stood taller than that. So today we get another butcher's bill, he thought angrily.

He was always angry when the earth took its payment in mangled flesh and snapping bones. All the ingenuity of man and the experience gained in sixty years of deep mining on the Witwatersrand were used in trying to keep the price in blood as low as possible. But when you go down into the ultra-deep levels below 8,000 feet and from those depths you remove a quarter of a million tons of rock each month, mining on an inclined sheet of reef that leaves a vast low-roofed chamber thousands of feet across, then you must pay, for the stress builds up in the rock as the focal points of pressure change until the moment when it reaches breaking point and she bumps. That is when men die.

Rod's knees flexed under him as the cage braked and then yoyoed to a halt at the brightly lit station on 66 level.

Here they must trans-ship to the sub-main shaft. The door rattled up and Rod left the cage, striding out down the main haulage the size of a railway tunnel; concreted and

8

whitewashed, brightly lit by the bulbs that lined the roof, it curved gently away.

The emergency team followed Rod. Not running, but walking with the suppressed nervous energy of men going into danger. Rod led them towards the sub-main shaft.

There is a limit to the depth which you can sink a shaft into the earth and then equip it to carry men suspended on a steel cable in a tiny wire cage. The limit is about 7,000 feet.

At this depth you must start again, blast out a new headgear chamber from the living rock and below it sink your new shaft, the sub-main.

The sub-main Mary Anne was waiting for them, and Rod led them into it. They stood shoulder to shoulder, and the door rattled shut and again the stomach-swooping rush down into darkness.

Down, down, down.

Rod switched on his head lamp. Now there were tiny motes in the air – air that had been sterilely clean before.

Dust! One of the deadly enemies of the miner. Dust from the burst. As yet the ventilation system had been unable to clear it.

Endlessly they fell in darkness and now it was very hot, the humidity building up so the faces about him, both black and white, were shiny with sweat in the light of his head lamp.

The dust was thicker now, someone coughed. The brightly lit stations flashed past them – 76, 77, 78 – down, down. The dust was a fine mist now. 85, 86, 87. No one had spoken since entering the cage. 93, 94, 95. The deceleration and stop.

The door rattled up. They were 9,500 feet below the surface of the earth.

'Come on,' said Rod.

There were men cluttering the lobby of 95 station, a hundred and fifty, perhaps two hundred of them. Still filthy from their work in the stopes, clothing sodden with sweat, they were laughing and chattering with the abandon of men freshly released from frightful danger.

In a clear space in the centre of the lobby lay five stretchers, on two of them the bright red blankets were pulled up to cover the faces of the men upon them. The faces of the other three men looked as though they had been dusted with flour.

'Two' – grunted Rod – 'so far.'

The station was a shambles, with men milling aimlessly; each minute more of them came back down the haulages as they were pulled out of the undamaged stopes, which were now suspect.

Quickly Rod looked about him, recognizing the face of one of his mine captains.

'McGee,' he shouted. 'Take over here. Get them sitting down in lines ready to load. We'll start hauling the shift out immediately. Get onto the hoist room, tell them I want the stretcher cases out first.'

He paused long enough to watch McGee take control. He glanced at his watch. Two fifty-six. He realized with astonishment that only twenty-six minutes had passed since he felt the pressure burst in his office.

McGee had the station under a semblance of control. He was shouting into the hoist room telephone, on Rod's authority demanding priority to clear 95 station.

'Right,' said Rod. 'Come on.' And he led into the haulage.

The dust was thick. He coughed. The hanging wall was lower here. As he trudged on once more, Rod pondered the unfortunate choice of mining terminology that had named the roof of an excavation 'the hanging wall'. It made one think of a gallows, or at the best it emphasized the fact that there were millions of tons of rock *hanging* overhead.

The haulage branched, and unerringly Rod took the right fork. In his head he carried an accurate three-dimensional map of the entire 176 miles of tunnels that comprised the Sonder Ditch's workings. The haulage came to a T-junction and the arms were lower and narrower. Right to 42 section, left to 43 section. The dust was so thick that visibility was down to ten feet. The dust hung in the air, sinking almost imperceptibly.

'Ventilations knocked out here,' he called over his shoulder. 'Van den Bergh!'

'Yes, sir.' The leader of the emergency squad came up behind him.

'I want air in this drive. Get it on. Use canvas piping if you have to.'

'Right.'

'Then I want pressure on the water hoses to lay this dust.'

'Right.'

Rod turned into the drive. Here the foot wall – the floor – was rough and the going slower. They came upon a line of steel trolleys filled with gold reef abandoned in the centre of the drive.

'Get these the hell out of the way,' ordered Rod, and went on.

Fifty paces and he stopped abruptly. He felt the hair on his forearms stand on end. He could never accustom himself to the sound, no matter how often he heard it.

In the deliberately callous slang of the miner they called them 'squealers'. It was the sound of a grown man, with his legs crushed under hundreds of tons of rock, perhaps his spine broken, dust suffocating him, his mind unhinged by

11

the mortal horror of the situation in which he was trapped, calling for help, calling to his God, calling for his wife, his children, or his mother.

Rod started forward again, with the sound of it becoming louder, a terrifying sound, hardly human, sobbing and babbling into silence, only to start again with a blood-chilling scream.

Suddenly there were men ahead of Rod in the tunnel, dark shapes looming in the dust mist, their head lamps throwing shafts of yellow light, grotesque, distorted.

'Who is that?' Rod called, and they recognized his voice.

'Thank God. Thank God you've come, Mr Ironsides.'

'Who is that?'

'Barnard.' The 43 section shift boss.

'What's the damage?'

'The whole hanging wall of the stope came down.'

'How many men in the stope?'

'Forty-two.'

'How many still in?'

'So far we've got out sixteen unhurt, twelve slightly hurt, three stretcher cases and two dead 'uns.'

The squealer started again, but his voice was much weaker.

'Him?' asked Rod.

'He's got twenty ton of rock lying across his pelvis. I've hit him with two shots of morphine, but it won't stop him.'

'Can you get into the stope?'

'Yes, there is a crawling hole.' Barnard flashed his lamp over the pile of fractured blue quartzite that jammed the drive like a collapsed garden wall. On it was an aperture big enough for a fox terrier to run through. Reflected light showed from the hole, and faintly from within came the grating sounds of movement over loose rock and the muffled voices of men.

'How many men have you got working in there, Barnard?'

'I – ' Barnard hesitated, 'I think about ten or twelve.'

And Rod grabbed a handful of his overall front and jerked him almost off his feet.

'You think!' In the head lamps Rod's face was white with fury. 'You've put men in there without recording their numbers? You've put twelve of my boys against the wall to try and save nine?' With a heave Rod lifted the shift boss off his feet and swung him against the side wall of the drive, pinning him there.

'You bastard, you know that most of those nine are chopped already. You know that stope is a bloody killing ground, and you send in *twelve* more to get the chop *and* you don't record their numbers. How the hell would we ever know who to look for if the hanging fell again?' He let the shift boss free, and stood back. 'Get them out of here, clear that stope.'

'But, Mr Ironsides, the General Manager is in there, Mr Lemmer is in there. He was doing an inspection in the stope.'

For a moment Rod was taken aback, then he snarled. 'I don't give a good damn if the State President is in there, clear the stope. We'll start again and this time we'll do it properly.'

Within minutes the rescuers had been recalled, they came squirming out of the aperture, white with dust like maggots wriggling from rotten cheese.

'Right,' said Rod, 'I'll risk four men at a time.'

Quickly he picked four of the floury figures, among them an enormous man on whose right shoulder was the brass badge of a boss boy.

'Big King – you here?' Rod spoke in Fanikalo, the lingua franca of the mines which enabled men from a dozen ethnic groups to communicate.

'I am here,' answered Big King.

'You looking for more awards?' A month before, Big King had been lowered on a rope 200 feet down a vertical

13

orepass to retrieve the body of a white miner. The bravery award by the company had been 100 rand.

'Who speaks of awards when the earth has eaten the flesh of men?' Big King rebuked Rod softly. 'But today is children's play only. Is the Nkosi coming into the stope?' It was a challenge.

Rod's place was not in the stope. He was the organizer, the co-ordinator. Yet, he could not ignore the challenge, no Bantu would believe that he had not stood back in fear and sent other men in to die.

'Yes,' said Rod, 'I'm coming into the stope.'

He led them in. The hole was only just big enough to admit the bulk of Rod's body. He found himself in a chamber the size of an average room, but the roof was only three and a half feet high. He played his lamp quickly across the hanging wall, and it was wicked. The rock was cracked and ugly, 'a bunch of grapes' was the term.

'Very pretty,' he said, and dropped the beam of his lamp.

The squealer was within an arm's length of Rod. His body from the waist up protruded from under a piece of rock the size of a Cadillac. Someone had wrapped a red blanket around his upper body. He was quiet now, lying still. But as the beam of Rod's lamp fell upon him, he lifted his head. His eyes were crazed, unseeing, his face running with the sweat of terror and insanity. His mouth snapped open, wide and pink in the shiny blackness of his face. He began to scream, but suddenly the sound was drowned by a great red-black gout of blood that came gushing up his throat, and spurted from his mouth.

As Rod watched in horror, the Bantu posed like that, his head thrown back, his mouth gaping as though he were a gargoyle, the life blood pouring from him. Then slowly the head sagged forward, and flopped face downwards. Rod crawled to him, lifted his head and pillowed it on the red blanket.

There was blood on his hands and he wiped it on the front of his overalls.

'Three,' he said, 'so far.' And leaving the dying man he crawled on towards the broken face of the fall.

Big King crawled up beside him with two pinch bars. He handed one to Rod.

Within an hour it had become a contest, a trial of strength between two men. Behind them the other three men were shoring up and passing back the rock that Rod and Big King loosened from the face. Rod knew he was being childish, he should have been back in the main haulage, not only directing the rescue, but also making all the other decisions and alternative arrangements that were needed now. The company paid him for his brains and his experience, not for his muscle.

'The hell with it,' he thought. 'Even if we miss the blast this evening, I'm staying here.' He glanced at Big King, and reached forward to get his hands onto a bigger piece of rock in the jam. He strained, using his arms first, then bringing the power of his whole body into it – the rock was solid. Big King placed huge black hands on the rock, and they pulled together. In a rush of smaller rock it came away, and they shoved it back between them, grinning at each other.

At seven o'clock Rod and Big King withdrew from the stope to rest and eat sandwiches, and drink Thermos coffee while Rod spoke to Dimitri over the field telephone that had been laid up to the face.

'We've pulled shift on both shafts, Rod, the workings are clear to blast. Except for your lot, there are fifty-eight men in your 43 section.' Dimitri's voice was reedy over the field telephone.

'Hold on.' Rod revolved the situation in his mind. He worked it out slower than usual, for he was tired, emotionally and physically drained. If he stopped the blast on both shafts for fear of bringing down more rock in 43 section, it would cost the Company a day's production, 10,000 tons of gold reef worth sixteen rand a ton, the formidable sum of R160,000 or £80,000 or $200,000 whichever way you looked at it.

It was highly probable that every man in the stope was already dead, and the original pressure burst had de-stressed the rock above and around the 95 level, so there was little danger of further bumps.

And yet there might be someone alive in there, someone lying pinned in the womb-warm darkness of the stope with a bunch of loose grapes hanging over his unprotected body. When they hit all the blast buttons on the Sonder Ditch Mine, they fired eighteen tons of Dynagel. The kick was considerable, it would bring down those grapes.

'Dimitri,' Rod made his decision, 'burn all longwalls on No. 2 shaft at seven-thirty exactly.' No. 2 shaft was three miles away. That would save the Company R80,000. 'Then at precisely five-minute intervals burn south, north and west longwalls here on No. 1 shaft.' Spreading the blast would reduce the disturbance, and that put another R60,000 in the shareholders' pockets. The total monetary loss inflicted by the disaster was around R20,000. Not too bad really, Rod thought sardonically, blood was cheap. You could buy it at three rand a pint from the Central Blood Transfusion Service.

'All right,' he stood up, and flexed his aching shoulders. 'I'm pulling everybody back into the safety of the shaft pillar while we blast.'

5

After the successive earth tremors of the blast, Rod put them back into the stope, and at nine o'clock they uncovered the bodies of two machine boys crushed against the metal of their own rock drill. Ten feet further on they found the white miner; his body was unmarked, but his head was flattened.

At eleven o'clock they found two more machine boys. Rod was in the haulage when they dragged them out through the small opening. Neither of them were recognizable as human, they looked more like lumps of raw meat that had been rubbed in dirt.

A little after midnight Rod and Big King went into the stope again to take over from the team at the face, and twenty minutes later they holed through the wall of loose rock into another chamber that had been miraculously left standing.

The air in here was steamy with heat. Rod recoiled instinctively from the filthy moist gush of it against his face. Then he forced himself to crawl forward and peer into the opening.

Ten feet away lay Frank Lemmer, the General Manager of the Sonder Ditch Mine. He lay on his back. His helmet had been knocked from his head, and a deep gash split the skin above his eye. Blood from the gash had run back into his silver hair and clotted black. He opened his eyes and blinked owlishly in the dazzle of Rod's lamp. Quickly Rod averted the beam.

'Mr Lemmer,' he said.

'What the bloody hell are you doing with the rescue team?' growled Frank Lemmer. 'It's not your job. Haven't you learned a single goddamned thing in twenty years of mining?'

'Are you all right, sir?'

'Get a doctor in here,' replied Frank Lemmer. 'You're going to have to cut me loose from this lot.'

Rod wriggled up to where he lay, and then he saw what Frank Lemmer meant. From the elbow his arm was pinned under a solid slab of rock. Rod ran his hands over the slab, feeling it. Only explosive would shift the rock. As always Frank Lemmer was right.

Rod wriggled out of the opening and called over his shoulder.

'Get the telephone up here.'

After a few minutes delay he had the receiver, and was through to the station at 95 level which had been set up as an advance aid post and rest station for the rescuers.

'This is Ironsides, get me Doctor Stander.'

'Hold on.'

Then moments later, 'Hello, Rod, it's Dan.'

'Dan, we've found the old man.'

'How is he, conscious?'

'Yes, but he's pinned – you'll have to cut.'

'Are you sure?' Dan Stander asked.

'Of course I'm bloody well sure,' snapped Rod.

'Whoa, boy!' admonished Dan.

'Sorry.'

'Okay, where's he caught?'

'Arm. You'll have to cut above the elbow.'

'Charming!' said Dan.

'I'll wait here for you.'

'Right. I'll be up in five minutes.'

6

'It's funny, you see them chopped time and again, but you know it will never happen to you.' Frank Lemmer's voice was steady and even. The arm must be numb, Rod thought as he lay beside him in the stope.

Frank Lemmer rolled his head towards Rod. 'Why don't you go farming, boy?'

'You know why,' said Rod.

'Yes.' Lemmer smiled a little, just a twitching of the lips. With his free hand he wiped his mouth. 'You know, I had just three months more before I went on pension. I nearly made it. You'll end like this, boy, in the dirt with your bones crunched up.'

'It's not the end,' said Rod.

'Isn't it?' asked Frank Lemmer, and this time he chuckled. 'Isn't it?'

'What's the joke?' asked Dan Stander, poking his head into the tiny chamber.

'Christ, it took you long enough to get here,' growled Frank Lemmer.

'Give me a hand, Rod.' Dan passed his bag through, then as he crawled forward he spoke to Frank Lemmer.

'Union Steel closed at 98 cents tonight. I told you to buy.'

'Over-priced, over-capitalized,' snorted Frank Lemmer. Dan lay on his side in the dirt and laid out his instruments, and they argued stocks and shares. When Dan had the syringe full of pentathol and was swabbing Frank Lemmer's stringy old arm, Lemmer rolled his head towards Rod again.

'We made a good dig here, Rodney, you and I. I wish they'd give it to you now, but they won't. You're still too young. But whoever they put in my place, you keep an eye on him, you know the ground – don't let him balls it up.'

And the needle went in.

Dan cut through the arm in four and a half minutes, and twenty-seven minutes later Frank Lemmer died of shock and exposure in the Mary Anne on his way to the surface.

– 7 –

O nce he had paid Patti's alimony there was not too much of Rod's salary left for extravagances, but one of these was the big cream Maserati. Although it was a 1967 model, and had done nearly 30,000 miles when he bought it, yet the instalments still took a healthy bite out of his monthly pay cheque.

On mornings like this he reckoned the expense worthwhile. He came twisting down from the Kraalkop ridge, and when the national road flattened and straightened for the final run into Johannesburg he let the Maserati go. The car seemed to flatten against the ground like a running lion, and the exhaust note changed subtly, becoming deeper, more urgent.

Ordinarily, it was an hour's run from the Sonder Ditch Mine into the city of Johannesburg, but Rod could clip twenty minutes off that time.

It was Saturday morning, and Rod's mood was light and expectant.

Since the divorce Rod had lived a Jekyll and Hyde existence. Five days of the week he was the company man in top-line management, but on the last two days of the week he went into Johannesburg with his golf clubs in the boot of the Maserati, the keys to his luxury Hillbrow apartment in his pocket, and a chuckle on his lips.

Today the anticipation was keener than ever for, in addition to the twenty-two-year-old blonde model who was prepared to devote her evening to entertaining Rodney Ironsides, there was the mysterious summons from Dr Manfred Steyner to answer.

The summons had been delivered by a nameless female caller describing herself as 'Dr Steyner's Secretary'. It had come the day after Frank Lemmer's funeral, and was for Saturday at 11 a.m.

Rod had never met Manfred Steyner, but he had, of course, heard of him. Anyone who worked for any of the fifty or sixty companies that comprised the Central Rand Consolidated Group must have heard of Manfred Steyner, and the Sonder Ditch Gold Company was just one of the Group.

Manfred Steyner had a bachelor's degree in Economics from Berlin University, and a Doctor's degree in Business Administration from Cornell. He had joined CRC a mere twelve years previously at the age of thirty, and now he was the front runner. Hurry Hirschfeld could not live for ever, although he gave indications of doing so, and when he went down to make a takeover bid on Hades, the word was that Manfred Steyner would succeed him as Chairman of CRC.

Chairmanship of CRC was an enviable position, the incumbent automatically became one of the five most powerful men in Africa, and that included heads of state.

The betting favoured Dr Steyner for a number of good reasons. He had a brain that had earned him the nickname of 'The Computer'; no one had yet been able to detect in him the slightest evidence of a human weakness, and more than this he had taken the trouble ten years previously to catch Hurry Hirschfeld's only granddaughter as she emerged from Cape Town University and marry her.

Dr Steyner was in a strong position, and Rod was intrigued with the prospect of meeting him.

The Maserati was registering 125 miles an hour as he went under the over-pass of the Kloof Gold Mining Company property.

'Johannesburg, here I come!' Rod laughed aloud.

It was ten minutes before eleven o'clock when Rod

21

found the brass plaque reading 'Dr M. K. Steyner' in a secluded lane of the lush Johannesburg suburb of Sandown. The house was not visible from the road, and Rod let the Maserati roll gently in through the tall white gates, with their imitation Cape Dutch gables.

The gates, he decided, were a display of shocking taste but the gardens beyond them were paradise. Rod knew rock, but flowers were his weak suit. He recognized the massed banks of red and yellow against the green lawns as cannas, but after that he had no names for the blazing beauty spread about him.

'Wow!' he muttered in awe. 'Someone has done a hell of a lot of work around here.'

Around a curve in the macadamized drive lay the house. It also was Cape Dutch and Rod forgave Dr Steyner his gates.

'Wow!' he said again, and involuntarily braked the Maserati to a standstill.

Cape Dutch is one of the most difficult styles to copy effectively, where one line in a hundred out of place could spoil the effect; this particular example worked perfectly. It gave the feel of timelessness, of solidarity, and mixed it subtly with a grace and finesse of line. He guessed that the shutters and beams were genuine yellow wood and the windows hand-leaded.

Rod looked at it, and felt envy prickle and burn within him. He loved fine things, like his Maserati, but this was another concept in material possessions. He was jealous of the man that owned it, knowing that his own entire year's income would not be sufficient for a down payment on the land alone.

'So I've got my flat,' he grinned ruefully, and coasted down to park in front of the line of garages.

It was not clear which was the correct entrance to use, and he chose at random from a number of paved paths that all led in the general direction of the house.

Around a bend in this path he came on another spectacle. Though smaller it had, if anything, a more profound effect on Rod than the house had. It was a feminine posterior of equal grace and finesse of line, clad in Helanka stretch ski-pants, and protruding from a large and exotic bush.

Rod was captivated. He stood and watched as the bush shook and rustled, and the bottom wriggled and heaved.

Suddenly, in ladylike tones there issued from the bush a most unladylike oath and the bottom shot backwards and its owner straightened up with her forefinger in her mouth, sucking noisily.

'It bit me!' she mumbled around the finger. 'Damned stinkbug bit me!'

'Well, you shouldn't tease them,' said Rod.

And she spun round to face him. The first thing Rod noticed were her eyes, they were enormous, completely out of proportion to the rest of her face.

'I wasn't—' she started, and then stopped. The finger came out of her mouth. Instinctively one hand went to her hair, and the other began straightening her blouse and brushing off bits of vegetation that were clinging to her.

'Who are you?' she asked, and those huge eyes swept over him. This was fairly standard reaction for any woman between the ages of sixteen and sixty viewing Rodney Ironsides for the first time, and Rodney accepted it gracefully.

'My name is Rodney Ironsides. I've an appointment to see Dr Steyner.'

'Oh.' She was hurriedly tucking her shirt-tails into her slacks. 'My husband will be in his study.'

He had known who she was. He had seen her photographs fifty times in the Group newspaper; but in them she was usually in full-length evening dress and diamonds, not in a blouse with a tear in one sleeve nor pig-tails that were coming down. In the pictures her make-up was immaculate,

23

now she had none at all and her face was flushed and dewed with perspiration.

'I must look a mess. I've been gardening,' said Theresa Steyner unnecessarily.

'Did you do this garden yourself?'

'Only a very little of the muscle work, but I planned it,' she answered. She decided he was big and ugly – no, not really ugly, but battered-looking.

'It's beautiful,' said Rod.

'Thank you.' No, not battered-looking, she changed her mind, tough-looking, and the chest hair curled out of the V of his open neck shirt.

'This is a protea, isn't it?' He indicated the bush from which she had recently emerged. He was guessing.

'Nutans,' she said; he must be in his late thirties, there was greying at his temples.

'Oh, I thought it was a protea.'

'It is. "Nutans" is its proper name. There are over two hundred different varieties of proteas,' she answered seriously. His voice didn't fit his appearance at all, she decided. He looked like a prize fighter but spoke like a lawyer, probably was one. It was usually lawyers or business consultants who came calling on Manfred.

'Is that so? It's very pretty.' Rod touched one of the blooms.

'Yes, isn't it? I've got over fifty varieties growing here.'

And suddenly they were smiling at each other. 'I'll take you up to the house,' said Theresa Steyner.

24

'**M**r Ironsides is here, Manfred.'

'Thank you.' He sat at the stinkwood desk in a room that smelled of wax polish. He made no effort to rise from his seat.

'Would you like a cup of coffee?' Theresa asked from the doorway. 'Or tea?'

'No, thank you,' answered Manfred Steyner without consulting Rod who stood beside her.

'I'll leave you to it, then,' she said.

'Thank you, Theresa.' And she turned away. Rod went on standing where he was, he was studying this man of whom he had heard so much.

Manfred Steyner appeared younger than his forty-two years. His hair was light brown, almost blond, and brushed straight back. He wore spectacles with heavy black frames, and his face was smooth and silky-looking, soft as a girl's with no beard shadow on his chin. His hands that lay on the polished desk top were hairless, smooth, so that Rod wondered if he had used a depilatory on them.

'Come in,' he said, and Rod moved to the desk. Steyner wore a white silk shirt in which the ironing creases still showed, the cloth was snowy white and over it he wore a Royal Johannesburg Golf Club tie, with onyx cuff links. Suddenly Rod realized that neither shirt nor tie had ever been worn before; that much was true of what he had heard then. Steyner ordered his shirts hand-made by the gross and wore each once only.

'Sit down, Ironsides.' Steyner slurred his vowels slightly, just a trace of a Teutonic accent.

'Dr Steyner,' said Rod softly, 'you have a choice. You may call me Rodney or Mr Ironsides.'

There was no change in Steyner's voice nor expression.

'I would like to go over your background, please, Mr

Ironsides, as a preliminary to our discussion. You have no objection?'

'No, Dr Steyner.'

'You were born October 16th, 1931, at Butterworth in the Transkei. Your father was a native trader, your mother died January 1939. Your father was commissioned Captain in the Durban Light Infantry and died of wounds on the Po River in Italy during the winter of 1944. You were raised by your maternal uncle in East London. Matriculating from Queen's College, Grahamstown, in 1947, you were unsuccessful in obtaining a Chamber of Mines scholarship to Witwatersrand University for a B.Sc. (Mining Engineering) degree. You enrolled in the GMTS (Government Mining Training School) and obtained your blasting ticket during 1949. At which time you joined the Blyvooruitzicht Gold Mining Company Ltd as a learner miner.'

Dr Steyner stood up from his desk and crossing to the panelled wall he pressed a concealed switch and a portion of the panelling slid back to reveal a wash basin and towel rack. As he went on talking he began very meticulously to soap and wash his hands.

'In the same year you were promoted to miner and in 1952 to shift boss, 1954 to mine captain. You successfully completed the examination for the Mine Manager's ticket in 1959, and in 1962 you came to us as an Assistant Underground Manager, and in 1968 you achieved your present position as Underground Manager.'

Dr Steyner began drying his hands on a snowy white towel.

'You've memorized my company record pretty thoroughly,' Rod admitted.

Dr Steyner crumpled the towel and dropped it into a bin below the wash basin. He pressed the button and the panelling slid closed, then he came back to the desk stepping precisely over the glossy polished wooden floor, and Rod realized that he was a small man, not more than five and a half feet tall, about the same height as his wife.

'This is something of an achievement,' Steyner went on. 'The next youngest Underground Manager in the entire Group is forty-six years of age, whereas you are not yet thirty-nine.'

Rod inclined his head in acknowledgement.

'Now,' said Dr Steyner as he reseated himself and laid his freshly washed hands on the desk top. 'I would like briefly to touch on your private life – you have no objections?'

Again Rod inclined his head.

'The reason that your application for the Chamber of Mines scholarship was refused, despite your straight A matriculation, was the recommendation of your headmaster to the selection board in effect that you were of unstable and violent disposition.'

'How the hell did you know that?' ejaculated Rod.

'I have access to the board's records. It seems that once you had received your matric you immediately assaulted your former headmaster.'

'I beat the hell out of the bastard,' Rod agreed happily.

'An expensive indulgence, Mr Ironsides. It cost you a university degree.'

And Rod was silent.

'To continue: In 1959 you married Patricia Anne Harvey. Of the union was born a girl child in the same year, to be precise, seven and a half months after the wedding.'

Rod squirmed slightly in his chair, and Dr Steyner went on quietly.

'This marriage terminated in divorce in 1964. Your wife is suing you on the grounds of adultery, and receiving custody of the child, alimony and maintenance in the sum of R450.000 monthly.'

27

'What's all this about?' demanded Rod.

'I am attempting to establish an accurate picture of your present circumstances. It is necessary, I assure you.' Dr Steyner removed his spectacles and began polishing the lens on a clean white handkerchief. There were the marks of the frames on the bridge of his nose.

'Go on, then.' Despite himself, Rod was fascinated to learn just how much Steyner knew about him.

'In 1968 there was a paternity suit brought against you by a Miss Diane Johnson and judgement for R150.00 per month.'

Rod blinked and was silent.

'I should mention two further actions against you for assault, both unsuccessful on the grounds of justification or self-defence.'

'Is that all?' asked Rod sarcastically.

'Almost,' admitted Dr Steyner. 'It is only necessary to note further recurrent expenditure in the form of a monthly payment of R150.00 on a continental sports car, and a further R100.00 per month rental on the premises 596 Glen Alpine Heights, Corner Lane, Hillbrow.'

Rod was furious, he had believed that no one in CRC knew about the flat.

'Damn you! You've been prying into my affairs!'

'Yes,' agreed Dr Steyner levelly. 'I am guilty, but in good cause. If you bear with me, you'll see why.'

Suddenly Dr Steyner stood up from the desk, crossed the room to the concealed wash basin, and again began to wash his hands. As he dried them, he spoke again.

'Your monthly commitments are R850. Your salary, after deduction of tax, is less than one thousand Rand. You have no mining degree, and the chances of your taking the next step upwards to General Manager without it are remote. You are at your ceiling, Mr Ironsides. On your own ability you can go no further. In thirty years' time you will not be

28

the youngest Underground Manager in the CRC Group, but the oldest.' Dr Steyner paused. 'That is, provided that your rather expensive tastes have not landed you in a debtors' prison, and that neither the quickness and heat of your temper, nor the matching speed and temperature of your genitalia have gotten you into really serious trouble.'

Steyner dropped the towel in the bin and returned to his seat. They sat in absolute silence, regarding each other for a full minute.

'You got me all the way up here to tell me this?' asked Rod, his whole body tense, his voice slightly husky. It needed only an ounce more of provocation to launch him across the desk at Steyner's throat.

'No.' Steyner shook his head. 'I got you up here to tell you that I will use all my influence, which I flatter myself is considerable, to secure your appointment – and I mean immediate appointment – to the position of General Manager of the Sonder Ditch Gold Mining Company Ltd.'

Rod recoiled in his chair as though Steyner had spat in his face. He stared at him aghast.

'Why?' he asked at last. 'What do you want in exchange?'

'Neither your friendship, nor your gratitude,' Dr Steyner told him. 'But your unquestioning obedience to my instructions. You will be my man – completely.'

Rod went on staring at him while his mind raced. Without Steyner's intervention he would wait at the very least ten years for this promotion, if it ever came. He wanted it, my God, how he wanted it. The achievement, the increase in income, the power that went with the job. His own mine! His own mine at the age of thirty-eight – and an additional 10,000 rand per annum.

Yet Rod was not gullible enough to believe that Manfred Steyner's price would be cheap. When the instruction came that he was to follow with unquestioning obedience, he knew it would stink like a ten-day corpse. But once he had the job he could refuse the instruction. Get the job first, then decide once he received the instruction whether to follow it or not.

'I accept,' he said.

Manfred Steyner stood up from the desk.

'You will hear from me,' he said. 'Now you may go.'

– 9 –

Rod crossed the wide-flagged stoep without seeing or hearing; vaguely he wandered down across the lawns towards his car. His mind was harrying the recent conversation, tearing it to pieces like a pack of wild dogs on a carcass. He almost bumped into Theresa Steyner before he saw her, and abruptly his mind dropped the subject of the General Managership.

Theresa had changed her clothing, made up her face and eyes, and the pig-tails were concealed under a lime-coloured silk scarf, all this in the half hour since their last meeting. She was hovering over a flower bed with a flower basket on one arm, as bright and pleasing as a hummingbird.

Rod was amused and flattered, vain enough to realize that the change was in his honour, and connoisseur enough to appreciate the improvement.

'Hello.' She looked up, contriving successfully to look both surprised and artless. Her eyes were really enormous, and the make-up was designed to enhance their size.

'You are a busy little bee.' Rod ran a knowledgeable appraisal over the floral slack suit she wore, and saw the colour start in her cheeks as she felt his eyes.

'Did you have a successful meeting?'

'Very.'

'Are you a lawyer?'

'No. I work for your grandfather.'

'Doing what?'

30

'Mining his gold.'

'Which mine?'

'Sonder Ditch.'

'What's your position?'

'Well, if your husband is as good as his word, I'm the new General Manager.'

'You're too young,' she said.

'That's what I thought.'

'Pops will have something to say on the subject.'

'Pops?' he asked.

'My grandfather.' And Rod laughed before he could stop himself.

'What's so funny?'

'The Chairman of CRC being called "Pops".'

'I'm the only one who calls him that.'

'I bet you are.' Rod laughed again. 'In fact I'd bet you'd get away with a lot of things no one else would dare.'

Suddenly the underlying sexuality of his last remark occurred to them both and they fell silent. Theresa looked down and carefully snipped the head off a flower.

'I didn't mean it that way,' apologized Rod.

'What way, Mr Ironsides?' She looked up and enquired with mischievous innocence, and they laughed together with the awkwardness gone again.

She walked beside him to the car, making it seem a completely natural thing to do, and as he slipped behind the steering-wheel she remarked:

'Manfred and I will be coming out to the Sonder Ditch next week. Manfred is to present long service and bravery awards to some of your men.' She had already refused the invitation to accompany Manfred, she must now see to it that she was re-invited. 'I shall probably see you then.'

'I look forward to it,' said Rod, and let in the clutch.

Rod glanced in the rear view mirror. She was a remarkably provocative and attractive woman. A careless man could drown in those eyes.

'Dr Manfred Steyner has got himself a big fat problem there,' he decided. 'Our Manfred is probably so busy soaping and scrubbing his equipment, that he never gets round to using it.'

– 10 –

Through the leaded windows Dr Steyner caught a glimpse of the Maserati as it disappeared around the curve in the driveway, and he listened as the throb of the engine dwindled into silence.

He lifted the receiver of the telephone and wiped it with the white handkerchief before putting it to his ear. He dialled and while it rang he inspected the nails of his free hand minutely.

'Steyner,' he said into the mouthpiece. 'Yes – yes.' He listened.

'Yes . . . He has just left . . . Yes, it is arranged . . . No, there will be no difficulty there, I am sure.' As he spoke he was looking at the palm of his hand, he saw the tiny beads of perspiration appear on his skin and an expression of disgust tightened his lips.

'I am fully aware of the consequences. I tell you, I know.'

He closed his eyes and listened for another minute without moving as the receiver squawked and clacked, then he opened his eyes.

'It will be done in good time, I assure you. Goodbye.'

He hung up and went to wash his hands. Now, he thought, as he worked up lather, to get it past the old man.

11

He was old now, seventy-eight long hard years old. His hair and his eyebrows were creamy white. His skin was folded and creased, freckled and spotted, hanging in unexpected little pouches under his chin and eyes.

His body had dried out, so he stood gaunt and stooped like a tree that has taken a set before the prevailing winds; but there was still the underlying urgency in the way he held himself, the same urgency that had earned him the name of 'Hurry' Hirschfeld when first he bustled into the gold fields sixty years ago.

On this Monday morning he was standing before the full length windows of his penthouse office, looking down on the city of Johannesburg. Reef House stood shoulder to massive shoulder with the Schlesinger Building on the Braamfontein ridge above the city proper. From this height it seemed that Johannesburg cowered at Hurry Hirschfeld's feet, as well it should.

Long ago, even before the great depression of the 'thirties, he had ceased to measure his wealth in terms of money. He owned outright a little over a quarter of the issued share capital of Central Rand Consolidated. At the present market price of R120 per share, this was a staggering sum. In addition, through a complicated arrangement of trusts, proxy rights and interlocking directorates, he had control of a further massive block of twenty per cent of the company's voting rights.

The overhead intercom pinged softly into this room of soft fabrics and muted colours, and Hurry started slightly.

'Yes,' he said, without turning away from the window.

'Dr Steyner is here, Mr Hirschfeld,' his secretary's voice whispered, ghostly and disembodied into the luscious room.

'Send him in,' snapped Hurry. That goddamned intercom

always gave him the creeps. The whole goddamned room gave him the creeps. It was, as Hurry had said often and loudly, like a fairy brothel.

For fifty-five years he had worked in a bleak uncarpeted office with a few yellowing photographs of men and machinery on its walls. Then they had moved him in here – he glanced around the room with the distaste that five years had not lulled. What did they think he was, a bloody ladies' hairdresser?

The panelling door slid noiselessly aside and Dr Manfred Steyner stepped neatly into the room.

'Good morning, Grandfather,' he said. For ten years, even since Terry had been bird-brained enough to marry him, Manfred Steyner had called Hurry Hirschfeld that, and Hurry hated it. He remembered now that Manfred Steyner was also responsible for the design and decor of Reef House, and therefore the author of his recent irritation.

'Whatever it is you want – No!' he said, and he moved across to the air-conditioning controls. The thermostat was already set at 'high', now Hurry turned it to 'highest'. Within minutes the room would be at the correct temperature for growing orchids.

'How are you this morning, Grandfather?' Manfred seemed not to have heard, his expression was bland and neutral as he moved to the desk and laid out his papers.

'Bloody awful,' said Hurry. It was impossible to disconcert the little prig, he thought, you might as well shout insults at an efficiently functioning piece of machinery.

'I am sorry to hear that.' Manfred took out his handkerchief and touched his chin and forehead. 'I have the weekly reports.'

Hurry capitulated and went across to the desk. This was business. He sat down and read quickly. His questions were abrupt, cutting and instantly answered, but Manfred's handkerchief was busy now, swabbing and dabbing. Twice he removed his spectacles and wiped steam from the lenses.

'Can I turn the air-conditioning down a little, Grandfather?'

'You touch it and I'll kick your arse,' said Hurry without looking up.

Another five minutes and Manfred Steyner stood up suddenly.

'Excuse me, Grandfather.' And he shot across the office and disappeared into the adjoining bathroom suite. Hurry cocked his head to listen, and when he heard the taps hiss he grinned happily. The air-conditioning was the only method he had discovered of disconcerting Manfred Steyner, and for ten years he had been experimenting with various techniques.

'Don't use all the soap,' he shouted gleefully. 'You are the one always on about office expenses!'

It did not seem ludicrous to Hurry that one of the richest and most influential men in Africa should devote so much time and energy to baiting his personal assistant.

At eleven o'clock Manfred Steyner gathered his papers and began packing them carefully in his monogrammed pigskin briefcase.

'About the appointment of a new General Manager for the Sonder Ditch to replace Mr Lemmer. You will recall my memo regarding the appointment of younger men to key positions—'

'Never read the bloody thing,' lied Hurry Hirschfeld. They both knew he read everything, and remembered it.

'Well—' Manfred went on to enlarge his thesis for a minute, then ended, 'In view of this, my department, myself concurring entirely, urges the appointment of Rodney Barry Ironsides, the present Underground Manager, to the position. I hoped that you would initial the recommendation and we can put it through at Friday's meeting.'

Dexterously Manfred slid the yellow memo in front of Hurry Hirschfeld, unscrewed the cap of his pen and offered it to him. Hurry picked the memo up between thumb and forefinger as though it were someone's dirty handkerchief and dropped it into the waste-paper bin.

'Do you wish me to tell you in detail what you and your planning department can do?' he asked.

'Grandfather,' Manfred admonished him mildly, 'you cannot run the company as though you were a robber baron. You cannot ignore the team of highly trained men who are your advisers.'

'I've run it that way for fifty years. You show me who's going to change that.' Hurry leaned back in his chair with vast satisfaction and fished a powerful-looking cigar out of his inner pocket.

'Grandfather, that cigar! The doctor said—'

'And I said Fred Plummer gets the job as Manager of the Sonder Ditch.'

'He goes on pension next year,' protested Manfred Steyner.

'Yes,' Hurry nodded. 'But how does that alter the position?'

'He's an old dodderer,' Manfred tried again, there was a desperate edge to his voice. He had not anticipated one of the old man's whims cutting across his plans.

'He's twelve years younger than I am,' growled Hurry ominously. 'How's that make him an old dodderer?'

12

Now that the weekend was over, Rod found the apartment oppressive, and he longed to get out of it.

He shaved, standing naked before the mirror, and he caught a whiff of the reeking ashtrays and half-empty glasses in the lounge. The char would have her customary Monday-morning greeting when she came in later today. From Louis Botha Avenue the traffic noise was starting to build up and he glanced at his watch – six o'clock in the morning. A good time to examine your soul, he decided, and leaned forward to watch his own eyes in the mirror.

'You're too old for this type of living,' he told himself seriously. 'You've had four years of it now, four years since the divorce, and that's about enough. It would be nice now to go to bed with the same woman on two consecutive nights.'

He rinsed his razor, and turned on the taps in the shower cabinet.

'Might even be able to afford it, if our boy Manfred delivers the goods.' Rod had not allowed himself to believe too implicitly in Manfred Steyner's promise; but during the whole of these last two days the excitement had been there beneath the cynicism.

He stepped into the shower and soaped himself, then turned the cold tap full on. Gasping he shut it off and reached for his towel. Still drying himself, he went through and stood at the foot of the bed; as he towelled himself he examined the girl who lay among the tousled sheets.

She was tanned dark toffee brown so she appeared to be dressed in white transparent bra and panties where the skin was untouched by the sun. Her hair was a blonde-gold flurry across her face and the pillow, at odds with the jet black triangle of body hair. Her lips in sleep were fixed in a soft pink pout, and she looked disquietingly young. Rod had to make a conscious effort to remember her name, she was not the companion with whom he had begun the weekend.

'Lucille,' he said, sitting down beside her. 'Wake up. Time to roll.'

She opened her eyes.

'Good morning,' he said and kissed her gently.

'Mmm.' She blinked. 'What time is it? I don't want to get fired.'

'Six,' he told her.

'Oh, good. Plenty of time.' And she rolled over and snuggled down into the sheets.

'Like hell.' He slapped her bottom lightly. 'Move, girl, can you cook?'

'No—' She lifted her head. 'What's your name again?' she asked.

'Rod,' he told her.

'That's right – Piston Rod,' she giggled. 'What a way to die! Are you sure you aren't powered by steam?'

'How old are you?' he asked.

'Nineteen. How old are you?'

'Thirty-eight.'

'Daddy, you're vintage!' she told him vehemently.

'Yes, sometimes I feel that way.' He stood up. 'Let's go.'

'You go. I'll lock up when I leave.'

'No sale,' he said, the last one he had left in the flat had cleaned it out – groceries, liquor, glasses, towels, even the ashtrays. 'Five minutes to dress.'

Fortunately she lived on his way. She directed him to a run-down block of flats under the mine dumps at Booysens.

'I'm putting three blind sisters through school. You want to help?' she asked as he parked the Maserati.

'Sure.' He eased a five-rand note out of his wallet and handed it to her.

'Ta muchly.' And she slipped out of the red leather seat, closed the door and walked away. She did not look back

38

before she disappeared into the block, and Rod felt an unaccountable wave of loneliness wash over him. It was so intense that he sat quiescent for a full minute before he could throw it off, then he hit the gears and screeched away from the kerb.

'My little five-rand friend,' he said. 'She really cares!'

He drove fast, so that as he topped the Kraalkop ridge the shadows were still long, and the dew lay silver on the grass. He pulled the Maserati into a layby and climbed out. Leaning against the bonnet he lit a cigarette, grimacing at the taste, and looked down at the valley.

There was no natural surface indication of the immense treasure house that lay below. It was like any of the other countless grassy plains of the Transvaal. In the centre stood the town of Kitchenerville, which for half a century had rejoiced in the fact that Lord Kitchener had camped one night here in pursuit of the wily Boer: a collection of three dozen buildings which had expanded miraculously into three thousand, around a magnificent town hall and shopping complex. Dressed in public lawns and gardens, wide streets and bright new houses, all of it paid for by the mining houses whose lease areas converged on the town.

Out of the bleak veld surrounding the town their headgears stood like colossal monuments to the gold hunger of man. Around the headgears clustered the plants and workshops. There were fourteen headgears in the valley. The field was divided into five lease areas, following the original farm titles, and was mined by five separate companies. Thornfontein Gold Mining, Blaauberg Gold Mining, West Tweefontein Mining, Deep Gold Levels, and the Sonder Ditch Gold Mining Company.

It was to this last that Rod naturally directed his attention.

'You beauty,' he whispered, for in his eyes the mountainous dumps of blue rock beside the shafts were truly beautiful. The complex but carefully thought out pattern of the works buildings, even the sulphur-yellow acres of the slimes dam, had a functional beauty.

'Get it for me, Manfred,' he spoke aloud. 'I want it. I want it badly.'

On the twenty-eight square miles of the Sonder Ditch's property lived 14,000 human beings, 12,000 of them were Bantu who had been recruited from all over Southern Africa. They lived in the multi-storied hostels near the shaft heads, and each day they went down through two small holes in the ground to depths that were scarcely credible, and came up again out of those same two holes. 12,000 men down, 12,000 up. That was not all: out of those two same holes came 10,000 tons of rock daily, and down them went timber and tools and piping and explosive, ton upon ton of material and equipment. It was an undertaking that must evoke pride in the men who accomplished it.

Rod glanced at his watch, 7.35 a.m. They were down already, all 12,000 of them. They had started going down at three-thirty that morning and now it was accomplished. The shift was in. The Sonder Ditch was breaking rock, and bringing the stuff out.

Rod grinned happily. His loneliness and depression of an hour ago were gone, swallowed up in the immensity of his involvement. He watched the massive wheels of the headgears spinning, stopping briefly, and then spinning again.

Each of those shafts had cost fifty million rand, the surface plant and works another fifty million. The Sonder Ditch represented an investment of 150 million rand, 220 million dollars. It was big, and it would be his.

Rod flicked away the butt of his cigarette. As he drove down the ridge, his eyes moved eastward down the valley. All mining activity ceased abruptly along an imaginary north-south line, drawn arbitarily across the open grassland.

There was no surface indication why this should be so, but the reason was deep down.

On that line ran a geological freak, a dyke, a wall of hard serpentine rock that had been named 'the Big Dipper'. It cut through the field like an axe stroke, and beyond it was bad ground. The gold reef existed in the bad ground, they knew this; but not one of the five companies had gone after it. They had prospected it tentatively and then shied away from it, for the boreholes that they sank were frightening in their inconsistency.

A big percentage of the Sonder Ditch lease area lay on the far side of the Dipper, and there was a diamond-drilling team working there now. They had already completed five holes.

Rod could remember accurately the results:-

Borehole SD No. 1.	Abandoned in water at 4,000 ft.
SD No. 2.	Abandoned in dry hole at 5,250 ft.
SD No. 3.	Intersected carbon leader reef at 6,600 ft.
Assay valve	27,323-inch penny-weights.
First deflection	6,212-inch penny-weights.
Second deflection	2,114-inch penny-weights.
SD No. 4.	Abandoned in artesian water at 3,500 ft.
SD No. 5.	Intersected carbon leader at 8,116 ft.
Assay valve	562-inch penny-weights.

And they were drilling the deflections on that one now.

The problem was to build up a picture from results like that. It looked like a mess of faulted and waterlogged ground with the gold reef fragmented and fluky, showing unbelievably high values at one spot, and then more than likely pinching out fifty feet away.

They may mine it one day, thought Rod, but I hope to hell I'm on pension by the time they do.

In the distance beyond the slimes dam he could just make out the spidery triangle of the drilling rig against the grown grass.

'Go to it, boys,' he muttered. 'Whatever you find there won't make much difference to me.'

And he went in through the imposing gates at the entrance to the mine property, halting carefully at the stop sign where the railway line crossed the road and he forked two fingers at the traffic policeman lurking behind the gates.

The traffic cop grinned and waved; he had caught Rod the previous week, so he was still one up.

Rod drove down to his office.

– 13 –

That Monday morning Allen 'Popeye' Worth was preparing to drill his first deflection on the SD No. 5. borehole. Allen was a Texan – not a typical Texan. He stood five feet four inches tall, but was as tough as the steel drill with which he worked. Thirty years before he had started learning his trade on the oilfields around Odessa and he had learned it well.

Now he could start at the surface and drill a four-inch hole down 13,000 feet through the earth's crust, keeping the hole straight all the way, an almost impossible task if you took into account the whippiness and torque in a jointed rod of steel that long.

If, as happened occasionally, the steel snapped and broke off thousands of feet down, Allen could fit a fishing tool on the end of his rig, and patiently grope for the stump, find it, grapple it and pull it out of the borehole. When he hit the reef down there, he could purposely kick his drill off the line and pierce the reef again and again to sample it over an area of hundreds of feet. This was what was meant by deflecting.

Allen was one of the best. He could command his own salary and behave like a prima donna, and his bosses would still fawn on him, for the things he could do with a diamond drill were almost magical.

Now he was assessing the angle of his first deflection. The previous day he had lowered a long brass bottle to the end of his borehole and left it overnight. The bottle was half filled with concentrated sulphuric acid, and it had etched the brass of the bottle. By measuring the angle of the etching he knew just how his drill was branching off from his original hole.

In the tiny wood and iron building beside the drilling rig he finished his measurements and stood back from the work bench, grunting with satisfaction.

From his hip pocket he drew a corncob pipe and pouch. Once he had stuffed tobacco into the pipe and lit it, it became very clear as to why his nickname was 'Popeye'. He was a dead ringer for the cartoon character, aggressive jaw, button eyes, battered maritime cap and all.

He puffed contentedly, watching through the single window of the shack as his gang went about the tedious business of lowering the drilling bit down into the earth. Then he took the pipe from his mouth and spat accurately through the window, replaced the pipe and stooped to minutely check his measurements.

His foreman driller interrupted him from the doorway.

'On bottom, and ready to turn, boss.'

'Huh!' Popeye checked his watch. 'Two hours forty to get down, you don't reckon to rupture a gut do you?'

'That's not bad,' protested the foreman.

'And it sure as hell isn't good either! Okay, okay, cut the cackle and let's get her turning.' He bounced out of the shed and set off for the rig, darting quick beady little glances about him. The rig was a fifty-foot-high tower of steel girders and within it the drill rod hung down until it disappeared into the collar. The twin 200-horsepower diesel engines throbbed expectantly, waiting to provide the power, their exhausts smoking blue in the early morning sunlight. Beside the rig lay a mountainous heap of drilling rods, beyond them the 10,000-gallon puddling reservoir to provide water for the hole. Water was pumped into the hole continuously to cool and lubricate the tool as it cut into the rock.

'Stand by to turn her,' Popeye called to his gang, and they moved to their stations. Dressed in blue overalls, coloured fibreglass helmets, and leather gloves, they stood ready and tensed. This was an anxious moment for the whole team: power had to be applied with a lover's touch to the mile and a half length of rod, or it would buckle and snap.

Popeye climbed nimbly up onto the collar, and glanced about him to make sure all was in readiness. The foreman driller was at the controls, watching Popeye with complete absorption, his hands resting on the levers.

'Power up!' shouted Popeye and made the circular motion with his right hand. The diesels bellowed harshly, and Popeye reached out to lay his left hand on the drilling rod. This was how he did it, feeling the rod with his bare hand as he brought in the power, judging the tension by ear and eye and touch.

His right hand gestured and the foreman delicately let in the clutch, the rod moved under Popeye's hand, he gestured again and it revolved slowly. He could feel it was near breaking point and he cut down the power instantly, then let it in again. His right hand moved eloquently, expressively as an orchestral conductor, and the foreman followed it, the junior member of a highly skilled team.

Slowly the tension of the gang relaxed as the revolutions

of the drill built up steadily, until Popeye gave the clenched fist 'okay' and jumped down from the collar. They scattered casually to their other duties, while Popeye and the foreman strolled back to the shed, leaving the drill to grind away at a steady four hundred revolutions a minute.

'Got something for you,' said the foreman, as they entered the shed.

'What?' demanded Popeye.

'The latest *Playboy*.'

'You're kidding!' Popeye accused him delightedly, but the foreman fished the rolled magazine out of his lunch box.

'Hey, there!' Popeye snatched it from him and turned immediately to the coloured foldout.

'Isn't that something!' He whistled. 'This dolly could get a job in a stockyard beating the oxen to death with her boo-boos!'

The foreman joined the discussion of the young lady's anatomy, and so neither of them noticed the change in the sound of the drill until two minutes had passed. Then Popeye heard it through an erotic haze. He flung the magazine from him, and went through the door of the shed white-faced.

It was fifty yards from the shed to the rig, but even at that distance Popeye could see the vibration in the drilling rod. He could hear the labouring note of the diesels as they carried increased load, and he ran like a fox terrier, trying to reach the controls and shut off the engines before it happened.

He knew what it was. His drill had cut into one of the many fissures with which this badly faulted ground was criss-crossed. The puddling water from his borehole had drained away leaving the bit to run dry against dry rock. The friction head had built up, the dust from the cut was not being washed away – and in consequence the rod had jammed. It was being held tightly at one end while at the other the two big diesels were straining to turn it. The whole rig was seconds away from a twist-off.

There should have been an operator at the controls to meet just such an emergency, but he was a hundred yards away, just emerging from the wood and iron latrine beyond the puddling dam. He was desperately trying to hoist his pants, clinch the buckle of his belt and run all at the same time.

'You whore's chamberpot!' roared Popeye, as he ran. 'What the hell you goofing off—'

The words choked off in his throat, for as he reached the door of the engine room there was a report like a cannon shot as the rod snapped, and immediately the diesels screamed into over-rev as they were relieved of the load. Just too late, Popeye punched the earth buttons on the magnetos, and the engines spluttered into silence.

In that silence Popeye was sobbing with exertion and frustration and anger.

'A twist-off,' he sobbed. 'A deep one. Oh no! God, no!' It might take two weeks to fish out the broken rod, pump cement into the fissure to seal it, and then start again.

He removed the cap from his head, and with all his strength hurled it on the engine room floor. He then proceeded to jump on it with both feet. This was standard procedure. Popeye jumped on his cap at least once a week, and the foreman knew that when he had finished doing that he would then assault anybody within range.

Quietly the foreman slipped behind the wheel of the Ford truck, and the rest of the gang scrambled aboard. They all bumped away down the rutted track. There was a roadhouse on the main road where they went for coffee at times like this. When the mists of rage had dispersed sufficiently from his mind for Popeye to start seeking a human sacrifice, he looked about to find the drilling area strangely still and deserted.

'Stupid bunch of yellow-bellied baboons!' he bellowed in

46

frustration after the retreating truck, and, as the next best thing, went into the shed to phone his Managing Director.

This gentleman sitting in the air-conditioned offices of 'Hart Drilling and Cementation' high above Rissik Street in Johannesburg was a little taken aback to learn from Popeye Worth that he, the Managing Director, was directly responsible for the twist-off of an expensive diamond drill at the Sonder Ditch No. 5 hole.

'If you used that sack of custard that passes for a brain, you'd fight shy of trying to sink holes into this bunch of knitting,' Popeye yelled into the mouthpiece. 'I'd prefer to stick my old man into a meat grinder than put a drill into this ground. It stinks, I tell you! It's really ugly down there. God help the poor son of a bitch who tries to mine it!'

He slammed down the phone and stuffed his pipe with trembling fingers. Ten minutes later his breathing had returned to normal and his hands were steady. He picked up the phone again and dialled the number of the road-house. The proprietor answered.

'José, tell my boys it's okay, they can come home now,' said Popeye.

– 14 –

For Rod Ironsides there was more excitement than usual in meeting and solving the dozen paper problems that lay on his desk to welcome him back to the office. As he worked he kept remembering that Manfred Steyner might be able to do it, might just be able to do it.

The Sonder Ditch might really belong to him soon. He dispatched the last problem and lay back in his swivel chair. His mind was clear of the last cobwebs of dissipation and, as always, he felt purged and cleansed.

If I get her, I'll make her the star performer in the whole field, he thought greedily, they'll talk about the Sonder

Ditch from Wall Street to the Bourse, and about the man who is running her. I know how to do it too. I'll cut the costs to the bone, I'll tighten her up solid. Frank Lemmer was a good man, he could get the stuff out of the ground, but he let it creep up on him. It cost him almost nine rand a ton to mill it.

Well, I'll get it out as well as he did *and* I'll get it out cheaper. An operation takes its temperament from the man at the head. Frank Lemmer would talk about costs every now and then, but he didn't mean it and we knew he didn't mean it. We have become a wasteful operation because we are on a rich reef, we have become big spenders. Well, I'm going to talk costs, and I'll skin the arse of anybody who thinks I'm joking.

Last year Hamilton at Western Holdings kept his working costs per ton milled down to just a touch over six rand. I could do the same here! I could jump our profits twelve million Rand in one year, if only they give me the job I'll shout the Sonder Ditch's name across the financial markets of the world.

The problem that Rod was pondering was the nightmare of the gold mining industry. Since the 1930s the price of gold had been fixed at $35 a fine ounce. Each year since then the cost of mining had crept up steadily. In those days they reckoned four penny-weights of gold in a ton of ore was payable value. Now around eight penny-weights was the marginal value.

So in the interim all those millions of tons of ore whose values fell between four and eight penny-weights had been placed beyond the reach of man until such time as they increased the price of gold.

There were many mines with vast reserves of goldbearing ore, millions in bullion, whose values lay just below the magical number eight. Those mines stood deserted and forlorn, rust reddening their headgears, and the corrugated iron roofs of the buildings collapsing wearily. Rising costs had shot the guts out of them, they were condemned by the single word 'UNPAY'.

The Sonder Ditch was running twenty to twenty-five penny-weights per ton. She was fat, but she could be fatter, Rod decided.

There was a knock at the door.

'Come in!' called Rod, and looked at his watch. It was nine o'clock already. Time for the Monday meeting of his mine captains.

They came in singly and in pairs, twelve of them. These were Rod's front-line men, his combat officers. They went down there each day, each to his own section, and directed the actual assault on the rock.

While they chatted idly, waiting for the meeting to begin, Rod looked them over surreptitiously and was reminded of a remark that Herman Koch of Anglo American had made to him once.

'Mining is a hard game, and it attracts a hard breed of men.'

These were men of the hard breed, physically and mentally tough, and Rod realized with a start that he was one of them. No, more than one of them. He was their leader, and with a fierce affection and pride he opened the meeting.

'Right, let's hear your gripes. Who is going to be first to break my heart?'

There are some men with a talent for controlling, and getting the very best results out of other men. Rod was one of them. It was more than his physical size, his compelling voice and hearty chuckle. It was a special magnetism, a personal charm and unerring sense of timing. Under his chairmanship the meeting would erupt, voices crackle and snap, then subside into chuckles and nods as Rod spoke.

They knew he was as tough as they were, and they respected that. They knew that when he spoke it made sense, so they listened. They knew that when he promised, he delivered, so they were placated. And they knew that when he made a decision or judgement, he acted upon it, so every man knew exactly where he stood.

If asked, any one of these mine captains would have admitted grudgingly that 'there was no bulldust in Ironsides'. This was the equivalent of a presidential citation.

'Very well then.' Rod terminated the meeting. 'You have spent a good two hours of the company's time beating your gums. Now, will you kindly haul arse, go down there and start sending the stuff out.'

– 15 –

As these men planned the week's operation, so their men were at work in the earth below them.

On 87 level, Kowalski moved like a great bear down the dimly-lit drive. He had switched off the lamp on his helmet, and he moved without sound, lightly for a man of such bulk. He heard their voices ahead of him in the dimly-lit tunnel, and he paused, listening intently. There was no sound of shovel crunching into loose rock, and Kowalski's Neanderthal features convulsed into a fearsome scowl.

'Bastards!' he muttered softly. 'They think I am in stopes, hey? They think it all right if they sit on fat black bum, no move da bloody rock, hey?'

He started forward again, a bear on cat's feet.

'They find plenty different from what they bloody think, soon!' he threatened.

He stepped round the angle of the drive and flashed his lamp. There were three men Kowalski had put on lashing, shovelling the loose stuff from the footwall into waiting cocopans. Two of them sat against the cocopan, smoking contentedly while the third regaled them with an account of a beer drink he had attended the previous Christmas.

Their shovels and sledge hammers leaned unemployed against the side wall of the drive.

All three of them froze into rigidity as the beam of Kowalski's lamp played over them.

'So!' The word burst explosively from Kowalski, and he snatched up a fourteen-pound hammer in one massive fist, reversed it and struck the butt of the handle against the foot wall. The steel head of the hammer fell off and Kowalski was left with a four-foot length of selected hickory in his hand.

'You, boss boy!' he bellowed, and his free hand shot out and fastened on the throat of the nearest Bantu. With one heave he jerked him off his feet onto his knees and began dragging him away up the drive. Even in his rage, Kowalski was making sure there were no witnesses. The other two men sat where they were, too horrified to move, while their companion's wails and cries receded into the darkness.

Then the first blow reverberated in the confined space of the drive, followed immediately by a shriek of pain.

The next blow, and another shriek.

The crack, thud, crack, thud, went on repeatedly, but the accompanying shrieks dwindled into moans and soft whimperings, then into complete silence.

Kowalski came back down the drive alone, he was sweating heavily in the lamp light, and the handle of the hammer in his hand was black and glistening with wet blood.

He threw it at their feet.

'Work!' he growled, and was gone, big and bearlike, into the shadows.

16

On 100 level, Joseph M'Kati was hosing down and sweeping the spillings from under the giant conveyor belt. Joseph had been on this job for five years, and he was a contented and happy man.

Joseph was a Shangaan approaching sixty years of age; the first frost was touching his hair. There were laughter lines around his eyes and at the corner of his mouth. He wore his helmet pushed to the back of his head, his overalls were hand-embroidered and ornamentally patched in blue and red, and he moved with a jaunty bounce and strut.

The conveyor was many hundreds of yards long. From all the levels above the shattered gold reef was scraped from the stopes and trammed back down the haulages in the cocopans. Then from the cocopans it was tipped into the mouths of the ore-passes. These were vertical shafts that dropped down to 100 level, hundreds of feet through living rock to spew the reef out onto the conveyor belt. A system of steel doors regulated the flow of rock onto the conveyor, and the moving belt carried it down to the shaft and dumped it into enormous storage bins. From there it was fed automatically into the ore cage in fifteen-ton loads and carried at four-minute intervals to the surface.

Joseph worked on happily beneath the whining conveyor. The spillings were small, but important. Gold is strange in its behaviour, it moves downwards. Carried by its own high specific gravity it works its way down through almost any other material. It would find any crack or irregularity in the floor and work its way into it. It would disappear into the solid earth itself if left long enough.

It was this behaviour of gold that accounted in some measure for Joseph M'Kati's contentment. He had worked his way to the end of the conveyor, washing and sweeping, and now he straightened, laid his bast broom aside and rubbed his kidneys with both hands, looking quickly around to make certain that there was no one else in the conveyor tunnel. Beside him was the ore storage bin into which the conveyor was emptying its load. The bin could hold many thousands of tons.

Satisfied that he was alone, Joseph dropped onto his hands and knees and crawled under the storage bin, ignoring the continuous roar of rock into the bin above him, working his way in until he reached the holes.

It had taken Joseph many months to chisel the heads off four of the rivets that held the seam in the bottom of the bin, but once he had done it, he had succeeded in constructing a simple but highly effective heavy media separator.

Free gold in the ore that was dumped into the storage bin immediately and rapidly worked its way down through the underlying rock, its journey accelerated by the vibration of the conveyor and bin as more reef was dropped. When the gold reached the floor of the bin, it sought an avenue through which to continue its downward journey, and it found Joseph's four rivet holes, beneath which he had spread a square of polythene sheet.

The gold-rich fines made four conical piles on the sheet of polythene, looking exactly like powdered black soot.

Crouched beneath the bin, Joseph carefully transferred the black powder to his tobacco pouch, replaced the polythene to catch the next filtering, stuffed the pouch into his hip pocket, and scrambled out from under the bin. Whistling a tribal planting tune Joseph picked up his broom and returned to the endless job of sweeping and hosing.

17

Johnny Delange was marking his shot holes. Lying on his side in the low stope of 27 section he was calculating by eye the angle and depth of a side cutter blast to straighten a slight bulge in his longwall.

In the Sonder Ditch they were on single blast. One daily, centrally fired, blast. Johnny was paid on *fathomage*, the cubic measure of rock broken and taken out of his stope. He must, therefore, position his shot holes to achieve the maximum disruption and blow-out from the face.

'So,' he grunted, and marked the position of the hole in red paint. 'And so.' With one bold stroke of the paint brush he set the angle on which his machine boy was to drill.

'Shaya, madoda!' Johnny clapped the shoulder of the black man beside him. 'Hit it, man.'

Machine boys were selected for stamina and physique; this one was a Greek sculpture in glistening ebony.

'Nkosi!' The machine boy grinned an acknowledgement, and with his assistant lugged his rock drill into position. The drill looked like a gargantuan version of a heavy-calibre machine gun.

The noise as the big Bantu opened the drill was shattering in the low-roofed, constricted space of the stope. The compressed air roared and fluttered into the drill, buffeting the eardrums. Johnny made the clenched-fist gesture of approval, and for a second they smiled at each other in the companionship of shared labour. Then Johnny crawled on up the stope to mark the next shot hole.

Johnny Delange was twenty-seven years old, and he was top rock breaker on the Sonder Ditch. His gang of forty-eight men were a tightly-knit team of specialists. Men fought each other for a place on 27 section, for that's where the money was. Johnny could pick and choose, so each month when the surveyors came in and measured up, Johnny Delange was way out ahead in fathomage.

Here was the remarkable position where the man at the lowest point of authority earned more than the man at the top. Johnny Delange earned more than the General Manager of the Sonder Ditch. Last year he had paid super-tax on an income of R22,000. Even a miner like Kowalski, who brutalized and bullied his gang until he was left with the dregs of the mine, would earn eight or nine thousand rand a year, about the same salary as an official of Rod Ironsides' rank.

Johnny reached the top of his longwall and painted in the last shot holes. Down the inclined floor of the stope below him all his drills were roaring, his machine boys lying or crouching behind them. He lay there on one elbow, removed his helmet and wiped his face, resting a moment.

Johnny was an extraordinary-looking young man. His long jet black hair was swept back and tied with a leather thong at the back of his head in a curlicue. His features were those of an American Indian, gaunt and bony. He had cut the sleeves out of his overalls to expose his arms – arms as muscular and sinuous as pythons, tattooed below the elbows, immensely powerful but supple. His body was the same, long and sinewy and powerful.

On his right hand he wore eight rings, two on each finger, and it was clear from the design of the rings that they were not merely ornamental. They were heavy gold rings with skull and cross-bones, wolves' heads and other irregularities worked into them, a mass of metal that formed a permanent knuckleduster. Of the big eyes in the one skull's head Rod Ironsides had once asked: 'Are those real rubies, Johnny?' And Johnny had replied seriously:

'If they aren't, then I've sure as hell been gypped out of three rand fifty, Mr Ironsides.'

Johnny Delange had been a really wild youngster, until

eight months ago. It was then he had met and married Hettie. Courtship and marriage occupying the space of one week. Now he was settling down very well. It was all of ten days since he had last fought anybody.

Lying in the stope he allowed himself five minutes to think about Hettie. She was almost as tall as he was, with a wondrously buxom body and chestnut red hair. Johnny adored her. He was not the best speech-maker in Kitchenerville when it came to expressing his affection, so he bought her things.

He bought her dresses and jewellery, he bought her a deep-freezer *and* a fifteen cubic foot Frigidaire, he bought her a Chrysler Monaco with leopard-skin upholstery and a Kenwood Chef. In fact, it was becoming difficult to enter the Delange household without tripping over at least one of Johnny's gifts to Hettie. The congestion was made more acute by the fact that living with them was Johnny's brother, Davy.

'Hell, man!' Happily Johnny shook his head. 'She's a bit of all-right, hey!'

There was an eye-level oven he had spotted in a furniture store in Kitchenerville the previous Saturday.

'She'll love that, man,' he muttered, 'and it's only four hundred rand. I'll get it for her on pay day.'

The decision made, he clapped his helmet onto his head and began crawling out of the stope. It was time now to go up to the station and collect the explosives for the day's blast.

His boss boy should have been waiting for him in the drive, and Johnny was furious to find no sign of him nor the piccaninny who was his assistant.

'Bastard!' he grunted, playing the beam of his lamp up and down the drive. 'He's been acting up like hell.'

The boss boy was a pock-marked Swazi, not a big man, but powerful for his size and highly intelligent. He was also a man of mean disposition; Johnny had never seen him smile, and for an extrovert like Johnny it was galling to work with someone so sullen and taciturn. He tolerated the Swazi because of his drive and reliability, but he was the only man in the gang that Johnny disliked.

'Bastard!' The drive was deserted, the roar of the rock drills was muted.

'Where the hell is he?' Johnny scowled impatiently. 'I'll skin him when I find him.'

Then he remembered the latrine.

'That's where he is!' Johnny set off down the drive. The latrine was a rock chamber cut into the side of the drive. A flap of canvas served as a door; beyond was a regular four-holer over sanitary buckets.

Johnny pulled the canvas aside and stepped into the cubicle. The boss boy and his assistant were there. Johnny stared in surprise, for a moment not understanding what they were doing. They were so absorbed they were unaware of Johnny's presence.

Suddenly realization dawned, and Johnny's face tightened with revulsion and disgust.

'You filthy—' Johnny snarled, and catching the boss boy by the shoulders pulled him backwards and pinned him against the wall. He lifted his heavily metalled fist and drew it back ready to hurl it into the boss boy's face.

'Strike me and you know what happens,' said the boss boy softly, his expression flat and neutral, looking steadily into Johnny's eyes. Johnny hesitated. He knew the Company rules, he knew the Government labour officers' attitude, he knew what the police would do. If he hit him, they would crucify him.

'You are a pig!' Johnny hissed at him.

'You have a wife,' said the boss boy. 'My wife is in Swaziland. Two years I have not seen her.'

Johnny lowered his fist. Twelve thousand men, and no women. It was a fact. The actuality sickened him, but he understood why it happened.

'Get dressed.' He stepped back, releasing the boss boy. 'Get dressed both of you. Come to the station. I will meet you there.'

– 18 –

For a week now, since the fall of hanging in 43 section, Big King had been out of the stopes.

Rod had ordered it that way. The excuse was that Big King's white miner had been killed in the fall and now he must await an allocation to another section. In reality Rod wanted to rest him. He had seen the strain both physical and emotional that Big King had undergone during the rescue. When together they had unearthed the miner's corpse, the man with whom Big King had worked and laughed, Rod had seen the tears roll unashamedly down Big King's cheeks as he picked up the body and held it easily against his chest.

'Hamba gahle, madoda,' Big King had muttered. 'Go in peace, man.'

Big King was a legend on the Sonder Ditch. They boasted about him; how much Bantu beer he could drink in a sitting, how much rock he could lash single-handed in a shift, how he could dance any other man off his feet. He had been awarded a total of over a thousand rand in bravery awards. Big King set the pace, others tried to equal him.

Rod had put him in charge of a transport team. For the first few days Big King had enjoyed the opportunity of showing off his strength and socializing, for the transport team moved about the workings allowing Big King to visit most of his numerous friends during a shift. But now Big King was becoming bored. He wanted to get back into the stopes.

'This,' he told his transport team contemptuously, 'is

58

work for old men and young women.' And with one snatch and lift he picked up a forty-four-gallon drum of dieseline and unaided placed it on the platform of the loco.

A forty-four-gallon drum of dieseline weighs a little over 800 lbs avoirdupois.

– 19 –

All this fuss for that. Davy Delange paused in his labour of tamping the Dynagel into the shot holes. He leaned forward to inspect the reef. In the face of the stope it was a black line, drawn against the blue quartz rock.

The carbon leader reef, it was called. A thin layer of carbon never more than a few inches thick, more often half an inch. Black soot, that's what it was. Davy shook his head thoughtfully. You could not even see the gold in it.

Davy was two years older than his brother Johnny, and there was no physical or mental resemblance between the two of them. Davy's sandy hair was cropped into a conventional 'short back and sides'. He wore no personal jewellery, and his manner was quiet and reserved.

Johnny was tall and lean, Davy squat and muscular. Johnny was extravagant, Davy careful beyond the point of meanness. Their only common trait was that they were both first-class miners. If Johnny broke more rock than Davy, it was only because Davy was more careful than Johnny; he did not take the same chances, he observed all the safety procedures which Johnny frequently flouted.

Davy earned less money than Johnny, but saved every penny he could. It was for his farm. Davy was going to buy a farm one day. Already he had saved a little over R49,000 towards it. In five more years he would have enough. Then he could get himself a farm and a wife to help run it. Johnny, on the other hand, spent every penny he earned. He was usually in debt to Davy by the end of each month.

'Lend us a hundred till pay day, Davy.' Disapprovingly, Davy lent him the money. Davy disapproved of Johnny, his appearance, attire and habits.

Abandoning his microscopic inspection of the carbon leader reef, Davy resumed tamping in the explosive, working carefully and precisely on this highly dangerous procedure. The sticks of explosive were charged with detonators and ready to burn. By law, nobody but the miner-in-charge could perform this operation, but Davy did it automatically while he thought about Johnny's latest trespass. He had raised Davy's rent.

'A hundred rand a month!' Davy protested aloud. 'I've got a good mind to move out and find my own digs.'

But he knew he would do no such thing. Hettie's cooking was too good, and her presence too feminine and alluring. Davy would stay on with them.

– 20 –

'Rod.' Dan Stander's voice was serious and low. 'I've got a nasty one for you.'

'Thanks for nothing.' Rod made his own voice weary and resigned as he spoke into the telephone. 'I'm just going on my underground tour. Can't it wait?'

'No,' Dan assured him. 'Anyway, it's on your way. I'm speaking from the first-aid station at the shaft head. Come across.'

'What is it?'

'Assault. White on Bantu.'

'Christ.' Rod jerked upright in his chair. 'Bad?'

'Ugly. Worked him over with the handle of a fourteen-pound hammer. I've put in forty-seven stitches, but I am worried about a fracture of the skull.'

'Who did it?'

'Miner by the name of Kowalski.'

'Him!' Rod was breathing heavily. 'All right, Dan. Can he make a statement?'

'No. Not for a day or two.'

'I'll be there in a few minutes.'

Rod hung up the phone and crossed the office.

'Dimitri.'

'Boss?'

'Pull Kowalski out of the stopes. I want him in my office soonest. Put someone in to finish his shift.'

'Okay, Rod, what's the trouble?'

'He beat up one of his boys.'

Dimitri whistled softly, and Rod went on.

'Call personnel, get them onto the police.'

'Okay, Rod.'

'Have Kowalski here when I get back from my tour.'

Dan was waiting for him in the first-aid room.

'Take a look.' He indicated the figure on the stretcher. Rod knelt beside him, his mouth tightening into a thin pale line.

The catgut stitches lay neatly across the dark swollen gashes in the man's flesh. One ear had been torn off, and Dan had sewn it back on. There was a black gap where teeth had been behind the swollen purple lips.

'You will be all right now.' Rod spoke gently, and the Bantu's eyes swivelled towards him. 'The man who did this will be punished.'

Rod stood up. 'Let me have a written report on his injuries, Dan.'

'I'll fix it. See you for a drink at the Club after work?'

'Sure,' said Rod, but underneath he was seething with anger, and it stayed with him during the whole of his underground tour.

21

Rod dropped straight down to 100 level. His first duty was to get the stuff out, and he wanted to check the reserve in the ore storage bins. He came into the long brightly-lit tunnel beneath the ore passes, and paused. The loaded conveyor belt whined monotonously, speeding the broken reef towards the bins.

The tunnel was deserted, except for the lonely figure of the sweeper at the far end. It was one of the phenomena of a well-run gold mine that in a tour through the workings you encountered so few human beings. Mile after mile of haulage and drive were silent and devoid of life, and yet there were 12,000 men down here.

Rod set off towards the bins at the shaft end of the tunnel.

'Joseph,' he greeted the old sweeper with a smile.

'Nkosi.' Joseph ducked and bobbed with shy pleasure.

'All is well?' Rod asked. Joseph was one of Rod's favourites, he was always so cheerful, so uncomplaining, so patently honest and without guile. Rod always made a point of stopping to chat to him.

'It is well with me, Nkosi. Is it well with you?'

Rod's smile died suddenly, he had noticed the fine white powdering of dust on Joseph's upper lip.

'You old rogue!' he scolded him. 'How often must I tell you to hose down before you sweep? Water! You must use water!'

This was part of the ceaseless battle of the miner to keep down the dust.

'The dust will eat your lungs!'

Phthisis, the dread incurable occupational disease of the miner, caused by silica particles being drawn into the lungs and there solidifying.

Joseph grinned shamefaced, shifting from one foot to the

other. He was always embarrassed by Rod's childish obsession with dust. In Joseph's opinion this was one of the few flaws in Rod Ironsides' character. Apart from this weird delusion that dust could hurt a man, he was a good boss.

'It is much harder to sweep wet dirt than dry dirt,' Joseph explained patiently. Rod never seemed to understand this self-evident fact, Joseph had to point it out to him every time they had this particular discussion.

'Listen to me, old man, without water the dust will enter your body.' Rod was exasperated. 'The dust will kill you!'

Joseph bobbed again, grinning at Rod to placate him.

'Very well, I will use plenty water.'

To prove it he picked up the hose and began spraying the floor with enthusiasm.

'That is good!' Rod encouraged him. 'Use plenty of water.' And Rod went on down to the storage bins.

When Rod was out of sight, Joseph turned off the hose and leaned on his broom.

'The dust will kill you!' he mimicked Rod, and chuckled merrily, shaking his head in wonder at the childishness of it.

'The dust will kill you!' he repeated, and burst into delighted laughter, slapping his thigh.

He did a few shuffling dance steps, it was so funny.

The dance steps were awkward, for under his trousers, strapped to the calves of both legs, were heavy polythene bags filled with gold fines from under the bins.

22

Rod stepped out of the Mary Anne at 85 level, and paused to watch Big King loading a baulk of timber onto the loco while his transport team stood back respectfully and watched him. Turning from his task Big King saw Rod standing on the station landing and marched up to him.

'I see you,' he greeted Rod. Big King was not one to make hasty judgements, it was only after the rescue operations in 43 section that he had decided Rod was a man. He was now ready to accept him as an equal.

'I see you also, King Nkulu.' Rod returned the greeting.

'Find me work with men. I sicken of this.'

'You will be back in the stopes before the week is ended,' Rod promised.

'You are my father,' Big King thanked him and went back to the transport team.

23

Johnny Delange saw the Underground Manager coming up the haulage towards him. There was no mistaking that tall wide-shouldered silhouette, nor the man's free swinging stride.

'Whee!' Johnny whistled with relief, grateful for the premonition that had warned him to pack the fifty-pound cardboard cartons of Dynagel into the explosives locker of the railway truck, rather than, as he usually did, pile them haphazard onto the platform in defiance of safety standards.

'Stop!' Johnny commanded the boss boy and his assistant who were pushing the truck, and it trundled to a halt beside Rod.

'Morning, Johnny.'

'Hello, Mr Ironsides.'

'How's it going?'

Johnny hesitated before replying, and immediately Rod was aware of the tension between the three men. He glanced at the two Swazis, they were sullen and apprehensive.

'There's been trouble,' he thought. 'Not like Johnny, he's too clever to let tension cut down his fathomage.'

'Well—' Johnny paused again. 'Look, Mr Ironsides, get rid of this bastard for me.' He jerked his thumb at the boss boy. 'Give me someone else.'

'What's the trouble?'

'No trouble, I just can't work with him.'

Rod raised an eyebrow in disbelief, but turned to the boss boy.

'Are you happy in this section, or do you want transfer?'

'I want transfer!' growled the boss boy.

'Right.' Rod was relieved, sometimes in a case like this the Swazi would refuse transfer. 'Tomorrow you will be told your new section.'

'Nkosi!' The boss boy glanced sideways at his assistant. 'It is the wish of my friend that he transfers with me.'

So that's it, Rod thought, the ever-present spectre which we must ignore because we can find no way to lay it. Johnny had probably caught them at it.

'Your friend shall go with you,' Rod nodded, telling himself that this was not condonation, but merely practical politics. If he separated them, the boss boy would pick on someone else who might not be receptive. Then there would be more trouble, stabbings, faction fighting.

'I'll get you a replacement,' he told Johnny, and then suddenly a thought occurred to him. My God, yes! What a team they would make!

'Johnny, how would you like Big King?'

'Big King!' Johnny's gaunt bony features split into a wide smile. 'Now you're talking, boss!'

24

At three o'clock Rod had finished his tour and was in the cage on the way to the surface. The cage was crowded, men pressed shoulder to shoulder, the stench of sweat almost overpowering. They were hauling shift now, the day's work was over, the stopes were scraped and washed down, the shot holes drilled and charged, the fuses connected into the electrical circuit.

The men were out of the stopes now, falling back in orderly companies and battalions along the haulages to the stations. There to wait patiently for their turn to enter the cages and be whisked to the surface.

Rod was mulling over the myriad problems he had encountered during the day, and the solutions he had dreamed up. He had opened a new section in the back pages of his notebook and headed it simply 'COSTS'.

Already there were two entries there. Let them give me the job, he thought fervently, just let me have it one month and I'll move the world.

'Mr Ironsides.' The man beside him spoke. Rod glanced down at him recognizing him.

'Hello, Davy.' It was remarkable how dissimilar the two brothers were.

'Mr Ironsides, my boss boy has worked his ticket. He's going home at the end of the month. Can you see that I get a good man to replace him?'

'Your brother's boss boy has asked for transfer. Will you take him?'

'Ja!' Davy Delange nodded. 'I know him, he's a good boy.'

And that takes care of one more detail, thought Rod, as he stepped out of the cage into a bright summer's afternoon and tasted the fresh sweet air with pleasure. Now there are only the butt ends of the day's work to tidy up. Then I can go and fetch the drink that Dan promised me.

Dimitri met him in the passage outside the office.

'I've got Kowalski in my office.'

'Good,' said Rod grimly. He went into his own office and sat on the edge of his desk.

'Send him in,' he called through to Dimitri.

Kowalski came through the door and stopped. He stood very still, his long arms hanging slackly at his side, his belly bulging out over his belt.

'You call me,' he muttered thickly, his English hardly intelligible. It was a peasant's face, coarse-featured, dull-eyed. He had not shaved, dirt from the stopes clung in the thick black stubble of beard.

'You beat a man today?' Rod asked softly.

'He no work,' Kowalski nodded. 'I beat him. Maybe next time his brothers they work. No bloody nonsense!'

'You're fired,' said Rod. 'Pull your time and get the hell off this property.'

'You fire?' Kowalski blinked in surprise.

'There will be criminal charges pressed against you by the Company.' Rod went on. 'But in the meantime I want you off the property.'

'Police?' Kowalski growled. There was expression on his face now.

'Yes,' said Rod, 'police.'

The spade-sized hands at the end of Kowalski's arms balled slowly into massive fists.

'You call da bloody police!' He took a step towards the desk, big, menacing.

'Dimitri,' Rod called sharply, 'close the door.'

Dimitri had been listening intently, now he jumped up from his desk and closed the interleading door. He stood with his ear pressed to the panelling. For thirty seconds more there was the growl and mutter of voices, then

67

suddenly a thud, a bellow, another thud and a shattering crash.

Dimitri winced theatrically.

'Dimitri!' Rod's voice, and he pushed the door open.

Rod sat on the edge of his desk, swinging one leg casually, he was sucking the knuckle of his right hand.

'Dimitri, tell them not to put so much polish on the floor. Our friend slipped and hit his jaw on the desk.'

Dimitri clucked sympathetically as he stood over the reclining hulk of the big Pole. Kowalski was snoring loudly through his mouth.

'Gave himself a nasty bump,' said Dimitri. 'Shame!'

– 25 –

D r Steyner worked on quietly for the remainder of Monday morning. He favoured the use of a tape recorder, for this cut out human contact which Manfred found vaguely repellent. He disliked having to speak his thoughts to a female who sat opposite him with skirts up around her thighs, squirming her bottom and touching her hair. However, what he really could not abide was the odour. Manfred was very sensitive to smells, even his own body smell of perspiration disgusted him. Women, he found, had a peculiar cloying odour that he could detect beneath their perfume and cosmetics. It nauseated him. This was why he had insisted on separate bedrooms for Theresa and himself. Naturally he had not told her the reason, but had insisted instead that he was such a light sleeper that he could not share a room with another person.

His office was in white and ice-blue, the air clean and cold from the air-conditioning unit, his voice was crisp and impersonal, the whirr of the recorder subdued, and with the conscious portion of his mind Manfred was happily absorbed in his conjuring tricks with figures and money, past performance and future estimates, a three-dimensional structure of variables and contingencies which only a super-normal brain could visualize. But beneath it was a sense of disquiet; he was waiting, hanging in time, and the outward sign of his agitation was the way the fingers of his right hand ran up and down his thigh as he worked, a caressing narcissistic gesture.

A few minutes before noon the unlisted direct telephone on his desk rang, and the movement of his hand stilled. Only one caller could reach him here, only one caller had that number. For a few seconds he sat unmoving, delaying the moment, then deliberately he switched off the recorder and lifted the telephone.

'Dr Manfred Steyner.' He identified himself.

'You have got our man in?' the voice enquired.

'Not yet, Andrew.'

There was silence from the other end, a dangerous crackling silence.

'But there is no cause for alarm. It is nothing. A delay merely, not a setback.'

'How long?'

'Two days – at the latest by the end of the week.'

'You will be in Paris next week?'

'Yes.' Manfred was an adviser to the Government team which was to meet the French for gold price talks.

'He will meet you there. It would be best for you that your side of the bargain were completed by then. You understand?'

'I understand, Andrew.'

The discussion was ended, but Manfred interjected to prevent the caller from hanging up.

'Andrew!'

'Yes.'

'Will you ask him if—' Manfred's tone had changed almost imperceptibly, there was an obsequious edge in it. 'Ask him if I may play tonight, please, Andrew.'

'Wait.'

The minutes drifted by, and then the voice came back on the line.

'Yes, you may play. Simon will inform you of your limits.'

'Thank you. Tell him, thank you.'

Manfred made no effort to conceal his relief as he cradled the receiver. He sat beaming at the ice-blue paper on the far wall of his office, even his spectacles seemed to sparkle.

– 26 –

There were five men in the opulently furnished room. One of the men was subservient to the others, he was younger than they, attentive to their moods and wishes. Clearly he was a servant. Of the remaining four, one was just as obviously the host. He was seated at the focus of all their attention. He was fat, but not excessively so, the fat of good living not of gluttony. He was speaking, addressing himself to his three guests.

'You have expressed doubts as to the reliability of the tool I intend using in the coming venture. I have arranged a demonstration which I hope will convince you that your concern is groundless. That is the reason for the invitation that Andrew here conveyed to you this afternoon.'

The host turned to the younger man. 'Andrew, would you be good enough to go through and wait for Dr Steyner to arrive; as soon as that happens, please let Simon seat him while you come through and inform us.' He gave his orders with dignity and courtesy, a man accustomed to command.

'Now, gentlemen, while we wait may I offer you a drink?'

The conversation that sprang up between the four of them as they sipped their drinks was knowledgeable, and extraordinarily well informed. At its root was one subject:

wealth. Mineral wealth, industrial wealth, the harvest of the land and the sea. Oil, steel, coal, fish, wheat and – gold.

There were clues to the stature of these men in the cut and quality of the cloth they wore, the sparkle of a stone on a finger, the tone of authority in a voice, the casual unaffected use of a high name.

'He is here, sir,' Andrew interrupted them from the doorway.

'Oh! Thank you, my boy.' The host stood up. 'Would you mind stepping this way, please, gentlemen.'

He crossed the room and drew aside one of the gold and maroon drapes. Behind it was a window.

The four men clustered about the window and looked through into the room beyond. It was a gaming room of an expensive gambling establishment. There were men and women sitting about a baccarat table, and none of them so much as glanced up at the window overlooking them.

'This is a one-way glass, gentlemen,' the host explained. 'So you need not worry about being seen in such a den of iniquity.'

They chuckled politely.

'What kind of profit does this place show you?' one of them asked.

'My dear Robert!' The host feigned shock. 'You don't for a moment believe that I would be in any way associated with an illegal undertaking?'

This time they chuckled with genuine amusement.

'Ha!' exclaimed the host. 'Here he is.'

Across the gaming room Dr Manfred Steyner was being ushered to a seat at the table by a tall sallow-faced young man, who in his evening dress looked like an undertaker.

'I have asked Simon to place him so that you may watch his face as he plays.'

They were intent now, leaning forward slightly, scrutinizing the man as he arranged the plaques that Simon had stacked at his elbow.

Dr Manfred Steyner began to play. His face was completely devoid of expression, but the pallor was startling. Every few seconds the pink tip of his tongue slipped out between his lips, then disappeared again. In the intervals between each coup, there was a reptilian stillness about him, the stillness of a lizard or an iguana. Only a pulse beat steadily in his throat and his spectacles glittered like a snake's eyes.

'May I direct your attention to his right hand during the play of this coup,' the host murmured, and all their eyes flicked downwards.

Manfred's right hand lay open beside the pile of his chips, but as his card was laid before him so his fingers closed.

'*Carte.*' Soundlessly he mouthed the word, and now his hand was a fist, the knuckles whitened, the tension was so fierce that his fist trembled. Yet, still his face was neutral.

The banker flipped his card.

'*Sept!*' The croupier's mouth formed the number. He faced Manfred's card, then he swept Manfred's stake away. Manfred's hand flopped open and lay soft and hairless as a dead fish on the green baize.

'Let us leave him to his pleasures,' suggested the host and drew the curtains across the window. They returned to their chairs, and they were strangely subdued.

'Jesus,' muttered one of the guests. 'That was ugly. I felt like a peeping Tom, like watching someone, you know, pulling his pudding.'

The host glanced at him quickly, surprised at his perception.

'In effect, that is exactly what you were watching,' he told him. 'You will excuse me playing the role of lecturer, but I know a little about this man. It cost me nearly four hundred rand for an analytic report on him by one of our leading psychiatrists.'

The host paused, assuring himself of their complete attention.

'The reasons are obscure, probably arising from an event or series of events during the period in which Dr Steyner was an orphan wandering through the smoking ruins of war-torn Europe.' The host coughed, deprecating his own flight of oratory. 'Be that as it may. The results are there for all to see. Dr Manfred Kurt Steyner's intelligence quotient is a genius rating of 158. He neither smokes nor drinks. He has no hobbies, plays no sport, has never made so much as an improper remark to any woman other than his wife, and there is some doubt as to just how often or to what extent she is favoured by his attentions.' The host sipped his drink conscious of their intense interest. 'Mechanically, if that is the correct term, Dr Steyner is neither impotent nor deficient in his manhood. However, he finds all bodily contact, and especially the secretions that may arise from such contact, to be utterly loathsome. For arousal he relies on the baccarat cards, for release he might endure a brief contact with a member of the opposite sex, but more likely he would – oh, what was the expression you used, Robert?'

They absorbed this in silence.

'He is, to be precise, a compulsive gambler. He is also a compulsive loser.'

They stirred with disbelief.

'You mean he tries to lose?' demanded Robert incredulously.

'No.' The host shook his head. 'Not on the conscious level. He believes he is trying to win, but he lays bets against odds that, with his magnificent brain, he must realize are suicidal. It is a deep-seated subconscious need to lose, to be humiliated. A form of masochism.'

The host opened a black leather notebook and checked its contents.

'During the period from 1958 to 1963 Dr Steyner lost

the total sum of R227,000 at this table. In 1964 he was able to arrive at an arrangement with his sole creditor to discharge the debt plus the accumulated interest.'

You could see the faces change as they rapidly searched their memories for a set of circumstances which would fit the dates and principals. Robert reached the correct deduction first. In 1964 their host had sold his majority holdings in the North Maun Copper Co. to CRC at a price that could only be considered advantageous. Just prior to this Dr Steyner had been made head of finance and planning at CRC.

'North Maun Copper,' said Robert with admiration. That is how he had done it, the cunning old fox! He had forced Steyner to buy well above market value.

The host smiled softly, deferentially, neither confirming nor denying.

'Since 1964 to the present Dr Steyner has continued to patronize this establishment. His gambling losses for this further period amount to—' He consulted his notebook again, pretending surprise at the figure, 'to a touch over R300,000.'

They sighed and moved restlessly. Even to these men it was a very large sum of money.

'I think we can rely on him.' The host closed his notebook with a snap, and smiled around at them.

– 27 –

Theresa lay in the dark. The night was warm, the stillness spoiled only by the klonking of a frog down at the fishpond. The moonlight came in through the window, playing shadow pictures through the branches of the Pride of India tree onto the wall of her bedroom.

She threw back the single sheet, and swung her legs off the bed. She could not sleep, it was too warm, her nightdress kept binding under her armpits. She stood up and on a sudden reckless impulse she drew the nightdress off over her head and tossed it through the open door of her dressing-room, then, naked, she walked out onto the wide veranda. Into the moonlight, with the cool stone flags under her bare feet, and the warm night air moving like the touch of fairy hands on her skin.

She felt suddenly devilish and daring, she wanted to run down across the lawns and to have someone catch her doing it. She giggled, uncertain of this mood. It was so far removed from Manfred's conception of a good German Hausfrau's behaviour.

'He'd be furious,' she whispered with wicked delight, and then she heard the motor of the car.

She froze with horror, the headlights flicked through the trees as the car came up the driveway and she darted back into her room; in panic she dropped to her knees and searched for her nightgown, found it and ran to the bed as she dragged it on over her head.

She lay in the darkness and listened to the car door slam. There was silence until she heard him pass her door. His heels clacked on the yellow wood floor, he was almost running. Theresa knew the symptoms, the late night return, the suppressed urgency, and she lay rigid in her bed, waiting.

The minutes passed slowly, and then the interleading door from Manfred's suite swung open silently.

'Manfred, is that you?' She sat up and reached for the switch of the bedside lamp.

'Don't put the light on.' His voice was breathless, slurred as though he had been drinking but there was no trace of liquor on his breath as he stooped over her and kissed her. His lips were dry and tightly closed, as he slipped off his dressing-gown.

Two and a half minutes later he stood up from the bed, turning his back to Theresa as he quickly shrugged into the silk dressing-gown.

'Excuse me a minute, Theresa.' The breathlessness was gone from his voice. He went through the door of his own suite, and seconds later she heard the hiss of the shower and the tinkling splash of water.

She lay on her back and her fingernails cut into the palms of her hands. Her body was trembling with a mixture of revulsion and desire, it had been so fleeting a contact – enough to stir her, but so swift as to leave her with a feeling of having been used and sullied. She knew that the rest of the night would pass infinitely slowly, with restless burning tension, remorse and self-pity alternating with wild elation and half-crazed erotic fantasy.

'Damn him,' she screamed silently within her skull. 'Damn him! Damn him!'

She heard the shower stop, and then Manfred returned to her room. He smelt of 4711 Eau de Cologne, and he sat down carefully on the end of the bed.

'You may turn on the light, Theresa.'

It required a conscious effort for her to unclench her hand and reach out for the lamp switch. Manfred blinked behind his spectacles at the flood of light. His hair was damp and freshly combed, his cheeks shone like ripe apples.

'I hope you had an enjoyable day?' he asked, and listened seriously to her reply. Despite her tension, Theresa found herself falling under the almost hypnotic influence he wielded over her. His voice precise, almost monotonous. The glitter of his spectacles, the reptilian stillness of his body and features.

As she had so many times before, she thought of herself as a warm fluffy rabbit sitting tense and fascinated before the cobra.

'It is late,' he said at last and he stood up.

Looking down at her as she lay cuddled into the white silk sheets, he asked with as little emphasis as if he were requesting her to pass the sugar: 'Theresa, could you raise three hundred thousand rand without your grandfather knowing?'

'Three hundred thousand!' She sat up startled.

'Yes. Could you?'

'Good Lord, Manfred, that's a small fortune.' She truly saw nothing unusual in her choice of adjective. 'You know it's all in the Trust Fund, well, most of it. There is the farm and the – no, I couldn't find half of that without Pops knowing.'

'Pity,' murmured Manfred.

'Manfred, you aren't in – difficulties?'

'No. Good Lord, no. It was just a thought. Forget that I asked. Good night, Theresa, I hope you sleep well.'

Involuntarily she lifted her hands towards him in invitation.

'Good night, Manfred.'

He turned and left the room, she let her hands fall to her sides. For Theresa Steyner the long night had begun.

– 28 –

'Ladies and Gentlemen, it is customary for the General Manager to introduce the distinguished guest who presents our special service awards. Last week, in tragic circumstances, our General Manager, Mr Frank Lemmer, was killed in the Company's service, a loss which we all bitterly regret, and I am sure you all join me in sincere condolence to Mrs Eileen Lemmer.' Rod paused for the acknowledging murmur from his audience. There were 200 of them packed into the Mine Club hall. 'It falls upon me, therefore, as Acting General Manager, to introduce to you Dr Manfred Steyner who is a senior Director of Central Rand Consolidated, our parent company. He is also head of the Departments of Finance and Planning.'

Sitting beside her husband, Theresa Steyner had noticed

Manfred's irritation at Rod's mention of Frank Lemmer. It was company policy not to draw public attention to accidental death or injury inflicted on employees by the Company's operation. She liked Rod the better for his small tribute to Frank Lemmer.

Theresa was wearing sunglasses, for her eyes were swollen and red. In the dawning, after a sleepless night, she had succumbed suddenly to a fit of bitter weeping. The tears were without cause, or reason, and had left her feeling strangely lightheaded and with a brittle sense of well-being. However, her enormous eyes always showed up badly for hours after she had wept.

She sat with her legs demurely crossed, immaculate in a suit of cream shantung, a black silk scarf catching her hair and then letting it fall in a dark glossy brown cascade onto her shoulders. She leaned forward in polite attention to the speaker, one elbow on her knee, her chin cupped in her palm, one long tapered finger against her cheek. A lady with diamonds on her fingers and pearls at her throat, smiling an acknowledgement at Rod's reference to 'the lovely granddaughter of our Chairman'.

Except for the slight incongruity of the sunglasses, she was the perfect image of the young matron. Polished, poised, cosseted, secure in her unassailable virtue and duty.

However, the thoughts that were running through Theresa Steyner's head, and the flutterings and sensations that were prickling and tickling her, had they been known, would have broken up the assembly in disorder. All the formless fantasy and emotional disturbance of the previous night were now directed at one target – Rodney Ironsides. Suddenly, with a start of amusement and alarm, she was aware of a phenomenon that she had last experienced many years ago. She moved quickly, shifting her seat, for the cream shantung marked so easily with any moisture.

'Terry Steyner!' she thought, deliciously shocked at

herself, and found with relief that Rod had finished speaking and Manfred was standing up to reply. She joined in the applause enthusiastically to distract her errant fancy.

Manfred briefly mentioned the six gentlemen sitting in the front row of seats whose courage and devotion to duty they had come to honour, he then went on into an exploration of the prospects of an increase in the price of gold. In measured, carefully considered terms, he set out the advantages and benefits that would accrue to the industry, the nation and the world at large. It was an erudite and convincing dissertation, and there was a large contingent of newspaper men to record it. The press had been alerted by the public relations department of CRC to the text of Dr Steyner's speech and all the leading dailies, weeklies, financial gazettes and journals were represented.

At intervals a photographer would come to crouch below the platform and pop a flash bulb up at Dr Steyner. On the eve of the gold price talks with France this would make good copy, for Steyner was the boy genius in the South African team.

The six heroes sat uncomfortably, forlorn in their best suits, scrubbed like schoolboys at a prize-giving ceremony, staring up at the speaker, not understanding a single word of the foreign language, but maintaining expressions of grave dignity.

Rod caught Big King's eye and winked at him. Solemnly Big King's right eyelid drooped and rose in reply, and quickly Rod averted his gaze to prevent himself laughing out loud.

He looked straight into Theresa Steyner's face, taking her completely off her guard. Not even the dark glasses could conceal her thoughts, they were as clear as if she had spoken them aloud. Before she could drop her eyes to examine the hem of her skirt, Rod knew with a stomach swoop of excitement how it could be if he chose.

With a new awareness he examined her from the corner

of his eye, seeing her for the first time as an accessible woman, a highly desirable woman, but nevertheless still the granddaughter of Hurry Hirschfeld and the wife of Manfred Steyner. This made her as dangerous as a force ten pressure burst, he knew, but the desire and temptation were hard to deny, inflamed perhaps rather than dampened by the danger.

He saw that she was blushing now, her fingers picking nervously at the hem of her skirt. She was as agitated as a schoolgirl, she knew he was watching her. Rod Ironsides, who until five minutes before had been thinking of nothing but his speech, now found himself impelled into a completely new and exciting dimension.

After the awards had been made, tea had been drunk, biscuits consumed and the crowd had dispersed, Rod escorted the Steyners down across the vivid green lawns of Kikuyu grass to where the chauffeur was holding the Daimler.

'What a magnificent physique that Shangaan has, what was his name – King?' Terry was walking between the two men.

'King Nkulu. Big King, we call him.'

Rod found his speech unsteady, he had stuttered slightly. This thing between the two of them was suddenly overpowering, it hummed like a turbine, making the space between them crackle with tension. Unless he was deaf, Manfred Steyner must be aware of it.

'He is pretty special. There is nothing he can't do, and do it far and away better than his nearest rival. My God, you should see him dance.'

'Dance?' enquired Terry with interest.

'Tribal dancing, you know.'

'Of course.' Terry hoped the relief in her voice was not obvious; she had been racking her badly flustered brain for an excuse to visit the Sonder Ditch again or have Rod Ironsides come to Johannesburg. 'I have a friend who is absolutely mad keen on seeing the dances. She pesters me every time I see her.'

Quickly she selected a name from her list of friends, she must have one ready should Manfred ask.

'They dance every Saturday afternoon, bring her out any time.' Rod fielded the ball neatly.

'What about this Saturday?' Terry turned to her husband, 'Would that be all right, Manfred?'

'What's that?' Manfred looked at her vaguely, he had not been following the conversation. Manfred Steyner was a worried man, he was pondering his obligation to gain control of the management of the Sonder Ditch within two days.

'May we come out here on Saturday afternoon to watch the tribal dancing?' Terry repeated her question.

'Have you forgotten that I fly to Paris on Saturday morning, Theresa?'

'Oh, dear.' Terry bit her lip thoughtfully. 'It *had* slipped my mind. What a pity, I would have enjoyed it.'

Manfred frowned slightly, irritated.

'My dear Theresa, there is no reason why you shouldn't come out to the Sonder Ditch without me. I am sure you will be safe enough in Mr Ironsides' hands.'

His choice of words brought the colour to Terry's cheeks again.

– 29 –

After the award ceremony, Big King's first stop was the Recruiting Agency office at the entrance to the No.1 shaft hostel. There were men clustered about the counter, but they stood aside for Big King and he acknowledged the courtesy by slapping their backs indiscriminately and greeting them with:

'Kunjane, madoda. How is it, men?'

The clerk behind the counter hurried to serve him. Up at the Mine Club Big King might be a little out of his depth, but here he was treated like a reigning monarch.

In two neat bundles Big King placed the award money on the counter.

'Twenty-five rand you will send to my senior wife.' He instructed the clerk. 'And twenty-five rand you will put to my book.'

Big King was scrupulously fair. Half of all his earnings was remitted to the senior of his four wives, and half was added to the substantial sum already credited in his savings bank passbook.

The Agency was the procurer of labour for the insatiably man-hungry gold mines of the Witwatersrand and Orange Free State. Its representatives operated across the southern half of the continent. From the swamps and fever lagoons along the great Zambesi, from among the palm groves fringing the Indian Ocean, out of these simmering plains that the bushmen called 'the big dry', down from the mountains of Basutoland and the grass lands of Swaziland and Zululand they gathered the Bantu, the men themselves completing the first fifty or sixty miles of the journey on foot. Individuals meeting on a footpath to become pairs, arriving at a little general dealer's store in the bleak scrub desert to find three or four others already waiting, the arrival of the recruiting truck with a dozen men and their luggage aboard, the long bumping grinding progress through the bush. The stops at which more men scrambled aboard, until a full truck load of fifty or sixty disembarked at a railway siding in the wilderness.

Here the tiny trickle of humanity joined a stream, and at the first major centre they trans-shipped and became part of the great flood that washed towards 'Goldi'.

However, once they had reached Johannesburg and been allocated to one of the sixty major gold mines, the Agency's obligations towards its recruits were not yet discharged.

Between them the employing mine and the Agency must provide each man with employment, training, advice and comfort, maintain contact between him and his family, for very few of them could write, reassure him when he worried that his goats were sick or his wife unfaithful. They must provide a banking and savings service with a personal involvement unknown to any commercial banking institute. They had, in short, to make certain that a man taken from an environment that had not changed in a thousand years and deposited into the midst of a sophisticated and technological society would retain his health, happiness and sanity, so that at the end of his contract he would return to the place from which he had come and tell them all how wonderful it was at 'Goldi'. He would show them his hard helmet, and his new suitcase crammed with clothes, his transistor radio and the little blue book with its printed figures, inflaming them also with the desire to make the pilgrimage, and keep the flood washing towards 'Goldi'.

Big King completed his business transactions and went in through the gates of the hostel. He was going to take advantage of the fact that he had missed the shift and would be among the first at the ablutions and dining-hall.

He went down across the lawns to his block. Despite the size of an establishment that housed 6,000 men, the Company had tried to make it as attractive as possible. The result was an unusual design, halfway between a motel and an advanced penitentiary.

As a senior boss boy, Big King rated a room of his own. An ordinary labourer would share with five others.

Carefully Big King brushed down his suit and hung it in the built-in cupboard, wiped down his glossy shoes and racked them, then with a towel around his waist he set off for the ablution block and was irritated to find it already filled with new recruits up from the acclimatization centre.

Big King ran an appraising eye over their naked bodies and judged that this batch must be nearing the completion of their eight-day acclimatization. They were sleek and shiny, the muscle definition showing clearly through the skin.

You could not take a man straight out of his village, probably suffering from malnutrition, and put him down a gold mine to lash and bar and drill in a dry bulb heat of 91° Fahrenheit and 84% relative humidity, without running a serious risk of killing him with heat stroke or exhaustion.

Every recruit judged medically fit to work underground went into acclimatization. For eight days, eight hours a day, he and hundreds of others stood with only a loin cloth about his middle in a vast barn-like hall stepping up onto and down from a platform. The height of the platform was carefully matched to the man's height and body weight, the speed of his movements was regulated by a flashing panel of lights, the temperature and humidity were controlled at 91° and 84%, every ten minutes he was given water and his body temperature was registered by the half dozen trained medical assistants in charge of the room.

At the end of the eighth day he emerged as fit as an olympic athlete, and quite able to perform heavy physical labour in conditions of high temperature and humidity without discomfort or danger.

'Gwedeni!' growled Big King, and the nearest recruit, still white with soap suds, hurriedly vacated his shower with a respectful 'Keshle!' in deference to Big King's rank and standing. Big King removed his towel and stepped under the shower, revelling as always in the rush of hot water over his skin, flexing the great muscles of his arms and chest.

The messenger found him there.

'King Nkulu, I have word for thee.' The man used Shangaan, not the bastard Fanikalo.

'Speak,' Big King invited, soaping his belly and buttocks.

'The Induna bids you call at his house after you have eaten the evening meal.'

'Tell him I will attend his wishes,' said Big King and held his face up into the rush of steaming water.

Dressed in a white open-necked shirt and blue slacks, Big King sauntered down to the kitchens. Again the recruits were ahead of him, queueing with bowls in hand outside the serving hatches. Big King walked past them through the door marked 'No Admittance – Staff Only'.

The kitchens were cavernous, glistening with white porcelain tiles and stainless steel cookers and bins that could serve 18,000 hot meals a day.

When Big King entered a room, even one as large as this, no one was unaware of his presence. One of the assistant cooks snatched up a bowl not much smaller than a baby's bath, and hurried across to the nearest stainless steel bin. He opened the lid and looked expectantly at Big King. Big King nodded and the cook ladled about two litres of steaming sugar beans into the bowl, before passing on to the next bin where he again looked for and obtained Big King's approval. He added an equal quantity of mixed vegetables to the bowl, slammed down the lid and scampered across to where a second assistant waited with a spade beside yet another bin.

The spade was the same as those used for lashing gold reef underground, but the blade of this one had been polished to gleaming cleanliness. The second cook dug into the bin and came up with a spadeful of white maize porridge, cooked stiff as cake, the smell of it as saliva-making as the smell of new bread. This was the staple of Bantu diet. He deposited the spadeful in the bowl.

'I am hungry.' Big King spoke for the first time, and the second cook dug out another spadeful and added it to the bowl. They passed on to the end of the kitchens and at their approach another cook lifted the lid on a pressure cooker the size of a washing machine. From it arose a cloud of fragrant steam.

Apologetically the cook held out his hand and Big King produced his meat ticket. Meat was the only food that was rationed. Each man was limited to one pound of meat a day; the Company had long ago discovered to its astonishment and cost that a Bantu, offered unlimited supplies of fresh meat, was quite capable of eating his own weight of it monthly.

Having ascertained that Big King was entitled to his daily pound, the cook proceeded to ladle at least five pounds of it into the bowl.

'You are my brother,' Big King thanked him, and the little procession moved on to where yet another cook was filling a half-gallon jug of thick, gruel-like, mildly alcoholic Bantu beer from one of the multiple spiggots beneath the thousand-gallon tank.

The bowl and jug were ceremonially handed to Big King and he went out onto the covered terraces where benches and tables were set out for alfresco dining in mild weather.

While he ate, the terrace began to fill, for the shift was out of the mine now. Every man who passed his table greeted Big King, but only a few privileged persons took the liberty of seating themselves at the same table. One of them was Joseph M'Kati, the little old sweeper from 100 level.

'It has been a good week, King Nkulu.'

'You say so.' Big King was non-committal. 'I go now to a meeting with the Old One. Then we shall see.'

The Old One, the Shangaan Induna, lived in a Company house. A self-contained residence with lounge and dining-room, kitchen and bathroom. He was handsomely paid by the Company, provided with servants, food, furniture and all the other appurtenances of his rank and station.

He was the head of the Shangaan community on the Sonder Ditch. A chief of the blood, a greybeard and member of the tribal councils. In similar houses and with the same privileges and in equal style lived the Indunas of the other tribal groups that made up the labour force of the

Sonder Ditch. They were the paternal figureheads, the tribal jurists, ruling and judging within the framework of law and custom. The Company could not hope to maintain harmony and order without the assistance of these men.

'Baba!' Big King greeted his Induna from the doorway of his house, touching the forehead in respect not only for the man but also for what he represented.

'My son.' The Induna smiled his greeting. 'Come and sit by me.' He gestured for his servants to leave the room, and Big King went to squat at the feet of the old man. 'Is it true you go now to work with the mad one?' That was Johnny Delange's nickname.

They talked, the Induna questioning him on fifty matters that affected the welfare of his people. For Big King this was a comforting and nostalgic experience, for the Induna stood in the place of his father.

At last, satisfied, the Induna went on to other matters.

'There is a parcel ready tonight. Crooked Leg waits for you.'

'I shall go for it.'

'Go in peace then, my son.'

On his way through the gates of the hostel Big King stopped to chat with the guards. These men had the right to search over any person entering or leaving the hostel. Particularly they were concerned with preventing either women disguised as men or bottles of spirits entering the premises, both of which tended to have a disruptive effect on the community. As an afterthought they were also instructed to look out for stolen property entering or leaving. Big King had to ensure that none of them would ever, under any circumstances, take it into his head to search Big King.

While he stood at the gates, the last glow of the sunset faded and the lights began to come on across the valley. The clusters of red aerial warning lights atop the headgears, the massed yellow squares of the hotels, the strings of street lamps and the isolated pinpricks of the residential areas up on the ridge.

When it was truly dark, Big King left the guards and sauntered down the main road, until a bend in the road took him out of their sight. Then Big King left the road and started up the slope. He moved like a night animal, swiftly and with certainty of the path he followed.

He passed the ranch-type split-levels of the line management officials with their wide lawns and swimming-pools, pausing only once when a dog yapped nearby, then moving on again until he was into the broken rock and rank grass of the upper ridge; he crossed the skyline and started down the far side until he made out the grass-covered mound of rubble in the moonlight. He slowed and moved cautiously forward until he found the rusty barbed wire fence that guarded the entrance. He vaulted it easily and went on into the black mouth of the tunnel.

Fifty years before, a long-defunct mining company had suspected the existence of a gold reef in this area and had driven prospecting adits into the side of the ridge, exhausting its funds in the process, and finally abandoning the network of tunnels in despair.

Big King paused long enough to draw an electric torch from his pocket before going on into the tunnel, flashing the beam ahead of him. Soon the air stank of bats and their wings swished about his head. Unperturbed, Big King went on deeper and deeper into the side of the hill, taking a turning and fork in the tunnel without hesitation. At last there was a faint glow of yellow light ahead and Big King switched off his torch.

'Crooked Leg!' he called, his voice bounced and boomed along the tunnel. There was no reply.

'It is I, Big King!' he shouted again, and immediately a shadow detached itself from the sidewall and limped towards him, sheathing a wicked-looking knife as it came.

'All is ready.' The little cripple came to greet him. 'Come, I have it here.'

Crooked Leg had earned his limp and his nickname in a rockfall a dozen years ago. Now he owned and operated the concession photographic studio on the mine property, a flourishing enterprise, for dearly the Bantu love their own image on film. Not, however, as profitable as his nocturnal activities in the abandoned workings beyond the ridge.

He led Big King into a small rock chamber lit by a suspended hurricane lantern. Mingled with the bat stench was the acrid reek of sulphuric acid in high concentration.

On a wooden trestle table that occupied most of the chamber were earthenware jars, heavy glass bowls, polythene bags, and a variety of shoddy and very obviously second-hand laboratory equipment. In a clear space amongst all this clutter stood a large screw-topped bottle. The bottle was filled with a dirty yellow powder.

'Ha!' Big King exclaimed his pleasure. 'Plenty!'

'Yes. It has been a good week,' Crooked Leg agreed.

Big King picked up the bottle, marvelling once again at the unbelievable weight of it. This was not pure gold, for Crooked Leg's acid reduction methods were crude, but it was at least sixteen carats fine.

The bottle represented the week's collection of fines and concentrates by men like Joseph M'Kati from a dozen vulnerable points along the line of production; in some cases carried out from the company reduction works itself under the noses of the heavily armed guards.

All the men involved in this surreptitious milking off of the company's gold were Shangaans. There was only one man in whom was vested sufficient authority and prestige to prevent the greed and hostility which gold breeds from destroying the whole operation. That was the Shangaan Induna. There was only one man with the physical presence and necessary command of the Portuguese language to negotiate the disposal of the gold. That was Big King.

Big King placed the bottle in his pocket. The weight pulled his clothing out of shape.

'Run like a gazelle, Crooked Leg.' He turned back into the dark tunnel.

'Hunt like a leopard, King Nkulu,' chuckled the little cripple, as he disappeared into the moving shadows.

– 30 –

'A packet of Boxer tobacco,' said Big King. The eyes of José Almeida, the Portuguese owner of the mine concession store and the local roadhouse, narrowed slightly. He took down the yellow four-ounce packet from the shelves and handed it across the counter, accepted Big King's payment and counted the change into his palm.

He watched as the giant Bantu wandered down between the loaded shelves and racks of merchandise to disappear through the front door of the store into the night.

'Take charge,' he muttered in Portuguese to his plump little wife with her silky dark moustache, and she nodded in understanding, moving into José's place in front of the cash register. José went through into his storerooms and living quarters behind the store.

Big King was waiting in the shadows. When the back door opened he slipped through and José closed the door behind him. José led him through into a cubicle of an office, and from a cupboard he took down a jeweller's balance. Under Big King's watchful eye he began to weigh the gold.

José Almeida purchased the gold from the unofficial outlet of each of the five major mines on the Kitchenerville field, paying five Rands an ounce and selling again for sixteen. He justified the large profit margin he allowed himself by the fact that mere possession of unregistered gold was a criminal offence in South Africa, punishable by up to five years' imprisonment.

Almeida was a man in his middle thirties with lank black hair that he continually pushed back from his forehead, bright brown inquisitive eyes and dirty fingernails. Despite his grubby and well-worn clothing and unkempt hairstyle, he was a man of substance.

He had been able to pay in cash the 40,000 rand demanded by the Company for the monopoly concession to trade on the mine property. He had, therefore, an exclusive clientele of 12,000 well-paid Bantu, and had recovered his 40,000 during his first year of trading. He did not really need to run the risk of illicit gold buying, but gold is strange material. It infects most men who touch it with a reckless greed.

'Two hundred and sixteen ounces,' said José. His scale was set to record a twenty per cent error – in José's favour.

'One thousand and eighty rand,' agreed Big King in Portuguese, and José went to the big green safe in the corner.

– 31 –

Terry Steyner entered the 'Grape and Gable' bar of the President Hotel at 1.14 p.m. precisely, and as Hurry Hirschfeld stood to greet her he reflected that fourteen minutes was hardly late at all for a beautiful woman. Terry's grandmother would have considered herself to be early if she was only that late.

'You're late,' growled Hurry. No sense in letting her get away with it unscathed.

'And you are a big, cuddly, growly, lovable old bear,' said Terry and kissed him on the tip of his nose before he could duck. Hurry sat down quickly scowling thunderously with pleasure. He decided he didn't give a good damn if Marais and Hardy, who further down the bar were listening and trying to cover their grins, repeated the incident to the entire membership of the Rand Club.

'Good day, Mrs Steyner.' The scarlet-jacketed barman smiled his greeting. 'Can I mix you a Manhattan?'

'Don't tempt me, Thomas. I'm on a diet. I'll just have a glass of soda water.'

'Diet,' snorted Hurry. 'You're skinny enough as it is. Give her a Manhattan, Thomas, and put a cherry in it. Never was a Hirschfeld woman that looked like a boy, and you'll not be the first of them.' As an afterthought, he added: 'I've ordered your lunch also, you'll not starve yourself in my company.'

'You are a shocker, Pops,' said Terry fondly.

'Now, young lady, let's hear what you've been up to since I last saw you.'

They talked together as friends, very dear and trusted friends. The affection they felt for each other went beyond the natural duty of their blood tie. There was a kinship of the spirit as well as the flesh. They sat close, heads together, watching each other's face as they talked, completely lost in the pleasure of each other's company, the murmur of their voices interrupted by a tinkling burst of laughter or a deep chuckle.

They were so absorbed that Peter, the headwaiter, came through from the Transvaal Room to find them.

'Mr Hirschfeld, the chef is in tears.'

'Good Lord.' Hurry looked at the antique clock above the bar. 'It's almost two o'clock. Why didn't someone tell me?'

The oysters had been flown up from Mossel Bay that morning, and Terry sighed with pleasure after each of them.

'I was out at the Sonder Ditch with Manfred on Wednesday.'

'Yes, I saw the photograph in the paper.' Hurry engulfed his twelfth and final oyster.

'I must say I like your new General Manager.'

Hurry laid down his fork and a little flush of anger started in his withered old cheeks.

'You mean Fred Plummer?'

'Don't be silly, Pops, I mean Rodney Ironsides.'

'Has that cold fish of yours been briefing you?' Hurry demanded.

'Manfred?' She was genuinely puzzled by the question, Hurry could see that. 'What's he got to do with it?'

'All right, forget it.' Hurry dismissed Manfred with a shake of his head. 'Why do you like Ironsides?'

'Have you heard him speak?'

'No.'

'He's very good. I'm sure he must be a first-class mining man.'

'He is.' Hurry nodded, watchful and non-commital.

Peter whisked Terry's plate away, giving her the respite she needed to gather her resources. In the previous few seconds she had realized that Rodney Ironsides was not, as she had believed, a certainty for the job. In fact, Pops had already chosen old plum-faced Plummer for the General Managership. It took another moment for her to decide that she would use even the dirtiest in-fighting to see that Rod was not overlooked.

Peter laid plates of cold rock lobster in front of them, and when he had withdrawn Terry looked up at Hurry. She had perfected the trick of enlarging her already enormous eyes. By holding them open like this she could flood them with tears. The effect was devastating.

'Do you know, Pops, he reminds me so much of the photographs of Daddy.'

Colonel Bernard Hirschfeld, Terry's father, had burned to death in his tank at Sidi Rezegh. She saw Hurry

Hirschfeld's expression crack with pain, and Terry felt a sick little flutter of guilt. Had it been necessary to use such a vicious weapon to achieve her ends?

Hurry pushed at the rock lobster with his fork, his head was bowed so she could not see his face. She reached out to touch his hand.

'Pops—' she whispered, and he looked up. There was a restrained excitement in Hurry's manner.

'You know, you're bloody well right! He does look a bit like Bernie. Did I ever tell you about the time when your father and I—'

Terry felt dizzy with relief. I didn't hurt him, she told herself, he likes the idea, he really does. With a woman's instinct she had chosen the only form of persuasion that could have moved Hurry Hirschfeld from his decision.

– 32 –

Manfred Steyner fastened his safety belt and lay back in the seat of the Boeing 707, feeling slightly nauseated with relief.

Ironsides was in, and he was safe. Hurry Hirschfeld had sent for him two hours before to wish him farewell and good luck with the talks. Manfred had stood before him, trying desperately to think of some way in which he could bring up the subject naturally. Hurry saved him the trouble.

'By the way, I'm giving Ironsides the Sonder Ditch. Reckon it's about time we had some young blood in top management.'

It was as easy as that. Manfred had difficulty in persuading himself that those threats which had kept him lying awake during the past four nights were no longer of consequence. Ironsides was in. He could go to Paris and tell them. *Ironsides is in. We are ready to go.*

94

The note of the jets changed, and the Boeing began to roll forward. Manfred twisted his head against the neck rest and peered through the Perspex porthole. He could not distinguish Terry's figure amongst the crowd on the observation balcony of Jan Smuts Airport. They taxied past a Pan Am Boeing which cut off his view and Manfred looked straight ahead. Instantly his nostrils flared, he looked around quickly.

The passenger in the seat beside him had stripped to his shirtsleeves. He was a big beefy individual who very obviously did not use deodorant. Almost in desperation Manfred looked about. The aircraft was full, there would be little chance of changing seats and beside him the beefy individual produced a pack of cigarettes.

'You can't smoke,' cried Manfred. 'The light's on.' The combination of body odour and cigarette smoke would be unbearable.

'I'm not smoking,' said the man, 'yet.' And placed a cigarette between his lips, his lighter ready in the other hand.

Nearly two thousand miles to Nairobi, thought Manfred, with his stomach starting to heave.

– 33 –

'Terry darling, why on earth should I go all the way out to Kitchenerville to watch a lot of savages prancing around?'

'As a favour to me, Joy,' Terry pleaded into the telephone.

'It means mucking up my whole weekend. I've got rid of the kids to their grandmother, I've got a copy of A Small Town in Germany and I was going to have a lovely time reading and—'

'Please, Joy, you're my last hope.'

'What time will we be home?' Joy was weakening. Terry sensed her advantage and pressed forward ruthlessly.

'You might meet a lovely man out at the mine, and he'll sweep you—'

'No, thanks.' Joy had been divorced a little over a year ago, some people took longer than others to recover. 'I've had lovely men in big fat chunks.'

'Oh, Joy, you can't sit around moping for ever. Come on, I'll pick you up in half an hour.'

Joy sighed with resignation. 'Damn you, Terry Steyner.'

'Half an hour,' said Terry and hung up before she could change her mind.

'I'm playing golf. It's Saturday, and I'm playing golf,' said Doctor Daniel Stander stubbornly.

'You remember when I drove all the way to Bloemfontein to—' Rod began, and Dan interrupted quickly.

'All right, all right, I remember. You don't have to bring that up again.'

'You owe me plenty, Stander,' Rod reminded him. 'All I am asking is one of your lousy Saturday afternoons. Is that so much?'

'I can't let the boys down. It's a long-standing date.' Dan wriggled to escape.

'I've already phoned Ben. It will be a pleasure for him to take your place.'

There was a long gloomy silence, then Dan asked, 'What's this bird like?'

'She's a beautiful, rich nymphomaniac, and she owns a brewery.'

'Yeah! Yeah!' said Dan sarcastically. 'All right, I'll do it. But I hereby declare all obligations and debts to you fully discharged.'

'I'll give you a written receipt,' Rod agreed.

Dan was still sulking when the Daimler came up the drive and parked in the front of the Mine Club. He and Rod were standing at the Ladies' Bar, watching for the arrival of their guests.

Dan had just ordered his third beer.

'Here they come,' said Rod.

'Is that them?' Dan's depression lifted magically as he peered through the coloured-glass windows. The chauffeur was letting the two ladies out of the Daimler. They were both in floral slack suits and dark glasses.

'That's them.'

'Jesus!' said Dan with rare approval. 'Which one is mine?'

'The blonde.'

'Ha!' Dan grinned for the first time since their meeting. 'Why the hell are we standing here?'

'Why indeed?' asked Rod, his stomach was tied up in knots that twisted tighter as he went down the front steps toward Terry.

'Mrs Steyner. I'm so glad you could come.' With a wild lift of elation he saw it was still there, he had not imagined it, it was there in her eyes and her smile.

'Thank you, Mr Ironsides.' She was like a schoolgirl again, uncertain of herself, flustered.

'I'd like you to meet Mrs Albright. Joy, this is Rodney Ironsides.'

'Hello.' He smiled at her as he clasped her hand. 'It's gin time, I think.'

Dan was waiting at the bar for them, and Rod made the introductions.

'Joy is so excited at the chance of watching the dancing,' said Terry as they sat down on the bar stools. 'She's been looking forward to it for days.' And for an instant Joy looked stunned.

'You'll love it,' agreed Dan, moving in to take up a position at Joy's elbow. 'I wouldn't miss it for anything.'

97

Joy was a tall slim girl with long straight golden hair that hung to her shoulders, her eyes were cool green but her mouth when she smiled was soft and warm. She smiled now full into Dan's eyes.

'Nor would I,' she said, and with relief Rod knew he could devote all his attention to Terry Steyner. Joy Albright would be more than adequately looked after. He ordered drinks, and all four of them promptly lost further interest in tribal dancing.

At one stage Rod told Terry Steyner, 'I am going up to Johannesburg this evening. There is no point in your unfortunate chauffeur sitting around all afternoon. Let him go, and I'll take you home.'

'Good,' Terry agreed immediately. 'Would you tell him, please?'

The next time Rod looked at his watch it was half past three.

'Good Lord!' he exclaimed. 'If we don't hurry, it will be all over.' Reluctantly Joy and Dan, who had their heads close together, drew apart.

The overflow from the amphitheatre pressed about them, a merry jostling throng, all inhibitions long since evaporated in the primeval excitement of the dance, much like the crowd at a bull ring.

Rod and Dan ran interference for the girls, ploughing a path through the main gateway and down to their reserved seats in the front row. All four of them were laughing and flushed by the time they were seated, the excitement about them was infectious and the liquor had heightened their sensibilities.

An expectant hum of voices.

'The Shangaans!' And the audience craned towards the entrance from which pranced a dozen drummers, their long wooden drums hung on rawhide straps about their necks, they took up stations around the circular earthen stage.

Tap, tap. Tap, tap – from one of the drummers, and silence gripped the amphitheatre.

Tap, tap. Tap, tap. Naked, except for their brief loin cloths, stooped over the drums that they clasped between their knees, they began to lay down the rhythm of the dance. It was a broken, disturbing beat, that jerked and twitched like a severed nerve. A compelling, demanding sound, the pulse of a continent and a people.

Then came the dancers, shuffling, row upon row, head-dresses dipping and rustling, the animal tail kilts swirling, war rattles at the wrists and ankles, black muscles already oiled with the sweat of excitement, coming in slowly rank upon majestic rank, moving as though the drums were pumping life into them.

A shrill blast on a duiker horn and the ranks whirled like dry leaves in a wind, they fell again into a new pattern, and through the opening in their midst came a single gigantic figure.

'Big King!' The name blew like a sigh through the audience, and immediately the drums changed their rhythm. Faster, demanding, and the dancers hissed in their throats a sound like storm surf rushing up a stony beach.

Big King flung his arms wide, braced on legs like black marble columns, his head thrown back. He sang a single word of command, shrilling it, and in instantaneous response every right knee was brought up to the level of the chest. Half a second's pause and then 200 horny bare feet stamped down simultaneously with a crash that shook the amphitheatre to its foundations. The Shangaans began to dance, and reality was gone in the moving, charging, swirling, retreating ranks.

Once Rod tore his eyes from the spectacle. Terry Steyner was sitting forward on the bench, eyes sparkling, lips slightly parted, completely lost in the erotic turmoil and barbaric splendour of it.

Joy and Dan had a firm hold on each others' hands, their shoulders and the outside of their thighs were pressed tightly together, and Rod was stabbed by a painful thrust of envy.

Afterwards, back in the Ladies' Bar of the Club, there was very little conversation but they were all of them tensed up, restless, moved by strange undercurrents and interplays of primitive desires and social restraints.

'Well,' said Rod at last, 'if I am to get you two ladies back to Johannesburg at a decent hour—'

Dan and Joy spoke together.

'Don't worry, Rod, I'll—'

'Dan says he will—' Then they stopped and grinned at each other sheepishly.

'I take it that Dan has suddenly remembered that he has to go to Johannesburg this evening also, and he has offered to give you a lift?' asked Rod dryly, and they laughed in confirmation.

'It looks as though we are on our own, Mrs Steyner.' Rod turned to Terry.

'I'll trust you,' said Terry.

'If you do that, you're crazy,' said Dan.

Outside the Maserati, darkness was falling swiftly. The horizon blending into the black sky, isolated lights winking at them out of the surrounding veld.

Rod switched on the headlights, and the instrument panel glowed softly, turning the interior into a warm secluded place, isolating them from the world. The wind whispered, and the tyres and the engine hummed a gentle intimate refrain.

Terry Steyner sat with her legs curled up under her, cuddled into the soft maroon leather of the bucket seat.

She was staring ahead down the path of the headlights, and she seemed withdrawn and yet very close. Every few minutes Rod would take his eyes from the road and study her profile briefly. He did so again, and this time she met his gaze frankly.

'You realize what is happening?' she asked.

'Yes,' he answered as frankly.

'You know how dangerous it could be for you?'

'And you.'

'No, not me. I am invulnerable. I am a Hirschfeld – but you, it could destroy you.'

Rod shrugged.

'If we counted the consequences before every action, nobody would do anything.'

'Have you thought that I might be a spoiled little rich girl amusing myself? I might do this all the time.'

'You might,' Rod agreed. They were silent for a long while, then Terry spoke again.

'Rod?' She used his given name for the first time.

'Yes?'

'I don't, you know, I really don't.'

'I guessed that.'

'Thank you.' She opened her bag. 'I need a cigarette. I feel as though I'm standing poised on the edge of a cliff and I've got this terrible compulsion to hurl myself over the edge.'

'Light me one, Terry.'

'You need one also?'

'Badly.'

They smoked in silence again, both of them staring ahead, then Terry rolled down the window and flicked the cigarette butt away.

'You've got the job, you know.' All day she had wanted to tell him, it had been bubbling inside her. Watching his face, she saw his lips stiffen, his eyes crease into slits.

'Did you hear me?' she asked at last, and he braked the

Maserati, swinging it off onto the shoulder of the road. He pulled on the hand brake and turned to face her.

'Terry, what did you say?'

'I said, you've got the job.'

'What job?' he demanded harshly.

'Pops signed the instruction this morning. You'll receive it on Monday. You're the new General Manager of the Sonder Ditch.' She wanted to go on and say – *and I got it for you. I made Pops give it to you.*

I never will, she promised, I will never spoil it for him. He must believe he won it fairly, not as my gift.

– 34 –

It was Saturday night, the big night in Dump City.

The Blaauberg Mine was the oldest producer on the Kitchenerville field. There were sections of its property which had been worked out completely, and the old waste dumps were now abandoned and overgrown. Among the scrub and head-high weed in the valleys between these man-made hills had grown up a shanty town. Dump City, the inhabitants had named it. The buildings were made of discarded galvanized iron sheets and flattened oil drums, there was no sanitation or running water.

Remote from the main roads, the residential communities of the neighbouring mines or the town of Kitchenerville, hidden among the dumps, accessible only to a man on foot, never visited by members of the South African Constabulary, it was ideally suited to the purposes for which its 300 permanent inhabitants had chosen it.

Every one of the shacks was a shebeen, a clip joint where watered liquor was sold at inflated prices, where dagga*

* Marijuana.

102

was freely obtainable and where men from the surrounding mines gathered to carouse.

They came not so much for the liquor. Each of the mine hostels had a bar where a full range of liquor was on sale at club prices. Very few of them came for the dagga. There was little addiction amongst these well-fed, hard-worked and contented men. What they came for were the women.

Five mines in the area, each employing ten or twelve thousand men. Here at Dump City were 200 women, the only available women within twenty miles. It was not necessary for the young ladies of Dump City to solicit custom; even the fat, the withered, the toothless, could behave like queens.

Big King came down the path that skirted the mine dump. With him were two dozen of his fellow tribesmen, big Shangaans wearing their regalia, carrying their fighting sticks and still tensed up from the dancing. They came at a trot, Big King leading them. They were singing, not the gentle planting or courting melodies, not the work chant nor the song of welcome.

They were singing the fighting songs, those their forefathers had sung when they carried the spear in search of cattle and slaves. The driving inflammatory rhythm, the fiercely patriotic words wrought so mightily on the delicate susceptibilities of the average Shangaan that the Company had found it necessary to ban the singing of these songs.

Like a Scot hearing the pipes, when a Shangaan began singing these warlike chants, he was ready for violence.

The song ended as Big King led them down to the nearest shanty, and pushed aside the sacking that acted as a door. He stooped through the opening, and his comrades crowded in behind him.

A brittle electric silence fell on the large room. The air was so thick with smoke, and the light from the suspended hurricane lamps so feeble, that it was impossible to see the far wall. The room was filled with men, forty or fifty of them, the smell of humanity and bad liquor was solid. Among this press of men were half a dozen bright spots of the girls' dresses, but with their curiosity aroused by the singing more girls were coming through from the interleading doorways at the back, some of them had men with them and were still shrugging into their clothing. When they saw Big King and his warriors in full war kit, they fell silent and watchful.

At Big King's shoulder one of his Shangaans whispered:

'Basutos! They are all Basutos!' He was right, Big King saw that they were all men of that mountainous little independent state.

Big King started forward, swaggering just enough to make his leopard tail kilt swing and swirl and the heron feathers of his head-dress rustle. He reached the primitive bar counter.

'Flying Bird,' he told the crone who owned the house, and she placed a bottle of Eagle Brandy on the counter.

Big King half filled a tumbler, conscious that every eye was on him, and drained it.

Slowly he turned and surveyed the room.

'What is it,' he asked in a voice that carried to every corner, 'that sits on top of a mountain and scratches its fleas. Is it a baboon, or a Basuto?'

A roar of delight went up from his Shangaans.

'A Basuto!' they shouted, crowding forward to the bar, while a growl and a mutter went up from the rest of the room.

'What is it,' shouted a Basuto jumping to his feet, 'that has feathers on its head and crows from a dungheap? Is it a rooster, or a Shangaan?'

Without seeming to move, Big King picked up the bottle of Eagle Brandy and hurled it. With a crack it burst against the Basuto's forehead and he went over backwards taking two of his companions with him.

The old crone snatched up her cash register and ran as the room exploded into violent movement.

There was not enough space in which to use the fighting sticks, Big King realized, so he lifted a section of the bar counter off its trestles and, holding it in front of him like the blade of a bulldozer, he charged across the room, flattening all and everything before him.

The crash of breaking furniture and the yelp and squeal of men being struck down drove Big King beyond the frontiers of sanity into the red atavistic fury of the berserker.

Basuto is also one of the fighting tribes of the N'guni group. These wiry mountaineers rushed into the conflict with the same savage joy as the Shangaans, a conflict that raged and roared out of the single room to engulf the entire population of Dump City.

One of the girls, her dress ripped from her back so she was left with only a tattered pair of bloomers, had climbed on top of the remains of the bar counter from where, with her big melon breasts swinging in the lamp light, she shrilled that peculiar ululation that Bantu women used to goad their menfolk into battle frenzy. A dozen of the other girls joined in, trilling, squealing, and the sound was too much for Big King.

With the bar top held ahead of him he charged straight through the flimsy wall of the shack, bursting it open like a paper bag. The roof sagged down wearily, and Big King raged on unchecked down the narrow dirt street, striking down any man who crossed his path, scattering chickens and yelping dogs, roaring like a bull gorilla.

He turned at the end of the encampment and came back, his frustration mounting as he found the street deserted except for a few prostrate bodies; through the gaping hole in the wall he entered the shebeen once more to find that here also the fighting had died down. A few of the participants were crawling, or moaning as they lay on the carpet of broken glass.

Big King glared about him, seeking a further outlet for his wrath.

'King Nkulu!' The girl was still on the trestle table, her eyes bright with excitement, her legs trembling with it.

Big King let out another roar, and hurled the bar top from him. It clattered against the far wall and Big King started towards her.

'You are a lion!' She shrieked encouragement at him, and she took one of her big black velvety breasts in each hand and pointed them at him, squeezing them together, shaking with excitement.

'Eat me!' she screamed, as Big King swept her off the table and, lifting her high, ran with her out into the night. Carrying her into the scrub below the mine dumps, holding her easily with one arm, ripping the leopard-tail kilt from his own waist as he ran.

– 35 –

It was Saturday night in Paris also, but there were men who were still working, for there were lights burning in the upstairs rooms of one of the big embassies in the rue Royale.

The fat man who had been the host in the gambling establishment in Johannesburg was now the guest. He sat at ease in a leather club easy chair, his corpulence and the steel-grey hair at his temples giving him dignity. His face heavy, tanned, intelligent. His eyes glittery and hard as the diamond on his finger.

He was listening intently to a man of about the same age as himself who stood before a projected image on a screen that covered one wall of the room. There was that in the man's bearing and manner that marked him as a scholar, he was speaking now, addressing himself directly to the listener in the easy chair, pointing with a marker to the screen beside him.

'You see here a plan of the working of the five producing gold mines of the Kitchenerville fields in relation to each other.' He touched the screen with the marker. 'Thornfontein, Blaauberg, Tweefontein, Deep Gold Levels and Sonder Ditch.'

The man in the chair nodded. 'I have seen and studied this diagram before.'

'Good, then you will know that the Sonder Ditch property sits in the centre of the field. It has common boundaries with the other four mines and here,' he tapped the screen again, 'it is intersected by the massive serpentine dyke which they call the Big Dipper.'

Again the fat man nodded.

'It is for these reasons we have selected the Sonder Ditch as the trigger point.' The lecturer touched a button on the wall panel and the image on the screen changed.

'Now, here is something you have not seen before.'

The man in the chair crouched forward.

'What is it?'

'It is an underground map based on the borehole results of the five companies who have been exploring the ground to the east of the Big Dipper. These results have been pooled and interpreted by some of the finest brains in the fields of geology and hydrophysics. You have here a carefully considered representation of exactly what lies on the far side of the Big Dipper fault.'

The big man moved uncomfortably in his chair.

'It's a monster!'

'Yes, a monster. Lying just beyond the fault is an underground lake, no, that is not the correct word. Let us call it an underground sea, the size of, say, Lake Eyrie. The water is held in a vast sponge of porous dolomite rock.'

'My God.' For the first time the fat man had lost his

poise. 'If this is right, why don't the mining companies arrive at the same conclusion and keep well away from it?'

'Because,' the lecturer switched off the image and the overhead lights came on, 'because of their highly competitive attitude none of them has access to the findings of the others. It is only when all the results are studied that the picture becomes clear.'

'How did your government come to be in possession of *all* the results?' demanded the fat man.

'That is not important.' The lecturer was brusque, impatient of the interruption. 'We are also in possession of the findings of a certain Dr Peter Wessels who is at present head of a research team in Rock Mechanics based on the Sonder Ditch mine property. It is Company classified information and consists of a paper that Dr Peter Wessels has written on the shatter patterns and stresses of rock. His researches are directly related to the Ventersdorp quartzites which comprise the country rock of the Sonder Ditch workings.'

The lecturer picked up a pamphlet from his desk.

'I will not weary you by asking you to wade through its highly technical findings. Instead I will give it to you in capsule form. Dr Wessels arrives at the conclusion that a column of Ventersdorp quartzite 120 feet thick would shatter under a side pressure of 4,000 pounds per square inch.'

The lecturer dropped the pamphlet back on the desk.

'As you know, by law, the gold mining companies are bound to leave a barrier of solid rock 120 feet thick along their boundaries. That is all that separates one mine's working from another, just that wall of rock. You understand?'

'Of course. It is very simple.'

'Simple? Yes, it is simple! This Dr Steyner, over whom you have control, will instruct the new General Manager of the Sonder Ditch to drive a tunnel through the Big Dipper dyke. The drive will puncture the vast underground reservoir and the water will run back and flood the entire Sonder Ditch workings. Once they are flooded, the pressure delivered by a 6,000-foot head of water at the lower levels will be in excess of 4,000 pounds per square inch. That is sufficient to burst the rock walls, and flood the Thornfontein, the Blaauberg, Deep Gold Levels and Tweefontein gold mines.'

'The entire Kitchenerville gold fields would be effectively and permanently put out of production. The consequences for the economy of the Republic of South Africa would be catastrophic.'

The fat man was visibly shaken.

'Why do you want to do it?' he asked, shaking his head in awe.

'My colleague here,' the lecturer indicated a man who was sitting quietly in one corner, 'will explain that to you presently.'

'But – people!' the fat man protested. 'There will be people down there when it bursts, thousands of them.'

The lecturer smiled, raising one eyebrow. 'If I were to tell you that six thousand men would drown, would you refuse to proceed, and forfeit the million-dollar payment my government has offered you?'

The fat man looked down, embarrassed, and muttered barely audibly, 'No.'

The lecturer chuckled. 'Good! Good! However, you may salve you aching conscience by assuring yourself that we do not expect more than forty or fifty fatalities from the flooding. Naturally, those men actually working on the face will be killed. But that tremendous volume of water under immense pressure should make it a merciful death. For the rest of them, the mine can be evacuated swiftly enough to allow them excellent chances of survival. The surrounding mines will have days to evacuate before the water pressure builds up sufficiently to burst through the boundary walls.'

There was silence then in the room for nearly a minute.

'Have you any questions?'

The fat man shook his head.

'Very well, in that case I will leave it to my colleague to complete the briefing. He will explain the necessity for this operation, will arrange the terms of payment and conditions upon which you will proceed.' The lecturer gathered up the pamphlet and other papers from the desk. 'It remains only for me to wish you good luck.' He chuckled again and left the room quickly.

The little man, who up until them had remained silent, suddenly bounced out of his chair and began pacing up and down the wall-to-wall carpeting. He spoke rapidly, shooting occasional sideways glances at his audience, his bald head shining in the fluorescent lighting, wriggling his moustache like rabbit whiskers, puffing nervously at his cigarette.

'Reasons first. I'll make it short and sweet, right? The South Africans and the Frogs have got together. They're here in Paris now cooking up mischief. We know what they're up to, they're going to launch an all-out attack on my government's currency. Gold price increase, you know. Very complicated and very nasty for us, right? They might just be able to do it, South Africa is the world's biggest gold producer. With the Frogs helping her, they might just be able to force an increase.'

He stopped in front of the fat man and thrust out an accusing finger.

'Are we going to sit back and let them have a free run? No, sir! We are going to throw down our own curve ball! In three months time the Syndicate will be ready to attack. At that precise moment we will kick the chair out from under the South Africans by cutting their gold production in half. We will flood the Kitchenerville goldfields and the attack will fizzle out like a damp squib, right?'

'As simple as that?' asked the fat man.

'As simple as that!' The bald head nodded vigorously.

'Now, my next duty is to make clear to you that the agreed million dollars is *all* the reward you receive. Neither you nor your agents may indulge in any financial transactions that might, in retrospect, show that this was a planned operation, right?'

'Right.' The fat man nodded.

'You give your assurance that you will not deal in any of the shares of the companies involved?'

'You have my solemn word.' The fat man told him earnestly, and not for the first time in his life reflected how easily and painlessly a promise could be given.

With the assistance of the three men who had watched Manfred Steyner that night at the gambling club in Johannesburg, he intended launching a bear offensive on the stock exchanges of the world.

On the day that they drilled into the Big Dipper dyke he and his partners would sell millions of the shares of the five mining companies for one of the biggest financial killings in the history of money.

'We are agreed then.' The bald head bobbed. 'Now, as for this Dr Steyner, we have had a screening and personality analysis and we believe that, despite the secure hold you have on his loyalties, he would jib at giving the order to drive on the Big Dipper if he were aware of the consequences. Therefore we have prepared a second geological report,' he produced from his brief case a thick manila folder, 'incorporating those figures which he will recognize. In other words the drilling results of the CRC exploration teams, but the other figures are fictitious. This report purports to prove the existence of a fabulously rich gold reef beyond the fault.' He crossed to the fat man and handed him the folder. 'Take it. It will help you convince Dr Steyner, and he in turn to convince the new General Manager of the Sonder Ditch gold mine.'

'You have been thorough,' said the fat man.

'We try to give a satisfactory service to our customers,' said the bald man.

– 36 –

The game was five-card stud poker, and there were two big winners at the table, Manfred Steyner and the Algerian.

Manfred had timed his arrival in Paris to ensure himself an uninterrupted weekend before the rest of the delegates came in on the Monday morning flight.

He had checked in at the Hotel George Cinq on Saturday afternoon, bathed and rested for three hours until eight in the evening, then he had set out for the Club Chat Noir by taxi.

He had been playing now for five hours, and a steady succession of strong cards had pushed his winnings up to a formidable sum. It lay piled in front of him, a fruit salad of garish French bank notes. Across the table sat the Algerian, a slim dark-skinned Arab with toffee eyes and a silky black moustache. His teeth were very white against the creamy brown skin. He wore a turtle-neck shirt in pink silk, and a linen jacket of baby blue. With long brown fingers he kept smoothing and stacking his own pile of bank notes.

A girl sat on the arm of his chair, an Arab girl in a skin-tight gold trouser suit. Her hair was shiny black and hung onto her shoulders, her eyes were disconcertingly level as she watched Manfred.

'Ten thousand.' Manfred's voice was explosive, like that of a teutonic drillmaster. He was betting on his fourth card which had just been dealt to him. He and the Algerian were the remaining players in the game. The others had folded their hands and were sitting back watching with the casual interest of men no longer involved.

The Algerian's eyes narrowed slightly and the girl leaned down to whisper softly in his ear. He shook his head, annoyed, and drew on his cigarette. He had a pair of queens and a six showing and he leaned forward to study Manfred's cards.

The dealer's voice prodded. 'The bet is ten thousand francs, from four, five, seven of clubs. Possible straight flush.'

'Bet or drop,' said one of the uncommitted players. 'You're wasting time.'

The Algerian flashed him a venomous glance.

'Bet,' he said, and counted out ten thousand-franc notes into the pool.

'*Carte.*' The dealer slid a card face down in front of each of them. Quickly the Algerian lifted one corner of his card with his thumb, glanced at it and then closed the face.

Manfred sat very still, the card lying inches from his right hand. His face was pale, calm, but he was seething internally. Far from a possible straight flush, Manfred was holding four, five, seven of clubs and the eight of hearts. A six was the only card that could improve his hand and one six was already showing among the Algerian's cards. His chances were remote.

His lower belly and loins were tight and hot with excitement, his chest constricted. He drew out the sensation, wanting it to last for ever.

'Pair of queens still to bet,' murmured the dealer.

'Ten thousand.' The Algerian pushed the notes forward.

He has found another queen, thought Manfred, but he is uncertain of my flush or straight.

Manfred placed his smooth white hand over his fifth card, cupping it. He lifted it.

'Table,' said Manfred calmly, and there was a gasp and rustle from the watchers. The girl's hand tightened on the Algerian's sleeve, she stared with hatred into Manfred's face.

'The gentleman has made a table bet,' intoned the croupier. 'House rules. Any player may bet the entire stake he has upon the table.' He reached across and began to count the notes in front of Manfred.

Minutes later he announced the total. 'Two hundred and twelve thousand francs.' He looked across at the Algerian. 'It is now up to you to bet against the possible straight flush.'

The girl whispered urgently into the Arab's ear, but he snapped a single word at her and she recoiled. He looked about the room, as if seeking guidance, then he lifted and examined his hole cards again.

Suddenly his face hardened, and he looked steadily across at Manfred.

'Call!' he blurted, and Manfred's clenched right hand fell open upon the table.

The Arab faced his hand. Three queens. The whole room looked expectantly at Manfred.

He flicked over his last card. Two of diamonds. His hand was worthless.

With a birdlike cry of triumph the Algerian leaped from his seat and reaching across the table began raking Manfred's stake with both arms towards him.

Manfred stood up from the table, and the Arab girl grinned maliciously at him, taunting him in Arabic. He turned quickly away and almost ran down the steps that led to the cloakrooms. Twenty minutes later, feeling weak and slightly dizzy, Manfred slipped into the back seat of a Citroën taxi cab.

'George Cinq,' he told the driver. As he entered the lobby of the hotel he saw a tall figure rise from one of the leather armchairs and follow him across to the lifts. Shoulder to shoulder they stepped into the lift and as the doors slid closed the tall man spoke.

'Welcome to Paris, Dr Steyner.'

'Thank you, Andrew. I presume you have come to give me my instructions?'

'That is correct. He wishes to see you tomorrow at ten o'clock. I will call for you.'

– 37 –

It was Saturday night in Kitchenerville and in the men's bar of the Lord Kitchener Hotel the daily-paid men from the five gold mines were bellying up to the counter three deep.

The public dance had been in progress for three hours. At tables along the veranda the women-folk sat primly sipping their port and lemonade. Although they all were admirably ignoring the absence of the men, yet a constant and merciless vigil was kept on the door to the men's bar. Most of the wives already had the automobile keys safely in their handbags.

In the dining-hall, cleared of its furniture and sprinkled liberally with French chalk, the local four-piece band who played under the unlikely name of the 'Wind Dogs' launched without preliminaries into a lively rendition of 'Die Ou Kraal Liedjie', and from the men's bar, in various stages of inebriation, answering the call to arms came the troops.

Many of them had shed their jackets, the knots of their ties had slipped, their voices were boisterous and legs were a little unsteady as they led their women onto the dance floor and immediately showed to which school of the dance they belonged.

There was the cavalry squadron which tucked partner under one arm, very much like a lance, and charged. At the other end of the scale were those who plodded grimly around the perimeter, looking neither left nor right, speaking to no one, not even their partners. Then there were the sociables who reeled about the floor, red in the face, their movements completely unrelated to the music, shouting to their friends and attempting to pinch any feminine posterior that came within range. Their unpredictable progress interfered with the revolutions of the dedicated.

The dedicated took up their positions in the centre of the floor and twisted. A half dozen years previously the twist had swept like an Asian 'flu epidemic through the world and then faded out. Gone, forgotten, except in places like Kitchenerville. Here it had been taken and firmly entrenched into the social culture of the community.

Even in this stronghold of the twist, there was one master. 'Johnny Delange? Gott man, but he can twist, hey!' they murmured with awe.

With the sinuous erotic movements of an erect cobra, Johnny was twisting with Hettie. His shiny rayon suit caught the light and the lace ruffles of his shirt fluttered at his throat. There was a fierce grin of pleasure on his hawk features, and the jewelled buckles of his pointed Italian shoes twinkled as he danced.

A big girl with copper hair and creamy skin, Hettie was light on her feet. She had a tiny waist and a swelling regal bottom under the emerald-green skirt. She laughed as she danced, a full healthy laugh to match her body.

The two of them moved with the expertise of a couple who have danced together often. Hettie anticipated each of Johnny's movements, and he grinned his approval at her.

From the veranda Davy Delange watched them. He stood in the shadows, clutching a tankard of beer, a squat, lonely figure. When another dancing couple cut off his view of Hettie's luscious revolving buttocks he would exclaim with irritation and move restlessly.

The music ended and the dancers spilled out onto the veranda, laughing and breathless, mopping streaming faces;

girls squealing and giggling as the men led them to their seats, deposited them and then headed for the bar.

'See you.' Johnny left Hettie reluctantly, he would have liked to stay with her, but he was sensitive about what the boys would say if he spent the whole evening with his wife.

He was absorbed into the masculine crowd, to join their banter and loud laughter. He was deeply involved in a discussion of the merits of the new Ford Mustang, which he was considering buying, when Davy nudged him.

'It's Constantine!' he whispered, and Johnny looked up quickly. Constantine was a Greek immigrant, a stoper on the Blaauberg Mine. He was a big strong black-haired individual with a broken nose. Johnny had broken his nose for him about ten months previously. As a bachelor Johnny would fight him on the average of once a month, nothing serious, just a semi-friendly punch-up.

However, Constantine could not understand that nowadays Johnny was forbidden by his brand new wife from indulging in casual exchanges of fisticuffs. He had developed the erroneous theory that Johnny Delange was afraid of him.

He was coming down the bar room now, holding his glass in his massive hairy right hand with the little finger extended genteely. On his hip rested his other hand and he minced along with a simpering smile on his blue-jowled granite-textured features. Stopping in front of the mirror to pat his hair into place, he winked at his cronies and then came on down to where Johnny stood. He paused and ogled Johnny heavily, fluttering his eyelids and wriggling his hips. His colleagues from the Blaauberg Mine were weak with laughter, gurgling merrily, hanging onto each other's shoulders.

Then with a bump and grind that raised another howl of laughter Constantine disappeared into the lavatories, to emerge minutes later and blow Johnny a kiss as he went back to join his friends. They plied liquor on the Greek in appreciation of his act. Johnny's smile was a little strained as he resumed the discussion on the Mustang's virtues.

Twenty minutes and half a dozen brandies later, Constantine repeated his little act again on the way to the latrine. His repertoire was limited.

'Hold it, Johnny,' whispered Davy. 'Let's go and sit on the veranda.'

'He's asking for it. I'm telling you!' Johnny's smile had disappeared.

'Come on, Johnny, man.'

'No, hell, they'll think I'm running. I can't go now.'

'You know what Hettie will say,' Davy warned him. For a moment longer Johnny hesitated.

'The hell with what Hettie says.' Johnny bunched his right fist with its array of gold rings as he moved down to Constantine and leaned beside him on the counter.

'Herby,' he called the barman, and when he had his attention he indicated the Greek. 'Please give the lady a port and lemonade.'

And the bystanders scattered for cover. Davy shot out of the door onto the veranda to report to Hettie.

'Johnny!' he gasped. 'He's fighting again.'

'Is he!' Hettie came to her feet like a red-headed Valkyrie. But her progress to the men's bar was delayed by the crowd of spectators that jammed the doorway and all the windows. The crowd was tiptoeing and climbing onto the chairs and tables for a better view, every thud or crash of breaking furniture was greeted with a roar of delight.

Hettie had her handbag clutched in her right hand, and like a jungle explorer hacking his way through the undergrowth with a machete, she opened a path for herself to the bar room door.

At the door she paused. The conflict had reached a critical stage. Among a litter of broken glass and shattered stools, Johnny and the Greek were circling each other warily, waving and feinting, all their wits concentrated upon each other. Both of them were marked. The Greek was bleeding from his lip, a thin red ribbon of blood down his chin that dripped onto his shirt. Johnny had a shiny red swelling closing one eye. The crowd was silent, waiting.

'Johnny Delange!' Hettie's voice cracked like a Mauser rifle-fired from ambush. Johnny started guiltily, dropping his hands, half turning towards her as the Greek's fist crashed into the side of his head. Johnny spun from the blow, hit the wall and slid down quietly.

With a roar of triumph Constantine rushed forward to put the boot into Johnny's prostrate form, but he pitched forward to sprawl unconscious beside Johnny. Hettie had hit him with the water bottle snatched up from one of the table tops.

'Please help me get my husband to the car,' she appealed to the men around her, suddenly helpless and little-girlish.

She sat beside Davy in the front of the Monaco, fuming with anger.

Johnny lay at ease upon the back seat. He was snoring softly.

'Don't be angry, Hettie.' Davy was driving sedately.

'I've told him, not once, a hundred times.' Hettie's voice crackled like static. 'I told him I wouldn't put up with it.'

'It wasn't his fault. The Greek started it,' Davy explained softly and placed his hand on her leg.

'You stick up for him, just because he is your brother.'

'That's not true,' Davy soothed her, stroking her leg. 'You know how I feel about you, Hettie.'

'I don't believe you.' His hand was moving higher. 'You men are all the same. You all stick together.'

Her anger was fast solidifying into a burning resentment of Johnny Delange, one in which she was willing to take a calculated revenge. She knew that Davy's hand was no longer trying to comfort her and quench her anger. Before she married Johnny Delange, Hettie had had every opportunity to learn about men, and she had been an enthusiastic and receptive pupil. She placed no special importance on an act of the flesh, dispensing her favours as casually as someone might offer a cigarette-case around.

'Why not?' she thought. 'That will fix Mr Johnny Delange! Not all the way, of course, but just enough to get my own back on him.'

'No, Hettie. It's true – I tell you.' Davy's voice was husky, as he felt her knees fall apart under his hand. He touched the silky-smooth skin above her stocking top.

The Monaco slowed to almost walking pace, and it was ten minutes more before they reached the company-owned house on the outskirts of Kitchenerville.

In the back seat Johnny groaned. Immediately Davy's hand jerked back to the steering-wheel, and Hettie sat up in the seat, straightening her skirt.

'Help me get him inside,' she said, and her voice was shaky and her cheeks flushed. She was no longer angry.

– 38 –

They were both a little tipsy. They had stopped to celebrate Rod's promotion at the Sunnyside Hotel. They had sat side by side in one of the booths, drinking quickly, excitedly, laughing together, sitting close but not touching.

Terry Steyner could not remember when she had last behaved this way. It must have been all of ten years ago, her last term at Cape Town varsity, swigging draught beer in the Pig and Whistle at Randall's Hotel and talking the most inane rubbish. All the matronly dignity that Manfred insisted she maintain was gone, she felt like a freshette on a first date with the captain of the rugby team.

'Let's get out of here,' Rod said suddenly, and she stood

up unquestioningly. He took her arm down the stairs, and the light touch of his fingers tingled on her bare skin.

In the Maserati again she experienced the feeling of isolation from reality.

'How often do you see your daughter, Rod?' she asked as he settled into the seat beside her, and he glanced at her, surprised.

'Every Sunday.'

'Tomorrow?'

'Yes.'

'How old is she?'

'Nine next birthday.'

'What do you do with her?'

Rod pressed the starter.

'How do you mean?'

'Where do you take her, what do you do together?'

'We go rowing on Zoo Lake, or eat ice cream sundaes. If it's cold or raining we sit in the apartment and we play mah-jong.' He let in the clutch, and as they pulled away he added, 'She cheats.'

'The apartment?'

'I keep a hideaway in town.'

'Where?'

'I'll show you,' said Rod quietly.

She sat on the studio couch and looked about her with interest. She had not expected the obvious care that he had taken in furnishing the apartment. It was in wheatfield gold, chocolate brown and copper. There was a glorious glowing autumn landscape on the far wall that she recognized as a Dino Paravano.

She noticed a little ruefully how Rod stage-managed the lighting for full romantic effect, and then moved automatically to the liquor cabinet.

121

'Where is the bathroom?' Terry asked.

'Second left, down the passage.'

She lingered in the bathroom, opening the medicine cabinet like a thief. There were three toothbrushes hanging in the slots, and below them an aerosol can of Bidex. Quickly she shut the cabinet. Feeling disturbed, not sure if it was jealousy or guilt at her own prying.

The bedroom door was open and so she could not help seeing the double bed as she went back to the lounge. She stood in front of the painting.

'I love his work,' she said.

'Not too photographic for your taste?'

'No. I love it.'

He gave her the drink and stood beside her, studying the painting. She tinkled the ice in her glass, and he turned towards her. The feeling of unreality was still holding Terry as she felt him take the glass from her hand.

She was conscious of his hands only, they were strong and very practised. They touched her shoulders, and then moved onto her back calmly. She felt a voluptuous shudder shake her whole body, and then his mouth came down over hers and the sense of unreality was complete. It was all warm and misty, and she let him take control.

She never knew how long afterwards she jerked back to complete, chilling reality. They were on the couch. She lay in his arms. The front of her slack suit was open to the waist and her bra was unhooked. His head was bowed over her and with a handful of thick springy hair she was directing his lips in their quest. His mouth was warm and sucky on her breast.

'I must be mad!' she gasped, and struggled violently from his arms. She was trembling with fright, horrified with herself. Nothing like this had ever happened to her before.

'This is madness!' Her eyes were great dark pools in her pale face, and her fingers were frantic as she buttoned her blouse. As the last button slipped into its hole, anger replaced her fright.

'How many women have you seduced on that couch, Rodney Ironsides?'

Rod stood up, reaching out a hand to reassure her.

'Don't touch me!' She stepped back. 'I want to go home!'

'I'll take you home, Terry. Just calm down. Nothing happened.'

'That's not your fault,' she blazed.

'No, it's not,' he agreed.

'If you had your way, you'd have—' she bit it off.

'Yes, I would have.' Rod nodded. 'But only if you wanted the same thing.'

She stared at him, starting to recover her temper and her control.

'I shouldn't have come up here, I know. It was asking for trouble, but please take me home now.'

– 39 –

The telephone woke Rod. He checked his wrist watch as he tottered naked and half asleep through to the lounge. Eight o'clock.

'Ironsides!' He yawned into the mouthpiece, and then came fully awake as he recognized her voice.

'Good morning, Rodney. How's your hangover?'

He had not expected to hear from her again.

'Just bearable.'

'I called to thank you for an amusing and – instructive evening.'

'Hark at the girl!' He grinned and scratched his chest. 'She changes with the wind. Last night I expected a bullet between the eyes.'

'Last night I got one big fright,' she admitted. 'It comes

as a bit of a shock to discover suddenly that you are quite capable of acting the wanton. Not all the names I called you were meant.'

'I am sorry for my contribution to your distress,' Rod said.

'Don't be, you were very impressive.' Then quickly, changing the subject, 'You are picking up your daughter today?'

'Yes.'

'I'd like to meet her.'

'That could be arranged.' Rod was cautious.

'Does she like horses?'

'She's crazy about them.'

'Would you like to take her and me out to my stud farm on the Vaal river?'

Rod hesitated. 'Is it safe? I mean, being seen together?'

'It's my reputation, I'll look after it.'

'Fine!' Rod agreed. 'We'd love to visit your farm.'

'I'll meet you at your apartment. When?'

'Half past nine!'

Patti was still in her dressing-gown and she offered Rod her cheek casually to be pecked. There were curlers in her hair and from her eyes he could tell she'd had a late night.

'Hello, you're getting thin. Melly is dressing. Do you want some coffee? Your maintenance cheque was late again this month.' And she took a swipe at the spaniel pup as it squatted on the carpet. 'Damn dog pees all over the place. *Melanie.*' She raised her voice. 'Hurry up! Your Papa is here.'

'Hello, Daddy!' Melanie's voice shrieked delightedly from the interior of the apartment.

'Hello, baby.'

'You can't come in, Daddy, I haven't got any clothes on.'

'Well hurry up! I've come a million miles to see you.'

'Not a *million*!' You couldn't fool Melanie Ironsides.

'Did you say you wanted coffee? It's no trouble, it's made already.' Pattie led him through into the sitting-room.

'Thanks.'

'How are things?' she asked as she filled a cup and gave it to him.

'They've made me General Manager of the Sonder Ditch.' He could not prevent himself, it was too good. He had to boast.

Patti looked at him, startled.

'You're joking!' she accused, and then he saw her mind beginning to work like a cash register.

He almost laughed out loud. 'No. It's true.'

'God!' She sat down limply. 'It will nearly *double* your salary.'

He looked at her dispassionately, and not for the first time felt a great wash of relief as he realized he was no longer shackled to her.

'It's usual to offer congratulations,' he prompted her.

'You don't deserve it.' She was angry now. 'You are a selfish, philandering bastard, Rodney Ironsides, you don't deserve the good things that keep happening to you.' He had cheated her. She could have been the General Manager's wife, first lady of the goldfields. Now she was a divorcée, stuck with a miserable four fifty a month. It had seemed good before, but not now.

'I hope you will have enough conscience to make a suitable adjustment for Melanie and me. We are entitled to a share.'

The door burst open and Melanie Ironsides arrived at a gallop to wrap herself around Rod's neck. She had long blonde hair and green eyes.

'I got nine out of ten for spelling!'

'You're not clever, you're a genius. Also you're beautiful.'

'Will you carry me down to the car, Daddy?'

'What's wrong? Your legs in plaster?'

'Please, please, pretty please times three.'

Patti interrupted the love feast. 'Have you got your jersey, young lady?'

And Melanie flew.

'I'll have her back before seven,' said Rod.

'You haven't answered my question.' Patti was surly. 'Do we get a share?'

'Yes, of course,' said Rod. 'The same big juicy four fifty you've had all along.'

They had been in Rod's apartment ten minutes when the doorbell announced Terry's arrival. She was in jeans and a checked shirt with her hair in a plait, and she greeted Rod self-consciously. When he introduced her to Melanie, she did not look much older than his daughter.

The two girls summed each other up solemnly. Melanie was suddenly very demure and refined, and Rod was relieved to see that Terry had the good sense not to gush over the child.

They were in the Maserati and half way to the village of Parys on the Vaal River before Melanie had completed her microscopic scrutiny of Terry.

'Can I come up front and sit on your lap?' she asked at last.

'Yes, of course.' Terry was hard put to conceal her relief and pleasure. Melanie scrambled over the seat and settled on Terry's lap.

'You are pretty,' Melanie gave her considered opinion.

'Thank you. So are you.'

'Are you Daddy's girlfriend?' Melanie demanded. Terry glanced across at Rod, then burst out laughing.

'Almost,' she gurgled, and then all three of them were laughing.

They laughed often that day. It was a day of sunshine and laughter.

Terry and Rod walked together with fingers almost touching through the green paddocks along the willow-lined bank of the Vaal. Melanie ran ahead of them shrieking with glee at the antics of the foals.

They went up to the stables where Melanie fed sugar lumps to a winner of the Cape Metropolitan Handicap and then kissed his velvety muzzle.

They swam in the pool beside the elegant whitewashed homestead, laughter mingling with the splashes, and when they drove back to Johannesburg in the evening Melanie curled in exhausted slumber on Terry's lap, her head cushioned on Terry's bosom.

Terry waited in the Maserati while Rod carried the sleeping child up to her mother, and when he returned and slipped into the driver's seat, Terry murmured, 'My car is at your apartment. You'll have to take me with you.'

Neither of them spoke until they were back in Rod's sitting-room. Then he said, 'Thank you for a wonderful day.' And he took her to his chest and kissed her.

In the darkness she lay pressed to his sleeping body, clinging to him, as though he might be taken from her. She had never felt such intensity of emotion before, it was a compound of awed wonder and gratitude. She had just been admitted to a new level of human experience she had never suspected existed.

The sheets were still damp. She felt bruised internally, aching, a slow voluptuous pulse of pain that she cherished.

Lightly she touched his body, not wanting to wake him, running her fingertips through the coarse curls that covered his chest, marvelling still at the infinity that separated this from what she had known before.

She shuddered with almost unbearable pleasure as she remembered his voice describing her body to her, making her proud of it for the first time in her life. She remembered the words he had used to tell her exactly what they were doing together, and the feel of his hands, so gentle, sure, so lovingly possessive upon her.

He was so unashamed, taking such obvious joy in her, that the reserves which the barren years of her marriage had placed in her mind were swept away and she was able to go with Rodney Ironsides beyond the storm into that tranquil state where mind and body are completely at peace.

She became aware of him awakening beside her, and she touched his face, his lips and his eyes with her fingertips.

'Thank you,' she whispered, and he seemed to understand, for he took her head and drew it gently down into the hollow of his shoulder.

'Sleep now,' he told her softly, and she closed her eyes and lay very still and quiet beside him, but she did not sleep. She would not miss one moment of this experience.

– 40 –

R od's letter of appointment lay on his desk when he arrived at his office at seven-thirty on the Monday morning.

He sat down and lit a cigarette. Then he began to read it slowly, savouring each word.

'Duly instructed by the Board of Directors,' it began, and ended, 'it remains only to tender the congratulations of the Board, and to voice their confidence in your ability.'

Dimitri came through from his office, distracted.

'Hey! Rod! Christ what a start to the week! We've got a fault in the main high voltage cable on 90 level, and—'

'Don't come squealing to me,' Rod cut him short. 'I'm not the Underground Manager.'

Dimitri gaped at him, taken by surprise.

128

'What the hell, have they fired you?'

'Next best thing,' said Rod and flipped the letter across the desk. 'Look what the bastards have done to me.'

Dimitri read and then whooped, 'My God, Rod! My God!' He shot down the passage to carry the news to the other line managers. Then they were all in his office, shaking his hand. He judged most of their reactions as favourable, though occasionally he detected a false note. A twinge of envy here, one there who had recently had his ears burned by the Ironsides tongue, and an incompetent who knew his job was now in danger. The phone rang. Rod answered it, his expression changed and he cleared his office with a peremptory wave.

'Hirschfeld here.'

'Morning, Mr Hirschfeld.'

'Well, you've got your chance, Ironsides.'

'I'm grateful for it.'

'I want to see you. I'll give you today to sort yourself out. Tomorrow morning at nine o'clock, my office at Reef Buildings.'

'I'll be there.'

'Good.'

Rod hung up, and the day dissolved into a welter of activity and reorganization, constantly interrupted by a stream of well-wishers. He was still running the Underground Manager's job in addition to the General Manager's. It would be some considerable time before a new Underground Manager was transferred in from one of the other group mines. He was trying to arrange his move to the big office in the main Administrative Block up on the ridge, when he had another visitor, Frank Lemmer's secretary, Miss Lily Jordan, looking like a wardress from Ravensbruck in a severe grey flannel suit.

'Mr Ironsides, you and I have not seen eye to eye in the past.'

This was the understatement of the year. 'It is unlikely that we will in the future. Therefore, I have come to tender my resignation. I have made arrangements.'

The phone rang. Dan Stander's voice, breezy and carefree.

'Rod, I'm in love.'

'Oh Christ, no!' Rod groaned. 'Not this morning.'

'I've got to thank you for introducing me to her. She's the most wonderful—'

'Yeah, yeah!' Rod cut him short. 'Look, Dan, I'm rather busy. Some other time, all right?'

'Oh yes, I forgot. You are the new General Manager they tell me. Congratulations. You can buy me a drink at the Club. Six o'clock.'

'Right. By then I'll need one.' Rod hung up, and faced the hanging-judge expression of Miss Lily Jordan.

'Miss Jordan, in the past our interests have conflicted. In the future they will not. You are the best private secretary within a hundred miles of the Sonder Ditch. I need you, the Company needs you.'

That was the magic word. Miss Jordan had twenty-five years' service with the Company. She wavered visibly.

'Please, Miss Jordan, give me a chance.' Shamelessly Rod switched on his most engaging smile. Miss Jordan's femininity was not so completely atrophied that she could resist that smile.

'Very well, then, Mr Ironsides. I'll stay on initially until the end of the month. We'll see after that.' She stood up. 'Now, I'll get your things moved up to the new office.'

'Thank you, Miss Jordan.' With relief he let her take over, and tackled the problems that were piling up on his desk. One man, two jobs. Now he was responsible for surface operation as well as underground. The phone rang, men queued up in the passage, memos kept coming through from Dimitri's office. There was no lunch hour, and by the time she rang he was exhausted.

'Hello,' she said. 'Do I see you tonight?' Her voice was as refreshing as a wet cloth on the brow of a prizefighter between rounds.

'Terry.' He simply spoke her name in reply.

'Yes or no. If it's *no*, I intend jumping off the top of Reef Building.'

'Yes,' he said. 'Pops has summoned me to a meeting at nine tomorrow morning, so I'll be staying overnight at the apartment. I'll call you as soon as I get in.'

'Goody! Goody!' said she.

At five-thirty Dimitri stuck his head around the door.

'I'm going down to No. 1 shaft to supervise the shoot, Rod.'

'My God, what time is it?' Rod checked his watch. 'So late already.'

'It gets late early around here,' Dimitri agreed. 'I'm off.'

'Wait!' Rod stopped him. 'I'll shoot her.'

'No trouble.' Dimitri demurred. Company standard procedure laid down that each day's blast must be supervised by either the Underground Manager or his assistant.

'I'll do it,' Rod repeated. Dimitri opened his mouth to protest further, then he saw that expression on Rod's face and changed his mind quickly.

'Okay then. See you tomorrow.' And he was gone.

Rod grinned at his own sentimentality. The Sonder Ditch was his now and, by God, he was going to shoot his own first blast on her.

They were waiting for him at the steel door of the blast control room at the shaft head. It was a small concrete room like a wartime pillbox, and there were only two keys to the door. Dimitri had one, Rod the other.

The duty mine captain and the foreman electrician added their congratulations to the hundreds he had received during the day, and Rod opened the door and they went into the tiny room.

'Check her out,' Rod instructed, and the mine captain began his calls to the shaft overseers at both No. 1 and No. 2 for their confirmation that the workings of the Sonder Ditch were deserted, that every human being who had gone down that morning had come out again this evening.

Meanwhile, the foreman electrician was busy at the electrical control board. He looked up at Rod.

'Ready to close the circuits, Mr Ironsides.'

'Go ahead,' Rod nodded and the man touched a switch. A green light showed up on the board.

'No. 1 north longwall closed and green.'

'Lock her in,' Rod instructed and the electrician touched another switch.

'No. 1 east longwall closed and green.'

'Lock her in.'

The green light showed that the firing circuit was intact. A red light would indicate a fault and the faulty circuit would not be locked into the blast pattern.

Circuit after circuit was readied until finally the foreman stood back from the control board.

'All green and locked in.'

Rod glanced at the mine captain.

'All levels clear, Mr Ironsides. She's ready to burn.'

'Cheesa!' said Rod, the traditional command that had come down from the days when each fuse had been individually lit by a hand-held igniter stick.

'Cheesa' was the Bantu word for 'burn'.

The mine captain crossed to the control board and opened the cage that guarded a large red button.

'Cheesa!' echoed the mine captain and hit the button with the heel of his hand.

Immediately the row of green lights on the control board was extinguished, and in its place showed a row of red lights. Every circuit had been broken by the explosions.

The ground under their feet began to tremble. Throughout the workings the shots were firing. In the stopes the head charges fired at the top of the inclines, then in succession the other shots went off behind them. Each charge taking a ten-ton bite of rock and reef out of the face.

At the end of the development drives, a more complicated pattern was shooting. First a row of *cutters* went off down the middle of the oval face. Then the *shoulder charges* at the top corners, followed by the *knee charges* at the bottom corners. A moment's respite with the dust and nitrous fumes swirling back down the drive, then a roar as the *easers* on each side shaped the hole. Another respite and then the *lifters* along the bottom picked up the heap of broken rock and threw it back from the face.

Rod could imagine it clearly. Though no human eye had ever witnessed the blast, he knew exactly what was taking place down there.

The last tremor died away.

'That's it. A full blast,' said the mine captain.

'Thank you.' Rod felt tired suddenly. He wanted that drink, even though their brief exchange that morning had warned him that Dan would probably be insufferable. He could guess the conversation would revolve around Dan's new-found love.

Then he smiled as he thought about what waited for him in Johannesburg later that night, and suddenly he wasn't all that tired.

They sat facing each other.

'Only three things worry me,' Terry told Rod.

'What are they?' Rod rubbed soap into the face flannel.

'Firstly, your legs are too long for this bath.'

Rod rearranged his limbs, and Terry shot half out of the water with a squeak.

'Rodney Ironsides, would you be good enough to take a bit more care where you put your toes!'

'Forgive me.' He leaned forward to kiss her. 'Tell me what else worries you.'

'Well, the second thing that worries me is that I'm not worried.'

'What part of Ireland did you say you were from?' Rod asked. 'County Cork?'

'I mean, it's terrible but I'm not even a little conscience-stricken. Once I believed that if it ever happened to me I would never be able to look another human being in the eyes, I'd be so ashamed.' She took the flannel from his hands and began soaping his chest and shoulders. 'But, far from being ashamed, I'd like to stand in the middle of Eloff Street at rush hour and shout "Rodney Ironsides is my lover".'

'Let's drink to that.' Rodney rinsed the soap from his hands and reached over the side of the bath to pick up the two wine glasses from the floor. He gave one to Terry and they clinked them together, the sparkling Cape burgundy glowed ruby red.

'Rodney Ironsides is my lover!' she toasted him.

'Rodney Ironsides is your lover,' he agreed and they drank.

'Now, I give you a toast,' he said.

'What is it?' She held her glass ready, and Rod leaned

forward and poured the red wine from the crystal glass between her breasts. It ran like blood down her white skin and he intoned solemnly:

'Bless this ship and all who sail in her!'

Terry gurgled with delight.

'To her captain. May he keep a firm hand on the rudder!'

'May her bottom never hit the reef!'

'May she be torpedoed regularly!'

'Terry Steyner, you are terrible.'

'Yes, aren't I?' And they drained their glasses.

'Now,' Rod asked, 'what is your third worry?'

'Manfred will be home on Saturday.'

They stopped laughing, Rod reached down for the burgundy bottle and refilled the glasses.

'We still have five days,' he said.

– 42 –

It had been a week of personal triumph for Manfred Steyner. His address to the conference had been the foundation of the entire talks, all discussion had revolved upon it. He had been called upon to speak at the closing banquet which General de Gaulle had attended in person, and afterwards the General had asked Manfred to take coffee and brandy with him in one of the ante-rooms. The General had been gracious, had asked questions and listened attentively to the answers. Twice he had called his finance minister's attention to Manfred's replies.

Their farewells had been cordial, with a hint of state recognition for Manfred, a decoration. In common with most Germans, Manfred had a weakness for uniforms and decorations. He imagined how a star and ribbon might look on the snowy front of his dress shirt.

There had been a wonderful press both in France and at

home. Even a bad-tempered quarter column in *Time* magazine, with a picture, de Gaulle stooping over the diminutive Manfred solicitously, one hand on his shoulder. The caption read: 'The huntsman and the hawk. To catch a dollar?'

Now standing in the tiny cloakroom in the tail of the South African Airways Boeing, Manfred was whistling softly as he stripped his shirt and vest, crumpled them into a ball and dropped them into the waste bin.

Naked to the waist, he wiped his upper body with a wet cloth and then rubbed 4711 Eau de Cologne into his skin. From the briefcase he took an electric razor. The whistling stopped as he contorted his face for the razor.

Through his mind ran page after page of the report that Andrew had delivered that morning to his hotel room. Manfred had total recall when it came to written material. Although the report was in the briefcase beside him, in his mind's eye he could review it word for word, figure for figure.

It was a stupendous piece of work. How the authors had gained access to the drilling and exploration reports of the five Kitchenerville field companies he could not even guess, for the gold mining companies' security was as tight as that of any national intelligence agency. But the figures were genuine. He had checked those purporting to be from CRC carefully. They were correct. So therefore the other four must also be genuine.

The names of the authors of the report were legend. They were the top men in the field. Their opinions were the best in Harley Street. The conclusion that they reached was completely convincing. In effect it was this:

If a haulage was driven from 66 level of the Sonder Ditch No. 1 shaft through the Big Dipper dyke, it would pass *under* the limestone water-bearing foundations, and just beyond the fault it would intersect a reef of almost unbelievable value.

It had not needed the lecture that Manfred had received

from his corpulent creditor to show him the possibilities. The man who gave the order to drive through the Big Dipper would receive the credit. He would certainly be elected to the chairmanship of the Group when that office fell vacant.

There was another possibility. A person who purchased a big packet of Sonder Ditch shares immediately before the reef was intersected would be a very rich man when he came to sell those shares later. He would be so rich that he would no longer be dependent on his wife for the means to live the kind of life he wanted, and indulge his own special tastes.

Manfred blew the hairs from his razor and returned it to his brief case. Then as he took out a fresh shirt and vest, he began to sing the words to the tune:

> 'Heute ist der schönste Tag
> In meinem Leben.'

He would telephone Ironsides from Jan Smuts Airport as soon as he had passed through customs. Ironsides would come up to the house on Sunday morning and receive his orders.

As he knotted the silk of his tie Manfred knew that he stood at the threshold of a whole new world, the events of the next few months would lift him high above the level of ordinary men.

It was the chance for which he had worked and waited all these years.

Circumstances had changed completely since his last visit, Rod reflected, as he took the Maserati up the drive towards the Dutch gabled house.

He parked the car and switched off the ignition, sitting a while, reluctant to face the man who had sponsored his career and whom Rod in return had presented with a fine pair of horns.

'Courage, Ironsides!' he muttered and climbed out of the Maserati and went up the path across the lawns.

Terry was on the veranda in a gay print dress, with her hair loose, sprawled in a canvas chair with the Sunday papers scattered about her.

'Good morning, Mr Ironsides,' she greeted him as he came up the steps. 'My husband is in his study. You know the way, don't you?'

'Thank you, Mrs Steyner.' Rod kept his voice friendly but disinterested, then as he passed her chair he growled softly, 'I could eat you without salt.'

'Don't waste it, you gorgeous beast,' Terry murmured and ran the tip of her tongue over her lips.

Fifteen minutes later, Rod sat stony-faced and internally chilled before Manfred Steyner's desk. When at last he forced himself to speak, it felt as though the skin on his lips would tear with the effort.

'You want me to drive through the Big Dipper,' he croaked.

'More than that, Mr Ironsides. I want you to complete the drive within three months, and I want a complete security blanket on the development,' Manfred told him primly. Despite the fact that it was Sunday he was formally dressed, white shirt and dark suit. 'You will commence the drive from No. 1 shaft 66 level and make an intersect on reef at 6,600 feet with the SD No. 3 borehole 250 feet beyond the calculated extremity of the serpentine intrusion of the Big Dipper.'

'No,' Rod shook his head. 'You can't go through that. No one can take the chance. God alone knows what is on the other side, we only know that is bad ground. Stinking rotten ground.'

'How do you know that?' Manfred asked softly.

'Everybody on the Kitchenerville field knows it.'

'How?'

'Little things.' Rod found it hard to put into words. 'You get a feeling, the signs are there and when you've been in the game long enough you have a sixth sense that warns you when—'

'Nonsense,' Manfred interrupted brusquely. 'We no longer live in the days of witchcraft.'

'Not witchcraft, experience,' Rod snapped angrily. 'You've seen the drilling results from the other side of the fault?'

'Of course,' Manfred nodded. 'SD No. 3 found values of thousands of penny-weights.'

'And the other holes went dry and twisted off, or had water squirting out of them like a pissing horse!'

Manfred flushed fiercely. 'You will be good enough not to employ bar-room terminology in this house.'

Rod was taken off balance, and before he could answer Manfred went on.

'Would you put the considered opinions of,' Manfred named three men, 'before your own vague intuitions?'

'They are the best in the business,' Rod conceded reluctantly.

'Read that,' snapped Manfred. He tossed a manila folder onto the desk top, then stood up and went to wash his hands at the concealed basin.

Rod picked up the folder, opened it and was immediately engrossed. Ten minutes later, without looking up from the report, he fumbled a pack of cigarettes from his pocket.

'Please do not smoke!' Manfred stopped him sharply.

Three-quarters of an hour later, Rod closed the folder. During that time Manfred Steyner had sat with reptilian stillness behind his desk, with the glitter of his eyes the only signs of life.

'How the hell did you get hold of those figures and reports?' Rod asked with wonder.

'That does not concern you.' Manfred retrieved the folder from him, his first movement in forty-five minutes.

'So that's it!' muttered Rod. 'The water is in the limestone near the surface. We go in under it!' He stood up from the chair abruptly and began to pace up and down in front of Manfred's desk.

'Are you convinced?' Manfred asked, and Rod did not answer.

'I have promoted you above older and more experienced men,' said Manfred softly. 'If I tear you down again, and tell the world you were not man enough for the job, then, Rodney Ironsides, you are finished. No one else would take a chance on you again, ever!'

It was true. Rod knew it.

'However, if you were to follow my instructions and we intersected this highly enriched reef, then part of the glory would rub off on you.'

That was also true. Rod stopped pacing, he stood with shoulders hunched, in an agony of indecision. Could he trust that report beyond his own deep intuition? When he thought about that ground beyond the dyke, his skin tickled with gooseflesh. He almost had the stink of it in his nostrils. Yet he could be wrong, and the weight of the opposition was heavy. The eminent names on the report, the threats which he knew Manfred would not hesitate to put into effect.

'Will you give me a written instruction?' Rod demanded harshly.

'What effect would that have?' Manfred asked mildly.

'As General Manager, the decision to work certain ground or not to work it is technically yours. In the very unlikely event that you encountered trouble beyond the fault, it would be no defence to produce a written instruction from me. Just as if you murdered my wife you could not defend yourself by producing a written instruction from me to do so.'

This again was true. Rod knew he was trapped. He could refuse, and wreck his career. Or he could comply and take the consequences whatever they may be.

'No,' said Manfred, 'I will not give you a written instruction.'

'You bastard,' Rod said softly.

Manfred answered as gently. 'I warned you that you would not be able to refuse to obey me.'

And the last twinge of remorse that Rod felt for his association with Terry Steyner faded and was gone.

'You've given me three months to hit the Big Dipper. All right, Steyner. You've got it!'

Rod turned on his heel and walked out of the room.

Terry was waiting for him among the protea plants on the bottom lawn. She saw his face and dropped all pretence. She went to meet him.

'Rod, what is it?' Her hand on his arm, looking up into his eyes.

'Careful!' he warned her, and she dropped her hand and stood back.

'What is it?'

'That bloody Gestapo bastard,' Rod snarled, and then, 'I'm sorry, Terry, he's your husband.'

'What has he done?'

'I can't tell you here. When can I see you?'

'I'll find an excuse to get away later today. Wait for me at your apartment.'

141

Later she sat on the couch below the Paravano painting and listened while he told her about it. All of it, the report, the threat and the order to pierce the Big Dipper.

She listened but expressed neither approval nor disapproval of his decision.

Manfred turned away from the window and went back to his desk. Even at that distance there had been no doubt about his wife's gesture. The hand outstretched, the face turned up, the lips parted in anxious enquiry, and then the guilty start and withdrawal.

He sat down at his desk, and laid his hands neatly in front of him. For the first time he was thinking of Rodney Ironsides as a man and not a tool.

He thought how big he was, tall and as wide across the shoulders as a gallows. Any reprisal on Ironsides could not be physical, and it could not be immediate. It must be after the drive to the Big Dipper.

I can wait, he thought coldly, there is time for everything in this life.

– 44 –

Johnny and Davy Delange sat in the two chairs before Rod's desk. They were both awkward and uncomfortable up here in the big office with picture windows looking out over the Kitchenerville valley.

I don't blame them, Rod thought, even I am not accustomed to it yet. Wall-to-wall carpeting, air-conditioning, original paintings on the wood-panelled walls.

'I have sent for you because you two are the best rock breakers on the Sonder Ditch,' Rod began.

'Tin Ribs wants something,' thought Davy, with all the suspicion of the union man for management.

'We will now have a few words from our sponsor,' Johnny grinned to himself. 'Before we start the programme.'

Rod looked at their faces and knew exactly what they were thinking. He had been on daily pay himself once. Cut out the compliments, Ironsides – he advised himself – these are two tough cookies and they are not impressed.

'I am pulling you out of the stopes and putting you onto a special development end. You will take it in turns to work day and night shift. You will be directly responsible to me and there will be a security blanket on your activity.'

They watched him without reaction, their expressions guarded. Johnny broke the short silence.

'One end, one blast a day?' He was thinking of his pay. Calculated on the amount of rock broken, he would earn little more than basic salary with a blast on one small face daily.

'No.' Rod shook his head. 'Ultra-fast, multi-blast, and shaft sinkers' rates.'

And both the Delange brothers sat forward in their chairs.

'Multi-blast?' Davy asked. That meant that they could shoot just as soon as they were ready. A good team could blast three – maybe four times a shift.

'Ultra-fast?' Johnny demanded. That was language Johnny understood. It was a term employed only in emergency, as when driving in to rescue trapped men after a fall. It was tacit approval from management to waive standard safety procedure in favour of speed. Christ, Johnny exulted, I can shoot her four – maybe five times a shift.

'Shaft sinkers' rates?' they asked together. That was a 20 per cent bonus on stopers' rates. It was a fortune they were being offered.

Rod nodded affirmative to their questions, and waited for the reaction which he knew would follow. It came immediately.

The Delange brothers now began to look for the catch.

They sat stolidly turning the deal over in their minds, like two cautious housewives examining a tomato for blemishes because the price was too cheap.

'How long is this drive?' Johnny asked. If the drive was short, a few hundred feet, then it was worth nothing. They would hardly get into their stride before it was completed.

'Close on six thousand feet,' Rod assured him. They looked relieved.

'Where is it headed?' Davy discovered the rub.

'We are going to drive through the Big Dipper to intersect on reef at 6,000 feet.'

'Jesus!' said Johnny. 'The Big Dipper!' He was awed but unafraid. It excited him, the danger, the challenge. Had he been born earlier, Johnny Delange would have made a fine Spitfire pilot.

'The Big Dipper,' Davy murmured, his mind was racing. Nothing in this world or beyond would entice Davy Delange to drive through the Big Dipper. He had an almost religious fear of it. The name alone conjured up all sorts of hidden menace and unspeakable horror. Water. Gas. Friable ground, faults. Mud-rushes. All a miner's nightmare.

There was no question of him doing it, yet the money was too good to pass up. He could net ten or eleven thousand rand on those terms.

'All right, Mr Ironsides,' he said. 'I'll take the first night shifts. Johnny can start the day shifts.'

Davy Delange had made his decision. He would work until his drills hit the greenish-black serpentine rock of the dyke. He would then walk out of the drive and quit. He would go up to, but not beyond the dyke.

Afterwards, any of the other mines would snap him up, he had an impeccable record and he would force Johnny to follow him.

'Hey, Davy!' Johnny was delighted, he had expected Davy to turn the deal down flat.

Now he would be able to buy the Mustang for certain –

and perhaps an MGB GT for Hettie – and take a holiday to Durban over Christmas, and . . .

Rod was puzzled by Davy's easy agreement. He studied him a moment and decided that he had ferrety eyes. He's a sneaky little bastard, Rod decided, I'll have to watch him.

– 45 –

It took one shift only to prepare for the development. Rod selected the starting point. The main haulage curved away from the shaft on 66 level. 1,000 feet along this tunnel there was a chamber that had been cut out as a loco repair station but which was now out of use. Two large batwing ventilation doors were fitted to the opening of the chamber to provide privacy and behind them the chief underground surveyor set up his instruments and marked out the head of the tunnel that would fly arrow straight a mile and more through the living rock to strike through the Big Dipper into the unknown.

The area surrounding the head chamber was roped off band sign-posted with warnings.

DANGER

INDEPENDENT BLASTING

The mine captains were instructed to keep their men well away, and all loco traffic was rerouted through a secondary haulage.

On the doors of the chamber another notice was fixed.

FIERY MINE PROCEDURE IN FORCE

NO NAKED LIGHTS BEYOND THIS POINT

Owing to small deposits of coal and other organic substance in the upper stratas of rock, the Sonder Ditch was classed as a fiery mine and subject to the government legislation covering this subject. No matches, lighters or other spark-generating devices were allowed into a new development end, because the presence of methane gas was always suspected.

Colourless, odourless, tasteless, detectable only by test with a safety lamp, it was a real and terrifying danger. A nine per cent concentration in air was highly explosive. Stringent precautions were taken against accidental triggering of methane that may have oozed out of a fissure or cavity in the rock.

From the main compressed air-pipes running down the corners of the shaft were taken leads to air tanks in the haulage, ensuring that sixty pounds per square inch of pressure was available for the rock drills. Then drills, pinchbars, hammers, shovels, and the other tools were unloaded from the cage at 66 level and stored at the shaft head.

Lastly, explosive was placed in the red lockers at the head of the development, and on the evening of October 23rd 1968, thirty minutes after the main blast, Davy Delange and his gang disembarked from the cage and went to the disused loco shop.

Davy, with the surly little Swazi boss boy beside him, stood before the rock wall on which the surveyor had marked the outline of the tunnel. Behind him his gang had fallen unbidden to their labour, each man knowing exactly what was expected of him.

Already the machine boys and their assistants were lugging their ungainly tools forward.

'You! You! You! You!' Davy indicated to each of them the hole on which he was to begin and then stepped back.

'Shaya!' he commanded. 'Hit it!' And with a fluttering bellow that buffeted the eardrums the drive began.

The drilling ceased and Davy charged the holes. The

fuses hung like the tails of white mice from their holes. Each length carefully cut to ensure correct firing sequence.

'Clear the drive!' The boss boy's whistle shrilled, the tramp of heavy boots receded until silence hung heavy in the chemically cleaned air.

'Cheesa!' Davy and the boss boy, with the igniters burning like children's fireworks in their right hands, touched them to the hanging tails until the chamber was lit by the fierce blue light of the burning fuses. The shadows of the two men flickered gigantic and distorted upon the walls.

'All burning. Let's go!' And the two men walked quickly back to where the gang waited along the haulage.

The detonations sucked at their ears, and thrust against their lungs, so that afterwards the silence was stunning.

Davy checked his wristwatch. By law there was a mandatory thirty minutes' wait before anyone could go back to the face. There may be a hang-fire waiting to blow the eyes out of someone's head. Even if there were not, there was still the cloud of poisonous nitrous fumes that would destroy the hair follicles in a man's nostrils and render him still more vulnerable to the fine particles of rock dust that would seek to enter his lungs.

Davy waited those thirty minutes, by which time the ventilation had sucked away the fumes and dust.

Then, alone, he went up the haulage. With him he carried his safety lamp, its tiny blue flame burning behind the screen of fine brass wire mesh. That mesh was flash proof and insulated the flame from any methane in the air.

Standing before the raw circular wound in the rock wall, Davy tested for methane gas. Watching the blue flame for the tell-tale cap. There was no sign of it, and satisfied he extinguished the lamp.

'Boss boy!' he yelled, and the Swazi came up uncoiling the hose behind him.

'Water down!'

Only when the rock face and all the loose rubble below it were glistening and dripping with water was Davy satisfied that the dust was laid sufficiently to bring up his gang.

'Bar boys!' he yelled, and they came up, carrying the twelve-foot-long pinchbars, a tool like a giant crowbar.

'Bar down. Make safe!' And the bar boys attacked the bunches of loose rock that were flaking and crumbling from the hanging wall. Two of them manipulating one bar between them, with the steel point striking sparks from the rock. The dislodged fragments rained down, heavily at first and then less and less until the rock above their heads was solid and clean.

Only then did Davy scramble over the pile of rubble to reach the face and begin marking in the shot holes.

Behind him his gang were lashing the stuff into the waiting cocopans, and his machine boys were dragging the drills up to the face.

Davy's gang made three blasts that first night. As he rode up in the cage into a pink, sweet-smelling dawn, Davy was satisfied.

'Perhaps tonight we will get in four blasts,' he thought.

In the Company change house he showered, running the water steaming hot so his skin turned dull angry red, and he worked up a fat white lather of soap suds over his head and at his armpits and crotch.

He rubbed down with a rough thick towel and dressed quickly. Crossing the parking lot to his battered old Ford Anglia he felt happy and good-tired; hungry and ready for bed.

He drove into Kitchenerville at a steady forty miles an hour, and by this time the sun was just showing over the Kraalkop ridge. The dawn was misty rose, with long shadows against the earth, and he thought that this was how it would be in the early mornings on the farm.

On the outskirts of the town Johnny's Monaco roared past him going in the opposite direction. Johnny waved and blew the horn, shouting something that was lost in the howl of wind and motor.

'They'll catch him yet.' Davy shook his head in disapproval. 'The speed limit is forty-five along here.'

He parked the Anglia in the garage and let himself in through the kitchen door. The Bantu maid was busy over the stove.

'Three eggs,' he told her and went through to his bedroom. He shrugged off his jacket and threw it on the bed. Then he returned to the door and glanced quickly up and down the passage. It was deserted, and there was no sound besides the clatter of the maid in the kitchen.

Davy sidled into the passage. The door to Johnny's bedroom was ajar, and Davy moved quietly down to it. His heart was pounding in his throat, his breathing was stifled by his guilt and excitement.

He peered around the edge of the door and gasped aloud. This morning it was better than usual.

Hettie was a sound sleeper. Johnny always maintained it would take a shot of Dynagel to wake her. She never wore night clothes and she never rose before ten-thirty in the morning. She lay on her stomach, hugging a pillow to her chest, her hair a joyous tangle of flaming red against the green sheets. The morning was warm and her blankets had been kicked aside.

Davy stood in the passage. A nerve in his eyelid began to twitch, and under his shirt a drop of perspiration slid from his armpit down along his flank. On the bed Hettie mumbled unintelligibly in her sleep, drew her knees up and rolled slowly onto her back. One arm came up and flopped limply over her face, her eyes were covered by the crook of her elbow.

She sighed deeply. The twin mounds of her bosom were pulled out of shape by their own weight and the angle of her arm. The hair in her armpit and at the base of her belly was bright shiny red-gold. She was long and smooth and silky white, crowned and tipped with flame.

She moved her body languorously, voluptuously, and then settled once more into slumber.

'Breakfast ready, master,' the maid called from the kitchen. Davy started guiltily, then retreated down the passage.

He found with surprise that he was panting, as though he had run a long way.

– 46 –

Johnny Delange leaned against the sidewall of the haulage, his hard helmet tilted at a jaunty angle and a cigarette dangling from his lips.

Down at the face the shots began to fire. Johnny recognized each detonation, and when the last dull jar disrupted the air about them, he pushed himself away from the wall with his shoulder.

'That was the *lifters*,' he announced. 'Come on Big King!'

Not for Johnny Delange a thirty-minute waste of time. As he and Big King set off down the haulage together they were binding scarves over their noses and mouths. Ahead of them a bluey-white fog of dust and fumes filled the tunnel, and Big King had the hose going, using a fine mist spray to absorb the fumes and particles.

They pushed on up to the face, Johnny stooping over the safety lamp. Even he had a healthy respect for methane gas.

'Bar boys!' he bellowed, not waiting for Big King to finish watering down. They came up like ghosts in the fog. Hard behind them the machine boys hovered with their drills.

Taking calculated risks Johnny had his drills roaring

150

forty-five minutes sooner than Davy Delange would have in the same circumstances.

When he came back to the face from cutting fuses and priming his explosives, he found his lashing gang struggling with a massive slab of rock that had been blown intact from the face. Five of them were beating on it with fourteen-pound hammers in an attempt to crack it into manageable pieces. As Johnny reached them, Big King was berating them mercilessly.

'You look like a bunch of virgins grinding millet.'

The hammers clanged and struck sparks from the slab. Sweat oozed from every pore of the hammer boys' skin, greasing their bodies, flying from their heads in sparkling droplets with each blow.

'Shaya!' Big King goaded them on. 'Between you all you wouldn't crack the shell of an egg. Hit it, man! Hit it!'

One by one the men fell back exhausted, their chests heaving, gulping air through gaping mouths, blinded by their own sweat.

'All right,' Johnny intervened. The rock was holding up the whole blast. It warranted drastic measures to break it up.

'I'll pop her,' he said, and any government inspector or mine safety officer would have paled at those words.

'Stand far back and turn your faces away,' Big King instructed his gang. From the forehead of one of his men he took a pair of wire mesh goggles, designed to shield the eyes from flying splinters and rock fragments. He handed them to Johnny who placed them over his eyes.

From the canvas carrying bag he took out a stick of Dynagel. It looked like a candle wrapped in yellow greased paper.

'Give me your knife.' Big King opened a large clasp knife and handed it to Johnny.

Carefully Johnny cut a coin-shaped sliver of explosive from one end of the stick, a piece twice as thick as a penny.

He returned the remains of the stick to the bag and handed it to Big King.

'Get back,' he said and Big King moved away.

Johnny eyed the slab of rock thoughtfully and then placed the fragment of Dynagel in the centre of it. He adjusted the goggles over his eyes, and picked up one of the fourteen-pound hammers.

'Turn your eyes away,' he warned and took deliberate aim. Then with a smooth overhead two-handed swing he brought the hammer down on the Dynagel.

The explosion was painful in the confined space of the drive, and afterwards Johnny's ears hummed with it. A tiny drop of blood ran down his cheek from the scratch inflicted by a flying splinter. His wrists ached from the jolt of the hammer in his hands.

'Gwenyama!' grunted Big King in admiration. 'The man is a lion.'

The explosion had cracked the slab into three wedge-shaped segments. Johnny pushed the goggles onto his forehead and wiped the blood from his cheek with the back of his hand.

'Get it the hell out of here,' he grinned, then he turned to Big King.

'Come.' He jerked his head towards the end of the tunnel. 'Help me charge the holes.'

The two of them worked quickly, sliding the sticks of Dynagel into the shot holes and tamping them home with the charging sticks.

For anyone who was not in possession of a blasting licence, to charge up was an offence punishable by a fine of one hundred rand or two months' imprisonment, or both. Big King had no licence, but his assistance saved fifteen minutes on the operation.

Johnny and his gang blew the face five times that day, but as they rode up in the cage into the cool evening air he was not satisfied.

'Tomorrow we'll shoot her six times,' he told Big King.

'Maybe seven,' said Big King.

Hettie was waiting for him in the lounge when he got home. She flew to him and threw her arms about his neck.

'Did you bring me a present?' she asked with her lips against his ear, and Johnny laughed tantalizingly. It was very seldom that he did not have a gift for her.

'You did!' she exclaimed, and began to run her hands over his pockets.

'There!' She thrust her hand into the inside pocket of his jacket, and brought out the little white jeweller's box.

'Oh!' She opened it, and then her expression changed slightly.

'You don't like them?' Johnny asked anxiously.

'How much did they cost?' she enquired as she examined the porcelain and lacquer earrings, representing two vividly coloured parrots.

'Well,' Johnny looked shamefaced, 'you see, Hettie, it's the end of the month, you see, and well, like I'm a bit short till pay day, you see, so I couldn't—'

'How much?'

'Well, you see,' he took a breath, 'two rand fifty.'

'Oh,' said Hettie, 'they're nice.' And she promptly lost interest in them. She tossed the box carelessly onto the crowded mantelpiece and set off for the kitchen.

'Hey, Hettie,' Johnny called after her. 'How about we go across to Fochville? There's a dance there tonight. We go and twist, hey?'

Hettie turned back, her expression alive again.

'Gee, yes, man!' she enthused. 'Let's do that. I'll go and change, hey!' And she ran up the passage.

Davy came out of his bedroom, on his way to work.

'Hey, Davy.' Johnny stopped him. 'You got any money on you?'

'Are you broke again?'

'Just till pay day.'

'Hell, man, Johnny, you got a cheque for eleven hundred the beginning of the month. You spent it all?'

'Next month,' Johnny winked, 'I'm going to get a cheque for two or three thousand. Then watch me go! Come, Davy, lend me fifty. I'm taking Hettie dancing.'

– 47 –

For Rod the days flicked past like telegraph poles viewed from a speeding automobile. Each day he gained confidence in his own ability. He had never doubted that he could handle the underground operation and now he found that he had a firm grasp on the surface as well. He knew that his campaign to reduce working costs was having effect, but its full harvest would only be apparent when the quarterly reports were drafted.

Yet he lay awake in the big Manager's residence on the ridge in which he and his few sticks of furniture seemed lost and lonely, and he worried. There were always myriad nagging little problems, but there were others more serious.

This morning Lily Jordan had come through into his office.

'Mr Innes is coming up to see you at nine.'

'What's he want?' Herbert Innes was the Manager of the Sonder Ditch Reduction works.

'He wouldn't tell me,' Lily answered. The end of the month had come and gone and Lily was still with him. Rod presumed that he had been approved.

Herby Innes, burly and red-faced, sat down and drank the cup of tea that Lily provided, while he regaled Rod with a stroke by stroke account of his Sunday afternoon golf round. Rod interrupted him after he had hit a nine-iron short at the third and shanked his chip.

'Okay, Herby. What's the problem?'

'We've got a leak, Rod.'

'Bad?'

'Bad enough,' Herby grunted. To him the loss of a single ounce of gold during the process of recovery and refinement was catastrophic.

'What do you reckon?'

'Between the wash and the pour we are losing a couple hundred ounces a week.'

'Yes,' Rod agreed. 'That is bad enough.'

20,000 rand a month, 120,000 a year.

'Have you any ideas?'

'It's been going on for some time, even in Frank Lemmer's day. We have tried everything.'

Rod was a little hazy about the workings of the reduction plant, not that he would admit that, but he was. He knew that the ore was weighed and sampled when it reached the surface, from this a fairly accurate estimate of gold content was made and compared with actual recovery. Any discrepancy had to be investigated and traced.

'What is your recovery rate for the last quarter?'

'Ninety-six point seven-three.'

'That's pretty good,' Rod admitted. It was impossible to recover all the gold in the ore that was surfaced but Herby was getting most of it out. 96.73 per cent of it, to be precise. Which meant that very little of the missing 200 ounces was being lost into the dumps and the slimes dam.

'I tell you what, Herby,' Rod decided. 'I'll come down to the plant this afternoon. We'll go over it together, perhaps a fresh eye may be able to spot the trouble.'

'May do.' Herby was sceptical. 'We've tried everything else. We are pouring this afternoon. What time shall I expect you?'

'Two o'clock.'

They started at the shaft head, where the ore cage, the copie, arrived at the surface every four minutes with its cargo of rock which it dumped into a concrete shute. Each load was classified as either 'reef' or 'waste'.

The reef was dropped into the massive storage bins, while the waste was carried off on a conveyor to the wash house to be sluiced down before going to the dump. Tiny particles of gold sticking to the waste rock were gathered in this way.

Herby put his lips close to Rod's ear to make himself heard above the rumbling roar of rock rolling down the chute.

'I'm not worried about this end. It's all bulk here and very little shine.' Herby used the reduction plant slang for gold. 'The closer we get to the end, the more dangerous it is.'

Rod nodded and followed Herby down the steel ladder until they reached a door below the storage bins. They went through into a long underground tunnel very similar to the ore tunnel on 100 level.

Again there was a massive conveyor belt moving steadily along the tunnel while ore from the bins above was fed onto it. Rod and Herby walked along beside the belt until it passed under a massive electromagnet. Here they paused for a while. The magnet was extracting from the ore all those pieces of metal which had found their way into the ore passes and bins.

'How much you picking up?' Rod asked.

'Last week fourteen tons,' Herby answered, and taking Rod's arm led him through the door beside them. They were in an open yard that looked like a scrap-metal merchant's premises. A mountain of pinchbars, jumper bits, shovels, steel wire rope, snatch blocks, chains, spanners, fourteen-pound hammers, and other twisted and unrecognizable pieces of metal filled the yard. All of it was rusted, much of it unusable. It had been separated from the ore by the magnet.

Rod's mouth tightened. Here he was presented with indisputable evidence of the carelessness and it-belongs-to-the-company attitude of his men. This pile of scrap represented a waste that would total hundreds of thousands of rand annually.

'We will see about that!' he muttered.

'If one of those hammers got into my jaw mills it would smash it to pieces,' Herby told him dolefully and led him back into the conveyor tunnel.

The belt angled upwards sharply and they followed the catwalk beside it. They climbed steadily for five minutes and Herby was puffing like a steam engine. Through the holes in the honeycomb steel plate under his feet, Rod could see that they were now a few hundred feet above ground level.

The conveyor reached the head of a tall tower and dumped its load of ore into the gaping mouths of the screeners. As the rock fell down the tower to ground level again it was sorted for size, and the larger pieces diverted to the jaw crushers which chewed it into fistsize bites.

'See anything?' Herby asked, barely concealing the sarcasm.

Rod grinned at him.

They climbed down the steel ladders that seemed endless. The screeners rattling and the crushers hammering, until Rod's eardrums pleaded for mercy.

At last they reached ground level and went through into the mill room. This was a cavernous galvanized-iron shed the size of a large aircraft hangar. At least one hundred yards long and fifty feet high, it was filled with long rows of the cylindrical tube mills.

Forty of them in all, they were as thick as the boiler of a steam locomotive and about twice as long. Into one end of them was fed the ore which had been reduced in size by the jaw crushers. The tube mills revolved and the loose steel balls within them pounded the rock to powder.

If the noise before had been bad, it was hideous in the mill room. Rod and Herby made no effort to speak to each other until they had walked through into the comparative quiet of the first heavy-media separator room.

'Now,' Herby explained. 'This is where we start worrying.' He indicated the rows of pale blue six-inch piping that came through the wall from the mill room.

'In there is the powdered rock mixed with water to a smooth flowing paste. About forty per cent of the gold is free.'

'No one can get into those pipes and you've checked for any possible leak?' Rod asked. Herby nodded.

'But,' he said, 'have a look here!'

Along the far wall was a series of cages. They were made of heavy steel mesh, the perforations would not allow a man's finger through. The heavy steel doors were barred and locked. Outside each battery of cages stood a Bantu attendant in clean white overalls. They were all concentrating on the manipulation of the turncock that obviously regulated the flow of the powdered ore through the pipes.

Herby stopped at one of the cages.

'Shine!' He pointed. Beyond the heavy guard screen the grey paste of rock powder was flowing from a series of nozzles over an inclined black rubber sheet. The surface of the rubber sheet was deeply corrugated, and in each corrugation the free gold was collecting, held there by its own weight. The gold was thick as butter in a Dagwood sandwich, greasy yellow-looking in the folds of rubber.

Rod laid hold of the steel screen and shook it.

'No,' Herby laughed. 'No one will get in that way.'

'How do you clean the gold off that sheet? Does someone have access to the separator?' Rod asked.

'The separator cleans itself automatically,' Herby answered. 'Look!'

Rod noticed for the first time that the rubber sheet was moving very slowly, it was also an endless belt running round two rollers. As the belt inverted, so fine jets of water washed the gold from the corrugations into a collection tank.

'I'm the only one who has access. We change the collection tanks daily,' said Herby.

It looked foolproof, Rod had to admit.

Rod turned and glanced down the row of four Bantu attendants. They were all intent on their duties, and Rod knew that each of them had a high security rating. They had been carefully selected and screened before being allowed into the reduction works.

'Satisfied?' Herby asked.

'Okay,' Rod nodded, and the two of them went out through the door in the far wall. Locking it behind them.

Immediately they had gone the four Bantu attendants reacted. They straightened up, the scowls of concentration smoothed out to be replaced by grins of relief. One made a remark and they all laughed, and opened the waist bands of their tunics. From inside each trouser leg they drew a length of quarter-inch copper wire and began probing them through the steel screen.

It had taken Crooked Leg, the photographer, almost a year to work out a means of milking gold from the heavily screened and guarded separators. The method which he had discovered was, like all workable plans, extremely simple.

Mercury, quicksilver, absorbs gold the way blotting paper sucks up moisture. It will suck in any speck of gold that comes in contact with it. Mercury has a further property, it can be made to spread on copper like butter on bread. This layer of mercury on copper retains its powers of absorbing gold.

Crooked Leg had devised the idea of coating lengths of copper wire with mercury. The wire could be inserted through the apertures in the steel mesh and the wire laid across the corrugated rubber sheet, where it set about mopping up every speck of gold that flowed over it. The lengths of wire could be quickly slipped down the trouser leg at the approach of an official, and they could be smuggled in and out of the reduction works the same way.

Every evening Crooked Leg retrieved the gold-thickened wire, and issued his four accomplices with newly coated lengths. Every night in the abandoned workings beyond the ridge he boiled the mercury to make it release its gold.

'Now,' Herby could speak normally in the blessed quiet of the cyanide plant, 'we have skimmed off the free gold – and we are left with the sulphide gold.' He offered Rod a cigarette as they made their way between the massive steel tanks that spread over many acres. 'We pump this into the tanks and add cyanide. The cyanide dissolves the gold and takes it into solution. We tap it off and run it through zinc powder. The gold is deposited on the zinc, we burn away the zinc and we are left with the gold.'

Rod lit his cigarette. He knew all this but Herby was giving him a Cooks' tour for visiting VIPs. He flicked his lighter for Herby. 'There is no way anyone could swipe it when it's in solution.'

Herby shook his head, exhaling smoke. 'Apart from anything else, cyanide is a deadly poison.' He glanced at his watch. 'Three-twenty, they'll be pouring now. Shall we go across to the smelt house?'

The smelt house was the only brick building among all the galvanized iron. It stood a little isolated. Its windows were high up and heavily barred.

At the steel door Herby buzzed, and a peephole opened in the door. He and Rod were immediately recognized and the door swung open. They were in a cage of bars which could only be opened once the door was closed behind them.

'Afternoon, Mr Ironsides, Mr Innes.' The guard was apologetic. 'Would you sign, please?' He was a retired policeman with a paunch and a holstered revolver on his hip.

They signed and the guard signalled to his mate on the steel catwalk high above the smelt room floor. This guard tucked his pump action shotgun under one arm, and threw the switch on the walk beside him.

The cage door opened and they went through.

Along the far wall the electric furnaces were set into the brickwork. They resembled the doors of the bread ovens in a bakery.

The concrete floor of the room was uncluttered, except for the mechanical loader that carried the gold crucible in its steel arms, and the moulds before it. The half dozen personnel of the smelt house barely looked up as Rod and Herby approached.

The pour was well advanced, the arms of the loader tilted and a thin stream of molten gold issued from the spout of the crucible, and fell into the mould. The gold hissed and smoked and crackled, and tiny red and blue sparks twinkled on its surface as it cooled.

Already forty or fifty bars were laid out on the rubber-wheeled trolley beside the mould. Each bar was a little smaller than a cigar box. It had the knobby bumpy look of roughly cast metal.

Rod stopped and touched one of the bars. It was still hot and it had the slightly greasy feeling that new gold always has.

'How much?' he asked Herby, and Herby shrugged.

'About a million rand's worth, perhaps a little more.'

So that's what a million rand looks like, Rod mused, it's not very impressive.

'What's the procedure now?' Rod asked.

'We weigh it, and stamp the weight and batch number into each bar.' He pointed to a massive circular safe deposit door in the near wall. 'It's stored there overnight, and tomorrow a refinery armoured car will come out from Johannesburg and pick it up.' Herby led the way out of the smelt house. 'Anyway, that's not the trouble. Our leak is sucking off the shine before it ever reaches the smelt house.'

'Let me think about it for a few days,' Rod said. 'Then we'll get together again, try and find the solution.'

He was still thinking about it now. Lying in the darkness and smoking cigarette after cigarette.

There seemed to be only one solution. They would have to plant Bantu police in the reduction works.

It was an endless game involving all the mining companies and their reduction plant personnel. An inventive mind would devise a new system of sucking off the shine. The Company would become aware of the activity by comparison of estimated and actual recovery and they would work on the leak for a week, a month, sometimes a year. Then they would break the system. There would be prosecutions, stiff gaol sentences, and the Company would circularize its neighbours, and they would all settle back and wait for the next customer to appear.

Gold has many remarkable properties, its weight, its non-corruptibility and, not least, the greed and lust it conjures up in the hearts of men.

Rod stubbed his cigarette, rolled onto his side and pulled the bedclothes up over his shoulders. His last thought before sleep was for the major problem that, these days, was never very far from the surface of his mind.

The Delange brothers had driven almost 1,500 feet in two weeks. At this rate they would hit the Big Dipper seven weeks from now, then even the theft of gold would pale into insignificance.

At the time that Rod Ironsides was composing himself for sleep, Big King was taking a little wine with his business associate and tribal brother Philemon N'gabai, alias Crooked Leg.

They sat facing each other in a pair of dilapidated cane chairs with a lantern and a gallon jug of Jeripigo set between them. The bat stench of the abandoned workings did little to bring out the bouquet of the wine, which was of small concern to either man, for they were drinking not for taste but for effect.

Crooked Leg refilled the cheap glass tumbler that Big King preferred, and as the wine glug-glugged from the jar he continued his attack on the character and moral fibre of José Almeida, the Portuguese.

'For many months now I have had it in my heart to speak to you of these matters,' he told Big King, 'but I have waited until I could set a deadfall for the man. He is like a lion that preys upon our herds, we hear him roar in the night and in the dawn we see his spoor in the earth about the carcasses of our animals, but we cannot meet him face to face.'

Big King enjoyed listening to the oratory of Crooked Leg and while he listened he drank the Jeripigo as though it were water, and Crooked Leg kept refilling the tumbler for him.

'In counsel with myself I spoke thus: "Philemon N'gabai, it is not enough that thou should suspect this white man. It is necessary also that you see with your own eyes that he is eating your substance".'

'How, Crooked Leg?' Big King's voice was thickening, the level of the jug had fallen steadily and now showed less than half. 'Tell me how we shall take this man.' Big King showed a fist the size of a bunch of bananas. 'I will . . .'

'No, Big King.' Crooked Leg was scandalized. 'You must not hurt the man. How then would we sell our gold? We must prove he is cheating us and show him we know it. Then we will proceed as ever, but he will give us full measure in the future.'

Big King thought about that for some time, then at last he sighed regretfully. 'You are right, Crooked Leg. Still, I would have liked to . . .' He showed that fist again, and Crooked Leg went on hurriedly.

'Therefore, I have sent to my brother who drives a delivery van for SA Scale Company in Johannesburg, and he has taken from his Company a carefully measured weight of eight ounces.' Crooked Leg produced the cylindrical metal weight from his pocket and handed it to Big King who examined it with interest. 'Tonight, after the Portuguese has weighed the gold you take to him, you will say, "Now, my friend, please weigh this for me on your scale," and you will watch to see that his scale reads the correct number. Each time in the future he will weigh this on his scale before we sell our gold.'

'Hau!' Big King chuckled. 'You are a crafty one, Crooked Leg.'

Big King's eyes were smoky and blood-shot. The Jeripigo was a raw rough fortified wine, and he had drunk very nearly a gallon of it. He sat opposite the Portuguese store-keeper in the back room behind the concession store, and watched while he poured the gold dust into the pan of the jeweller's scale. It made a yellow pyramid that shone dully in the light from the single bare bulb above their heads.

'One hundred and twenty-three ounces.' Almeida looked up at Big King for confirmation, a strand of greasy black hair hung onto his forehead. His face was pale from lack of sun so that the blue stubble of beard was in heavy contrast.

'That is right,' Big King nodded. He could taste the

liquor fumes in the back of his throat, and they were as strong as his distaste for the man who sat opposite him. He belched.

Almeida removed the pan from the scale and carefully poured the dust back into the screw-top bottle.

'I will get the money.' He half rose from his chair.

'Wait!' said Big King, and the Portuguese looked at him in mild surprise.

Big King took the weight from the pocket of his jacket. He placed it on the desk.

'Weigh that on your scale,' he said in Portuguese.

Almeida's eyes flicked down to the weight, and then back to Big King's face. He sank back into his seat, and pushed the strand of hair off his forehead. He began to speak, but his voice cracked and he cleared his throat.

'Why? Is there something wrong?' Suddenly he was aware of the size of the man opposite him. He could smell the liquor on his breath.

'Weigh it!' Big King's voice was flat, without rancour. His face was expressionless, but the smoky red glare of his eyes was murderous.

Suddenly Almeida was afraid, deadly, coldly afraid. He could guess what would happen once the error in his balance was disclosed.

'Very well,' he said, and his voice was forced and off key. The pistol was in the drawer beside his right knee. It was loaded, with a cartridge under the hammer. The safety-catch was on, but that would only delay him an instant. He knew it would not be necessary to fire, once he had the weapon in his hand he would have control of the situation again.

If he did have to fire, the calibre was .45 and the heavy slug would stop even a giant like this Bantu. *Self-defence*, he was working it out feverishly. A *burglar*, I surprised him and he attacked. *Self-defence*. It would work. They'd believe it.

But how to get the pistol? Try and sneak it out of the drawer, or make a grab for it?

There was a desk between them, it would take a few seconds for the Bantu to realize what he was doing, a few more for him to get around the desk. He would have plenty of time.

He snatched the handle of the drawer, and it flew open. His fingernails scrabbled against the woodwork as he clawed for the big black U.S. Navy automatic, and with a surge of triumph his hand closed over the butt.

Big King came over the top of the desk like a black avalanche. The scale and the jar of gold dust were swept aside to clatter and shatter against the floor.

Still seated in his chair, with the pistol in his hand, Almeida was borne over backwards with Big King on top of him. Many years before, Big King had worked with a safari outfit in Portuguese East Africa, and he had seen the effect of gunshot wounds in the flesh of dead animals.

In the instant that he had recognized the weapon in Almeida's hand, he had been as afraid as the Portuguese. Fear had triggered the speed of his reaction, it was responsible for the savagery of his attack as he lay over the struggling body of the Portuguese.

He had Almeida's pistol hand held by the wrist and he was shaking it to force him to drop the firearm. With his right hand he had the Portuguese by the throat, and instinctively he was applying the full strength of his arms to both grips. He felt something break under his right hand, cracking like the kernel of a nut, and his fingers were suddenly without strength, and the gun skittered across the floor to come up against the far wall with a thump.

Only then did Big King begin to regain the sanity that fear had scattered. Suddenly he realized that the Portuguese was lying quietly under him. He released his grip and scrambled to his knees. The Portuguese was dead. His neck was twisted away from his shoulders at an impossible angle. His eyes were wide and surprised, and a smear of blood issued from one nostril over his upper lip.

Big King backed away towards the door, his gaze fixed in horror on the sprawling corpse. When he reached the door, he hesitated, fighting down the urge to run. He subdued it, and went back to kneel beside the desk. First he picked up the controversial cylindrical weight and placed it in his pocket, then he began sweeping up the scattered gold dust and the shattered fragments of the screw-topped container. He placed them into separate envelopes that he found among the papers on the desk. Ten minutes later he slipped out through the back door of the concession store, into the night.

– 49 –

At the time Big King was hurrying back towards the mine hostel, Rod Ironsides thrashed restlessly in a bed in which the sheets were already bunched and damp with sweat. He was imprisoned in his own fantasy, locked in a nightmare from which he could not break away. The nightmare was infinite and green, quivering, unearthly, translucent. He knew it was held back only by a transparent barrier of glass. He cowered before it, and he knew it was icy cold, he could see light shining through it, and he was deadly afraid.

Suddenly there was a crack in the glass wall, a hairline crack, and through it oozed a single drop. A large, pear-shaped drop, as perfect as though it had been painted by Tretchikoff. It glittered like a gemstone.

It was the most terrifying thing that Rod had ever seen in his life. He cried out in his sleep, trying to warn them, but the crack starred further, and the drop slid down the glass, to be followed by another and another. Suddenly a jagged slab of glass exploded out of the wall, and Rod screamed as the water burst through, in a frothing jet.

With a roar the entire glass wall collapsed, and a mountain high wave of green water hissed down upon him, carrying a white plume of spray at its crest.

He awoke sitting upright in his bed, a cry of horror on his lips and his body bathed in sweat. It took minutes for him to steady the wild racing of his heart. Then he went through to the bathroom. He ran a glass of water and held it up to the light. 'Water. It's there!' he muttered. 'I know it's there!' He drank from the tumbler.

Standing naked, with his sweat drying cold on his body, the tumbler held to his lips, the idea came to him. He had never heard of anyone trying it before, but then nobody he knew would be crazy enough to drive into a death trap like the Big Dipper.

'I'll drill and charge a matt of explosive into the hanging wall of the drive. I'll get the Delange boys on to it right away. Then at any time I choose I can blast the whole bloody roof in and seal off the tunnel.'

Rod was surprised at the strength of the relief that flooded over him. He knew then how it had been worrying him. He went back to the bedroom and straightened out his bedclothes. However, sleep would not come easily to him. His imagination was overheated, and a series of events and ideas kept playing through his mind, until abruptly he was presented with the image of Terry Steyner.

He had not seen her for almost two weeks, not since their meeting just after Manfred Steyner's return from Europe. He had spoken to her twice on the telephone, hasty, confused conversations that left him feeling dissatisfied. He was increasingly aware that he was missing her. His one attempt to find solace elsewhere had been a miserable failure. He had lost interest halfway through the approach manoeuvres and had returned the young lady to the bosom of her family at the unheard-of hour of eleven o'clock on a Saturday night.

Only the unremitting demands of his new job had prevented him from slipping away to Johannesburg and taking a risk.

'You know, Ironsides, you'd better start bracing up a little, don't lose your head over this woman. Remember our vow – *Never Again!*'

He punched the pillow into shape and settled into it.

Terry lay quietly, waiting for it. It was after one o'clock in the morning. It was one of those nights. He would come soon now. As never before she was filled with dread. A cold slimy feeling in the pit of her stomach. Yet she had been fortunate. He had not been near her since his return from Paris. Over two weeks, but it could not last. Tonight.

She heard the sound of the car coming up the drive and she felt physically ill. I can't do it, she decided, not any more, not ever again. It wasn't meant to be like this, I know that now. It's not dirty and furtive and horrible, it's like . . . like . . . it's the way Rod makes it.

She heard him in his bedroom, suddenly she sat up in bed. She felt desperate, hunted.

The door of her room opened softly.

'Manfred?' she asked sharply.

'It's me. Don't worry.' He came briskly towards her bed, a dark impersonal shape and he was undoing the cord of his dressing-gown.

'Manfred,' Terry blurted. 'I'm early this month, I'm sorry.'

He stopped. She saw his hands fall back to his sides, and he stood completely still.

'Oh!' he said at last, and she heard him shuffle his feet into the thick pile of the carpet. 'I just came to tell you,' he hesitated, seeking an excuse for his visit, 'that . . . that I'll be going away for five days. Leaving on Friday. I have to go to Durban and Cape Town.'

'I'll pack for you,' she said.

'What? Oh, yes – thank you.' He shuffled his feet again. 'Well, then.' He hesitated, then stooped quickly and brushed her cheek with his lips. 'Good night, Theresa.'

'Good night, Manfred.'

Five days. She lay alone in the darkness and gloated. *Five whole days alone with Rod.*

– 50 –

Detective Inspector Hannes Grobbelaar of the South African Criminal Investigation Department sat on the edge of the office chair with his hat tipped onto the back of his head and spoke into the telephone, which he held in a handkerchief-covered hand. He was a tall man with a long sad face and a mournful-looking moustache that was streaked with grey.

'Gold buying,' he said into the receiver, and then in reply to the obvious question, 'There's gold dust spilled all over the place and a jeweller's scale, and a .45 automatic with a full magazine and the safety-catch still on, dead man's prints on it.' He listened. 'Ja. Ja. All right, ja. Broken neck, looks like.' Inspector Grobbelaar swivelled his chair and looked down at the corpse that lay on the floor beside him. 'Bit of blood on his lip, but nothing else.'

One of the finger-print men came to the desk and Grobbelaar stood up to give him room to work, the receiver still held to his ear.

'Prints?' he asked in disgust. 'There are finger prints on everything, we have isolated at least forty separate sets so far.' He listened a few seconds. 'No, we will get him, all right. It must be a Bantu mine worker and we have got all the finger prints of the men from outside the Republic. It's just a matter of checking them all out and then questioning. Ja, we'll have him within a month, that's for sure! I'll be back at John Vorster Square about five o'clock, just as soon as we finish up here.' He hung up the receiver, and stood looking down at the murdered man.

'Ugly bastard,' said Sergeant Hugo beside him. 'Asked for it, buying gold. It's as bad as diamonds.' He drew attention to the large envelope he carried in his hand. 'I've got a whole lot of glass fragments. Looks like the container the gold was in. The murderer tried to clean up, but he didn't make a very good job. These were under the desk.'

'Prints?'

'Only one piece big enough. It's got a smeary print on it. Might be of use.'

'Good,' Grobbelaar nodded. 'Get cracking on that, then.'

There was a feminine wail from somewhere in the interior of the building, and Hugo grimaced.

'There she starts again. Hell, I thought she'd exhausted herself. Bloody Portuguese women are the end.'

'You should hear them having a baby,' grunted Grobbelaar.

'Where did you hear one?'

'There was one in the ward next door to my old girl at the maternity home. She nearly brought the bloody roof down.'

Grobbelaar's moustache took on a more melancholy droop as he thought about the work that lay ahead. Hours, days, weeks of questioning and checking and cross-checking, with a succession of sullen and uncooperative suspects.

He sighed and jerked a thumb at the corpse. 'All right, we've finished with him. Tell the butcher boys to come and fetch him.'

It had taken Rod almost two days to design his dropblast matt. The angle and depth of the shot holes were carefully placed to achieve maximum disruption of the hanging wall. In addition he had decided to drill and charge the side walls of the drive with charges timed to explode *after* the hanging wall had collapsed. This would kick in on the rubble filling the tunnel and jam it solid.

Rod was fully aware of the power of water under pressures of 2,000 pounds per square inch and more and he had decided it was necessary to block at least 300 feet of the tunnel. His matt blast was designed to do so, and yet he knew that this would not seal off the water completely. It would, however, reduce the flow sufficiently to allow cementation crews to get in and plug the drive solid.

The Delange brothers did not share Rod's enthusiasm for the project.

'Hey man, that's going to take three or four days to drill and charge,' Johnny protested when Rod showed him his carefully drawn plan.

'Like hell it will,' Rod growled at him. 'I want it done properly. It will take at least a week.'

'You said ultra-fast. You didn't say nothing about drilling the hanging wall with more holes than a cheese!'

'Well, I'm saying it now,' Rod told him grimly. 'And I'm also saying that you will drill, but you won't charge the holes until I come down and make sure that you've gone in as deep as I want them.'

He didn't trust either Johnny or Davy to spend time drilling in twenty feet, when he could go in six feet, charge up and nobody would know the difference. Not until it was too late.

Davy Delange spoke for the first time.

'Will you credit us bonus fathomage while we fiddle around with this?' he asked.

'Four fathoms a shift.' Rod agreed to pay them for the removal of fictitious rock.

'Eight?' said Davy.

'Hell, no!' Rod exclaimed. That was robbery.

'I don't know,' Davy murmured, watching Rod with sly ferrety little eyes. 'Maybe I should talk to Brother Duivenhage, you know, ask his advice.'

Duivenhage was No. 1 shaft shop steward for the Mine Workers' Union. He had driven Frank Lemmer to the edge of a nervous breakdown and was now starting on Rodney Ironsides. Rod was pleading with Head Office to offer Duivenhage a fat job in management to get him out of the way. The last thing in the world that Rod wanted was Brother Duivenhage snooping around his drive on the Big Dipper.

'Six,' he said.

'Well . . .' Davy hesitated.

'Six is fair, Davy,' Johnny interrupted, and Davy glared at him. Johnny had snatched complete victory from his grasp.

'Good, that's agreed.' Quickly Rod closed the negotiations. 'You'll start drilling the matt right away.'

Rod's design demanded nearly 1,200 shot holes to be filled with two and a half tons of explosive. It was 1,000 feet down the drive from the main haulage on 66 level to where the matt began.

The drive now was a spacious, well lit and freshly ventilated tunnel, with the vent piping, the compressed air pipe, and the electrical cable bolted into the hanging wall, and a set of steel railway tracks laid along the floor.

All work on the face ceased while the Delange brothers set about drilling the matt. It was light work that demanded little from the men. As each hole was drilled, Davy would insert his charging rod to check the depth and then plug the entrance with a wad of paper. There was much time for drinking Thermos coffee and for thinking.

There were three subjects that endlessly occupied Davy's mind as he sat at ease, waiting for the completion of the next shot hole. Sometimes for half an hour at a time Davy would hold the image of that 50,000 rand in his mind. It was his, tax paid, painstakingly accumulated over the years and lovingly deposited with the local branch of the Johannesburg Building Society. He imagined it bundled and stacked in neat green piles in the Society's vault. Each bundle was labelled 'David Delange'.

Then his imagination would pass automatically on to the farm that the money would buy. He saw how it would be in the evenings when he sat on the wide stoep, with the setting sun striking the peaks of the Swart Berg across the valley, and the cattle coming in from the paddocks towards the homestead.

Always there was a woman sitting beside him on the stoep. The woman had red hair.

On the fifth morning Davy drove home in the dawn, he was not tired. The night's labours had been easy and unexacting.

The door of Johnny and Hettie's bedroom was closed. Davy read the newspapers with his breakfast; as always the cartoon strip adventures of Modesty Blaise and Willie Garvin intrigued him completely. This morning Modesty was depicted in a bikini and Davy studied her comparing her to the big healthy body of his brother's wife. The thought of her stayed with him as he rolled onto his bed, and he lay unsleeping, daydreaming an adventure in which

Modesty Blaise had become Hettie, and Willie Garvin was Davy.

An hour later he was still awake. He sat up and reached for the towel which lay across the foot of his bed. He wrapped the towel around his waist as he went down the passage to the bathroom. As he reached for the handle of the bathroom door, it opened under his hand and he was face to face with Hettie Delange.

She wore a white lace dressing-gown with ostrich-feather mules on her feet. Her face was innocent of make-up and she had brushed her hair and tied it with a ribbon.

'Oh!' she gasped with surprise. 'You gave me a fright, man.'

'I'm sorry, hey.' Davy grinned at her, holding the towel with one hand. Hettie let her eyes run quickly over his naked upper body.

Davy was muscled like a prizefighter. His chest hair was crisp and curly. On both arms the tattoos drew attention to the thickness and weight of muscle.

'Gee, you *are* built,' Hettie murmured in admiration, and Davy sucked in his belly reflexively.

'You think so?' His grin was self-conscious now.

'Yes.' Hettie leaned forward and touched his arm. 'It's hard too!'

The movement had allowed the front of her dressing-gown to gape open. Davy's face flushed as he looked down into the opening. He started to say something, but his voice had dried up on him. Hettie's fingers stroked down his arm, and she was watching the direction of his eyes. Slowly she moved closer to him.

'Do you like me, Davy?' she asked, her voice throaty and low, and with an animal cry Davy attacked her.

His hands ripping at the opening of her gown, pinning her to the wall of the bathroom with his mouth frantically hunting hers. His body pressing hard and urgent, his eyes wild, his breathing ragged.

Hettie was laughing, a breathless gasping laugh.

This was what she loved. When they lost their heads, when they went mad for her.

'Davy,' she said, jerking loose his towel. 'Davy.'

She kept wriggling away from his thrusting hips, knowing that it would inflame him further. His hands were tearing at her body, his eyes were maniacal.

'Yes!' she hissed into his mouth. He threw her off balance and she slid down the wall onto the floor.

'Wait,' she panted. 'Not here – the bedroom.'

But it was too late.

Davy had spent the afternoon locked in his bedroom, lying on his bed in an agony of black all-pervading remorse and guilt.

'My brother,' he kept repeating. 'Johnny is my brother.'

Once he wept, each sob tearing something in his chest. The tears squeezed out between burning eyelids, leaving him feeling exhausted and weak.

'My *own* brother,' he shook his head slowly in horrified disbelief. 'I cannot stay here,' he decided miserably. 'I'll have to go.'

He went to the washbasin and washed his eyes. Stooping over the basin, water still dripping from his face, he decided.

'I will have to tell him.' The burden of guilt was too heavy. 'I'll write to Johnny. I'll write it all, and then I'll go away.'

Frantically he searched for pen and paper, it was almost as though he could wipe away the deed by writing it down. He sat at the table by the window and wrote slowly and laboriously. When he had finished it was three o'clock. He felt better.

He sealed the four closely written pages into an envelope and slipped it into the inside pocket of his jacket. He dressed quickly, and crept out of the house, fearful of meeting Hettie, but she was nowhere about. Her big white Monaco was not in the garage, and with relief he turned out of the driveway and took the road out to the Sonder Ditch. He wanted to reach the mine before Johnny came off shift.

Davy listened to his brother's voice, as he kidded and laughed with the other off-duty miners in the company change house. He had locked himself in one of the lavatory closets to avoid meeting his brother, and he sat disconsolately on the toilet seat. The sound of Johnny's voice brought his guilt flooding back in its full strength. His letter of confession was buttoned into the top pocket of his overalls, and he took it out, broke open the flap and reread the contents.

'So long, then.' Johnny's voice sang out gaily from the change room. 'See you bastards tomorrow.'

There was an answering chorus from the other miners, then the door slammed.

Davy went on sitting alone for another twenty minutes in the stench of stale bodies and urine, dirty socks and rank disinfections from the foot baths. At last he tucked the letter away in his pocket and opened the closet door.

Davy's gang were at their waiting place at the head of the drive. They were sitting along the bench laughing and chatting. There was a holiday spirit amongst them for they knew it would be another shift of easy going.

They greeted Davy cheerfully, as he came down the haulage. Both the Delange brothers were popular with their gangs and it was unusual that Davy did not reply to the chorused greeting. He did not even smile.

The Swazi boss boy handed him the safety lamp, and Davy grunted an acknowledgement. He set off alone down the tunnel, trudging heavily, not conscious of his surroundings, his mind encased in a padding of guilt and self-pity.

177

A thousand feet along the drive he reached the day's work area. Johnny's shift had left the rock drills in place, still connected to the compressed air system, ready for use. Davy came to a halt in the centre of the work area, and without a conscious command from his brain his hands began the routine process of striking the wick of the safety lamp.

The little blue flame came alight behind the protective screen of wire mesh, and Davy held the lamp at eye level before him and walked slowly along the drive. His eyes were watching the flame without seeing it.

The air in the tunnel was cool and refrigerated, scrubbed and filtered, there was no odour nor taste to it. Davy walked on somnambulantly. He was wallowing in self-pity now. He saw himself in a semi-heroic role, one of the great lovers of history caught up in tragic circumstances. His brain was fully occupied with the picture. His eyes were unseeing. Blindly he performed the ritual that a thousand times before had begun the day's shift.

Slowly in its wire mesh cage the blue flame of the safety lamp changed shape. Its crest flattened, and there formed above it a ghostly pale line. Davy's eyes saw it, but his brain refused to accept the message. He walked on in a stupor of guilt and self-pity.

That line above the flame was called 'the cap', it signified that there was at least a five per cent concentration of methane gas in the air. The last shot hole that Johnny Delange's gang had drilled before going off shift had bored into a methane-filled fissure. For the previous three hours, gas had been blowing out of that hole. The ventilation system was unable to wash the air fast enough and now the gas had spread slowly down the drive. The air surrounding Davy's body was heavy with gas, he had breathed it into his lungs. It needed just one spark to ignite it.

Davy reached the end of the drive and snapped the snuffer over the wick, extinguishing the flame in the lamp.

'All safe,' he muttered, not realizing that he had spoken. He went back to his waiting men.

'All safe,' he repeated, and with the Swazi boss boy leading them the forty men of Davy Delange's gang trooped gaily into the mouth of the drive.

Moodily Davy followed them. As he walked he reached into his hip pocket and took out a pack of Lexington filter tips. He put one between his lips, returned the pack and began patting his pockets to locate his lighter.

Davy went from team to team of his machine boys, directing them in the line and spot to be drilled. Every time he spoke, the unlit cigarette waggled between his lips. He gesticulated with the hand that held his cigarette-lighter.

It took twenty minutes for him to set all his drills to work. And he stood and looked back along the tunnel. Each machine boy and his assistant formed a separate sculpture. Most of them were stripped to the waist. Their bodes appeared to be carved and polished in oiled ebony, as they braced themselves behind the massive rock drills.

Davy lifted his cupped hands, holding the cigarette-lighter near his face, and he flicked the cog wheel.

The air in the tunnel turned to flame. In a flash explosion, the flame reached the temperature of a welding torch. It seared the skin from the faces and exposed bodies of the machine boys, it burned the hair from their scalps. It turned their arms to charred stumps. It roasted their eyeballs in their sockets. It scorched their clothing, so as they fell the cloth smouldered and burned against their flesh.

In that instant, as the skin was licked from his face and hands, Davy Delange opened his mouth in a great gasp of agony. The flame shot down his throat into his gas-drenched lungs. Within the confines of his body the gas exploded and his chest popped like a paper bag, his ribs fanning outward about the massive wound like the petals of a sunflower.

Forty-one men died at the same moment. In the silence

after that whooshing, sucking detonation, they lay like scorched insects along the floor of the drive. One or two of them were moving still, an arched spine relaxing, a leg straightening, charred fingers unclenching, but within a minute all was absolutely still.

Half an hour later Doctor Dan Stander and Rodney Ironsides were the first men into the drive. The smell of burned flesh was overpowering. Both of them had to swallow down their nausea as they went forward.

– 52 –

Dan Stander sat at his desk and looked out over the car park in front of the mine hospital. He appeared to have aged ten years since the previous evening. Dan envied his colleagues the detachment they could bring to their work. He had never been able to perfect the trick. He had just completed forty-one examinations for issue of death certificates.

For fifteen years he had been a mine doctor, so he was accustomed to dealing with death in its more hideous forms. This, however, was the worst he had ever encountered. Forty-one of them, all victims of severe burning and massive explosion trauma.

He felt washed out, exhausted with ugliness. He massaged his temples as he examined the tray of pathetic possessions that lay on the desk before him. This was the contents of the pockets of the man Delange. Extracting them from the scorched clothing had been a filthy business in itself. Cloth had burned into the flesh, the man had been wearing a cheap nylon shirt under his overalls. The fabric had melted in the heat and had become part of his blistered skin.

There was a bunch of keys on a brass ring, a Joseph Rogers pen-knife with a bone handle, a Ronson cigarette-lighter which had been clutched in the man's clawed and charred right hand, a springbok skin wallet, and a loose envelope with one corner burned away.

Dan had already passed on the effects of the Bantu victims to the agent of the Bantu Recruiting Agency, who would send them on to the men's families. Now he sighed with distaste and picked up the wallet. He opened it.

In one compartment there were half a dozen postage stamps, and five rands in notes. The other flap bulged with paper. Dan glanced through salesmen's cards, dry-cleaning receipts, newspaper cuttings offering farms for sale, a folded page from the *Farmer's Weekly* on the planning of a dairy herd, a JBS savings book.

Dan opened the savings book and whistled when he saw the total. He fanned the remaining pages.

There was a much-fingered envelope, unsealed and tucked behind the cardboard cover of the savings book. Dan opened it, and pulled a face. It contained a selection of photographs of the type which one found offered for sale in the dock area of the Mozambique port of Lourenço Marques. It was for this type of material that Dan was searching.

When the man's possessions were returned to his grieving relatives, Dan wanted to spare them this evidence of human frailty. He burned the photographs and the envelope in his ashtray and then crushed the blackened sheets to powder before spilling it into his waste-paper bin.

He went across to the window and opened it to let the smell of smoke escape. He stood at the window and searched the car park for Joy's Alfa Romeo. She had not arrived as yet and Dan returned to his desk.

The remaining envelope caught his eye and he picked it up. There was a smear of blood upon it, and the corner was burned away. Dan removed the four sheets of paper and spread them on the desk:

Dear Johnny,

When Pa died you were still little – and I always reckoned you were more like my son, you know, than my brother.

Well, Johnny, I reckon now I've got to tell you something . . .

Dan read slowly, and he did not hear Joy come into the room. She stood at the door watching him. Her expression fond, a small smile on her lips, shiny blonde hair hanging straight to her shoulders. Then she moved up quietly behind his chair and kissed his ear. Dan started and turned to face her.

'Darling,' Joy said and kissed him on the mouth. 'What is so interesting that you ignore my arrival?'

Dan hesitated a moment before telling her.

'There was a man killed last night in a ghastly accident. This was in his pocket.'

He handed her the letter and she read it slowly.

'He was going to send this to his brother?' she asked, and Dan nodded.

'The bitch,' Joy whispered, and Dan looked surprised.

'Who?'

'The girl – it's her fault, you know.' Joy opened her purse and took out a tissue to dab her eyes. 'Damn it, now I'm messing my make-up.' She sniffed, and then went on. 'It would serve her right if you gave that letter to her husband.'

'You mean I shouldn't give it to him?' Dan asked. 'We have no right to play God.'

'Haven't we?' asked Joy, and Dan watched quietly as she tore the letter to tiny shreds, screwed them into a ball, then dropped them into the waste bin.

'You are wonderful,' he said. 'Will you marry me?'

'I've already answered that question, Dr Stander.' And she kissed him again.

53

Hettie Delange was in a turmoil.

It had started with the phone call that had roused Johnny from their bed. He had said something about trouble at the shaft as he pulled on his clothes, but she had come only briefly awake and then drifted off again as Johnny hurried out into the night.

He had come in hours later and sat on the edge of the bed, his hands clasped between his knees and his head bowed.

'What's wrong, man,' she had snapped at him. 'Come to bed. Don't just sit there.'

'Davy's dead.' His voice had been listless.

There was a moment's shock that had convulsed the muscles of her belly, and brought her fully awake. Then, immediately, she had felt a swift cleansing rush of relief.

He was dead. It was as easy as that! All day she had worried. She had been stupid to let it happen. Just that moment of weakness, that self-indulgent slip and she had been dreading the consequences all that day. She had imagined Davy trailing after her with puppy eyes, trying to touch her, making it so obvious that even Johnny would see it. She had enjoyed it but just the once was enough. She wanted no repeat performance and certainly no complications to follow the original deed.

Now it was all taken care of. He was dead.

'Are you sure?' she had asked anxiously, and Johnny heard the tone as concern.

'I saw him!' Johnny had shuddered, and wiped the back of his hand across his mouth.

'Gee, that's terrible.' Hettie had remembered her role, and sat up and put her arms about Johnny. 'That's terrible for you.'

She had not slept again that night. Somehow the

thought of Davy going directly from her to his violent death was exciting. It was like in the movies, or a book, or something. Like he was an airman and he had been shot down, and she was his girl. Perhaps she was pregnant and all alone in the world, and she would have to go to Buckingham Palace and get his medal for him. And the Queen would say . . .

The fantasies had played out in her mind until the dawn, with Johnny tossing and muttering beside her.

She woke him when it was first light in the room.

'How was he?' she asked softly. 'What did he look like, Johnny?'

Johnny shuddered again, and then he started to tell her. His voice was husky, and the sentences broken and disconnected. When he stumbled into silence, Hettie found herself trembling with excitement.

'How terrible,' she kept repeating. 'Oh, how awful!' And she pressed against him. After a while Johnny made love to her, and for Hettie it was better than she had ever known it to be.

All that morning there were phone calls, and four of her friends came over to drink coffee with her. A reporter and photographer from the *Johannesburg Star* called and asked questions. Hettie was the centre of attraction, and again and again she repeated the story with all its grisly details.

After lunch Johnny came home with a little dark-haired man in a charcoal suit and black Italian shoes, with a matching black briefcase.

'Hettie, this is Mr Boart. He was Davy's lawyer. He's got something to tell you.'

'Mrs Delange. May I convey to you my sincere condolences in the tragic bereavement you and your husband have suffered.'

'Yes, it's terrible, isn't it?' Hettie was apprehensive. Had Davy told this lawyer about them? Had this man come to make trouble?

'Your brother-in-law made a will of which I am the executor. Your brother-in-law was a wealthy man. His estate is in excess of fifty thousand rand.' Boart paused portentously. 'And you and your husband are the sole beneficiaries.'

Hettie looked dubiously from Boart to Johnny.

'I don't – what's that mean? Beneficiary?'

'It means that you and your husband share the estate between you.'

'I get half of fifty thousand rand?' Hettie asked in delighted disbelief.

'That's right.'

'Gee,' exulted Hettie. 'That's fabulous!' She could hardly wait for Johnny and the lawyer to go before she phoned her friends again. All four of them returned to drink more coffee, to thrill again and to envy Hettie the glamour and excitement of it.

'Twenty-five thousand,' they kept repeating the sum with relish.

'Hell, man, he must really have liked you a lot, Hettie,' one of the girls commented with heavy emphasis, and Hettie lowered her eyes and contrived to look bereft and mysterious.

Johnny came home after six, unsteady on his feet and reeking of liquor. Reluctantly Hettie's four friends left to rejoin their waiting families, and almost immediately after that a big white sports car pulled up in the driveway and Hettie's day of triumph was complete. Not one of her friends had ever had the General Manager of the Sonder Ditch Gold Mining Company call at their home.

She had the front door open the instant the doorbell rang. Her greeting had been shamelessly plagiarized from a period movie that had recently played at the local cinema.

'Mr Ironsides, how good of you to come.'

When she led Rod through into the over-furnished lounge, Johnny looked up but did not get to his feet.

'Hello, Johnny', said Rod. 'I have come to tell you that I'm sorry about Davy, and to . . .'

'Don't give me that bull dust, Tin Ribs,' said Johnny Delange.

'Johnny,' gasped Hettie, 'you can't talk to Mr Ironsides like that.' And she turned to Rod, laying a hand on his sleeve. 'He doesn't mean it, Mr Ironsides. He has been drinking.'

'Get out of here,' said Johnny. 'Get into the bloody kitchen where you belong.'

'Johnny!'

'Get out!' roared Johnny, rising from his chair, and Hettie fled from the room.

Johnny lurched across to the chrome and glass liquor cabinet that filled one corner. He sloshed whisky into two glasses and handed one to Rod.

'God speed to my brother,' he said.

'To Davy Delange, one of the best rock hounds on the Kitchenerville field,' said Rod, and tossed the drink back in one gulp.

'The best!' Johnny corrected him, and emptied his own glass. He gasped at the sting of the whisky, then leaned forward to speak into Rod's face.

'You've come to find out if I'm game to finish your bloody drive for you, or if I'm going to quit. Davy didn't mean nothing to you and I don't mean nothing to you. Only one thing worrying you – you want to know about your bloody drive.' Johnny refilled his glass. 'Well, hear this, friend, and hear it well. Johnny Delange don't quit. That drive ate my brother but I'll beat the bastard, so you got nothing to worry about. You go home and get a good night's sleep, 'cos Johnny Delange will be on shift and breaking rock tomorrow morning first thing.'

54

A Silver Cloud Rolls-Royce was parked amongst the trees in the misty morning. Ahead was the practice track with the white-painted railings curving away towards the willow-lined river. The mist was heavier along the river and the grass was very green against it.

The uniformed chauffeur stood away from the Rolls, leaving its two occupants in privacy. They sat on the back seat with an angora wool travelling rug spread over their knees. On the folding table in front of them was a silver Thermos of coffee, shell-thin porcelain cups, and a plate of ham sandwiches.

The fat man was eating steadily, washing each mouthful down with coffee. The little bald-headed man was not eating, instead he puffed quickly and nervously at his cigarette and looked out of the window at the horses. The grooms were walking the horses in circles, nostrils streaming in the morning chill, blankets flapping. The jockeys stood looking up at the trainer. They wore hard caps and polo-necked jerseys. All of them carried whips. The trainer was speaking urgently, his hands thrust deep into the pockets of his overcoat.

'It's a very fine service,' said the little man. 'I particularly enjoyed the stop in Rio. My first visit there.'

The fat man grunted. He was annoyed. They shouldn't have sent this agent out. It was a mark of suspicion, distrust, and it would seriously hamper his market operation.

The conference between trainer and jockeys had ended. The diminutive riders scattered to their mounts, and the trainer came towards the Rolls.

'Good morning, sir.' He spoke through the open window, and the fat man grunted again.

'I'm giving him a full run,' the trainer went on. 'Emerald Isle will make pace for him to the five, Pater Noster will take over and push him to the mile, I've Tiger Shark to pace him for the run in.'

'Very well.'

'Perhaps you'd like to keep time, sir.' The trainer proffered a stop-watch, and the fat man seemed to recover his urbanity and charm.

'Thank you, Henry.' He smiled. 'He looks good, I'll say that.'

The trainer was pleased by the condescension.

'Oh! He's red-hot! By Saturday I'll have him sharpened down to razor edge.' He stood back from the window. 'I'll get them off, then.' He walked away.

'You have a message for me?' asked the fat man.

'Of course.' The other wriggled his moustache like a rabbit's whiskers. It was an annoying habit. 'I didn't fly all this way out here to watch a couple of mokes trotting around a race-track.'

'Would you like to give me the message?' The fat man hid his affront. What the agent had called a moke was some of the finest horseflesh in Africa.

'They want to know about this gas explosion.'

'Nothing.' The fat man dismissed the question with a wave of his hand. 'A flash explosion. Killed a few men. No damage to the workings. Negligence on the part of the miner in charge.'

'Will it affect our plans?'

'Not one iota.'

The two horses had jumped away from the start, shoulder to shoulder, with the wreaths of mist swirling in their wake. The glossy bay horse on the rails ran with an easy floating action while the grey plunged along beside it.

'My principals are very concerned.'

'Well, they have no need to be,' snapped the fat man. 'I tell you it makes no difference.'

'Was the explosion due to an error of judgement on the part of this man Ironsides?'

188

'No.' The fat man shook his head. 'It was negligence of the miner in charge. He should have detected the gas.'

'Pity.' The bald man shook his head regretfully. 'We had hoped it was a flaw in the Ironsides character.'

The grey horse was tiring, while the bay ran on smoothly, drawing away from him. From the side rail a third horse came in to replace the grey, and ran shoulder to shoulder with the bay.

'Why should the character of Ironsides concern you?'

'We have heard disturbing reports. This is no pawn to be moved at will. He is taking the job of General Manager by the throat. Already our sources indicate that he has reduced running costs on the Sonder Ditch by a scarcely believable two per cent. He seems to be tireless, inventive – a man, in short, to reckon with.'

'Well and good,' the fat man conceded. 'But I still fail to see why your – ah, principals – are alarmed. Do they expect that this man will hold back the flood waters by the sheer force of his personality?'

The second pacemaker was faltering, but still the big bay ran on alone. A far figure in the mist, passing the mile post, joined at last by the third pacemaker.

'I know nothing about horses,' said the bald man watching the two flying forms. 'But I've just seen that one,' he pointed with his cigarette at the far-off bay. 'I've just seen him run the guts out of the other two. One after the other he has broken their hearts and left them staggering along behind him. We would call him an imponderable, one who cannot be judged by normal standards.' He puffed at his cigarette before going on. 'There are men like that also, imponderable. It seems to us that Ironsides is one of them, and we don't like it. We don't like them on the opposing team. It is just possible that he could upset the entire operation, not, as you put it, by sheer force of personality, but by suddenly doing the unexpected, by behaving in a manner for which we have not allowed.'

Both men fell silent watching the galloping horses come round the last bend and hit the straight.

'Watch this.' The fat man spoke softly, and as though in response to his words the big bay lengthened his stride, reaching out, driving strongly away from the other horse. His head was going like a hammer, twin jets of steam shot from wide flaring nostrils, and thrown turf and dirt flew from his hooves. Five lengths clear of the following horse he went slashing past the finish line and the fat man clicked his stop watch.

He scrutinized the dial of the watch anxiously and then chuckled like a healthy baby.

'And he wasn't really being extended!'

He rapped on the window beside him, and immediately the uniformed chauffeur opened the driving door and slid in behind the wheel.

'To my office,' instructed the fat man, 'and close the partition.'

When the sound-proof glass panel had slid closed between driver and passengers, the fat man turned to his guest.

'And so, my friend, you consider Ironsides to be an imponderable. What do you want me to do about him?'

'Get rid of him.'

'Do you mean what I think you mean?' The fat man lifted an eyebrow.

'No. Nothing that drastic.' The bald head bobbed agitatedly. 'You have been reading too much James Bond. Simply arrange it that Ironsides is far away and well occupied when the drive holes through the Big Dipper Dyke, otherwise there is an excellent chance that he will do something to frustrate our good intentions.'

'I think we can arrange that,' said the fat man and helped himself to another ham sandwich.

55

As he had promised, Manfred caught the Friday evening flight for Cape Town. On the Saturday night Rod and Terry took a wild chance on not being recognized and spent the evening at the Kyalami Ranch Hotel. They danced and dined in the Africa Room, but were on their way back to the apartment before midnight.

In the dawn a playful slap with the rolled-up Sunday papers which Rod delivered to Terry's naked posterior as she slept triggered off a noisy brawl in which a picture was knocked off the wall by a flying pillow, a coffee table overturned and the shrieking and laughter reached such a pitch that it called down a storm of indignant thumping from the apartment above them.

Terry made a defiant gesture at the ceiling, but they both subsided gasping with laughter back onto the bed to indulge in activity every bit as strenuous if not nearly so noisy.

Later, much later, they collected Melanie and once again spent the Sunday at the stud farm on the Vaal. Melanie actually *rode* a horse, a traumatic experience which bade fair to alter her whole existence. After lunch they launched the speedboat from the boat house on the bank of the river and water-skied down as far as the barrage, Terry and Rod taking turns at the wheel and on the skis. It occurred to Rod that Terry Steyner looked good in a white bikini. It was dark before Rod delivered his sleeping daughter to her mother.

'Who is this *Terry* that Melanie talks about all the time?' demanded Patti; she was still sulking about Rod's promotion. Patti had a memory like a tax collector.

'Terry?' Rod feigned surprise. 'I thought you knew.' And he left Patti glaring after him as he went back down the stairs.

Terry was curled up in the leather bucket seat of the Maserati, just the tip of her nose protruding from the voluminous fur coat she wore.

'I love your daughter, Mr Ironsides,' she murmured.

'It would appear that the feeling is reciprocated.'

Rod drove slowly towards the Hillbrow ridge, and Terry's hand came out of the wide fur sleeve and lay on his knee.

'Wouldn't it be nice if we had a daughter of our own one day?'

'Wouldn't it,' Rod agreed dutifully, and then found to his intense amazement that he really meant it.

He was still investigating this remarkable phenomenon as he parked the Maserati in the basement garage of his apartment and went round to open Terry's door.

Manfred Steyner watched Terry climb out of the Maserati and lift her face towards Rodney Ironsides. Ironsides stooped over her and kissed her, then he slammed and locked the door of the Maserati, and arm in arm the two of them crossed to the elevator.

'Peterson Investigations always delivers the goods,' said the man at the wheel of the black Ford parked in the shadows of the garage. 'We will give them half an hour to get settled in comfortably, then we will go up and knock on the door of his apartment.'

Manfred Steyner sat very still and unblinking on the seat beside the private detective. He had arrived back in Johannesburg three hours previously in answer to the summons from the investigation bureau.

'You will leave me here. Drive the Ford out and park at the corner of Clarendon Circle. Wait for me there,' said Manfred.

'Hey? Aren't you going to . . . ?' The detective was taken aback.

'Do as I tell you.' Manfred's voice stung like thrown vitriol, but the detective persisted.

192

'You will need evidence for the court, you need me as a witness . . .'

'Get out,' Manfred snapped, and opening the door of the Ford he climbed out and closed the door behind him. The detective hesitated a moment longer, then started the engine and drove out of the garage leaving Manfred alone.

Manfred moved slowly towards the big shiny sports car. From his pocket he took a gold-plated pen-knife and opened the large blade.

He had recognized that the car was of special significance to the man. It was the only form of retaliation he could make at the moment. Until Rodney Ironsides completed the drive on the Big Dipper Dyke, he could not confront him nor Theresa Steyner. He could not let them know he even suspected them.

Such human emotions as love and hate and jealousy Manfred Steyner seldom experienced, except in their mildest manifestations. Theresa Hirschfeld he had never loved, as he had never loved any woman. He had married her for her wealth and station in life. The emotion that gripped him was neither hatred nor jealousy. It was affront. He was affronted that these two insignificant persons should conspire to cheat him.

He would not rush in blindly now with threats of physical violence and divorce. No, he would administer an anonymous punishment that would hurt the man deeply. This would be part payment. Later, when he had served his purpose, Manfred would crush him as coldly as though he were stepping on an ant.

As for the woman, he was aware of a mild relief. Her irresponsible behaviour had placed her completely at his mercy, both legally and morally. As soon as the strike beyond the Big Dipper had made him financially secure and independent, he could throw her aside. She would have served her purpose admirably.

The journey which he had interrupted by this hurried return to Johannesburg was connected with the purchase of Sonder Ditch shares. He was touring the major centres arranging with various firms of stock brokers that on a given date they would commence to purchase every available scrap of Sonder Ditch script.

As soon as he had completed this business he would tell the private detective to drive him out to Jan Smuts Airport where he had a reservation on the night plane to Durban where he would continue his preparations.

It had all worked out very well, he thought, as he slipped the knife blade through the rubber buffer of the triangular side window of the Maserati. With a quick twist he lifted the window catch, and pushed the window open. He reached through and turned the door handle. The door clicked open and Manfred climbed into the driver's seat.

The blade of the pen-knife was razor sharp. He started on the passenger seat and then the driver's seat, ripping the leather upholstery to shreds before moving to the back seat and repeating the process there. He slid the panel that concealed the tray of tools each in their separate foam rubber padded compartment, and selected a tyre lever.

With this he smashed all the dials on the dashboard, broken glass tinkling and falling to the carpeted floor. With the point of the tyre lever he dug into the rosewood panelling and tore out a section, splintering and cracking the woodwork into complete ruin.

He climbed out of the Maserati and struck the windshield with the tyre lever. The glass starred. He rained blows on it, unable to shatter it but reducing it to a sagging opaque sheet.

Then he dropped the tyre lever and groped for his pen-knife again. On his knees he slashed at the front offside tyre. The rubber was tougher than he had allowed. Annoyed, he slashed again. The knife turned in his hand, the blade folding against the blow. It sliced the ball of his thumb, a deep stinging cut. Manfred came to his feet with a cry, clutching his injured thumb. Blood spurted from the wound.

'Mein Gott! Mein Gott!' Manfred gasped, horrified by his own blood. As he staggered wildly from the basement garage, he was wrapping a handkerchief around his thumb.

He reached the waiting Ford, hauled the door open and fell into the front seat beside the detective.

'A doctor! For God's sake, get me to a doctor. I'm badly hurt. Quickly! Drive quickly!'

– 56 –

Terry's husband is due back in town today, Rod thought, as he sat down at his desk. It was not a thought that gave him strength to work through a day he knew would be filled with hectic activity.

The quarterly reports were due at Head Office tomorrow morning. In consequence the entire administration was in its usual last-minute panic. Already there was a mob in the waiting-room outside his office that Lily Jordan would soon need a stock whip to control. At three o'clock he was due at a consultants' meeting at Head Office, but before that he wanted to go underground to check the drop-blast matt that Johnny Delange had now completed and charged up.

The phone went as Lily led in his first visitor, a tall, thin, sorrowful-looking man with a droopy moustache.

'Mr Ironsides?' said the voice on the phone.

'Yes.'

'Porters Motors here. I've got an estimate on the repairs to your Maserati.'

'How much?' Rod crossed his fingers.

'Twelve hundred rand.'

'Wow!' Rod gasped.

'Do you want us to go ahead?'

'No, I'll have to contact my insurance company first. I'll call you.' He hung up. That act of unaccountable vandalism still irked him terribly. He realized that he would be reduced to the Company Volkswagen for a further indefinite period.

He turned his attention to his visitor.

'Detective Inspector Grobbelaar,' the tall man introduced himself. 'I am investigating officer in the murder of José Almeida, the concession store proprietor on this mine.'

They shook hands.

'Have you any ideas on who did it?' Rod asked.

'We have always got ideas,' said the Inspector, so sadly that for a moment Rod had the impression that his name was on the list of suspects. 'We believe that the murderer is employed by one of the mines in the district, probably the Sonder Ditch. I have called on you to ask for your co-operation in the investigation.'

'Of course.'

'I will be conducting a great number of interrogations amongst your Bantu employees. I hoped you might find a room for me to use on the premises.'

Rod lifted his phone and while he dialled he told Grobbelaar, 'I'm calling our Compound Manager.' Then he transferred his attention to the mouthpiece. 'Ironsides here. I am sending an Inspector Grobbelaar down to see you. Please see that an office is placed at his disposal and that he receives full co-operation.'

Grobbelaar stood up and extended his hand.

'I won't take up more of your time. Thank you, Mr Ironsides.'

His next visitor was Van der Bergh, his Personnel Officer, brandishing his departmental reports as though they were a winning lottery ticket.

'All finished,' he announced triumphantly. 'All we need is your signature.'

As Rod uncapped his pen, the telephone squealed again.

'My God,' he muttered with pen in one hand and telephone in the other. 'Is it worth it?'

It was well after one o'clock when Rod fled his office, leaving Lily Jordan to hold back the tide. He went directly to No. 1 shaft where he was welcomed like the prodigal son by Dimitri and his old Line Managers. They were all anxious to know who would be replacing him as Underground Manager. Rod promised to find out that afternoon when he visited Head Office, and changed into his overalls and helmet.

At the spot where Davy Delange had died, Rod found a gang fixing a screen of wire mesh over the hanging wall to protect the fuses of his drop-blast. The electric cable that carried the blasting circuit to the surface was covered with a distinctive green plastic coating and securely pegged to the roof of the drive.

In the concrete blast room at the shaft head, his electrician had already set up a separate control for this circuit. It would be in readiness at all times. He could fire it within minutes. Rod felt as though a great weight had been lifted from his shoulders as he passed through the swinging ventilation doors and tramped on up the drive to speak to Johnny Delange.

Halfway to the face he met the gigantic figure of Big King coming back towards him with a small gang of lashing boys under his command. Rod greeted him, and Big King stopped and let his gang go on out of earshot before he spoke.

'I wish to speak.'

'Speak then.' Rod noticed suddenly that Big King's face was gaunt, his eyes appeared sunken and his skin had the dusty greyish look of sickness so evident in an ailing Bantu.

'I wish to return to my wives in Portuguese Mozambique,' said Big King.

'Why?' Rod was dismayed at the prospect of losing such a valuable boss boy.

'My blood is thin.' This was as non-committal an answer as any man has ever received. In essence it meant, 'My reasons are my own, and I have no intention of disclosing them.'

'When your blood is thick again, will you return to work here?' Rod asked.

'That is with the gods.' An answer signifying no more than the one preceding it.

'I cannot stop you if you wish to go, Big King, you know that,' Rod told him. 'Report to the Compound Manager and he will mark your notice.'

'I have told the Compound Manager. He wants me to work out my ticket, thirty-three more days.'

'Of course,' Rod nodded. 'You know that it is a contract. You must work it out.'

'I wish to leave at once,' Big King replied stubbornly.

'Then you must give me your reason. I cannot let you break contract except if there is some good reason.' Rod knew better than to set a dangerous precedent like that.

'There is no reason.' Big King admitted defeat. 'I will work out the ticket.'

He left Rod and followed his gang down the drive. Since the night he killed the Portuguese, Big King had slept little and eaten less. Worry had kept his stomach in a turmoil of dysentery, he had neither danced nor sung. Nothing that Crooked Leg nor the Shangaan Induna could say comforted him. He waited for the police to come. As the days passed, so the flesh melted from his body, he knew that they could come before the thirty-three days of his contract expired.

His approach to Rod had been a last despairing effort. Now he was resigned. He knew that the police were inexorable. One day soon they would come. They would lock the silver chains on his wrists and lead him to the closed van. He had seen many men led away like that and he had heard what happened to them after that. The white man's law was the same as the tribal law of the Shangaans. The taking of life must be paid for with life.

They would break his neck with the rope. His ancestors would have crushed his skull with a war club, it was the same in the end.

Rod found Johnny Delange drinking cold tea from his canteen while his gang barred down the face.

'How's it going?' he asked.

'Now we have finished messing about, it has started moving again.' Johnny wiped cold tea from his lips and recorked the canteen. 'We have broken almost fifteen hundred feet since Davy died.'

'That's good going.' Rod ignored the reference to the methane explosion and the drop-blast matt.

'Would have been better if Davy were still alive.' Johnny disliked Campbell, the miner who had replaced Davy on the night shift. 'The night shift aren't breaking their fair ground.'

'I'll chase them up,' Rod promised.

'You do that.' Johnny turned away to shout an order at his gang.

Rod stood and stared at the end of the drive. Less than a thousand feet ahead lay the dark hard rock of the Big Dipper – and beyond it . . . ? Rod felt his skin creep as he remembered his nightmare. That cold green translucent thing waiting for them beyond the dyke.

'All right, Johnny, you are getting close now.' Rod tore his imagination away from that green horror. 'As soon as you hit the serpentine rock you are to stop work immediately and report to me. Is that understood?'

'You'd better tell that to Campbell also,' said Johnny. 'The night shift may hit the Big Dipper.'

'I'll tell him,' Rod agreed. 'But you make sure you

remember. I want to be down here when we hole through the dyke.'

Rod glanced at his watch. It was almost two o'clock. He had an hour to get to the consultant's meeting at Head Office.

'You are late, Mr Ironsides.' Dr Manfred Steyner looked up from the head of the boardroom table.

'My apologies, gentlemen.' Rod took his seat at the long oak table. 'Just one of those days.'

The men about the table murmured sympathetic acknowledgement, and Dr Steyner studied him for a moment without expression before remarking, 'I would be obliged for a few minutes of your time after this meeting, Mr Ironsides.'

'Of course, Dr Steyner.'

'Good.' Manfred nodded. 'Now that Mr Ironsides has graced the table with his presence, the meeting can come to order.' It was the closest any of them had ever heard Dr Steyner come to making a joke.

It was dark outside when the meeting ended. The participants shrugged on their coats, made their farewells and left Manfred and Rod sitting at the table with its overflowing ashtrays and littered pencils and note pads.

Manfred Steyner waited for fully three minutes after the door had closed on the last person to leave. Rod was accustomed to these long intent silences, yet he was uneasy. He sensed a new hostility in the man's attitude. He covered his awkwardness by lighting another cigarette and blowing a series of smoke rings at the portrait of Norman Hradsky, the original chairman of the Company. Flanking Hradsky's portrait were two others. One of a slim blond man, with ravaged good looks and laughing blue eyes. The caption read: 'Dufford Charleywood. Director of CRC from 1867–1872.' The other portrait in its heavy gilt frame depicted an impressively built man with mutton-chop whiskers and black Irish features. 'Sean Courtney' said the caption, and the dates were the same as Charleywood's.

These three had founded the Company, and Rod knew a little of their story. They had been as pretty a bunch of rogues as would be found in any convict settlement. Hradsky had ruined the other two in an ingenious bear raid on the stock exchange, and had virtually stolen their shares in the Company.*

We have become a lot more sophisticated since then, thought Rod. He looked instinctively towards the head of the long table and met Dr Steyner's level, unblinking stare. *Or have we?* he wondered. Just what devilment has our friend in mind?

Manfred Steyner was examining Rod with detached curiosity. So remote from any emotional rancour was Manfred, that he intended using the relationship that had developed between this man and his wife to further the instructions he had received that morning.

'How far is the end of the drive from the dyke?' he asked suddenly.

'Less than a thousand feet.'

'How much longer before you reach it?'

'Ten days. No more, possibly less.'

'As soon as the dyke is reached, all work on it must cease immediately. The timing of this is important, do you understand?'

'I have already instructed my miners not to hole through without my specific orders.'

'Good.' Manfred lapsed into silence for another full minute. Andrew had called him that morning with instructions from the man. Ironsides was to be well away from the Sonder Ditch when they pierced the dyke. It was left to Manfred to engineer his absence.

* Read *When the Lion Feeds*.

'I must inform you, Mr Ironsides, that it will be at least three weeks before I give the order to drill through. When you reach the dyke, it will be necessary for me to proceed to Europe to make certain arrangements there. I will be away for at least ten days during which time no work of any type must be allowed in the drive to the Big Dipper.'

'You will be away over Christmas?' Rod asked with surprise.

'Yes,' Manfred nodded, and could read Rod's mind.

Terry will be alone, Rod thought quickly, she will be alone over Christmas. The Sonder Ditch goes onto *essential services only* for a full seven days over Christmas. Just a skeleton crew to keep her going. I could get away for a week, a whole week away together.

Manfred waited until he knew that Rod had reached the decision to which he had been steered, then he asked: 'You understand? You will await my order to hole through. You need not expect that order until the middle of January.'

'I understand.'

'You may go.' Manfred dismissed him.

'Thanks,' Rod acknowledged drily.

There was a coffee bar in the ground-floor shopping centre of Reef Building. Rod beat a bearded hippie to the telephone booth, and dialled the Sandown number. It was safe enough, he had just left Manfred upstairs.

'Theresa Steyner,' she answered his call.

'We've got a week to ourselves,' he told her. 'One whole glorious week.'

'When?' she demanded joyously.

And he told her.

'Where shall we go?' she asked.

'We'll think of somewhere.'

At 11.26 a.m. on December 16th, Johnny Delange blasted the face of the drive, and went forward in the fumes and dust.

In the beam of his lantern, the new rock blown from the face was completely different from the blueish Ventersdorp quartzite. It was a glassy, blackish green, veined with tiny white lines, more like marble than country rock.

'We are on the dyke.' He spoke to Big King, and stooped to pick up a lump of the serpentine rock. He weighed it in his hand.

'We've done it, we've beaten the bastard!'

Big King stood silently beside him. He did not share Johnny's elation.

'Right!' Johnny tossed the lump of rock back onto the pile. 'Bar down, and make safe. Then pull them out of the drive. We are finished here until further orders.'

'Well done, Johnny,' applauded Rod. 'Clean her up and pull out of the drive. I don't know how much longer it will be till we get the order to hole through the dyke. But take a holiday in the meantime. I'll pay you four fathoms of bonus a day while you are waiting.' He broke the connection with his finger, keeping the receiver to his ear. He dialled and spoke to the switch-board girl at Head Office. 'Get me Dr Steyner, please. This is Rodney Iron-sides.' He waited a few seconds and then Manfred came on the line.

'We've hit the Big Dipper,' Rod told him.

'I will leave for Europe on tomorrow morning's Boeing,' said Manfred. 'You are to do nothing until I return.' Manfred cradled the receiver and depressed the button on his intercom.

'Cancel all my appointments,' he told his secretary. 'I am unavailable.'

'Very well, Dr Steyner.'

Manfred picked up the receiver of his unlisted, direct-line telephone. He dialled.

'Hello, Andrew. Will you tell him that I am ready to discharge my obligations. We have intersected the Big Dipper.' He listened for a few seconds, then spoke again. 'Very well, I will wait for your reply.'

Andrew replaced the telephone and went out through the sliding glass doors onto the terrace. It was a lazy summer's day, hushed with heat, and the sun sparkled on the crystal clear waters of the swimming-pool. Insects murmured languidly in the massed banks of blooms that surrounded the terrace.

The fat man stood before an artist's easel. He wore a blue beret and a white smock that hung like a maternity dress over his jutting stomach.

His model lay face down on an air mattress by the edge of the pool. She was a dainty, dark-haired girl with a pixy face and a doll-like body. Her discarded bikini lay in a damp bundle on the flags of the terrace. Drops of water caught the sun and bejewelled her creamy buttocks, giving her a paradoxical air of innocence and oriental eroticism.

'That was Steyner,' said Andrew. 'He reports that they have hit the Big Dipper.'

The fat man did not look up. He went on laying paint upon the canvas with complete concentration.

'Please lift your right shoulder, my dear, you are covering that utterly delightful bosom of yours,' he instructed, and the girl obeyed him immediately.

Finally he stepped back and regarded his own work critically.

'You may have a break now.' He wiped his brushes while the naked girl stood up, stretched like a cat and then dived into the pool. She surfaced with the water slicking her short dark hair against her head like the pelt of an otter, and swam slowly to the far end of the pool.

'Cable New York, Paris, London, Tokyo and Berlin the code word "Gothic",' he instructed Andrew. This was the word which would unleash the bear offensive on the financial markets of the world. On receipt of those cables, agents in the major cities would begin to sell the shares of the companies mining the Kitchenerville field, sell them by the millions.

'Then instruct Steyner to get Ironsides out of the way, and hole through the dyke.'

Manfred answered Andrew's return call on the unlisted line. He listened to, and acknowledged, his instructions. Afterwards he sat still as a lizard, running over his preparations. Reviewing them minutely, examining them for flaws. There were none.

It was time to begin the purchase of Sonder Ditch shares. He called his secretary on the intercom and instructed her to place calls to numbers in Cape Town, Durban and Johannesburg itself. He wanted the purchase orders to come through a number of different brokers, so that it would not be obvious that there was only one buyer in the market. There was also the question of credit; he was not covering the purchase orders with banker's guarantees. The stock brokers were buying for him simply on his name and reputation and position with CRC Manfred could not place too large a buying order with any one firm lest they ask him to provide surety. Dr Manfred Steyner had no surety to offer.

So, instead, he placed moderate orders with dozens of different firms. By three o'clock that afternoon Manfred had ordered the purchase of three quarters of a million rand's worth of shares. He had no means of paying for those shares but he knew he would never be called upon to do so. When he sold them again in a few weeks' time they would have doubled in value.

A few minutes after his final conversation with the firm of Swerling and Wright in Cape Town, his secretary came through on the intercom.

'SAA have confirmed your reservation on the Boeing to Salisbury. Flight 126 at nine a.m. tomorrow. You are booked to return to Johannesburg on the Rhodesian Airways Viking at 6 p.m. tomorrow evening.'

'Thank you.' Manfred grudged this wasted day but it was imperative that Theresa believed he had left for Europe. She must see him depart on the SAA flight. 'Please get my wife on the phone for me.'

'Theresa,' he told her, 'something important has come up. I have to fly to London tomorrow morning. I am afraid I will be away over Christmas.'

Her display of surprise and regret was unconvincing. She and Ironsides had made their own arrangements for the time he was away, Manfred was convinced of this.

It was all working out very well, he thought as he cradled the receiver, very well indeed.

– 58 –

The Daimler drew up under the portico of Jan Smuts Airport and the chauffeur opened the door for Terry and then for Manfred.

While the porter removed his luggage from the boot of the Daimler, Manfred swept the car park with a quick scrutiny. So early in the morning it was less than half filled. There was a cream Volkswagen with a Kitchenerville number plate parked near the far end. All the line and senior members of the Sonder Ditch had cream Volks-wagens as their official vehicles.

'The bee has come to the honeypot,' thought Manfred, and smiled bleakly. He took Terry's elbow into the main concourse of the airport.

Terry waited while Manfred went through his ticket and immigration formalities. On the outside she was a demure and dutiful wife, but she also had seen the Volkswagen and inside she was itching and bubbling with excitement. Darting surreptitious glances from behind her sunglasses, looking for that tall broad-shouldered figure among the crowds.

It seemed a lifetime until she stood alone on the observation balcony with the wind whipping her piebald calfskin coat around her legs, and blowing her hair into a snapping, dancing tangle. The long shark-like shape of the Boeing jet crouched at the far end of the runway and as it started forward Terry turned from the balcony rail and ran back into the main building.

Rod was waiting for her just inside the doors, and he swung her off her feet.

'Gottcha!'

With her feet dangling, she put her arms around his neck and kissed him.

The watchers paused and then smiled, and there was a minor traffic jam at the head of the stairs.

'Come on,' she entreated, 'let's not waste a minute of it.'

He put her on her feet, and they ran down the staircase hand in hand. Terry paused only to dismiss the chauffeur, and then they ran through the car park like children let out of school, and clambered into the Volkswagen. Their luggage was on the back seat.

'Go,' she said, 'go as fast as you can!'

Twenty minutes later Rod pulled the Volkswagen to a tyre-squealing halt in front of the hangars at the private airfield.

The twin-engined Cessna stood on the tarmac. Both engines were ticking over in readiness, and the mechanic climbed down from the cockpit when he recognized Terry.

'Hello, Terry, right on time,' he greeted her.

'Hello, Hank. You've got her warmed up already. You are a sweety!'

'Filed your flight plan also. Nothing too good for my most favourite customer.' The mechanic was a chunky grizzled little man, and he looked at Rod curiously.

'Give you a hand with the bags,' he said.

By the time they had the luggage stowed away in its compartment, Terry was in the cockpit speaking to the control tower.

Rod climbed up into the passenger seat beside her.

Terry switched off her radio and leaned over Rod's lap to speak to Hank.

'Thanks, Hank.' She paused delicately, and then went on with a rush. 'Hank, if anyone asks you, I was on my own today, okay?'

'Okay.' Hank grinned at her. 'Happy landings.' And he closed the cockpit door, and Terry taxied out onto the runway.

'Is this yours? Rod asked. It was a 100,000 rand's worth of aircraft.

'Pops gave it to me for my birthday,' Terry replied. 'Do you like it?'

'Not bad,' Rod admitted.

Terry turned upwind and applied the wheel brakes while she ran the engines up to peak revs, testing their response.

Suddenly Rod realized that he was in the hands of a woman pilot. He fell silent and his nerves began to tighten up.

'Let's go,' said Terry and kicked off the brakes. The Cessna surged forward, and Rod gripped the arm rests and froze with his gaze fixed dead ahead.

'Relax, Ironsides,' Terry advised him without taking her eyes off the runway, 'I've been flying since I was sixteen.'

At 3,000 feet she levelled out and banked gently onto an easterly heading.

'Now that didn't hurt too much did it?' She smiled sideways at him.

'You are quite a girl,' he told her. 'You can do all sorts of tricks.'

'You just wait,' she warned him. 'You ain't seen nothing yet!'

They flew in silence until the Highveld had fallen away behind them, and they were over the dense green mattress of the Bushveld.

'I'm going to divorce him.' She broke the silence, and Rod was not surprised that they were experiencing the mental telepathy of closely attuned minds. He had been thinking about her husband also.

'Good,' he said.

'You think I'd have a chance with you if I did?'

'If you played your cards right, you might get that lucky.'

'Conceited swine,' she said. 'I don't know why I love you.'

'Do you?' he asked.

'Yes.'

'And I you.'

They relapsed into a contented silence, until Terry put the Cessna in a shallow dive.

'What's wrong?' Rod asked with alarm.

'Going down to have a look for game.'

They flew low over thick olive-green bush broken by veils of golden brown grass.

'There,' said Rod, pointing ahead. A line of fat black bugs moving across one of the open places. 'Buffalo!'

'And over there.' Terry pointed left.

'Zebra and wildebeeste,' Rod identified them. 'And there

is a giraffe.' Its long stalk of a neck stuck up like a periscope. It broke into an awkward stiff-legged run as the aircraft roared overhead.

'We have arrived.' Terry indicated a pair of round granite koppies on the horizon ahead. They were as symmetrical as a young girl's breasts, and as they drew nearer Rod made out the thatched roof of a large building standing in the hollow between the koppies. Beyond it a long straight landing-strip had been cut from the trees, and the fat white sausage of a wind sock flew from its pole.

Terry throttled back and circled the homestead. On the lawns half a dozen tiny figures waved up at the Cessna, and as they watched, two of the figures climbed into a toy Land Rover and set off for the landing-strip. A ribbon of white dust blew out from behind it.

'That's Hans,' Terry explained. 'We can go down now.'

She lined the Cessna up for its approach, and then let it sink down with the motors bumbling softly. The ground came up and jarred the undercarriage, then they were taxiing to meet the racing Land Rover.

The man who piled out of the Land Rover was white-haired, and sunburned like old leather.

'Mrs Steyner!' He was making no attempt to conceal his pleasure. 'It's been much too long. Where have you been?'

'I've been busy, Hans.'

'New York? What the hell for?' said Hans surprisingly.

'This is Mr Ironsides.' Terry introduced them. 'Rod, this is Hans Kruger.'

'Van Breda?' asked Hans as they shook hands. 'You related to the van Bredas from Caledon?'

'I don't think so,' Rod muttered weakly and looked at Terry appealingly.

'He is stone deaf,' Terry explained. 'Both his ear drums blown out by a hangfire in the 1930s. He won't admit it though.'

'I'm glad to hear it,' Hans nodded, happily. 'You always

were a healthy girl. I remember when you were a little piccaninny.'

'He is an absolute darling though, so is his wife. They look after the shooting lodge for Pops,' Terry told Rod.

'Good idea!' Hans agreed heartily. 'Let's get your bags in the Land Rover and go up to the house. I bet Mr van Breda could use a drink also.' And he winked at Rod.

The lodge had thatch and rough-hewn timber roofing, stone-flagged floors covered with cured animal skins and Kelim rugs. There was a walk-in fireplace flanked by gun racks on which were displayed fifty fine examples of the gunsmith's art. The furniture was massive and masculine, leather-cushioned and low. The Spanish plaster walls were hung with trophies, horned heads and native weapons.

A vast wooden staircase led up to the bedrooms that opened off the gallery above the main room. The bedrooms were air-conditioned, and after they had got rid of Hans and his fat wife, Rod and Terry tested the bed to see if it was suitable.

An hour and a half later the bed had been judged eminently satisfactory, and as they went down to pass further judgement on the gargantuan lunch that fat Mrs Hans had spread for them, Terry remarked, 'Has it ever occurred to you, Mr Ironsides, that there are parts of your anatomy other than your flanks which are ferrous in character?' Then she giggled and added softly, 'And thank the Lord for that!'

Lunch was an exhausting experience and Terry pointed out that there was little sense in going out before four o'clock as the game would still be in thick cover avoiding the midday heat, so they went back upstairs.

After four o'clock Rod selected a .375 magnum Holland and Holland rifle from the rack, filled a cartridge belt with ammunition from one of the drawers, and they went out to the Land Rover.

'How big is this place?' Rod asked as he turned the Land

Rover away from the gardens and took the track out into the virgin bush.

'You can drive for twenty miles in any direction and it's all ours. Over there our boundary runs against the Kruger National Park,' Terry answered.

They drove along the banks of the river, skirting sandbanks on which grew fluffy-headed reeds. The water ran fast between glistening black rocks, then spread into slow lazy pools.

They saw a dozen varieties of big game, stopping every few hundred yards to watch some lovely animal.

'Pops obviously doesn't allow shooting here,' Rod remarked, as a kudu bull with long spiral horns and trumpet-shaped ears studied them with big wet eyes from a range of thirty feet. 'The game is as tame as domestic cattle.'

'Only family are allowed to shoot,' Terry agreed. 'You qualify as family, however.'

Rod shook his head. 'It would be murder.' Rod indicated the kudu. 'That old fellow would eat out of your hand.'

'I'm glad you feel like that,' Terry said, and they drove on slowly.

The evening was not cool enough to warrant a log fire in the cavernous fireplace of the lodge. They lit one anyway because Rod decided it would be pleasant to sit in front of a big, leaping fire, drink whisky and hold the girl you love.

– 59 –

When Inspector Grobbelaar lowered his teacup, there was a white scum of cream on the tips of his moustache. He licked it off carefully, and looked across at Sergeant Hugo.

'Who have we got next?' he asked.

Hugo consulted his notebook.

'Philemon N'gabai.' He read out the name, and Grobbelaar sighed.

'Number forty-eight, only sixteen more.' The single smeary fingerprint on the fragment of glass from the gold container had been examined by the fingerprint department. They had provided a list of sixty-four names any one of which might be the owner of that print. Each of them had to be interrogated, it was a lengthy and so far unrewarding labour.

'What do we know about friend Philemon?' Grobbelaar asked.

'He is approximately forty years old. A Shangaan from Mozambique. Height 5' 7½", weight 146 lb. Crippled right leg. Two previous convictions. 1956: 60 days for bicycle theft. 1962: 90 days for stealing a camera from a parked car,' Hugo read from the file.

'At one hundred and forty-six pounds I don't see him breaking many necks. But send him in, let's talk to him,' Grobbelaar suggested and dunked his moustache in the tea cup again. Hugo nodded to the African Sergeant and he opened the door to admit Crooked Leg and his escort of an African constable.

They advanced to the desk at which the two detectives sat in their shirt sleeves. No one spoke. The two interrogators subjected him to a calculated and silent scrutiny to set him at as great a disadvantage as possible.

Grobbelaar prided himself on being able to sniff out a guilty conscience at fifty paces, and Philemon N'gabai reeked of guilt. He could not stand still, he was sweating heavily, and his eyes darted from floor to ceiling. He was guilty as hell, but not necessarily of murder. Grobbelaar did not feel the slightest confidence as he shook his head sorrowfully and asked, 'Why did you do it, Philemon? We have found the marks of your hand on the gold bottle.'

The effect on Crooked Leg was instantaneous and

dramatic. His lips parted and began to tremble, saliva dripped onto his chin. His eyes for the first time fixed on Grobbelaar's face, wide and staring.

'Hello! Hello!' Grobbelaar thought, straightening in his chair, coming completely alert. He sensed Hugo's quickening interest beside him.

'You know what they do to people who kill, Philemon? They take them away to . . .' Grobbelaar did not have an opportunity to finish.

With a howl Crooked Leg darted for the door. His crippled gait was deceptive, he was fast as a ferret. He had the door open before the Bantu Sergeant collared him and dragged him gibbering and struggling back into the room.

'The gold, but not the man! I did not kill the Portuguese,' he babbled, and Grobbelaar and Hugo exchanged glances.

'Pay dirt!' Hugo exclaimed with deep satisfaction.

'Bull's eye!' agreed Grobbelaar, and smiled, a rare and fleeting occurrence.

– 60 –

'You see it has a little light that comes on to show you where the keyhole is,' said the salesman pointing to the ignition switch on the dashboard.

'Ooh! Johnny, see that!' Hettie gushed, but Johnny Delange had his head under the bonnet of the big glossy Ford Mustang.

'Why don't you sit in her?' the salesman suggested. He was very cute really, Hattie decided, with dreamy eyes and the most *fabulous* sideburns.

'Ooh! Yes, I'd love to.' She manoeuvred her bottom into the leather bucket seat of the sports car. Her skirt pulled up, and the salesman's dreamy eyes followed the hem all the way.

214

'Can you adjust the seat?' Hettie asked, innocently looking up at him.

'Here, I'll show you.' He leaned into the interior of the Mustang and reached across Hettie's lap. His hand brushed over her thigh, and Hettie pretended not to notice his touch. He smelled of Old Spice after-shave lotion.

'That's better!' Hettie murmured, and wriggled into a more comfortable position, contriving to make the movement provocative and revealing.

The salesman was encouraged, he lingered with his wrist just touching a sleek thigh.

'What's the compression ratio on this model?' Johnny Delange demanded as he emerged from the engine, and the salesman straightened up quickly and hurried to join him.

An hour later Johnny signed the purchase contract, and both he and Hettie shook the salesman's hand.

'Let me give you my card,' the salesman insisted, but Johnny had returned to his new toy, and Hettie took the cardboard business card.

'Call me if you need anything, anything at all,' said the salesman with heavy significance.

'Dennis Langley. Sales Manager,' Hettie read out aloud. 'My! You're very young to be Sales Manager.'

'Not all that young!'

'I'll bet,' Hettie murmured, and her eyes were suddenly bold. She ran the tip of a pink tongue over her lips. 'I won't lose it,' she promised, and placing the card in her handbag, walked to the Mustang, leaving him with a tantalizing promise and a memory of swaying hips and clicking heels.

They raced the new Mustang as far as Potchefstroom; Hettie encouraging Johnny to overtake slower vehicles with inches to spare for oncoming traffic. With horn blaring he tore over blind rises, forking ringed fingers at the protesting toots of other drivers. They had the speedometer registering

120 mph on the return run, and it was dark as they pulled into the driveway and Johnny hit the brakes hard to avoid running into the back of a big black Daimler that was parked outside their front door.

'Jesus,' gasped Johnny. 'That's Dr Steyner's bus!'

'Who is Dr Steyner?' Hettie demanded.

'Hell, he's one of the big shots from Head Office.'

'You're kidding!' Hettie challenged him.

'Truth!' Johnny affirmed. 'One of the real big shots.'

'Bigger than Mr Ironsides?' The General Manager of the Sonder Ditch was as high up the social ladder as Hettie had ever looked.

'Tin Ribs is chicken feed compared to this joker. Just look at his bus, it's five times better than Tin Ribs's clapped-out old Maserati.'

'Gee!' Hettie could follow the logic of this line of argument. 'What's he want with us?'

'I don't know,' Johnny admitted with a twinge of anxiety. 'Let's go and find out.'

The lounge of the Delange home was not the setting which showed Dr Manfred Steyner to best advantage.

He sat on the edge of a scarlet and gold plastic-covered armchair as stiff and awkward as the packs of china dogs that stood on every table and shelf of the show cabinet, or the porcelain wild ducks which flew in diminishing perspective along the pale pink painted wall. In contrast to the tinsel Christmas decorations that festooned the ceiling and the gay greeting cards that Hettie had pinned to strips of green ribbon, Manfred's black homburg and astrakhan-collared overcoat were unnecessarily severe.

'You will forgive my presumption,' he greeted them without rising. 'You were not at home and your maid let me in.'

'You're welcome, I'm sure,' Hettie simpered.

'Of course you are, Dr Steyner,' Johnny supported her.

'Ah! So you know who I am?' Manfred asked with satisfaction. This would make his task so much easier.

'Of course we do.' Hettie went to him and offered her hand. 'I am Hettie Delange, how do you do?'

With horror Manfred saw that her armpit was unshaven, filled with damp ginger curls. Hettie had not bathed since the previous evening. Manfred's nostrils twitched and he fought down a queasy wave of nausea.

'Delange, I want to speak to you alone.' He cowered away from Hettie's overwhelming physical presence.

'Sure.' Johnny was eager to please. 'How about you making us some coffee, honey,' he asked Hettie.

Ten minutes later Manfred sank with relief into the lush upholstery of the Daimler's rear seat. He ignored the two Delanges waving their farewells, and closed his eyes. It was done. Tomorrow morning Johnny Delange would be on shift and drilling into the glassy green rock of the Big Dipper.

By noon Manfred would own quarter of a million shares in the Sonder Ditch.

In a week he would be a rich man.

In a month he would be divorced from Theresa Steyner. He would sue with all possible notoriety on the grounds of adultery. He no longer needed her.

The chauffeur drove him back to Johannesburg.

It began on the floor of the Johannesburg Stock Exchange.

For some months nearly all the activity had been in the industrial counters, centring about the Alex Sagov group of companies and their merger negotiations.

The only spark of life in the mining and mining financials had been Anglo American Corporation and De Beers Deferred rights issues, but this was now old news and the prices had settled at their new levels. So it was that nobody was expecting fireworks when the call over of the gold mining counters began. The brokers' clerks crowding the floor were quietly spoken and behaved, when the first squib popped.

'Buy Sonder Ditch,' from one end of the hall.

'Buy Sonder Ditch,' a voice raised.

'Buy!' The throng stirred, heads turned.

'Buy.' The brokers suddenly agitated swirled in little knots, broke and reformed as transactions were completed. The price jumped fifty cents, and a broker ran from the floor to confer with his principal.

Here a broker thumped another on the back to gain his attention, and his urgency was infectious.

'Buy! Buy!'

'What the hell's happening?'

'Where is the buying coming from?'

'It's local!'

The price hit ten rand a share, and then the panic began in earnest.

'It's overseas buying.'

'Eleven rand!'

Brokers rushed to telephone warnings to favoured clients that a bull run was developing.

'Twelve fifty. It's only local buying.'

'Buy at best. Buy five thousand.'

Clerks raced back onto the floor carrying the hastily telephoned instructions, and plunged into the hysterical trading.

'Jesus Christ! Thirteen rand, sell now. Take your profit! It can't go much higher.'

'Thirteen seventy-five, it's overseas buying. Buy at best.'

In fifty brokers' offices around the country, the professionals who spent their lives hovering over the tickers regained their balance and, cursing themselves for having been taken unawares, they scrambled onto the bull wagon. Others, the more canny ones, recognized the makings of a sick run and off-loaded their holdings, selling industrial shares as well as mining shares. Prices ran amok.

At ten-fifteen there was a priority call from the offices of the Minister of Finance in Pretoria to the office of the President of the Johannesburg Stock Exchange.

'What are you going to do?'

'We haven't decided. We won't close the floor if we can possibly help it.'

'Don't let it go too far. Keep me informed.'

Sixteen rand and still spiralling when at eleven o'clock South African time, the London Stock Exchange came in. For the first fifteen wild minutes the price of Sonder Ditch gold mining rocketed in sympathy with the Johannesburg market.

Then suddenly and unexpectedly the Sonder Ditch shares ran head-on into massive selling pressure. Not only the Sonder Ditch, but all the Kitchenerville gold mining companies staggered as the pressure increased. The prices wavered, rallied a few shillings and then fell back, wavered again, and then crashed downwards, plummeting far below their opening prices.

'Sell!' was the cry. 'Sell at best!' Within minutes freshly-made paper fortunes were wiped away.

When the price of the Sonder Ditch gold mining shares

fell to five rand seventy-five cents, the committee of the Johannesburg Stock Exchange closed the door in the interests of the national welfare, preventing further trading.

But in New York, Paris and London the investing public continued to beat South African gold mining shares to death.

In the air-conditioned office of a skyscraper building, the little bald-headed man was smashing his balled fist onto the desk top of his superior officer.

'I told you not to trust him,' he was almost sobbing with anger. 'The fat greedy slug. One million dollars wasn't enough for him! No, he had to blow the whole deal!'

'Please, Colonel,' his chief intervened. 'Control yourself. Let us make a fair and objective appraisal of this financial activity.'

The bald-headed man sank back into his chair, and tried to light a cigarette with hands that trembled so violently as to extinguish the flame of his lighter.

'It sticks out a mile.' He flicked the lighter again, and puffed quickly. 'The first activity on the Johannesburg Exchange was Dr Steyner being clever. Buying up shares on the strength of our dummy report. That was quite natural and we expected it, in fact we wanted that to happen. It took suspicion away from us.' His cigarette had gone out, the tip was wet with spit. He threw it away and lit another.

'Fine! Everything was fine up to then. Dr Steyner had committed financial suicide, and we were on the pig's back.' He sucked at his new cigarette. 'Then! Then our fat friend pulls the big double-cross and starts selling the Kitchener-ville shares short. He must have gone into the market for millions.'

'Can we abort the operation at this late date?' his chief asked.

'Not a chance.' The bald head shook vigorously. 'I have

sent a cable to our fat friend ordering him to freeze the work on the tunnel, but can you imagine him obeying that order? He is financially committed for millions of dollars and he will protect that investment with every means at his disposal.'

'Could we not warn the management of the Sonder Ditch company?'

'That would put the finger squarely on us, would it not?'

'Hmm!' the chief nodded. 'We could send them an anonymous warning.'

'Who would put any credence on that?'

'You're right,' the chief sighed. 'We will just have to batten down our hatches and ride out the storm. Sit tight and deny everything.'

'That is all we can do.' The cigarette had gone out again, and there were bits of tobacco in his moustache. The little man flicked his lighter.

'The bastard, the fat, greedy bastard!' he muttered.

– 62 –

Johnny and Big King rode up shoulder to shoulder in the cage. It had been a good shift. Despite the hardness of the serpentine rock that cut down the drilling rate by fifty per cent, they had been able to get in five blasts that day. Johnny reckoned they had driven more than half-way through the Big Dipper. There was no night shift working now. Campbell had gone back to the stopes, so the honour of holing through would be Johnny's. He was excited at the prospect. Tomorrow he would be through into the unknown.

'Until tomorrow, Big King,' he said as they reached the surface and stepped out of the cage.

They separated, Big King heading for the Bantu hostel, Johnny to the glistening new Mustang in the car park.

221

Big King went straight to the Shangaan Induna's cottage without changing from his working clothes. He stood in the doorway and the Induna looked up from the letter he was writing.

'What news, my father?' Big King asked.

'The worst,' the Induna told him softly. 'The police have taken Crooked Leg.'

'Crooked Leg would not betray me,' Big King declared, but without conviction.

'Would you expect him to die in your place?' asked the Induna. 'He must protect himself.'

'I did not mean to kill him,' Big King explained miserably. 'I did not mean to kill the Portuguese, it was the gun.'

'I know, my son.' The Induna's voice was husky with helpless pity.

Big King turned from the doorway and walked down across the lawns to the ablution block. The spring and swagger had gone from his step. He walked listlessly, slouching, dragging his feet.

– 63 –

Manfred Steyner sat at his desk. His hands lay on the blotter before him, one thumb wearing a turban of crisp white bandage. His only movement was the steady beat of a pulse in his throat and a nerve that fluttered in one eyelid. He was deathly pale, and a light sheen of perspiration gave his features the look of having been sculptured from washed marble.

The volume of the radio was turned high, so the voice of the announcer boomed and reverberated from the panelled walls.

'The climax of the drama was reached at eleven forty-five South African time when the President of the Johan-

222

nesburg Stock Exchange declared the floor closed and all further trading suspended.

'Latest reports from the Tokyo Stock Exchange are that Sonder Ditch gold mining shares were being traded at the equivalent of four rand forty cents. This compares with the morning's opening price of the same share on the Johannesburg Stock Exchange of nine rand forty-five cents.

'A spokesman for the South African Government stated that although no reason for these extraordinary price fluctuations was apparent, the Minister of Mines, Doctor Carel De Wet, had ordered a full-scale commission of inquiry.'

Manfred Steyner stood up from his desk and went through into the bathroom. With his flair for figures he did not need pen and paper to compute that the shares he had purchased that morning had depreciated in value by well over one million rand at the close of business that evening.

He knelt on the tiled floor in front of the toilet bowl and vomited.

– 64 –

The sky was darkening rapidly, for the sun had long ago sunk below a blazing horizon.

Rod heard the whisper of wings, and strained his eyes upwards into the gloom. They came in fast, in V-formation, slanting down towards the pool of the river. He stood up from the blind and swung the shotgun on them, leading well ahead of the line of flight.

He squeezed off both barrels. Wham! Wham! And the duck broke formation and rocketed upwards, whirring aloft on noisy wings.

'Damn it!' said Rod.

'What's wrong, dead-eye Dick, did you miss?' asked Terry.

'The light's too bad.'

'Excuses! Excuses!' Terry stood up beside him, and Rod pushed a balled fist lightly against her cheek.

'That's enough from you, woman. Let's go home.'

Carrying the shotguns and bunches of dead duck, they trudged along the bank in the dusk to the waiting Land Rover.

It was completely dark as they drove back to the lodge.

'What a wonderful day it's been,' Terry murmured dreamily. 'If for nothing else, I will always be grateful to you for teaching me how to enjoy my life.'

Back at the lodge, they bathed and changed into fresh clothes. For dinner they had wild duck and pineapple, with salads from Mrs Fat Hans' vegetable garden. Afterwards, they sprawled on the leopard-skin rugs in front of the fireplace and watched the log fire without talking, relaxed and happy and tired.

'My God, it's almost nine o'clock.' Terry checked her wristwatch. 'I fancy a bit of bed myself, how about you, Mr Ironsides?'

'Let's hear the nine o'clock news first.'

'Oh, Rod! Nobody ever listens to the news here. This is fairyland!'

Rod switched on the radio and the first words froze them both. They were 'Sonder Ditch'.

In horrified silence they listened to the report. Rod's expression was granite-hard, his mouth a tight grim line. When the news report ended, Rod switched off the radio set and lit a cigarette.

'There is trouble,' he said. 'Big trouble. I'm sorry, Terry, we must go back. As soon as possible. I have to get back to the mine.'

'I know,' Terry agreed immediately. 'But Rod, I can't take off from this landing-strip in the dark. There is no flare path.'

'We'll leave at first light.'

Rod slept very little that night. Whenever she woke, Terry sensed him lying unsleeping, worrying. Twice she heard him get up and go to the bathroom.

In the very early hours of the morning she woke from her own troubled sleep and saw him silhouetted against the starlit window. He was smoking a cigarette and staring out into the darkness. It was the first night they had spent together without making love. In the dawn Rod was haggard and puffy-eyed.

They were airborne at eight o'clock and they landed in Johannesburg a little after ten.

Rod went straight to the telephone in Hank's office and Lily Jordan answered his call.

'Miss Jordan, what the hell is happening? Is everything all right?'

'Is that you, Mr Ironsides. Oh! Thank God! Thank God you've come, something terrible has happened!'

– 65 –

Johnny Delange blew the face of the drive twice before nine o'clock, cutting thirty feet further into the glassy green dyke.

He had found that by drilling his cutter blast holes an additional three feet deeper, he could achieve a shatter effect on the serpentine rock which more than compensated for the additional drilling time. This next blast he was going to flout standard regulations and experiment with double-charging his cutter holes. He would need additional explosives.

'Big King,' he shouted to make himself heard above the roar of drills. 'Take a gang back to the shaft station. Pick up six cases of Dynagel.'

He watched Big King and his gang retreat back down the drive, and then he lit a cigarette and turned his attention to his machine boys. They were poised before the rock face, sweating behind their drills. The dark rock of the dyke absorbed the light from the overhead electric bulbs. It made the end of the drive a gloomy place, filled with a sense of foreboding.

Johnny began to think about Davy. He was aware suddenly of a sense of disquiet, and he moved restlessly. He felt the hair on his forearms come slowly erect, each on a separate goose pimple. *Davy is here*. He knew it suddenly, and surely. His flesh crawled and he went cold with dread. He turned quickly and looked over his shoulder. The tunnel behind him was deserted, and Johnny gave a sickly grin.

'Shaya, madoda,' he called loudly and unnecessarily to his gang. They could not hear him above the roar of the drills, but the sound of his own voice helped reassure him.

Yet the creepy sensation was still with him. He felt that Davy was still there, trying to tell him something.

Johnny fought the sensation. He walked quickly forward, standing close to his machine boys, as though to draw comfort from their physical presence. It did not help. His nerves were shrieking now, and he felt himself beginning to sweat.

Suddenly the machine boy who was drilling the cutter hole in the centre of the face staggered backwards.

'Hey!' Johnny shouted at him, then he saw that water was spurting in fine needle jets from around the drill steel. Something was squeezing the drill steel out of its hole, like toothpaste out of a tube. It was pushing the machine boy backwards.

'Hey!' Johnny started forward and at that instant the heavy metal drill was fired out of the rock with the force of a cannon ball. It decapitated the machine boy, tearing his head from his body with such savagery that his carcass was thrown far back down the drive, his blood spraying the dark rock walls.

226

From the drill hole shot a solid jet of water. It came out under such pressure that when it caught the machine boy's assistant in the chest it stove in his ribs as though he had been hit by a speeding automobile.

'Out!' yelled Johnny. 'Get out!' And the rock face exploded. It blew outwards with greater force than if it had been blasted with Dynagel. It killed Johnny Delange instantly. He was smashed to a bloody pulp by the flying rock. It killed every man in his gang with him, and immediately afterwards the monstrous burst of water that poured from the face picked up their mutilated remains and swept them down the drive.

Big King was at the shaft station when they heard the water coming. It sounded like an express train in a tunnel, a dull bellow of irresistible power. The water was pushing the air from the drive ahead of it, so that a hurricane of wind came roaring from the mouth of the drive, blowing out a cloud of dust and loose rubbish.

Big King and his gang stood and stared in uncomprehending terror until the head of the column of water shot from the drive, frothing solid, carrying with it a plug of debris and human remains.

Bursting into the T-junction of the main 66 level haulage, the strength of the flood was reduced, yet still it swept down towards the lift station in a waist-deep wall.

'This way!' Big King was the first to move. He leapt for the steel emergency ladder that led up to the level above. The rest of his gang were not fast enough, the water picked them up and crushed them against the steel-mesh barrier that guarded the shaft. The crest of the wave burst around Big King's legs, sucking at him, but he tore himself from its grip and climbed to safety.

Beneath him the water poured into the shaft like bath

water into a plug hole, forming a spinning whirlpool about the collar as it roared down to flood the workings below 66 level.

– 66 –

Leaving Terry at the airfield to solicit transport from Hank, the mechanic, Rod drove directly to the head of No. 1 shaft of the Sonder Ditch. He jumped from the Volkswagen into the clamouring crowd clustered above the shaft head.

Dimitri was wide-eyed and distracted, beside him Big King towered like a black colossus.

'What happened?' Rod demanded.

'Tell him,' Dimitri instructed Big King.

'I was at the shaft with my gang. A river leaped from the mouth of the drive, a great river of water running faster than the Zambesi in flood; roaring like a lion the water ate all the men with me. I alone climbed above it.'

'We've hit a big one, Rod,' Dimitri interrupted. 'It's pouring in fast. We calculate it will flood the entire workings up to 66 level in four hours from now.'

'Have you cleared the mine?' Rod demanded.

'All the men are out except Delange and his gang. They were in the drive. They've been chopped, I'm afraid,' Dimitri answered.

'Have you warned the other mines we could have a burst through into their workings?'

'Yes, they are pulling all their shifts out.'

'Right.' Rod set off for the blast control room with Dimitri trotting to keep up with him. 'Give me your keys, and find the foreman electrician.'

Within minutes the three of them were crowded into the tiny concrete control room.

'Check in the special circuit,' Rod instructed. 'I'm going to shoot the drop-blast matt and seal off the drive.'

The foreman electrician worked quickly at the control panel. He looked up at Rod.

'Ready!' he said.

'Check her in,' Rod nodded.

The foreman threw the switch. The three of them caught their breath together.

Dimitri said it for them: 'Red!'

On the control panel of the special circuit the red bulb glared balefully at them, the Cyclops eye of the god of despair.

'Christ!' swore the foreman. 'The circuit is shot. The water must have torn the wires out.'

'It may be a fault in the board.'

'No.' The foreman shook his head with certainty.

'We've had it,' whispered Dimitri. 'Goodbye the Sonder Ditch!'

Rod burst out of the control room into the expectant crowd outside.

'Johnson!' He singled out one of his mine captains. 'Go down to the Yacht Club at the dam, get me the rubber rescue dinghy. Quick as you can, man.'

The man scurried away, and Rod turned on the electrician foreman as he emerged from the control room.

'Get me a battery hand-operated blaster, a reel of wire, pliers, two coils of nylon rope. Hurry!'

The foreman went.

'Rod.' Dimitri caught his arm. 'What are you going to do?'

'I'm going down there. I'm going to find the break in the circuit and I'm going to blast her by hand.'

'Jesus!' Dimitri gasped. 'You are crazy, Rod. You'll kill yourself for sure!'

Rod completely ignored his protest.

'I want one man with me. A strong man. The strongest there is, we will have to drag the dinghy against the flood.' Rod looked about him. Big King was standing by the banksman's office. The two of them were tall enough to face each other over the heads of the men between them.

'Will you come with me, Big King?' Rod asked.

'Yes,' said Big King.

– 67 –

In less than twenty minutes they were ready. Rod and Big King were stripped down to singlets and bathing-trunks. They wore canvas tennis shoes to protect their feet, and the hard helmets on their heads were incongruous against the rest of their attire.

The rubber dinghy was ex-naval disposal. A nine-foot air-filled mattress, so light that a man could lift it with one hand. Into it was packed the equipment they would need for the task ahead. A water-proof bag contained the battery blaster, the reel of insulated wire, the pliers and a spare lantern. Lashed to the eyelets along the sides of the dinghy were two coils of light nylon rope, a small crowbar, an axe and a razor-sharp machete in a leather sheath. To the bows of the dinghy were fastened a pair of looped nylon towing lines.

'What else will you need, Rod?' Dimitri asked.

Rod shook his head thoughtfully. 'That's it, Dimitri. That should do it.'

'Right!' Dimitri beckoned and four men came forward and carried the dinghy into the waiting cage.

'Let's go,' said Dimitri and followed the dinghy into the cage. Big King went next and Rod paused a second to look up at the sky. It was very blue and bright.

Before the onsetter could close the shutter door, a Silver Cloud Rolls-Royce came gliding onto the bank. From the rear door emerged first Hurry Hirschfeld and then Terry Steyner.

'Ironsides!' roared Hurry. 'What the hell is going on?'

'We've hit water,' Rod answered him from the cage.

'Water? Where did it come from?'

'Beyond the Big Dipper.'

'You drove through the Big Dipper?'

'Yes.'

'You bastard, you've drowned the Sonder Ditch,' roared Hurry, advancing on the cage.

'Not yet, I haven't,' Rod contradicted.

'Rod.' Terry was white-faced beside her grandfather. 'You can't go down there.' She started forward.

Rod pushed the onsetter aside and pulled down the steel shutter door of the cage. Terry threw herself against the steel mesh of the guard barrier, but the cage was gone into the earth.

'Rod,' she whispered, and Hurry Hirschfeld put his arm around her shoulders and led her to the Rolls-Royce.

From the back seat of the Rolls, Hurry Hirschfeld was conducting a Kangaroo Court Trial of Rodney Ironsides. One by one he called for the line managers of the Sonder Ditch and questioned them. Even those who were loyal to Rod could say little in his defence, and there were others who took the opportunity to level old scores with Rodney Ironsides.

Sitting beside her grandfather, Terry heard such a condemnation of the man she loved as to chill her to the depths of her soul. There was no doubt that Rodney Ironsides, without Head Office sanction, had instituted a new development so risky and contrary to company policy as to be criminal in concept.

'Why did he do it?' muttered Hurry Hirschfeld. He seemed bewildered. 'What could he possibly achieve by driving through the Big Dipper? It looks like a deliberate attempt to sabotage the Sonder Ditch.' Hurry's anger began to seethe within him. 'The bastard! He has drowned the Sonder Ditch and killed dozens of men.' He punched his fist into the palm of his hand. 'I'll make him pay for this. I'll break him, so help me God, I'll smash him! I'll bring criminal charges against him. Malicious damage to property. Manslaughter. Culpable homicide! By Jesus, I'll have his guts for this!'

Listening to Hurry ranting and threatening, Terry could keep silent no longer.

'It wasn't his fault, Pops. Truly it wasn't. He was forced to do it.'

'Ha!' snorted Hurry. 'I heard you at the pithead a few minutes ago. Just what is this man to you, Missy, that you spring to his defence so nobly?'

'Pops, please believe me.' Her eyes were enormous in her pale face.

'Why should I believe you? The two of you are obviously up to mischief together. Naturally you will try and protect him.'

'Listen to me at least,' she pleaded, and Hurry checked the run of his tongue and breathing heavily he turned to face her.

'This better be good, young lady,' he warned her.

In her agitation she told it badly, and halfway through she realized that she wasn't even convincing herself. Hurry's expression became more and more bleak, until he interrupted her impatiently.

'Good God, Theresa, this isn't like you. To try and put the blame for this onto your own husband! That's despicable! To try and switch the blame for this . . .'

'It's true! As God is my witness.' Terry was almost in tears, she was tugging at Hurry's sleeve in her agitation. 'Rod was forced to do it. He had no option.'

'You have proof of this?' Hurry asked drily, and Terry fell silent, staring at him dumbly. What proof was there?

– 68 –

The cage checked and slowed as it approached 65 level. The lights were still burning, but the workings were deserted. They lugged the dinghy out onto the station.

They could hear the dull waterfall roar of the flood on the level below them. The displacement of huge volumes of water disturbed the air so that a strong cool breeze was blowing up the shaft.

'Big King and I will go down the emergency ladder. You will lower the dinghy to us afterwards,' Rod told Dimitri. 'Make sure all the equipment is tied into it.'

'Right.' Dimitri nodded.

All was in readiness. The men who had come down with them in the cage were waiting expectantly. Rod could find no reason for further delay. He felt something cold and heavy settle in his guts.

'Come on, Big King.' And he went to the steel ladder.

'Good luck, Rod.' Dimitri's voice floated down to him, but Rod saved his breath for that cold dark climb downwards.

All the lights had fused on 66 level, and in the beam of his lamp the water below him was black and agitated. It poured into the mouth of the shaft, bending the mesh barrier inwards. The mesh acted as a gigantic sieve, straining the floating rubbish from the flood. Amongst the timber and planking, the sodden sacking and unrecognizable objects, Rod made out the water-logged corpses of the dead pressed against the wire.

He climbed down and gingerly lowered himself into the water. Instantly it dragged at his lower body, shocking in its power. It was waist-deep here, but he found that by bracing his body against the steel ladder he could maintain his footing.

Big King climbed down beside him, and Rod had to raise his voice above the hissing thunder of water.

'All right?'

'Yes. Let them send down the boat.'

Rod flashed his lamp up the shaft, and within minutes the dinghy was swaying slowly down to them. They reached up and guided it right side up to the surface of the water, before untying the rope.

The dinghy was sucked firmly against the wire mesh, and Rod checked its contents quickly. All was secure.

'Right.' Rod tied a bight of the nylon rope around his waist, and climbed up the wire mesh barrier until he could reach the roof of the tunnel. Behind him Big King was paying out the nylon line.

Rod leaned out until he could get his hands on the compressed air pipes that ran along the roof of the tunnel. The pipes were as thick as a man's wrist, bolted securely into the hanging wall of the drive; they would support a man's weight with ease. Rod settled his grip firmly on the piping and then kicked his feet free from the barrier. He hung above the rushing waters, his feet just brushing the surface.

Hand over hand, swinging forward with feet dangling, he started up the tunnel. The nylon rope hung down behind him like a long white tail. It was 300 feet to where the water boiled from the drive into the main haulage, and Rod's shoulder muscles were shrieking in protest before he reached it. It seemed that his arms were being wrenched from their sockets, for the weight of the nylon rope that was dragging in the water was fast becoming intolerable.

There was a back eddy in the angle formed by the drive and the haulage. Here the flood swirled in a vortex, and

Rod lowered himself slowly into it. The water buffeted him, but again he was able to cower against the side wall of the haulage and hold his footing. Quickly he began tying the rope onto the rawlbolts that were driven into the sidewall to consolidate the rock. Within minutes he had established a secure base from which to operate, and when he flashed his lamp back down the haulage he saw Big King following him along the compressed air piping.

Big King dropped into the waist-deep water beside Rod, and they gripped the nylon rope and rested their burning arm muscles.

'Ready?' asked Rod at last, and Big King nodded.

They laid hold of the rope that led back to the dinghy and hauled upon it. For a moment nothing happened, the other end might just as well have been anchored to a mountain.

'Together!' grunted Rod, and they recovered a foot of rope.

'Again!' And they drew the dinghy inch by inch up the haulage against the rush of water.

Their hands were bleeding when they at last pulled the laden dinghy up to their own position and anchored it to the rawlbolts beside them. It bounced and bobbed with the water drumming against its underside.

Neither Rod nor Big King could talk. They hung exhausted on the body lines with the water ripping at their skin and gasped for breath.

At last Rod looked up at Big King, and in the lamp light he saw his own doubts reflected in Big King's eyes. The drop-blast matt was 1,000 feet up the drive. The strength and speed of the water in the drive was almost double what it was in the haulage. Could they ever fight their way against such primeval forces as these that were now unleashed about them?

'I will go next,' Big King said, and Rod nodded his agreement.

The huge Bantu drew himself up the rope until he could reach the compressed air pipe. His skin in the lamplight glistened like that of a porpoise. Hand over hand he disappeared into the gaping black maw of the drive. His lamp threw deformed and monstrous shadows upon the walls of rock.

When Big King's lamp flashed the signal to him, Rod climbed up to the pipe and followed him into the drive. Three hundred feet later he found Big King had established another base. But here they were exposed to the full force of the flood, and they were pulled so violently against the body lines that the harsh nylon smeared the skin from their bodies. Together they dragged the dinghy up to them and anchored it.

Rod was sobbing softly as he held his torn hands to his chest and wondered if he could do it again.

'Ready?' Big King asked beside him, and Rod nodded. He reached up and placed the raw flesh of his palms onto the metal piping, and felt the tears of pain flood his eyes. He blinked them back and dragged himself forward.

Vaguely he realized that should he fall, he was a dead man. The flood would sweep him away, dragging him along the jagged side walls of the drive, ripping his flesh from the bone, and finally hurling him against the mesh surrounding the shaft to crush the life from his body.

He went on until he knew he could go no farther. Then he selected a rawlbolt in the side wall and looped the rope through it. And they repeated the whole heart-breaking procedure. Twice as he strained against the dinghy rope Rod saw his vision explode into stars and pinwheels. Each time he dragged himself back from the brink of unconsciousness by sheer force of will.

The example that Big King was setting was the inspiration which kept Rod from failing. Big King worked without change of expression, but his eyes were bloodshot with exertion. Only once Rod heard him grunt like a gut-shot lion, and there was bright blood on the rope where he touched it.

Rod knew he could not give in while Big King held on.

Reality dissolved slowly into a dark roaring nightmare of pain, wherein muscles and bone were loaded beyond all endurance, and yet continued to function. It seemed that for all time Rod had hung on arms that were leadened and slow with exhaustion. He was inching his way along the compressed air pipe for yet another advance up the drive. Sweat running into his eyes was blurring his vision, so at first he did not credit what he saw ahead of him in the darkness.

He shook his head to clear his eyes, and then squinted along the beam of his lamp. A heavy timber structure was hanging drunkenly from the roof of the drive. The bolts that held it were resisting the efforts of the water to tear it loose.

Rod realized abruptly that this was what remained of the frame which had held the ventilation doors. The doors were gone, ripped away, but the frame was still in position. He knew that just beyond the ventilation doors the drop-blast matt began. They had reached it!

New strength flowed into his body and he swung forward along the pipe. The timber frame made a fine anchor point and Rod secured the rope to it, and flashed back the signal to Big King. He hung in the loop of rope and rested awhile, then he forced himself to take an interest in his surroundings. He played the beam over the distorted timber frame and saw instantly why the blasting circuit had been broken.

In the lamp light the distinctive green plastic-coated blasting cable hung in festoons from the roof of the drive; clearly it had become entangled in the ventilation doors and been severed when they were ripped away. The loose end of the cable dangled to the surface of the racing water.

Rod fastened his eyes on it, drawing comfort and strength from the knowledge that they would not have to continue their agonized journey down the drive.

When Big King came up out of the gloom, Rod indicated the dangling cable.

'There!' he gasped, and Big King narrowed his eyes in acknowledgement; he was unable to speak.

It was five minutes before they could commence the excruciating business of hauling the dinghy up and securing it to the door frame.

Again they rested. Their movements were slowing up drastically. Neither of them had much strength left to draw upon.

'Get hold of the end of the cable.' Rod instructed Big King, and he dragged himself over the side of the dinghy and lay sprawled full-length on the floor boards.

His weight forced the dinghy deeper, increasing its resistance to the racing water, and the rope strained against the wooden frame. Rod began clumsily to unpack the battery blaster. Big King stood waist-deep clinging with one arm to the wooden frame, reaching forward with the other towards the end of the green-coated cable. It danced just beyond his fingertips, and he edged forward against the current, steadying himself against the timber frame, placing a greater strain on the retaining bolts.

His fingers closed on the cable and with a grunt of satisfaction he passed it back to Rod.

Working with painstaking deliberation, Rod connected the crocodile clips from the reel of wire to the loose end of the green cable. Rod's plan was for both he and Big King to climb aboard the dinghy, and, paying out the nylon rope, let themselves be carried back down the drive. At the same time they would be letting the wire run from its reel. At a safe distance they would fire the drop-blast matt.

Rod's fingers were swollen and numbed. The minutes

passed as he completed his preparations and all that while the strain on the wooden frame was heavy and constant.

Rod looked up from his task, and crawled to his knees.

'All right, Big King,' he wheezed as he knelt in the bows of the dinghy and gripped the wooden frame to steady the dinghy. 'Come aboard. We are ready.'

Big King waded forward and at that instant the retaining bolts on one side of the heavy timber frame gave way. With a rending, tearing sound the frame slewed across the tunnel. The beams of timber crossed each other like the blades of a pair of gigantic scissors. Both Rod's arms were between the beams. The bones in his forearms snapped with the loud crackle of breaking sticks.

With a scream of pain Rod collapsed onto the floorboards of the dinghy, his arms useless, sticking out at absurd angles from their shattered bones. Three feet away Big King was still in the water. His mouth was wide open, but no sound issued from his throat. He stood still as a black statue and his eyes bulged from their sockets. Even through his own suffering Rod was horrified by the expression on Big King's contorted features.

Below the surface of the water the bottom timber beams had performed the same scissor movement, but this time they had caught Big King's lower body between them. They had closed across his pelvis and crushed it. Now they held him in a vicelike grip from which it was not possible to shake them.

The white face and the black face were but a few feet apart. The two stricken companions in disaster looked into each other's eyes and knew that there was no escape. They were doomed.

'My arms,' whispered Rod huskily. 'I cannot use them.'

Big King's bulging eyes held Rod's gaze.

'Can you reach the blaster?' Rod whispered urgently. 'Take it and turn the handle. Burn it, Big King, burn it!'

Slow comprehension showed in Big King's pain-glazed eyes.

'We are finished, Big King. Let us go like men. Burn it, bring down the rock!'

Above them the rock was sown with explosive. The blaster was connected. In his agitation Rod tried to reach out for the blaster. His forearm swung loosely, the fingers hanging open like the petals of a dead flower, and the pain checked him.

'Get it, Big King,' Rod urged him, and Big King picked up the blaster and held it against his chest with one arm.

'The handle!' Rod encouraged him. 'Turn the handle!'

But instead Big King reached into the dinghy once more and drew the machete from its sheath.

'What are you doing?' Rod demanded, and in reply Big King swung the blade back over his shoulder and then brought it forward in a gleaming arc aimed at the nylon rope that held the dinghy anchored to the wooden frame. Clunk! The blade bit into the wood, severing the rope that was bound around it.

Freed by the stroke of the machete, the dinghy was whisked away by the current. Lying in the dancing rubber dinghy, Rod heard a bull voice bellow above the rush of the water.

'Go in peace, my friend.'

Then Rod was careening back along the drive, a hell ride during which the dinghy spun like a top and in the beam of his lamp the roof and walls melted into a dark racing blur as Rod lay maimed on the floor of the dinghy.

Then suddenly the air jarred against his ear drums, a long rolling concussion in the confines of the drive and he knew that Big King had fired the drop-blast matt. Rodney Ironsides slipped over the edge of consciousness into a soft warm dark place from which he hoped never to return.

Dimitri squatted on his haunches above the shaft at 65 level. He was smoking his tenth cigarette. The rest of the men waited as impatiently as he did; every few minutes Dimitri would cross to the shaft and flash his lamp down the hundred-foot hole to 66 level.

'How long have they been gone?' he asked, and they all glanced at their watches.

'An hour and ten minutes.'

'No, an hour and fourteen minutes.'

'Christ, call me a liar for four minutes!'

And they lapsed into silence once more. Suddenly the station telephone shrilled, and Dimitri jumped up and ran to it.

'No, Mr Hirschfeld, nothing yet!'

He listened a moment.

'All right, send him down then.'

He hung up the telephone, and his men looked at him enquiringly.

'They are sending down a policeman,' he explained.

'What the hell for?'

'They want Big King.'

'Why?'

'Warrant of arrest for murder.'

'Murder?'

'Ja, they reckon he murdered the Portuguese store-keeper.'

'Jeez!'

'Big King, is that so!' Delighted to have found something to pass the time, they fell into an animated debate.

The police inspector arrived in the cage at 65 level, but he was disappointing. He looked like a down-at-heel under-taker, and he replied to their eager questions with a sorrowful stare that left them stuttering.

For the fifteenth time Dimitri went to the shaft and peered down into it. The blast shook the earth around them, a long rumbling that persisted for many seconds.

'They've done it!' yelled Dimitri, and began to caper wildly. His men leapt to their feet and began beating each other on the back, shouting and laughing. The police inspector alone took no part in the celebrations.

'Wait,' yelled Dimitri at last. 'Shut up all of you! Shut up! Damn it! Listen!'

They fell silent.

'What is it?' someone asked. 'I can't hear anything.'

'That's just it!' exulted Dimitri. 'The water! It has stopped!'

Only then did they become aware that the dull roar of water to which their ears had become resigned was now ended. It was quiet; a cathedral hush lay upon the workings. They began to cheer, their voices thin in the silence, and Dimitri ran to the steel ladder and swarmed down it like a monkey.

From thirty feet up Dimitri saw the dinghy marooned amongst the filth and debris around the shaft. He recognized the crumpled figure lying in the bottom of it.

'Rod!' he was shouting before he reached the station at 66 level. 'Rod, are you all right?'

The floor of the haulage was wet, and here and there a trickle of water still snaked towards the shaft. Dimitri ran to the stranded dinghy and started to turn Rod onto his back. Then he saw his arms.

'Oh, Christ!' he gasped in horror, then he was yelling up the ladder. 'Get a stretcher down here.'

Rod regained consciousness to find himself covered with blankets and strapped securely into a mine stretcher. His arms were splinted and bandaged, and from the familiar rattle and rush of air he knew he was in the cage on the way to the surface.

He recognized Dimitri's voice raised argumentatively.

'Damn it! The man is unconscious and badly injured, can't you leave him alone?'

'I have my duty to perform,' a strange voice answered.

'What's he want, Dimitri?' Rod croaked.

'Rod, how are you?' At the sound of his voice Dimitri was kneeling beside the stretcher anxiously.

'Bloody awful,' Rod whispered. 'What does this joker want?'

'He's a police officer. He wants to arrest Big King for murder,' Dimitri explained.

'Well, he's a bit bloody late,' whispered Rod, and even through his pain this seemed to Rod to be terribly funny. He began to laugh. He sobbed with laughter, each convulsion sending bright bursts of pain along his arms. He was shaking uncontrollably with shock, sweat pouring from his face, and he was laughing wildly.

'He's a bit bloody late,' he repeated through his hysterical laughter as Dr Dan Stander pushed the hypodermic needle into his arm and shot him full of morphine.

– 70 –

Hurry Hirschfeld stood in the main haulage on 66 level. There was bustle all around him. Already the crews from the cementation company were manhandling their equipment up towards the blocked drive.

These were specialists from an independent contracting company. They were about to begin pumping thousands of tons of liquid cement into the rock jam that sealed the drive. They would pump it in at pressures in excess of 3,000 pounds per square inch, and when that concrete set it would form a plug that would effectively seal off the drive for all time. It would also form a burial vault for the body of Big King, thought Hurry, a fitting monument to the man who had saved the Sonder Ditch.

He would arrange to have a commemorative plaque placed on the outer wall of the cement plug with a suitable inscription describing the man and the deed.

The man's dependants must be properly taken care of; perhaps they could be flown down for the unveiling of the plaque. Anyway he could leave that to Public Relations and Personnel.

The haulage stank of wetness and mud. It was dank and clammy cool, and it would not improve his lumbago. Hurry had seen enough; he started back towards the shaft. Faintly he was aware of the muted clangour of the mighty pumps which in a few days would free the Sonder Ditch of the water that filled her lower levels.

The laden stretchers with their grisly blanket-covered burdens stood in a row under the hastily rigged electric lights along one wall of the tunnel. Hurry's expression hardened as he passed them.

'I'll have the guts of the man responsible for this,' he vowed silently as he waited for the cage.

Terry Steyner rode in the rear of the ambulance with Rod. She wiped the mud from his face.

'How bad is it, Dan?' she asked.

'Hell, Terry, he'll be up and about in a few days. The arms of course are not very pretty, that's why I'm taking him directly to Johannesburg. I want a specialist ortho-paedic surgeon to set them. Apart from that he is suffering from shock pretty badly and his hands are superficially lacerated. But he will be fine.'

Dan watched curiously as Terry fussed ineffectually with the damp hair of the drugged man.

'You want a smoke?' he asked.

'Light me one, please Dan.'

He passed her the cigarette.

'I didn't know that you and Rod were so friendly,' he ventured.

Terry looked up at him quickly.

'How very delicate you are, Dr Stander,' she mocked him.

'None of my business, of course.' Hurriedly Dan withdrew.

'Don't be silly, Dan. You're a good friend of Rod's and Joy is mine. You two are entitled to know. I am desperately, crazily in love with this big hunk. I intend divorcing Manfred just as soon as possible.'

'Is Rod going to marry you?'

'He hasn't said anything about marriage but I'll sure as hell start working on him,' Terry grinned, and Dan laughed.

'Good luck to you both, then. I'm sure Rod will be able to get another job.'

'What do you mean?' Terry demanded.

'They say your grandfather is threatening to fire him so high he'll be the first man on the moon.'

Terry relapsed into silence. Proof was what Pops had asked for, but what proof was there?

'They'll be waiting on the X-ray reports.' Joy Albright gave her opinion. Since her engagement to Dan, Joy had suddenly become something of a medical expert. She had rushed down to the Johannesburg Central Hospital at Dan's hurried telephonic request. Dan wanted her to keep Terry company while she waited for Rod to come out of emergency. They sat together in the waiting-room.

'I expect so,' Terry agreed. Something Joy had just said had jolted in her mind, something she must remember.

'It takes them twenty minutes or so to expose the plates

and develop them. Then the radiologist has to examine the plates and make his report to the surgeon.'

There, Joy had said it again. Terry sat up straight and concentrated on what Joy had said. Which word had disturbed her?

Suddenly she had it.

'The report!' she exclaimed. 'That's it. The report, that's the proof.'

She leapt out of her chair.

'Joy! Give me the keys of your car,' she demanded.

'What on earth?' Joy looked startled.

'I can't explain now. I have to get home to Sandown urgently, give me your keys. I'll explain later.'

Joy fished in her handbag and produced a leather key folder. Terry snatched it from her.

'Where are you parked?' Terry demanded.

'In the car park, near the main gate.'

'Thanks, Joy.' Terry dashed from the waiting-room, her high heels clattered down the passage.

'Crazy woman.' Joy looked after her bewildered.

Ten minutes later Dan looked into the waiting-room.

'Rod's fine now. Where's Terry?'

'She went mad—' And Joy explained her abrupt departure. Dan looked grave.

'I think we'd better follow her, Joy.'

'I think you're right, darling.'

'I'll just grab my coat,' said Dan.

There was only one place where Manfred would keep the geological report on the Big Dipper that Rod had told her about. That was in the safe deposit behind the panelling in his study. Because her jewellery was kept in the same safe, Terry had a key and the combination to the lock.

Even in Joy's Alfa Romeo, taking liberties with the traffic regulations, it was a thirty-five-minute drive out to

Sandown. It was after five in the evening when Terry coasted down the long driveway and parked before the garages.

The extensive grounds were deserted, for the gardeners finished at five, and there was no sign of life from the house. This was as it should be, for she knew Manfred was still in Europe. He was not due back for at least another four days.

Leaving the ignition keys in the Alfa, Terry ran up the pathway and onto the stoep. She fumbled in her handbag and found the keys to the front door. She let herself in, and went directly to Manfred's study. She slid the concealing panel aside and set about the lengthy business of opening the steel safe. It required both key and combination to activate the mechanism, and Terry had never developed much expertise at tumbling the combination.

Finally, however, the door swung open and she was confronted by the voluminous contents. Terry began removing the various documents and files, examining each one and then stacking them neatly on the floor beside her.

She had no idea of the shape, size nor colour of the report for which she was searching, it was ten minutes before she selected an unmarked folder and flicked open the cover. 'Confidential Report on the geological formations of the Kitchenerville gold fields, with special reference to those areas lying to the east of the Big Dipper Dyke.'

Terry felt a wonderful lift of relief as she read the titling for she had begun doubting that the report was here. Quickly she thumbed through the pages and began reading at random. There was no doubt.

'This is it!' she exclaimed aloud.

'I'll take that, thank you.' The dreaded familiar voice cut into her preoccupation, and Terry spun around and came to her feet in one movement, clutching the file protectively to her breast. She backed away from the man who stood in the doorway.

She hardly recognized her own husband. She had never

seen him like this. Manfred was coatless, and his shirt was without collar or stud. He appeared to have slept in his trousers, for they were rumpled and baggy. There was a yellow stain down the front of his white shirt.

His scanty brown hair was dishevelled, hanging forward wispily onto his forehead. He had not shaved, and the skin around his eyes was discoloured and puffy.

'Give that to me.' He came towards her with hand outstretched.

'Manfred.' She kept moving away from him. 'What are you doing here? When did you get back?'

'Give it to me, you slut.'

'Why do you call me that?' she asked, trying for time.

'Slut!' he repeated, and lunged towards her. Terry whirled away from him lightly.

She ran for the study door, with Manfred close behind her. She beat him into the passage and raced for the front door. Her heel caught in one of the Persian carpets that covered the floor of the passage, and she staggered and fell against the wall.

'Whore!' He was on her instantly trying to wrestle the report out of her hands, but she clung to it with all her strength. Face to face they were almost of a height, and she saw the madness in his eyes.

Suddenly Manfred released her. He stepped back, bunched his fist and swung it round-armed into her cheek. Her head jerked back and cracked against the wall. He drew back his fist and hit her again. She felt the quick warm burst of blood spurt from her nose, and staggered through the door beside her into the dining-room. She was dizzy from the blows and she fell against the heavy stink-wood table.

Manfred was close behind her. He charged her, sending her sprawling backwards onto the table. He was on top of her, both his hands at her throat.

'I'm going to kill you, you whore,' he wheezed. His thumbs hooked and pressed deep into the flesh of her throat. With the frenzied strength of despair, Terry clawed at his eyes with both hands. Her nails scored his face, raking long red lines into his flesh. With a cry Manfred released her, and backed away holding both hands to his injured face, leaving Terry lying gasping across the table.

He stood for a moment, then uncovered his face and inspected the blood on his hands.

'I'll kill you for that!'

But as he advanced towards her, Terry rolled over the table.

'Whore! Slut! Bitch!' he screamed at her, following her around the table. Terry kept ahead of him.

There were a matched pair of heavy Stuart crystal decanters on the sideboard, one containing port, the other sherry. Terry snatched up one of them and turned to face Manfred. She hurled the decanter with all her remaining strength at his head.

Manfred did not have time to duck. The decanter cracked against his forehead, and he fell backwards, stunned. Terry snatched up the report and ran out of the dining-room, down the passage, out of the front door and into the garden. She was running weakly, following the driveway towards the main road.

Then behind her she heard the engine of an automobile roar into life. Panting wildly, holding the report, she stopped and looked back. Manfred had followed her out of the house. He was behind the steering wheel of Joy's Alfa Romeo. As she watched he threw the car into gear and howled towards her, blue smoke burning from the rear tyres with the speed of the acceleration. His face behind the windscreen was white and streaked with the marks of her nails, his eyes were staring, insane, and she knew he was going to ride her down.

She kicked off her shoes and ran off the driveway onto the lawns.

Crouched forward in the driver's seat of the Alfa, Manfred watched the fleeing figure ahead of him.

Terry ran with the full-hipped sway of the mature woman, her long legs were tanned and her hair flew out loosely behind her.

Manfred was not concerned with the return of the geological report, its existence was no longer of significance to him. What he wanted was to completely destroy this woman. In his crazed state, she had become the symbol and the figurehead of all his woes. His humiliation and fall were all linked to her, he could exact his vengeance by destroying her, crushing that revolting warm and clinging body, bruising it, ripping it with the steel of the Alfa Romeo's chassis.

He hit second gear and spun the steering-wheel. The Alfa swerved from the driveway, and as its rear wheels left the tarmac, they skidded on the thick grass. Deftly Manfred checked the skid and lined up on Terry's running back.

Already she was among the protea bushes on the lower terrace. The Alfa buck-jumped the slope, flying bird-free before crashing down heavily on its suspension. Wheels spun and bit, and the sleek vehicle shot forward again.

Terry looked back over her shoulder, her face was white and her eyes very big and fear-filled. Manfred giggled. He was aware of a sense of power, the ability to dispense life or death. He steered for her, reckless of all consequences, intent on destroying her.

There was a six-foot-tall protea bush ahead of him, and Manfred roared through it, bursting it asunder. Scattering branches and leaves, giggling again, he saw Terry directly ahead of him. She was still looking back at him, and at that moment she stumbled and fell onto her knees.

She was helpless. Her face streaked with tears and blood,

her hair falling forward in wild disorder, kneeling as though for the headsman's stroke. Manfred felt a flood of disappointment. He did not want it to end so soon, he wanted to savour this sadistic elation, this sense of power.

At the last possible moment he yanked the wheel over and the car slewed violently. It shot past Terry with six inches to spare, and its rear wheels pelted her with clods of turf and thrown dirt.

Laughing aloud, wild-eyed, Manfred held the wheel hard over, bringing the Alfa around in a tight skidding circle, crackling sideways through another protea bush.

Terry was up and running again. He saw immediately that she was heading for the changing rooms of the swimming-pool among the trees on the bottom lawn and she was far enough ahead to elude him, perhaps.

'Bitch!' he snarled, and crash-changed into third gear, with engine revs peaking. The Alfa howled in pursuit of the running girl.

Had Terry thrown the bulky report aside, she might have reached the brick change rooms ahead of the racing sports car, but the report hampered and slowed her. She still had twenty yards to cover, she was running along the paved edge of the swimming-pool, and she sensed that the car was right on top of her.

Terry dived sideways, hitting the water flat on her side, and the Alfa roared past. Manfred trod heavily on the brakes, the Michelin metallic tyres screeched against the paving stones, and Manfred leapt out of the driver's seat the moment the Alfa stopped.

He ran back to the pool side. Terry was floundering towards the far steps. She was exhausted, weak with exertion and terror. Her sodden hair streamed down over her face, and she was gasping open-mouthed for air.

Manfred laughed again, a high-pitched, almost girlish giggle, and he dived after her, landing squarely between

Terry's shoulder blades with his full weight. She went under, sucking water agonizingly into already aching lungs, and when she surfaced she was coughing and gagging, blinded with water and her own wet hair.

Almost immediately she felt herself seized from behind and forced face down into the water. For half a minute she struggled fiercely, then her movements slowed and became weaker.

Manfred stood over her, chest deep in the clear water, gripping her around the waist and by a handful of her sodden hair, forcing her face deep below the surface. He had lost his spectacles, and he blinked owlishly. The wet silk of his shirt clung to his upper body, and the water had slicked his hair down.

As he felt the life going out of her, and her movements becoming sluggish and slow, he began to laugh again. The broken, incoherent laughter of a madman.

'Dan!' Joy pointed off through the trees. 'That's my car down there, parked by the swimming-pool!'

'What the hell is it doing there?'

'There's something wrong, Terry wouldn't drive through her beloved garden, unless there was!'

Dan braked sharply and pulled his Jaguar to the side of the driveway.

'I'm going to take a look.' He slid out of the car and started off across the lawns. Joy opened her own door and trotted after him.

Dan saw the man in the water, fully dressed, intent on what he was doing. He recognized Manfred Steyner.

'What the hell is he up to?' Dan started running. He reached the edge of the pool, and suddenly he realized what was happening.

'Christ! He's drowning her,' he shouted aloud, and he sprang into the water.

He did not waste time struggling with Manfred. He hit him a great open-handed, round-armed blow, that cracked against the side of Manfred's head like a pistol shot and sent him lurching sideways, releasing his grip on Terry.

Ignoring Manfred, Dan picked Terry from the water like a drowned kitten and waded to the steps. He carried her out and laid her face down on the paving. He knelt over her and began applying artificial respiration. He felt Terry stir under his hands, then cough and retch weakly.

Joy came up at the run and dropped on her knees beside him.

'My God, Dan, what happened?'

'That little bastard was trying to drown her.'

Dan looked up from his labours without interrupting the rhythm of his movement over Terry. She spluttered and retched again.

On the far side of the pool Manfred Steyner had dragged himself from the pool. He was sitting on the edge with his feet still dangling into the water, his head was hanging and he was fingering the side of his face where Dan had hit him. On his lap he held a wet pulpy mess that had been the geological report.

'Joy, can you take over here? Terry's not too far gone, and I want to get my hands on that little Hun.'

Joy took Dan's place over Terry's prostrate form, and Dan stood up.

'What are you going to do to him?' Joy asked.

'I'm going to beat him to a pulp.'

'Good show!' Joy encouraged him. 'Give him one for me.'

Manfred had heard the exchange and as Dan ran around the edge of the pool he scrambled to his feet, and staggered to the parked Alfa. He slammed the door and whirred the engine to life. Dan was just too late to stop him. The car shot forward across the lawns, leaving Dan running, futile, behind it.

'Look after her, Joy!' Dan shouted back.

By the time Dan had run up the terrace to his Jaguar and reversed it to point in the opposite direction, the Alfa had disappeared through the white gates with a musical flutter of its exhaust.

'Come on, girlie,' Dan spoke to his Jaguar. 'Let's go get him.'

The rear wheels spun as he pulled away.

Without his spectacles Manfred Steyner's vision was blurred and milky. The outlines of all objects on which he looked were softened and indistinct.

He instinctively checked the Alfa at the stop street at the bottom of the lane. He sat undecided, water still streaming from his clothing, squelching in his shoes. Beside him on the passenger seat lay the sodden report, its pages beginning to disintegrate from its soaking and the rough handling it had received.

He had to get rid of it. It was the shred of incriminating evidence. That was the only clear thought Manfred had. For the first time in his life the crystalline clarity of his thought processes was interrupted. He was confused, his mind jerking abruptly from one subject to another, the intense pleasure of inflicting hurt on Terry mingled with the sting and smart of his own injuries. He could not concentrate on either sensation for overlying it all was a sense of fear, of uncertainty. He felt vulnerable, hunted, hurt and shaken. His brain flickered and wavered as though a computer had developed an electrical fault. The answers it produced were nonsensical.

He looked in the rear view mirror, saw the Jaguar glide out between the white gates and turn towards him.

'Christ!' he panicked. He rammed his foot down on the accelerator and engaged the clutch. The Alfa screeched out into the main highway, swerved into the path of a heavy truck, bounded over the far kerb and swung back into the road.

Dan watched it tear away towards Kyalami.

He let the truck pass and then swung into the traffic behind it. He had to wait until the road was clear ahead before he could overtake the truck, and by that time the Alfa was a dwindling cream speck ahead of him.

Dan settled back in the leather bucket seat, and gave the Jaguar its head. He was furious, outraged by the treatment he had seen Manfred meting out to Terry. Her swollen and bruised face had shocked him and his feet were firmly set upon the path of vengeance.

His hands gripped the steering-wheel fiercely, he was muttering threats of violence as the speedometer moved up over the hundred mile per hour mark and he began relentlessly overhauling the cream sports car.

Steadily he moved up behind the Alfa until he was driving almost on its rear bumper. The Alfa was held up by a green school bus. Dan could not pass, however, for there was a steady stream of traffic coming in the opposite direction.

He fastened his attention on the back of Manfred's head, still fuming with anger.

Dan dropped down a gear, ready to pull out and overtake the Alfa when the opportunity arose. At that moment Manfred looked up into his rear view mirror. Dan saw the reflection of his white face with disordered damp hair hanging onto the forehead, saw his expression change immediately he recognized Dan and the Alfa shot out into the face of the approaching traffic.

There was a howl and blare of horns, vehicles swerved to make way for Manfred's wild rush. Dan glimpsed frightened faces flicking past, but the Alfa had squeezed around the green bus and was speeding away.

Dan dropped back, then sent the Jaguar like a thrown javelin through the gap between bus and kerb, overtaking on the wrong side and ignoring the bus driver's yell of protest.

The Jaguar had a higher top speed, and on the long straight Pretoria highway Dan crept up steadily on the cream Alfa.

He could see Manfred glancing repeatedly into his driving-mirror, and he grinned mirthlessly.

Ahead of them the highway rose and then dipped over a low rounded ridge. A double avenue of tall blue gum trees flanked each side of the road.

Travelling in the same direction as the two high performance sports cars was a Mini of a good vintage year. Its elderly driver was triumphantly about to overtake an overloaded vegetable truck. Neck and neck they approached the blind rise at twenty-five miles per hour, between them they effectively blocked half the road.

The horn of the Alfa wailed a high-pitched warning, and Manfred pulled out to overtake both slower vehicles. He was level with them, well out over the white dividing line, when a cement truck popped up over the blind rise.

Dan stood on his brake pedal with all the strength of his right leg, and watched it happen.

The cement truck and the Alfa came head on towards each other at a combined speed of well over a hundred miles per hour. At the last moment the Alfa began to turn away but it was too late by many seconds.

It caught the heavy cement truck a glancing blow and was hurled across the path of the two slower vehicles, miraculously touching neither of them; it skidded sideways leaving reeking black smears of rubber on the tarmac, and hurdled the low bank. It struck one of the blue gums full on, with a force that shivered the giant tree trunk and brought down a rain of leaves.

Dan pulled the Jaguar into the side of the road, parked it, and walked back.

He knew there was no hurry. The drivers of the Mini

and the vegetable truck were there before him. They were attempting to talk each other down, both of them excited and relieved by their own escapes.

'I'm a doctor,' said Dan, and they fell back respectfully.

'He doesn't need a doctor,' said one of them. 'He needs an undertaker.'

One look was sufficient. Dr Manfred Steyner was as dead as Dan had ever seen anybody. His crushed head was thrust through the windscreen. Dan picked up the sodden bundle of paper from the seat beside the huddled body. He was aware that some particular importance was attached to it.

Dan's anger had evaporated entirely, and he felt a twinge of pity as he looked into the wreckage at the corpse. It appeared so frail and small – of such little consequence.

– 71 –

The sunlight was sparkling bright, broken into a myriad eyestinging fragments by the rippling surface of the bay.

The breeze was strong enough for the Arrow class yachts to fly their spinnakers as they came down on the wind. The sails bulged out blue and yellow and bright scarlet against the sombre green of the great whale-back bluff above Durban Bay.

Under the awning on the afterdeck of the motor yacht it was cool, but the fat man wore only a pair of white linen slacks with his feet thrust into dark blue cloth espadrilles.

Sprawled in a deck-chair, his belly bulged smooth and hard over the waistband of his slacks; he was tanned a dark mahogany colour and his body-hair grew thick and curly from chest to navel.

'Thank you, Andrew.' He extended his empty glass, and the younger man carried it to the open-air bar. The fat man watched him as he mixed another Pimms No. 1 cup.

A white-clad crew member clambered down the companion way from the bridge. He touched his cap respectfully to the fat man.

'Captain's respects, sir, and we are ready to sail when you give the order.'

'Thank you. Please tell the captain we will sail as soon as Miss du Maine comes aboard.' And the crew man ran back to the bridge.

'Ah!' The fat man sighed happily as Andrew placed the Pimms in his outstretched hand. 'I have really earned this break. The last few weeks have been nerve-racking, to say the least.'

'Yes, sir,' Andrew agreed dutifully. 'But, as usual, you snatched victory from the ashes.'

'It was close,' the fat man agreed. 'Young Ironsides gave us all a nasty fright with his drop-blast matt. I was only just able to make good my personal commitments before the price shot up again. The profit was not as high as I had anticipated, but then I have never made a habit of peering into the mouths of gift-horses.'

'It was a pity that our associates lost all that money,' Andrew ventured.

'Yes, yes. A great pity. But rather them than us, Andrew.'

'Indeed, sir.'

'In a way I am glad it worked out as it did. I am a patriotic man, at heart. I am relieved that it was not necessary to disrupt the economy of the country to make our little profit.'

He stood up suddenly, his interest quickening as a taxi cab came down onto the Yacht Club jetty. The cabby opened a rear door and from it emerged a very beautiful young lady.

'Ah, Andrew! Our guest has arrived. You may warn the captain that we will be sailing within minutes; and send a man to fetch her luggage.'

He went to the entry port to welcome the young lady.

In mid-summer in the Zambesi Valley the heat is a solid white shimmering thing. In the noonday nothing moves in the merciless sunlight.

At the centre of the native village grew a baobab tree. A monstrous bloated trunk with malformed branches like the limbs of a polio victim. The carrion crows sat in it, black and shiny as cockroaches. A score of grass huts ringed the tree, and beyond them lay the tilled fields. The millet stood tall and green in the sun.

Along the rude track towards the village came a Land Rover. It came slowly, lurching and jolting over the rough ground, its motor growling in low gear. Printed in black on its sides were the letters ARC, African Recruiting Corporation.

The children heard it first, and crawled from the grass huts. Naked black bodies, and shrill excited voices in the sunlight.

They ran to meet the Land Rover and danced beside it, shrieking and laughing. The Land Rover came to a halt in the meagre shade under the baobab tree. An elderly white man climbed from the cab. He wore khaki safari clothes and a wide-brimmed hat. Complete silence fell, and one of the oldest boys fetched a carved stool and placed it in the shade.

The white man sat on the stool. A girl came forward, knelt before him and offered a gourd of millet beer. The white man drank from the gourd. No one spoke, none would disturb an honoured guest until he had taken refreshment, but from the grass huts the adult members of the village came. Blinking into the sunlight, winding their loin clothes about their waists. They came and squatted in a semi-circle before the white man on his stool.

He lowered the gourd and set it aside. He looked at them.

'I see you, my friends,' he greeted them, and the response was warm.

'We see you, old one,' they chorused, but the expression of their visitor remained grave.

'Let the wives of King Nkulu come forward,' he called. 'Let them bring each their first-born son with them.'

Four women and four adolescent boys left the crowd and came shyly into the open. For a moment the white man studied them compassionately, then he stood and stepped forward. He placed a hand on the shoulder of each of the two eldest lads.

'Your father has gone to *his* fathers,' he told them. There was a stirring, an intake of breath, a startled cry, and then, as was proper, the eldest wife let out the first sobbing wail of mourning.

One by one each wife sank down onto the dry musty earth and covered her head with her shawl.

'He is dead,' the white man repeated against the background of their keening lament. 'But he died in such honour as to let his name live on forever. So great was his dying that for all their lives money will each month be paid to his wives, and for each of his sons there is already set aside a place at the University that each may grow as strong in learning as his father was in body. Of Big King there will be raised up an image in stone.

'The wives of Big King and his sons will travel in a flying machine to I'Goldi, that their eyes also may look upon the stone image of the man who was their husband and their father.' The white man paused for breath, it was a lengthy speech in the midday heat of the valley. He wiped his face and then tucked the handkerchief into his pocket.

'He was a lion!'

'Ngwenyama!' whispered the sturdy twelve-year-old boy standing beside the white man. The tears started from his eyes and greased down his cheeks. He turned away and ran alone into the millet fields.

– 73 –

D ennis Langley, the Sales Manager of Kitchenerville Motors who were the local Ford agents, stretched his arms over his head luxuriously. He sighed with deep contentment. What a lovely way to spend a working-day morning.

'Happy?' asked Hettie Delange beside him in the double bed. In reply Dennis grinned and sighed again.

Hettie sat up and let the sheet fall to her waist. Her breasts were big and white, and damp with perspiration. She looked down on his naked chest and arm muscles approvingly.

'Gee, you're built nicely.'

'So are you,' Dennis smiled up at her.

'You're different from the other chaps I've gone out with,' Hettie told him. 'You speak so nicely – like a gentleman, you know.'

Before Dennis Langley could decide on a suitable reply, the front door bell shrilled, the sound of it echoing through the house. Dennis shot into an upright position with a fearful expression on his face.

'Who's that?' he demanded.

'It's probably the butcher delivering the meat.'

'It may be my wife!' Dennis cautioned her. 'Don't answer it.'

'Of course I've got to answer it, silly.' Hettie threw back the sheet, and rose in her white and golden glory to find her dressing-gown. The sight was enough to momentarily quiet Dennis Langley's misgivings, but as she belted her gown and hid it from view he urged her again.

'Be careful! Make sure it's not her before you open the door.'

261

Hettie opened the front door, and immediately drew her gown more closely around her with one hand, while the other she tried to pat her hair into a semblance of order.

'Hello,' she breathed.

The tall young man in the doorway was really rather dreamy. He wore a dark business suit and carried an expensive leather briefcase.

'Mrs Delange?' he enquired. He had a nice soft dreamy voice.

'Yes, I'm Mrs Delange.' Hettie fluttered her eyelashes. 'Won't you come in?'

She led him through to the lounge, and she was pleasantly aware of his eyes on the opening of her gown.

'What can I do for you?' she asked archly.

'I am your local representative of the Sanlam Insurance Company, Mrs Delange. I have come to express my company's condolences on your recent sad bereavement. I would have called sooner, but I did not wish to intrude on your sorrow.'

'Oh!' Hettie dropped her eyes, immediately adopting the role of the widow.

'However, we hope we can bring a little light to disperse the darkness that surrounds you. You may know that your husband was a policy-holder with our Company?'

Hettie shook her head, but watched with interest while the visitor opened his briefcase.

'Yes, he was. Two months ago he took out a straight life policy with double indemnity. The policy was ceded to you.' The insurance man extracted a sheaf of papers from his case. 'I have here my company's cheque in full settlement of all claims under the policy. If you will just sign for it, please.'

'How much?' Hettie abandoned the role of the bereaved.

'With the double indemnity, the cheque is for forty-eight thousand rand.'

Hettie's eyes flew wide with delight.

'Gee!' she gasped. 'That's *fabulous*!'

– 74 –

Hurry's original intentions had expanded consider-ably. Instead of a plaque on the cement plug at 66 level, the monument to Big King had become a life-sized statue in bronze. He sited it on the lawns in front of the Adminstrative offices of the Sonder Ditch on a base of black marble.

It was effective. The artist had captured a sense of urgency, of vibrant power. The inscription was simple, just the name of the man – 'King Nkulu' – and the date of his death.

Hurry attended the unveiling in person, even though he hated ceremonies and avoided them whenever possible. In the front row of guests facing him his granddaughter sat beside Doctor Stander and his very new blonde wife. She winked at him and Hurry frowned lovingly back at her.

From the seat beside Hurry, young Ironsides stood up to introduce the Chairman. Hurry noted the expression on his granddaughter's face as she transferred all her attention to the tall young man with both his arms encased in plaster of Paris and supported by slings.

'Perhaps I should have fired him, after all,' thought Hurry. 'He is going to cut one out of my herd.'

Hurry glanced sideways at his General Manager, and decided with resignation, 'Too late'. Then he went on to cheer himself. 'Anyway he looks like good breeding stock.'

His line of thought switched again. 'Better start making arrangements to transfer him up to Head Office. He will need a lot of grooming and polishing.'

Without thinking he fished a powerful-looking cigar from his breast pocket. He had it halfway to his mouth when he caught Terry's scandalized glare. Silently her lips formed the words: 'Your doctor!'

Guiltily Hurry Hirschfeld stuffed the cigar back into his pocket.